Praise for Judith Tarr

"*Pillar of Fire* is a tremendous historical fantasy brought to life. . . . Judith Tarr, already renowned for her previous works in this genre, provides her readers with a puissant, entertaining, and insightful reading experience."
—*Affaire de Coeur*

"An exhilarating ride, powerfully written, through a lost world of chariot races, royalty, revolt, and enduring loyalty."
—*Booklist* on *Pillar of Fire*

"With her usual skill, Tarr combines fact and fiction to create yet another remarkably solid historical novel set in ancient Egypt. . . . This is a highly entertaining blend of romance, drama, and historical detail."
—*Publishers Weekly* on *Pillar of Fire*

"This is a sumptuous work, bristling with action, intrigue, and more than a little subterfuge. *Queen of Swords* will provide many an enjoyable hour."
—*The Washington Post*

D0451738

PILLAR OF FIRE

JUDITH TARR

TOR ®

A TOM DOHERTY ASSOCIATES BOOK
NEW YORK

This is a work of fiction. All the characters and events portrayed in this book are either products of the author's imagination or are used fictitiously.

PILLAR OF FIRE

Cover art by Donato

A Tor Book
Published by Tom Doherty Associates, Inc.
175 Fifth Avenue
New York, NY 10010

Tor Books on the World Wide Web:
http://www.tor.com

Tor® is a registered trademark of Tom Doherty Associates, Inc.

ISBN: 0-812-53903-6
Library of Congress Card Catalog Number: 95-6315

First edition: June 1995
First mass market edition: December 1997

Printed in the United States of America

0 9 8 7 6 5 4 3 2 1

A NOTE ON THE PRONUNCIATION

▲

Names in the most ancient languages, such as Egyptian and Hittite, can seem daunting to the eye of a reader accustomed to English names. The simplest rule to remember is that spelling is phonetic: every syllable is pronounced separately. Vowels (often a matter of extreme uncertainty in these languages written down chiefly by their scribes as collections of consonants) are perhaps most easily pronounced in the European fashion: A as in *father*, E as in *set*, I as in *pique*, O as in *most*, and U as in *put*.

Hence, Ankh-e-sen-pa-a-ten, and Tut-ankh-a-mon, and Akh-en-a-ten, and Smenkh-ka-re, and Sup-pi-lu-li-u-mas, and Lu-pak-ki, and so on.

The reader can of course, if all else fails, resort to the simple expedient of referring to all unpronounceabilities as "Fred." The author, doomed by her subject matter to inflict these names on her readers, is fully sympathetic.

PART ONE

HORIZON OF THE ATEN

You rise in beauty upon the horizon,
O living Aten, Creator, beginning of life.
When you come with the dawn on the eastern horizon,
All the earth is full of your beauty.

—THE GREAT HYMN TO THE ATEN

CHAPTER ONE

▲

THE queen was the most beautiful woman in the world. The king was one of the oddest of men, both to look at and to listen to. They sat side by side on their golden thrones under the golden canopy in the desert outside of their city, where the sun's light was pure molten gold. The whole world had come to them here, to fall at their feet and offer them tribute.

Some of the tribute had not yet been presented. A mighty queen of servants, a woman of massive bulk and dignity, was instructing it in duty, propriety, and the language it was now and forever after to speak. "Khemet," she said, "the Black Land, the fertile land, the land that comes as a gift with the river's inundation. Deshret, the Red Land, the barren land, the desert that embraces and completes the Black Land. These are the Two Lands to which you have been given."

"But I thought," said one of the lesser bits of tribute, "that the Two Lands were Upper Egypt—that's the south—and Lower Egypt, which is the north. Look, he's wearing a crown for each, one inside the other. He looks remarkably . . ." She trailed off. She was a monument to insouciance, but the royal servant, whose name was Seni, had a truly appalling glare. It silenced her, though it could never teach her to repent.

The rest of the girls and young women in the tribute party from Mitanni were suitably awed, if not simply prostrated by the heat. They had insisted on keeping to their Asiatic modesty, wrapping themselves in bright wool and embroidered linen, plaiting their hair with such gauds as they could manage. Their faces were crimson and streaming. Two had fainted already, and it was a long way yet to the king's feet, where they were to fling themselves and beseech him to accept them.

The one who dared to speak was different. She had seen how servants dressed in this country—quite simply they did not, except for a string about the hips and an array of amulets hung about the neck or plaited into the hair. The others had been shocked, had called her immodest and worse. She had been delighted to come to the place of tribute and to see that the king's daughters—all six of them, from budding woman to weanling child—went as bare as they were born.

She sat clasping her knees in the shade of their guardian, watching a great procession of coal-black Nubians presenting the king with gifts of gold and ivory, furs, feathers, a spotted cat that slipped its leash and sprang after one of the little princesses' pet gazelles. The cat was caught before it could fell its prey, the gazelle restored to its weeping mistress. It was grandly entertaining.

"Your name," Seni bellowed in her ear. "Your *name*, child!"

She started nigh out of her bare sun-brown skin. Her mouth opened.

"No!" cried Seni. "Not that mouthful of foreign cat-spit that passes for a name in your country. Your name here.''

She glowered. And how did this woman know what her birthname sounded like? She had never told it, nor had Seni heard it. That was part of the vow she had sworn to herself when she was taken out of her own country and carried off to be a slave to her people's enemies. With teeth-gritted and excessively conspicuous obedience she said, ''My name in captivity is Nofret.''

''Your name in the Two Lands is Nofret,'' said Seni, smiling a broad white crocodile's smile. ''Every other name that you have had, forget. It means nothing here.''

''Someday,'' said the tribute-offering called Nofret, ''I shall be the chief of the queen's servants. Then I can call myself whatever I please.''

''You will call yourself whatever their royal majesties please,'' said Seni with awful mildness. ''Now, Kawit, tell us—what is it that a servant does before the face of the queen?''

Nofret left bland milk-faced Kawit to Seni's tender mercies and went back to watching the processions. The Nubians had gone away, leaving the king's people to contend with the leopard. Now the king received an embassy from Nofret's own country. There was no mistaking those tall full-fleshed men with their splendid arched noses and their hair falling long and thick from clean-shaved foreheads and clean-shaved faces. They were paler than people in Egypt, taller in the main, and much broader and thicker-set.

She blinked hard. Her head wanted to bow to her knees, her face to hide itself, but she stayed where she was, with her chin defiantly lifted. Only the shape of the faces and the fashion of clothes and hair were familiar. None of them was a man she knew.

And well enough for her that they were strangers. She was long gone from Great Hatti, and all her honor was dead. That had died the day she went hunting by herself because her brothers refused to be encumbered with a girl, and met a raiding-party from Mitanni.

They had been looking for whatever prey was most convenient. A fierce-tongued girlchild with an unstrung bow, tracking a deer from covert to covert, was worth a few scratches and some screeching, though the man she had stabbed with his own dagger had not been greatly happy. The others might have held out for a ransom, since the quality of her clothes and her ornaments made it clear enough that she was a lord's child—daughter of a commander of a thousand, if anyone had asked, which no one did. But the man she had stabbed was feeling vindictive. The wound was not deadly but it was deep and it was bloody, and it pained him considerably. He argued that she should be sold for the best price she could fetch. The others gave in after a while, bound and gagged her and carried her away to Mitanni.

She fetched a decent price in the slave market, bought by a lord whose senior wife needed a maid to fetch and carry for her. Nofret was not the prettiest of children, but she was tall for her age and strong, what with an indulgent father and a tribe of brothers and more freedom to run wild in the woods than might have been regarded as proper for a Hittite lady.

She had decided, well before she was set up naked and furious on the block, that she would make the best of what the gods had done to her. Mostly it was anger at herself and at the gods, because she had been hunting too far from home and she had known it, as she had known that there were raiders on the border with Mitanni. It was shame, too, and stubbornness. She did not want her father or her brothers to know how foolish she had been. If they thought her dead, so be it. Better dead than a slave. Better even a slave than prey to her brothers' mockery and her father's wrath.

Once, the night after she was taken, she had tried to kill herself. She had gone for a dagger again, but this time her captors were ready for her. They laughed as they tied her more securely and set a guard on her. Their laughter did a strange thing: it drove her anger deep inside her and turned it cold.

She would live, she swore then. She would live and prosper and be altogether a new thing. Her name in Great Hatti was forgotten. She would not speak it then or ever. Let them call her what they pleased—which, mostly, was *You There* or *Hittite Bitch* or something uncomplimentary in gutter Mitanni. None of them mattered. None of them touched or changed her.

Her new mistress was easy enough to wait on, once she learned how to do it. It was crashingly dull, being a maid to a lady in Mitanni. The only distraction was the son of the house, the darling of his mother's eye, a plump and pretty youth possessed of the conviction that he was irresistible to anything female. Nofret found him wonderfully easy to resist.

She had been an innocent, and no mistake. She thought that a clear and often repeated *No* ought to be enough. But a slave, his young lordship made clear to her, was not allowed to say no.

He let her live, in the end, chiefly because he was afraid of his mother's tears and reproaches. His mother was very soft-hearted; she hated to see anything die, even a slave. The greater wonder was that he let her live unmaimed after what she had done and said to him. He had enough wits left—and enough low cunning—to realize that he could rid himself of her the more quickly if he let her keep her ears and her nose and her breasts.

She smiled to herself, thinking of him; how he had flung her at his father's steward and bidden the man send her with the rest of the king's tribute-train to Egypt. His voice had broken like a boy's.

Astonishing how excellent an education it was to grow up a girl in a houseful of boys. One learned just what to say—and just where, and when, to sink one's teeth.

Her smile alarmed the delicate flower of Mitanni who crouched next to her, and made the child snivel. Nofret sighed. Women in Great Hatti were nothing like these feeble creatures. They kept their heads up; they walked with pride, even when they were slaves.

The Hittites had gone past without ever noticing the lone Hittite in the knot of slaves from Mitanni. One of the many officials who kept the processions moving was striding toward them. His wig was askew, baring his shaven skull; it looked as if he had thrust it aside absentmindedly. He looked only mildly ridiculous. Men in Egypt, Nofret had been noticing, were not ill to look at, for foreigners. One could even become accustomed to men as slender as boys, and brown smooth bodies.

The king's minister was much too busy to think any such thoughts of her, even if he had noticed her. "Come, in your ranks," he said brusquely. "Seni, when you've presented this lot, Lady Kiya bids you attend her."

Seni, who despite her Egyptian name was as much of Mitanni as any of these children except Nofret, inclined her head. The steward had turned away already, intent on the party behind them. Seni took them briskly in hand, lined them up according to age and size and prettiness— which left Nofret well in the back, since she was tall and leggy like a wild filly-foal—and marched them forth like an army into battle.

Nofret had heard about battles. There was a great deal of waiting about in the hot sun, and very little actual fighting. Seni's ordering of the ranks had removed Nofret from her shadow, which was a nuisance. Nofret envied the princelings with their canopies or their parasols, and the king in his great golden pavilion. Such amenities were not given to slaves. They had to brave the naked sun, and stand in it until they were given leave to advance.

"The sun is his god," said one of the girls near Nofret. She was a dreamer; she should have been a priestess, but her family thought itself better served to send her to the Egyptian king. He was a dreamer himself, people said, when they did not say outright that he was mad.

"He worships the sun," the dreamer murmured. "He sets no other gods before it. Oh, they are angry, the myriad gods of Egypt!"

"Hush," said the girl on the other side of her from Nofret. "*She* will hear you."

They all, even Nofret, glanced warily at Seni. The woman was preoccupied with keeping her troops in order. The youngest and smallest were inclined to straggle if they were bold, and to whimper if they were not.

Nofret did not intend to do either. There was too much to see. The whole world was here, come to pay homage to the king of Egypt, Amenophis who had changed his name to Akhenaten for the glory of his god. He had been king a dozen years already, but in the Two Lands of Egypt they often had two kings, an old one and a young one, two courts and two palaces, even—in this age of the world—two cities from which to rule. Now the old king was dead and Akhenaten ruled alone, he and his queen whose beauty was sung even in Great Hatti.

This was the festival of his ascent to sole kingship. It was both coronation and feast of renewal, both declaration of the new reign and affirmation that he was king and had been king since the days of his youth. All these crowding armies of people, lords of the Two Lands and princes and ambassadors from the wide world, were here in the honor of his name. From Libya to Nubia to Asia, west to south to east to north, everyone knew who was king over kings, who was both ruler and god.

Nofret had never seen so many people together, or so much gold in a single place. Everywhere she looked, it dazzled her. And there in front of her, where the king was, was nothing but gold. She wondered briefly if he swam in it when he was in his palace, just because he could.

Maybe he would not be so frivolous. The closer she came to him, the more clearly she saw his face. It was a strange face, so ugly it was almost beautiful, with its long chin and its long nose and its long, heavy-lidded dreamer's eyes under the weight of the two tall crowns. He held crook and flail crossed over his narrow chest, as if he had been used to hold them so since he was a child, and could not imagine doing anything else. The strip of false beard strapped to his chin looked both ridiculous and peculiarly royal: an absurdity that only a king would dare.

Nofret did not succumb to awe even before the gods. None of them had ever had any particular use for her that she had noticed. Gods were for kings, or for snivelers like the infant who dropped in a dead faint as soon as she saw the king's face.

Even so, and with all her defenses armed and ready, Nofret knew a moment's cold stillness that had nothing to do with the shade of the king's pavilion. This was not a man as other men were—even men who were kings.

No one near him was like him, either. People surrounded him: his queen, his daughters, his ladies of the palace, a great crowd of lords and ladies, princes, princesses, servants and stewards and hangers-on, overflowing the dais and the pavilion and streaming out into the sun. They were all focused on him. He was their center. And he was, somehow, utterly alone.

■ ■ ■

Seni led her charges to the dais' foot. A herald with a brazen voice named them and their purpose, tribute from Tushratta of Mitanni to the king of Egypt. The king of Egypt regarded them as he must regard everything that was not his god: with a kind of absent benevolence. He did not speak. Probably it was beneath his dignity.

Nofret made her obeisance in turn, as Seni had taught her. She was not supposed to stare at the king, or at the queen who was as coldly beautiful as her lord was odd to look at. But Seni had said nothing about not staring at the rest of the king's family.

He had six daughters. Seni had named their names, but Nofret did not remember them. The three eldest stood in a row beside and behind their mother, linked hand to hand. The three youngest sat at their father's feet. Two had pet gazelles, which seemed to be trained to lie quietly while the king went about his business. Nofret wondered if the elder three had sore feet from standing there all day long. The one in the middle looked as if she would have liked to sit down.

The one on the end met Nofret's stare with a stare just as bold and rather more sure of itself. She had long eyes like her father's, but neither narrow nor heavy-lidded as his were. She, like all her sisters—and fortunate for them, too—took after her mother. She was very long-headed, which was easy to see, since her skull was shaved but for the sidelock that marked her a child and a princess; but she only seemed the more elegant for it, and not at all grotesque. If she grew her hair, Nofret thought, she would not look odd at all. In fact she would be quite pretty.

It did not seem to matter to her whether she was as beautiful as her mother or as odd as her father. Probably beauty was a common thing to her; her family had so much of it. She made Nofret feel large and coarse and clumsy.

That made Nofret angry. The princess did not flinch from Nofret's glare. She smiled a little—sneering, Nofret thought. Amused by the gape-mouthed foreigner.

Painted lids lowered over the long eyes. The princess whispered to her sisters. The middle one frowned. The one nearest the queen, who was also the eldest and the closest to being a woman, whispered back. The third princess persisted. The eldest sighed at last—to the evident disapproval of the princess in the middle—and bent toward the queen.

Nofret discovered that she was holding her breath. Seni was almost done with presenting Mitanni's fairest tribute, as she put it. No one was listening that Nofret could discern. The king was lost in dreams of his god. The court was bored. The queen was inclining toward her eldest daughter, while the princess whispered in her ear.

Nofret had to breathe or suffocate. Seni gathered her charges together and herded them away from the dais. Nofret tried to hang back. The queen and the princesses were talking about her, she knew it. She refused to think that they wanted her put to death or served for dinner, or anything so dreadful.

But there was no saying any such thing to Seni. They were dismissed. Seni had duties waiting. The newest of the royal servants were handed over to a harried steward, who handed them to a company of guards, who quickmarched them away from the plain of tribute and into the king's city.

They were not delivered to the palace. Nofret knew where that was. She had asked, and it was clear enough on the city's horizon: only the Aten's temple and the towers of the gates were taller. Seni's erstwhile charges were housed in an inn for foreigners. The palace was full, said the guard whom Nofret bullied into speech, and so were all the lords' houses—overflowing with gifts and tribute. When there was room, the ladies from Mitanni would be taken into the palace. Or else, he said, they would go to one of the other palaces. "Thebes, you can hope," he said. "Thebes is best of all. Not like this place." He spat. "So new it creaks, and so raw you can't take a breath without gagging on stone dust."

"It's not that bad," said one of the others with a meaning glance at the captain, who was settling the reckoning with the innkeeper—mostly with the blade of his sword and the keener blade of his smile. "The pay's good and the barracks're clean. More than you can say for a lot of places."

Nofret had a little trouble understanding their speech—she had been taught to speak Egyptian like a lady, not a soldier—but she made enough sense of it to go on with. "You aren't happy here?" she asked. "In Akhetaten?" She said the name carefully, as she had been taught.

"We are happy wherever the king is, may he live long in health and prosperity," said the cautious guard—and none too soon, either. His captain was approaching, ordering him back to duty in the king's festival.

Which the king's possessions—or these portions of it at least—were not to see, now that they had played their part in it. They had orders. They would remain where they were until their master summoned them. However long that might be.

■ ■ ■

The inn was a crashingly dull place. Everyone who might have livened it with drunken song was out carousing at the feast laid out in all the markets. The king's servants were not allowed to go. They ate barley bread and drank thin barley beer under the innkeeper's jaundiced eye. Then, because there was nothing else to do, they made what comfort they could in the sleeping-room, and drowsed or chattered or wept the day away.

Norfret did none of those things. She had plans. The gods meant her to be a slave: so be it. She was going to make the best of it. She would turn her shame into triumph.

How she would go about it she did not yet know, but she would find a way. She sat in a corner with her back to the cool stucco of the wall and propped her chin on her knees, and told herself how it would be when she was the chief of the queen's servants.

CHAPTER TWO

▲

IN the morning the festival was still going on, and the king's servants were still relegated to the inn. Toward mid-morning more came in: a chattering flock of girlchildren from Libya and Nubia. Some were as wild as desert falcons, and their faces were marked with blue swirls and scars. Only one or two spoke any Egyptian. They had not had the good offices of a royal lady to give them Seni for a teacher.

Nofret envied them. She was thinking of running away to the festival, the tables laden with good things to eat and replenished every morning and evening, the spectacles that went past as the high ones celebrated their king and god. She had heard people saying that the king was coming himself after he had run the course of his rebirth in the court of the temple, dressed as a runner and giving his strength to the people. She wanted to see that tall narrow soft-bellied man running. He would be knock-kneed, she thought, and run like a woman. But a woman could run very fast, if she had reason.

She was just done with plotting the routes of her escape when someone new appeared in the inn. Nofret regarded her with mild interest. She wore a gown like a lady but had to be a servant: no lady would stoop to appear here, and without servants or a palanquin besides.

She picked her way fastidiously through the crowd. Her feet in their delicate sandals looked barely fit to touch the earth, let alone tramp the streets of the city. Nofret remembered the naked princesses with their supple bodies and their well-callused feet. Everything in Egypt was turned about, it seemed. Princesses going naked like slaves, slaves dressed and jeweled like princesses.

The woman halted in front of Nofret and regarded her with fastidious distaste. Nofret smiled sweetly back. The woman frowned. "You are summoned," she said. "You will come with me."

"Who summons me?" Nofret asked.

The thin nostrils pinched thinner. "A slave asks whom she serves? Come with me."

Nofret followed because she was curious, and because she was fool enough to hope for something wonderful. Something royal, maybe. Something that would separate her from the lot of a common slave and set her at the feet of queens.

■　■　■

The disdainful servant led Nofret to the palace, to the high royal house beside the temple of the Aten. As raw as the rest of the city was, this part of it was more nearly finished, and more finely made. People who lived here did not have to live in the midst of scaffolding, half-laid bricks, plaster barely dry. The walls were straight and tall and clean, and the paint on them was brilliant, as new as the morning and almost as splendid.

Nofret was not sure what to think of the way people's images were painted on every wall and gatepost. They all looked like the king, but stretched to grotesquerie—even likenesses of a woman who must be the queen, because she wore the queen's crown, and naked children who had to be the princesses. They looked like nothing truly human. Their eyes were stretched long and narrow, their chins drawn vast, their breasts hanging low whether they were the king or the queen or his children, their bellies huge and their thighs immensely round. They were most peculiar, and rather disturbing.

And yet, like the king, they were oddly beautiful, marching in procession through the halls of the palace, bearing their gifts of tribute to the god or embracing one another in a garden of flowers and palm trees or sitting on golden thrones while dancers whirled about them. The king waged no wars here, destroyed no enemies. No bound captives abased themselves at his feet. In Hatti, that would have made him a very unkingly king.

Nofret's guide left her in a room with nothing in it but a table, a reed mat, and a chest that held a few flower petals and a length of undyed linen. Light came from the portico, for the room was less a closed place than an alcove that opened on a courtyard full of trees and flowers.

Nofret could not imagine what the room was supposed to be used for. Its walls were painted with river-scenes, people in boats, fishers with nets, hunters shooting at birds in the reeds. They were all shaped like caricatures of the king, with the king's long dreamer's face.

She amused herself counting images of the king. There was a lady on the river, and she wore the queen's crown; she too had that face. Nofret, who had seen the queen's true face only yesterday, felt sorry for the lady. How terrible to be so beautiful, and to see oneself painted over and over as a grotesque.

Maybe the queen did not mind. She looked endlessly serene, as if nothing ever troubled her. Maybe being queen meant being able to endure anything, even a blow to one's vanity.

Nofret traced the line of the queen's hair—a wig, really, in the style that Seni had called Nubian: short, with curls. It was wonderfully drawn. "I wonder," she said aloud, "what the painters thought when they were told to draw people like this."

No one answered her. She was all alone but for the chittering of a bird in a branch just outside. The whole city was at the festival.

It was quiet here. Nofret liked it, rather, or told herself

she did. It was nothing at all like anything she had known in either Hatti or Mitanni. Her old mistress' garden had been a crowded, chattering place, full of flowers that made her sneeze. This was serene, and strangely austere in its splendor.

Nofret wandered into the courtyard, since no one seemed likely to stop her. The trees were fig trees, heavy with green fruit. There was a hive, too, and bees in it. Nofret shied from that.

Just as she was about to explore the gate at the court's far end, it opened. A small body slipped through, supple and perfectly free of itself without the encumbrance of clothes.

Nofret recognized the third princess, the one who had whispered to the others at the giving of tribute. Nofret was a little disappointed. She was been wagering on the queen, or on the eldest princess at least.

The third princess would do if no other was to be had. Nofret studied her with what no doubt was shocking frankness. She returned the favor. She had an air that Nofret could not begin to imitate, as if she was born so far above anyone else that she had no need to condescend. When she clearly judged that she had seen enough, she said, "Come with me."

"That's what the servant said," said Nofret. "Are you a servant, too?"

"No," said the princess. She turned on her heel and walked through the gate.

Nofret thought about staying where she was, but curiosity got the better of her. On the other side of the gate was a garden with a pool in it, full of lilies. A pair of gazelle fawns were drinking from the pool. At sight of Nofret they raised their heads but did not run away.

The princess was sitting by the pool. There were fish in it: she fed them bits of barley bread, which they took from her hands. She did not glance at Nofret till the bread was gone.

Nofret sat on her heels a little distance away. She should fall on her face, she supposed, but she did not see the use in that. There was someone on guard: she saw a shadow among the flowers, with wary eyes. But shadows did not care if one bowed properly to a princess of the Two Lands.

Nor, it seemed, did the princess. While she fed the fish, Nofret tried to coax one of the gazelles to come and be petted. The gazelles were easy enough in her presence, but not as easy as that. They browsed by the water's edge, nibbling on the lilies, ignoring Nofret's importunings. Just as she reached to pluck a lily for bait, the princess said, "Tell me your name."

"Tell me yours," Nofret almost shot back, but she was feeling suddenly circumspect. Instead she said, "I was told to call myself Nofret."

"That's not your name," said the princess.

"The one I had before is gone," Nofret said. "I let it go. It's little loss, I suppose. Seni says all my people's names sound like the start of a catfight."

"You're not from Mitanni," the princess said. "Names in Mitanni sound like bubbles underwater."

Nofret drew herself up on her knees. "Do I *look* as if I come from Mitanni?"

"You look foreign," the princess said. Her tone was indifferent.

"I come from Great Hatti," Nofret said, stung in her pride, "where the Great King bows to no one—no, not even to the king of Egypt. He calls your father Brother, not Father or Lord or Master."

"He is presumptuous," the princess said. She tilted her head so that the sidelock swung, brushing her shoulder. "Are you loyal to him?"

"My loyalty belongs to myself," said Nofret.

"You will be loyal to me," said the princess. "You're

mine now. Mother says that if you try anything in the least treacherous, I'm to have you flayed and bathed in salt and hung from a spike. I might not be so drastic. I might only feed you to a crocodile."

Nofret laughed. It was more a gasp than real mirth. "You're very bloody-minded."

"I'm the king's daughter," said the princess. "My name is Ankhesenpaaten. You will call me Lady. And Princess."

"What do your sisters call you?" Nofret asked.

The princess narrowed her long eyes. She looked like a cat in the sun, both wary and serene. "You are not my sister. You are my servant."

"I'll wager they call you Minnow," said Nofret. "Or Kitten."

"Kitten is my eldest sister," the princess said: "Meritaten. Meketaten is Fawn."

"And you?"

"I see you are a Hittite," the princess said. She did not look angry. Bemused, yes. Even amused. "You imitate your king's presumption."

"So it is Minnow," said Nofret.

"It is not," said the princess. "It is Lotus, and you are not to call me that."

Nofret bent her head. "Yes, lady," she said, as meek as she could manage.

She slanted a glance. She had not caught the princess off balance after all. The princess had expected obedience. She did not even thank Nofret for granting it.

The princess had plucked a lily and tucked it behind her ear and bent to peer at her reflection in the pool. It was not as if she was vain; it was more a game, to see how clear her image would show itself before the fish came darting to shatter it.

Nofret crouched beside her, not too close. Her own reflection was larger and broader and wilder, with hair in exuberant curling tangles, and eyes glaring out of it like a lion from a covert.

The princess was not even on her guard against the half-wild slave. She said, "You will wait on me alone. If my sisters ask you to serve them, you will tell them that you belong to me and not to them. Do be polite when you say it. My sisters aren't as forbearing as I am."

"I thought you shared everything," Nofret said.

"Oh, no," said the princess. "That's for show, because we're the king's children, and the king wants us to seem perfectly in harmony. And so we are, because we don't have to share anything but each other's company. My older sisters have their maids. My younger sisters have their nurses, each her own. My nurse died. Now I have a maid, and you belong to me."

"But," said Nofret, coming to heart of it at last, "why me?"

"Because," said the princess.

That was all she was going to say, too. Nofret could see it. Nofret had been forgetting how young a child this was—eight, nine summers at most. She talked and acted much older, mostly; as old as Nofret, and Nofret had been a woman since before the last harvest.

But the princess was still a child, and like any child she could choose to be infuriating.

Nofret smiled at her. "I think you think I'm fascinating. I don't look anything like anybody else who came in from Mitanni, and I don't look much like the Hittite princelings, either. They aren't bringing their own women to give to the Egyptian king."

"No, they'll sell their sisters and daughters to him for anything he'll pay." The princess' smile was as bland as the one Nofret struggled not to lose. "Great Hatti has a king. The Two Lands have a god."

"Does that make you a god, too?"

"My lineage is royal," said the princess, "and descends from the gods."

"I'm awed," Nofret said.

"You are impertinent," said the princess. "Is that why you were given away? Because you couldn't keep a civil tongue in your head?"

"Partly," said Nofret. And in sudden ferocity: "And because I wouldn't bed a fat louse with fleas in his beard."

The princess' eyes widened slightly: her only sign of startlement. "You were given a choice?"

"I bit him," said Nofret, snapping off the words with relish. "He's glad he's got a pack of sons to start with."

"You won't be biting me," the princess said after a perceptible pause.

"You won't be trying to rape me, either," said Nofret.

"Not if you behave yourself properly," the princess said, "and save your tongue's freedom for when we're alone. You are very . . ." She paused. "You are refreshing. But everyone isn't as odd as I am."

Nofret had no reason to doubt her. Seni's education of her charges had been as thorough as time permitted. It had had much to say of royal manners and of the behavior expected of servants. Silence, obedience, and perfect effacement were the virtues she proclaimed most often.

Nofret had never learned to be quiet, was only as obedient as she could remember to be, and had never been able to efface herself. But she had become maid to a princess, and not, she thought, because she had kept her head down and her eyes fixed on her feet like a proper servant.

"Play a game with me," the princess said. "When anyone's about, pretend that you're the very perfection of servitude. When we're alone, you may chatter as you will."

"Is that a bargain?" Nofret asked.

The princess stiffened perceptibly. "I'm the king's daughter. I never bargain."

"Of course you do," said Nofret. "You just don't call

it that. Let's say we play the game, then. And you don't have me flayed for whatever I say when there's no one else about.''

"That depends on what you say," said the princess.

CHAPTER THREE

▲

THE life of a maid in the palace of Akhetaten was not unlike that of a maid in a middling great house in Mitanni, in that one waited about a great deal, and spent a remarkable amount of one's time being expected to divine one's mistress' wishes from hints so subtle as to be imperceptible. Otherwise it was profoundly different—and it was anything but dull.

The accommodations were better to begin with than the cramped and perfume-reeking women's quarters that Nofret had known. She was required to sleep at the princess' feet, and hence to spread a reed mat in the room that all the princesses shared, wide and airy, with tall bright-painted pillars and frescoed walls and a floor of richly woven rugs over jeweled tiles.

The food was better, too. Nofret's first duty under her new mistress was to taste everything before the princess ate it, and afterwards she could dine on the leavings. The shiver in the gut, the fear that this time there might be poison, never quite went away, but Nofret was the daughter of a fighting man—she was raised to be brave, and to sneer at cowards.

But although she lived and ate as much like a princess as anyone could, she was still but the newest of servants in a palace teeming with them. As soon as she had met the princess she was handed over to a linen-gowned palace lady who looked her over as fastidiously as the messenger had in the inn, and taken to be bathed and inspected and, as her guide put it, cleansed.

Cleansing meant losing her hair, her beautiful hip-long curly mane that was black in the shade but deep red in the light. It meant being plucked and shaved all over, and then rubbed with something ghastly and stinging that would kill the rest of the vermin with which these arrogant Egyptians imagined she was infested. It meant standing truly naked and shivering and trying to cover herself with her inadequate hands, while rude fingers prodded in places they had no business to be.

"She's a virgin," her tormentor declared.

The bath-servants snickered. "That won't last long," one of them said. Nofret would have gone for the creature's eyes, but they had taken her claws, too, trimmed her nails almost to the quick.

When they were done with her she ached and stung inside and out. She looked like a peeled wand with a white tip—they had laughed at that, too, seeing her skull bare and pallid above the sun-browning of the rest of her. She would get revenge, she swore to herself. Somehow. When she could.

Stay with the princess she well might, serve her and follow her orders, but she was subject to the rule of the chief of servants, and to the steward of the palace above that. She was also subject to the whim of whichever older and more powerful servant chose to notice her—beginning with the one delegated to escort her to the bath and then to teach her what she must know in order to wait on a princess. Seni had taught well in what time she had had, but there was much more to know, and Nofret was expected to know all of it at once. Servants who failed to learn quickly felt the sting of the rod.

There was nothing fair about it, and little that was honestly interesting. The weakling in Nofret begged her to complain to the princess, but the soldier's daughter stiffened her back and set her chin and endured. Even if the princess cared, after all, what could she do? Her intervention would only make it harder for Nofret when the servants had her alone again.

Escape she did not think of, nor would she let it vex her dreams. She was not going to escape. She was going to show the gods, or the Powers, or whatever had set her here, that she was more stubborn than they.

The first thing Nofret learned after she was shown the ways of the palace and informed that she would be her mistress' taster at every meal, was a bewildering array of highborn names and faces. Not only the king and queen, either, or even their six daughters, from the beautiful Meritaten to the baby Sotepenre. The king had other ladies, the daughters of allies who were sent to him as gifts and as hostages. Chief of them was Seni's Lady Kiya—Tadukhipa of Mitanni, princess in her own right and a great beauty. The king favored her although she had borne him no child. Nor would she, people muttered, with veiled glances at the queen. Queen Nefertiti did not expect her husband to devote himself to her alone as lesser men were supposed to do—that was not allowed a king—but neither would she wish another woman to do what she had not, and give him a son to rule after him. Nofret wondered how the queen did it, if she did. It might be useful to know.

The king's mother was in the city for the festival, the widowed queen who commanded whomever she chose. Even Nofret was informed that she might be asked to wait on her. Nofret did not say that her princess had forbidden her to serve anyone else. Everyone was in awe of Queen Mother Tiye. Even, perhaps, the queen's granddaughter Ankhesenpaaten.

And no wonder, too, Nofret thought as she stood in the shadow of a colonnade, watching the court in its stately dance of precedence. The king sat on his throne with his

queen beside him, as Nofret had seen them before. The
queen mother was standing just behind her son, robed and
crowned. She was a small figure, very erect, with a vitality
that struck Nofret even across the width of that great hall.
Her face was almost too strong for beauty, but beauty it
had, with all the passion the queen's cold perfection
lacked.

It was not an Egyptian face. Not quite. Tiye was half a
foreigner. Her eyes were rounder, her nose more distinctly
arched, her lips fuller than anyone's here. She looked as
if she might be partly of Mitanni, or maybe of Canaan.
Her eyes were green like Nofret's own, and the hair that
she let grow under her wig was red, like cedarwood—
Nofret saw a strand of it that had escaped—and her skin
had a different pallor than that of Egyptian ladies who
seldom braved the sun. Egyptians were yellow-pale when
they were not a deep sun-baked red-brown. Queen Mother
Tiye was blue-pale, milk-pale, almost like Nofret herself.
Her father had been a foreigner from Asia, a Master of
Horse to one of the old kings. He was dead not long since,
but people remembered him.

Her brother Ay was a great man in the Two Lands, with
a wife of the royal lineage herself, and a house almost as
big as the palace. He looked even more foreign than Tiye
did, tall and elegantly narrow, with his sharp hawk's face
and his odd light eyes, like the sea whipped green-grey in
a storm. He was Queen Nefertiti's father, in the way these
Egyptians had of breeding kin to kin, and father to the
Lady Mutnodjme. That lady was less splendidly beautiful
than the queen but still very lovely, and if anything more
coldly haughty.

The queen mother had other sons than the king, and two
daughters no older than the king's daughters. Those were
all here. The daughters were nothing in particular: pretty
children with none of their mother's fire. The sons, two of
them, were so wide apart in age that at first Nofret thought

the younger must be the son of the elder. Prince Smenkh-kare was tall and lithe and quite dazzlingly beautiful, more beautiful than the queen, to Nofret's mind—strange to see him beside the odd and decidedly unpretty king, and to realize that they came of the same mother.

Their brother Tutankhaten was hardly more than a baby still, a plump black-eyed child who showed promise of becoming as slenderly elegant and fully as handsome as Smenkhkare. At the moment he was just weaned and inclined to be restless. He had adopted the princess Ankhesenpaaten, which meant that Nofret saw a great deal of him. He followed them both with tireless persistence, imitated whatever they did, insisted that he sit with Ankhesenpaaten at dinner, and made a general nuisance of himself.

Ankhesenpaaten sighed and endured it. She well might: it was Nofret who had to run after the brat when he strayed, and make sure he was fed, and wonder where in the world his nurses had got to. They were in the kitchens, probably, swilling beer and taking their ease.

Ease was not a word Nofret knew the meaning of. She had to be her princess' taster and her tamer of small uncles, and she was expected to know everyone, too, and to give each his proper degree of respect. The king's family, the king's lords, his ladies, his guests and allies, blurred into a mass of disconnected names and faces. Ipy the steward, Pentu the king's physician, Tutu the chamberlain, Ani the royal secretary, Mahu who kept the peace in the king's name, the governor of the city whose name Nofret could not say without either a stumble or a giggle: Neferkheperuhersekheper. Such a vast name for so small and round a man, of such undistinguished family—as if the size of his name could make up for the lack of the rest. She said the names over when she lay on her mat at night, made a learning-chant of them, and matched them to faces as best she might, not for fear of the rod, but because she was too proud to fail.

Simplest of course was to bow low to anyone who looked remotely lordly, and to address him as "my lord" or her as "my lady." But Nofret wanted to be a power in the palace. She needed to know who everyone was, what he did, how he could be used or avoided.

It was dizzying, but exhilarating in its way. Nofret wished her brothers could see her now: their little sister in the palace in Egypt, speaking and being spoken to by whole courts of princes. Most of that was what one would expect of slavery: orders to fetch this or that, demands for services that Nofret was not about to perform, and the inevitable groping in dark corners. But some of it was worth bragging about. The king was pleasant to her when he noticed, and the king's brother Smenkhkare actually smiled at her as if he thought her pretty—scraped pale skull and all.

Above it all, she was in love. She knew about being in love. People were always singing about it. This was what they sang about: these wobbling knees, this melting inside, the absolute conviction that Prince Smenkhkare was the most beautiful male creature she had ever seen, and that included the king of Hatti's white herd stallion.

Being Nofret, and being practical, she knew that he was not really very intelligent nor very strong in the spirit. But she did not care. He was beautiful, and that was enough. He might even turn his eye toward her someday. Princes were known to do that. They were even known to marry foreign women, though not to make them the Great Royal Wife. That was only for a daughter of daughters of the royal line.

Nofret considered Nefertiti and Tadukhipa, and ventured, in such moments as she could manage, to dream.

■　■　■

Nofret's princess could be demanding, but then she could be all gracious ease, letting Nofret go to watch the soldiers' games or to see a procession of priests among the temples. She saw the king perform sacrifice in the Aten's great temple, making a mighty offering for the prosperity of the Two Lands. He did it as he did everything else, with a dreamer's intensity.

He was a strange man, and seemed stranger the more she saw of him. Only he saw his god clearly, or so he said. Everyone else was deaf and blind and must trust him to show them what the god wanted.

The god did not even have a face. It was the Sun-disk, pure light. The painters drew it round and golden, with a multitude of arms that were its rays, and hands giving gifts of the god's grace to the king. Nofret, remembering the sturdy solid human-bodied divinities of Great Hatti and Mitanni and everywhere else—even Egypt—thought this Aten an odd ungraspable thing.

So did everybody else. In the palace it was never spoken of, but as Nofret took to wandering in the city when her princess gave her leave, she heard much that the palace would not have been pleased to hear. Akhetaten had been built a bare handful of years ago and was still raw and new. People lived in it not because they had been born and expected to die here, but because the king had need of them. They paid tribute to the Aten because he required it. But he could not make them worship the Aten as their only god, nor trust him to protect them from ill omens and night spirits. They kept on wearing amulets of every god in Egypt, and they prayed to those gods, though there were no temples in the Aten's own and only city except the great temple to the Aten.

They called the Aten the king's god. They had gods of their own, whom they worshipped as they could. They muttered about priests in other cities, who had no love for the king and none at all for his god. One god in particular, Amon of Thebes, was fiercely jealous. His priests would harm the king if they could. The king had stopped their rites and driven them out, and called them enemies of the Aten.

"He tries to force us," said a seller of beer in the market, more outspoken than most, probably because she partook liberally of her own wares. "He thinks he can make his god the only god, and himself the only speaker for the god, because he's king and god and no one ever told him he couldn't do whatever he likes. But we can't change what we are. I was born on Taweret's knees, I grew up praising Hathor, I pray to Mother Isis when I need anything. Should I give them up for a bauble with hands?"

"You came here," one of her customers pointed out. "You could have stayed in—wherever you came from."

"Memphis," the beer-seller said robustly, "and proud of it too. But there's plenty of people brewing beer in Memphis, and there weren't as many here. So I came to see what was doing in the new city the king made."

What was doing, as the woman put it, was the building and shaping of a new city in a land where new could mean a mere thousand years old. The god had led the king to this place midway between Thebes and Memphis. For long leagues the great river of Egypt ran through lofty walls of stone—save here, where the cliffs opened their arms to embrace the plain and the river. This was a clean place, an empty place—holy, the king said. Across the river were cities of appropriate longevity and considerable prosperity. Here, before the king came, had been only desert.

Beyond the gardens of its princes it was still the Red Land. At night Nofret heard the cries of jackals, sounding as if they came from just outside the walls. Desert falcons hunted in the garden, and once Nofret could have sworn she saw a lioness sunning herself on a roof on the city's edge.

Nofret had been reluctant before that to wander past the city's walls. After, she had her Hittite pride to contend with—she had to go out as far as the workers' village in the place of tombs. That was set apart and starkly so, a huddle of houses in a hollow where the roads met, and past them the steep cliffs and the narrow wadis that clove them, and here and there the open maw of a tomb as yet hardly begun. Only a few were tenanted. Not many of the noble or the rich had seen fit as yet to die in Akhetaten.

The poor of course had no such houses to live in for eternity. A grave dug in the sand had to suffice.

The workers on the tombs lived apart and kept apart. The priests who looked after the tombs once they were built and inhabited were apart even from those. None of them had any welcome for a stranger, but Nofret was quiet and she was adept at fading into shadows. She was only driven off if she made a noise, or if she spied on something the priests wanted kept secret.

The house of the embalmers, which the Egyptians called the house of purification, was so secret it stood right in the open, with a door that was bolted against scavengers but not sealed. Nofret skirted it every time she came, but she eyed it sidelong. Her fingers, moving of themselves, shaped a sign of protection against ill spirits.

In the far corner of the village, where the land was most stony and barren, the foreigners had their huts and their little stone houses. Nofret heard about them from mutters here and there, even in the city: the Apiru, people called them, though they were little like the robbers and reivers who carried that name in Mitanni. They had come to the Two Lands with Yuya the queen's father, following him from drought and famine into a country where they could be fed and looked after.

He had done well for himself, married a lady of the line of queens and fathered a daughter who herself became queen. His clansmen had been less fortunate. Separated from their flocks and herds, robbed of their tents, they knew nothing better to do than become makers of bricks and carvers of stone for the tombs.

For all of that, they were a stiff proud people. They all seemed to have the face of the Lord Ay, like a gathering of falcons. The men grew their hair long and wound it in plaits and covered it with a cap or a bit of cloth, and grew their beards to their breasts. The women were modest but not to absurdity, going about in robes and veils and covering their faces in front of strangers. Their gods were few and strict, and their songs were all of desert places.

Nofret understood a little of their language. It was like the patois of the desert people in Mitanni, which Nofret had learned in bits and pieces in the marketplace and from one of the slaves in her master's house.

She did not know why she kept going back to the workmen's village in particular. There were places cooler and sweeter-smelling and more alluring to wander to. But this was as far as she could get from the palace and still be in the valley of the king's city. She could try to scale the cliff, she supposed, or explore the steep narrow wadis that cleft the hills. One day she would. Now she was content to seek out the place she had found, an outcropping of rock past the houses of the Apiru. She could not see the city from there, only desert. There was a stump of tree on it, clinging stubbornly to life in that barren place, under which she could sit with her back against the trunk, and plan and ponder and dream—all the things she had no time to do while she waited on the princess.

There were goats in a pen near her rock, next to a house of respectable size for hereabouts. It was built of brick, and it had an actual door, a wooden panel that must have been rejected by builders in the city: it was cracked down the middle but still serviceable. Nofret, sitting on her rock, could see who came and went by that door. There was a woman with grey hair under her veil, and a man who was neither young nor old, and a boy. A youth, more like—he must be a little older than Nofret. He had the faint downy beginnings of a beard, and his voice cracked when he spoke, reducing the girls in the village to fits of the giggles. He was really dreadfully homely, long and gangly, with a vast beak of a nose and a rat's nest of black hair under a striped cap.

None of them seemed to notice the stranger on the rock. They never looked in that direction, nor acknowledged anything much but each other, their family's god, and the he-goat that was given to breaking its tether and rampaging through the village.

The goat had a demon in him. His yellow slotted eye was endlessly wicked and evilly wise. He waited till everyone was well occupied in the house or in the tombs before he crouched low, gathered his every muscle, and lunged with ferocious intent, snapping the rope and leaving him free to strike terror in the street. The pen's wall, sufficient though it was to keep in his harem and his young, was but a stepping-stone for him, a leap to the top, a pause to contemplate his freedom, a spring down into the village.

He never offered to join her on her rock, which was a mercy. She had seen what he did to people who got in his way.

The second time the goat escaped, Nofret had been to the rock several times. She thought of it as her dreaming place, the place where she was free. The goat's leap for freedom startled her out of a daydream in which she was both the queen and the chief of the queen's servants, and was laying down the law to the servitors in the palace, all of whom wore Hittite robes and Hittite faces. The goat made her think of one of the king's advisors, a great droner on about trifles and a terrible groper of maidservants in corners. She laughed at the thought—and laughed even harder when she saw the boy bolt from the house in pursuit of the goat.

It was a grand chase. She saw some of it, heard the rest: shrieks, curses, a shattering crash, and a flurry of yelping. The goat had got into a workshop and horrified the artisan's dog. It had wrought havoc among the workbenches, too, from the sound of it.

A rumble of hoofs presaged the goat's return at the gallop, pursued by an irate throng. Among them they herded it into a corner by the wall—not without casualties—and watched openmouthed as the goat sprang up onto the wall, farted loudly in their faces, and leaped back down among his ladies.

Nofret's sides ached with laughter. She lay on the rock under the stump of tree and took a deep breath, and held it against an attack of hiccoughs.

A shadow darkened the sun. She squinted. After a moment the shape came clear: long bony body, wild mane of hair, fierce scowl over the vast arch of nose. "You saw him go," the boy accused her.

His Egyptian was notably better than hers. There was nothing, in fact, to distinguish it from the Lord Ay's own, except perhaps a certain vicious brevity.

Nofret yawned. It was deliberate and very rude. It also stopped the hiccoughs—except for one last persistent catch of breath.

The boy set hands on hips and glared. "You watched our goat get out. Why didn't you say something?"

"I didn't know I was your servant," Nofret said.

The boy made a disgusted noise. "You must belong to Pharaoh. Nobody's as arrogant as his servants are. Even Pharaoh himself."

No doubt he thought he was being clever. Nofret took pleasure in saying sweetly, "I belong to Pharaoh's daughter. Who do you belong to? The goat?"

"I belong to no one but my god," the boy said haughtily.

"I fall down in awe," said Nofret with a curl of the lip. "You belong to the king. All the laborers here do. I'll wager you've never seen him face to face."

"Of course I have," said the boy. "He's my cousin,

and the husband of my cousin. And who are you beside that?''

"A warrior's daughter from Great Hatti," she said, "which is better than a king's slave in Egypt—whether he be kin or no.''

He had the full measure of his people's pride. She wondered if he would try to climb up on the rock and hit her. But he only glared so fiercely that she felt scorched where she sat.

But then he laughed. It was honest laughter, and it went on for quite a long time.

By the time he stopped, she was sure that he was mad. What he said next did little to dissuade her. "Did you see how everybody ran after the goat? Wasn't it splendid?''

"Well," Nofret said after a pause, "yes.''

He came up on the rock in a flurry of bare brown legs and striped coat. Nofret schooled herself not to flinch. She would cast him off if she must.

He did not threaten her. He sat cross-legged in what shade her presence left him, and grinned at her. He did not look like a madman, only a boy in an antic humor, regarding her with lively interest. "You're wonderfully rude," he said. "What are you really?''

"I told you the truth," said Nofret. "I'm the third princess' servant. She calls me Nofret.''

"That's not a Hittite name," he said.

"No," said Nofret.

There was a silence. Before it could stretch too thin he said, "My name is Johanan.''

Nofret looked at him unblinking.

"You hide your true name," he said. "Are you afraid of magic?''

"No!" Nofret snapped.

"You are," he said. "You don't want anybody to know who you are, so that no one has power over you.''

"I'm not afraid of magic," said Nofret, "no matter what

it can do to me. My name is still my own."

"There's no such thing as magic, you know," he said. "It's only superstition. Only the god has such power, and he doesn't waste it on such as you. Only the god is real."

"Which god?" Nofret demanded. "The king's Aten?"

"The god," said Johanan. "Our god. The one who led us here, and will lead us home again."

"Why? Did you forget the way?"

"Never," he said. "But we're bound to Pharaoh. We serve him as our fathers did, to pay the debt from the famine."

"That debt's long paid, I should think," said Nofret.

"You aren't one of us," he said. "You don't understand. We have long memories. We pay well for whatever we're given—good or bad."

"You are strange," she said.

"We're our god's people," he said, as if that was all that needed to be said.

CHAPTER FOUR

▲

THE king's kin in the laborers' village and the king in his palace were very much alike. They were both convinced that their god was the only right one. And they were both extraordinarily odd.

The king had no sons. He had daughters—six of them, all born of his queen. His concubines had never conceived. It was rumored that they could not; that the queen made sure of it, for fear of a son who must be the king's heir. She would bear him that son, or no woman would.

It was beginning to seem that there would be no son at all, then, because the queen bore only daughters.

"Six of them," said the princess Meritaten's maid, fitting new strings to her harp in a corner of the princesses' sleeping room. The princesses were in the temple with their mother, giving the morning offering to the Aten. Servants were airing the beds and folding linen into presses and sweeping the floor.

Nofret had been going to take her freedom in the city, but Tama wanted to gossip. Tama was a Nubian, as tall as a man in great Hatti and broad with it, but beautifully delicate with the strings of her gilded harp. She loved to chatter, and she did not approve of Nofret's expeditions. They were not fitting, she said.

She was keeping Nofret from one now, and deliberately, too. Nofret indulged her out of caution, because the princesses, except for Nofret's own, did not know what Nofret did when she went away, and Nofret did not want them to know. Meritaten, like her maid, would reckon it not fitting.

So Nofret lingered, mending a necklace that her princess had broken. It was exacting work, stringing the beads in precise order, making sure that none was lost or forgotten. Tama's voice ran on like water.

"He has six daughters," she said, "and no interest in any woman but the queen."

"He's fond of Lady Kiya," said Nofret. She was not being loyal. She was remembering how that lady had sat beside the king at dinner, feeding him morsels from her plate, when the queen was not there—indisposed, the servants knew, because she had failed to conceive again and was ill with her courses. The king seemed much pleased with Kiya. He smiled at her, a slow dreamer's smile that yet had a spark in it. He had left not long after she did, with intent that everyone could see.

Tama remembered, too. But she said, "He's under a bewitchment. He's only potent with the queen. Even Kiya—she may try, but she can't raise his shaft for anything she does. Kisses and fondlings are all she gets from him.''

Nofret pursued a bead of lapis across the bowl in her lap. When she had caught it and strung it beside its brothers, she said, ''People whisper that the king can't do anything with his queen, either. That the daughters are all hers and none of his.''

''That's slander,'' said Tama. ''Who do they say fathered them? Lord Ay?''

''Lord Ay is her brother,'' Nofret said.

''That's no difference to these princes. They keep the futtering in the family.''

''I don't believe it,'' said Nofret. ''There's probably a groom somewhere who could tell tales if he would. Or one of the princes who nurses a long passion for the queen.''

Tama snorted. ''Nonsense. The queen has great arts. She manages with her husband, and well enough for daughters if not for sons. Even she can't make his seed strong enough for that. Nor will, my bones tell me.''

Tama did not mean the bones in the big meaty arm that moved so daintily to tighten a harpstring. She had a handful of polished sheep's knuckles in a pouch, that she brought out when the spirit moved her, and cast into patterns that she read as if they meant something. Sometimes her oracles even made sense. Nofret had never noticed that her prophecies came true any sooner or more exactly than Nofret's own blind guesses.

But Tama was a seer of sorts, and it did not do to offend one who claimed the power. Nofret widened her eyes as she had seen her princess do, and asked ingenuously, ''Your bones speak to you? What do they tell?''

''That he'll have no sons,'' said Tama.

''But does it really matter?'' Nofret asked. ''The right to be king comes from the princesses—from the daughters of the daughters of Queen Nefertari, who was a god's child. He could find a good man willing to marry a princess and be king. Any hundred men both good and bad would leap at the chance.''

"That's not how the king thinks," Tama said as if she could know. "Any other king, yes. This king is bound to his god, and his god tells him that *he* is a god. He has to have a son of his own blood and loins, or the god's line fails.''

"That's difficult," said Nofret.

"Oh, for a fact it is," Tama said. "He'll have to do something if he's to do what he thinks his god wants.''

■ ■ ■

The king did indeed do something. He summoned his daughters to him in the evening, long after the festival of his coronation was over. The throngs had left the city, the queen mother returned with her younger children to Thebes, the foreigners left, all but those who had been given as tribute to the king.

Akhetaten was not a quiet city, with all the people who lived in it for the king's service, and all the builders raising new houses, and the king's messengers coming and going at the gallop or the run. But in the evening it grew quieter. Laborers left their labors and trudged toward home. Princes abandoned the court for one another's houses, to sleep or to drink the night away. People in the palace prepared for sleep, except the young bloods, who would dance till dawn in a haze of wine.

The princesses were accustomed to sit together in their big airy chamber, with lamps lit and shadows in the corners, telling stories or gossiping or hearing Tama sing and play her harp till it was time to sleep. That evening Tama was singing a love song from Nubia, mournfully passionate and rather beyond the princesses' comprehension, but they called it pretty. The king's messenger waited courteously till the song was done. When it was, he bowed low and summoned them all into the king's presence.

Nofret took that to mean the maids, too. She affixed herself to her lady's shadow and followed in silence, and no one stopped her.

She had not been to the king's palace before. The ladies and the queens and the princesses lived in the palace proper, but the king had a house apart, bound to the rest by a bridge over the grand processional way that was the spine of Akhetaten. Mere mortals walked below if they were allowed so far at all. Royalty walked aloft into the king's own house.

Royalty, and Nofret. The other maids had not come, even endlessly curious Tama. None of them was bold enough to do as Nofret had done.

The king waited in a room that must be a reception room. Its lamps were lit, softening the hard bright colors of the painted walls. There were woven mats on the floor, and rugs over them.

He sat with his queen on a couch with crimson cushions. Its arms and back were carved and painted with images of the king and his family. Its legs were the bodies of lions, and they had the unmistakable deep sheen of solid gold.

The king and queen were not robed and crowned here as Nofret had always seen them. The queen wore a linen gown and a pectoral like the wings of the Horus falcon, gold and lapis and chalcedony, and the short-cropped curls of the Nubian wig. The king wore a kilt, and a pectoral the near kin of his queen's, and a striped headdress that Nofret thought must be notably cooler and more comfortable than a wig.

He looked almost human here, odd though his long face was, and his body with its narrow shoulders and soft belly. His eyes actually seemed to see what was in front of him, and to take note of it, and to care that it was there. He was at ease, or undertaking to seem so, with his arm about the queen's shoulders, close and familiar as long-married Egyptians so often seemed to be.

Even the queen did not seem so coldly perfect as she did on the throne or in the temple. Nofret could see the living flesh beneath the mask that was her beauty. It seemed tired, drawn, no longer in the first of youth: there were faint, fine lines at the corners of the wonderful eyes and about the lovely mouth. This was a woman who had borne six daughters alive, whose breasts and belly were richly fruitful—but not of sons.

The princesses made reverence one by one, kissed each parent and were kissed in turn, and settled in the royal laps or at the royal feet. It was a pretty picture, the image of familial affection. The king smiled at all his daughters, then beckoned to Meritaten and said, "Here. Sit between us."

The king's eldest daughter looked as if she might ask why, but she smiled instead and nestled between the two of them, not without a glance of triumph at her sisters. They were always contesting for their parents' favor. Meketaten, the second princess, made a face at her sister under cover of a feather fan.

The king laid his arm about Meritaten's shoulders as, a little before, he had done with his queen. Meritaten leaned against him, conspicuously content.

"Your mother and I have been taking counsel with one another," he said. His voice was thin and rather high, and he stammered. He rarely spoke in public, people had told Nofret, and never since she had come to Akhetaten.

He went on in that unprepossessing voice, "I have no son, my daughters. No prince to take the Two Crowns after me. No one to rule beside me till the Aten takes me to himself."

The princesses listened without speaking. The queen stared straight ahead. Her mask was on again, no more yielding than stone.

"Your mother will bear me no more children," he said. "The god has said it, and her heart agrees."

"Then," said the third princess, rashly intervening, "is the Lady Kiya going to be allowed to have a baby? She wants one badly, you know."

The queen's glance was quelling. Ankhesenpaaten flushed faintly and became very interested in her bare brown toes.

The king seemed not to have heard. He had his dreamer's look again, as if nothing mattered, and no one except the god who spoke in his heart. When he spoke again his voice was different. Stronger. Less hesitant. "The god tells me that I must have a son, that there must be a god of his lineage to continue when I have been taken into his embrace. There must be a son. There must be an heir."

No one said anything. The princesses must not like to hear that they were insufficient—that six of them could not begin to equal a single puling manchild.

The king stroked a hand down Meritaten's cheek, along the curve of her neck to her budding breasts. She shivered lightly, pleasurably: her nipples were erect, her eyes soft, almost as dreamridden as the king's. Meritaten was devout. She heard the god sometimes, or so she said. It was her right, she also said, as the eldest princess, from whom the next king would take his right to rule.

She regarded her father with calm too pure for arrogance. "If I were to marry," she said, "I could pray the god to give me a son. I'm old enough now. My courses have begun. I can carry a child."

"Ah," said the king, "but whom can you marry, who would keep the god's line pure? It must be a son of mine who inherits. My son, of my loins. The god has told me this."

The god was an idiot, in Nofret's estimation. Otherwise he would know that his beloved and peculiar offspring was not likely to get a son on anyone if he had not done it already.

Nofret did not say so. She was air and shadow, ears and eyes and teeth-gritted silence.

"It must be so," said the king as if to himself. "Do you understand? It must be so."

"I understand," the queen said. They were the first words she had spoken. Her voice was nigh as deep as the king's, and much more beautiful.

"For the Aten," he said. "For the world that he will make. A son."

"If the Aten wills it," the queen said, "then so be it."

She sounded cold and lost, and tired beyond bearing. The king did not notice. His smile was loving and completely oblivious. He bent it on Meritaten, who blinked in the radiance of it. "I will marry you," he said. "You will bear a son to the god, and the god will heap his blessings on you."

The only sound was the beating of Nofret's heart in her ears. She had stopped breathing, because if she did not, she would cry aloud, and that cry would win her a flaying.

The princesses were mute. The youngest were too young to know what was happening. The elder ones stared at their father, and at their sister. Meritaten seemed dazzled by the god's light.

"There must be a son," the king said. "The blood must not be weakened and scattered. Only our line is worthy. Only you."

Meritaten blinked. She was coming to herself, surely. She was stiffening in horror. Father to wed daughter, to beget a child on her . . .

She smiled. "Yes," she said. "Yes. Only we are worthy."

The king returned her smile. The queen sat like a carven image. The princesses watched like hangers-on at a festival, taking no part in it.

The king bent to kiss his daughter. It was not the kiss

of a bridegroom. It was warm but not hot; chaste, without passion.

■ ■ ■

"It is mad," Nofret cried, but softly, because she was not alone with her princess. "*He* is mad. How can he do that? How can he even think it?"

"The god wills," said Ankhesenpaaten. She was coolly serene. Uncomprehending, Nofret would have thought, but her lady understood a great deal. She knew what was between men and women. She knew what was natural, and what was not.

"The lion will beget young on its own young," she said. "The stallion mounts his daughter when she comes into her season. The god knows. He asks it of us because no one else is fit. Only a god may wed a god."

"You're as mad as he is," gritted Nofret. She went on rubbing sweet ointment into her lady's skin, the ritual of each evening, meant to keep her beautiful as her mother was, even when she began to grow old. The other princesses were asleep in their beds or being tended by their own maids or nurses. None was listening to Nofret.

"You're not a god," the princess said, "or a god's child. You don't understand."

"I don't want to." Nofret worked in ointment with her fingers, hard enough that the princess flinched. Nofret lightened her touch but not the force of her voice. "I know kings are always desperate to have sons. They need them, after all. But there's no need for this king to commit an abomination. He has a whole harem full of princesses from anywhere he pleases. He can take one every night, and pray as hard as his god could ever want, and get himself a whole army of sons."

"No," said Ankhesenpaaten. "They are common blood. The heir must be the god's own."

"Gods bed with mortals. Often. Every day. They even

have children by them. Amon himself and Queen Nefertari—"

"He was her father," said Ankhesenpaaten, "and her lover."

"I thought he was a false god," Nofret said with vicious precision, "and all his teachings were lies."

"They are," said Ankhesenpaaten.

"And yet the throne-right comes from him, through the queen whose sire and lover he was. If he existed."

"It's a mystery," said Ankhesenpaaten. "It's for gods to understand."

Nofret could not tell if she was piercing the armor at all. It was not canny that a child so young should be so completely able to mask herself—so evidently, uncompromisingly convinced that her father was a god, and therefore incontestable.

The princesses slept, each in her bed, with her maid snoring at her feet. All the maids but Nofret, who lay in the nightlamp's light, remembering how the queen had stared into the dark. The air was warm as it always was in Egypt, but Nofret was cold. Cold inside, and to the bone.

CHAPTER FIVE
▲

THE king was the king, and could do as he pleased. Even to take his daughter to wife, to wed her with ceremony before the altar of the Aten, and bed her as a husband must if he wishes to get sons. She did not supplant the queen nor rule as queen. She was the god's servant, the vessel of his will.

She was a woman now completely. Her bed was taken

out of the princesses' chamber and set in a room of the
harem near Queen Nefertiti's. Tama went with her, keeping close by her side.

The evenings were hardly empty of music: they could
all sing, some even well, and the princesses could play on
harp and tambour and sistrum. But Tama's rich voice, her
touch on the harp that had anchored them, was gone.

Nofret went looking for her one afternoon while the
princesses slept in the day's heat. The princesses' chambers—sleeping room and robing room and chapel and
bath—were on one side of a garden court, the queens'
rooms on the other. The garden was empty of either gar-
deners or basking ladies. Everyone drowsed who could,
even servants if their masters would allow.

So might Nofret if she were minded. But she wanted to
visit Tama.

She had been in the queens' house before, waiting on
her lady or running errands for her. She knew her way
about. The scents of perfume were richer here than in the
princesses' chambers. The rooms were the province of
queens, or of the king's most royal or most favored ladies.

Queen Nefertiti had the largest suite, of course, and the
richest. Princess Meritaten's was nearly as large. She had
many more servants than Tama now, maids and guards and
ladies in waiting. Her bed was in a room of its own, and
she had her own morning room and her own reception hall,
even her own throne on a low dais.

Nofret had known how many the rooms would be, and
how large: she had seen the queen's, after all. But she had
not thought to understand that, like the queen, the princess
would be surrounded by servants, walled in them. Lovely
Meritaten who had claimed the best corner of the princesses' sleeping room was now a queen, and a lofty one
at that.

She was lying on a couch in the room that was coolest
at this time of day, listening while Tama played on the

harp. She looked as Nofret remembered, as all the princesses did, delicate bones and lovely pointed face and long
eyes painted longer with kohl. There was no burden of
guilt on her, no shadow of misery that Nofret could see.
If anything she looked exalted, as the bride of a god should
look.

Nofret was going to wait till Tama was done, then lure
her away. She meant to do it. She poised to wait, to listen
to the song as the rest of the maids and attendants were
doing.

She found herself turning and walking, striding away,
faster and faster, till she was running.

People called out. She had a vague memory of a guard's
spear dropped to bar her way. She leaped over it and ran
blindly on.

Time was when she could have run for half the day and
still had strength to dance with the warriors at evening.
But she had become a tamed creature, an ornament for a
palace. Pain stabbed her side before she was well out of
the queens' house. She slowed to a walk, but a swift one,
breathing as runners learned to do, deep and consciously
slow.

She should go back to her own princess. She kept walking, straight out of the palace and into the city and out
past the walls of the city proper, toward the cliffs and the
tombs.

The desert was bleak, but it was clean. There were no
kings claiming godhood here, no princesses submitting to
the will of the god. Only sand, stone, things that grew
sparse and grew tough and had thorns to stab the awkward
or the unwary. The sun beat down on it, slanting long
across the roofs and walls of the city. Beyond the first
glance, she did not look back.

She was thirsty. Her feet hurt. She kept walking, because if she stopped she would fall.

The workmen's village had never seemed so far before,

or so well hidden in the broken land. Just as she wondered if she had mistaken the way, she saw it in front of her, bare of green thing or rich thing, bleak and barren and yet somehow blessed—maybe because it was not in Akhetaten, nor cared aught for the city.

As she stood wavering in the road, she heard a clatter of hoofs. They were too small, too quick for a horse, much too quick for an ox. Her wits were so scattered that she did not even guess what came till it hurtled toward her, horns lowered, running as blindly as she had, but maybe with better heart.

Just before it was too late, she stumbled out of its way. Something lashed her leg. She struck at it, caught hold of what felt like—was—a rope, wheeled and fell sprawling. Idiot that she was, she kept her grip on the rope. The he-goat lunged against it. Nofret clung for grim obstinacy, her light weight against the goat's wicked strength.

Arms locked about her middle. A second, slightly less inconsiderable weight added itself to hers. It was light but wiry strong, cursing in a boy's voice, consigning the goat and all its ancestors and all its descendants to the pits of the netherworld.

Between the two of them they hauled the goat in hand over hand, the goat snorting and tossing its horns but yielding to the rope about its neck. The boy—Johanan, Nofret remembered, that was his name—caught it as it came in reach, dodging a last, rebellious slash of horns. Once it was caught and closely held, the goat followed docilely enough, as if its whole pleasure had been in the chase, and now it was ready to rest.

Nofret walked with them. Her sides and buttocks stung where the goat had dragged her. The rope had burned her palms. She was, for all of that, almost lighthearted.

"You should build his wall higher," she said.

"He'd climb it," Johanan muttered. He was still breathless with running. There was dust on his striped coat, and sand in his wild curly hair.

"Kill him and eat him for dinner!" a woman called from a doorway.

"I'd break my teeth on him!" Johanan shot back.

Others' advice was less practical and more fanciful. Johanan's glower broke into laughter. The goat trotted beside him, meek as if it had never defied a human soul. But its eyes were as wicked as they had ever been.

Everyone knew the goat, as one might expect. Its escapes were a game of sorts. There was more laughter than cursing along its path, people emerging into safety, dogs creeping out from hiding to snap boldly at the conquered enemy. The goat's horns caught one that ventured too close, and sent it yelping back into its lair.

"They aren't angry at all," Nofret said, surprised.

"What, the dogs?" Johanan flashed a grin at her glare. "No more they aren't. This blasted goat will be sacrificed yet. I'll wear its skin for a coat."

"Why haven't you already?"

Johanan shrugged. "We haven't. That's all."

Nofret thought of pressing him, but it was easy enough to see what the answer was. One did not slaughter family, even on the altar of one's god.

As they approached his house, she began to hang back. He spared a hand from leading the goat to seize her wrist and pull her along with him. She tried to dig in her heels, to protest. He took no notice. "You're bleeding," he said.

"Scratches," said Nofret. "I really should—"

"No," said Johanan.

It took both of them to get the goat through the gate in the wall and to secure him on his tether. The rope was much knotted and mended, Nofret noticed. "You could use a chain," she said.

"We could," said Johanan. Now that the goat was tied again, with a heap of fodder in front of it and its ladies watching in mild-eyed interest, he took Nofret's hand and dragged her, will she, nill she, into the house.

It was tiny after the palace, large as houses went in this village. The front of it was goatpen and storehouse. The back, through a heavy wall of curtains, was a dwelling place for human people.

They had made it like a tent in the desert, the floor deep-piled and the walls hung thick with rugs, and rolls of rugs to sit on or recline against, and a low table here and there. A chest against a wall must hold treasure: it was made of wood, rare and precious in the desert, carved with a procession of gazelles and ibexes and bound with bronze. A bronze ewer stood on its lid, and bronze cups, and a basin.

At first Nofret thought the room was empty. It was dim, no lamp lit, the only light slanting wan through a narrow window. Under the window, what at first seemed another, larger roll of carpets raised a veiled head. It was the old woman whom Nofret had seen before, old but strong, with eyes as dark and clear as a girl's.

Johanan bent his knee in front of her as if she had been a queen. "Grandmother," he said. "We brought the goat back."

The old woman nodded. "This too," she said in a soft sweet voice, in pure and unaccented Egyptian, "you bring back. Is it ours? Will you keep it?"

Johanan laughed and shook his head. "This calls herself Nofret, but her true name is something else. She belongs to one of the princesses."

"The queen," said the old woman.

"No, Grandmother," Johanan said. "A princess. The one with the name that goes on and on."

"Ankhesenpaaten," said Nofret, tired of being spoken of as if she were not there. "The third princess. The one who is—still—"

"She will be," the old woman said. "He's cursed them, you know: the king. He's done the thing that no right-minded man does, not even in Egypt. There will be payment for that.''

Nofret shuddered so hard that she nearly fell. Johanan propped her up. ''Grandmother,'' he said, not quite in reproof. ''She's taken wounds of honor in capturing the goat. She needs to be tended.''

''Bathed, too,'' the old woman said. ''The water is hot, the basin filled. See that she uses it first.''

''Of course, Grandmother,'' said Johanan.

There was a servant, Nofret discovered, or a woman who carried herself sufficiently like one, mute and meek. She must have brought the water that filled the great basin set in the back of the house, and heated it over the kitchen fire and poured it in. None of which needed the services of an oracle, either: anyone with wits would have expected that Johanan had come back needing a bath.

Nofret had it first, by the old woman's order. She had never had a bath first before, or had clean water to herself. It was wonderful, though it stung fiercely in her cuts and scratches—more of those than she had known, and more painful. She was actually bleeding in a place or two.

The servant had light hands, and a salve that cooled the scratches. The worst of them she bound up in soft cloths, with Nofret twisting to peer, and getting in the way. She brought out a robe, too, and insisted that Nofret put it on.

Nofret might not have obliged, but something about the old woman made her want to be covered. Armor, she thought, and a shield: a robe of plain white linen, embroidered along the hem.

These people were not as poor as she might have expected. They had vessels of bronze, good linen and finely dyed wool. The beer in the jar was as good as the palace had. The bread was fresh and well baked.

Nofret was given both, and in courtesy she had to accept them. It was not difficult. She was hungry and thirsty. With the bread was cheese made from goats' milk, and a bit of honeycomb.

The grandmother did not share the feast, but Johanan ate everything that Nofret would let him have, and looked about for more. He was one of those whipcord youths who could eat till a lesser man would burst, and still be hungry.

While Johanan investigated the bottom of the jar in hopes that there would somehow, by some miracle, be another drop for him to drink, a man came through the curtain from the outer room. He was vastly tall, richly bearded, dressed in a striped coat like Johanan's but filling his as Johanan barely began to. He was warrior-powerful, and warrior-graceful, too. And yet he could not be anything more noble than a layer of brick or a cutter of stone.

He regarded Nofret without hostility, if without cordiality, either. She wondered if she should rise and do him reverence. But she had not done it for the grandmother, whose age made her worthy of it; she did not see that she should do it for this man, Johanan's father or uncle or whatever he was.

She kept on sitting at the low table, propped against a roll of carpet, comfortable as a cat and nearly as insouciant.

"Father," said Johanan, proving her first surmise correct, "this is Nofret. Nofret, this is my father. His name is Aharon."

Nofret could think of nothing better to do than incline her head in greeting. As soon as she had done it, she went hot with shame. She was acting like a queen, as if she had any right to it.

Aharon did not seem to mind. He smiled, bowed as the desert people did, and said, "Well met, my lady."

"I'm not a lady," Nofret said sharply. "I'm a princess' maid."

There. She was rude. She could not help herself.

"It's courtesy," he said unruffled, "and no more. Will you please to indulge it?"

She flushed hotter than ever. He had a beautiful voice, rich and deep, and a way with words that would have done justice to a courtier.

It was much of a piece with the rest of this surprising place. These were the king's kin, she knew that: the tribe that had come into Egypt with the king's maternal grandfather. But Nofret had not expected them to speak Egyptian as well as princes ever did, or to show court manners in the middle of the laborers' village. That would be their pride, to be always princely even in exile, even as little better than slaves.

Somewhere between the bath and the beer, the sun had gone down. The silent maid lit the lamps and effaced herself, making an island of light in the dusk. Good smells wafted in from the kitchen, savory smells, meat roasting, cakes baking. What Nofret had thought to be a fair feast now showed itself for beginning only, appeasement of hungry stomachs till dinner itself was ready.

"You eat like princes," she said when Aharon had gone to bathe.

Johanan lay back on the carpets, sighing in anticipation of roast kid and honey sweets. "Sometimes we do. This is a festival for us: the return of the goat to the fold."

"And the arrival of a guest," his grandmother said in her gentle voice.

"But," said Nofret, "you couldn't have known—"

The old woman smiled.

Nofret shivered. It was sweet, that smile, and kind, and perfectly terrifying.

"Grandmother always knows," Johanan said.

"She has the eyes that see," said Aharon, coming damp and fresh from the bath. His beard was curling with wet; with the stone dust washed out of it, it was glossily black, no grey to be seen. He was wearing a handsomer robe than he had before, fine crimson wool with an embroidered belt. It made him look more princely than ever.

"You are very strange people," Nofret said.

"We are our god's people," said Aharon. "He has given my mother the gift that is rarest of all, to see all that is to be seen, and to know what it signifies."

"A prophet," said Nofret, fixing her eyes anywhere but on the old woman. "An oracle."

"A voice for the god," Aharon said.

"By which token," said the old woman, "I'm no more than wind. There's no need to be afraid of me. What I see, I never tell, unless I'm given leave."

"You won't see me," Nofret said with sudden fierceness. "I don't know your god. I don't believe in him."

"It doesn't matter," the old woman said. "He guided you to us. Didn't you feel him steadying your steps?"

"I felt nothing but that I must be away from—from my duties."

"From your duties," the old woman said. "Yes."

She could see even that: when Nofret shifted course from what she had begun to say, to something that was the truth but not all the truth. Nofret tensed to bolt. But she had run away already, as a coward will, and found herself here. There was nowhere else to run, unless she fled into the desert—and that way was death. She was neither brave enough nor craven enough for that.

"The king is not loved," the old woman said. Nofret began to wonder what her name was. Whether she had one.

"My name is Leah," she said, driving Nofret into silence of mind and body both. She smiled a little sadly. "It was in your face, child. Nothing more arcane than that."

"I don't believe you," Nofret muttered.

"No," said Leah. "The truth can be difficult. As any king knows."

"Does it matter if people hate him?" asked Nofret. "He's the king. He's a god. No one can touch him."

"He may think so," Leah said, "but he has guards and tasters, and spies in every tavern."

"Then he knows," said Nofret.

"He may not choose to," Leah said. "He took down their great god, the lord of Thebes, Amon the mighty. Amon's temples are closed, his name forbidden—and the king himself was named for him, Amenophis, before he became Akhenaten. The people didn't like that, nor the way he turned his back on Thebes and on every city in his kingdom, to build a city where none had ever been before."

"They won't kill him," said Nofret. "They won't do that to their king."

"You think not? He killed their gods. He abandoned their cities. Now he tells them, as clear as ever he may, that no woman of theirs is fit to be the mother of his heir—only his own seed. When she fails, the second will make the attempt, and fail even more terribly than she. That will curse him surely."

Nofret had nothing to say. The same conviction had driven her from the palace, the same surety that what the king did would in the end destroy him. She did not know what the word was for a man who defied his people's gods, but it was a terrible word, a word that meant only and ever ill.

"You have the eyes to see," said Leah.

"No," Nofret said. "I don't dream dreams or see visions."

"You see truth," Leah said.

"I don't want to." Nofret huddled where she sat, clenched about her cold and knotted middle. "The king is dreadful enough. I don't want to be like that."

"Oh, the king is mad," Leah said, "or close enough. You're sane. That's your trouble."

"What will become of him?"

Leah sighed. "I don't know. I fear too much. He'll die

or be deposed, as a king must be who runs too strongly counter to his people's will.''

"Kings in Egypt are never deposed," said Aharon, startling Nofret, who had forgotten that there was anyone else in the room but herself and Leah. "No more than a god can be. They die, and become gods of the dead."

"Or they die altogether, and their names are forgotten, effaced from every wall and image." Leah had that blind look again, the look she had when she saw, as she put it, truth.

"It may be," Aharon mused, "that the queen can rein him in. She's Yuya's granddaughter. She's not a fool, nor is she mad."

"She said not one word of protest," said Nofret, "when she saw her husband married to their daughter."

"She said nothing that you could hear," Aharon said. "She wouldn't. She's too perfectly the queen. What she said when they were alone—"

"He didn't listen," Nofret said. "And if they quarreled, he won."

"Necessity won," said Leah. "She would want no other woman's son to supplant her daughters. A son of her daughter—that, she might endure."

"She would never countenance it," Aharon said.

"She did," said his mother. Her voice, always so gentle, took on a hint of impatience. "Enough. Whatever was in her mind when she submitted to his will, the consequences are for all of us to face."

"Why?" Nofret demanded. "You're safe enough here. The princes will fight as they please, and leave the common folk alone."

"Not if they drive Akhenaten from the throne and raze his city to the ground." Aharon's big hands clenched and unclenched in front of him. "Our livelihood is here. We have none elsewhere in Egypt, and the desert, the home of our ancestors, is farther than most of us can go. If he fails, we have nothing left.''

"The queen should protect you," Nofret said. "You're her kin.''

"We hope for that," said Aharon.

CHAPTER SIX
▲

LEAH was too true a prophet. The Aten blessed the princess Meritaten, and she conceived.

But the king saw in that blessing the promise of doubled blessing: on the day when it was known that Meritaten was with child, the second princess, Meketaten, came to her woman's courses. When she had finished the days of purification, he took her to wife in the Great Temple in the morning.

They stood in front of the altar in the sixth of the courts, in the inmost house of the Aten. The Aten's splendor shone on them both. The king was wholly given up to it. The princess stood straight and tall as a princess should, but to Nofret she seemed small and frightened.

Nofret was there in the train of the princesses, standing behind Ankhesenpaaten. The third princess was still a child. Nofret kept glancing at her, making sure of it. Was that a suggestion of rounding to the child-flat chest? Was there the faintest furze of down between those child-thin legs?

Ankhesenpaaten was next after Meketaten, born in the next year, between the river's flood and the harvest. It could not be long before she was a woman. And when she came to it, she would go the way of her sisters.

Unless Meritaten's child was a son. Nofret saw her beside the queen. They were robed and crowned alike, beautiful alike, the daughter a smaller image of her mother. It was too early to see that Meritaten was bearing; she was as slender as ever.

Nofret could not read their expressions. Were they jealous? Perturbed? Afraid?

There was no telling. They would betray nothing to strangers.

Nofret wondered when they learned to mask themselves so. The littlest princesses were as children always were, better behaved than most, certainly, but boisterous and fretful in season. When they were distressed, they cried. When they were afraid, one or another of them might come to Nofret and beg for the comfort of her embrace.

They did not understand what all this was. Neferneferuaten, who was old enough to ask questions, wanted to know in a clear and carrying voice when she could wear a gown like Meketaten and stand in the sun. Her nurse hushed her.

A wedding should be joyful; should be full of laughter and song, bawdry and merriment. This was no more mirthful than any rite in the temple, and less lively than most. The king's family were quiet, subdued, all but the king, who was exalted. The high ones who were there with their attendants were wearing the same mask the queen wore. An interesting number were not present at all. Those were the boldest, or the ones who could invent pretexts: illness, or duties that could not wait, that took them far away in the Two Lands.

Nofret by now had learned the names and faces of all the high ones who were often in the king's company. Not all were here by any means. There was one stranger, a man dressed and attended like a prince, but Nofret had never seen him before. He had a face that would not be easy to forget.

Princes in Egypt, even those who were vigorous in the

hunt and in the exercises of war, had a look that would have won scorn from a Hittite soldier. They were soft, sleek. They never failed to paint their eyes in the fashion that Egypt so loved, making them long with kohl. If they ever went to war—which they had not done since Akhenaten's father was king—they would surely manage to bathe every day and to keep their bodies plucked and shaved clean.

This man was clean enough for Egyptian fastidiousness, and dressed with care that must be due to his servants. His wig was the Nubian wig that men and women wore when they would be practical. His jewels were plentiful, but somehow plain: bracelets and armlets of bright beaten gold, a necklace of amber beads as big as ducks' eggs, a fillet of silver that was rare in Egypt. His face was a strong face, a hard face, its lines carved as if in granite. His body was a soldier's body. Nofret knew the look of it from her father's house: the knotted muscle, the sun-beaten skin, the scars.

She leaned toward her lady. "Who is that?" she said in the princess' ear.

The princess did not move or turn, but she answered, just barely loud enough for Nofret to hear. "That's General Horemheb. He commands the armies in the Delta."

"Why did he come here now?"

The princess frowned. Maybe she did not want to answer. Maybe she could not. They had begun the hymn to the Aten, the king singing first and strongly. He did not stammer when he sang. His voice was thin as it always was, but clear, and his ear was true.

The others followed him, the priests in trained chorus, the rest more raggedly. The general from the Delta did not sing, Nofret noticed, nor pretend to sing as many were doing. He stood like a rock, feet braced as a soldier will stand on parade or a general in a chariot. Nofret could imagine him riding behind two swift horses, with the reins in his hands, the wind in his face. He would love that, if he could love anything. Such men did.

Her father had been a man like this. There was no other likeness between them, to be sure. This was an Egyptian, a burly man but lighter boned than a Hittite, with a full-lipped, straight-nosed, firm-chinned Egyptian face. Her father was bigger, broader, his nose a great hooked blade.

She stared too long. The general felt the heat of her eyes on him and turned his own on her, cold black eyes like stones. They found her, measured her, knew her for exactly what she was. Then they dismissed her. She was nothing that he needed or could use.

■　■　■

The wedding feast was duly and dully splendid. Like the rite in the temple, it lacked passion or even conviction. The king was put to bed with his bride as soon as decently possible, well before the wine had finished flowing from the jars.

The four younger princesses left directly after their father, set free of tedium to do as they or their nurses pleased. For Ankhesenpaaten that was to sleep, for she had slept badly in the night. She would not tell Nofret what it was, but Nofret knew the marks of nightmare.

She seemed to be sleeping well this evening, curled with thumb in mouth as she sometimes did. Nofret watched her and sighed. She was afraid. No wonder, too, if she was to be the next bride for the king. Nofret could foresee him taking each daughter in turn as she came of age to conceive a child, trying again and again to get himself a son.

■　■　■

All the princesses were asleep with their nurses beside them. Nofret had no sleep in her. She used the chamberpot, but was too restless to go back to her mat. She prowled instead.

There were still revellers in the great hall. The cones of scented fat set on their heads to stave off drunkenness would be melting and streaming about their faces and shoulders, raising a reek of perfume to mingle with those of wine and sweat and flowers. Nofret heard echoes of singing, the pounding of a drum not quite in time, the usual noise of a feast in the court. The hardiest would be at it till dawn. The rest would leave when their attendants carried them out.

She was glad that her princess was a child, and was not expected to roister through the night. It would have been different for a prince. Smenkhkare had been dedicated in pursuit of that duty while he was in Akhetaten.

The moon was high, shining down into the queen's garden. The fruit trees were heavy with ripening fruit. The roses from Asia, tended lovingly by a gardener who devoted himself only to them, were in full bloom. Their scent made Nofret faintly dizzy. It made her think she saw things. One thing. A man walking from moonlight to shadow and back again.

It was only the moonlight catching a treetrunk just so. Or one of the monkeys from the menagerie had got loose. That had happened before. They liked to come in here and steal fruit from the trees.

Nofret paused by the fountain and bent to drink. The moon was brilliant in the water, a disk of white silver. She saw the shadow of her own head, the hair grown back in a curly tangle, making her look as if she herself wore the Nubian wig.

The shadow shifted. Yet she had not moved. She heard the hiss of breath behind her and froze.

Yes, there was someone there. Something. And nothing as small as a monkey, either.

She turned slowly, braced to fight or flee, whichever seemed wisest. And froze again.

There was no way not to know him. No one else looked

like that, even in moonlight, even without crown and crook and flail, and away from his throne. His head was bare. The moon gleamed on it.

Nofret's head was empty of words.

The king smiled at her. "Do I know you?" he asked in his light voice with its suggestion of a stammer. Before she could think of an answer he said, "No, I remember now. You're my Lotus' maid. The Hittite. Are you happy here?"

Nofret gaped at him. She had never expected him to know who she was. As for whether she was happy . . .

"No," she said. "Yes. Majesty. I—"

"I understand," he said. That was well, for she did not. He bent over the fountain, dipped water in his long hands, drank. It was a very human thing for him to do, very ordinary. Not what she might expect of a god-king who drank wine only from golden cups, and beer never, that she had ever seen.

He straightened with water dripping from his chin and sighed. "Oh, that is good. Pure water from the rock—it comes from there, you know. In the beginning."

"Yes," said Nofret, since he seemed to be expecting an answer.

"Everything comes from the god," he said, "in the end. Beginning is the earth. We are all born of it."

Nofret nodded.

His eyes sharpened, glittering in the moonlight. "You think I'm mad, don't you? They all do, even the ones who believe in the god. No one understands. How strong he is. How he burns. He blinds me. I see him even at night, even in the dark. Even now. The moon is his child, you know. Its light is the offspring of his."

"The moon is the blind eye of Horus," Nofret said.

"Who told you that?"

She bit her tongue. She should know better than provoke

a madman. "It's what they believe in this country. Isn't it?"

"Not I," he said. "I know the truth."

"Yes," said Nofret.

"You don't need to humor me," the king said irritably. "If I were anything but the king, I'd be scoffed at for a fool."

"But you are the king," said Nofret. She was no less dismayed to be standing here under the moon talking to the king, but he was beginning to intrigue her. He was not at all what she would have expected, either as a madman or as a king.

"I am the king," he said with a regal inclination of the head, as if he sustained the weight of the Two Crowns. Then he laughed, short and bitter. "I know how little my people love me. Even my children. But the god drives me. No one hears him but me. He deafens me to anything else."

"It might," said Nofret with breathtaking boldness, "be no god at all, but your own heart speaking."

He did not leap on her and strangle her where she stood. He sank to the ground beside the fountain, long legs folding as awkwardly as a foal's, long hands trailing limply on the paving. "So I thought when it first began. So I ventured to hope. But I'm not so fortunate. The Aten has made me his instrument. I'm powerless to be anything but that."

He was both pitiful and terrifying, crouching there, with his long strange face and his long strange body and that soft hesitant voice. The raising of this man's hand could lay a nation low. And yet he was only a man, whether mad or truly god-ridden.

"He will consume me," the king said. "Already when I stand in his temple in the morning I feel my body become a pillar of fire. My heart is charred and will wither to ash. Then I will be nothing but his instrument."

"Is that why you do what you do?" Nofret demanded. "Because he makes you?"

"Yes," he said. "Everything is as he wills."

"Your bride today," said Nofret, "was trying her hardest to obey the god, but she was terrified. Did the god bed her, too? Or did he let you be gentle with the poor frightened child?"

He lowered his head to his knees. His voice came muffled and infinitely tired. "She is so young. So tender. So very brave."

"You could have let her be. Or waited. She's a baby. She shouldn't have been ready for bedding for years yet."

"She must be ready now," said the king, still huddled into himself. "The god says she must. There must be a son, or it all fails; all falls. Akhetaten sinks back to desert again, to sand and stone. The Aten's glory is forgotten. All the old false gods return to power in the Two Lands."

"For that you take your children's lives and make them serve you with body and soul?"

He raised his head. His eyes were clear, clearer than Nofret had ever seen them: as if prophecy brought him back to the world instead of taking him away from it. "You have a dangerous tongue, child of Hatti. Were you exiled for it?"

"Twice," she said. "I was in Mitanni before I came here."

"You won't be exiled from the Two Lands," said the king. "Not while I am lord of them. You have my word on it."

The word of a king, thought Nofret. That was worth either more or less than most.

CHAPTER SEVEN

▲

THE king in daylight was as he had ever been, dreamer and god. If he remembered the night in the garden, he gave no sign of it to Nofret. Nor did she try to remind him. Best if he forgot, or pretended to forget.

Egypt was a strange country even apart from its strange king. People here loved life and laughter, lived for the sun, drove away the night with lamps and revelry. Because they loved life so much, they never forgot that life must end; that even a god, as they believed, must die.

Death's country for them was a frightening place, as it was everywhere that Nofret knew of. They set it in the west, behind the setting sun. They filled it with demons and with souls of the unquiet dead. But for those who were fortunate, who were kings or who aspired to the wealth of kings, and lately even for the lesser luminaries with wherewithal to build the tomb and pay the priests to keep the rites, there was a country within death's country that offered all the pleasures of earthly life. The way to it was hard, the paths marked by magic. There was a book to guide them, a book as old as Egypt, that the fortunate man took with him to his tomb.

The tomb was the house of everlasting, the place of rest for the body. That was the peculiarity of death in Egypt: that the body must remain and the name be remembered, or that part of the soul which went to the death-country could not endure. Every king and every prince and every man or woman of wealth or note began to build his tomb while he was young. He furnished it as richly as his palace;

he filled it with images of the life that he hoped for in the otherworld, life exactly as it was in life.

The place of tombs was known, but each tomb that was built was kept a secret, as much as anything could be in crowds of workmen. But the workmen kept to themselves, likewise the priests in their mantles of awe, and while the temples for the dead might be difficult to conceal, the tomb and treasure-house of the body was buried deep and well hidden from thieves.

It was common for a prince to watch over the building of his tomb and the tombs of his family. The temple of the king's death, where he would be worshipped after he had died, was in Akhetaten, but the tomb of his body was being built in the desert, deep in the mountain wall, in a wadi as remote as it was difficult to enter. Its door faced the east, toward the rising sun. He wanted the first rays of the Aten to fall full on the hidden door, to bless him in death as they had blessed him every morning of his life.

■ ■ ■

When the princess—Nofret could never bring herself to say queen—Meritaten was great with child and her sister Meketaten was rounding in the belly, for by the god's blessing she had conceived as soon as she was bedded, the king and his family made a pilgrimage to his tomb. He went there at least once each season, inspected the work, conferred with the chief of the workmen, inevitably bethought himself of a change here, an improvement there. The workmen, accustomed to royal whims, sighed and did as they were told, even if it were to destroy the last season's worth of work and begin anew.

This time the pilgrimage was twofold, since the Lord Ay was also minded to visit his tomb. He was vigorous for a man late in middle years, but he was more likely than some to need it soon. They all rode out of Akhetaten in a procession of chariots, each with his attendant clinging precariously behind. The king rode in front under his golden parasol, wearing the Blue Crown that was most practical for riding out in the wind. The queen rode behind him, and the rest in back of them. A company of guards brought up the rear.

Somehow—Nofret did not know how—the general Horemheb was in command of the guards. He had left Akhetaten after Meketaten's wedding, but he had come back. Rumor had it among the servants that he was there to protect the king. Akhetaten was at peace, but it was a taut peace, a watchful stillness. Affairs elsewhere were not so quiet. The Two Lands were not in charity with the king or with his god.

But it was difficult to fret out there in the sun, with the chariot rattling and lurching under her, and the wind in her face. Ankhesenpaaten was her own charioteer, an indulgence that her father allowed and her mother did not refuse. Her horses, a pair of pretty bays, each with a star on its forehead, were soft-mouthed and gentle. They loved to stretch their stride on the broad level road, and the princess loved to encourage them. Once or twice she even sped past her father, who smiled at her, holding his own team of chestnuts to a more sedate pace.

She always fell back to her proper place, and she never let out the whoop that Nofret knew was in her. She was too much the princess for that. Sometimes Nofret wished that she would let herself be a child while she could, before she had no choice but to be a lady and a queen.

This was close enough. To an Egyptian there was nothing grim or sad about a visit to a tomb in the building. It was life to them, a promise of life after life, past the place of judgment and the demons and the trials, in the Field of Reeds that was west of the west.

Lord Ay's attendants were singing. The words were demure but Nofret knew the tune. It was a very bawdy song indeed in the taverns. They knew it, too: they were laughing much harder than the song seemed to warrant.

Royalty had to pretend to ignore such indecorum. The king probably did not even notice. He was full of his god.

■ ■ ■

The gaiety grew muted as they left the broad way and ventured onto the desert track. The horses slowed on the rougher road. The riders in the chariots clung tightly lest they fall. Nofret wished she were the charioteer and not her lady. Then she could balance in the middle of the chariot, feet braced, poised and graceful as the princess was doing, and as the king did with grace that he never had else. As it was, she gripped the gilded side and did her best not to slip.

The road ran as straight as it might to the place of tombs, passing the workmen's village and the house of the embalmers. As bleak as the village was, it was a garden of delights beside the wilderness of crag and stone in which so many noble bodies would rest for eternity.

The king's tomb was far up in the hills, the road steep and narrow between high walls that clove the region of tombs into north and south. Lord Ay parted from them at the foot of the cliff to turn south where his own tomb was, begun later than some and still little more than a rough tunnel in the rock. Nofret had not seen it, of course, but her lady had, and she shook her head as she watched her grandfather's party clatter away. "He doesn't believe," she said. "He builds a tomb in Thebes, too, to placate Amon."

"Is that treason?" Nofret asked.

The princess shot a glance over her shoulder. There was nothing of the child in it. "That depends on who is king."

Nofret shut her mouth tight. This child was not supposed to think such things, or say them to her servant. Maybe it was the freedom of the air and the noise of hoofs and chariot wheels that let her speak more openly than she ever had before.

■ ■ ■

The way to the king's tomb was even more difficult than Nofret had imagined. It was narrow, little more than a passage in the rock, and stony, and ghastly steep. They had to leave the chariots and scramble the rest of the way.

When they came at too long last to the king's tomb, Nofret was worn to a rag, footsore and thirsty and itching with sweat. She was ready to collapse before she even began the last grueling slope, the one that led up to the tomb. And yet the builders walked this road every day, morning and evening, and spent the long day carving a house of everlasting from the living rock.

There were laborers at work within the tomb. She saw the mouth of it yawning open, and a flicker of lamplight. The chief of the workers was standing outside in front of a canopy, clearly a shelter for the more delicate tools of his trade, but set in order for the king's use.

Nofret blinked. She knew that man. For an instant she did not remember where. It had been a long while since she wandered to the workmen's village—not, she realized with a small shock, since the night she heard Leah's prophecies.

The man who built the king's tomb under the orders of the king and of the king's master artificer was the foreigner Aharon. He looked much less princely here than he did in his own house. His coat was drab, his beard greyed with dust. His hands were thick with it, as if he had been carving stone and had not had opportunity to wash himself for the king's arrival. Maybe for him it was a point of pride. He was a maker and a builder. He had no shame of it.

He bowed to the king and the queen and the princesses, not to the ground as an Egyptian might, but from the waist and with peculiar grace, in the manner of the desert. The king did not bridle at it, although the queen's lips tightened infinitesimally. So, thought Nofret. Nefertiti stood on ceremony with her own kin. That was interesting. Was she ashamed of them?

It could be awkward in this country, Nofret supposed, to be a queen and to be in part a foreigner. She came of the royal line through her mother and her mother's mother, but that might not be enough for Egypt, where princes reckoned their lineage back three thousand years. A foreigner, a parvenu, even wedded to a royal lady as Yuya and Ay both had been, would be a matter of subtle scorn.

Maybe that was why the king had built Akhetaten—to show what he thought of such snobbery. Did his princes sneer at his wife and her kin? He would show them what a truly new thing was, a city built where no human habitation had ever been.

Nofret started back to herself. Her lady was already halfway toward the tomb, clambering like a she-goat up the steep stony slope. The maids were assisting Meritaten, who truly should not have come: she was too big with child, and clearly in discomfort. Meketaten, less advanced in pregnancy, trailed behind. When her maid offered a hand, she shook it off irritably.

That was brave of her, but Nofret did not like the look of her face. It was tight and drawn, and it had a greenish pallor.

Nofret glanced at her own princess. Ankhesenpaaten moved strongly, lightly, as a healthy child should. If Nofret were a proper courtier she would assist regardless, but Nofret was anything but that. She thrust herself upward toward Meketaten.

Someone else reached Meketaten even as Nofret did. This time Nofret knew him at once, even without his handsome striped coat. Johanan was taller, that struck her first, and even more gangly than ever. He was starting a beard: a furze of down on his upper lip and a patch or two on his cheeks. He looked ridiculous. She would tell him so at the earliest opportunity.

Meketaten might not be willing to accept help from her own maid, but she was no match for two determined foreigners, both of whom were notably larger than she. Her hand in Nofret's was cold, and it trembled.

Nofret stopped. Meketaten halted perforce: Johanan held her, tight but gentle, when she tried to go on. "You're ill," said Nofret. "Come in under the canopy. Johanan, is there wine? Beer at least?"

"We have water," he said, "from a spring in the hills. It's as pure as a princess could wish."

"I wish," said Meketaten tightly, "to do my duty in my father—my husband's tomb."

"Do that," Nofret said, "and you'll have the baby at his feet."

Meketaten's hands flew to her swelling middle. "I can't. It's too soon."

"Babies don't always know that," said Johanan. "Here, lady. Come into the shade. I'll call the maids. They can fan you while I fetch a cup fit for a queen, and the water-jar."

"I don't want—" Meketaten began.

"Hush," said Nofret with rough gentleness that tended to work with children and animals.

It worked with Meketaten, queen though she might be. Nofret got her under the canopy, heaped rugs for her to rest on, found a roll of plans in a leather case that would do admirably for a bolster. The maid with the fan was glad to be let out of attending the queen in the tomb. "Bury us alive, it will," she said under her breath to Nofret, fanning the princess as she had been trained to do, slow but strong, raising a breeze that felt blessedly cool.

Johanan left at the run and came back at the run, balancing a tall clay jar on his shoulder. He halted panting just out of the shade, produced a gilded cup from his robes, filled and presented it with a flourish.

Meketaten was recovering. She laughed, if weakly, at Johanan's display, and took the cup with good grace, and sipped. Her eyes widened. "Oh, this is good!"

"Drink deep, princess," Johanan said. "There's more if you want it."

She drank the whole cup, and a sip of another. Then she insisted that he have the rest, and Nofret, and the maid with the fan.

"She's a gracious little thing," Johanan observed. Having drunk, and having refused what refreshment Johanan could produce—a hamper of bread and goat cheese, and a basket of figs—Meketaten had fallen asleep on her heap of rugs.

"She's not well," said Nofret, frowning. Even in sleep the princess looked ill. There were deep shadows under her eyes, and a pallor about her lips that Nofret did not like.

"She's too young to have a baby." Johanan's voice was fierce, though he kept it down lest he wake Meketaten. "She's a baby herself."

"Yes." Nofret turned her back on Meketaten and glared out into the sun. Her eyes watered. It was the light—it was too bright after the shade of the canopy.

Johanan let the silence stretch. After a while, in a studiedly ordinary tone, he said, "You haven't visited us lately. Did Grandmother scare you off?"

"No," Nofret said. "I've been busy. That's all."

"You're welcome to come," he said. "Any time you can. Grandmother promises not to say anything too shocking."

"She can't help it," said Nofret.

"When you come," he said, "come at dinnertime if you can. We have a lamb we've been raising. We're going to slaughter it for a feast, come the new moon."

Nofret's brows went up. "Is it a festival of your god?"

"Mostly," he said. "And a wedding."

Her heart thudded once, sharply. "Yours?"

He gaped. "What—" His voice cracked, then dropped to a rumble. "Of course not! Rahotep the limner's marrying old Benavi's daughter. We'll have wine," he said, almost as if he wheedled. "And honey. You like honey, I can see you do."

"I don't know," she said, "if I can—"

"I'll ask your princess," he said.

"No!"

He grinned and would not listen. And when the king came out of the tomb with his family behind him, Johanan waited till they were all drinking water from the jar and clucking over Meketaten—too little too late, in Nofret's opinion—to walk boldly up to Ankhesenpaaten. Nofret could not leap fast enough to stop him. He bowed in desert fashion. "Lady," he said, "would you, of your grace, grant your servant leave to visit us on the night of the new moon?"

The princess looked him up and down. Nofret had not said anything of him, and yet she said, "You must be Johanan ben Aharon. We're cousins, I think."

"Yes, lady," said Johanan. "There's a wedding among us, you see, and your servant would like the feast and the dancing. Will you let her come?"

"Are you friends?" the princess asked.

Johanan never even flinched. "I think we are. My grandmother approves of her."

"Your grandmother . . ." The princess frowned. "Leah? Is that her name?" He nodded. She half-smiled. "My grandfather told me about her. She's a seeress, isn't she? Her god talks to her as the Aten talks to my father."

"Not . . . quite . . . as compellingly as that," Johanan said. "But she does see clearer than most."

"I think I pity her," said the princess. "Yes, you may

borrow my maid on the night of the new moon. Be sure that she comes back in the morning, and that she's fit to wait on me.''

Nofret opened her mouth, shut it again. Not once had her lady glanced at her, nor, worse yet, had Johanan. She might have been a shadow on the wall for all the notice they took of her. They disposed of her with grand disregard for whether she would care to be consulted.

And she could not say a word. She was a slave. She was the instrument of her mistress' will, with neither mind nor will of her own, nor right of argument. Too often she forgot that. She had an indulgent mistress, most times. This was not one of them. Though the princess might think differently in setting her free to dance at a stranger's wedding.

CHAPTER EIGHT

▲

THE night of the new moon came much too quickly to suit Nofret. Worse, her lady was in an antic mood, convinced that Nofret wanted to go, and determined to see that she put on as brave a show as a princess' servant should. She had a gown made of the finest linen, so fine it was transparent, and gave Nofret jewels to adorn it, armlets and earrings and pectoral of lapis and gold, carnelian and malachite. A wig Nofret would not endure, but the queen's own hairdresser arranged her crop of curls into a reasonable semblance of a lady's wig.

Nofret felt like an idol set up in a temple. She turned in the clinging gown, tried a step, came up short. ''How in the world am I supposed to walk to the village in this?''

"You're not," said the princess. "You're going in a chair."

"I am not!" Nofret stamped her foot. "They'll think I'm haughty. They'll stare. They'll hate the sight of me."

"I don't think so," said the princess. She paused, frowning. "Well. Maybe not a chair. Can you drive a chariot?"

"Can I—" Nofret caught her breath. "That's even worse!"

"I should think you'd like it," the princess said. "I'll wager Johanan would. He looked the sort of young man who would love to try the sport."

"At night? With no moon?"

"Well," said the princess. "There is that." She sighed the sigh of the lover of spectacle denied her heart's desire. "Well then. Take the dress off. You'll carry it with you. You can put it on when you come to the village."

That was practical enough to be worth doing. Nofret found herself actually thinking that—and wanting to see Johanan's face when she came to the feast looking like a lady of the palace.

The princess helped Nofret out of the gown, taking care not to disarrange her hair, and made a bundle of gown and jewels and the afterthought, a pair of delicate sandals with gilded straps. "You don't know what you'll be dancing on," she said, wrapping the whole in a mantle of coarser linen and tying it.

"There," she said in satisfaction. "Carry this on your head, and no one will know you for anything but a maid-servant on an errand."

"You are too clever by half," muttered Nofret.

The princess only laughed.

■ ■ ■

Nofret walked through Akhetaten as a servant walks, with her bundle on her head. No one took note of her. The sun was sinking low, the light falling long across the walls and roofs of the city. It did not look so raw in that gold-red light, nor so unfinished. The shadows filled the open places, gilded the skeletal walls, raised pillars where none had yet been built.

Even the desert seemed a gentler place, its harsh angles softened by sunset. Nofret's shadow stretched long ahead of her, all legs and spidery arms and misshapen head. There was no one else on that road. The workmen would be coming down another way from the tombs. The people of the city did not go into the desert so close to nightfall. She found herself wishing that she had taken the chair or, better yet, the chariot.

But she did not want the attention that would have won her, the mistrust, the conviction that she was her princess' spy. Slaves would think such things, being slaves. And no matter that Johanan would deny vehemently that he was anything but a free man. His freedom was entirely at the king's pleasure—just as was Nofret's.

By the time she came to the village, it was dusk. Her bundle had grown heavy on her head, but she forgot it in the light of lamps and torches, in the wholly unlooked-for splendor of that squalid little place in the dimness.

If sunset had made Akhetaten more beautiful, night made the laborers' village almost lovely. The square in the middle, by day a market and a gathering place, was full of light. A canopy was set at one end of it like a king's pavilion. Tables were raised on the other, weighed down with bowls and platters and jars. Women brought more as Nofret came in: bread, cheese, cakes, meat, fruits of the garden and the orchard. It was a rougher wealth than a king's banquet, but richer than one might ever expect of such a place.

Nofret's mouth was watering. The bread was freshly baked and richly fragrant, and somewhere a lamb was roasting: its scent coiled about her, drawing her in through a crowd of shadowy people.

"Nofret!"

That was Johanan, calling her name. He appeared out of the confusion of shadow and light, grinning all over his beaky face, and half pulled her off her feet. By the time she knew where she was going, she was most of the way there.

"You have to put something on," he was saying. She had to strain to hear him. People were singing. There were drums, timbrels, what sounded like a shepherd's pipe, all making a shocking clamor.

Just at the door of his house she dug in her heels. "I have something. If you would let me go, I could put it on."

"What, in the street?" He laughed when she scowled, damnably like her lady, and pulled her inside.

As swift as he made her move, she still dreaded meeting his grandmother. But there was no one in the house. Johanan showed her a room behind a curtain, a place where she could dress in modesty—absurd since he had never seen her in more than a string about her middle, but she was not in a mood to quarrel.

It was harder to get into the gown and jewels by herself than it had been with the princess to help, but Nofret managed. She hoped that her hair was not too badly disarrayed. Still smoothing the disconcerting tightness of the skirt, she slipped through the curtain, nearly into Johanan's arms.

His blush was worth every bit of the rest. After the first astonished glance, he patently did not know where to look.

Now she could laugh at this boy who saw her naked without a moment's discomfort, and yet one glimpse of her in clothes and he was struck speechless. "What," she said, "you didn't think I could be as civilized as this?"

"I didn't think—" he said thickly. "I didn't know—I didn't—"

"What, am I hideous?"

"No!" He had startled himself: he shut his mouth with a snap. But then, finding at last his wits and his courage, he said, "You are beautiful. I never expected that."

"You're blind," she said.

"No," he said. "You are." He held out his hand. "Come, we'll be late."

His fingers were wiry thin and surprisingly strong. They were cold, too: he was not as calm as he pretended. But neither was she. "I'm only Nofret," she said.

"Yes," said Johanan. Whatever he meant by that.

■　■　■

Now this, thought Nofret, was a wedding. Not that sad strange rite in the king's house. This, with dancing and laughter, flowers and torches, bride blushing and laughing and being now kept apart, now driven into the arms of her bridegroom. He was a handsome man, as Egyptian as the bride was of the Apiru: slender, graceful, quick on his feet. She was a little taller than he, a little broader, but he swung her up easily in the most energetic of the dances, whirling her about him till her long hair flew free of its pins and veils. He crowned her with flowers and worshipped her with kisses—such passion as no prince ever let himself show before his people.

The bride's eyes grew smoky, looking at him. People laughed and shouted encouragement. She was blushing still, but not as one who intended to give way to it. Her arms linked about her bridegroom's neck. She swayed toward him.

Someone lurched forward, it seemed to pull them apart. Someone else stopped him. People were dancing, singing, feasting, but where those two were, was quiet. This was the wedding. This was the rite of which the king's marriages were pale shadows.

"So should it always be," said Leah the prophetess.

Nofret had not seen her till now. She was standing beside Nofret, she and her grandson hemming Nofret in.

And yet somehow there was nothing fearful in it, no sense that she was trapped. She was safe, rather. Protected as in walls.

Leah smiled, mostly at the lovers but somewhat at Nofret. "This you should have," she said, "and will, if the god is kind. The king does what he does because he can see no other way. We who were never kings, nor wished to be . . . we're the ones who are fortunate."

"Is this my lesson? Am I to learn such things as a priestess does, as mysteries?" Nofret meant to mock, but it was harder than she expected. Leah seemed harmless, only an elderly woman of the desert people, and yet she was so powerful, and saw so much.

"Every woman is a priestess," said Leah. "Every maiden, every bride, every mother. Yes, even the grandmother who should keep her place but who never quite knows how."

"Her place is to be the one who sees," Johanan said. "That's a woman's mystery, but I know it well enough."

"You know too much," Nofret muttered.

Leah laughed, startlingly sweet. "Doesn't he? Boys do. Men learn to be properly ignorant." She took Nofret by the hand. "Come, child. It's time to dance for the bride."

And dance they did, all the women, the girls down to the smallest who clung to their mothers' hands, the mothers big-bellied with child, the grandmothers long since grown past childbearing. They all danced round the bridegroom and his bride.

The dance was the binding. Maybe the men thought the words had done that, the priest uttering blessings over them, the lamb sacrificed on the altar that faced the morning sun. The women knew better—even Nofret the foreigner, the princess' slave. Words were only words. The dance bound soul to soul and life to life.

The women who were fruitful, who were bearing or giving suck to children, gave of their strength. The women who had not yet borne fruit, or who would bear it no longer, offered what had been and what was to come. They set none of it in words. Words would break the spell. The music was drumbeat, heartbeat, and the pounding of feet on the earth's breast.

They made magic in their god's name, the first true magic that Nofret had seen in Egypt. And it was not even Egyptian magic. It was the magic of the desert, of earth and blood and living flesh.

It was clean, as the desert was. It was wonderful. It was all the palace was not, nor now could ever be.

■ ■ ■

And yet Nofret went back to the palace. It was not fear of punishment. It was duty, and what Leah called necessity: the god calling her where she must go. As she had walked away from the setting sun, now she walked away from the sunrise. Her bundle was on her head, her steps light for all her weariness, marking the pattern of the dance in the road's dust. A little of the magic lingered in her, or so she fancied. It carried her into the city and through the palace gate and into her lady's presence.

The princess barely saw her, except as a shadow in her shadow. "Meritaten is brought to bed," she said. "It's early—too early, no one dares to say. Pray to what gods you know. Pray she doesn't die."

CHAPTER NINE

▲

NOFRET had not yet come to Akhetaten when Queen Nefertiti bore the sixth of the king's daughters. She wondered if it had been the same then and whenever the queen came to childbed—if the palace went about its business, but with a distracted air, an ear cocked toward the room from which came now and then the sound of a woman's cry, but not yet a baby's.

She was not supposed to notice or to admit that she noticed. She waited on her princess. Her princess had rites in the temple to assist in, duties to perform, lessons in dancing and singing and in the reading of the sacred writing, but her mind was not on any of them. When she made complete nonsense of a passage from the Tale of the Doomed Prince, had the prince giving birth to a crocodile instead of being menaced by one, the scribe who was her tutor sent her away to do something less taxing to mind and wits.

The princess had her chariot made ready and ordered Nofret into it. This was not something she had done before, but she had never been forbidden, either, that Nofret knew of. Certainly she did not act as if she expected anyone to stop her.

Just as Nofret settled herself behind her lady, as the princess took up the reins to drive out of the stableyard, a broad figure set itself in front of the horses. The horses, trusting creatures that they were, lowered their heads to search the obstacle's hands for bits of honey-sweet. He rubbed their noses absently, but his eyes were on the princess. "Would you go out all alone, highness?" he asked. His voice was rough and sweet at once, a soldier's voice but with a hint of the courtier.

The princess lifted her chin. "General Horemheb," she said, "you are in my way."

"You are unattended, highness," he said.

She did not glance at Nofret. That, Nofret knew, would have been an admission of weakness. One did not do such a thing with such a man. "I am as I wish to be."

General Horemheb took each horse by the bridle, lightly, not to threaten, but quite enough to keep them from going forward. "I'll accompany you, highness. Come, my horses are ready and standing in the outer court.''

So they were: a pair of stallions, much more restless and eager than the princess' gentle mares, with a look to them that spoke of a long morning's run already. But they were more than willing to go out again, tossing their heads and snorting and nigh pulling off his feet the groom who held them.

Horemheb took whip and reins and sprang into the chariot in one swift graceful movement. The groom leaped out of the way. Horemheb had the stallions in hand. They champed and fretted but held still. He bowed with no irony that Nofret could detect. "After you, highness."

Haughty as the queen and fully as cold, the princess urged her mares forward. They trotted out willingly, disdainful of the fretting, pawing stallions.

Where the princess would have gone without escort, Nofret did not know. Maybe to the king's tomb. Maybe ever farther out into the desert, away from any human thing, though not from human fear.

As it was, the princess ventured no such escape. She drove sedately down the processional way, keeping a pace far slower than she would have done if left to herself—slow enough that the general was much beset to hold his stallions in. Ankhesenpaaten seemed oblivious. People stopped to stare as she drove by. Those who were Egyptian dropped down in homage. Those who were not, once apprised of who she was, bowed each in the fashion of his country. It was a little like wind in a field of barley, all those heads bent and bodies lowered for the princess' passing.

She drove from one end of the great road to the other, from gate to gate and back again. Then, still at that maddening, leisurely pace, she drove back into the palace. Her mares were not even warm. Horemheb's stallions were sodden with sweat, white-flecked with foam. He himself was grim about the mouth, and yet his eyes were laughing.

When both chariots stood in the stable court, the mares calmly standing, the stallions close to rearing with frustration, Horemheb bowed over the rail of his chariot. "A fair match, highness," he said, "and a fair victory."

The princess raised her brows. "It was a game? I had no idea." She stepped down from the chariot, turned her back on her would-be guardian, and walked away.

■   ■   ■

Once they were safe in the princesses' house again, she let the mask fall. She wheeled on Nofret, half in laughter, half in rage. "Oh, that man! How *dared* he?"

"I don't know," said Nofret. "What did he dare? To protect you? That was wise, I thought."

"Oh," said her lady, disgusted. "Protection. From what? This is my father's own city. No one would dare touch me here."

"You don't know that. Nor does he."

"I do know it," the princess said sharply. "I know I'm safe. How dared he imply that I'm not?"

"Maybe," said Nofret, "because he knows something you don't."

The princess was notably smaller than Nofret, but she could loom as tall as any warrior. It was sheer royal arrogance, and refusal to be cowed by anything so insignificant as size or strength or length of arm. She stood loftily upright and fixed Nofret with a fierce black stare. "What does he know that the king's own spies don't?"

"Very little, probably," said Nofret. "But they're not telling your father everything, and he's telling you even less. He has enemies. Many of them. They aren't always going to let this city be. Not when most of the people in it still secretly worship other gods than his."

The princess drew a slow breath. "You shouldn't have told me that. Not if I'm not to be trusted."

"I trust you," Nofret said. "Besides, what will the king

do? Massacre everybody who still says a prayer to Bes or Hathor or even Amon when there's need of a god's ear? He closed temples, struck out the names of the gods—but he hasn't had anyone killed.''

"Except the gods," said the princess. She sighed. She seemed to shrink, to become the delicate-boned child again, the king's third and still unwedded daughter. "It's not that he did it. You should understand that. It's that *he* did it."

"You don't like General Horemheb," said Nofret.

"It has nothing to do with liking or disliking," the princess said. "The man is a commoner. He has his eye on higher things—and he means to get them."

"Higher things?" Nofret asked. "Such as a princess for a wife?"

"That will not happen," the princess said.

She was sure of that and of herself. Nofret hoped she would not be disappointed. Kings—even, possibly, a king who married his own daughters to keep the king-right in the family—were slaves to expedience. And it might be expedient to give a daughter to a strong fighting man, a general of armies who might, once bound, assure that those armies did not muster in support of other gods than the king's.

It could be coming to that. Nofret did not know, could only guess: nor had she seen the temples that were closed, or heard the cries of the priests. But what she had heard was clear enough. The people in Akhetaten were not well content with their king. If they were less than pleased, who had the benefit of his living and constant presence, than the rest of Egypt must be unhappy indeed.

"If the general has his eye on you," Nofret said, "then you could do worse than to indulge his fancy. There's no need to say you'll marry him, or even indicate that you know he's thinking of it. But you can let him think he has some hope someday, when you're old enough to contemplate such things. He's a strong man. He'll keep anyone else from troubling you.''

"What, I should lead him on?" The princess looked ready to slap Nofret, but it seemed that she thought better of it. "He's a dreadful man. He's old. He smells of horses."

"Horses smell lovely," said Nofret.

"*Old* horses," the princess said. "Filthy, sweaty horses. Horses that haven't been washed since they were foaled."

"That's still better than some priest with bloody hands from the sacrifice. Or," said Nofret, "the king."

That was ill judged. The princess, who had been hovering on the edge between child and queen, became again all royal. "The king is king and god. And," she said, "he is always clean."

"But what he *does* isn't—" Nofret stopped herself. Her lady was Egyptian, and royal Egyptian at that. She had never understood, and never would, how deep a revulsion was in Nofret. That much she and all her kin had made clear. Her fear was the child-bride's fear of being brought to womanhood too soon, not the fear of any god's curse.

Nofret's stomach was knotting again. She cursed it wearily and said, "You won't marry him as long as the king lives—you can be sure of that. Your father would never allow it, even if you wanted it. But he doesn't have to know that. He's strong, he has soldiers, he can guard you against anyone who thinks to threaten you. Isn't that worth a little inconvenience?"

"There is nothing to protect me against," said Ankhesenpaaten, calmly and royally stubborn.

■　■　■

There was nothing more to be said—not, at least, just then. Nofret did not intend to give up the fight. But she could withdraw for a while, and wait.

It was a calmer waiting than the vigil over the princess

Meritaten. This baby had been in a fever of haste to begin its arrival, but now that its mother had taken to her bed, it decided to take its time. Nor did it help that she was young and small. When she was a grown woman she would have her mother's wonderful wide hips and bountiful breasts. But she was hardly more than a child.

Ankhesenpaaten, thwarted of her escape from the city, went to sleep instead. Nofret envied her that facility. She herself, as always, was wide awake and fretting. She did not love the princess Meritaten or even greatly like her. But Meritaten was in pain and fear, as strong as smoke in the air.

Nofret thought of running away as she had before. Her lady had tried it and failed. Nofret, who might have better luck, found herself unable to move so far, but unable to rest.

There was nothing she could do for Meritaten. She could not even go as far as the princess' door. There were guards at the gates of the queens' house, and no one went in who did not have clear and present purpose.

Nofret, as the third princess' maid, belonged with that princess and not, the guards made it very clear, with the princess within. She did not even know why she pressed for admittance. She knew a little of midwifery, but Meritaten had whole companies of physicians and midwives to attend her. Nofret would only have been an encumbrance.

Still she hung about. The garden court was hot as the sun bent toward the west, the air still, with that flavor of dust and dung which was distinctly Egypt. Even the heavy scent of flowers could not quite obscure it.

Through the humming of bees, she thought she heard a sound. A gardener, probably, venturing the day's heat to perform some mystery of his trade. Everyone else who could be was asleep or resting.

The sound came again. It was like a catch of breath. It could be one of the monkeys. Or a cat. Or, thought Nofret as she moved toward it, a child trying to cry quietly.

She trod softly down the line of fruit-trees, past the pool with fish in it, to the rose garden. Inside that prickly wall, under an arch of blossoms, huddled the child who had been weeping.

And yet, in the king's mind, this was no child at all. This was his second daughter, his second child-queen, Meketaten. She was robed, jeweled, wigged as a queen, but the face that turned upward at Nofret's approach was that of a young girl, a child, eleven years old. The eyepaint that even children wore, the paint of cheeks and lips, had all run and smeared.

Nofret had never been adept at soothing crying children. Practicality suited her better. She looked about for something to wipe Meketaten's face clean, found nothing more useful than the princess' own gauzy shawl. Meketaten sat mute while Nofret scrubbed away the paint, not wincing though the linen was inclined to scratch.

Once the paint was gone, or mostly, her face was starkly pale. Her body looked odd, misshapen, like the image of her father carved or painted on every wall. She was protecting her middle, Nofret realized, with her odd huddled posture, half sitting, half lying among the roses.

"Let me guess," Nofret said, deliberately rough, to startle Meketaten awake. "Nobody's paying any attention to you, they're all caught up with Meritaten, and you hurt, and you're scared. Is the baby coming?"

Meketaten's face did not change, but her body stiffened. "You have no elegance of expression," she said.

"Gods forbid I ever should," said Nofret. She laid hands on the bulge of belly. Meketaten uncoiled like a cobra, striking hard and viciously fast.

But Nofret was a warrior's daughter, and she had had brothers who meant to be warriors. She was faster, and stronger, too. And she had a gift that her father called the warrior's gift, to see slow and clear even in the heat of action. She saw what Meketaten maybe wished least for her to see.

There was blood on the fine white gown, blood that could only come from something very wrong with the child that Meketaten carried. Nofret did not pause to think, even to recover from the force of Meketaten's attack. As Meketaten sank with a gasp—pain, shock, something of both—Nofret caught her and lifted her. She was a light weight for Nofret's sturdiness, all bones and skin like a bird.

Once Nofret had her in hand, she stopped struggling and lay breathing hard, with a catch in it that Nofret did not like. When she shut her eyes and let her head fall back, Nofret nearly dropped her. She looked like a dead thing.

But she was still breathing, still conscious. She said in a thread of a voice, "Let me lie in the sun. The sun will make me strong. The sun will—stop—"

"You don't need a sunbath," Nofret said. "You need a midwife. And quickly."

"No," said Meketaten. "This is the king's son. He will be born when his proper time comes. He won't be born now."

"I don't think he's listening to you," Nofret said, striding away from the roses toward the queens' house.

■   ■   ■

This time the guards let her pass. Meketaten was her surety. A glance at the princess' face persuaded the chief of the guards to send a man at the run for a midwife or at the very least a healer-priest. Nofret did not waste time in thanking him for having eyes in his head. She walked straight through the guards, who at the last instant had the wits to open the door before she ran into it, and made what speed she could to a room with a bed in it.

The bed probably belonged to someone other than Meketaten: it was smaller and much plainer than a princess would insist on. It was big enough for the purpose. Anyone who came to remonstrate, Nofret put to work opening shutters, wielding fans, fetching necessities.

One servant had the wits to bring wine still cool from its jar, thinned with good water. Nofret saw her at first only as a shadow, a hand with a cup in it, holding the cup to Meketaten's lips. Then, abruptly, she came into focus. "Tama!" said Nofret, startled. "Why aren't you—"

"They don't need me," said Princess Meritaten's maid, "nor want to hear what anyone knows, that she's killing herself to give the king another daughter."

"I am not," said Meketaten, startling them both. Nofret at least had thought her too racked with pain to hear.

"Not you, highness," said Tama. "Your sister."

"Not I," said Meketaten. "I won't die. I'll have a son."

Someone small, wiry, and preoccupied thrust Nofret aside. Nofret noticed the amulet of Taweret, whose province was childbirth. No one else seemed to, or would admit it.

She was being crowded away from the bed. There were more midwives than the one. And blood. There was always blood in a birthing, but should there be so much?

Tama, larger and better placed, held her ground at the princess' side. Nofret pressed against the wall. Tama's dark face was clear in a shaft of light, intent, almost rapt. Slowly Nofret understood its expression. It was grief.

The first wail brought Nofret bolt upright. It was like no infant's she had ever heard. Tama's head was thrown back. She was keening as mourners did before the dead.

"No," said Nofret. "No, she's not. She hasn't even made a sound."

No one heard her. The midwives worked feverishly. One chanted what must have been a spell. It made no sense otherwise. They had knives. They would cut—were cutting—

Not only Tama was keening. Other servants, silly sheep,

were yowling, too. None of them was doing anything useful.

Nofret leaped on them, slapping, thrusting, cursing, driving them out. They went like the fools they were, weeping and caterwauling. "Princess Meketaten!" they wailed. "Princess Meketaten is dead!"

CHAPTER TEN

▲

PRINCESS Meketaten was dead. Her child, the daughter whom she never saw, tiny and perfectly formed, turned its face to the light of the lamps and died, too young and small to live beyond the womb.

In a room much richer, by the light of many more lamps, Princess Meritaten delivered herself of a daughter. The child was small, but never as small as Meketaten's, and frail; but she lived and she breathed, and she bore without flinching the prayers and magic of the priests. For all anyone knew, they succeeded in making her stronger.

Her father named her, taking her up in his hands: "Meritaten," he said. "Meritaten as her mother is, Meritaten-ta-Sherit."

What joy anyone had in her, another daughter born in the hour of sister-aunt and cousin-sister's death, Nofret could not imagine. The shrieking and wailing below seemed not to have impinged on anyone in Meritaten's presence until after the child was born and named. Then someone troubled to listen, or someone else dared to approach the king with news that he could not have looked for. No one had feared for Meketaten. No one had taken great notice of her, except to sacrifice her to her father's craving for a son. Now that she was dead, she was a stronger presence than she had ever been in life.

Nefertiti came first to the room where Meketaten was lying, walking with grace as she always did, but carrying herself as if she would shatter. People who had come to stare, to shriek, to fling themselves to their knees and beat their thighs in grief, fell back before the queen's coming. For all the notice she took of them, she might have been alone.

She bent over the small shrunken figure in the bed, the even smaller and more shrunken one laid beside it. One long delicate finger brushed first one cheek, then the other. The beautiful eyes closed.

Nofret half-stepped forward, ready to catch the queen if she fainted. But she was stronger than that. Her face was stark white under its paint. Her body swayed, but she kept her feet.

She did not speak. That was for the king, coming soon after her. He had run as she had been too dignified to do, straight from the living daughters to the two who were dead. He dropped to his knees beside the bed, took Meketaten's hand as gently as if she had been alive, and said, "My child. Oh, my child. Could you not have waited for the god to come for you?"

And what else had the god done, Nofret wondered, but that?

She bit her tongue till it bled, before she said something that would see her flayed alive. Soon enough she had sufficient to do: her lady came trailing servants and sisters. Their wailing rang within those narrow walls. It tried to seize Nofret, to sweep her away with it, but she was too solidly stubborn.

The princess was purely out of her head. Every fear that had ever beset her, every anxiety she had had from the moment her father made her sisters his wives, was gathered in this one place. If Nofret had not caught and held her, she would have rent her cheeks and her breast, then flung herself—at her sister who was dead, at her father whose folly had killed her, Nofret did not know and did not greatly care. She fought blindly and with dismaying strength, but Nofret was stronger.

If the queen saw, she gave no sign of it. She seemed to see only the dead. The king knelt and rocked from side to side, a silent, senseless dance of grief.

One would think, Nofret thought, that no royal child had ever died before. Had the king thought that by building his city all new and giving it a new god, he could keep death from touching him?

Ankhesenpaaten might have thought it, if the king had not. She sagged in Nofret's arms, weeping helplessly. Nofret's own eyes were dry, but her throat ached with the tears that refused to be shed.

Someone was going to have to turn practical very soon. It was night now, and cool as nights were in the desert, even in high summer. But the sun would rise, and with it the heat.

Even as Nofret thought of that and wondered who would have the sense to send for the embalmers, someone spoke. He did not speak loudly, and yet his voice cut through the wailing, muting it. "You there, fetch the embalmers. You—see that the bodies are washed and readied. You, tend the queen; you, the king. Where are the children's nurses? Fetch them." And when obedience was not instant: *"Move!"*

That bellow had been honed to pierce the clamor of a battlefield. Here in the palace it shook the walls, cut off the wailing, and put most of the crowding people to flight.

Nofret found that she was clinging to her lady nigh as tightly as her lady clung to her. Her ears were ringing.

General Horemheb surveyed the remnants of the field with a grim eye. Nofret could almost hear him wondering what anyone would do if he had not been there to rouse them. Soft pampered feckless fools. No warrior would be as weak as they were.

And yet, whatever he might be thinking, to the king he was softly polite, easing him away as the embalmers came with their bier. The king was docile, surprisingly so. Nofret might have expected him to fight, to cling to his daughter's body. But he yielded without a struggle. He was weeping unashamedly.

Nofret took Horemheb for an example and half-carried, half-dragged her own princess away. Ankhesenpaaten was notably less willing than her father. Nofret set her teeth and firmed her grip and kept on.

■   ■   ■

She got as far as the princesses' chambers before Ankhe-senpaaten broke free and bolted. Nofret sped after her, but she was lighter, faster, and more agile. It was all Nofret could do to keep her in sight.

She did not run, as Nofret had expected, toward the queens' rooms. For all her blindness of grief, she was aware of what she did: she darted round guards and ser-vants, eluded any who snatched at her.

She seemed to have a purpose. She ran straight and she ran swift, out of the palace, into the vast chain of courts and shrines that was the Great Temple of the Aten. It was deep night there, but the priests were getting ready for the dawn. Already many were awake and in the shrines, mourning the death of the king's child-wife.

The princess turned not toward the great altar with its heaps of offerings and its lamps that burned from dark to dawn, but toward one of the lesser shrines. It was little more than a pavilion in a courtyard, such as a prince might set up beside the pool in which he bathed; but instead of water, the bather bathed in light.

There was no light now, except that of a lamp beside the pavilion. The princess flung herself on the couch there, drew into a knot and lay breathing hard but otherwise still.

Nofret stood swaying, half furious, half afraid, but her lady did not move or speak. Slowly Nofret sank to the pavement beside the couch. If the princess got up, she would have to step over Nofret to escape. But she seemed to have come where she meant to come, and to be content to lie there. Even, after a while, to sleep.

Nofret slid in and out of a drowse. Each time she started awake, Ankhesenpaaten lay as before, coiled about her middle, asleep or skillfully feigning it.

No one came to disturb her. The night passed with dragging slowness. The stars faded. Little by little the sky lightened: Egypt's endless sky, pure empty vault, not even a cloud to mar it. Nofret was forgetting how the sky could be in Hatti and Mitanni, forgetting the touch of rain, the memory of cold and snow and the knife-edge of wind in the uplands of Hatti. Only Egypt was real, the river and the sand, the rain that fell so seldom as to be a marvel when it came.

This that she lay in was a sunrise pavilion, a place of worship and of drawing in strength from the sun's first rays. As the sun came at last, reaching long fingers over the temple's wall, the princess stirred and uncoiled.

Nofret tensed. But the princess only lay on her back after so long on her side, and stretched out her arms as if to embrace the sun. It washed her in light.

She lay for a long while, so long that Nofret almost drowsed again. But some instinct kept Nofret awake, held her on watch.

The princess convulsed. Nofret sprang. She sat upright, rigid in Nofret's hands, oblivious to them. When after a long moment she made no other move, Nofret drew back, but slowly.

The princess was not aware of her maid at all. She stared straight into the sun, strong as it was even so close to the horizon. "Father Aten," she said. "Father Aten, you lied.

You gave my sisters no sons. You took Meketaten. You *lied.*"

"Your father lied," said Nofret, "or heard what he wanted to hear, what the god never meant to say."

"The Aten lied," said the princess. "He killed my sister."

"Your father—" Nofret began, but she stopped. Ankhesenpaaten was not listening. She did not want to listen. Idiot. It was not her god who was at fault, but her fool of a father.

"Maybe," said the princess, "there is no Aten. Maybe there is nothing more than Amon-Re, and Amon-Re is angry with my father. So he gives him lies."

Since Nofret had never been a devotee of the Aten, she could hardly defend him to her lady. She held her tongue.

"Lies," said the princess. "The god lies. What if he lies to me? What if I can't tell? What if he kills me?"

"Not if I can help it," said Nofret grimly.

The princess turned to stare. Nofret was startled. She had been thinking herself unregarded, but those eyes with their bruise-dark shadows were piercingly keen and very much aware of her. "What can you do?" the princess demanded.

"Whatever I can," Nofret said.

"Why? You don't love me. If I died you could escape."

"Where would I go? Back to Hatti on foot, naked and alone?"

"You don't love me at all," said the princess.

"Does that matter?" asked Nofret. "As long as I look after you, do you care what I think of you?"

"Yes," said the princess. "I want you not to hate me."

"I never hated you," Nofret said.

"You hate us all. I see how you look at us, how you run away to be with your Apiru. Are they more to your taste than we are, with their beards and their robes and their reek of goats?"

That was grief, Nofret told herself. Grief and anger, striking at the one target that could not properly strike back.

"I don't hate you," Nofret said carefully. "I don't—admire—your father for what he's done, and yes, I've run away from that, but I came back."

"Because you had nowhere else to go."

"Princess," said Nofret. "Highness. Do you want a screaming argument? Do you think that would bring Meketaten back?"

For a moment Nofret was sure that her lady would leap on her. The princess did not move, did not look at Nofret, but glared into the fierce glare of the sun. "I wish I had died instead of Meketaten."

"You do not," said Nofret. "You wish Meketaten had never died at all."

"I wish—" The princess closed her eyes. Tears ran from beneath the lids. "I wish no one ever died! Why did she have to? We were all busy worrying about Meritaten. Nobody saw that Meketaten wasn't well. Why didn't we see? Why didn't someone say something?"

Nofret had tried, but no one had listened. She did not say so. There was no use in it.

Her lady wept sitting up with her eyes shut, rocking slightly, back and forth, back and forth. Her father had done the same thing on his knees by Meketaten's body. She did not seem any more aware of it than he had been.

Nofret crouched where she had been for so long, saying nothing, powerless to offer anything but her presence. Maybe that was enough. Maybe it did not matter at all.

CHAPTER ELEVEN

▲

MERITATEN'S daughter lived and seemed to thrive, and Meritaten herself recovered her strength, if slowly. Much of that slowness, surely, was grief.

The six daughters of Akhenaten and Nefertiti had been the six pillars on which the world of Akhetaten rested—so the songs said. Now one was broken and the rest tottered, unable to stand.

Queen Mother Tiye came down the river from Thebes to be with her children in their sorrow. She brought the princes with her, Smenkhkare more beautiful than ever, Tutankhaten now old enough to wait on the god in the temple, and very proud of it, too. The palace was livelier for their presence, the blackness of grief a little lighter, at least in Nofret's mind.

Nofret had not noticed till Tiye came, how muddled the palace had become. Nor had she known till it was gone, how light but firm a rein the queen had kept on the servants and on the workings of the king's household. When Meketaten died, Nefertiti simply, quietly stopped noticing anything or anyone but her daughter who was dead and her daughters who were alive. She did not even, as far as Nofret knew, notice her husband. The king was going to Lady Kiya every night, or so it was said among the servants. Some had a wager on whether, with Nefertiti so distracted, Kiya would conceive at last, and give the king a son.

Tiye's coming did not remove the Lady Kiya from the king's bed—Tiye in fact was heard to observe that he was well served to take such fruitful consolation—but it kept the servants too busy to gossip overmuch. Queen Nefertiti had ruled with the soft relentlessness of water. Queen Mother Tiye was iron and stone: hard, unsparing, but fair enough in her judgments.

Nofret did her best to keep her head down, to do her duties, to escape the queen mother's notice. She thought she was succeeding, until she came back from a morning of running about the city with Johanan and found her lady being hurried into a gown by one of the younger princesses' nurses. "You," said Ankhesenpaaten as soon as Nofret crossed the threshold, "come with me."

Nofret was not even given time to make herself presentable. Sweating, street-dusty, still clutching the bit of scarf that she had found and coveted in the market, she trotted in her princess' wake. She managed as she went to twist the scarf into a fillet and bind it about her brows. It looked rakish, no doubt, and detestably foreign, but her lady did not say anything.

Tiye had set up court in the queen's house, in the hall that the queen favored for audiences within the household. She sat small and very erect in Nefertiti's gilded chair, the one with legs like columns of papyrus, and the back carved and gilded and inlaid with ivory. Nefertiti had needed no footstool although she affected one shaped like a cluster of lilies. Tiye's delicate sandaled feet just rested on it. She was crowned with golden plumes, but her wig was of a style that Nofret had not seen before: loose curling locks that were not black but a wonderful deep red.

Nofret realized that the queen mother was not wearing a wig; that the hair was her own, thick and beautiful. She was at ease, then, Nofret thought, in privacy such as queens knew, with attendants crowding about and courtiers clustering at the door. Nofret was not unduly comforted. The eyes that examined her and her princess impartially and with minute attention were grey like iron, and like iron they were cold, with a deadly edge. The warmth that glimmered in them as they rested on her granddaughter was a thin and transitory thing, like the sheen of sunset on the river.

Ankhesenpaaten rose from her knees to sit at the queen mother's feet. The queen mother rested a hand on her head, stroking the child's shaved skull, the glossy thickness of the sidelock. The princess sighed and leaned against her grandmother's knee.

"Has it been so terrible, then?" Tiye asked her.

She shook her head. But she said, "It will never be the same again."

"That is the way of time and the gods," Tiye said. "All things change and pass."

"But not so soon!" the princess cried. "Not like this!"

"This of all ways that the gods may choose," said Tiye. "The gods are cruel, child."

"The gods are false. All but the Aten. Father says so."

"The Aten is a god," Tiye said.

The princess shook her head and buried her face in her grandmother's knees. Tiye petted her as if she had been a cat. She shivered and clung tighter.

Nofret, kneeling, sitting on her heels, invisible as a servant should be, kept her eyes down as best she could. But they were always the least servile of her body's possessions. They kept wanting to look about, to see who was there. Not Prince Smenkhkare; he would be in the king's house as a young man should. Prince Tutankhaten was there, with a nurse to make sure of it—he looked as if he would have liked to leap into the princess' lap.

His nurse let her guard slip; or, Nofret thought nastily, saw a convenient way to escape her duty. Tutankhaten slipped free and flung himself on Nofret. She was braced for him, and prepared for his young strength, too. His baby softness was all but gone; he was a limber child, light-boned as his brother's daughters were, but sturdy and wiry and strong. He was as imperious as ever, too. "Take me to visit the horses," he said.

Away from his mother's eye Nofret would have slapped him lightly to get his attention. Here she could only say, "Not now. Hasn't anybody taught you to be polite when your mother has guests?"

"You aren't guests," he said. "You're family."

"I am not," said Nofret.

"You are too," he said. "When will you take me to see the horses?"

"Young Reed-in-the-River," said Tiye with tenderness that she did not spare for her grandchildren, "hush your rattling. You will see the horses when I give you leave."

"I want to see them now," said Tutankhaten.

The princess raised her head. "I will take you for a ride in my chariot," she said. "Tomorrow. Just as the sun comes up. Can you be ready that early?"

"I can be ready all night," said Tutankhaten. "Why can't I go now?"

"Because I'm not going now," the princess said.

"But why—"

"He is now," said his mother, "wishing to know the why of everything. He has a tutor whose sole duty is to answer his questions. To tell him why. You may," she said to her son, "go and ask Ptahmose. Now, if it pleases you."

"Ptahmose is asleep," said Tutankhaten. "I want to stay with Nofret. And Lotus Blossom," he said, with a glance at the princess. "I'll be quiet. I promise."

Nofret bit her lip. How like this race of kings to find a cure for the young child's siege of whys: to give him a servant who could answer, or feign to, until he wearied of the game. She wondered if the king had had such a servitor. And if he had, had he gained his notions of godhead from some answer meant simply to shut him up?

If she was not careful she would begin to giggle. And once she started she would not be able to stop. She made herself look at Tiye. That strong beautiful face sobered her admirably, and stilled her like a mouse under an owl's eye.

When Tiye spoke, it was to her granddaughter, but Nofret wondered if some of it was meant for her. "You have to be strong," she said. "As terrible as these days are, as little as your mother and father can bear them, someone is needed who can go on, who can think and plan and rule even in grief."

"I'm not old enough," the princess said.

"That is whining," said her grandmother. "You are old enough to be angry that your sister is dead, and old enough to be troubled that your mother is taking it so badly."

"Mother didn't want Father to marry Meketaten," the princess said. "She gave in because it was the god's will. Now the god has taken Meketaten. Mother won't forgive him for that."

"Nor will you," said Tiye, "and maybe that is as it should be. But you cannot afford to break, simply because your mother has chosen to."

"Meritaten can be strong," said the princess. "She's older than I am."

"She never had the strength that you have," Tiye said, "and she has her own fears and her own pain, and the baby to look after. No, child. You can't evade this duty. No more than I can."

"I'll never be as strong as you," said the princess.

Tiye bent toward her and lowered her voice. "I tell you a secret, child. I'm not strong, either. But someone has to keep her wits about her, and no one else seems likely to."

The princess frowned. Nofret could see her mind coming to itself. So, Nofret judged, could Tiye. Tiye wisely did not press her, but let her do her own thinking.

Tutankhaten began to wriggle in Nofret's grip. Nofret shook him to make him stop. For a wonder he obeyed.

At length, slowly, the princess said, "I can't be strong for me, but I can help you, and be as strong as you need me to be. Unless you want me to forgive the Aten for taking Meketaten.''

"I would rather you forgave your father for it,'' Tiye said.

''Father only did what the Aten made him do,'' said the princess.

''Yes,'' said Tiye, but distantly, as if she believed it no more than Nofret did.

The princess did not hear, or if she heard, did not heed. She drew herself up and firmed her chin. ''Majesty. What would you have me do?''

Tiye's approval was a subtle thing: a warming of the eyes, an inclination of the head. ''First,'' she said, ''see that your younger sisters are properly looked after. Then come to me in the hall of audience. It's time you knew what exactly it is that a queen does.''

The princess knew long since, of course. She had sat or stood beside her mother's throne since she was old enough to stand on her own. But this time she would not be allowed to idle about, drowsing or playing with a monkey or a gazelle, while her mother said and did things that she barely took notice of. She would listen and maybe even respond as a queen should, as Tiye clearly meant to teach her.

Nofret wondered if she knew what that meant. Tiye was instructing her in the art of being a ruling queen—as her mother had never precisely done. Ankhesenpaaten had been the third princess, the one who would come late if at all to queenship. Now she was second, and her elder sister might prove as frail as Meketaten had. Then the princess would have to be queen in truth, and swiftly, however potent her grief.

■　■　■

Often in that year after Meketaten died, Nofret wondered if Tiye had a gift of foresight. She was not a prophet as

Leah was, not that Nofret ever saw, but she saw clearly and she saw true—and everything she saw that year was ill.

Meketaten and the daughter that she had borne were buried after the threescore days and ten of the embalming, laid in the king's tomb in its remote and desolate valley. The king had a carving made for her in the tomb, showing himself and his queen and the rest of his daughters mourning their dead. She would see that for all the days of her death, and know that she was loved.

Nofret would have preferred her to know it while she lived, or even in the hour when she died. But no one was asking Nofret. No one but Johanan, and Leah who always asked the hard questions.

"You always *ask*," Nofret said to her one evening after Meketaten's burial, "but you never answer. Except when you speak in riddles."

"I make perfect sense to myself," Leah said.

Nofret laughed in spite of herself.

"There," said Leah. "You see. There's laughter in you still."

"It hurts," Nofret said. "Like a muscle I haven't used in years."

"You should train in laughter as a soldier trains in war," said Leah. "For when it gets too dark to see, when you most need light."

Nofret did not see how that could be. All at once she was empty of mirth, cold and scared—and for no reason that she could name. "Something's coming, isn't it? Something horrible. Queen Mother Tiye sees it, too. She's training my princess to be a queen."

"Queen Mother Tiye has been living in Thebes, where Amon once was sole lord and god. She knows what Egypt thinks of her so-eccentric son. She prepares for whatever comes—however dreadful that may be."

"Queens," said Nofret, "or kings, and prophets. They're much the same. Aren't they?"

"I suppose," said Leah. "I can't see myself in a crown or sitting on a throne, all in gold and jewels. I'm too plain a creature for that."

Nofret looked at her with her head crowned with silver braids under the plain black veil, sitting in the chair that no one else ever presumed to claim, and discovered that she did, after all, remember how to laugh.

▪ ▪ ▪

That was the night, though Nofret did not know it till long after, when the plague came to Akhetaten. It struck first in the poorer quarter, riding in on a boat from the Delta or brought by a traveler from the north who fell ill in his lodging and died before his landlord could cast him into the street. It was slow to begin, creeping insidiously from house to house, taking a sickly child, an old man, a woman weakened in childbirth.

The weak always died. Even the palace knew that, as it mourned even yet for Meketaten. But this new sickness was not content to fell only the feeble. It tasted the blood and living spirit of the strong, and found them good, and settled to the feast.

The queen mother had been intending to return to Thebes after Meketaten's funeral. The weakness that she found in the king's palace and in the queen's will had kept her in Akhetaten; the plague bound her there. Thebes, south of Akhetaten, was not yet beset. Memphis in the north suffered terribly: hundreds dead, the messengers said; thousands, rumor declared, and more every hour. The houses of the embalmers, even in refusing to take any who could not pay and pay high, were filled to overflowing. They were scanting the rite, people said, dipping the dead in natron for a day or two and thrusting them aside till they could be wrapped in haste and buried with meager ceremony.

Some of those people were highborn, passing swiftly through Akhetaten on their way south to what they fancied was safety. Some were already ill: already fevered, already coughing, blaming the sun and the desert dryness. They urged the king to flee with them.

But the king was convinced that the Aten would protect him. He said so with unwearying patience, smiling his dreamer's smile, which his daughters' death had done little to dim. Lady Kiya, rumor had it among the servants, was ill in the mornings of late. She had sworn her maids to silence, but her bath-servants were under no such stricture. Nofret hoped that she concealed her condition successfully till it was too late for even a queen's magic to harm the child. A son, Nofret prayed to any god who would hear. A son to keep the king away from Nofret's princess.

If the gods heard, they were too busy to answer. Little Sotepenre had a restless night, fretting and whining as she had not done since she was very small. Her nurse, deep asleep, paid no attention. Nofret got up at last, speeded on her way by her lady's sleepy irritation, and stepped over the soddenly sleeping nurse to shake the child into quiet.

Even as she took hold of Sotepenre's shoulders, she went cold and still inside. Not only the nightlamp's glow made the child seem flushed. She was burning hot, and yet she shivered.

It could be a simple fever, Nofret told herself. It did not need to be the plague.

That was foolish, and she knew it. The nurse was drunk on barley beer: a trick to keep sickness at bay. Maybe for her it succeeded.

The other young princesses were not ill. Not yet, Nofret thought. Her lady was awake and minded to be thoroughly unreasonable. "Can't you shut her *up?*"

"Be quiet," said Nofret, so sharp and short that the

princess obeyed out of sheer indignation. Nofret lowered
her voice. "Your sister is sick. If it pleases your royal
highness, would you deign to send for a physician?"

The princess was out of bed, braced to confront Nofret,
but a long look at Sotepenre brought her fully to her
senses. The other children's nurses were awake and blinking sleepily, all but the woman who was supposed to be
tending Sotepenre. Carefully, calmly, Ankhesenpaaten
said, "Take the children to the queens' house. They can
sleep in one of the ladies' rooms for tonight. You, Nofret,
fetch someone to look after my sister. Preferably not someone who will shriek and run from a bit of fever."

Nofret had not intended to be sent out, but there was no
denying the need. The plague had entered the palace. It
would not leave till it had fed.

CHAPTER TWELVE

▲

THE plague had come to the palace. Sotepenre was only
the first to fall ill of it. The servants succumbed one by
one to the fever. So too the princesses. And the queen.
And the queen mother.

But not the king. Nor, as far as it could matter, Nofret.
The queen mother sent her younger sons away to Thebes
as soon as she knew that Sotepenre was ill. Her eldest son
would not move, nor would he cease to repeat, "The god
protects me."

"Only you," said Tiye with rare bitterness. She was
barely ill yet, holding everything in those small and de-
ceptively delicate hands. The king spent all his hours in
the temple, lying by day in the sun till he burned as brown
as a farmer in the fields, sleeping at night before the altar

of the Aten, making his every moment a prayer. That left him no time to be king; so Tiye was king in his name.

She kept Ankhesenpaaten by her. The rest of the princesses, and Queen Nefertiti already swaying with fever, had gone into the temple with the king. He would have had them lie in the sun to be made strong as he was strong, but the healer-priests forbade. They lay in the courts of the sun under canopies wetted often with water, bathed and soothed and plied with healing draughts by priests whose art was the cooling of fever.

The priests themselves fell ill as so many others had, but pressed on, waging war against the plague. So did everyone who could stand. One tended the sick or one buried the dead, or one did what one could to keep the living alive with food, drink, rest.

Rest was most difficult of all. No one servant could be spared for a single princess, not with so many sick or dying or dead. Nofret did whatever she was bidden to do, which was most often the queen mother's will; or else she did what needed doing, as she saw the need.

Her lady caught the fever, but lightly. Maybe the force of stubborn will was enough to hold it at bay. But if that had been so, then Queen Mother Tiye would not have taken sick at all.

Maybe the queen mother failed of her strength. She was the mother of a grown son. She had granddaughters and a great-granddaughter. Maybe her heart judged that she had lived and fought and ruled enough.

Her will resisted. When Ankhesenpaaten grew flushed and irascible, Tiye saw the child put to bed and a guard set on her, and called for healers to tend her. Nofret should have stayed with her, but Tiye's eyes had a glitter that Nofret did not like.

The princess was being looked after as well as anyone could be. No one was looking after Tiye.

Strange to think such a thing of so great a queen. But

she did not seem so mighty on this day in the midst of the plague. Only a tired, aging woman in whose hands the whole of the Two Lands had come to rest.

Messengers kept coming, most with pleas for aid from the lords of the Delta and the north. Embassies still came, though only, after a while, from the south. There were still petitions to hear, audiences to hold, a city and a palace to watch over. There were so many dead, so many dying, so few to carry out her commands.

Nofret did not try to leave the palace. Sometimes she climbed to the top of the wall and looked out across the city. It looked much as it always had, save that the streets were all but empty. It smelled of sun and dust, and dung, and death.

■ ■ ■

Sotepenre died in the dark before dawn, the seventh day after she fell ill. Her sisters whom Nofret had always called the Beauties, because they were named for the beauty of the god, Neferneferuaten and Neferneferure, died within an hour of one another on the evening that their youngest sister died.

Nefertiti did not know that she had lost three more of her daughters, that they would follow Meketaten so soon through the lands of the dead. She was deep in a dream of fever, a dream that deepened into sleep, and from sleep into death.

She was beautiful upon her bier: beautiful and cold as she had ever been alive. For a long while no one knew that she had died. Her healer-priests were all ill themselves, or strove to tend Meritaten and her baby, who were tossing in delirium.

The baby's wailing was thin and piercing. Nofret heard it even in the outer court as she came in on the queen mother's errand, to tell the king that the embalmers must take his children. She found the king lying in the sun as always, the dead princesses borne away out of the light and heat, the living princesses insensible to anything but their own burning dreams, and the queen lying utterly still.

There was a strange and ringing clarity in it. The sunlight was blinding, and yet Nofret saw perfectly well. She saw every pillar of that courtyard, every stone of its paving, every thread in the canopy of the pavilion. So much gold, she thought. Egyptians would clothe themselves completely in it if they could.

Cold comfort in the face of death. She had a fever, she realized. It did not matter much. She could walk, and do as she was told.

The baby's cries hiccoughed into silence. She was sucking at the breast of a tired but seemingly hale nurse—only a little and with much fretting, but Nofret knew a glimmer of hope. Maybe the little one, frail as she appeared to be, would get well.

There was no such hope for the queen. Nofret bent over the bed on which she lay. In the heat of the day, even under the canopy, her hand was warm. But there was no life in it. Her face for all its beauty had the look that death brings: the skull drawn close beneath the skin, the living spirit gone out of it, leaving it empty and cold.

Nofret straightened slowly. There should have been more people about. She only saw the handful tending Meritaten and the baby, and the king lying in the sun, blind to everything but that.

He was not dead. He was not even sick. He recoiled from the prodding of Nofret's foot, drawing into a knot like a child waked irascible from sleep.

She had no patience left, and no fear of him, either as king or as god. He was only a man, and a fool at that.

"Wake up," she said roughly. "Get up. The queen is dead."

The king blinked at her. "No one is dead. The god protects me."

"The queen is dead," Nofret said again.

"No," said the king.

She dragged him to his feet. He was a tall man, but soft, and meeker than a king should be, yielding to her fierce impatience. "Wake up!" she shouted at him. "Look about you! While you prayed your god to protect your miserable carcass, your whole city is dying or dead. Your daughters are dead. Your queen is dead. *Look* at her!"

The king looked. He looked long and long. Then he began to sway. "No," he said. "Oh, no. No, no, no."

Fool, and mad. Nofret turned from him in disgust.

He would stay there, rocking and moaning his denial, until the embalmers came. He was good for nothing else. His mother would have to be king, and queen too, unless Lady Kiya could be persuaded to come out of the room in which she had barricaded herself. If she was still alive. Nofret had not looked, to be sure.

The king could stay where he was. Nofret should go back to the queen mother. Tiye must know that Nefertiti was dead.

Something hurtled past Nofret. She thought it a shadow till she felt the wind of its speed. It was a man, naked, bareheaded, stripped of anything that could mark him for a king.

He still ran like a woman, knock-kneed, ill-balanced. But a woman could run fast enough for the purpose; so could the king. He ran too fast for Nofret to catch.

She did not care at all, and yet she followed him. The guards were all sick or fled. No one would look after him if she did not, unless she reckoned on his god.

He was still the king. Even naked, even out of his head with the cold shock of truth.

He had a good turn of speed for a man who never stood when he could sit, nor walked when he could ride. She was staggering and gasping when he slowed to an ungainly trot. He had run right out of the city, past the living who did not know him and the dead who knew nothing.

He was running toward his tomb, Nofret thought, insofar as she had mind to think. Better if he had sought the river, to drown in it. She would have welcomed that. Cool water closing over her head, cool darkness covering her eyes.

Instead she had the sun beating down and the dust of the road on her tongue. The king had slowed, but she could not lengthen her stride to catch him. Not till he stumbled and fell.

She had a little malice left in her. She did not leap to catch him. But when he lifted himself up she was there, pulling at his arm, getting him to his feet. He was smeared with dust and sweat and tears. His hands and knees were torn. A rivulet of blood ran down his shin.

The sun was a hammer on her skull. She could barely think, let alone see. She pulled the king with her toward the one place she could conceive of to go, that was close and cool, and quiet.

Later it would occur to her that she might have brought the sickness into the workmen's village. But that was foolish. The dead of means had come here to the house of the embalmers. Their sickness must have come with them.

The village was quiet, but then it always was at midday. The men and boys labored among the tombs. The women kept to the cool of their houses. Evening would find them gossiping at the well or gathering in the market.

Nofret heard no wailing, no sounds of mourning. There were no sick lying in the street, no dead to be carried away to a common grave. A dog or two followed her, fascinated by the man she brought with her. They sniffed at his heels but did not offer to nip.

He took no more notice of them than he did of anything else. He was sniveling again. Tears ran down his long peculiar face and dripped from his chin.

Leah was sitting in the doorway of Aharon's house, spinning thread with gnarled deft hands, winding it on a spindle. Johanan sat cross-legged with the basket of wool on his lap and a young goat trying to clamber in.

They received Nofret with a blessed lack of surprise. Her companion made Johanan roll his eyes like a startled colt, but Leah was unshakably serene. She led them within, gave them cool water to wash in and cool water to drink, clothed them in robes of the desert people, and coaxed them to rest on the heaped rugs of the room where Nofret had sat or dined so often.

Slowly Nofret came to herself. The king was half lying, half sitting opposite her, blinking as if he had roused from sleep. Johanan tried desperately hard not to stare, but his eyes kept darting under lowered brows.

Finally he could not contain himself. He hissed at Nofret. "That isn't—really—"

"Of course it is," his grandmother said, flinging him into worse confusion.

"But what is he doing—"

"I ran away," the king said. Even Nofret was surprised, though maybe Leah was not. He sounded as sane as she had ever heard him, and he barely stammered at all. "It is true, isn't it? The Beautiful One is dead."

"Yes," said Nofret.

His face tightened, but he was in command of himself. "Even as a child I never ran away. It's a peculiar sensation."

"You should have done it then," said Nofret, "instead of leaving it for when your people need you. Your mother has been ruling in your name. Isn't it time you did it for yourself?"

"But," he said perfectly reasonably, "how can I? My beloved is dead."

Nofret opened her mouth, then shut it again.

It was Leah who said, "While she lived she was your pillar and prop, and much of your intelligence, too."

He took no offense. He nodded. It was strange to see

that his eyes were dry, his face calm, his voice level, and to know that that in him was grief beyond endurance. "There's no time, you see. The god takes everything, leaves nothing. She was the half of me that could act and rule and think."

"In your name," muttered Nofret. "Always in your name."

"No," he said. "For herself, too. For the children. And always, always for the god." He wrapped his arms about himself and rocked. "Oh, I burn, I burn."

Johanan went white. His grandmother said, "No, it's not the plague. His god protects him from that—and afflicts him with another fever altogether. A fire in the dark, yes, Lord Pharaoh?"

"A fire always," he said. "My beloved is dead. My children—the son who never comes—they will say that Amon is angry. That this is a visitation upon us and upon me."

"Isn't it?" Nofret demanded.

"No," he said. "The god tests me. If I have not the strength, and I fear I do not—"

"You have to," said Leah, sounding so much like the queen mother that Nofret blinked. But they were kin, after all, of the spirit as well as the body. "The Beautiful One is gone. Her king must be king in more than name."

He looked about. His mouth twisted.

Leah's smile had a sword's edge. "What do I know of kings and kingship? Why, nothing, Lord of the Two Lands. But I know the ruling of a household, and I know what it is that a strong woman does when her man is weak. I know what a weak man does when his prop is taken away."

"Why, so do I," he said. "He totters. He falls."

"I do not think," said Leah, "that you are weak. God-ridden, yes, beyond all help or mercy. But weak you are not. And your god created you to be king."

"My god created me to serve him," said the king. "It suited his whim to set me in the Great House."

"Which you have fled," said Leah, "now that your life of ease has grown hard."

For the first time Nofret saw a spark of temper in the placid king. "It was never easy! The jewels, the gold, the rich banquets, the people bowing, scraping, worshipping at my feet . . . those are all any commoner sees of what it is to be king. But jewels are cold lovers, and gold glitters but has no warmth of its own."

"And the banquets cloy in the stomach, and the wine turns foul by morning." Leah shook her head sharply. "What of the people, Lord Pharaoh? What of the grovelers at your feet? Do you even know their names?"

"I know what is fitting for me to know," he said stiffly.

"You know nothing," said Leah. "Have you ever spoken to a commoner face to face, as a man and not a petition, a human spirit and not a pair of hands meant only to serve you? Have you ever cared what anyone feels or thinks or sees, except in your service?

"Your god," said Leah, "is a god for you and no other—Akhenaten, who alone can hear him speak. How easy for you; how convenient, since no one else can know when you err, or when you lie."

"It is the truth," he said.

"It is the truth you want to see," said Leah. And at the curl of his lip: "Ah, so others have said the same, have they? Did they ever go so far as to tell you what this truth has done? People want their gods. *Their* gods, Lord Pharaoh. Gods whom they can speak to, beg favors of, even revile when their luck is bad. They don't want a god who can only talk to one man, and that man patently cares nothing for any of them."

"I love my people," said the king. "My every prayer is on their behalf."

"You pray for your own power, your own family, your

own body's protection. You think that that is enough, that when you're done with the god's favors, your people will be content with the leavings. If those leavings are sickness and death while you go on untouched, do you imagine that anyone will love you for them?''

''I tell the truth,'' he said. ''I say what the god bids me say.''

''Then your god is a fool,'' said Leah. ''Amon whom you hate so much, from whose attributes you took your own god—Amon knows what your Aten seems not to understand. A god may begin in one man's heart, but if that god is to live, he must be fed and nourished on the people's belief. Many people, Lord Pharaoh. Not only one man and his dutiful wife and his children who know no better.''

''I have commanded,'' he said. ''I have made the Aten chief and only god in the Two Lands.''

''No king can command a man's heart,'' Leah shot back. ''No, not even you. Not with words and edicts, or ever with the breaking down of temples. You took away the gods whom they knew and gave them one whom only you can know. That's no god they can worship. Not where it matters. Not in their hearts.''

Nofret had forgotten to breathe. She was breathtakingly bold, she knew that very well, but Leah had no fear at all, and no mercy either. Nofret knew somehow that if Leah had been standing in front of the king in his hall of audience, with him sitting crowned on his throne and an army of guards about him, she would still have said what she said to him in her own house. Things that even Nefertiti, even Tiye, had never dared to say.

The king was too shocked, maybe, to be angry. Princes, Nofret had noticed, were not punished as lesser children were. Kings were not punished at all, unless they were deposed; then they paid high for their arrogance.

''Your god is a good god,'' Leah said, ''a useful god, even a true one. But without a people to worship him, he's as mortal as you are. He lives and dies with you, because no one else can know him.''

"But if everyone knew him," the king protested, "everyone would be blinded by the light. Then who would be left to do what needs doing?''

"Maybe," said Leah, "if more people knew him, the light would be gentler and people better able to think, even when the god's attention is on them.''

The king's face brightened at that. He was like a child, Nofret thought, with a child's mingling of stubborn purpose and malleable will. He did not lack intelligence. God-ridden or merely mad though he might be, he was no simpleton. "Do you think," he asked Leah, "that people would—'' Then he darkened. "No, not my people. If I let them choose, they'll only go back to their old gods.''

"Some wouldn't," Leah said. "Some would come to him of their own accord. Those would bring others, who would bring others. It would grow as living things do, and endure past a mortal lifetime.''

"No," said the king. "Your people maybe can do this. Mine have so many thousand years of gods. One who comes new, who comes alone, is like a child against an army.''

"What then when you die?" Leah asked. "Your god will die, too, with no one but you to believe in him.''

"My god is, whether the world believes, or one man. Or," said the king, "one woman. I'll leave a son to be his voice among men. I leave daughters—'' He faltered.

"Meritaten lives, and Meritaten-ta-Sherit," Nofret said, "and Ankhesenpaaten.''

"My beautiful ones? My little Sotepenre?''

"Dead," said Nofret.

His head bowed as if suddenly it was too heavy for his neck. "The Aten tests me," he said. "Oh, how he tests me.''

"He kills your children," Nofret snapped. "Can't you

tell him to stop? People are saying it's not the Aten at all, not any false god, but all the true gods of Egypt rising up against the usurper.''

"No one compels my god," said the king.

"You can't even ask?" Nofret had had enough. The incongruity of it twisted in her like pain, the king dressed like an Apiru of the desert and arguing the niceties of divine will with Leah the prophet while in the palace his children lay dying or dead. "You may be free to run away. I am going back to my duties. The queen mother needs any of us who can walk or stand. May you have joy of your leisure, my lord king."

She had shocked him maybe more than Leah had. She did not know why. Leah had told him the truth unadorned. Nofret simply told him what she meant to do. Maybe that was why he looked so stunned. Akhenaten the king was not a man who liked to act if he could dream instead.

He rose, unfolding himself like a long-legged bird. The robe he wore must have been Aharon's: it was long enough and more than wide enough. He ignored it except to shake the sleeves away from his hands. They fell back at once. He thrust them aside with an irritable gesture, rolled them up as a laborer would, and then appeared to forget them. "You cannot go," he said to Nofret. "I forbid you."

Nofret faced him. Her heart was beating hard. "I serve your daughter and the queen mother. They both need me far more than you do. Majesty."

"I have no other attendant here," he said. He sounded haughty and yet oddly frightened. Probably he had never been alone in his life, never been anywhere without at least a dozen people crowded into his shadow.

Here was only Nofret, and Leah who served no man that Nofret knew of, and Johanan big-eyed and silent. Johanan had been tongue-tied ever since he recognized the king. Nofret had never taken him for the sort to be awed speechless by any man, even Akhenaten. It seemed she did not know him as well as she thought she had.

"These people," she said to the king, "are friends to me. I trust them. They'll look after you till it pleases you to come back to your palace."

His back was stiff; so were his lips as he spoke. "My palace and my people and my duties. I understand you very well. You will escort me back to them."

That was not what Nofret wanted at all. It was what she had done, no question of that. She had issued a challenge. The king was man enough after all: he had risen to it.

"Come then," she said ungraciously, "and be quick. Night will catch us before we get to the gate."

"And the gate closes at sunset." He met her stare. "Yes, there are a few things I do notice."

The king was not a man whom Nofret could like, nor would he have cared if she had. She certainly did not admire him. Yet she had to grant that he was interesting. He seldom did or said what one would expect.

She said what was polite to Leah, and Leah smiled, understanding. The king of course did not say anything. Kings did not thank commoners for kindness that was only their royal due.

Walking stiffly, face to the setting sun, Nofret led the king back to Akhetaten.

CHAPTER THIRTEEN

▲

THE king returned to his palace but did not, as far as Nofret could see, become any stronger a king for his lessoning at Leah's knee. He did devote only his days to the temple, returning at night to his own bed, often with Lady Kiya in it. He mourned Nefertiti, there was no doubt of that. But mourning had never, that Nofret had observed, kept a man from taking pleasure where he could get it.

Queen Nefertiti and her children were given the full seventy days of embalming. The embalmers might lessen the time to nothing for a mere prince of the Two Lands, but for the queen and the princesses they spared no tiniest detail of their rite.

Well before the time was ended, Queen Mother Tiye was laid beside them in the vats of natron.

She concealed her sickness with the skill of a woman accustomed to the sleights of courts, ruling as she had since the plague began, until she rose from the throne after a long day of audience, staggered and fell into Ankhesenpaaten's arms.

The princess braced against the sudden weight. "Grandmother," she said. "Lady." She touched palm to the queen mother's cheek and recoiled.

Nofret did not need to touch Tiye to know how she burned. Most who died of this plague caught fire slowly and sank by degrees into ash. A few went up like torches, from weakness and swelling fever to death in a day or a night.

For Tiye it was not even so long. Nofret shouted for guards, servants, anyone who would come. Two pale and frightened guards and a single servant who had come forth alive from the fever came to her call, took up the queen mother and carried her to her bed.

The princess would not let go her hand. She was awake and aware: once she was laid in bed with a maid easing crown and robe and jewels from her and bathing her with cool water, she said in a husk of her old strong voice, "Listen to me. Don't interrupt."

The princess opened her mouth to do just that, but Tiye overrode her. "You must look after your father. He is not capable of ruling alone, nor can he discipline his mind to do everything that must be done. You must do it, little

Lotus Blossom: you and your sister, if she's of any more use than your father. Seek out wise counselors. Lord Ay, if he lives, is loyal and circumspect and will serve you well. Most of your father's toadies and parvenus are useless if not worse. Avoid them as you can. The priests of the old gods are dangerous. They fear your father not at all, although I taught them to respect the divinity of his kingship. You must continue to teach them. Never let them forget. Never let them grow too bold. Kings have died before for causes that were less than certain—and no king has ever been as truly hateful to them as this.''

The princess tried more than once to speak. But Tiye would not hear her. Time was short, the fever mounting, her voice sinking as she told over all the lessons in queenship that she had given this child since the plague began.

The princess received them as if they had been blows. At first she wept. But as Tiye went on, the tears dried. Her face went white, her body rigid. Her hand that gripped the queen mother's hand looked fair to break those fragile bones, until with a gasp she forced her fingers to unlock.

She did not, as Nofret had more than half expected, beg Tiye not to die. Death on death had taught them all the uselessness of such follies.

Tiye held souls to body by raw will. Nofret heard the death-rattle through the words she spoke, the last of them forced through it. ''Look after my little one, my Tutankhaten. See that he remembers me.''

The princess bent her head. Tiye smiled faintly as the life slipped out of her. Nofret saw it go, like the passing of a shadow in an empty room.

The princess gasped, caught at air. If anything had winged past her, it was too insubstantial for mortal hands to catch. ''Grandmother,'' she said. ''Tiye.''

But the power of names was not enough to bring back the dead. The princess sucked in a breath. Now, thought Nofret, she would howl her grief.

She surprised Nofret. She pushed herself to her feet. There was no one here but the two of them. Everyone else was dead or fled. She smoothed the coverlet over the lifeless body, kissed the brow that must be fever-warm still.

She straightened. She moved as if her every bone and muscle ached. "Fetch a guard," she said, "or a servant. Someone to watch over her. Someone must still be alive here."

Someone was: a guard almost too sodden with beer to stand up sobered remarkably quickly for the dashing of a half-jar of beer in his face. While he gasped and sputtered, Nofret said in a voice like a slap, "Get up and move. Queen Tiye is dead. She needs a man to guard her body."

The man was too befuddled to bolt, or even to disobey. Propped up against a wall with his spear for a brace, reeking of beer, he was at least a breathing body to watch over the one that would never breathe again.

"When morning comes," said the princess in a still, cold voice, "there will be order in this palace. No more drunken guards. No more servants running for no one knows where."

Nofret did not say anything. Somewhere in the long ordeal of the plague, the child had become a woman. A woman who must be a queen.

She walked, and Nofret walked in her shadow, through the queens' palace to the rooms in which Meritaten had shut herself. To keep her daughter safe, her messenger had said; to escape the plague. As far as Nofret knew, she might have died, and no one had sent word because no one was left alive.

Meritaten's rooms were strange after the emptiness of the rest. The guard at the door was awake, aware, and much upon his dignity. The servants within were as they should be, maids to wait on the young and now only queen, and an elderly steward to conduct the visitors to his mistress.

She had been asleep. Her daughter was in the bed still, nested in cushions. She sat in a chair, dressed in a light, transparent robe. Her body was little less childlike than her sister's. Her face was much the same, delicately lovely, but softer, less clean-drawn.

She had her father's capacity for ignoring the inconvenient or the unpleasant. She did not even seem perturbed by the plague that raged beyond her safe and solid walls. She greeted her sister warmly as these princes would think of it, cool to indifference to Nofret's foreign-born eye.

Ankhesenpaaten endured the niceties, the dance of politeness that would have made Nofret scream with impatience. She sat in a chair across from her sister's, she sipped date wine and pretended to nibble a bit of cake, she listened to Meritaten's inconsequential chatter and murmured inconsequentialities of her own.

Well after Nofret would have ended the game, well before Meritaten might have chosen to, Ankhesenpaaten said, "Grandmother is dead."

Meritaten paled but kept her composure. "I grieve for her," she said.

Ankhesenpaaten inclined her head. "So do we all. The whole world is sick with grief. So many dead. So many who still could die."

Meritaten was stark white. "Not I. Not my Meritaten-too."

"May the god grant it," said Ankhesenpaaten. "Father lives and is well. Everyone else——" Her voice broke, but she mastered it. "Everyone else is gone."

"Lady Kiya?"

That was more perceptive, and more to the point, than Nofret might have expected. Ankhesenpaaten did not seem startled by it. "She keeps Father warm of nights."

As Meritaten did not. Neither sister remarked on it. Meritaten said, "Then we are all that is left. Is Father . . . awake?"

"As much as he ever is," said Ankhesenpaaten. "We have to do something, Mayet. No one else can or will."

Meritaten closed her eyes. "I'm very weary," she said. "I need to sleep."

"We are all weary," said Ankhesenpaaten. But her flash of temper faded fast. She tried again, sweetly, with just the proper degree of quiver in her voice. "Mayet, won't you help me? I'm so much younger, I know so little, and I'm not a queen. I was never supposed to be. It was always you and Meketaten. I was the afterthought. Won't you help me think on what to do?"

"I can't think," said Meritaten. "Lotus Blossom, I have to sleep. Can't you come back tomorrow? The dead will be no less dead then, and the sickness no less dreadful."

And Meritaten, thought Nofret, would be no more help then. Ankhesenpaaten seemed inclined to press harder, but she was no fool. She knew her sister. She left almost indecently quickly—before, maybe, she throttled the lovely idiot.

■　■　■

"Meritaten," she said to Nofret as they left the door and the guard behind, "had the great fortune to inherit our mother's beauty and our father's mind."

"Whereas you take after your grandmother Tiye," said Nofret.

The princess slid her a glance. The name was pain, Nofret could see. Nofret did not try to unsay it. "I look more like our mother," her lady said.

"You think as Tiye thought."

"As she taught me to think."

"She taught you because she knew you could learn. The others were all too young or too nearly witless."

The princess shrugged, quick, almost angry. "I am what I am. My sister is the queen, insofar as anyone is. If she can't or won't do what's necessary, then I'll do it for her.

That's what I'm for. To do what the others won't do.''

"You're too young to be that bitter," said Nofret.

"I am so old as Cheops," said the princess. She had stopped under a torch that flickered and tried to go out. She reached up and twisted it free of its mooring, sweeping it in a long arc to set it flaring. It was a very childlike thing to do, and yet very much like a woman grown, if a woman could be a warrior.

The bright unsteady light made the shadows leap and dance. Some of them, maybe, had eyes: spirits of the night or of the dead, come to wonder at these two walkers in the dark. For all Nofret knew, one of them was Tiye.

She shivered in her skin. No, not Tiye. Tiye would haunt her son if she haunted anyone.

The princess began to walk swiftly, almost to run. Nofret had to stretch her stride to keep up. At first Nofret thought she must be going to beat sense into the king, but she went deeper into the queens' palace instead of escaping from it. She went up into rooms that Nofret had never seen, wide and airy, with the moon shining in. Someone had omitted to shield the windows against the spirits of the night.

There were people alive here as there had been below. Nofret knew a surge of dizziness. The faces here, the garments, the furnishings and rugs and hangings, flung her back into a life she had willed to forget. This was Egypt, she told herself. Not Mitanni.

And yet Mitanni was here, in these rooms. The maids with their arched noses and their waving hair confined in braids and veils, the eunuchs murmuring in corners, the blind harper singing a song that Nofret had not heard since she came to Egypt, were all strangers to this place. Their manners too were strange, the fashion of their courtesy.

Lady Kiya had not been sleeping, nor had she been warming the king's bed. The harper sang to soothe her spirit, but she seemed hardly to be listening. She lay on a couch heaped with cushions, her great dark eyes intent, but not on the song.

At the princess' coming she rose and performed obeisance gracefully despite the growing bulk of the child she carried. The princess seated herself on the end of the couch and gestured, a little imperiously Nofret thought. "Come, lie down again. Be at ease."

Kiya laughed with a catch of pain. "Ease is nothing that we know in these days, highness."

"Some of us might not think so," said the princess. She was not being polite, she was not being patient. She had exhausted that in contending with Meritaten. "Lady Tadukhipa whom the king loves, listen to me. There is now no queen regnant in the Two Lands. The Beautiful One is dead. Queen Mother Tiye has died."

"Queen Meritaten is young and has little skill as yet." Kiya met the princess' eyes directly, without the studied shyness that Nofret had always seen in her. "So you come to me. I do not want to be queen, highness. My ambition has never stretched so far."

"Well for you it hasn't," the princess said. "And well you know it. I never took you for a fool, lady, nor did the queen mother. Is it your urging that keeps the king lost in a dream of the god?"

"How would that serve me?" asked Kiya.

"Since you ask," said the princess, "it keeps him docile. It allows him to be ruled by anyone with wits and will to command him."

"Have I done so?" Kiya asked gently.

"No," said the princess. "But it's not so long since my mother died. You might simply be biding your time."

"I might," said Kiya. "I might be content to wait till my child is born. If it's a son, then I'm mother to the heir."

"If it's a daughter, you're no worse off than you were before." The princess sighed. She had not relaxed by any fraction that Nofret could see. "My mother was never fond of you, but she always told me that you had more and better wits than anyone gave you credit for. My grandmother told me the same thing. Neither ever had need of you; they were strong enough in themselves.

"I," said the princess, "am not. I need an ally. You are loyal to my father. I don't ask you to be loyal to me or to Meritaten, but for his sake I ask you to help me decide what to do. He can't rule by himself. Meritaten won't help him or me."

"And only I am left," Kiya said. She seemed unoffended, which was more than Nofret could have managed. No doubt she was inured to Egyptian arrogance, from having been so long the brunt of it. "I thank you for coming to me. That took great courage."

"It took great desperation," said the princess. "You are a foreigner, but you belong to the king. Your son may be king after him. That's all very well, but your son hasn't been born yet, and he might be a daughter. What then?"

"I try again," said Kiya, "and again, till the gods grant me a son."

"Admirable," said the princess. "It does nothing for us now. Someone has to hold the reins of kingship while Father communes with the god."

"Is there not," mused Kiya, "an expedient that might suit? Your father ruled from youth to full manhood while his own father lived and was strong in Thebes. For a dozen years the Two Lands had two kings, the old king and the young. Might that not be done again?"

"But the old king had a son," said Ankhesenpaaten. "He had more than one. He had . . ." She trailed off. "Oh, I am a fool! Smenkhkare."

Kiya nodded. "Smenkhkare," she said.

"You understand," said the princess, "that if Smenkhkare is crowned Lord of the Two Lands beside my father, then your son, if son you bear, may never take the throne."

"My son, if son I bear," said Kiya, "will be very young

for a very long time. And Prince Smenkhkare is a man already.''

''He would have,'' said the princess, ''to marry a princess who carries the king-right, in order to be king himself.''

''Yes,'' said Kiya.

The princess' fingers knotted in her lap. ''There are only two princesses left alive. One is already a queen.''

''Yes,'' said Kiya again.

The princess drew a breath that shook her where she sat. She looked pale and small and cold. ''I . . . am still a child. But it won't be long before I'm a woman.''

''I wish you could wait till you are much older, more truly a woman,'' Kiya said with unusual and rather surprising feeling. ''But the kingdom has no mercy. It needs you now.''

''I know,'' said the princess. ''Do you think . . . we can persuade Father to allow a coregency?''

''I think we can,'' Kiya said.

''That would mean,'' said the princess, ''that my son would rule instead of yours. Are you sure you want that?''

Kiya looked her in the face. ''Princess,'' she said in something close to anger, ''you would never have come to me unless you trusted me at least a little. Or are you planning to slip poison in my cup, once you've taken from me everything I know or can advise?''

Ankhesenpaaten went stiff with wounded pride, but her lessons with Tiye had taught her much. She spoke softly, choosing the words with care. ''Lady Tadukhipa, I believe that you esteem my father. You may even love him. For his sake you will do what is necessary. Your honor is bound up in it.''

''Women have no honor,'' said Kiya. ''Women have their men and their children. They do whatever they must in order to protect them.''

"That's what I hope," said the princess. "That's what I fear, too."

"I give you my word," said Kiya, "that I will do nothing to harm the king—even if that king is Smenkhkare."

The princess paused, eyes narrowed, thinking hard. Kiya sat still and waited. At length the princess said, "I trust you. I think you'll act honorably for your own pride's sake. I would welcome alliance with you."

Nofret supposed that that was as close as an Egyptian princess could come to friendship. Kiya, princess of Mitanni that she was, did not seem disconcerted by the coolness of the sentiment. She bowed her head. "I will not shame the bond," she said.

"Nor I," said Ankhesenpaaten.

CHAPTER FOURTEEN

▲

ANKHESENPAATEN'S alliance with Kiya was well considered, but it reckoned without the king. Even as the princess rose to leave Kiya, a flurry at the door brought her about.

The king was wide awake and only slightly vague about the eyes. He greeted his daughter with no surprise at all, and his favorite with a murmured politeness that was like a caress. Nofret had the peculiar urge to withdraw discreetly from what was clearly a private thing, but she could hardly do that while her mistress lingered.

He sat on the couch with the air of one who has done it often before and is comfortable, and looked from Kiya to his daughter. "Do I understand," he inquired, "that you are disposing of kingdoms in my absence?"

Kiya paled just visibly. Ankhesenpaaten maintained her composure, saying levelly, "You know very well, Father, that the god keeps you too busy for anything else.''

"So I've been told,'' he said mildly. "And what are you going to do, my ladies?''

Ankhesenpaaten glanced at Kiya. Kiya pressed her lips together. Ankhesenpaaten said, "A coregency, Father, with Prince Smenkhkare. He's old enough, and he'll do until you have a son of your own.''

"Which may be never,'' he said. "Are you intending to offer him your hand in marriage? That would be required, since no man in himself carries the king-right.''

"There's no one else,'' said Ankhesenpaaten.

"There is Meritaten,'' he said.

"But—''

He reached for her hands and took them, and held them. "Meritaten is the eldest. The king-right is hers first.''

"But she is already—''

His eyes had their wild look again, their look of dreamer and prophet. "The god tells me that she has given me all that is in her to give. Smenkhkare is young, he is beautiful, he has the art of making a woman smile. I should like to see our Mayet smile again. She's been so sad.''

"You'll give her up?'' The princess' voice was thin with strain. "Father, that's generous beyond belief.''

"It's the god's bidding,'' he said. "And not so generous. Mother meant you to be queen, to rule as she ruled, with her strength and, as you grow, her wisdom. You'll do well on the throne at my side.''

Nofret was not hearing this. No, she was not. Her lady was safe. She would marry the beautiful prince whose lack of intelligence would leave her free to rule as she saw fit. Meritaten would continue, weak queen to a weak king. It was ridiculous, it was folly to pass her to Smenkhkare like an outworn sandal. The two of them together had no more capacity to rule than a pair of kittens.

The king could not see it at all. His god blinded him as always with the light of his own selfishness.

The princess could not say a word. Kiya, who could have spoken, chose not to. She was as useless as the princess for beating sense into the king's head.

But then no one had ever succeeded in that, not even Nefertiti or Tiye. The king was the king. His ladies might rule while he occupied himself with the god, but when he spoke, none of them could do anything but listen.

There was something wrong with that. An Egyptian maybe could not see it. Nofret, foreigner that she was, could not fail to see. But there was nothing she could say. She was a servant, a slave. She had no power to speak in the king's presence, except by the king's leave.

Even so, she opened her mouth to say what she thought. But her lady spoke first. "If the god wills, then we all must yield."

■ ■ ■

"You can see your father as the useless layabout he is, and you can still fall flat on your face when he lifts a finger?"

Nofret was beside himself. She had held it all in till they were in the princesses' room, now her lady's alone, with only the one bed in it, and a whisper of echoes that recalled the sisters who were dead. There were lamps lit about the bed, as many as Nofret could find oil for, to keep the dark away.

The princess stood like an image of herself, waiting for Nofret to ready her for bed. She barely seemed to see her maid at all. "The god wills," she murmured, hardly louder than the spirits in the shadows.

"Your father wills!" Nofret made a ripe sound of disgust. "We've had this argument before. Can't you see what he's doing? He's completely off his head. He killed Meketaten with his desperate urge to get a son. Meritaten has little enough will at the best of times, and now she has none. You were the strong one. How can you let him make you his slave?''

''What choice do I have?'' The princess swayed gently with exhaustion, but shook off Nofret's hands. ''I have to marry someone. The line has to go on.''

''You could insist that he give you to Smenkhkare.''

''What, your Hittite conscience objects to a father but not to a father's brother? Aren't they sons of the same mother? Does it matter which of them calls me his wife?''

''Yes!'' cried Nofret. ''He'll kill you, too. That's what he wants. To see you all dead and himself alone, king over nothing.''

''Stop it,'' said the princess, soft and tired but stone-hard beneath. ''It is not your place to judge the Lord of the Two Lands. Nor have you the right or authority to tell me what I should do. I would prefer Smenkhkare if I am to have anyone. But Father is king and god and servant of the god, and Father commands me to do this. I have no choice but to obey.''

''You could run away,'' said Nofret.

''No,'' said the princess. ''That's the coward's way.''

''But this is wrong,'' Nofret persisted. She did not know why she bothered. It was a griping in her middle, a buzzing in her ears: a horror that ran to the bone, and no reason in it. She was too foreign. She could not live here, among these people.

Once before, she had run away. She had found sanctuary of a sort with the Apiru. It would be there now if she sought it out.

But what then of her lady? She would be all alone.

She had Kiya. She had her father, madman that he was. She could find another maid and other servants—she would have to once she was queen, for the honor of her rank. She did not need Nofret.

Nofret found herself folding back the coverlets, sprinkling the rose petals from the jar, straightening the headrest that Egyptians used instead of a pillow. It was a simple thing, carved of cypress wood with a gilded foot. It was cool and smooth under her hands.

Her lady lay down with a sigh that held all the weariness in the world. She was so small, so thin, so fragile to bear such burdens as had been laid on her. She was only a child, not even yet a woman.

Not quite yet, but soon. Her breasts were budding. A faint soft shadow of down darkened her loins. Her father had seen it, or his god had, and claimed her for his own.

Nofret lay on her mat at the bed's foot. She would go. She swore it to herself. But not now. Not till her lady had other servants to look after her.

■   ■   ■

Ankhesenpaaten woke from the heavy sleep of exhaustion to the stain of blood on her thighs. Her dismay turned to laughter, and briefly to tears. "He knew," she said. "The god knew."

Nofret helped her to bathe and tend herself. The princess cut her own sidelock, chose a gown from the chest, and a wig that had been made for one of her elder sisters. She put them all on like armor, and went out to rule as Tiye had taught her.

She summoned every servant who was yet alive or in the palace, and set each one to work restoring the palace to its former order. Some she sent to find their fellows who had fled but who might linger in the city, and to bring them back without fear of punishment. "The work they've left undone," she said, "will be punishment enough."

Once that was done, she had the captain of guards brought to her. The one who came was no other than General Horemheb. The princess, sitting on the chair that had been Tiye's, attended by as many guards and servants as she could spare, received him with no visible tremor. "Lord general," she said, "we thank you for your aid in this terrible time. It was most generous of you to take on duties so far beneath your rank and station.''

Horemheb did not look on the princess with mockery. He well might have, child that she was, robed and seated like a queen. But his words and his expression held only rough respect. ''Someone had to do it, highness, and I was here and knew what to do. I was a captain of guards before I was a general of armies.''

''You've done well,'' she said levelly, ''in the circumstances. I summoned you to ask if you could do better. Everything that we can restore to its old place and use, we must. The sickness may go on, but so does the kingdom.''

Horemheb bowed. ''That's good sense, highness. Better, if I may say so, then your grandmother had.''

''My grandmother set first things first,'' the princess said stiffly. ''The kingdom sustains itself through her doing. All I do here is finish what she begun.''

''Yes, she did tie the steering oar and turn the bow into the waves, didn't she? I'm glad to see you steering again, and into a safe harbor, too.''

The princess set her chin. She was angry enough to show it, which was very angry indeed. ''I am glad that our actions meet with your approval. Can you see your way, perhaps, to returning all guards to their duties, and bringing in new guards to replace those who were lost to the plague?''

Horemheb was impervious to irony. He bowed again. ''As you wish, highness. May I have your leave to summon men of my own from the Delta? They're trained men, and will serve more readily than new recruits.''

''Ah,'' said Ankhesenpaaten with sweet reason, ''but the Delta was devastated by the plague, was it not? It needs every man who can stand. Send to Thebes, lord general, where the plague was less terrible than it was here, and much less so than in the Delta.''

''As your highness wishes,'' said Horemheb. If he was

dismayed to find this child princess so clearly able to see through him, he did not show it. Nor did he press to bring his own men, loyal to him, to a city that chafed under a lunatic king. There would be time for that, his manner said.

■ ■ ■

"That man is dangerous," Nofret said when she could.

Her lady, resting in the little room behind the hall of audience and sipping barley water, closed her eyes and sighed. "Why, because he wants to be king? He can't be. He's a commoner."

"He could seize a royal bride and dispose of the king and claim the throne by force of arms," said Nofret.

"In Great Hatti he could," said the princess. "Not here."

"Which is exactly why he could do it. No one would believe it till it was done. Most of Egypt would even help him."

"It would not."

"It would," said Nofret. "They want their gods back."

"Servants' gossip," said the princess. She set down her cup still half-full of barley water, and lay back on the couch that had been Tiye's. "I think I should move into the queen's palace today, and not wait till after I'm married. It would be simpler, don't you think? We can close these rooms and save the servants the effort of looking after them."

"Which rooms will you take?" Nofret asked. This was a blatant change of subject, but she was as tired as her lady. She lacked the strength to argue.

"I had thought," the princess said, "to take the rooms that were Mother's." Her breath caught slightly, but she went on with determined placidity. "The others that are left are small, and not suitable for my station. I can't ask Meritaten to give up hers, nor Lady Kiya. Mother's rooms are lying empty. I'll have new furniture brought in. I might even have the walls repainted. I never did like the temple scenes. What would you think of something different, a hunt for birds by the river, maybe, or something with horses and chariots?''

"That would be very Hittite," said Nofret. "All that hunting and galloping."

The princess smiled. It was faint, but it was genuine. "Well then, maybe not. Maybe just birds, or people dancing."

"Whatever you like," Nofret said. "Should I tell the king's painter you want to see him?"

"Maybe," said the princess drowsily. "Tomorrow. I need to think on it. And get the rooms ready." She yawned. "Oh, I could sleep till Osiris lives again."

"Sleep for an hour," Nofret said. "No one needs you more desperately than that."

"No," the princess said. "I should go—the embassy from Lagash—"

"Their excellencies can wait," said Nofret firmly. "I'll have them fed and plied with wine. By the time you're awake, they'll be ready to give you anything you ask."

The princess sighed and did not answer, did not even smile at Nofret's attempt at wit. She had fallen asleep.

■ ■ ■

Nofret did as she had promised, saw that the ambassadors were kept well content in a lesser banqueting hall, and had the steward put off further audiences until the morrow. She did not think till afterward that she was commanding grave and august persons much older than she—that, after all and without even noticing it, she was what she had meant to be on that first day in Akhetaten: chief servant to a queen.

Well, and the queen was not a queen yet, only a very tired, very young princess whose royal father was no use at all for anything but praying in the temple and fathering daughters. She was only doing what she had to do, since no one else would do it. So too was Nofret.

Many of Queen Nefertiti's servitors were dead, but some were still alive and still in the palace. Without orders to the contrary, they kept to the queen's rooms and did no more there than they must. Nofret roused them in her lady's name.

The chief of them, a eunuch of middling age and massive girth, ventured to curl his lip at her. She set hands on hips and showed him her teeth in what was only by remotest courtesy a smile. "Ah, Setnef. I'd wondered where you were keeping yourself. Her highness has sore need of assistance, and I'm both young and inexperienced. If you could advise . . ."

He was not going to give way to such blatant flattery, not that veteran of the court, but he softened to it. Just a little. Just enough to take command of the queen's rooms, to order their refurbishing and to send for the king's painter. Nofret, he made clear, was in his way.

She went away well satisfied. Giving orders, she was discovering, was a heady pleasure. But it was even sweeter to convince people that they were somehow winning the fight by doing what she wanted. It took a little more time, a little more effort to begin, but much less of both thereafter.

Kings could study that art, she thought. Not that they needed it much. A king commanded and was obeyed. A slave had to be more circumspect.

CHAPTER FIFTEEN

▲

PRINCE Smenkhkare sailed down the river from Thebes in a golden boat, in such state as if he were already king and god. He came ostensibly to fetch his mother's body to her tomb. But by then everyone knew that while he was in

Akhetaten he would be married to the princess Meritaten and crowned king beside the elder king in the Two Lands.

His bride waited for him on the river's bank. When her father and her sister came to tell her what had been decided for her, she had bowed her head and murmured, "The god's will be done." But Nofret had caught the gleam of eyes under the painted lids. Meritaten was not sorry to be forsaking her father-husband for her uncle.

Smenkhkare was as beautiful as ever, and as vain of his looks, sitting in his flawlessly pleated kilt on the deck of his ship, surrounded by attendants carefully chosen to be almost, but not quite, as beautiful as he. He wore the Nubian wig that he, like Nefertiti, had always favored. His jewels were gold and lapis and turquoise of Sinai, his pectoral an image of the protector of the south, Nekhbet the vulture-goddess with her wings spread from shoulder to shoulder. The width of those shoulders was much to be admired, and the narrowness of waist and hips, and the perfection of each calf and ankle and foot. He made certain that he sat in order to show them all to best advantage.

Nofret did not know when or how she had become so weary of the world. Maybe in the plague, when so many died and she did not even take sick. Somehow, imperceptibly, she had fallen out of love with the beautiful prince. He was too sleek, too untouched by grief, even though his mother was dead. All he could see was the crown that waited for him and maybe, a little, the bride who was his right to it.

Meritaten did not appear to have Nofret's cursed clarity of vision. She watched the prince coming toward her over the water, and blinked as if dazzled. The sun was strong and the gilding of the boat shone blinding bright, but her eyes were fixed on Smenkhkare.

Why, thought Nofret, she was besotted with him. She and half the ladies of the court. He was unutterably pretty, as pretty as Meritaten herself.

Ankhesenpaaten stood behind her sister. She had been very quiet since this choice was made, a quiet that Nofret had stopped trying to break. If she was dazzled by her uncle's splendor, she did not show it. Her eyes were narrowed against the glare of sunlight, that was all.

Her father drove forward in his chariot sheathed in electrum, a vision of splendor to rival the one that approached on the water. He wore the Two Crowns, and his ornaments were all pure gold.

He had no head for the myriad duties of kingship, but spectacle he loved. He descended from his chariot at the end of the quay, left his horses to the princely groom who ran forward to tend them, and set himself at the foot of the boarding-plank just as it came to rest. Prince Smenkhkare could not in courtesy linger on his boat for the crowds to admire. He had to rise, make his way from the boat, and bow low before the man who was still, and until the burials of queen and queen mother and princesses, king over him.

"Well met in both joy and sorrow, brother," said the king, hardly stumbling over the words.

"My royal brother," said Smenkhkare. His voice was deeper than the king's, and clearer, no stammer to mar it. "Is all well in Akhetaten?"

"Now it will be well," the king said, raising his brother and embracing him.

Meritaten waited her turn as a lady should, patient, with eyes lowered. When Smenkhkare took her hands she looked up. She did not smile, but her eyes were bright.

He was much taller than she. He smiled down at her. "Little Kitten," he said. "How lovely you've grown!"

She blossomed under that simple flattery. When he lifted her into the chariot that waited for him, and stepped up behind her so that she had to stand pressed against him while he took up the reins, no one said a word, least of all she. She shot a lone unreadable glance at her father before the horses began to move.

Everyone scrambled to form the procession. Smenkhkare led it, laughing, with his princess in his arms. The king seemed half baffled, half amused. He took with good grace his brother's insolence—for it was nothing less than that.

Poor plague-battered Akhetaten came out in such force as it could muster to see the great ones go by. The cheering was thin, the processional way wide; there were times when there was little more sound than the clatter of hoofs and the rattle of wheels and the occasional snorting of horses. Ankhesenpaaten, however, with Kiya's encouragement, had taken measures to avoid the humiliation of a king riding in silence to his palace: musicians both led and followed the procession, beating on drums, braying on horns, rattling timbrel and sistrum. They made a brave noise coming up from the river, and a brave sight in their golden splendor.

■   ■   ■

That night, for the first time in many days, no one died of the plague. "The god blesses us," the king said when word was brought to him.

With Smenkhkare here he actually paid attention to the work of a king's days, instead of leaving it to his ladies. Maybe Smenkhkare's presence shamed him into it. Maybe he had roused and seen that the kingdom needed a king.

He looked odder and frailer than ever beside his tall beautiful brother, but the drawn and weary look had faded from his face. The malaise of the spirit that had held him immobile seemed to have lifted, at least enough for him to put on a show of strength. He even held audience as he had not since before Nefertiti died.

It must have been difficult for him to mount the dais that first day, and to sit on the throne that stood alone where once had been two, and Nefertiti on the other. Where all his daughters had been were only Meritaten and Ankhesenpaaten. There were empty places among the court, princes and high officials who were ill, fled, or dead.

Lord Ay was there, gaunt and pale but determined to do his duty despite the death that had nearly taken him. He had gone all the way to the edge of the dark lands before his will and the will of the gods brought him back. He was still half among the dead, his eyes as strange almost as the king's, but Nofret saw the effort with which he made himself rouse. Lord Ay was a practical man. He had none of the divine madness that vexed the king.

Neither, Nofret took note, did Smenkhkare. He held the crown prince's place beside the king, looked beautiful as always, but was profoundly bored. Sometimes he cast glances at Meritaten, to see if he could make her blush.

She was different since Smenkhkare came to Akhetaten, more alive somehow. She was not more interesting for it. All her life and gaiety were focused on her husband-to-be. She went boating with him on the river. She went riding with him in his chariot. She sat with him in a pavilion in the garden, playing the harp and singing in her thin sweet voice.

He seemed less besotted with her than she was with him, but he was not averse to her attentions. She was a pretty creature, and trained to give pleasure to princes. No one ventured to remind him that another had been there before him. Her daughter was kept in the nursery, out of sight and mind. There was nothing to stand between prince and princess, and no one who would prevent them from doing as they pleased.

■　■　■

For once Ankhesenpaaten was the pale shadow of her sister. Where Meritaten was vivid, smiling, even learning to laugh, Ankhesenpaaten went quiet and slow, with her head lowered and her eyes downcast. Sometimes they flashed up in temper, but that was too rare for Nofret's liking.

The king did not try to woo her. He wanted her with him as she had always been, from morning greeting of the sun until the quiet of evening, when they sat in a chamber lit with lamps and listened to a singer or a storyteller; or if there was a feast she had to attend it, crowned with perfume and garlanded with flowers. In between she had a little time to herself, which she spent sleeping or pretending to, or sitting in the garden staring at nothing.

Nofret tried shaking, shouting, anything to rouse her from her listlessness. She took no notice. She had not said two words together, Nofret reckoned, since Smenkhkare came.

■   ■   ■

The burial of Nefertiti and her three youngest daughters fell on a day of brutal heat. The desert shimmered. The sun beat down like a hammer in the forge. The narrow wadi that led to the royal tomb seemed steeper and rockier than it had ever been, and searingly hot.

The mourners were not supposed to notice anything but the depth of their grief. They struggled behind the priests with the biers, wet with sweat and tears. Their wailing echoed to the molten sky.

Nofret wailed with them, because it kept her from having to think. She kept a wary eye on her lady. The princess stumbled behind her father, eyes blank, face blank, keening.

The rite of burial was a blur of heat. The feast in the tomb was hurried, and much more of it than usual left as sustenance for the spirits of the dead. The king was minded to linger, but Smenkhkare coaxed him away with soft words and gentle tugs.

He had not tried to fling himself on the coffins as Nofret had seen people do at other funerals. He had not eaten, either, nor joined in the keening. He kept his sorrow within, nourished it and treasured it, lest he forget.

The dead were at rest. That was a blessing. As many as had died, as untimely as they had fallen to the sickness, some surely must be haunting their kin. But Nofret had seen no restless spirits, nor heard them since people stopped dying. They were all gone away.

She said her own farewell to Queen Nefertiti and the three little princesses. There was no sense of them here, the children with their laughter and their silliness, the queen with her cold composure and her glimmer of hidden warmth. The four stone sarcophagi, shut up in the dark amid the wealth of kings, held nothing but dust and dried husks.

Wherever the spirits had gone, Nofret wished them well. They had never done harm to her.

Whereas if it had been the king . . .

She stumbled, following her princess back along the wadi. Her ankle twisted but held. She cursed the stones and her own clumsiness, but even in her fit of temper she knew that that was not why she had set her foot awry.

She hated the king.

No, not as strong as that. She despised him. She hated what he did in the name of his god, what he was doing to her princess, sucking all the life and spirit out of her and turning her into a mute shadow of a creature.

Ankhesenpaaten had tried to be strong. She had tried to be worthy of her grandmother's memory, to be a queen and not a half-grown child. But she was too young, the burden too great. She could not bear it.

It was the king's fault. He had killed one daughter already. He was killing this one.

Nofret's fists clenched. The king scrambled in front of her, awkward undignified figure in this cruel place. The guard behind him had a dagger in a sheath, bouncing at his hip as he descended the slope. One leap, that was all, one swift movement, and she could snatch the knife and plunge it into the king's narrow back.

It would not even be murder. Execution, rather. Disposal of a madman. Nofret would die for it, of course, but too quickly to feel the pain.

She measured the distance. She flexed her fingers, feeling already the shape of the hilt, the shock as the blade plunged home.

Ankhesenpaaten stumbled against Nofret. Her skin felt much too cool. Her face was greenish-pale. She was breathing much too fast and much too shallow.

"Water," said Nofret. Then louder: "Water, here, quick! Her highness is ill of the heat."

■　■　■

Ankhesenpaaten came to herself once she had had a sip of water. She shook off the solicitous, tried to shake off the sunshade that Nofret had wrested from a protesting slave, but Nofret ignored her. It was Nofret who drove the princess' chariot back to Akhetaten, while her lady rested as best she could under the sunshade.

And the king went on living. He would have said that the god had intervened to prevent Nofret from doing murder. Nofret preferred to attribute it to chance—and an opportunity that would not come again. She was a warrior's child. She could not kill a man, even this man, in cold blood.

"And that," she said to herself under cover of their entry into the city, "is a ghastly pity."

CHAPTER SIXTEEN

▲

AFTER the days of mourning for his queen and his children were over, the king led the court in grand processional up the river to Thebes. Prince Smenkhkare had gone ahead to prepare the city for a threefold feast: the funeral of Queen Mother Tiye, the triumph of the king and his god over the plague, and the wedding and crowning of the prince. The king also would be wedded to the third of his daughters, but more quietly.

Not, to be sure, because of any shrinking on his part from what he was doing. It was Smenkhkare's time, he said, and Smenkhkare who should stand in the light for all the people to admire. The king could be generous when it pleased him.

King and court, guards and servants and hangers-on, rowed in boats up the river, singing as they went. Prince Smenkhkare, soon to be king, shared his own glittering barge with his bride. He sat in his gilded chair, she stood leaning on its arm, until he pulled her laughing and protesting into his lap.

They were all light and laughter, all forgetful of the carved and painted coffin that rode on its barge far back in the procession, with its escort of priests and mourners. Even the king seemed to forget that he escorted his mother to her tomb, in contemplation of the two who lived so perfectly for the present.

People laughed too seldom in Akhetaten. The king was not a mirthful man, nor had his queen been. His children had learned their ways from him. But Meritaten had a new preceptor, and he lived in laughter. All the lightness, all the frivolity that his brother lacked, he had in abundance, as if the god had given all the dark to one and all the bright to the other.

The king was indulgent, lying on a couch under a canopy, with the breeze off the river cooling his cheeks. He felt it, Nofret could see. But Ankhesenpaaten did not.

The princess sat like an ivory image at her father's feet. She did not hear the laughter ringing over the water, nor see the flash of sun on gilded oars, nor catch the scent of river mud and fish, green reeds and flowers, that was the river of Egypt. Once a crocodile got among the servants' boats. It was driven off with oars and spears, with much shrieking and carrying on. She did not turn toward the sound. Her eyes were blank, like carven stones. The heart in her, for all that Nofret could see, was as dead as the queen mother in her coffin.

It was not only the wedding that she went to that drained the spirit out of her. Her mother the queen was dead, and her sisters, all but one, who had eyes and ears and mind for no one but her pretty prince. The queen mother whom she had loved was being taken to the tomb, had left her to be queen when she was no more than a child. It was all too much for her.

The king nibbled bits of fruit that Lady Kiya had peeled and cut for him, and sipped wine from a cup carved of pale chalcedony. The princess ate nothing, drank nothing. Nofret had got a bite or two of bread and a sip of water into her in the dawn before they left Akhetaten—hardly enough of either to keep a bird alive.

Nofret had seen much apathy before, but only in the very sick or the very old. Only in those who did not care to live.

Crouching at her lady's feet, staring up into that lifeless mask of a face, Nofret began to be afraid. If Ankhesenpaaten died, it was all to do again: gain the notice of a princess, become her favored servant, stand beside her when she became a queen. No delicate court lady would want a great gawk of a Hittite girl with barely a civil tongue in her head. Certainly she would never suffer a servant to speak as freely as Nofret did to Ankhesenpaaten.

Ankhesenpaaten was different. As careful as she was, as hard as she tried to be a perfect image of a queen, she honored plain speaking. She found Nofret interesting. She liked a servant to speak her mind.

Nofret had to do something. Something swift, before her lady withered and shrank to nothing. Something that would last, that she would not have to do all over again when the princess' courage failed.

Something, she thought. Something drastic. But what, she did not know, nor could she foresee. Her mind was as blank as her lady's eyes.

■   ■   ■

Nofret had grown up near Hattusas in Great Hatti. She had served an idiot of a lordling in Mitanni. She had seen the cities of Egypt when she came to be tribute to the king in Akhetaten. Memphis was very great. Akhetaten was new and raw, but mighty, and in places even beautiful.

Thebes was greater than any, and ancient, as old as Egypt. Older. Before the Two Lands were, Thebes had stood on the eastern bank of the river. Now it sprawled from east to west with the river between. East was the old city, the place of temples, the houses of princes, old palaces, and the uncounted dwellings of people whose ancestors had lived exactly as they did, for years out of count. West was the palace that the king's father had built, and a lesser, younger city, and beyond these, on the border to the land of the dead, the mighty tombs and temples of the old kings.

Everything in Thebes was older and higher and vaster than anything else that Nofret had known. Thebes loomed. Even its sky seemed immense, blue without cloud; no limit, no end to it but the roofs and walls of the city.

The king rode in processional from end to end of Thebes, from river to easternmost boundary and back across the river to his father's palace. The way was lined with cheering throngs and carpeted with flowers. Everything was bright, beautiful, splendid.

And yet the splendor rang hollow. Nofret saw the sealed gates of temples, the names of gods cut out, leaving raw wounds in paint and stone. She saw that the crowds pressed tight, but she also saw that they moved, flowing with the king in his processional. She, caught in the middle of it, clinging as always to the back of her lady's chariot, could not see the beginning or end of the throng. But she suspected that it was smaller than it looked, that it ended abruptly before and behind, and all about it was sullen silence.

In the most ancient part of the city, where the processional way was narrowest and the crowd most deafening, more than flowers rained down from rooftops and out of the crowd. Fruit ripe to rottenness, handfuls of dung, fell reeking on the king's attendants. Even as his guards scattered in pursuit of the miscreants, one of his chariot-horses bucked and squealed. Something had struck its flank: a stone or a bit of brick, hurled with stinging force.

The team's stately pace quickened to a trot. Guards closed in. The king did not flee, he was too dignified for that, but he did not linger, either.

Nofret never knew if the guards caught anyone with proof of his transgression clinging ripely to his hands. That one barrage seemed to be all the honesty that Thebes deemed necessary. All else was cheering and flowers, avid and well-paid loyalty, and silence ringing with echoes beneath.

■ ■ ■

The tombs that Aharon and his fellows were building out-side of Akhetaten were no more than burrows in the sand beside the great temples and houses of everlasting in the desert to the west of Thebes. Queen Mother Tiye's was far from the least of them, and far from the most easily dis-covered, far up in the valley of the tombs of kings. There she was laid in full and royal state, surrounded by all that she would need in the life beyond life: food, drink, fur-nishings, wigs and gowns and jewels, and servants to look after them, carved of wood and imbued with magical life, and a palace to live in, and words of magic carved and painted on all the walls, to give them life and substance.

When she was set on her way to the land of the blessed dead, her sons turned from the care of the dead to that of the living. She would not have minded. She had always been a practical woman.

Prince Smenkhkare was wedded to the princess Meri-taten in the great temple of the Aten that his father and his brother had built in Thebes. There too he was crowned with the Two Crowns, invested with the crook of a shep-herd and the flail of a master of slaves, and set upon the throne that had, in the last time of twofold kingship, be-longed to his brother.

The younger princess was married much more quietly, while the court was still recovering from the grand revel that had been her sister's wedding. A simple rite in the temple, a feast no greater than any that the court indulged in when the king was in residence, and she was a crowned queen.

It seemed to matter little to her. Thebes had not brought her to herself. On her first day in the city she was con-ducted to the queen's palace by a great concourse of the queen's servants and bidden to tell them her will. She could even disperse them and bring in her own people if she so desired: that was done more often than not when a new queen succeeded the old.

She roused enough to decline the privilege. "No," she said. "No, stay. Serve me as you served the queen before me."

That was as much as she would do. The palace could not run itself—Nofret had seen as much in Akhetaten after Queen Nefertiti died—but while it had a queen to look to, it could pretend that she cared what happened to it.

On the day of her wedding, she stayed at the feast exactly as long as was proper, before the queen's servants led her away to be prepared for what they called her blessed duty. She stood immobile while they bathed and anointed her and dressed her in a gown of linen so thin as to be transparent. Her wig was more extravagant than she would ever have chosen for herself, a mass of curls and braids woven with golden beads, with a beaded headdress over it, and perfume scattered on it till she smelled like a garden of spices.

"Ah," sighed the eunuch who had been her grandmother's house-steward, "how beautiful you are!"

She did not seem to hear him. They had painted her face and eyes far more heavily than she had been used to permit. She looked like a painting on a coffin, no more life or substance to her, and no will to protest, either.

Nofret could not bear it any longer. She was there on sufferance, those prigs of royal servants had made that very clear. But she was the younger queen's own maid, and for years her only one.

She slapped Ankhesenpaaten hard, backhanded, first one cheek and then the other. The servants gaped like idiots. There were no guards—those were all outside the door, where they could leer and lay wagers as they pleased.

Ankhesenpaaten rocked under the blows. Her eyes barely flickered.

Nofret whirled on the gaggle of servants. "Out!" she raged at them. "Out!"

Oh, they were fools. They had the habit of obedience,

and she had the voice of command that she had learned
from her father. They could never have heard a battlefield
bellow from a maidservant before.

They fled like the geese they were, flapping and honking
as geese always will. She slammed the door shut on the
last of them and faced her lady.

Ankhesenpaaten had not moved. Nofret planted herself
in front of her, taking advantage of superior height and
bulk, and set fists on hips. "Who took my lady away from
me and put a plaster doll in her place? It must be a great
magician, and evil, to do such a thing. But I'm not afraid
of magic. I want my lady back."

Ankhesenpaaten blinked once, slowly. Her arms were
warm as Nofret took hold of them, but cold inside, and
stiff. "Who took the heart out of you," Nofret demanded
of her, "and hid it in a dusty tomb? What happened to
your bravery? Who is this coward who wears my lady's
face?" Nofret shook her. "Where is my lady? Give her
back!"

Her lady drew a breath, quicker than the one that had
gone before. Her eyes closed, opened again. They were
flat, black, no warmer or more human than a snake's.

At least, thought Nofret, they were alive. She was beginning to regret gaining even that much. Maybe it was
better for the child if she stayed in the place to which she
had retreated, where she did not have to see or hear or
feel, or be anything to anyone but a living image set on a
throne.

She was not made to live without a heart. Already she
was fading. The thin and wanton gown hid nothing of her
budding body: sweet faint curve of breast and hip; jut of
ribs between.

Nofret sat her down roughly on what was nearest: the
end of a couch. There was food on a table, arrayed to tempt
a child-bride's nervous appetite, and a jarful of watered
wine. Nofret poured a cup of wine, seized a round of

bread, slapped cheese and a slice of roast goose onto it, rolled it up and thrust it at her lady. "I've had enough of your nonsense. Eat."

Ankhesenpaaten set her lips tight and turned her head away.

Nofret gripped her jaw as if she had been a recalcitrant filly, levered it open and shoved the bread-roll in. Ankhesenpaaten gasped, choked, fought. Nofret held on. "Eat," she said, "or strangle. I don't care which."

Ankhesenpaaten ate. Her heart might recoil, but her belly had a mind of its own, and it was hungry.

Nofret almost laughed. Having browbeaten her lady into eating, now she found herself refusing to feed her more than a bite or two, lest she sicken and vomit it up. "Wine now," she said, "and just a little."

Ankhesenpaaten glared through her mask of paint. She was awake at last, blessedly aware, and absolutely furious.

Fury was good. Fury was real. It was alive. It roused, it focused, it cleansed like fire.

"I hate you," said Ankhesenpaaten between the wine and the bread. She had enough sense to sip the one and nibble the other, now that she had come to herself.

Nofret laughed, half-choking. "I am so—glad—"

Gods. Her voice was breaking. Had she grown as weak as that?

"I was happy where I was," said Ankhesenpaaten. "It was peaceful. Nothing mattered. Nothing hurt. Now everything hurts. I hate you!"

"Life hurts," said Nofret. It was easy to be cruel—though not as easy as melting into tears of relief. "You'll die when your time comes. I'll even help you. But that's not yet, no matter how much pain you fancy you endure."

"You cannot imagine—"

"Oh, but I can," said Nofret. There was another cup beside the winejar, meant for the king no doubt, but Nofret took it and filled it to the brim and drank deep. It was good wine, well watered: heady. "You are a queen. I'm a slave. Slaves know a great deal about pain."

"I have never even struck you," said Ankhesenpaaten through clenched teeth. "Maybe I should begin."

"It's your right," said Nofret, "highness."

Ankhesenpaaten snatched the cup out of Nofret's fingers, spattering wine. She drained it with defiance that would cost her dear when her stomach took exception to the shock of too much wine after too long an abstinence.

It went swiftly to her head: her cheeks flushed under the thickness of paint. Her eyes glittered. "I'll have you flayed and bathed in salt."

"You would hate yourself for it," Nofret said.

Ankhesenpaaten stared at the bread in her hand as if she had forgotten it was there. She bit off a little, chewed it slowly. "You should not have roused me," she said.

"If you don't want to go through with this," said Nofret, "you can run away. I've found ways to go, places where no one will know us. If we went north, toward the desert—"

"Why would I run away?" asked Ankhesenpaaten.

"You said—" Nofret bit off the rest. "Why should I not have roused you? So that you could go to your marriage bed in blissful ignorance?"

"So that I would never have to feel anything, or remember."

"Including this?"

"Everything." Ankhesenpaaten closed her eyes. Her hands went to her face, felt of the paint. "This is horrible. I want it off."

Nofret was delighted to oblige. No Egyptian would abandon eyepaint for anything short of direst sickness, but the rest came off as it had gone on, thick as plaster on a wall. The face under it was, in Nofret's estimation, much the lovelier for it. A little color for the lips, that was all it needed. Another wig: one a good deal less gaudy, only lightly dusted with scent.

It would have been great pleasure to snatch her away altogether, but the princess would have none of that. "I know my duty," she said. She stood, small and lovely and very brave in her wisp of a gown. "I'm ready now."

Nofret drew breath to argue, but gave it up. Maybe it was the god's hand on her, or the weight of truth. This would be so whether she willed it or no. She could run away from it if she chose. She could not prevent it, or even alter it.

No Hittite liked to feel powerless. Even a Hittite slave. Someday, Nofret swore to herself, she would see that the king paid for what he did this night. Paid high. Paid, if possible, with everything that he held dear.

CHAPTER SEVENTEEN

▲

THE young queen's servant might prepare her bed, might see her settled in it, arrayed temptingly for her husband's delight. But once he came in, as awkward, as absurd, as arrogant as ever, Nofret was dismissed. She had to go: it was the king who commanded.

Her lady might have wanted her to stay. If so, she said nothing. Her eyes were fixed on her husband—her father, her king. They made Nofret think of small helpless creatures, and of cobras.

Nofret retreated, calm as one can be in an ice-cold rage.

She spent the night outside that door, sitting with her back to the wall, arms wrapped about knees. The door was heavy and well set on its hinges. No sound came from within. No shrieks of pain or of pleasure. No laughter; no sobbing. Nothing.

She felt in her skin the slow wheel of stars toward the dawn. The sun was a swelling warmth, a promise of fire. Once or twice she nodded, and for a little while she slept.

The guards stood watch outside the king's suite, three doors distant. The king's servants were abed or elsewhere. No one hovered or strained to hear, and no one tried to watch. There was no bawdry in this wedding, nor had there ever been when the king took a bride.

Smenkhkare's friends and favorites had tormented Meritaten till she nearly wept, but she had laughed, too, besotted with her husband and lover. Their wedding night had been one long raucous carouse, from bedding of the bride to her emergence at sunrise in the arms of her grinning husband.

For Ankhesenpaaten there was none of that. As soon as the sun cleared the horizon, Nofret tried the door. It was not, for a wonder, barred.

The room within was dim. Most of the lamps had burned out. Only one was still flickering, consuming the last of the oil. The air was close, still, heavily scented with perfumes and with something that made Nofret think of rutting goats. She gagged on it.

The king had drawn back curtains from a window. The shutter was open, first sunlight glimmering through. He lay in it, face down, praying as he always prayed, oblivious to anything about him.

Ankhesenpaaten was still asleep. She curled in the bed, thumb in mouth, looking even younger than she was. Nofret did not want to touch her or wake her, or see what might be in her eyes.

Maybe, Nofret thought. Maybe . . .

No hope of that. There was blood among the coverlets, blood on Ankhesenpaaten's thighs, dried and dark.

The anger that had slept in Nofret all night long drew

into a hard cold knot in her center. She settled herself on the floor beside the bed and waited till her lady sighed, stirred, opened eyes blurred with sleep.

There was nothing in them that had not been there before. No misery. No dullness of defeat. She was always irritable on first waking, frowning as she looked about, yawning and stretching each separate muscle, like a cat.

She saw the man on the floor. It was difficult not to see him: he took all the light to himself. Nothing changed in her expression. It did not soften, nor did it go stiff with anger. She sighed a little, that was all, and sat up. "I'll bathe this morning, I think," she said, perfectly calm, perfectly composed.

Foreign, thought Nofret. Utterly foreign.

■ ■ ■

Ankhesenpaaten the queen was no more or less than Ankhesenpaaten the princess had been. She did her duty in the marriage chamber, did it without complaint, and said nothing of it to Nofret. Nofret did not ask; did not want to know.

Maybe to Egyptians such things truly did not matter. Maybe Ankhesenpaaten was too much a child still to be troubled by them.

Nofret, enough the elder to know what women knew, did not know this that made a woman of a maiden. Since she disposed of her master in Mitanni, she had not let any man come close enough to threaten her innocence. It was easier than some people seemed to think. A slave was nothing and no one. A slave who belonged to a queen carried some of that queen's immunity, at least in Egypt.

And maybe Nofret was too ugly for Egyptian taste. Guards liked to vex her with catcalls and lewd suggestions, but guards were idiots. No one else ever looked at her, that she knew of.

She was glad. Bad enough that she had to deliver her

lady to that chamber every evening. She did not need a pack of panting males into the bargain.

■　■　■

The king lingered in Thebes long past both funeral and wedding. He was a lazy man, Nofret thought; once he had settled somewhere, he hated to move. It was a wonder that he had ever left Thebes to begin with, let alone built a whole city on virgin land between Thebes and Memphis. Maybe it truly was his god who had commanded it.

Nofret in Thebes found time as she had in Akhetaten, to explore the ways of the city. She did not explore the city of the dead, nor cultivate the acquaintance of the living priests and laborers who inhabited it. She had seen too much death—and, she could admit if she must, been too disconcerted by the Apiru in the laborers' village of Akhetaten. Here she turned face and mind to the city of the living.

No sudden friendship found her here. No goat escaped from captivity to gain her a friend. But wonders there were in plenty, and markets that had been open since Egypt was new.

There were gods in Thebes. In Akhetaten there had been none. Everything was burned away in the light of the Aten.

Here the Aten ruled by the king's decree, but Amon was only silenced. He was not destroyed, nor was he driven out. Nofret felt him in the paving stones under her feet, caught the scent of him in the air. It was a hot smell, like scorched linen, or like offerings burning on an altar.

The altars themselves were cold, the temples sealed, deserted. But Amon lived. His people did not forget him. They swore by him in the streets, invoked him with wails of mock anguish while they haggled in the market, called one another by his name or one of his secondary names: Rahotep, Merit-Amon, Neferure. Nofret, in a spirit of defiance against the king, bought an amulet from a vendor on the steps of a silent temple, a pretty thing of the blue glass that was called faience, shaped like a man with a ram's horns. It would make her fruitful, the seller said with a wary eye cocked for the king's guards, and give her strong sons, and protect her from importunate lovers. "And will it defend me against crocodiles?" she asked, meaning to be facetious.

The vendor rummaged through his tray of amulets, hesitated between a pair, chose the one of smooth greenish stone with a hole drilled through it for a string. It was another of the Egyptians' man-gods, but less manlike than some, a crocodile standing upright and grinning with remarkably lifelike expression. "Sobek," he said. "He rules the crocodile. Ask him when one menaces you, and he'll protect you."

Nofret was going to refuse a second amulet, but then she shrugged. Why not? She had a little barley left. She had been meaning to trade it for a sop of bread in honey. But she was not hungry, not really, and Sobek's grin made her want to grin in return.

Still she hesitated. "Isn't he a god of ill fortune?" she asked warily.

"He can be," the vendor said. He was an honest man, as his kind went. "But if you serve him well, he gives you fair return. He'll guard you against nightwalkers, too, and lay a curse on your enemies, if you invoke him properly."

"Not if it costs me extra," she said. She took both amulets in her hand. They did not seem angry to be thrown together. The Aten was enemy enough for both.

The vendor gave her a string for them and helped her plait them into her hair. She did not care if the king saw. Let him punish her if he pleased. She would rather welcome it.

Armed against crocodiles and importunate lovers, assured of fertility when she chose to exercise it, she wandered on through the city. When the sun touched the roof of Amon's temple, she would have to take the ferry back to the king's palace, but that was some time away yet. She had barely begun to explore the old city. The new would wait for another day, since it seemed that the king would not be leaving soon.

The gods were everywhere. People were as defiant as Nofret was, though maybe with lesser reason. How defiant, she saw with a shock of—not recognition, not exactly. Pleasure, that was it.

It was the mark of a city that while the houses of its gods and princes were lofty and splendid, most of it was simple to squalor. On a street in back of the street of temples, where even the temples were plain brick walls with here and there a low mean door, Nofret saw a gathering of men who looked suspiciously like bravos in a back street of Hattusas. They were young, they were large for Egyptians, they had a particular look that made her step backward quickly.

Before she could retreat, the way filled behind her. The young men ahead were, she realized with a small shock, priests. They were shaved clean, and they wore linen robes as priests did, and on each breast was a sigil in gold or electrum, remarkably like the amulet of Amon plaited into Nofret's hair. They carried wooden cudgels, which they looked as if they knew how to use.

The men behind her were older, some of them, and burlier. They wore the kilts and breastplates of the city guard. Some of them had swords. All had spears.

She knew the look of a battle in the making. And here was she, wearing Amon's amulet, naked and alone and temptingly female.

There was nowhere to escape. Her eye, casting frantically, found the niche of a doorway. It would not conceal her, but it might keep her out of the way.

She dived into the poor shelter even as the king's men ran toward the priests of Amon. Nobody spoke, even to bark a command. This was a battle they had fought before: spear and sword against cudgel and raw cold anger. The clack of wood on wood, the thud of wood on flesh, the sound of breath drawn quick, overwhelmed the sounds of the city.

This was war. She had known it before, heard it, seen it in people's eyes as they spoke of their gods against the Aten. Here she saw another face of it.

The fight swayed back and forth along the street. Nofret, alert for paths of escape, felt along the door behind her. It was wooden, cracked and old, with a string for a latch. Somewhat to her surprise the latch yielded to her tug on it.

Without stopping to think, she slipped through the opening and kicked the door shut. It had a bar. She thrust it home.

Then, and none too soon, she looked to see where she was. There was light ahead, a flicker of lamplight, showing her a narrow passage, no higher it seemed than the entrance to a tomb. She crept along it. The air reeked of old incense, rancid lamp-oil, long-dead flowers.

No doubt of it. She was in a temple. Its outer doors would be sealed, but someone was living inside and using the door she had come through, she supposed, to come and go. It was careless of the city guard to have left that door unblocked.

Maybe that was what the priests of Amon were fighting for. It seemed useless defiance else to engage in battle with the king's men. Maybe they were defending this place, and someone in it.

If so, she was no safer here than she had been in the street. There were whole companies of the city guard to reinforce the one that fought in the street. There might be armies of priests, too, but one or the other would come in here when the battle was over and find her. And she was the young queen's servant.

It was nothing she could help. Nor did she see the use in panic. She had to keep her wits about her if she was to get out of this unharmed.

It would not hurt, she decided, to say a prayer to Amon whose amulet she wore. He was not her god, but after all she had paid for his protection. She spoke in the barest breath of a whisper. "Amon, great god, look after me. I'm your enemy's servant's servant, but I'm none of his, not after what the king has done to his children. Guard me and I'll give you . . ." She paused. Here was a difficulty. Gods needed bribes, and she had nothing, not even the bag of barley that her mistress had given her to buy fripperies in the market.

She drew a deep breath. "I'll give you my thanks, and if I ever become the chief over all a queen's servants, I'll dedicate an offering of bread and barley beer to you."

There. That should be enough, and Egyptian enough, too. In Great Hatti it would have had to be a whole sheep at least.

Taking her courage in both hands and tugging at her amulets for luck—both of them: Sobek too, whose crocodile-teeth would be welcome against king's men and priests alike—she slipped with hunter's stealth toward the light.

CHAPTER EIGHTEEN

▲

THE light was lamplight in a room. It was a scribes' storeroom from the look of it. There were book-rolls everywhere, packed into cases along the walls, heaped on a table, piled like logs on the floor. Nofret, keeping cautiously to the shadows beyond the spill of light from the doorway, saw a scribe's palette on the table, and a scatter of pens and inks and paints.

Amid the clutter sat a pair of men in priests' robes. The lamp caught the sheen of a shaven skull, the glitter of an eye in its rim of paint. They were men of no particular age, neither young nor very old. One was fat and soft like a merchant in Great Hatti, the other whip-lean, with a sharp jut of cheekbones. They were drinking from a jar of what must be the ubiquitous barley beer, and ignoring a basket of bread and a bowl of dates.

The fat one drank in the morose silence of the suddenly drunk. The thin one watched him as a cat will watch a rathole, smiling slightly to himself when the other's eyes wandered away from him.

At length the fat man said, "See what we come to. A jug of beer in a back room, and young men brawling in the street."

"Even kings die," the thin man said coolly, as if he were speaking of nothing in particular.

The fat man drained his cup of beer and reached for the jar. It was nearly empty. He sighed. "Do you think it would do us any good to have him killed?"

"I doubt it," the thin man said.

"It hasn't done us any good to send people to court to speak for us to the young king. He's completely his brother's creature. Amon is dead, old friend. Dead and gone."

For the first time the thin man showed a flicker of emotion. It was not anger, Nofret realized. It was amusement. "You think so? No, no. He only waits, and bides his time. A king may be unassailable by the law and custom of the Two Lands, but one of the great gods is stronger in the end than any king and god."

The fat man, finding both cup and jar empty, flung them aside with a clatter. "What use is it? What use is any of

it? Unless that man dies, there will be no god in the Two
Lands but his fever-dream of divinity.''

"Patience," said the thin man. "Be patient."

"I have been patient!" cried the fat man. "Ever since
he built that city of his, ever since he sealed our temple, I
have been exquisitely patient."

"So was Thutmose," the thin man said, "and for longer
than we. Twenty years he waited for his stepmother to die.
All that while he nursed his hate and waited. But she was
king. Better to wait and suffer than to endure the god's
curse for the murder of a king."

"I believe in curses," the fat man muttered. "One lies
on us all. A curse of a king, that misshapen madman with
his harem of loyal daughters."

"Wait," said the thin man with maddening persistence.
"See what in the end the gods make of him."

"There are no gods left alive," the fat man said.

■   ■   ■

Nofret slid along the wall. The two men in the light
seemed intent on their litany of despair, but she was not
about to trust her life to chance. The passage beyond was
black dark, a torch flickering in a wall-socket where
seemed to be a corner. The wall was cold against her back,
and faintly rough: plaster over mudbrick, painted with images that were little more than shadows on shadow except
where the light struck them. There they were flashes of
sudden brilliance, the Egyptians' peculiar writing like
marches of beasts and birds and parts and wholes of human
bodies.

Magic lived in the holy writing, Nofret had heard. She
did not sense anything here but what one would expect in
a temple denied its god.

That was bad enough. Her spine was cold. She did not
know for a fact where she was going, except from torch
to torch through the shadows between. These were mur-

murs in the dark, faint voices, mew of cat, squeak of mouse, rustle of beetle in the wall. Or maybe those were the voices of ghosts, thin and bloodless.

She should have stayed in the palace. Oh, she should, indeed.

■ ■ ■

A temple was not a single building inside of its walls. There was the god's house, and there were the houses of the priests, and the scribes' workplaces and their houses. This temple, like the Great Temple of the Aten in Akhetaten, was as vast as a city, and all of it shut up, abandoned.

Nofret felt like a soul wandering lost among the houses of the dead. Doors were shut, but not all of them were barred. Outside of the scribes' house in which she had begun, there were no lamps or torches lit in the windowless places, no priests lingering where they were not supposed to be. She saw two cats fighting in a courtyard, and doves fluttering and cooing in a rank and wilting garden, but no other living thing.

Somehow she had got turned about. She did not know where she was, nor how long she had been trapped in this place. Maybe she was dead and had not known it. Maybe a god had cursed her.

She stumbled through yet another door, from yet another court in which the light was growing suspiciously golden, the sun sinking beyond the temple's walls. If night caught her here, she would go mad.

Here was another of the priests' houses, where they had slept while they did duty in the temple. Priests in Egypt were not like priests elsewhere: many of them lived the lives of ordinary men, except that for part of the year they were servants of their god. So were Amon's priests all sent back to their places in the world, and such of them as fought the king's men or drank themselves into a stupor in a storeroom were the bold and the recalcitrant, and the ones who would not accept any upstart god.

There were memories of them here. A sandal forgotten in a corner. A scattering of blue beads on a dusty floor. Nofret felt the presence of men who were not dead, and she knew it, but their spirits lingered nonetheless.

And their anger.

So much anger. Nofret was all raw to it. She thrust against a barred door, fell forward as it opened, caught herself up short against an obstacle that was warm; that breathed.

She recoiled. The obstacle did likewise, with an exclamation that made her ears burn. Soldier's crudity—and a soldier's voice, too, and a man she knew too well.

There was no telling if he knew her. She was nothing memorable, she did not think: a slave like a hundred other slaves, with amulets woven into her mane of hair.

Gods. If she could think . . .

"What are you doing here?" she heard herself say.

General Horemheb raised his brows. "Are you the porter of this gate, then?"

"It seems I must be," she said, tongue running ahead of wits, and dangerous in it.

"Well then," he said, "fetch your master, and be quick."

"What, the god?" she wanted to know.

That was in no way wise. She saw death in those flat black eyes, though the face barely changed expression.

Death she knew. It was an old friend, an old enemy. She grinned at it.

He raised a hand as if to strike. She did not flinch. "There are two priests getting blind drunk in a storeroom. Was it one of them you wanted?"

His hand lowered. For a moment she knew he knew her, but a frown's shadow flickered and passed. She was too far out of her place. He did not remember who she was.

"You are a poor servant," he said, but as if he had lost interest in her.

She stepped inside. "You can find your own way in. I have duties I can't shirk."

Truth, after its fashion. And breathtaking insolence. It seemed to shock him enough that he let her go.

The way out must be close if he had come in by it. She only needed to find it. ■

Instead she found herself shadow-creeping back the way she had come, following the general of the king's armies in the Delta, the commander of his guards in Akhetaten, the loyal servant of the king.

He went direct and without hesitation. Of course, she thought, he would know this place. He had served the old king. He would have worshipped Amon as everyone did in Thebes, and known the ways of his temple.

She was hard put both to keep up with him and to avoid being seen. She lost him at a turning where the priests' houses came close together, but before panic could possess her she heard the slap of his sandals. His long stride was firm, sure of itself. There was nothing furtive in him.

And yet he was alone. He was in Amon's temple, and he had come to speak to one who hid in it. If the king knew . . .

The king, in most things, would do nothing. But in this that touched his god, he could be deadly.

General Horemheb did not seem to care. Nofret had never noticed that he feared or greatly respected the king.

Caught up in her maundering, she nearly fell over him. He had stopped in a stone-paved court beside a statue of an old king. At the court's far end, just within the colonnade, a man stood waiting, evidently for him. It was not either of the priests whom Nofret had seen before.

She clutched at a column and at what shadow it could offer, crouching low to make herself smaller. She felt like a mouse in sight of a snake.

That was an old man who stood across the courtyard.
His linen robe glowed dimly in the fading sunlight. His
bare arms and his face were the color of the Red Land.
His eyes had the hard flat glitter of a cobra's.

If this was not the chief priest of fallen Amon, then it
was one who claimed that office and power by sheer
strength of will. He offered the king's general no gesture
of respect, still less of submission. The king's general
bowed in front of him, not too low, not too quick.

They did not waste time in greetings. No more did the
priest invite Horemheb inside, nor he insist on it. They
spoke as they began, he in the courtyard as the light died
about him, the priest in the deepening shadow of the colonnade. Nofret caught glimpses of light behind, and a
shifting of shadows. There were people listening, maybe
armed, maybe ready to strike if their master gave them
leave.

No one waited on Horemheb. No one stood guard over
him. His courage was breathtaking, and he wore it as easily
as he wore his kilt.

He spoke without raising his voice, but the walls and
pillars of the courtyard made it stronger, clear enough to
be heard no matter where one was. "Call off your dogs,"
he said. "They're winning out there, for the moment, but
the king has men to spend. You don't."

"What do you know of our numbers?" the priest asked.
He spoke softly. His tone was mild. It was the sound,
Nofret thought, of perfect and implacable hate.

"I know what all my spies tell me," said Horemheb,
"and what your own people will admit to. You can't win
while the king is in Thebes."

"And yet because he is in Thebes we must make it
known how little we either love or fear him."

"He doesn't care," said Horemheb.

"He should," the priest said. "It will be his downfall."

"But not yet." Horemheb set his feet apart and folded

his arms: a soldier's posture, at ease and yet poised to act if there was need. "You'd do best to kill him, you know. Poison's easy. A knife in the back is simple."

"No," said the priest, as soft as ever. "We do not kill the son of Horus, not though he be apostate. The gods would curse us and all our posterity."

"So they would," said Horemheb, "but wouldn't it be worth it? He'd be dead, and his god with him. The Two Lands would be free."

"But we would not," the priest said, "nor our god in whose name we did it."

"Then you'll wait him out? As your young men are waiting in the streets?"

"My young men convey a message to the king," the priest said. "When the dark falls, they will withdraw and be concealed. Your spies will find nothing but their blood on the paving stones."

"They won't bother to look," said Horemheb.

The priest's face by now was no more than a blur in the gloom, but Nofret thought he might have raised a brow. "And what do you ask in return?"

"What I've always asked," Horemheb answered. "That you wait, and that when the time comes, you support me. I'll get rid of your king for you."

"If you kill him," the priest said, "you will bear the curse of it. We will not—cannot—suffer your presence then."

"I," said Horemheb, "won't kill him. But I'll open the way for you to come back."

"How long?" the priest demanded, the first sign of emotion that Nofret had heard in him.

"As long as it takes," Horemheb said. "Call off your dogs and keep them kenneled. I'll get the king out of Thebes and see to it that he doesn't come back. The longer he stays away, the easier it will be for you to show the people how strong Amon still is."

The priest nodded slowly enough and deeply enough that Nofret saw the movement. "We will be patient again. We will wait. Only keep the king shut up in his city as we keep our young men under restraint in our own. And leave us free to do as we must here—as the god decrees that we should."

"As long as you don't go to war with the city guard," said Horemheb, "do the rest and welcome. And when the king is gone, I'll come to claim my reckoning."

"It will be waiting for you," said Amon's priest.

CHAPTER NINETEEN

▲

NOFRET had in her bones the memory of the way that Horemheb had taken to come to this place. She followed that memory backwards to the gate where she had collided with him, and found that the gate opened on a court, and the court ended in a wall, and in the wall was a door like the one through which she had come.

By then she could just see her hand in front of her face. The light that lingered in the sky made the earth below seem darker than it was. Her fingers, groping, found the latch. She tugged at it. For a moment she feared that the door was barred from without, but suddenly, so suddenly she nearly fell, it opened.

The street was all strange to her, dark and empty. She turned at random, not knowing which way was right, trusting to fate or chance or whatever god might happen to be watching. She brushed one of her amulets with a finger. It was cool, smooth, lifeless.

Briefly she hesitated. No. She would go on, and not turn back.

The narrow street gave way to a wider one. She refused to be afraid. It was night now, no question of it, and she was on the wrong side of the river from her lady. No one would ferry her across.

Unless . . .

General Horemheb must have a boat. He quartered in the palace with the king, on the sunset bank.

She could not name herself to him and demand to be returned to her mistress, or hope that she could hide on a boat as small as a lord's ferry, among the oarsmen and the attendants. She was not bold enough for either one.

Nor was she fool enough to think that she could sleep safe in the streets of Thebes, nor mad enough to swim the river. Crocodiles hid in the reeds, feeding on the leavings that the city cast into the water, with the odd stray cat or goose. Or, if fortune favored them, an idiot of a slave who stayed away too long and could not go home till morning.

The city was strange now that night lay on it. Lights were few and far between, in doorways mostly, or dancing along with companies of young bloods exploring the taverns or accompanying one another to a revel. In the darkness thieves crept, and slayers of the unwary, and other, darker things. Nightwalkers, drinkers of blood, souls of the dead in search of warmth and life.

She gripped her amulets tightly and made her way through the shadows. The stars were out, and a round-bellied moon, nearly full. It was the blind eye of Horus, the Egyptians said. It stared blankly down, casting cold white light that made the darkness darker. It did not see Nofret, nor would it have cared if it had.

Let thieves and footpads do the same. She made herself as invisible as she could, as negligible as a cat slipping from doorway to doorway. Her hands were cold. Her skin shuddered with the touch of the night air.

To shut off fear, she ran through over and over the things that she had heard in Amon's temple. The king's chief of guards wanted to be something more than he was, and he was not averse to a bit of petty treason. That much she could be sure of. Whether the priests of Amon would actually shrink from murdering a king for the sheer and holy terror of his office, she could not tell. Horemheb would do whatever he needed to get what he wanted. Even if it meant arranging for—but not exactly causing—the king to be killed.

A messenger who brought such news to the king might be rewarded richly—or she might be flayed and bathed in salt for afflicting his sacred ears with lies. The king trusted the general of his armies. Insofar as he could be said to like anyone at all, he liked—was fond of—General Horemheb. That soft awkward unbeautiful man with his stammering tongue might even envy the tall strong soldier who never failed in a speech, nor stumbled over a word.

Nofret was nothing to the king. She doubted that he even remembered her, for all the times he had seen or spoken to her since she came to serve the third princess in Akhetaten.

None of which would matter in the least if she fell prey to a footpad in midnight-darkened Thebes. She quickened her pace to a trot, aiming where she hoped the river was, where the heavy wet scent of water overcame the human reek of the city. If she was wrong she would wander the lightless ways till dawn, unless a nightwalker caught her and left her bloodless in a midden.

Her trot was almost a run. Her breath came in gasps. She steadied it by force of will. There was no slowing the pounding of her heart.

She stumbled into a wall, recoiled, flung herself through a gap between it and another. And there was the river, broad empty liquid-whispering expanse aflow with moonlight. Boats rocked empty at the piers and along the quays. On the other side Nofret saw a glimmer of light.

There was light on this side, too, some distance down

the riverbank. A torch flickered and swayed, riding on a boat that tugged at its tether. Shadowy shapes bulked beneath it: men asleep at the oars. She heard the rasp of a snore, and a curse as one of the others kicked the snorer into silence.

Nofret was a ghost, was shadow, was silence given substance. She crept toward the boat. No one on it kept watch. Her nostrils twitched at the scent of barley beer.

These could not be Horemheb's men, surely. He had no patience with drunkenness and none with guards who slept at their post.

And yet clearly they were waiting for someone. The torch would not have been lit else, making a beacon to guide any thief or murderer to unguarded prey.

In that open boat full of sleeping rowers there was still room for a woman to hide. The master's deck with its canopy and its gilded chair offered a niche of shadow behind the chair, a space just wide enough for Nofret to huddle with knees clasped to chest. There was even warmth to be had: the rug under her and the canopy hanging down behind, and a cloth—fine-woven rug or warm mantle—flung over the back of the chair. She appropriated that, wrapped herself in it and was remarkably comfortable.

Sleep stole up on her. She fought it for as long as she could. But the current rocked the boat on its mooring, and the snorer's racket had quieted to a gentle purr, and the warmth of the mantle about her did battle against the chill of the wind off the water. She curled tighter, to be less comfortable, and fell sound asleep.

■   ■   ■

Voices woke her, and a thunderous rattle that her stunned brain knew somehow to be the running out of oars. The deck creaked and shifted beneath her. Someone was standing on it.

She peered blinking from behind the chair, too sodden with sleep to be afraid. The man stood with his back to her, fists planted on hips, legs braced against the movement of the boat. The torch's light shone through his linen kilt. She could see the strong muscled shape of his thighs.

Her eyes closed. She had been right after all, or a god had guided her. She was in General Horemheb's boat, and General Horemheb stood in front of her, face turned to the night and the wind off the river. He did not sense her presence at all. No one did. She was as invisible as a living thing could be.

She took care to breathe lightly. Though her body cramped into a knot, she did not yield to the temptation to uncoil. The boat crawled toward the dark shore and the one light gleaming there. Bright as the moon was, she could see the shape of the palace and the faces of the cliffs behind, stark black, pale silver, that in the day were the sunstruck ruddy color of the Red Land.

As endless as the crossing had seemed in the magnitude of her discomfort, the arrival at the bank seemed to come in a moment, too quick for her wavering wits. Men ran along the gunwales of the boat, leaping to secure it to the pier. The others ran up the oars and stowed them, a rumble and clatter that sounded as loud as thunder in the night. But no one came to ask who crossed the river so late.

Nofret was trapped. Horemheb left the boat at his leisure, accompanied by the steersman and a handful of guards. The oarsmen and a pair of armored guards lingered endlessly. Not even a ship of the great sea, Nofret was sure, should take so long to secure itself after a voyage.

If she ever escaped this trap, she would have to do it on all fours like an animal. Her back would never unkink again. Her legs were cramped against her chest, her arms aching with holding them there.

She would burst out or scream, or do something to set at naught that endless hour of worsening discomfort. She would not be able to help herself. She was too certain of it even to regret it.

And yet somehow she held on. The boat's crew finished their interminable meandering duties. One by one they wandered off, followed by the guards. The last of them took the torch.

It did not matter. The moon was westering but bright enough to see by. Muscle by tormented muscle Nofret uncoiled. Gods oh gods it hurt. Wonderful hurt. Hurt of lying on her back, stretched straight and stiff as a corpse, and simply breathing.

Much later, but much too soon for her howling muscles, Nofret dragged herself to her feet. There was treason in Thebes. What she could do about it she did not know, but she had no particular desire to see her lady poisoned or killed. For one thing it would leave Nofret with nowhere safe to go.

There were no footpads in the palace, and the only robbers on this side of the river were those who robbed the dead. They cared nothing for the living. Nofret walked more steadily as she went on, as the pain in her body faded to an ache. She went in by a postern that was neither barred nor guarded, safe at last and too numb to notice.

■　■　■

Ankhesenpaaten was not asleep. Nofret did not think that she had slept at all that night. There were no signs that the king had been there. The young queen was lying in her royal bed on her sheets of finest white linen, with her headrest of ivory inlaid with gold. She was not the brown thinbodied child she had been when she made Nofret her maid. Her skin was golden still from her morning baths in the sun, but she had grown into a woman, and one who would be very beautiful when her growing was done.

She turned her head at Nofret's coming, her dark eyes washed clean of paint but seeming no less huge in her narrow face. She did not smile. She never smiled, Nofret thought. Not even when she drove her chariot, or when she played with Tutankhaten or with little Meritaten-too.

Nofret knelt beside her lady's bed. Ankhesenpaaten watched her but did not speak. That was a game she played sometimes: saying nothing, simply staring at a messenger, till the messenger blurted out everything at once.

Nofret often won that game by saying nothing at all and letting her lady go wild with curiosity, but tonight she was in no mood for silliness. She said, "Horemheb is talking treason with the high priest of Amon."

"So that was where you were," said the queen. No surprise. No shock. "You could have been killed."

"Would you have cared?"

The queen closed her eyes. "Probably. I don't know." She paused. "Amon is dead."

"He is not," said Nofret, not even thinking, but knowing it for the truth. "Your father's general is going to help Amon's priests get rid of your father."

"They won't do that," said the queen. "Father is the king. No priest can ever touch a king. He knows too well what the gods will do to him for sacrilege."

"He also knows who can be relied on to dispose of the king for him. I don't think," said Nofret, "that General Horemheb is a superstitious man."

"Superstition has nothing to do with it. The king is the king: Horus on earth, Osiris among the dead. The kingdom is as his own body. As he lives, it lives. If he grows ill or dies, it too fails, unless there is another to be king in his place."

"But there is!" cried Nofret. "Smenkhkare is exactly what they can use: beautiful, vain, and profoundly stupid."

The queen did not reprimand Nofret for that insolence. "Yes, he is stupid. That's why they won't be able to use him. He's styled himself the Beloved of Akhenaten, just as my mother did: the one who rules beside the king, the chosen of the god. He hasn't the wits to turn against Father. If they kill Father, they have to kill him, too. Then they'll see the Two Lands fall for lack of a king.''

''I don't think so,'' Nofret said. ''They'd find themselves a new king, one who would owe enough to Amon and the priests that he'd be paying the debt until he died.''

''There is no one who would do that,'' the queen said scornfully. She sat up and tucked her feet beneath her, frowning at Nofret. ''And even if he dared, he'd have to marry a royal lady in order to have a right to the crowns. None of us would do such a thing.''

''Wouldn't you?'' Nofret asked her. ''If one of you could be convinced that it was best for the kingdom or even for your own heart. Or,'' she said, ''if they got hold of Tutankhaten.''

''Tutankhaten would never let any mere mortal tell him what to do,'' said the queen. She no less than Nofret had reason to know. Her young uncle was, truth to tell, a bit of a terror. But then all boys were. They grew out of it, or else they became men like Horemheb—or like the king.

Which made Nofret think, and once she thought about it she knew. ''Horemheb might pretend to be any man's ally if it got him what he wanted. Then he'd have no scruples about disposing of the inconvenience.''

''Horemheb is loyal to the king,'' said the queen.

''He didn't sound loyal when I heard him telling the priest of Amon to hold off his troops while Horemheb gets your father out of Thebes,'' Nofret said, snapping off the words.

The princess sighed. ''Ah, so that's what the trouble is. You don't think a loyal man can treat with the enemy for his king's safety.''

''Safety!'' Nofret flung up her hands. ''Oh, you are a fool! He was buying and selling your king's life—but in his time, not in Amon's. He wants to be more secure, I suppose, before he moves on the throne. Don't you remember how he tried to fill Akhetaten with his own men?''

"Oh, but that was playing power. Any man worth his ambition will do that, to show that he's not to be trifled with. It's no threat to the king. Not even Amon is bold enough for that.''

Nofret could howl, or she could surrender. In the end she did a little of both. Muted howl, ferocious mutter. ''I don't understand you at all. Not . . . at . . . all.''

"Of course not,'' said the queen. She slipped out of bed and stood over Nofret. ''We do have to get Father out of Thebes. Horemheb is wise in that. No one will touch Father, but the rest of the court aren't safe, with the people so angry. They should go back to Akhetaten. Go, fetch the steward of the palace, and one of the maids. I should be dressed when he comes.''

And what was Nofret, then, if not a maid?

Shadow, Nofret thought as she ran on her errand. Runner at her lady's whim. Inveterate haunter of places in which she did not belong.

Better that than a betrayer of kings. Even such a king as Akhenaten.

CHAPTER TWENTY

▲

ANKHESENPAATEN might see sense after her own peculiar fashion, but the king was blind to anything resembling it. He would not move from Thebes. Lady Kiya was ill, he said with iron obstinacy, and much too near her time to travel. The court could do as it pleased. He would remain in Thebes until his lady was delivered of her child.

There was no shifting him. Not even Horemheb was strong enough to do it. Nofret wondered what Amon's high priest thought of that. She did not seek out the temple to learn. One evening in that terrible place was enough.

As Kiya kept to her rooms and her flock of maids and physicians, and the king attended her whenever he was not engrossed in praying to his god, the city grew more openly restless. Nofret did not hear of priests engaging in skirmishes with city guards, but she did hear of riots over this trifle and that, courtiers assaulted when they ventured to show their faces, seals on temples broken and rites celebrated there in defiance of the king's ban—but never in Amon's temple.

Amon's priest was keeping his word to Horemheb. No one came to kill the king. The west bank of the river was quiet, eerily so, although the eastern city snarled even in its sleep.

On a morning some days after Nofret's escape from city and temple, Nofret happened to be near the gate when a man in a priest's robe asked to be conducted to the king. He did not look like a madman, and yet it was mad for any priest of Amon to show himself openly in this place.

He had others with him, a handful of watchful-eyed young men, all tall and strongly built. Nofret recognized with a start the thin man whom she had seen in the temple. Maybe some of his guards were familiar, too, from the battle in the street.

The king's guards let them in without pause or objection. Nofret was astonished, but she should not have been. Horemheb was their commander.

Amon's priests were taken direct to the king, nor were they made to wait for more than half a day till he was disposed to speak with them. Nofret was there when they were brought in front of him, and properly so since her lady sat as queen on a throne beside the king's. Nofret kept her eyes fixed in front of her and refused to glance at the tall broad man among smaller, softer courtiers. Horemheb would not betray himself. Not he, who had been a soldier for so long.

Nor did he seem to know her. She was dressed as a royal servant and not as a slave wandering loose in the city. Her hair was tightly plaited, her body concealed in a gown of fine linen. She would, she hoped, look like another person altogether than the sharp-tongued maid in Amon's temple.

King and queen seemed oblivious to Horemheb or to any threat he might offer. They were at their most splendid and their most inhuman: all one blaze of gold like images of god and goddess. In the cavernous space of the great hall of audience, where echoes fluttered like bats beneath the roof, they seemed as brilliant as the sun, and as little concerned with mortal follies.

There had been other guests and petitioners before them, the long round of royal graciousness that the king could indulge in when it suited his whim. There would be others after, gratified to be granted the light of the king's own presence, and not merely that of his queen.

These emissaries—emissary, really, since all but one were simple bodyguards—paid homage to the king in due and proper form, as priests of one god to the living image of another. They made it clear by subtle flickerings of hand and eye that they offered their obeisance to the office and not to the man who held it; to the god whose living face he was, and not to him who had turned against all gods but the one of his own making.

Perhaps he understood what they were saying to him without words. Perhaps he did not. He did not seem to see them. His eyes gazed into the limitless distance of the hall. His mind was wherever it went when he was consenting to be, however briefly, king.

The thin priest's voice woke him out of his dream. It was the voice of a singer trained in the temple, pitched to fill that whole huge hall. It was neither loud nor strident, and yet it rattled Nofret's teeth in her skull.

"O king!" the priest intoned. Only the title, no softening of respect. "Lord of the Two Lands, apostate against its gods, hear the word of Amon who is from everlasting, who shall be lord and god when your bones are dust in the earth. Turn back to his ways. Forsake your falsehood. Serve him as your fathers served him before you, or suffer the force of his wrath."

The king had not moved on his throne, but his souls were all in his body, and his wits, too—more than Nofret had ever seen. Here was open threat to his god.

"If you fail of your duty," the priest said, "Amon will curse you and all your posterity. Your lineage will die before you. Your name will be cut out from among the names of kings, and be forgotten."

A movement caught Nofret's eye. Horemheb was signaling—to guards, to accomplices, who knew?

No one else could move. The priest's voice held them rapt. His words mastered them. He had made them remember fear: fear of the gods, fear of those who served the gods.

The king sat immobile. When he spoke he did not stammer at all. He lacked the priest's richness or strength of voice, but clarity he had, each word distinct as if limned in stone. "Who suffered this madman to come before my face?"

"Those," said the priest, "were the very words of Amon in speaking of you, O king."

"Remove him," said the king.

The guards who were nearest blanched and glanced at Horemheb. He twitched up his chin: *Go to it.* Reluctantly they moved to obey.

"No," the priest said. "No, I go by my own will and the will of my god. Remember, king. Come back to Amon or be forever cursed."

A murmur ran through the hall. Nofret felt the shudder in her skin. A priest's curse was a powerful thing. A king cursed tainted his whole realm, all his lands and people, their wars, their peace, their planting and harvest.

The king betrayed no fear of the curse or of the man who threatened it. "Amon is nothing to me," he said. "The Aten will protect me."

There could have been no doubt that he would say that. But Nofret watched the faces of the court, the glitter of their eyes, the fixity that had not been there before, or never so clear to see. They loved their king no more than did the people in the city or the priests in the temples.

He saw nothing but his god. He rose still gripping crook and flail. The flail, beads of gold and lapis lazuli on cords of gold, lashed the air. "Remove this man!"

The guards glanced again at Horemheb, again sought his leave to obey their lord and king. Horemheb scowled at it, but Nofret saw satisfaction in his eyes. He took his time in granting leave, while the king stood quivering and the priest regarded him with something close to scorn.

The king's guards closed about the priest. He shook off their hands. "If your god were a true god," he said to the king, "he would smite me now. I spit on him. I curse him to the nether realms, where Eater of Souls waits in hunger, and devouring Set remembers the savor of Osiris' blood."

"Your god is false," said the king, cold now and quiet. And to the guards yet again: "Remove him."

■ ■ ■

"You should have had him killed," said Horemheb.

The king, having seen the priest removed, had returned to the holding of audience. He had not seemed to notice that no one was paying attention to anything he said. The court was abuzz with Amon's stroke, the blow that had fallen at last and—or so they said—long expected. The king in Thebes had defied Amon to his face. Now he paid.

He would say that he paid nothing. The priest had pricked his temper, but the priest was gone, and the king was still in Thebes, still dispensing his justice in the hall of the palace.

Now that the audience was over, the king had thought to go to his rest. But Horemheb followed him into the retiring room where he was being soothed and anointed by his daughter-queen, attended by Nofret and a flock of maids and menservants.

"You should have had him killed," the general repeated when the king did not acknowledge him. "Now he's gone, and he'll tell the Two Lands that he cursed the king and escaped alive."

"His curse was nothing," said the king, "but wind and air." He yawned and patted his daughter-wife's cheek. "A little more of the flower scent, I think; a little less of the musk."

"My lord king," said Horemheb through gritted teeth, "a priest's curse is rather more than wind. It will sway the kingdom against you."

"The Aten protects me," the king said placidly.

"As he protected your queen and kin and kingdom in the plague?" Horemheb shot back. "Like that, lord king?"

The king stiffened slightly. Ankhesenpaaten rubbed sweet oil into his shoulders, easing him back into his complacency. She did not speak or offer to speak. The king said, "A god who is false has no power."

"He is not false to the people!" Horemheb muted his battlefield roar, but the walls of that small space shook, and maids squeaked and quailed. He ignored them. He spoke more softly but with all the force he could command. "The people cannot be told to stop worshipping the gods of their fathers simply because a king thinks he's found a better god to follow. If that god curses the king, the people remember—and every ill that falls on them, they set against his name. You are already hated, lord king.

Keep on and you'll be worse than hated. You'll be struck from the people's memory.''

"Do you too curse me?" the king asked mildly.

"I tell you the truth," said Horemheb.

"I will not bow to a god who is false," the king said, "nor leave this city until it pleases me to do so."

Horemheb widened his eyes. "What, did I ask you to go?"

"You were going to," said the king. "Everyone does. I am staying here. My son will be born in Thebes as kings' sons have been since the gods were young."

Horemheb bowed, stiffly correct, and took his leave. Neither he nor the king remarked that he had not been dismissed. The king sighed with relief, and to all appearances forgot him.

■ ■ ■

No one else could be so fortunate. With the king convinced that he was in no danger, the people in Thebes were emboldened. Courtiers clung to the palace or fled to their own estates. The king's servants and the servants of his ladies and queens went nowhere unguarded.

The young king and his queen, who had kept to their own palace in Thebes itself, had been refusing to leave the city that Smenkhkare reckoned to be his own. But in the blazing noon of the day when Lady Kiya was brought to bed of the child she carried, a golden boat rowed in haste across the river, and a straggle of lesser boats behind it, carrying whatever their passengers had been able to seize as they fled.

"Fire at the gates," said Smenkhkare, still breathless, though more with temper than with haste. "Men howling like dogs. Stones flying. Insolence beyond belief, brother. And all for a bit of holy nonsense."

Stupidity might be said to be Smenkhkare's greatest virtue. He had no conception of the hate that had driven him here, and nothing but astonishment that any man of Egypt would presume to do such a thing to his king. His fearlessness kept his queen from slipping into hysteria, which in Nofret's mind was a very good thing.

It fell to Ankhesenpaaten to see everyone housed and fed. That was not as difficult as it might have been, with so many of the court already gone, but there were still a myriad vexations. This princeling must be housed well apart from that petty lord lest there be murder committed, and this lady should not be suffered to look on the face of that rival of hers for some young idiot's favor, and everyone's servants were intriguing endlessly for their own and their masters' precedence.

Meritaten was no use. She only wanted to sit in her husband's lap while he idled in the garden. The thought of doing anything useful gave her the vapors.

She was really rather clever, thought Nofret, watching her poor lady try to be queen over two courts and two kingdoms. Of all the yattering crowd who had come across the river with Smenkhkare, Nofret was only glad to see Meritaten's chief of servants. Tama, unlike her mistress, was a great deal of use. She would of course never say it, but she made it clear in the way she looked at Ankhesenpaaten that she was pleased to find someone in Egypt who knew how to rule a kingdom.

■　■　■

That night there was music in the younger queen's chambers, Tama's harp and her deep sweet voice sounding as they had not since all the princesses were alive and living together in Akhetaten. Meritaten had gone to bed with her beloved. The king was in the palace temple praying for his lady, who labored still to produce his heir. There was only Ankhesenpaaten to listen, and a gaggle of maids, and a lady or two.

Nofret, crouched at her lady's feet, let her arm rest

across Ankhesenpaaten's knees and rested her chin on it. It was a familiarity, but Ankhesenpaaten did not rebuke it. She was watching Tama. As Nofret watched, a tear escaped the corner of her eye and slipped down her cheek.

Tama was weeping too as she sang. Nofret wondered if there was something wrong with herself. She did not want to cry, remembering the world as it had been when the king's daughters were children. She wanted to do something terribly painful to the king. Drag him behind a chariot. Rend him with hooks. Prove to him that his god was a lie.

▪ ▪ ▪

In the dark before dawn, Lady Kiya bore her king a daughter—the ninth that he had sired, big and lusty and strong. The mother was not so fortunate. The birth of so large a child tore her, and she bled, and nearly died.

There could be no leaving Thebes while the lady was still so ill. She, however, when she woke from the long sleep of one who has walked the edge of the dry land, among the souls of the newly dead, summoned the king and the king's younger daughter.

She looked like a corpse—a beautiful one, white as the bones under her delicate skin. Her body, which must be still shapeless from bearing the child, was artfully hidden under a coverlet of fine linen. Her hair lay in a plait on her shoulder. She seemed no older than Ankhesenpaaten.

She did not have much strength, but what she had, she put into her voice as the two whom she had summoned came to stand beside her bed. The king took her hand in both of his. The king's daughter stood a little apart. Kiya said to them both, "We must leave this city. Tomorrow, have the boats readied. Let us go back to Akhetaten."

"Beloved," the king said, "you cannot—"

"I want to go back home," she said with a quiver of the lip—masterful, Nofret thought.

Ankhesenpaaten apparently did not think so. "Who's been talking to you?" she asked, sharper maybe than she intended.

Kiya closed her eyes. "I have ears. I can hear. I know that the young king is here, and his queen. They would never have left their palace if it had been safe to stay."

"It's safe here," the king said.

Kiya kept her eyes closed, knowing maybe how frail she looked, and how enchanting. "I want to go home," she said, her voice growing faint.

She was not feigning her exhaustion. The king opened his mouth. He shut it again.

A sound made Nofret glance quickly toward the door. It was not so close. It sounded like thunder, or like the roar of the sea, muted by walls.

It was the city of Thebes massed along the eastern bank of the river, howling at the king in his palace. They were singing a hymn to Amon, with a command in it, and a promise. *Depart. Depart from my city, or I come to destroy you.*

That, Nofret learned later. Now she only heard it and shuddered. She knew the sound of the wolfpack closing in for the kill.

Ankhesenpaaten spoke very quietly, very steadily. "Have the boats made ready. We sail at dawn."

CHAPTER TWENTY-ONE

▲

DAWN was almost too late for the kings and their courts and queens. All night long the people of Thebes sang both hymns and curses, invoking each of the gods in turn, naming each as living truth. The king tried to counter them with his own people along the palace walls singing the hymns of the Aten, but they were too few and too scared. What he had conceived as a mighty lifting up of voices in the honor of his god, sounded thin and frightened, and died away almost as soon as it began.

He went on singing alone when the last of them had given up and fled. His voice was true, but it was weak and light, and barely audible a spearlength away. He stood in the waning moonlight, hands braced on the parapet of the palace wall, and sang the praises of the Aten into the clamorous dark.

■ ■ ■

In the morning the kings left Thebes in a golden ship, with as brave a show as their weary, frightened people could muster. The kings themselves were above anything so mortal as fear. They sat on a double throne on the deck of the ship in hieratic stillness, crowned each with the Two Crowns, and each clasping crook and flail. Their faces were immortally serene, their eyes masked in paint.

So too their queens on a second ship well warded in boats full of armored guards. Meritaten was stiff with terror, but Tama had coaxed her into gown and wig and crown and set her on the gilded throne, and given her the scepter to hold. She clutched it as if it were her only protection against an army of demons.

Ankhesenpaaten beside her was as calm as the kings were, but with more intelligence in it. Nofret saw how her eyes slid toward the eastern bank, toward the people linked arm in arm all along it, still singing, still mocking their king with their devotion to their gods.

No arrow flew from among them, no spear aimed to dispose of a king. They would not kill him, only defy him, and drive him out of their city.

He went not as one driven but as one who turns gladly toward home. Lady Kiya traveled in his boat: Nofret could see the crimson canopy under which the lady lay, and the servants who came and went, looking after their mistress. The wail of a child echoed over the water. Strong lungs, this latest of the king's failures had, and no reluctance to use them.

Long afterward she would remember that flight from Thebes: the golden boats, the frightened boatmen, the bank as thick with people as a marsh with reeds, and the rise and fall of voices in a hymn to ever-living Osiris. The strong sun of Egypt striking dazzle on the water might in the king's mind have been counter enough: hammer-force of living light against a god whom none could see.

The singing followed them far down the river. With wind in their sails and current to drive them, they sailed swiftly and in silence, the only sound the baby's wail and the song of the wind.

■   ■   ■

Akhetaten seemed strangely small after the magnificence of Thebes. Its beauties were all new beauties, without the life and soul that centuries could give them. Its mountain-walls closed in about it, shutting it away from the kingdom and its gods.

The kings were still kings, and the Two Lands still needed them. But they did not travel outside of Akhetaten. It was their choice, they proclaimed, to rest and to worship the Aten in the Aten's blessed city. But that choice was made perforce. They were not welcome in the rest of Egypt.

For a prison it was spacious and most luxurious. The court gave itself up to frivolity, inventing and discarding fashions by the hour. The kings conducted themselves each according to his nature: Akhenaten in prayer and visions, Smenkhkare in dalliance with his queen and his lesser ladies, or else on the hunt or at games among the young men.

They did not seem to notice that they had only this city and the desert about it and the river in sight of it to play in. Messengers came as they always had, embassies, letters from kings and princes. Nothing on the face of it had changed.

But Egypt had rejected its king. It suffered him to live because his office was sacred, but it would not accept his god or suffer his presence. His brother king, his Beloved, his younger and more beautiful image, was in no better case.

They were still kings. That to them was all that mattered.

▪   ▪   ▪

Nofret found herself seeking out a kind of imprisonment as if in echo of the kings. What had become habit in Thebes, not to leave the palace, lingered in Akhetaten where she was safe, where she knew all the roads and byways. She clung to the round of her days, waiting on her lady, chattering with Tama in the long drowsy afternoons while their ladies slept or idled with their husbands, becoming narrower and more circumscribed, till one morning she looked out of the window in her lady's chamber, and the courtyard without seemed intolerably vast.

That scared her. In the afternoon, although Tama wanted to settle in for a long delicious gossip, Nofret saw her mistress settled in the cool of the resting-room with a maid to fan her and another to fetch whatever her whim desired. Then she fled.

She was a woman of consequence now. She was a queen's personal maid, and entitled to wear a linen gown and a wig. She hated the wig but did not mind the gown. Her wild mane of hair she mostly tamed in plaits with beads on the ends, or wound in a cord and let hang down her back. Today she had braided it and coiled it about her head, to be cool. The amulets she had bought in Thebes hung on their string between her breasts, under the gown.

She walked boldly to the palace gate. It was open as it always was in daylight, a guard with a spear on either side of it, shining in armor of gilded bronze. They both knew her, and knew better than to grin at her as she went by. One of them still had the dent in his nose from the last—and only—time he had tried to force his attentions on her.

She strode past them into the city proper, and froze.

The world was too big. There were walls, but they were all too far away. The sky was unreachably high. She was falling into it.

She gasped and stiffened her knees before they buckled. The guards were staring straight ahead, conscientiously not watching her. She thanked them in her heart for that, though she would never say so. That would give them leave to take advantage.

As firmly as she could, but with beating heart, she made her way into the city. It was all strange, like a fever-dream. Was she cursed, then? Had some echo of the curse on the king come to torment her, to bind her within walls more of fear than of stone?

No, she told herself. She had been mewed up too long, that was all. The world looked too big and the sky too high. She had been the same way in Mitanni, when she had spent whole rounds of the moon in the same half-dozen rooms doing the same half-dozen things for the same handful of women. She only had to face it full and it would go away. Walls would be plain walls again, and the sky only sky.

She jostled through crowds in the market, too dizzy and befuddled to buy anything, although vendors sang for her, coaxed her, begged her to come and see their wares. She was going somewhere in particular. It had nothing to do with hot onion-pies or cheap baubles.

Walls again, and desert beyond them, the road that looked east to the cliffs and the tombs. Here the sky was

not so terrible, the air less full of empty fear. Her throat
was dry: she regretted, then, refusing to exchange a bit of
barley for a jar of beer.

She shrugged. Thirst would not kill her as quickly as
that. Part of her objected, but she did not listen to it. She
was going to the clean place, the place that had nothing to
do with kings or their gods.

■ ■ ■

The workmen's village was much the same as it had always been. The same dogs barked at her, the same naked
children played in the street. Where the Apiru were, the
women gossiped at the well or sat on doorsteps spinning
wool and dandling babies. They stared at Nofret as if she
had been a stranger: not hostile, but not friendly, either.

Some she knew by name, but she did not call to them.
Their eyes did not know her. The hurt of that was sharp.
It had not been so terribly long since she last came here.
Had it?

Maybe it had. A year, more . . . she did not remember.
Did she look that different, then, simply because she was
wearing a dress?

By the time she came to the house at the end of the
village, up against the rock with its stump of tree, she was
growing angry. She stopped in front of its door, ready to
hammer on it and demand to be let in. But she paused. If
truly it had been so long, then Leah and Aharon and Johanan might not live here at all. They could be dead, or—

She was being a fool. Leah was inside. She did not
know how she knew it, but that presence was distinct, and
it was waiting for her.

She walked in as if she had every right in the world,
into the heavy warmth and the smell of goats, and past
that to the curtain that was like the flap of a tent. It was a
little more worn than she remembered, a little more dusty,
but the room within was much the same.

So too the woman who sat in a shaft of light, weaving on a loom. The cloth was a handsome thing, stripes of red and black and fallow gold, woven tight and smooth. The gnarled fingers moved swiftly among the threads, not pausing even when Leah raised her head to smile at Nofret.

As if she had been there only the day before or had lived there always, Nofret folded herself at Leah's feet and rested her head on the wool-clad knees. Leah thrust the shuttle through warp and weft and straightened her back, and laid her hand on Nofret's head.

She did not say anything. Nofret was glad of that. If she had, Nofret would not have been able to keep from bawling like a baby.

After a long while Nofret sat up. She had not wept, but she felt as if she had: empty and clean. Leah was watching her with calm interest, offering nothing, taking nothing.

"I don't know what came over me," Nofret said, rough with the unshed tears. "To walk in like that—"

"You came where you needed to come," said Leah. "Is it so bad with your princess, then?"

"No!" said Nofret sharply. She sucked in a breath. "No. She's well. As well as she can be . . . considering . . ."

"Considering that she is barely thirteen years old, and going to have a baby."

Nofret gasped and lurched to her feet. "How did you— she isn't—"

"You know she is," said Leah. She clasped Nofret's hands and drew her down again so that they were face to face. "The good god was kind to her. He kept her from conceiving as quickly as her sisters."

"What's the good in it?" Nofret muttered bitterly. "It will only be another daughter."

"Only a daughter," Leah said. "Why, and so were you. So was I."

"But we weren't supposed to be a king's sons!" Nofret

stopped. The silence was enormous. "You weren't," she said.

"Oh, no," said Leah. "I was only to be priest and prophet. My poor father was dismayed to discover that I had the gifts without the blessing of being a man. None of the sons who came after me had the least calling to the god's ways. They all went for fighting men in Pharaoh's armies, or shepherds among his flocks. Our father died a disappointed man."

"So will this king do," said Nofret, "and none too soon for any of us."

"Maybe," Leah said. "Come, let me up. There's bread fresh from the baking, and cheese, and—"

"No," said Nofret. "No, I'll fetch it. I remember where you keep everything." She paused. "Your servant . . . ?"

"Zillah left us," said Leah. "She married Shem the goatherd, whose mother needed someone to look after her. There's a child who comes in in the mornings to learn to weave and sew and cook, but when the sun touches noon, she leaves me to my solitude. It's very satisfactory."

Nofret could barely imagine such luxury. To be alone every day, to do what she wanted, when she wanted it— astonishing.

Leah smiled. "Here, we'll both lay the table. Miriam gave me a basket of cakes that she'd baked. She tried something new with dates and honey, and it smells delectable."

"But won't Aharon and—" Nofret began.

"Oh, they'll come," said Leah serenely. "They don't see true, not as we do, but they both have a nose for their dinner."

Nofret laughed, and stopped, because it felt so strange. She had not laughed in—months? Years?

Since the last time she was among these people. She found herself chattering to Leah, telling her nothing in particular, and yet telling her a great deal: of Thebes and its splendors, of the young king, of her lady and of Tama, who was her friend, and of the court in its golden prison.

Leah had trivialities of her own to counter Nofret's: this woman married, that one widowed, and half a dozen either with child or just delivered of children. The goat was still lord of his kingdom, and all his harem had produced kids, to his considerable pride. "And yes," she said, "though he grows old and stiff in the joints, he still leaps the wall and thunders round the village on market days, for old times' sake."

Nofret was still laughing at that and arraying the last of the cups and bowls when the door-curtain parted and Aharon stooped to come in. He seemed bigger than ever, and stronger, with his dusty black hair and his—

Her mouth was hanging open. That was not Aharon at all, unless Aharon had misplaced a score of years and a span of beard. Which he had not, as she could see, for he came in behind the stranger, grinning white in his rich beard that had at last begun to show a thread or two of grey. "Nofret! Little fish. You've grown into a woman."

She blushed like a silly girl and nearly dropped the jar of goat's milk that she was holding. He laughed at that, relieved her of the jar and swept her into his embrace.

He had never welcomed her so before, never so much like family. She was too startled to resist, or to respond, either.

He held her at arm's length. "Ah," he said without undue regret. "I've embarrassed you." He shook his head. "I should learn to be more like a courtier."

"Don't do that!" Her vehemence made him laugh. He let her go, somewhat to her disappointment, and went to embrace his mother and to be embraced in turn.

That left the other, the young one. He was blushing bright red under his beard. By that, and by the noble arch of his nose, she knew him. "Johanan?"

His blush did not fade, but he laughed. His voice was

almost as deep as his father's. "I wouldn't have known you, either, if Grandmother hadn't said you'd come to-day."

She stared at him. He stared back, as bold as she, and as shy. "You aren't bad-looking," she said after a while.

"Nor are you," he said. "Are you a great lady now? I didn't see your chair outside. Did you send it home?"

"No," she said tartly. "I walked. Every step of the way, sir, just as I always have. Just because you finally noticed I'm female doesn't mean I've gone soft."

"I've always known you were female," he said. "I surprised you, didn't I? You never thought I'd grow up."

"You still haven't," she said. His coat was crooked. She tugged it straight and brushed stone-dust from it, brisk, annoyed for no good reason. Maybe because he let her do it. Maybe because he was there, and different, and yet the same. He was supposed to be as he had always been, or to be so changed that she did not know him. Not both at once.

Boys were like that. One season they were children, or nearly, with patchy beards and cracking voices. The next, they were men: tall and strong and deep-voiced and ineffably pleased with themselves, as if they had anything to do with it at all.

He was staring at her. She wanted to snap at him, to make him stop, but something held her back—maybe his grandmother and his father, waiting for them to sit, to eat. Both seemed much amused.

She glared at them all and sat in her old place at Aharon's right hand, where a guest would sit. But once she had sat, she leaped up again. There was no one to play the servant's part, no one to fetch the pot from the kitchen or—

"You sit," said Johanan with the authority of his new-minted manhood. "I'll play the maid." And at her half-voiced protest: "I've done it before." His grin was the same as it had always been, in that new and quite amazingly handsome face of his.

Who would ever have thought, Nofret mused to herself as he waited on them all like a well-trained servant, that gangly beaky-nosed Johanan would grow to look just like his father?

She drew a breath, let it out again. She was at ease here, more than she had ever been anywhere else. Yes, even in Hatti, in her father's house. And even though she had come in feeling like a stranger, and found strangers, but strangers who were kin.

■　■　■

Near sunset Nofret rose regretfully and readied to go. Aharon and Leah said their good-byes at the door of the house, but Johanan trailed after her, for all the world like a lost dog. Nofret said so, not slowing or turning, striding with grim purpose toward the road and the city.

A long step brought him level with her. "It will be dark by the time you get to the palace," he said.

"So?" said Nofret. "I used to go back in full night, and you never said a word."

"That was before," he said.

"Before what?"

He knew that tone: his brows were up, but he was not grinning as he might have before. "Before I really looked at you," he said.

"Why, do I have spots?"

"Well," he said. "One or two."

She checked and nearly stumbled, but caught herself. She was not going to let him take her off balance. No matter how hard he might try.

With teeth-gritted calm she said, "I am not fragile. You can stop hovering. Go home and feed the goats."

"I fed them before I came in," he said. "Can't I take

a walk in the evening? Is it cooler than it was yesterday, do you think?''

Nofret hissed. ''How old are you? Fifteen floods of the river? Shouldn't you be courting some sweet pink-faced girl in a striped veil?''

''I am sixteen,'' he said with dignity, ''and I don't like sweet pink-faced girls in striped veils. They're dull. And,'' he said, saving the worst for last, ''they giggle.''

Nofret did not know how to giggle. She wished she did. ''If I were in Hatti I would be married now, or about to be married.''

Gods. That was not what she should be talking about, and she certainly had not meant to say any such thing.

Johanan still walked with a bit of his old gangling awkwardness, as if parts of him were inclined to wander on their own. He tripped over a stone, righted himself, blushed furiously. The word he muttered in Apiru was not genteel at all.

When he spoke to Nofret, it could only be with as little control of himself as she had had. ''Have you—I mean, do you—did you ever—if there was someone who wanted—''

She understood him. It made her whitely angry. ''Why do you want to know? Because I'm a slave, and slaves are wanton? Because you want to tumble me under a bush?''

''No!''

His voice cracked on the word. He looked shocked, and then furious. ''What makes you think I would ever insult you like that?''

''Because you did.''

''I did not!''

''Did too!''

She stopped. So did he. Time was when they would have laughed, and the quarrel would have ended with them arm in arm, running wherever they would think to run to. But not any longer. They had grown up.

"I hate it," said Nofret. "I hate the way you look at me. As if you didn't know me. As if I were something—something horrible. Instead of—instead of—"

Oh, gods and goddesses. She was leaking like a sieve. Of course he would fold her in his arms as men were trained to do, and calm her and protect her and make her hate him even worse.

Except that he did not do that. He touched her, yes: laid a hand on her shoulder, lightly, as a friend does, to let her know he was there.

And she hated him for that, too, for not doing what a man would do with a woman.

She tried to shake him off, but all that did was persuade him to lay his arm about her shoulders. They were still walking through all of this. The sun was right in her eyes, dazzling her through the tears. Some idiot part of her reflected that Egyptian men walked like this with their wives, and had themselves carved so in their tombs, side by side, his arm about her shoulders. Saying for all eternity that they were friends as well as lovers.

Her courses were about to start. That was all it was. She grew weepy then, and irritable, and lately she had been thinking far too much of what men did with women. But never with her. She wanted to choose the man and the moment. Even if neither ever came.

This boy was a friend, that was all. Dear friend. Kin. He knew when to be quiet sometimes, as now.

She dug in her heels, stopping them both. He stood watching her. His eyes were big and dark, rounder than an Egyptian's, with long curling lashes like a girl's. She wondered what he saw in her. Puffy eyes, probably, and skin blotched with crying. Nothing for a man to dream of.

"Go back home," she said. "I can take care of myself."

"I know that," he said. "I want to walk with you."

"You do not. You were in the tombs at dawn, I know

that perfectly well, and you're so tired you can barely see straight. Go home and sleep.''

"No," said Johanan.

Johanan seldom said that word direct. When he did, he was unshakable. He began walking again, and so perforce did she.

After a few strides he said, "Maybe I missed you. Did you think of that? Maybe I want to see a little more of you before you go away for another year."

"Maybe I was in Thebes for most of that year," she retorted. "Maybe I was shut for so long in palaces that I forgot how to walk under the sky. Maybe I simply didn't want to hear you go on at me for never coming to see you, when you never came to see me at all, not while we were children, and not once in all that year and more. I don't belong to you that you can tell me when to come and go."

He barely flinched at what she had hoped would be a strong blow. "I came to the palace," he said, "after you came back. I asked for you. They told me to give it up. The queen's Hittite would never cast those eyes of hers on anything as worthless as I was. They made it sound as if you were grown immensely proud and high, much too high for the likes of me."

"So you turned around and left." Nofret wanted to curl her lip, but the demon of perversity that had been in her all this day made her soften instead. "You silly boy. You should have laughed at them and told them that you were a prince of a line of princes, and they would conduct you to me then and there or they would have my wrath to face. That's how it's done in palaces, when solitary strangers come asking after a queen's servants."

"I didn't know that," he said sulkily. "I was never raised in palaces."

"And well for you that you weren't." Her anger was gone, lost somewhere. So were her tears. Her arm was cramped against his side. She freed it and let it rest around his waist, thumb tucked into his sash, where it could be comfortable. She had never done that before, and yet it was as if she had always done it, as if it were only right and proper to walk this way, down the stony road to the Aten's city.

"The next time you come," she said, "tell the people who stop you that the queen's personal maid has asked for you. Be a prince to them. Make them listen, and make them do as you bid."

He thought about it for a while. The sulky look left his face; a smile crept across it. "I can do that. It's just like being a foreman in the tombs. I've been one for the past season, did you know that? I'm good at telling people what to do. Not so good," he added a little glumly, "at working stone. But orders, I can give."

"A leader of men," said Nofret, mocking him, but gently. She stopped yet again and worked herself free. "Now go home. Come and see me when you can—when you've a day to yourself. I can get away if I ask. My lady's reasonable about such things."

"I know that," said Johanan. "I'll come. And walk in like a prince, even if they laugh at me."

She looked at him in the sunset light. He looked nothing at all like an Egyptian: all that curling black hair, and the beard, and the immense authority of his nose. He was going to be tall, and strong too, from all his years of labor in the tombs. "They'll call you foreign," she said, "but they won't laugh at you. Not if they have any sense at all. After all," she pointed out, "you're taller than any of them, and strong as an ox."

He blushed. "Clumsy, too, I know. They *will* laugh."

"Idiot," said Nofret, pushing him back toward his village. "Get on with you. Come and see me. Promise."

"Promise," he said. Even if he was afraid of being laughed at.

CHAPTER TWENTY-TWO

▲

AMID the splendor and shallowness of the courts in Akhetaten, the king moved like a soul wandering apart from its body. He did not seem any madder than he ever had, or any more or less interested in royal duties, and yet to Nofret he seemed somehow more distant, less a part of anything about him.

When the new sickness came, they said it was Amon's curse. It struck only in the palace, and only the most royal. It killed Kiya, who had never recovered from the birth of her daughter. It seized and devoured Meritaten the younger, the frail milk-pale child going up like a torch within a night and a day. It took Kiya's daughter, though she had seemed the strongest of all the king's children, took her and left the lifeless body for the king to stare at as if he had never seen death before.

It almost took Ankhesenpaaten. She had been ill with pregnancy, but that had seemed to pass, and she settled to the long quiet waiting for the baby to be born. The waiting ended too soon, in fever that brought the baby wailing into the light. It was very young and small, but it seemed inclined to live nonetheless.

It was another daughter. Nofret ignored it, let someone else take it and wash it and do what needed to be done. She was Ankhesenpaaten's. She withstood the cold glare of the midwife and the colder one of the king's own physician, who had come to meddle when the women were done with their women's nonsense. She held her lady though she struggled, though her skin felt like papyrus stretched over a burning brand.

Priests came to chant prayers and work magic. The king's physician and his flock of assistants performed the dance of their trade. The king himself came and stared and went away.

Nofret was glad that he did not stay. Ankhesenpaaten did not know anyone, did not need to know him. Her spirit was wandering far away in the land of her childhood, or among the dead. She talked to her sisters and to her mother. She laughed and prattled as a small child will, but clinging always to Nofret, fretting if Nofret tried to move away.

Nofret preferred to think that although Ankhesenpaaten called her everything from Mother to Sotepenre, somewhere beneath the fever she knew that she spoke to Nofret. It was easier than admitting that she was altogether forgotten except as a body to clutch at.

■ ■ ■

The night was long, the day after longer still. Nofret heard wailing somewhere near and yet far away. Someone else had died. She did not trouble to ask who it was. Ankhesenpaaten was still alive. She lay on her bed, child-small, child-slight, what little flesh she had had seeming to have melted from her bones. Her breath rattled as she drew it in, caught as she let it out, over and over.

Priests and doctors had stopped trying to separate Nofret from her mistress. They made a space for her, a circle of quiet at Ankhesenpaaten's head where it lay in Nofret's lap. She was covered in amulets, reeking of the priests' spells and the physicians' doctoring. Dung was the least of it, and the most easily named.

Nofret gagged on the stink. One of the priests shot her a glance of pure annoyance.

Something in her snapped. "Out," she said, trembling with the effort of speaking softly. "Get out."

Of course they ignored her. A physician with flint and

steel ignited a bowlful of something ghastly: more dung, and the hair of something that had not lived clean.

Very carefully Nofret eased from beneath her lady's head. The queen was deep in fever-dream. Nofret was able to pry the thin fingers loose from her arm. The stripes and ache of bruises shocked her. She shut them out of her mind.

There was a feather fan in a stand beside the bed. It made a most effective broom. She swept them all out, priests and doctors, maids and ladies and hangers-on—all of them. She slammed the door on the last of them and shot the bolt, and stood breathing hard, the fan drooping in her hands.

"Oh," she said after a while. "Oh, gods." She dropped the fan, let it fall where it would, stumbled back to her lady.

Ankhesenpaaten lived still. She was not bleeding any more than a woman should after she has a baby. She was breathing. She was not aware, but when Nofret took her in her arms, she came as a child to its mother.

Hot, thought Nofret. So hot. She gathered her lady up, finding her a light burden, no more than bone and fragile skin. Walking as smoothly as she could, she carried Ankhesenpaaten to the pillared hall of the queen's bath.

There was no one there, but a lamp was always lit, and the pool was always filled with clear water. Nofret lowered herself into it, and the princess with her, and sat on the ledge in the lamp's glimmer.

It was like sitting in a pool in a forest somewhere far away, where Egypt's sand and heat were but a fever-dream. Somewhere in the mountains beyond Hattusas, in beauty and in quiet, where no one had ever heard of the Aten or known the king who worshipped him.

Somewhere, she thought, flowing with milk and honey: rich land, land that had never been Egypt. She made a song and sang it. Her voice was untrained but it was true, and in this half-dream of hers she remembered the tongue she had not spoken since she was a child, the language of Hatti.

She sang to the queen of Egypt a song of Hittite children, a simple song, rather silly, of a bear on a mountain. His adventures were many and absurd, and completely incomprehensible to one who did not speak Hittite.

Ankhesenpaaten lay quiet in Nofret's arms. Nofret stiffened. But she breathed. Was she less fever-hot? Nofret could not tell. She had a little fever herself, she realized. It did not matter very much. She was not going to die till she was old and wicked. She had informed the gods of that long ago.

The water lapped the edge of the pool. The lamp flickered. There were always whispers in the roof, especially at night. The dead were gathering, laying wagers on whether and when this lady would flutter among them. She was clinging to her body still, as the living persisted in doing.

"You won't have her," Nofret said to the dead. They were Egyptian dead: bird-bodied, human-headed. Some were like hawks, some like vultures, and a few, ruffling and cooing, like doves in the roofbeams. She did not look to see if she knew any of their faces.

"You can't have her," she said. "Your Two Lands need her. *I* need her."

Ankhesenpaaten stirred. She was slippery with wet. She began to slide in Nofret's grasp. Nofret snatched, gasped as her lady's head sank beneath the water.

Oh, she was dead. Nofret knew it. She did not struggle to breathe. She sank like a stone, and like a stone she was lifeless.

Nofret dived after her. Swimming was an art she barely knew, but she could paddle, and she was not afraid of water. She caught the inert body in her arms and flung herself out of the pool.

The touch of air, the coolness of it after the water, something, woke Ankhesenpaaten to thrashing, coughing life. Nofret nearly dropped her in shock. She flailed free, dropped, fell sprawling.

But she was awake. She rolled onto her back, gasping, coughing, choking. Nofret, helpless, could not even hold her—she would not allow it.

At last she stopped choking and lay still. Her breath came hard but steady. Her eyes were open. They flicked from pillar to ceiling to lamp to Nofret's face. There they held. "Nofret," she said.

A name was power. Nofret's old name, her Hittite name, was gone, forgotten. No one could wield it against her.

Somehow this Egyptian usename, this word that people used in speaking to her, had become a true name, too. Maybe because it was Egyptian, and Egyptians had first known the power of names. She felt it in herself: the closing of cords about her heart, gentle but inexorable, tugging, drawing her out of herself and into this lady's hand.

Such a frail lady, so thin, so racked with fever. But she was a king's daughter, and she had worn the crown of a queen. Holding fast to Nofret's hands, she pulled herself upright. "Tell me. Tell me—what—"

"You've been ill," Nofret said. "I think you're going to get better."

The dead chittered furiously in the roof. Ankhesenpaaten took no notice of them. She freed one hand to rest it on her middle. "I dreamed—" Her face went utterly still. "Is it dead?"

"Your daughter," said Nofret, "is—" The dead were shrieking—but not this time with rage. With laughter. "I saw her alive. I don't know if she lives. She was so young and so small . . ."

"She is dead," said Ankhesenpaaten. It did not seem to matter to her. She would not remember the birthing, nor the child when it was born. Before that it had not been real to her, nor had Nofret tried to make it so. It had been her way of fighting fear, the fear that every woman knew when she conceived a child. Birth could be death: of the child, of its mother.

It eased her way now, that numbness. Nofret was glad of it. Even if it meant that Ankhesenpaaten was numb to the heart and would never be otherwise—at least she was alive. At the very least she was that.

■ ■ ■

The child—Ankhesenpaaten-too, she was named—was not dead after all when her mother came to herself. But she did not live long. She was too small, too weak. While she lived she was like a newborn kitten, mewing as she groped for her nurse's breast; but when she found it she did not know how to suck.

Ankhesenpaaten saw her once, and once only, while she was alive. She was brought to her mother wrapped in linen swaddlings, so tiny within them that she was hardly to be seen. When the nurse tried to lay her in her mother's arms, Ankhesenpaaten pushed her away. The nurse drew back affronted. Ankhesenpaaten was oblivious. She looked for a long moment at the tiny red face in the white linen swathings, then turned her head to the wall.

The nurse was a foolish woman, and vain. She tried to press her burden once more on her lady. Nofret drove her out before Ankhesenpaaten could begin.

When Nofret came back to the bed, Ankhesenpaaten was lying on her back, staring at the ceiling. She had been looking better till then. Now she seemed little more than a dead thing. But she still had voice to speak. "I don't want to see her again. She came too soon. She's wrapped in death, did you see? She belongs to Osiris, not to anything living."

"I saw," said Nofret, very low. She tucked the coverlet about her lady, pleased to see that her hands were steady.

A horror of these people, of this place, rose up in her. It had not done that in a long while—longer than she could remember. It startled her enough that she almost turned and ran.

Almost. She was stronger now than cowardice, or else she was inured to it. She coaxed Ankhesenpaaten to drink the draught that the physician had mixed for her—nothing particularly vile this time, though it smelled bitter, and the princess grimaced at the taste. Nofret sat till her lady fell asleep. That was not very long. She was weak still, though strong enough to be exasperated by it.

When her lady's breathing had quieted, Nofret rose softly. There were always maids hovering. One slid to take Nofret's place. Nofret left her to it.

■　■　■

With the queen so ill and so many people trampling in and out, Nofret had to go elsewhere if she wanted to sleep. Rather than subject herself to a chattering flock of maids, she had spread a pallet in a small room not far from her lady's chamber. She kept her store of belongings there in a box that her lady had given her: her two linen gowns, a collar of faience and glass beads, a pair of sandals, a few oddments that had come to her from here and there. She was becoming quite the lady of property, she thought, dizzy with lack of sleep. She stumbled to the pallet without troubling to light the lamp, not needing to see where it was. She knew her own place even in the dark.

Something grunted as she dropped down, and something shifted under her. Something softer by far than a reed mat, and warmer.

She reacted in pure instinctive fury. She went for the face with claws full extended.

"Nofret!"

She knew that voice too late to keep from falling on top of him, soon enough not to claw his eyes out. The light from the doorway, now that she bothered to use it, was just bright enough to show her Johanan's face, his eyes white-rimmed, her clawed fingers a bare hand's thickness away from them.

She drew back carefully, on her knees, sitting on her heels. Johanan sat up just as carefully. His hands were shaking as he explored his face, making certain that everything was where it belonged.

"Don't worry," she said. "You're as ugly as ever."

He muttered something in Apiru. And then in Egyptian: "No thanks to you."

"Serves you right for sleeping in my bed."

"I wasn't—" A yawn caught him. As it passed, he admitted, "Well. Maybe I did. I was waiting for you. You were taking forever."

"I was keeping my lady alive."

"She can do that without you."

Nofret thought of glaring at him. Thought of shouting. Knew that if she tried either, she would burst into tears. She settled for a tight few words. "Maybe I need to think she can't."

"Maybe," said Johanan. He drew up his long legs and clasped his knees.

He looked superbly comfortable. Which was interesting considering that he had never been in this room before, still less sat on her bed. When he came to the palace past the grins of the guards, he had always visited her decorously in a garden or in one of her lady's chambers, or followed her on forays into the city.

"Who told you to come here?" she demanded of him.

He cocked a brow at her. "I don't know. Somebody. One of the maids. She said I could wait somewhere else if I liked, somewhere with her."

"I'll bet she did," muttered Nofret. The maids thought Johanan simply delightful. He knew it, too. He was grinning at her, and no doubt at the memory of the maid who had been so brazen.

She did her best to wipe the grin off his face. "Well. And why didn't you take her up on it?"

"Because I'm an idiot," he answered cheerfully. "And because I knew what you'd do to me if I tried."

"*I* don't own you," said Nofret.

"No," he said.

Suddenly Nofret was tired beyond words. She just managed to say what she needed to say. "Are you here for a reason, or just to keep me awake?"

"You can sleep," he said. "I won't mind."

She was sorely tempted to do just that. But curiosity was stronger in her than exhaustion. "What *did* you come for? I didn't forget that you were supposed to visit. Did I?"

"No," he said. "You didn't forget. I came to fetch you, to show you something, but it can wait. You need to sleep."

Oh, she did indeed. Her middle was cramped with it, her body aching. And yet . . .

"Sleep," said Johanan. "I'll be here when you wake."

"Don't you have a tomb to build? A wall to carve?"

"I have my father's leave," he said. "Sleep."

His voice was like a spell, an enchantment of sleep. He lifted her as she sagged, laid her on her pallet. The last thing she remembered was his face bending over her, black brows drawn together a little as if in worry. "I'm not," she tried to tell him. "I'm not sick." But the words did not come out, and sleep came flooding in.

CHAPTER TWENTY-THREE

▲

NOFRET fell asleep to Johanan's face, and woke to it, bending over her, watching her. Her dreams had been dark, full of flames and weeping. She raised a hand that seemed impossibly heavy, touched his cheek, ruffling the young curly beard. "I'm not sick, am I?"

"You were," he said. "All night long."

She breathed deep and carefully. No coughing racked her. She felt of her face. Hot, but not fever-hot. "Thank you," she said, "for not calling the doctors."

He grimaced. "I wouldn't do that to you. Here," he said, lifting her by the shoulders, holding a cup to her lips. "Drink. It's only water."

It was. She drank deep, and the last of it holding the cup in her own hands. She was wobbly, but she could sit up. She gave him back the empty cup and thought about standing. Her heart quailed. But she was stronger than cowardice. She made herself get up. Her head whirled. She stumbled against him. He was like a wall, solid and strong. He held her up till she could stand by herself, not trying to stop her, not rebuking her for being nine kinds of idiot.

The longer she stood, the easier it was. She had not been so very ill, then. A bit of fever, no more than a long night's sleep could cure.

Her heart stopped. "My lady! Gods. I forgot—"

She ran past Johanan. She was aware that he followed, but did not trouble to stop him.

■ ■ ■

Ankhesenpaaten was lying in her bed, motionless but visibly alive: her breast rose and fell with the deep breaths of sleep. Her face was pale and dreadfully thin, but there was a whisper of color in the cheeks. She was no warmer than a woman should be, sleeping in the warmth of Egyptian summer.

Nofret looked on her with a deep sigh of relief. She was well. She would live.

There were things to do, things that the queen's personal maid should see to while her lady slept. Nofret did them, with a second pair of hands to help. Johanan did not say anything. He simply did what he thought needed doing. The younger maids stared and covered giggles, which he ignored. Some of the older ones looked thunderous. A strange man in this place, however young he might be, was a shocking impropriety.

Nofret doubted that her lady would care. Johanan was no threat to any woman, unless she wanted him to be.

When everything was done as it should be, Nofret lingered, watching her lady. The queen was deep asleep. She would sleep the day through, Nofret suspected, and the night too, till she was healed of her sickness. Then, if the gods were kind, she would wake parched and ravenous, and be herself again, weak but growing stronger as she ate and drank and remembered how to be alive.

■　■　■

Nofret led Johanan out by the hand, and none too soon by the look of him. When they were outside the palace walls, under the sky, he shook himself all over and stretched till his bones cracked. "Lord of Hosts! How do you live in there? It's as close as a tomb."

"Not hardly," said Nofret. "Tombs are never that big."

"You haven't seen the tombs of kings in Memphis," he said. He stretched again, simply because he could do it, and drank deep breaths of city-reeking air. "Those are bigger than this. By far."

"I saw the Pyramids," Nofret said tartly, "when I came down from Mitanni. I heard what they're like inside. Solid stone, and a king in the middle."

"Just so," said Johanan. He caught her hand and pulled her after him. "Come on. It's just the time to see what I want you to see."

■   ■   ■

The road to the workmen's village had never seemed so long before, or the sun so strong, beating on her head. She was still a little fevered, and weak with it. Johanan insisted that he had to stop three times for water or a jar of beer, and once for a round of bread with meat rolled in it. She let him imagine that he deceived her. He was thirsty, she believed that, and hungry too—that big frame of his needed a great deal of provender—but he did not need to eat or drink as often as that. She, however, did: she could not take in much at once or her stomach revolted, but a little while later she needed more again.

From the last of the water-sellers he bought a skinful, and from a vendor a palmleaf basket filled with little cakes, which he carried with him as he went. Nofret trailed after him, breathless already, and they were not even out of the city.

He kept insisting that he needed to rest, too. When he paused just past the walls, claiming a mighty weariness, she snapped at him. "Stop pretending! I'm as weak as a rag and you know it."

"Well, and I'm lazy," he said, unruffled. "It's going to be hot today, don't you think?"

"Like fire in a forge," she sighed, letting temper drain away. She was not angry with him, not for being sensible, and understanding that she was still a little ill. She was furious at herself. Weakness was nothing that a Hittite ever learned to contend with. Among warriors, weak was dead. Even women were expected to be brave, and to be strong.

She got up somewhat before her body would have wanted to be ready, sipped from the waterskin, went on. It was a long walk to the village. She did the last of it leaning on Johanan, hating herself for it but rather liking it, too. He was sweating in the sun, a pungent smell, but clean. It smelled like him—like Johanan.

He did not lead her to his father's house as she had expected, but to another part of the village, where sturdy women ground barley between stones for the workers' bread, and bakers baked it in ovens, and brewers made beer of the bread that would not be eaten. Some of the bakers and brewers were Apiru, easy to see among the clean-shaven Egyptians, with their striped coats and their long curly beards. None of the Apiru women worked at grinding the flour or kneading the bread; those were Egyptians, naked or kilted, breasts bobbing as they ground stone on stone and grain between. One of them grinned at Johanan as he led Nofret past, a gap-toothed, snub-nosed, unbeautiful lump of a woman, but bright-eyed and full-breasted and altogether appealing.

Johanan grinned back, though Nofret noticed that he kept his eyes fixed carefully above the woman's chin. Apiru modesty was a peculiar thing.

Not all the people grinding grain were women. There were a few men, slaves too dull-witted or unskilled to work the ovens or the brewing vats, or boys of the village who were apprenticed to the trade. Among them knelt one with an Egyptian's shaved head and face but an Apiru's robe, deeply intent on his task, not even aware of the two who stood to watch him.

It dawned on Nofret slowly where she had seen that long skull before, and those long fingers. She was sunstruck and still slightly feverish, or she might have been quicker to understand. Or maybe not. It was simply too preposterous.

She sank wobbling to one knee, peering at the face that bent so diligently to the task. Long eyes, long nose, long chin. A certain habit of imperiousness that stamped it even in this impossible place.

The Great House of Egypt, the Lord of the Two Lands, the voice and servant of the Aten in the city that he had built, was grinding barley for bread and beer in the village of his slaves.

"But how could he—"

He did not seem to hear Nofret's voice. Johanan spoke quietly but without stealth, answering her. "He comes in most mornings, not long after sunup, and stays till noon. He never speaks. He grinds a great deal of flour, they say, enough for a day. Then he goes back . . . wherever he goes."

Nofret rounded on Johanan. "You know who he is!"

He pulled her with him away from the grinders of flour, toward the street. There was not much of anyone there: an old blind man snoring in the sun, a dog worrying a bone, a child gnawing with impunity on the dog's tail. Nofret got hold of Johanan's coat and shook it as hard as she could. It barely stirred the body inside. "How long has this been going on? How in the gods' name does anybody keep from knowing what he is?"

"Oh," he said, "everyone knows. One just doesn't ask. Do you see? The high ones do what they will do. It's not for us to wonder why."

"That's nonsense!" snapped Nofret. "Or you would never have dragged me out here when I should be dying in peace."

"You aren't dying," he said. "And you had to see. He's been coming here for a while—since Lady Tadukhipa took sick. He doesn't do any harm. No one bothers him. Maybe he thinks it's peaceful."

"Maybe he's lost his mind." Nofret turned back toward the place of the bakers. The king was easy to see once one knew what to look for: bald head and brown robe were unmistakable. "I can't believe no one's missed him."

"Why? If he's wanted for something kingly, everyone must suppose he's somewhere else. By the time they start to worry, there he is, praying in his temple or sitting on his throne or whatever he does when he goes away from here."

"Mostly," said Nofret, "he prays in the temple. Lying in the sun of his sunrise court, or lying in front of the altar, praying away Amon's curse."

"Maybe that's what he's doing here," said Johanan. "Praying."

Nofret would have hit him if she had heard any mockery, but there was none. Johanan the Apiru did not see anything odd at all about a king who might choose to pray while grinding flour for his servants' bread.

Apiru were strange beyond her comprehension.

She went back slowly along the line of men and women grinding flour. In front of the king she stopped and knelt again, sitting on her heels. He leaned on the grinding-stone, grinding steadily, back and forth, mute, utterly absorbed. Sweat ran down his face, but he kept it from staining the flour. She wondered why he did not simply shed the hot wool robe and go naked like the others.

More of his madness. And yet strangely he looked more sane in this than he ever did while he sat on his throne. His expression was calm, intent. His eyes fixed on his hands, and on the stone beneath him. He was not aware of anything else that she could see. Certainly not of her.

She glanced at the sun. It was some time yet to noon.

She settled to wait. Johanan hovered for a while outside, then came in and squatted beside her. He handed her the waterskin, now rather lighter than it had been when he bought it. She drank gratefully. The water was warm and tasted of leather, but it was wet. She took a little of it in her hand and laved her face.

A boy with a water-pail and a dipper went up and down among the workers. They paused at his coming to stretch, rest, chatter among themselves. Strangers' presence did not seem to constrain them. And why should it? Nofret was as much a slave as they. So was Johanan, for the matter of that, stiff pride and all. And the king, who could not be there, therefore was not.

He accepted water, but without raising his eyes and without pausing longer than was necessary before returning to his work. He scooped handfuls of barley from the basket beside him, spread them on the stone, ground them with as much concentration as before.

■   ■   ■

Just as the sun touched the zenith, he finished the last bit of barley and swept the flour into the bowl that waited for it. He had done his day's allotment in half a day—a feat worthy of a king. He rose stiffly, straightening each separate part of him, and turned his face to the sun. He smiled the smile of a man who has done well, and who knows it. Contentedly, still smiling, he left the place of the bakers.

Nofret followed him, with Johanan trailing after. He walked quickly but not in haste, his stride long and sure, as it never was when he was being king. He minced then in his tight kilt and his heavy, kingly adornments, balancing the lofty weight of the Two Crowns. Out here, bareheaded, stripped of everything but the raw self, he moved like a man who knew his way, and who was glad of it.

Nofret had to scramble to keep pace. To her astonishment, not to mention dismay, he glanced at her and said, "Blessings of the Aten on you, servant of my daughter."

Her tongue answered for her. "And on you, my lord of Egypt."

"Oh," he said, and she realized with a start that he had not stammered even once, "here I'm no such eminence. I'm only a servant among servants, except that they serve the king, and I serve the god who is above the king."

"You are quite mad," said Nofret.

"No doubt," said the king. "You do know, I suppose, that I'm cursed, or so everyone says. False Amon has damned me and all my blood, and killed as much of it as he could reach. But how can he do that if he is false? The Aten, who is true, says nothing. He only bids me come here and serve him as you saw, as a servant must who does his master's will."

"Then your god is mad," Nofret said. "No god makes his king labor like a slave."

"A god might," said the king, "if that king has displeased him. I failed, you see. I abandoned Thebes to Amon. I surrendered to the will of venal men, men who call themselves priests. But they are false, and their god is a lie."

"So you abase yourself by becoming a slave to slaves." Nofret shook her head in disgust. "No wonder your god wins no worshippers but you. Who will serve a god who makes his king a slave?"

"My god is like no gods that ever were," said the king. "I have much to learn, much to do, to serve him as he wills. And much . . . much to suffer." His whole body drooped, his face giving way to a wash of grief. The contentment that had been on him, that had seemed to be all of him, showed itself for the mask it was, like the mask of a king. He spread his arms wide to the blind glare of the sun. "O my god! So much sorrow. So many dead, so young, so beloved . . ."

If he wept in the road, she would do nothing to console him. But he was stronger than that, or madder. He clenched his hands into fists and shook them at the sky. "I will not give way! I will not fall! Do you hear me, O my god? Even if you take my life, I remain your servant."

"He won't take you," said Nofret bitterly. "He'll take

everything that belongs to you, but you he'll let live because he loves you.''

The king shot her a glance so clear and so piercing that she threw up a hand as if against a blow. ''Do you think he loves me? Do you call that love? All my ladies, all my children—all of them, he takes. Those that he leaves, he teaches to despise me, as he has taught my kingdom and all my people.'' He laughed, a terrible sound in that desert place. ''You think I don't know or care. You think I'm too much a fool to understand. They hate me. I taste their hate when I sit above them: bitter on my tongue, like gall. I smell it when they bow before me. I see it, hear it, feel it on my skin. Oh, how they hate me! They pray their gods that I will die, and dying, set them free.''

''Someday you'll do that,'' said Nofret. ''They won't speed you on your way. You don't have to be afraid of that.''

''I never was,'' he said. ''The king is the king. No man in the Two Lands will touch him. No matter how grim a horror he may be.''

''You aren't a horror.'' Nofret had to be honest; had to say that. ''You just aren't . . . what they want in a king.''

''They want a meek servant of their gods,'' he said. His voice held less venom than the words might have warranted. ''They want what they have had since the Two Lands took form in the mind of the Aten. They fear what is different, what will change all that they were, and all that they will be. They dread the truth: that all their gods are lies, shapes of their wanting, dreams, shadows of the One who made them.''

''*Adonai Elohenu,*'' said Johanan behind them. ''The Lord who is One. Did your mother teach you of him? He rules as lord in the desert where my people were born.''

''No one taught me,'' the king said. ''I knew him before I knew words to call him. He was in me from the womb.''

''Yes,'' said Johanan. ''That's how it is.''

"For you," the king said. "For your people. So fortunate, to know him clear, to hear him in the silence of the desert. No such gift is given us. The clamor of a thousand gods deafens us, dulls our senses, shuts us off from the truth that is One."

"But not you," Johanan said. "You heard him."

"He drowned out all the others," said the king. "I hear them sometimes even yet. Amon howls like a jackal under the moon, casting ill on those I love."

"But if he is false," Nofret said, "then how can he—"

Neither of them was listening. She had never seen Johanan look like that: stiff, erect, dark eyes burning with the same madness that was in the king's. Her skin shivered. That was the desert in him, and the god of the desert, like sun on the sand, like fire in the dark.

"You know," said this stranger-Johanan to the king, "what he's bidding you to do."

"No," said the king. It was not ignorance. It was refusal. "No."

"Then you are weak," said Johanan, "and a coward."

"I am king!" cried the king with sudden fury. "I was born to be king."

"You were born as we are all born, to be slave to the god. Your father was a king. Your mother was a queen. They too were born for the god's pleasure."

"It pleases the god that I be king in the Two Lands. I can be nothing else."

"So you say," said Johanan, turning on his heel.

They both gaped after him: the king astonished, furious, and Nofret empty of any emotion at all. She did not know which she should choose of the many that roiled in her. Rage was the least of them. Loss—that was strong, but not as strong as some of the others. Some did not even have a name.

It was the king who came to himself first, who took her

arm as if he were a simple man and she a simple woman, and said with weary practicality, "Come. We'll be late."

Late for what? she might have asked. But there was no voice in her. She let him lead her back to the city.

CHAPTER TWENTY-FOUR

▲

THE king's absences could not remain forever unnoticed. Inevitably, one day, servant would turn to servant and courtier to courtier, and the truth come clear: that the Lord of the Two Lands was nowhere in his palace, nor could he be found in the temple of his god.

Where he went, in Nofret's mind, was his secret. She only shared it with the one person who might reasonably be entitled to it.

Ankhesenpaaten knew no great grief when her daughter, after lingering for nearly a month, died quietly in her nurse's arms. Nofret did not think that any of it had been quite real to her, either pregnancy or birth, only a nightmare of sickness. Maybe she had been ill for longer than anyone knew, ill in the spirit.

Now, in the month after her daughter died, she was still fragile, but her eyes were clearer with each morning's waking. There was no more shadow in them than had been there since the first and more terrible of the plagues, a shadow that maybe would never go away. She could get up now, bathe and dress and put on the ornaments of a queen, and do the duties that were left to her by Kiya's death and Meritaten's persistent refusal to be anything but her young king's plaything.

"She has her evasions," Ankhesenpaaten said of her. "I have mine."

"Yours are a good deal more useful," Nofret said acidly.

Ankhesenpaaten only shrugged.

This was another day of many, with an audience to attend, and rites in the temple—more than one, since this was a festival day of the god—and court to hold. Meritaten and Smenkhkare were not in the city: they had gone up the river with a fleet of boats to hunt ducks in the reeds. Everyone knew what hunting ducks meant. There had been a great deal of grinning and nudging when the boatsful of near-naked young men and gauzily gowned young women pushed off from the quay in the early morning.

Ankhesenpaaten would not have known what to do if she had gone on such an expedition. She was still an innocent in the ways of women, though she had been a wife and borne a daughter. She was only beginning to look at some of Smenkhkare's handsomer princelings as if they were something more than annoyances.

Nofret, who had had a woman's eye for a man for a fair count of years, sometimes thought her lady was to be envied. A child's eye could be a great deal calmer and more dispassionate. A child never wanted to blush because some pretty boy had smiled at her.

Most of the court would have been astonished to know that Nofret thought such things of the elder king's queen. Ankhesenpaaten in crown and wig, robe and jewels and scepter, was universally acknowledged to be the image of her mother who was gone. She was even coming to that lady's height, tall for an Egyptian and willowy graceful. She was aware of her own beauty, as she could not help but be, but it mattered no more to her now than it ever had.

The person inside of that queenly image was still more child than woman. She was like spring in the mountains of Hatti, that could be as warm as summer in the morning, and by evening the snows had closed in again.

Nofret was growing sentimental in her old age. She shook off the shadow of regret for a country that she had barely known before she was shuffled off to Mitanni, and busied herself with the pleating of her lady's gown. It must be hung just so or it looked untidy: and that, in a queen, would never do.

The other maids were chattering and giggling as they saw to their lady's jewels. Nofret ignored them. She had never troubled to learn more of them than their names. Silly things, brought from everywhere in the world to wait on the queen of Egypt, and all they could think of was their next meal or their latest round of bedplay.

The queen was patient under Nofret's hands, letting herself be dressed like the image of a goddess in a temple. Nofret did not know what made her sit on her heels, look up at that mask of a face, and say, "I don't suppose you know where your father goes every day from full light till noon."

Maybe she said it to wake a response in her lady's eyes. Maybe she simply lacked discretion. Wherever the fault lay, she got what she wanted: her lady looked at her, actually looked, and seemed awake and aware. "He's always in the temple," she said.

"He's not," said Nofret.

"Of course he is," her lady said. "He stays there till the sun is high, and then he comes in and has his bath and puts on the crowns, and does what a king should do."

He did not do that either—his queen did it. But Nofret forbore to start that argument. She said, "He lets people think he's praying in the temple. He's somewhere else altogether. He goes to the village by the tombs, and does the work of a common laborer."

For the first time in much too long, the queen showed an honest emotion. It was a mingling of shock and scorn, and did her little credit, but Nofret decided to be glad of it. "You are raving. The Lord of the Two Lands would never—"

"This Lord of the Two Lands does. Every day. My friend Johanan—you remember him? He came and fetched me, and I saw. I talked to the man who grinds flour in the house of the bakers, and it was your father. There was no mistaking it."

"You must be mistaken," said the queen. "He is king and god. He would not do such a thing."

"He might if he'd lost what wits he had."

The queen moved so swiftly that Nofret, whose eye was famously quick, was caught flat-footed. The blow swept her off her feet.

She crouched with ringing ears and thudding heart, too astonished for anger.

"My father," said the queen, remote and icy cold, "is not to be judged by the likes of a slave."

Wisdom would have had Nofret crawl away, tongue between her teeth, the image of abject contrition. But Nofret was neither wise nor servile. She drew herself up. "If you don't believe me, come and see."

She knew as she spoke that her lady would strike her again. But the queen was more restrained than that. She turned her back on Nofret. The maids scrambled into their ranks to escort their lady to the hall of audience.

Nofret stayed where she was. She was too angry to be afraid. "You won't come, will you?" she called to the retreating back. "You're afraid. You don't want to see what's true."

The queen did not reply. Nofret had not expected her to. Therefore, she told herself, she was not disappointed. No. Not in the least.

■   ■   ■

Ankhesenpaaten did not speak to Nofret for a whole hand of days, not even to bid her do this or that. Nofret was shut out. Silence walled her. The other maids, whom she had never had much use for, were delighted to take their mistress' lead.

It was rather peaceful. Nofret might have been free to visit in the village or to wander in the city, but she lacked the inclination. She did her duties without speaking, attended her lady as the most distant and least regarded of her servants, and set herself to be grimly patient.

On the sixth day, something arose in audience that needed the king's ear. It was midmorning and he was supposedly deep in communion with his god, but this particular matter could not wait. Nofret did not even know what it was: she had been on the roof of the queens' palace, performing the delicate task of pleating her lady's new-washed gowns and pressing them with stones and laying them out to dry in the sun. She expected it to take all day, and she hated it, endless finicking thing that it was, each pleat exact, and hundreds of them in each gown.

The maid who came to fetch her was one of those who had been most pleased to relegate Nofret to nonentity. She was not delighted to address her now, and showed it with a spiteful jab of the foot at the gown Nofret had just finished pleating and spreading to dry. Nofret set her teeth and smoothed the gown as best she could.

The maid smiled a little, as if in satisfaction. She did not venture a second jab of the foot. She said with an audible sniff, in the tone she reserved for the lower orders, "Her majesty bids you come to her."

Nofret rose, straightening a kink in her back. "Does she, then?" She looked about. "Oh, dear. I can't go now. There's still the three court dresses, and the best one, the state robe . . ." She paused as if she had had a revelation. "Ah! What an idiot I am. Of course. You'll take my place."

Before the maid could protest, still less take flight, Nofret had thrust a damp bundle of linen into her arms and knocked her to her knees. "Be sure," Nofret said, "that every pleat is precise, and not one is missing. And make sure the linen stays white, not a smudge or a stain, or you'll have it all to do over."

She paused then, peered at the gown that the maid had kicked at, and shook her head. It gave her great pleasure to intone sadly, "Alas, this one is spoiled. It will need the pumice stone, and do be careful; it's the most fragile of them all, no more than gauze. If it's damaged, our lady will not be pleased."

Revenge was sweet, she thought as she went to obey her mistress' summons. The maid lacked even the sense to point out that Nofret had no authority to command her. She obeyed blindly as a slave will, in a mighty sulk to be sure, but too much a fool to refuse.

Such was the difference, Nofret thought, between a slave of necessity and a slave of the spirit.

■　■　■

The queen had left the hall of audience for the resting-room in which she could take her ease, put aside the weight of scepter and crown, even eat or drink if she was inclined. She had done none of those things. The scepter was still in her hand, the crown on her head. She was pacing with restlessness that Nofret had never seen in her.

As Nofret came in, her lady wheeled, scattering maids and servants. "Out!" she cried to them. "Get out!"

They were shocked enough to obey. She had never raised her voice to them—had never, that Nofret could remember, spoken loudly at all. Her mother had taught her too well to speak softly and sweetly and with queenly restraint.

Even when she spoke to Nofret the raw edge remained, though she was no longer shouting. "My father is nowhere to be found."

"You know where he is," said Nofret.

"No," her lady said. "I know where you think he is."

"So send someone to fetch him," Nofret said. She had little patience to spare at the best of times, which this certainly was not.

The queen dropped her scepter onto the wine-table. It clattered and rolled but forbore to fall. She took no notice. She seized Nofret's shoulders and shook her. Nofret braced against her. Her face was more animated than Nofret had seen it in a long while. "How can I send someone *there*? People will know!"

"Know what? That he's mad? The whole world knows that, has known it for years."

"No!" cried the queen. "That he would go—there. To do—that."

"Oh come," said Nofret impatiently. "I know he's a king and therefore useless for anything but warming his behind on a throne, but he really is very good at grinding flour for the workmen's bread. He manages a whole day's work between morning and noon."

"Oh," said the queen as if struck to the heart. "Oh, that is worse than unbearable. I can't possibly tell the courts of the Two Lands that their lord is unable to attend them because he's—gone to—to—"

"Then you had better lie to them, hadn't you? Tell them he's deep in trance, completely surrendered to his god. Which," said Nofret, "as a matter of fact is true. It's an eccentric way to pray, but prayer is what it is. There's no doubt of it."

The queen began to pace again, like a lioness robbed of her one cub. It struck Nofret that that was what her lady's father was to her: more child than man. She loved, indulged, even worshipped him. But no one, not even his own children, had ever regarded him as a man like other men.

As she paced she muttered to herself, almost too rapid for Nofret to catch. "Yes. Yes, I must dissemble. If anyone should learn—oh, if it's true, what shame to us! It's not kingly.''

"Anything is kingly," Nofret said, "if a king does it. Maybe he'll set a fashion. Can you see the ladies of the court tripping out in their tight little dresses to play at baking bread?''

"With their wigs on, and the perfume dripping in their faces.'' The queen was not even smiling. If she had been less careful of her eyepaint, Nofret suspected that she would have been in tears.

"There," said Nofret roughly. "There now. Come noon he'll be back, ready for his bath and his afternoon of being a proper kingly king. Surely you can hold off the inquisition till then. Can't you yourself be indisposed? It's hot, after all. You've been ill. You should be craving rest and coolness, and maybe a swim in the lotus pool.''

"Even when I do it because a queen must," said Ankhesenpaaten, "I hate to lie.'' She stopped pacing, looked about with a distracted air. Nofret retrieved the scepter and set it in her hand. She stared at it, and then at Nofret. "I wish I could run away, too. I'd be a worker in the fields by the river, with the cool green around me and the sun beating down.''

"But you can't do that," Nofret said, finishing the thought for her, "because a queen can't. And a king shouldn't indulge himself, either.''

"A king does whatever a king will do.'' She recited it like a lesson. She drew herself up as she had been taught to do, and went to lie barefaced to the courts of the two kingdoms.

■   ■   ■

What exactly Ankhesenpaaten said to the king of his eccentricity, Nofret did not know. When he came back as he did every day, his daughter-wife was at her coolest and most queenly, taking the throne beside him and saying nothing to him that was not prescribed by courtly ritual. That night she went to his chamber, her first such visit in a long while, and stayed there not much past the rising of a waning moon. When she came back she was silent, and her face told Nofret nothing.

Nofret had almost decided to press her and never mind the consequences, when she said, "You told the truth. He prays to the Aten as the Aten requires. He said . . ." It was hard for her to get it out, but in the end she did. "He said that it's a thing he must do. Because the god will no longer speak only to him, and won't speak to anyone princely. Maybe, he said, the god will speak to the least princely of all, to the people who are lowest."

"That is . . . unusual," Nofret said, "for a god in this country. Don't they give everything to kings, and kings give what they please to everyone else?"

"That is how gods are," said Ankhesenpaaten. "But Father says—not the Aten. Maybe. Not any longer." She drooped to her bed, for once forgetting to be either graceful or queenly. Then Nofret could see her as she might have been if she had been anyone else's child: neither child nor yet entirely a woman, all long limbs and big eyes. There were shadows under those eyes, and shadows in them.

"Nofret," she said with the calm of bone-deep fear, "I don't think he's thinking like anyone else any longer. Not even a little."

That was the closest she had ever come to confessing that her father was a madman. Nofret, who had been yearning for long and long to hear just such a thing, found herself saying, "Maybe he's starting to go sane. Any new god needs followers, and he hasn't won anyone to the Aten. The princes follow him because he's the king. If he can win the common people and turn them away from their other gods, then he's got numbers behind him, and strength to give his god, to set against Amon and the rest."

Ankhesenpaaten regarded Nofret in mingled pity and

exasperation. "Don't lie to me as I've been lying to myself. No king has ever done what my father has done—not any of it, not from the first. But this is a thing that even the Two Lands may balk at: a king who makes himself like a slave. If Amon's people learn of it, they'll have the proof they need that he should be disposed of."

"He's still the king," said Nofret, "no matter what he does."

"No," her lady said. "If he acts like a slave, some might think that he's become no better than a slave. And a slave can be got rid of. A slave can be killed."

There it was again: that strangeness which was Egypt. And royal Egypt at that. "True enough," said Nofret slowly, "if his enemies need a pretext—and any pretext will do . . ."

Her lady nodded. "I'm afraid. He says he can't hide. He can't keep it secret. If the Aten wants to be worshipped by a king in the guise of a slave, then the Aten must be worshipped so, and people will flock to his name. So Father says. He won't listen when I tell him he could die for it. 'The Aten will take me when the Aten wills,' he says. Nothing I say will make him change his mind."

"You never tried before, did you?" Nofret regretted that once she had said it: it won her a look of such pain that her own heart stabbed in sympathy. "I think maybe we need to ask for help. This isn't anything a single person can do, even a person who's a queen."

"There is no one," the queen said bleakly, "whom I can trust with this."

"Not even the Lord Ay? He's your uncle. His father was Apiru, and it's among the Apiru that your father goes. He might understand."

"I can't trust him," the queen said. "Not even him. He's loyal to the king, but this . . ."

Neither of them had mentioned the younger king, or the younger king's queen. Nofret did not expect that they would, either. Neither Smenkhkare nor Meritaten would understand, still less believe—no more than her lady had until she had proof.

"I have to bear this alone," the queen said. "I have no choice."

Nofret shook her head firmly. "You do not. Maybe you can't trust even your own kin in the palace, but there's someone—several someones—who I know can help. Or at least help hide him when he goes out."

"There is no one," said the queen with the gentle stubbornness that she had from her mother—and from her father, too.

"There are three," Nfreto said. "Leah the prophetess and her son and grandson. They're your kin, too, though you're too high-flown and they too modest to make much of it. Give me leave and I'll talk to them. Aharon's a leader of men after his fashion. He may know what we can do."

"You'll go whether I will or no," said the queen. "Why do you bother to ask my leave?"

"Because," said Nofret, "I like to be proper where I can."

The queen laughed, the laughter that comes through tears: the only kind she knew. But her words were somber. "If they betray us, then we have nothing. And Father may be dead."

"They won't betray us. And if they would, who would listen? They're only slaves, workers in the tombs, and foreigners besides. No prince will hear a word they say."

"Pray for that," said Ankhesenpaaten. "Pray with all your heart."

CHAPTER TWENTY-FIVE

▲

As terrible as Ankhesenpaaten had reckoned the king's eccentricity, it was only the faint beginning of a real and advancing lunacy. Or, as he would call it, an ever increasing urgency in his god's demands.

First he labored like a slave among the lowest of his people. Then he would not put on the Two Crowns to sit in his court, nor would he ride out in his chariot as he had done before, to show himself to his people. As he had in the year of the plague, he prayed in the temple by night and day. He did not eat. He drank only when his priests compelled him. He was wasting to sun-blackened flesh on hollow bones.

His younger king was no use at all. "My poor brother," Smenkhkare sighed. "So ill. So wasted. I fear he'll not live long."

He hoped it, Nofret thought nastily. It was a vague memory of childhood, and embarrassing at that, that she had ever thought him desirable. Even his beauty seemed to her overwrought, no more than prettiness, as shallow and silly as his whole court and all his mincing followers.

His queen was pregnant, and greensick with it. He was not as attentive to her as he had been. She pined after him like a street-cur after a bone. Occasionally he remembered to pet her and call her his pretty puss. More often he said with barely concealed impatience, "Oh, do take care of yourself! Go on, rest, play with your maids. You're making yourself ill trying to keep up with me."

So she was, but she lacked the wits to upbraid him. She

drooped and moped and even sank so far as to come weeping to her sister.

Ankhesenpaaten, beside herself with anxiety for her father, overburdened with the cares of being queen enough for all the rest of them, was far more patient with Meritaten than Nofret could have been. She petted and soothed and comforted her sister, saw her settled in a cool dark room with maids to fan her and eunuchs to lave her face with sweet-scented water, and summoned the king's physician in case she should decide to lose the baby that was still but the slightest bulge in her belly.

For herself the younger queen would take nothing but a sip of water and a bite of bread. She had too much to do. She was doing it from dawn till well into the night.

It was not that she had to do it completely alone. She might have fared better if she had. Advisors vexed her from every side. Stewards, chamberlains, lords of the nomes of Egypt, princelings of the court, priests and scribes and petty functionaries, all of them saw the young queen ruling where no one else would. And every one had his own certain path through her difficulties.

The king of course, they all agreed, was ill. Very ill. Maybe dying. The young king was preoccupied with his hunts and his fishing and his amusements. He could not be troubled to perform the duller duties of his office. When compelled, he performed them as briefly and perfunctorily as he could manage.

■ ■ ■

"This kingdom is not well served."

Horemheb said it, playing the blunt soldier as he best could. He had requested a private audience with the young queen, and been granted it to a degree. She was attended by a flock of servants, and of course by Nofret. She had summoned the Lord Ay to hear what the general of the Delta had to say to her.

The Lord Ay was the only one of the lot for whom Nofret had any use. She supposed that her lady knew better than she how far he was to be trusted, since her lady was princess and queen and also his granddaughter, daughter of his daughter Nefertiti. But Nofret liked him a great deal, maybe because he reminded her of Johanan. If Johanan were old enough to be a grandfather, his beard and his thick curly hair shaved clean in Egyptian fashion, his noble nose given leave to rule the strong-carved face, then he would look very much like the Lord Ay.

The Lord Ay's wife, the Lady Tey, was of the line of Nefertari, but she did not parade her lineage as many in the court might have done. She was not in fact Ankhe-senpaaten's grandmother; her lord had had another wife before her, who had been mother to Nefertiti. But she was fond of her husband's grandchild. Nofret did not often call a lady noble, with all that that meant, but the Lady Tey was both noble and gentle.

It was she who had persuaded the queen to receive her guest in some semblance of ease, after eating and drinking a little. Now she stood among the ladies not far from No-fret. Her lord stood at the queen's right hand, at ease there, and yet he too, like his lady, was on guard.

General Horemheb came into that scented and soft-lit place in a ringing of bronze and a scent of wind and sand and horses. He spared little time for preliminaries, less for politeness. He would not even sit in the chair that the queen had graciously ordered set out for him, nor partake of any refreshment, though he accepted a cup of water.

"I'll be honest, lady," he said. "This kingdom is not well served. Its elder king is ill or dying—no one is sure which, but everyone knows it's one of them. Its younger king does nothing but play like the child he seems never to have ceased to be. You do as well as you can, but you have neither the authority of a king nor the strength to be the queen that Tiye was before you. You're too young, and you've been ill. You're burdened beyond your strength.''

"I am stronger than I look," said the queen in the cold stillness that she had learned from her mother.

Horemheb was not one to be cowed by it. "You look like forged bronze. But you're hardly more than a child. You should never have been weighted with all of it—and you've been carrying it since Queen Tiye died. That's too bloody long."

His coarseness made some of the maids gasp, but the queen maintained her composure. "You are outspoken," she said.

"Someone has to be," he said. "Listen to me. Word's out that the king is sick. They're already celebrating in Thebes. The seals are off Amon's temple, and the other gods aren't far behind. They're singing in the streets that Amon cursed the apostate king, and the king is dying and will soon be dead."

"That is not true," the queen said with heat that seemed to startle him: his eyes widened a fraction. "My father is as well as he has ever been. He prays, that's all, and fasts, and hears the commandments of the Aten. He's not dying. He's not even ill."

"That," said Horemheb, "could be remedied."

Even the queen gasped at that. He shook his head, looked as if he would have liked to spit, clearly thought better of it. "You don't understand, do you? Even after Thebes. They wouldn't touch the king then, because he is king. But if enough people believe he's dying . . . they can make it so. Amon cursed him, after all. It may be left to mortal means to complete the curse."

"You mean," said Lord Ay in the monstrous silence, "that there may be attempts to slay the king."

"Not attempts," said Horemheb. "They'll succeed. Maybe not the first time, or the tenth, but they won't stop at that. They know they have their god's blessing."

"But my father is not ill," said the queen. She seemed in shock, unable to understand what Horemheb was saying. "They can't kill him if he's alive and well. He's the king."

"He's cursed by Amon and all the gods whom he named false. He no longer even walks outside of his god's temple. The people do what they can to forget him. And what's forgotten," said Horemheb, "has never been at all."

"He is ill," the Lord Ay said, drawing the heat of the queen's anger but keeping his eyes on Horemheb. "Ill in the spirit. In the body, too, maybe. Fasting as he does, praying, conducting himself more like a prophet of the desert than a lord of the Two Lands . . ."

"I do not hear this," said Ankhesenpaaten in her softest, clearest voice. "I will not hear it."

"Someone is going to have to," Horemheb said harshly. "The rest of your kin shut ears and eyes and pretend that the world is all golden joy. Yes, even your father, who's nothing by now but a shell full of a god that only he can see. You're the only one whom I could call either sane or sensible. You'd best listen, and think. The Two Lands are about to make themselves a new king, since neither of the ones they have is either willing or able to rule."

"They can't do that," said the queen. Her mask was cracking.

Horemheb wasted no time in satisfaction. "Lady," he said almost gently, "whether they can or no, they are going to do it. They've already begun."

"But there is no sign—"

"Then you're blind. You saw how he left Thebes. It's worse now. If he tried to go back there, he'd be torn from his boat and fed to the crocodiles. This city is cut off from the rest of Egypt. Cut off rather completely, as you'd know if you tried to leave it."

"That much is true," Lord Ay said. "The embassies are fewer than they were even half a year ago. The tribute that comes in is less than it used to be. And people are leaving the city. Parts of it are empty that once were full.''

"But," said the queen, "everything is quiet here. There's as much to do as ever.''

"Because there's only you to do it.'' Horemheb knelt beside her chair, maybe to give her tribute, maybe to address her directly, without the distraction of his looming over her. "Lady, you do your best, and that is very good indeed, but it's not enough. You can't be king and queen both. You can't hold together a kingdom that's falling apart. The heart's out of it, has been since the old king died.''

"Because of the Aten," she said. "That's what you're saying, isn't it? The old false gods are what held the Two Lands together. Without them they can't hold.''

"The old gods who may be true and may be false," said Horemheb, "but who are the heart of the Two Lands.''

"What you say," she said, "is defiance of the king's decree. By rights you should die for it.''

"Then I'll die for telling the truth.'' Horemheb gripped the arms of her chair, walling her in. "Lady, listen to me. This grand venture of the king's has failed. No one outside of Akhetaten worships the Aten, and precious few of the people here believe in their hearts that the Aten is the only true god. If he won't back down, if he won't at least let the temples be opened again, he'll pay. And that payment will likely be in blood.''

"Do you threaten us?'' The deadly softness was back, the intransigence that reminded Nofret forcibly of the king himself.

"I do whatever I need to do in order to protect the king. But, lady," said Horemheb, "my first oath is to the Two Lands. If the king's actions threaten the kingdom, then I must choose the kingdom.''

"Then you had best leave," she said, "or be arrested and tried for treason."

He rose slowly. Maybe his knees were stiff—he was not a young man, after all, though some distance yet from an old one. Or maybe the pain was in the heart. "If I leave, there will be no one to protect you."

"I have my people here," she said, "and my father's guards, who are an army."

"Not if I take them with me," he said.

There was a pause. Impasse, Nofret thought.

Horemheb broke it, but not as one who yielded to weakness. "Lady, I leave you to think on what I've said. If you can beat reason into his majesty's head, then all Egypt will be grateful. Only let him open the temples in law as in fact, and that will be enough, at least for the moment."

"And when the moment passes? What then, lord general? Will my father be found dead of something he ate?"

"Probably not," Horemheb answered her. "If they have their gods, they should be well content."

"But he won't allow that," she said. "He can't. The Aten doesn't allow it."

"Pray that the Aten has more sense," said Horemheb.

■　■　■

The queen sent everyone away, even Lord Ay. But Nofret did not count herself among the rest. She stayed, and her lady seemed not to mind it. Much.

Once alone, the queen rose from the chair in which she had been sitting. She put off her crown, laid aside her scepter, moving slowly, deliberately, as if too swift a motion would cause her to shatter.

Then she stopped and stood still, as one who does not know what to do next. She raised her hands, lowered them. She turned to stare at Nofret. "You always know what to do," she said. "What would you do now?"

Nofret was taken aback. "You ask me?"

"I seldom do," her lady said dryly, "but you always manage to tell me. You can't be as much at a loss as I am."

"But I am," Nofret said. "I'm not a queen, nor a princess either."

"That never mattered to you before. What do you see now? Do you think we'll ever persuade my father to open the temples, or my father's brother to care for anything but his pleasure?"

"No," said Nofret. "Not before the sun starts shining at night."

"It does," said her lady, "in the lands of the dead." She pressed her hands to her cheeks. "Oh, I wish I were there, with everyone else who could help me!"

Nofret let the echoes die before she spoke. "Be careful—you might just get what you wish for. Did you hear what General Horemheb wasn't saying? That's the next thing. Amon comes to Akhetaten and razes it, and disposes of the king and all his followers. That's what I see, lady. That's the best of what's to come."

The queen sank down where she stood, heedless of the gown that crumpled and lost its careful pleating. "I see it," she said. "I see it, too. Nofret, I'm afraid."

Nofret knelt beside her. She groped for Nofret's hands as a blind woman might, and held them tightly. Nofret felt the trembling in her, matching her own.

It was so peaceful here. There were no rioters in the streets, no attackers at the gates. The palace ran smoothly and quietly as it had since the queen made order out of the plague's confusion. Everything might have been as it was when Nofret first came to Akhetaten, the king strong on his throne, all his family alive and thriving, and the kingdom subdued if not perfectly happy under the rule of the Aten.

"Something happened," said the queen, following Nofret's thought as she sometimes could, or matching it with one of her own. "In the terrible year, when everyone died—no, even before that, when Father knew he wasn't going to have a son. Something broke in him, and in the Two Lands, too. It's never been mended. Now it never will. There's no one to do it. No one strong enough. No one great enough to work a miracle." She stopped to draw breath, to blink away tears that seemed to make her angry: she tossed her head till the stiff beaded plaits of her wig swung and danced. "I know. I shouldn't surrender. There must be something I can do. But I don't see anything. Not one thing."

Nor could Nofret, and that was painful to admit. She was resourceful, and famous if not notorious for it. For this she had nothing to offer. Despair lay on her like fog in the hills of Hatti, heavy and damp.

She said the only thing she could think of. "Let's go out. Let's go somewhere."

"Where? To grind flour out by the tombs?"

It was bitter and not meant to be taken at its word, but Nofret said, "Why not? It's better than sitting here wailing and gnashing our teeth. Besides," she said as the thought came to her, "you have kin there. Do you remember Leah the prophetess? A queen might consult her, if that queen were desperate enough."

"I don't know if I am," said the queen. But then: "Why not indeed? Let me go as a commoner, then, and consult the seer of the Apiru."

CHAPTER TWENTY-SIX

▲

ANKHESENPAATEN was not used to walking as far as she would have to, and her feet even in sandals were delicate, accustomed to walking on palace floors. But she did not complain, and Nofret did not try to coddle her.

It was no more difficult for the queen to escape the palace unnoticed than it was for the king. She simply walked out, wearing no crown and carrying no scepter, and no one knew her or tried to stop her. The few who might— Lord Ay, Lady Tey, General Horemheb—were nowhere to be seen. They would be conferring in private places, deciding what to do with a king who had become an embarrassment to them all.

The city was quiet, quieter than a city should be. It was emptying of people as sand seeps through a sieve, slower than water but just as sure. The seller of beer whom Nofret always passed on her way to the village was gone, her stall vanished. She must have gone back to Memphis, where competition was keener but custom more reliable.

That more than riots, invasions, assassins with knives, proved to Nofret that she was not lost in a fever-dream. Akhetaten was dying. Its people were scattering to the places from which they came. Rumor ran among them that the king was ill, or even that he was dead.

No one mourned him or troubled to discover the truth: that he was as well as he ever was.

She kept a grip on the queen's hand. Her lady was unaccustomed to walking as a common woman walks, and kept being offended that people would not give way as she passed. Fortunately she kept quiet.

By the time they reached the sunrise gate, she was footsore and tired and willing to follow blindly, saying nothing. Nofret bought her a skin of water—just as Johanan had when Nofret was ill, she thought with a stab half of amusement and half of sadness—and made her sip from it as she went. She did not like the taste or the warmth of water stored in a skin, but she had sense enough to drink when she was thirsty.

It took the two of them much longer to walk the distance from the gate to the village than it would have taken Nofret alone. Nofret throttled her impatience. If an army came after them with chariots to bring the queen back to her proper place, then so be it. The queen could not walk faster on those tender feet of hers.

■   ■   ■

The village, unlike the city, was much as it had always been. No one had left it, nor did the air seem full of dying voices. The people went on as they had since first Nofret knew them, raising their children, buying and selling in their market, going up to their work in the tombs.

Yet there was less work there, and more of the faces in the streets were men's faces. They gathered on doorsteps and in the market, idling and drinking beer. They leaned against walls, blank-eyed with boredom. They sat in the shade and called out to women who passed, who ignored them or gave as good as they got.

No one was sitting on Aharon's doorstep. Aharon and Johanan were not at home; they had work still, then, or could pretend that they did. Which was true of most of the Apiru in the village. All the men whom Nofret had seen on her way to Aharon's house had been Egyptians.

Leah was not in the house, either. It was not deserted, nor had she fled from it. Everything was in its place, the goats in their pen, and even a new thing, a cat sunning itself in front of the door. But there were no people either within or without.

The queen had sunk to the doorstep while Nofret went in to warn Leah of her coming. When Nofret came out, she was sitting with the cat in her lap, petting it while it purred. She looked more peaceful than Nofret had ever seen her, and not particularly tired, even as sore as her feet were.

Some of Nofret's anxiety seeped away, enough that she could put on a calm expression. "No one's home," she said. "You stay here while I see if I can find Leah. She's visiting the neighbors, I expect. Rahal's having a baby—maybe Leah's at the lying-in.''

The queen nodded. She did not sense that anything was wrong, Nofret hoped. Nofret put on a smile, glanced about to make sure that no one was coming to vex her lady, and walked away as purposefully as she could when she did not know where she was going.

Rahal's house first, then, since she had mentioned it. But Leah was not there. Rahal, huge with pregnancy and looking frayed about the edges, had not seen the prophetess at all. Nor had Miriam next door, nor Dina, who was visiting Miriam and who always knew where everyone was. "Maybe she's up at the tombs," Dina said, not to be caught in ignorance. "I saw her walking that way this morning, and didn't see her coming back."

That way also was the market, of course, but Nofret would have seen Leah there. She looked back from Miriam's door. The small figure in white linen was still sitting in front of Aharon's house, cat in lap, waiting as queens learned to wait. There would be no getting her up to the tombs, not as tired as she already was.

Nofret thanked Miriam and Dina and went back to her lady. "Come inside," she said, "and sit down. There's always water in the jar, and I know where they keep the bread and the cheese. I'm going to have to go up to the tombs. Leah's there with her men."

"I'll go with you," said the queen.

"You will not," said Nofret firmly. "It's a long way up there, and your feet are blistered raw as it is. You're safe here. Nobody comes in unless he's invited, and if anyone tries, go and let the he-goat out."

"But," said her lady, "how do I know which goat is a he?"

Nofret gaped at her. "You don't—" Of course she did not. Princesses did not commune with goats. Only with horses, and with pet gazelles, and with cats of varying sizes. Kingly animals. Goats were for commoners, and for princes of the desert.

Nofret gathered her wits. "It's simple enough. Follow your nose. See which one is the biggest and the rankest and wears a chain around its neck. Let him out, and I promise you, whoever invades this house will go out again as fast as his legs will take him—with the goat directly behind."

The queen frowned slightly. Then her brow cleared. "Oh! I had forgotten. The he-goat who always gets out, and everybody chases him everywhere, but he only comes when he's ready." She smiled, rare and wonderful. "May I see him now, before I go in? So I'll be sure which one he is?"

Nofret suppressed a sigh. It was worth the delay to see her lady smile.

It did not take so long for them to pause by the goats' pen. The he-goat was particularly redolent today; the queen held her nose, but she regarded him in delighted fascination. He stared back at her with his yellow slot-pupiled eyes, ancient and evil and wise.

Then he did a remarkable thing. He lowered his head with its great crooked horns, right to the ground, never taking his eyes from the queen's face. And she, little fool, climbed the gate and went to him and petted him, forgetting even that he reeked—and he butted up against her as gently as one of the kids.

She came out reluctantly, with many pauses to greet the she-goats and the young ones. When she was back outside the pen, Nofret finally remembered to breathe. The stench of he-goat came nigh to gagging her. And he, the incalculable creature, was watching her lady as if she had been the favorite of his harem.

Maybe after all there was something in the Egyptian conviction that their royalty were gods. Nothing else would explain the he-goat's infatuation.

The queen did not even know what she had done. She washed herself in the basin that Nofret showed her, let Nofret pour her a cup of water and fill a platter with bread and cheese and a handful of fruit, then lay on the heap of rugs where the men liked to sit in the evenings, and made it clear that she would rest. Nofret left her there, hoping to whatever gods would hear, that she would stay there and stay safe.

■ ■ ■

Without a delicate lady to impede her, Nofret could move as quickly as her legs would take her, up the steep way to the king's own tomb. She barely noticed how steep it was, or how far, or how rough and narrow the way could be. The sun, beating down, barely troubled her. Maybe she had a god with her, or a demon of haste. And no matter that her lady in Aharon's house was as safe as she had ever been in her life—safer by far than she could be in the palace, with servants who could poison her, guards who could draw their swords and stab her to the heart, courtiers who could cast her out for the mob to rend to pieces. Time, Nofret knew in her bones, was fearfully short.

The work on the king's tomb went on, and to Nofret it seemed more urgent than it had before: the urgency of work that must be finished, and soon. There were more men working than she remembered, and working deeper in, carving, painting, limning.

Aharon was in the place of the king's burial itself, down the long corridor and the two steep flights of stairs, laboring with the masons to carve a deeper chamber. Johanan was overseeing the plasterers along the wall, making certain that everything was done exactly. Of Leah there was no sign.

Nofret had to stop in the hot close air of the tomb, in the reek of sweat and lamp-oil, and remember how to breathe. The men, intent on their work, barely noticed her. But Johanan finished what he was doing, called one of the others to oversee the next bit, and made his way toward her through the crowded careful order of the workmen.

There was something about him as he came, taller and broader than ever, covered with plaster dust and stripped to his loincloth, that made her want to weep. She bit her tongue to stop the tears, and swallowed hard. By the time he reached her she was able to say with some semblance of steadiness, "I need to find your grandmother. Is she here?"

"Why, no," he said. "She was going to spend the day weaving the bridal veil for Levi the priest's daughter. Who sent you all the way up here?"

"Dina," said Nofret, too tired even to be angry. "I didn't know she disliked me that much."

Johanan led her out into the sun's heat that was stronger even than the heat of the tomb, but cleaner, like fire on the skin. He set her under the workmen's canopy and gave her water to drink, and crouched while she drank it. She, looking at him, began to laugh. She could not help it. He was so filthy, all grey and smeared with plaster, with sweat making runnels down it, streaking the grey with the warm brown of his skin.

He endured her laughter in remarkable patience. "I do look awful, don't I?" he said. "So do you. You look as if the hounds of Set are after you." He said it lightly, but then he sobered, abruptly, absolutely, as his own words had struck home. "What is it? What's wrong? Is the king dead?"

"Better for us all if he were," said Nofret. "He's not even ill. That's Amon and the priests, turning hope into prophecy. They'll kill him if they can. King or no king."

A second, slightly taller and broader shape loomed behind Johanan. Aharon's deep voice was like a hand on Nofret's head, calming her in spite of herself. "If he's not dead yet, he will be soon. We've had orders to finish the tomb before the moon wanes again.''

Nofret's mind would not take it in, could not count days or phases of the moon. But Johanan was quicker than she, or simply less tired. "Nine days. Give or take one." He turned to frown at his father. "That doesn't make sense. It takes them seventy days to embalm a body. Why are they—?"

"They want it well ready when he comes," Aharon answered. "It won't be. We'll barely get the king's chamber done as it is, and the new chamber will have to wait."

"So hasty," said Nofret. "It isn't like this in Thebes, is it? There you'd have years to do it right and finish everything."

"Thebes is old," said Aharon. "Akhetaten won't get much older, I don't think. It was built on barren land, and it will die before it bears fruit."

He was calm about it, without regret that she could see. That was the desert tribesman in him, she supposed: bred to move on always from desert place to desert place, pausing in the oases but calling no one place his home.

Johanan spoke briskly, calling them both back to the moment. "Why are you looking for Grandmother? You could have just waited at home till she came there."

"I did leave my lady there," Nofret said. And as his eyes widened: "She needed to know something. I thought your grandmother would be able to answer her."

"What—" Johanan caught his father's eye and did not say the rest of it. Instead he said, "We'll go back down with you."

Nofret did not object as both of them fetched their clothes, bundled and slung them over their shoulders, and brought one of the workmen's waterskins to sip from on the way. Desert practicality. She would never have it, not bred in the bone as these people did.

The way back was long and exhausting. None of them

spoke. Nofret was glad of the silence. There was comfort in their presence, and that was enough: two strong men whom she trusted, one in front of her, one behind, on that steep and narrow road.

■ ■ ■

After so much haste and so much struggle, Nofret was almost furious to find her lady in Aharon's house, sitting at Leah's feet, nibbling dates dipped in honey and looking as comfortable as if she had always been there. Nofret, footsore, breathless, covered with dust, simply stood and stared.

"Go and bathe," Leah said to her. There was no great force of command in the words, but Nofret could think of nothing better to do than obey.

When she came back, leaving the men to their own bathing, neither woman had moved. She sank to the heaped rugs, took the cup Leah handed her, found it full of heavily watered wine. It was cool in her throat, and the bread that came with it was fresh, and tasted better than anything she could remember eating. She had thought herself beyond hunger, but once she had taken a bite she found that she was ravenous.

The others waited patiently for her to eat and drink her fill. It was strange to see them together, and in such amity, too. Haughty Ankhesenpaaten should never have been so much at ease with a mere commoner, kin or no.

It seemed that Nofret did not know her lady as well as she had fancied.

The men came in just as the edge of Nofret's hunger began to grow blunt. They were clean, damp, and dressed in their best coats, looking more like brothers than like father and son. Johanan was clearly the younger: his eyes on the queen were frankly curious, his father's calmer, less taken aback by her presence here. Johanan, Nofret thought,

should be accustomed to it by now; the king himself had
sat in nearly the same place.

The men both ate as Nofret had, though maybe with
greater restraint. It was Leah who decided that courtesy
had been sufficiently observed. She said, "When you're
finished, get your sandals. We're going up to the palace."

Johanan gulped down a last bite so quickly that he
choked. His father and Nofret joined forces in pounding
his back. When he could breathe again, he sat back with
eyes streaming, scarlet-faced, staring at his grandmother.

She gave him no satisfaction. She rose without anyone's
help, a bit stiff but agile enough. Aharon was quick to
present her with sandals and shawl, a little less quick with
his own. Johanan, lagging last, hopped on one foot, tugging at his sandal-strap.

Nofret waited for him at the door. "You don't have to
run," she said. "You know the way."

He simply stared at her till he had to bend over or fall,
to fasten his sandal.

She grinned at him, though her heart was somewhat in
sympathy. She did not know what Leah had spoken of with
her lady, either. But she, at least as well as Johanan, knew
better than to ask. When it was time for them to know,
they would know. Until then, they could beg till they wept,
but she would not say a word.

CHAPTER TWENTY-SEVEN

▲

An Egyptian, a Hittite, and three Apiru walking together
into the city near sunset drew some notice from the guards,
but less than Nofret might have expected. She wondered,
not entirely facetiously, whether Leah had done some-

thing—a small working, a touch of magic—to distract them.

Probably not. Far stranger people had passed those gates, and in far greater state. Five people on foot, dusty and tired, were hardly worth noticing, unless they vexed a prince.

Leah led them, walking with a strong stride in spite of her years. She turned not toward the palace but toward the great temple of the Aten. She seemed to know her way, though as far as Nofret knew she had not left the workmen's village, except for the tombs, since it was built.

The others followed in silence. Nofret was stumbling on her feet. The first time Johanan held her up she snarled at him, but after that she let him be conspicuously stronger than she was. He was conspicuously bigger, after all. Let him carry half of her in addition to himself. He would tire of it soon enough.

Not that he seemed to. No more than Aharon did, carrying the queen in his arms when she faltered, and she allowing it, never too proud to let someone be her slave.

They were a peculiar procession through the courts of the temple, the big shaggy men in their woolen coats an outrage among the smooth-shaven, linen-clad priests. Those had clear thoughts of remonstrating, but the queen raised herself in her bearer's arms and said in a clear imperious voice, "These have my countenance. Go away."

They knew her then, bowed to the ground and did as she bade. She eased back against Aharon's shoulder, content as a cat is, in royal comfort. But there was a shadow in her eyes.

■ ■ ■

The king lay before the altar in the innermost temple. Offerings were heaped all about him, great banks and mounds of bread, jugs of beer, winejars, flowers withering in the day's heat, fruits of the earth arrayed on platters and in baskets, baked meats singing with flies. He was oblivious to them. Gaunt as he was in his linen kilt, Nofret wondered when he had eaten, if he had eaten at all, since the day began.

Aharon lowered the queen to her feet. She swayed, clutched at him, steadied. Nofret just behind her was no better.

Leah walked calmly among the offerings to stand over the king. "Get up," she said. She was brisk, matter-of-fact.

He rose slowly, blinking, peering at her as if he had been asleep.

"Come with me," she said.

She knew the temple as she knew the city, with a knowledge that could only be god-given. She led him to his sunrise-porch, now shadowed with evening, for the sun hung low on the other side of the temple. It was a quiet place, and kept the day's heat, but not so much as to be oppressive. No one hovered, no one strained to listen as priests had done in the inner temple.

The men were on guard, Nofret noticed. She had never seen either carry a weapon—slaves did not. But in Aharon's sash, somehow, a long dagger had appeared, and in Johanan's another. Concealed up their sleeves till now, she suspected, or under their coats. They were not mighty weapons beside a soldier's spear or a prince's bow or sword, but they were deadly enough. Her back was cold at the nearness of them. They made it real, and not a story. Death could come here. People could try to kill the king.

These people could—these who were his kin, whom she had trusted.

She had to trust them still. She had no choice. They were guarding the king, and not waiting to kill him.

Leah sat on the king's couch in the pavilion, leaving him nowhere to sit but on the pavement or on one of the steps. He chose to stand, swaying slightly. His long fingers twitched at his sides. He looked more than half entranced.

No one, Nofret observed, remarked that the prophetess of the slave-people usurped the place that belonged to a king. The king least of all.

He spoke before anyone else could, and not in particular to any of them. "The Aten has revealed himself to me," he said, "in words of fire."

"And what has he told you?" Leah asked, precise as a priest in a ritual.

"That I should . . ." The king faltered. He blinked, peered at her again, this time as if he honestly saw her. "You came. He said you would. Is it . . . is it then so late?"

"If anything," she said, "it's later. What did he say to you?"

"He said," said the king, "that I must die."

Someone's breath caught. Nofret did not think it was her own. Her lady's, maybe.

Neither king nor prophetess took the least notice.

"I must die," said the king, "but I must . . . not . . ." He shook his head as if to clear it. "I must die, but I must live. But not as Osiris who is forever risen. The god calls me. I must go up—I must go. Where the sun is, where it burns."

"He's raving," Nofret muttered, maybe to herself, maybe to Johanan who stood next to her.

He did not hear her. No one did. They were all watching the king.

"I must go," the king said, "into the desert. I must follow the god. By night he is a pillar of fire. By day he—is—"

Leah stood and did a thing that Nofret would never have dared, no, not if she had been a queen in Egypt. She struck the king hard on both cheeks, one blow and then another.

He rocked under them, but awareness came back into

his eyes, and something like sense into his face. He raised his hands to his cheeks. He looked perfectly and humanly astonished.

"There," said Leah, satisfied. "That should clear your head for you. So the god is calling you into the Red Land. Sensible of him, in the circumstances. The Black Land hasn't been delighted with your rule of it."

"I was not a good king," he said. He seemed to regret it in his vague and absent fashion. "Nor have I served my god well. He is angry. He calls me fool, weak servant, poor and stumbling slave. 'Out!' he commands me. 'Out into the desert! There in the land that I have made, bow down, worship me. Serve me as I wrought you to do, I who am, I who will always be.'"

"But," said Leah, "you are Pharaoh, Great House of Egypt."

"I am nothing!" he cried. "Dust and ashes, a breath of wind, a white bone in the red sand. I am a dead thing, a word unspoken. When I am gone I shall be all forgotten."

"If the god wills," said Leah, "then it shall be. But you've not died yet. You're still king, though your kingdom may wish it otherwise."

"I am dying," he said. "I will die. The god says so."

"He does," a new voice said. "He does indeed."

They all stared at Ankhesenpaaten, even the king. She lifted her chin under the weight of their eyes. "You don't see, do you? Even you, Father. You're too full of the god."

"I do," said Leah, "but it's not mine to say."

The queen nodded slightly. Nofret's belly tightened. This was what they had spoken of while she was clambering up to the king's tomb. It was something terrible. The queen was bearing it as she had learned to do, but her eyes had a look to them, a white shock, a horror of it that her bravery could not banish.

"You must die," she said to her father, "before the

Two Lands. You must die and be no longer king.''

Johanan's breath hissed between his teeth. He saw it, Nofret thought. So did she, and not before time. Horrible, yes—to an Egyptian. To a foreigner it made remarkable sense.

"The king will die," Leah said. "He's ill, the whole world knows it. His days are numbered. But the man who has been the king, the god's voice and servant—he will do as his god commands. He will go out into the desert, into the Red Land, under the burning eye of the god."

"And die there," the king said, "in all that he was, and be reborn." He smiled, a sweet smile, like a young child's. "Oh, yes! Yes, you see. You understand."

"I understand," said Leah, "that the king will lay down his office and become what he has always and more truly been, the prophet of his god."

"But to do that," the queen said, again as in a ritual, "the king must be seen to die, and be embalmed, and buried in his tomb."

"People die every day," said Aharon. "Priests can be bribed, and embalmers convinced to regard the body they're given as the king's own. The king will have to work his own deception on his physicians. Can he be ill, so ill that he's like to die, and seem to do even that?"

"The god will guide me," the king said. He was alight—exalted. And no wonder, too, if he was getting free of his kingship at last.

Nofret watched her lady carefully. Three Apiru and a Hittite could contemplate the abdication of a king with something resembling aplomb, and the king of course was mad. But her lady was Egyptian and a queen. No king ever abdicated in Egypt. He died, or his death was arranged, but he never laid down his crown and lived.

The queen seemed calm, seemed able and willing to face this that to an Egyptian was unthinkable. Still Nofret watched her. She must see that there was no choice in the circumstances, except to let the king be killed. His kingdom had repudiated him. Even his court was turning against him.

"This does mean," Leah said, as practical as ever, and sane in it—a sanity that these proceedings desperately needed—"that you yourself, girlchild, must play such a part as queen never played before. You'll have to watch him die where the world can see; and when he's known to be dead, it will fall to you to help him escape. Then you'll mourn over the body of a stranger, and see it buried. And when it's buried, you'll have to go on, to be queen, to take another king."

"But not yet," said the queen. "Smenkhkare is young, and if not strong in spirit, at least he's vigorous in body. He may outlive us all."

"He may not," said Leah. "You'll carry on with the secret in your heart, where it could eat away at your substance. Can you do that, child? Are you strong enough?"

"I'll have to be," she said.

Leah nodded. She seemed satisfied. Nofret was not— but Nofret had no say in this. She had had too much already. If she had not brought her lady to Leah—if Leah had not come here—

It would have happened no matter what Nofret did. Nofret was as much the god's slave as anyone else. Whichever god it was. Amon might not mind himself if the Aten's servant lived, if only the Aten was banished into the desert.

"But where will you go?" she heard herself say. "How will you keep yourself alive?"

The king answered her, somewhat to her startlement: she had not thought him aware of anything but his god and his escape from the tedium of being king. "I will follow the god, and go where he leads."

"He'll go north," Leah said, "and east, into the desert that was our homeland before we came here. Our kin are still there, the people who stayed behind when we came into Egypt. They'll look after him and keep him hidden. Egypt will never know that its king is a tribesman among the tribes of Sinai.''

Nofret shook her head so hard it made her dizzy. ''It will never work. Egypt rules in Sinai, or it did. He'll be found and killed.''

''The Aten will protect me,'' said the king: his old litany, as mindless as it had ever been, and as terribly true.

''Well then,'' she said. ''How will you get out of Egypt? There's a garrison at every river crossing, and agents of the priests in every village. If any of them even begins to suspect what you've done, you'll be caught. If you even get out of Akhetaten. You've no more sense of the world than a newborn kitten.''

The king blinked at her, too astonished to be offended. It was Aharon who said, ''Well, no, he doesn't, but he won't be alone. I'm going with him.''

''And I,'' said Johanan. ''We decided a long time ago. It would come to this, Grandmother saw it. We're to be what after all we are, tribesmen who've been living in Egypt and have a mind to go home. We'll get safe-conducts to pass the garrisons, and we'll have donkeys, and things to sell, to keep us fed and to keep people from being suspicious as we make our way north.''

''His majesty will be my brother,'' Aharon said, ''a bit feebleminded, you see, and apt to see visions. We keep him close for fear he'll take a fit.''

It was rather beautiful, as insanities went. ''It will never work,'' Nofret said. ''Someone will catch you. General Horemheb is nobody's fool. If he gets even a hint of what you're up to, he'll be after you with the whole of his army.''

''Then we'll have to see that he doesn't,'' said Aharon. He was as pleased with himself as Johanan was, like a boy plotting mischief.

''Don't you see?'' Johanan said to her, reading her with

damnable ease. "It's so ridiculously simple, it has to work. We'll walk out of here as if we have every right to do it, and we'll take our brother with us, leading him home."

"Home," said the king, hugging the word to his narrow breast. "Home to the Red Land, to my god's holy mountain. I'll build a temple there. I'll set it high, against the sky. Everyone will look at it and wonder."

"Yes," said Nofret sharply. "He'll wonder and he'll come there, and he'll recognize the late king of Egypt."

"Egypt's king will be dead," the king said. "He dies now. Do you hear him gasping? His span is shrunk to days—to hours. The Guide is waiting, the jackal-god who guards the paths of the dead."

Nofret threw up her hands. "Who will ever listen to me? You're all mad."

"We do what we must do," said Leah gently. "Yes, even you, who brought your lady to me, and gave me time to teach her what she must learn."

Nofret's lady nodded, still white about the eyes, but calm. "You do understand, though you don't want to. Like me. This is right, Nofret. This is what the god wants us to do."

But which god? Nofret wondered. The Aten, who professed to love the king—or Amon, who hated him? Or was there a difference?

CHAPTER TWENTY-EIGHT

▲

THE king's dying was a grand and terrible thing. He took to his bed with pomp and ceremony, attended by flocks of priests, physicians, slaves and servants, lords and hangers-on, as he had done everything for his life long. What should have been a long slow fading into dark was a royal spectacle, albeit not of gold and sunlight as so many others had been, but of white linen and the dark smoke of incense and the wailing of women and eunuchs.

None of them—not one—knew it for a lie. The king, fasting, taking no more than a sip of water or a bite of bread from day to day, looked sick unto death. Too convincingly so, in Nofret's mind. It would be like him to die in truth, simply because his god had bidden him to feign it.

She would not have wept more than duty required if he had been as ill as he seemed. He dragged it out interminably, though when she counted, it was no more than a single round of the moon from new to full and back to new again. The nine days of the tomb's completion passed, and he still lived, but as if on the edge of death. Even his enemies believed him; or else had resolved to be patient, to let the gods dispose of him.

In the dark of the moon, while his priests prayed and his physicians wrung their hands and his servants wailed in their chorus, he drew one great rattling breath, and then no more.

Nofret was there because her lady was there, playing the part of the grieving queen, and playing it as the king did: too well. It was in her arms that he died, or seemed to die. She who had been silent, who had spoken no word for days out of count, let out a great cry. The priests' drone stopped short. The physicians flocked toward the king's bed. The servants stood gaping, mute.

The queen would not let him go, though people tried to coax and then to compel her. The struggle impeded the physicians, as it was meant to. Their examination was distracted, their scrutiny less keen than it might have been.

If any of them might have remarked on this, he never spoke. Amid the flurry a new confusion burst in, Smenkhkare running naked from his bed, and Meritaten trailing behind, clumsy with her pregnancy. She saw the figure on the bed, pale and ghastly in the light of the lamps, and shrieked even more terribly than her sister had. Before anyone could stop her, she flung herself on her father's body.

Maybe he truly was dead. A living man would surely have leaped awake in shock, or gasped as she fell on top of him. She was quite out of her mind, shrieking, wailing, seizing and shaking him till her sister got a grip on her and pried her loose. There was great strength in the younger queen's slenderness, as they all knew who had tried to separate her from her father. She used it on her sister, flung her into Smenkhkare's arms. He caught her unthinking and held her as she struggled, staring at the bed, at the king, at Ankhesenpaaten.

He was stunned, and stupid with it. Maybe he had not believed that his brother was ill. Maybe it had not mattered to him: he had been too certain that there was no danger. People could be like that, particularly beautiful, young, spoiled princes. Death did not mean anything to them, not till they faced it; and then they forgot it till the next time it struck near them.

He had not been there when his mother died: he had been in Thebes, escaping from the plague. Nofret wondered where he had been at his father's death. Elsewhere, she supposed, convincing himself then as now that the king's illness was nothing. Had he been this startled then?

Maybe. Maybe not. She did not see any joy in him. He had not realized yet that this made him sole and uncontested king.

Meritaten kept him occupied, to be sure. She was wild beyond reason, struggling, yowling, carrying on as if she had never turned gladly from her father-husband to her beautiful uncle. Nor had she been there night and day as her sister was, except when duties required, the duties that no one else had troubled to perform.

"Take her out," the younger queen said in a soft, still, but carrying voice. "One of you healers, go with her. Prepare a draught for her, to make her sleep."

Meritaten's departure brought blessed silence. The servants, outdone by her hysterics, did not resume their wailing. The queen dismissed as many of the rest as she could, still in that quiet voice, sending some for the embalmers, others with messages for the lords and the court. Her composure calmed them, though they eyed it askance. Nofret hoped that they would ascribe it to exhaustion and to queenly strength, and not to the fact that—as far as the queen knew—her father was still alive. There was no telling it from the look of him. If he breathed, he breathed too shallowly to see. His face above the crimson coverlet was a corpse's face, skin sunk to skull, empty of life or of soul's presence.

Nofret had a duty of her own. She was forgetting it, or willing herself to forget. She did not want to leave her lady alone with an undead king and a frantic court, but there was no one else who could run this errand.

She gathered will and courage, slipped into the shadows and was gone.

■　■　■

Johanan and Aharon were awake though it was deep night, sitting in the gathering-room of their house. Leah drowsed in her place, but woke as Nofret came in. None of them needed to ask what had brought her. Johanan was already on his feet, reaching for his sandals. His father began to offer Nofret courtesy, even at such an hour, but she cut him off. It was rude, but she was past caring. "We need you now," she said. "The embalmers—"

"I'll see to it," said Johanan. He did not seem to move quickly, but he was gone before she was aware of it.

Nofret started to follow, but Aharon restrained her. "Stay here," he said. "Rest if you can. They won't bring him in till daylight. What we need to do . . . it isn't pleasant.''

Find a corpse, he meant, that was long enough and thin enough to be the king, if it were steeped in natron and wrapped in the mummy-wrappings. It did not need to be a fresh corpse, but fresh would be more convincing. The embalmers would swear more easily to its authenticity if they could say that they had embalmed it new on the day the king was brought to them.

They were already well bribed with royal gold. There was more for them in a box somewhere in Aharon's house, gold that he would never touch, but of which the embalmers would be most glad. They would receive some of it when they took the body into their house, and the rest when their task was done.

Nofret hoped that they would keep the secret. Everything hung on that. If they found more profit in crying fraud and scandal . . .

''Rest,'' said Leah. The word, though gently spoken, shattered the round of her fretting. She fell rather than lay on the heap of rugs and cushions that was nearest. Aharon left, she saw that: she was still awake. She had something she must tell him. She could not remember what. By the time she gathered her wits, he was gone.

''Don't,'' she said to the place where he had been. ''Don't kill anybody.''

''There will be no need,'' Leah said. ''The god looks after his own.''

''Which god?'' Nofret asked, or meant to ask. She never knew which. Sleep was taking her, bitterly though she fought it.

■ ■ ■

Aharon and Johanan found their corpse. Where and how, it was best not to ask. They delivered it to the embalmers and came back to their house, and scrubbed themselves over and over, not speaking, not looking at Nofret when she brought in each new tub of fire-warmed water. They had forgotten modesty, so intent were they on being clean again.

She could not help but notice that they were handsome men, and fair-skinned where the sun had not burned them brown. It was the kind of thing one noticed when one was too tired to be circumspect. Johanan had a small brown mark on his hip, like a flame, or like a spearhead. It would be reckoned a blemish in a place where people sacrificed their beautiful youths to rapacious gods. She thought it a fitting ornament for the spare clean lines of his body.

She was too tired not to look, but not so tired that she yielded to the temptation to touch. He would never have forgiven her. Not in front of his father.

When they had washed three times all over, hair and beards and all, they let her bring them the drying-cloths and their own clean clothes. The garments they had worn for the corpse-hunting, they burned. They still had not said anything. These Apiru, Nofret realized with a twisting of sickness that must be a faint echo of theirs, had a horror of handling the dead. And yet they had done it, because their kinfolk asked.

They were risking their lives now for one of them, the worst of them all. They would guide him out of Egypt, take him into the desert of Sinai, hide him among their own people. They would leave life and safety here, and maybe die on his behalf, because they were honorable, and he had no honor at all. Only his god and his royal whim.

She did not hate him any longer. Hate did nothing but cramp her belly. He was like the heat of Egyptian summer or the stink of dung or the snap of a crocodile in the reeds: present, and inescapable.

Even his departure would not change that. His memory would linger. His daughter would have to live with the lie of his death—and with his enemies, too, and without the

Aten to protect her as he protected her father.

It was like watching a storm roll toward them over the open desert, and no shelter anywhere, nor any hope of finding it. What little protection they had had, the king's office and his presence, was gone. Already she could feel the wind blowing. Egypt was waking, was discovering that the king whom it hated was king no longer. Its gods would rise now, its priests come out of hiding. Smenkhkare, even if he could resist, was not strong enough to stop them.

Nofret wondered if he would try. There was no telling. He might yield to the priests, or he might choose to be stubborn. He had been the Beloved of Akhenaten, the other half of the king: the half that was frivolous, the half that loved his pleasure and detested the duller duties of kingship.

Probably she should have tried to learn more, to discover what he would do. It had not occurred to her. She was too caught up in the king's deception, and in her lady's part in it.

For now, she had things that she must do. Aharon and Johanan, damp and pinkly raw with their threefold scouring, were getting ready to go out again. When the king came to the embalmers—the queen would make sure it was done in haste, because of the heat as she would insist, but in fact because the longer she waited, the greater risk of discovery—they must be there. They had their baggage, distressingly light for as great a journey as they had ahead of them: a small bundle for each, and a larger one for the king. Nofret knew what was in it; she had helped to fill it. Clothes, of course, and sandals, and a headdress and veil to cover the king's too-familiar face, his shaven head. Provisions for the way, all dried and hard and tightly wrapped. A few oddments that might be of use. No weapon for him, though the others had their long knives, and Johanan carried a bow in a case, and a quiver of arrows. Nofret felt oddly annoyed, looking at it. She had not known that Johanan was an archer.

She had to go back, to tell her lady that all was ready. She was reluctant to move. She would enter this house again, she supposed. Leah was staying, could not go lest she hinder the flight. But it would not be the same.

It was Johanan who startled her out of herself, tugged at the untidy plait of her hair and said, "Wake up, sleepyhead. Tell your lady we'll be waiting as we agreed, with food and drink, and a donkey for our sick brother who's going home to the desert to get well."

"Or to die," said Nofret.

"I don't think we'll be that lucky," he said.

He was keeping his heart light, even as horrible as it had been for him to hunt down a slave's corpse and carry it to the embalmers. She shamed him and herself with all her glooming and brooding. She did not put on a smile; it would have been a ghastly thing. But she said, "I'll go. I'll see you again. Before—"

"Yes," said Johanan, pushing her lightly toward the door. "Quick. It's almost sunup."

■　■　■

As tired as she was, as fuddled as her wits kept trying to be, she still managed to keep a decent pace back to the palace. She ran when she could. The rest of the time she walked quickly. The ache in her legs faded to a distant nuisance. She reached the sunrise gate just after it opened to the first light of the morning, passed through it into a city that had roused and found itself reft of a king. The sounds that she heard, passing through, might have passed for grief; but they were suspiciously like rejoicing.

The palace was in remarkably little disarray. The queen, wise with the lessons of the plague, had seen that everything would be taken care of when this moment came. There were still people running about without perceptible purpose, and other people wailing and beating their thighs where they could be seen and marked for loyal servants, but most of those whom Nofret saw were going about their business.

She was careful to be seen only after she came to the queens' palace, and then only when it could not be clear that she had come in from outside. Such caution might not be necessary. She chose to believe it was. The air was full of whispers and of wary eyes. The Aten's great servant was dead. No one knew yet what the young king would do. Maybe he himself had taken no thought for it, although his courtiers and his ministers most certainly had.

Nofret, hastening down a corridor toward her lady's chambers, nearly collided with the Lord Ay. She slipped aside and lowered her head as servants learned to do, making herself invisible.

But he had seen her. Worse, he stopped. She prayed that she did not show signs of her errand: dust on her feet, wind-tousle in her hair. His voice was soft over her head. "Ah, Nofret," he said. "Your lady is asking for you."

"I go to serve her," Nofret said, "my lord."

"Ah," he said. "Good."

He was barring her way. She waited for him to move, but he did not. Her teeth set. It would not be advisable to treat a man of his rank as she did the drunken young idiots who tried to back her against a wall, but she could not think of anything else to do. She was disappointed. She had thought him above such things.

She did not have the sensation now that she did with Smenkhkare's lordlings, that he was panting to sink his shaft in a convenient target. Quite the opposite. Lord Ay was calm. But he would not move to let her go.

She raised her head. "Sir," she said, "I would go to my lady, if I could."

"Yes," he said, still not moving. His face was expressionless. "Do persuade your lady to rest. She insists that

she must be queen now as always, however exhausted she
may be.''

Nofret swallowed a sigh of relief. He was fretting over
his granddaughter, that was all. He did not seem aware
that the king's death was a deception. Briefly, wildly, she
thought of telling him. But she was not as mad as that,
though she would have trusted him. Her lady did not, or
not enough.

She lowered her head in honest respect. ''I'll do what I
can, my lord.''

''Do that,'' said the Lord Ay. He sounded as if he believed her. Better yet, he moved aside so that Nofret could
pass.

Neither of them had mentioned the second queen, the
one who could have eased the burden. Nofret, walking
quickly but without unseemly haste to wait on her mistress,
decided not to think just yet about what would happen
when Meritaten was queen regnant and Smenkhkare was
one and only king—what would become of Ankhesenpaaten, whose husband was dead, who had no man to give
her a new and potent title.

CHAPTER TWENTY-NINE

▲

THE king's body was carried out of the city on a golden
bier borne by embalmer-priests and by priests of the Aten,
in wailing and in lamentation, as befit a king who went to
the house of the dead, or as they called it in Egypt, the
house of purification. The whole city seemed to follow him
and to grieve. They were doing again what Egyptians were
so adept at: dividing the man from the office, putting aside
the king whom they had hated for the king who was lord

in the Two Lands, whose body had been as the kingdom's body, and whose strength was the strength of Egypt.

They would mourn him so for seventy days. Then the king who yet lived would be the chief priest of his burial, and would take away from the tomb the whole power and strength of the kingship. So had kings' heirs done since Egypt was young, thousands and thousands of years, down to the morning of the world.

But the dead king's queen knew that the king was not dead. So did the queen's servant, and certain of the embalmers, and three Apiru in the laborers' village. Even that few might be too many. Nofret had forgotten sleep, had forgotten the meaning of ease. She would not rest till the king was far away from here, the slave's body embalmed and wrapped and laid in the tomb, and all threat of discovery past.

Ankhesenpaaten seemed much calmer than Nofret. She rent her cheeks and beat her thighs as a grief-stricken queen should, and maybe the grief was real. She was losing her father-husband, no matter whether he was alive or dead. She might never see him again.

The door to the house of purification was closed to any who was not an embalmer-priest. Even a queen had to stop there, to say her farewells until the body should emerge in its garments of eternity. For Ankhesenpaaten this was the true farewell, the last she would have. She allowed herself to break, there at the shadowed door, under a sky that was passing rare in Egypt: heavy with cloud and almost cold. There was rain in the wind.

She fell weeping on her father's breast. He lay motionless under her, no sign of life, no flicker of eyelid, no perceptible drawing of breath. Again Nofret wondered if he had died after all. She had not seen him move, not once, nor caught him in a breath.

Others of the servants moved past her to coax their lady away from the bier. Nofret let them do it. She was wrapped in a dark mantle against the unaccustomed chill. It was easy to wrap it tighter, to cover her head and face, to vanish amid the crush of people.

She saw Ankhesenpaaten lifted from the bier and carried sobbing away. The one who came to aid her, Nofret had time to notice, was the Lord Ay. She was glad of that. He would look after his grandchild and see that no one troubled her till she had cried herself out.

Nofret was not moved to weep. She was angry that her lady should be forced into this lie, that—yes, that two whom she called friends were going away and would maybe die for a worthless lunatic of a king.

The house of the embalmers swallowed the king's bier. Once it was gone, the crowd scattered, high ones seeking their servants or their allies, commoners trudging back to their houses or their work. No one lingered in the chilly wind. No one stayed to mourn the king with honest grief.

Nofret made her way quietly, shadow-fashion, round the house of purification. Not all the chill she felt was from the wind. This simple block of brick and stone was full of death, radiating cold and darkness as the sun radiated light.

Out of that darkness came two shrouded figures, and between them a third. They half-carried him, but he was walking, however feebly, stumbling and dragging feet that had not touched ground in a month and more. Stubborn fool. They had wrapped him in the robes of the desert, covered him to the eyes. Those, scoured of paint, were narrow, heavy-lidded, lifting to Nofret's face and fixing there with a peculiar intensity.

She stared back boldly, not caring what he saw: hatred, impatience, contempt. He was not the king any longer. The king was dead. This was a dead man walking, a shadow, a thing of air and emptiness.

The long eyes warmed, startling her. He was smiling.

She turned her back on him and led the way through the rough and tumbled country that backed against the workmen's village. This was their protection, this difficult land, where no one went unless he must.

The donkey was waiting up toward the pass, such as that was, a steep and narrow cleft in the cliffs that ringed the city. It bore a light burden, all the baggage that the Apiru would allow, and room enough for the king to sit on its back.

No, Nofret thought. Not the king any longer. Not Aten's Glory either, royal Akhenaten. This was a nameless man, Aharon's halfwit brother, sick and seeking healing in the northern desert.

They had had to carry him for most of the way, and a hard way it was, difficult even for men who were not burdened with deadweight. They set him gently on the donkey's back—more gently than Nofret would have managed. Aharon untied the leadrope from the stump of tamarisk that had kept the donkey from wandering. The man on the donkey slumped forward, near enough to unconscious that Johanan, muttering under his breath, drew a rope from the donkey's pack and lashed him in place.

Nofret, watching them, knew for a searing instant that she would go with them. She would not go back, she would not be a slave. She would go free into the desert. Her lady did not need her. Lord Ay would take care of his granddaughter. She could go—

No. Ankhesenpaaten had refused to flee with her father; had said simply and inarguably that if she disappeared it would look too suspicious. She belonged to Egypt. So, in spite of everything, did Nofret.

Johanan finished with the donkey's bindings. Aharon was waiting, watching Nofret. Nofret dipped her head to him. "May your god protect you," she said.

"And may he guard and guide you," said Aharon. Stiff words, but warm for all that, like the embrace Nofret did not dare ask for.

Johanan was less restrained than either of them. He

moved before Nofret knew it, seized her and held her so tightly that she could not breathe. She was too shocked to struggle.

He let her go as abruptly as he had caught her up, set her down breathless and staggering. His cheeks were flushed, his eyes more than a little wild. "I'll come back," he said. "I promise."

"Just don't come back dead," she said roughly.

"I promise that, too. Alive and breathing. And a free man."

She could not look at him any longer. If she did, she would burst into tears. "Go," she said. "Quickly. You don't know who might come up here. Thieves—soldiers—"

"And you have to go back," he said, appalled. "Father, I had better—"

"You will not," said Nofret. "I'll get back safe. That's my promise."

"Promise me you'll be in Egypt when I come back. Alive, and breathing."

Nofret could promise no such thing. She pushed him toward his father. "Go. Go! It's getting late."

He was going to protest, to drag it out, to delay them all. She stopped it by turning away, by walking back the way she had come. It was a steep, tumbled, stony way, and took all her skill and attention to keep from falling on her face. She could not look back. She could not catch a last glimpse of him—of them, scrambling and stumbling up the slope, toward the high desert and a long deadly road, and at the end of it, if the gods were kind, freedom.

■   ■   ■

There was no freedom for those who stayed behind in Akhetaten. Nofret nearly turned more than once, nearly ran after the ones who escaped. She would rather die on that road than live on the one she had chosen.

But choose it she did. She had a soldier's loyalty to his commander, bred in as inescapably as the arch of her nose, and worse maybe than that, a woman's irresistible compulsion to protect what was hers. Ankhesenpaaten was both of those.

Far down the road from the cliff, where it passed the laborer's village, a figure stood waiting. Nofret knew Leah even before she saw the face under the veil. It was the same face as always, no sadder or more bereft, though she had given her son and her grandson to a man whom she owed nothing. "One does what one must," she said, reading the thought in Nofret's eyes as she had always done.

"I should get back to my lady," said Nofret, uncomfortable. She did not want to go to Aharon's house, that now was only Leah's. It would be too empty. Too full of remembrance.

Leah nodded to all of it, spoken and unspoken. "I'm coming with you."

Nofret stopped short. "You can't—"

"And why not? The palace is full of idlers and do-nothings. What's one more? Particularly if she's kin to the queen."

"But—" Nofret bit her tongue. It was true, what Leah said. And yet, Leah in the palace . . .

Leah laughed wryly but without bitterness. "I may surprise you. Come, we're dallying. Your lady needs you."

Nofret thought of protesting further. It would do no good. Leah did as Leah chose, and if that was to become a queen's servant, then a queen's servant she would be. She would be no odder than the women from Mitanni who lingered wan and useless now that Lady Kiya was dead.

■ ■ ■

Leah came into the palace and made a place for herself among the queen's suite, so serenely and with such perfect assurance that no one presumed to ask who she was or

where she had come from. Either she had been a royal
servant in her youth or she was prescient beyond what
Nofret would have believed possible: she took over the
management of the queen's wardrobe as if she had been
born to it, and without discommoding anyone. It might be
coincidence, it might not, that her predecessor had left not
long before to marry a man of some little substance in
Thebes.

She did nothing to embarrass anyone. She uttered no
prophecies that Nofret heard. She was so perfectly a part
of the queen's following that the queen seemed not even
to know she was there.

Ankhesenpaaten had gone strange. It was not the apathy
that Nofret had dreaded. It was something both more
alarming and more reassuring. She had thrown herself into
the duties that had burdened her for so long, so much so
that she was in the temple at dawn performing the rites as
she had always done, and late at night she was still with
the scribes and the chamberlains, overseeing the affairs of
the kingdom. She grew gaunt and pale, and even the arts
of her maids were not enough to conceal the deep shadows
under her eyes.

She had no more help than she had ever had from either
Smenkhkare or Meritaten. Nor would she ask for any.

Lord Ay was bold enough to venture it. Nofret managed
to be there when he did it, chiefly by virtue of having had
wind of his errand and managed to escape duties that might
have detained her. She could not say why she went, except
that she was curious, and she did not object to looking at
Smenkhkare.

He had been exercising in his chariot and was being
bathed and fussed over by his wife and a flutter of maids
and courtiers. It was not unduly difficult for Nofret to vanish among the latter, most of whom had nothing better to
do than hang about and gossip and slide glances at the
king. He, knowing he was beautiful, made certain to pose

at his best advantage, standing water-sleeked and glistening clean while Meritaten stroked sweet ointment into his skin. She paused often for kisses, blind to anyone who watched, and deaf to the chatter of her court and servants.

Lord Ay came into this vision of royal ease as a grey wolf among a pack of house-dogs. His dignity was impeccable, his smile that of a man looking on the pleasures of children.

Meritaten did not even acknowledge his coming. Smenkhkare rolled his eyes and put on an expression of excruciating politeness underlaid with boredom. His manners had worsened, Nofret reflected, since his mother died.

Lord Ay said nothing of that, nor betrayed any distress at the coolness of the welcome. He had received it before, Nofret suspected. Smenkhkare acted so toward everyone who might hint to him of dull duty and duller obligation.

Lord Ay took his time in coming to the point. He greeted the king and his queen civilly, received a nod from the one and not even a glance from the other. He stood near but not among the courtiers who hung about, waiting with unruffled patience for the king to be done with his bath and his anointing.

Smenkhkare might have thought to outlast him, but the king was at heart an impatient man, and Lord Ay had learned long and in a hard school the art of waiting on royal whim. When Smenkhkare had had enough of his ladies' ministrations, Lord Ay was still there, still smiling slightly, in perfect and maddening calm.

"Well?" Smenkhkare said to him, a hint of sharpness in the languid tone. "Do you have a message for me?"

"In a manner of speaking, majesty," said the Lord Ay.

Smenkhkare waited, but Lord Ay did not go on. "Deliver it, then," he said, "and have done."

"As my lord wishes," said the Lord Ay. He paused, although a lesser man might have given way to the storm lowering on the royal brow. When he spoke, it was still at leisure, and mildly, with no suggestion of either anger or scorn. "My lord is no doubt aware that his brother the king is dead, and that he himself is king. Has my lord considered the precise meaning of this state of affairs?"

"Of course I have," said Smenkhkare. "Are you going to lecture me on duty and kingship and all the rest of it? If so, spare your breath. I'll not hear it."

"Perhaps," said Lord Ay. "Perhaps I may observe that your brother's wife is suffering greatly in order to spare you the ennui of royal duty."

"Ah," said Smenkhkare, "so you pity her. Poor little thing. It's all she has. She does seem to enjoy it. I'd hate to deprive her of that poor pleasure."

"She is doing the work of a man and a king," said Lord Ay. "Work that the king cannot be troubled to do."

Smenkhkare stepped closer to his uncle—for Ay was that, who had been brother to Queen Tiye. He was somewhat the smaller and much the lesser in intellect, but Nofret doubted that he was even aware of the latter. The former vexed him: she saw how he frowned, transparently considered stepping back again, realized that if he did he would seem to be in retreat. It was a fine dilemma for such a man.

It made him angry. Anger made him speak unwisely. "You are telling me that I am neither man nor king."

"I am telling you nothing, majesty," said the Lord Ay. "I am simply pointing out that your kinswoman is overwhelmed. She's hardly more than a child. Is it fitting that she do all that a king must, while the king takes his ease?"

Smenkhkare tried to laugh. It sounded like a snarl. "Did you deliver this same sermon to my dear departed brother? He left it all to the women, too. At least I am man enough to ride and hunt and dance among my princes, instead of living in a temple, groveling at the feet of my pet god."

"Certainly," said the Lord Ay, "a woman's feet are softer, and her presence more immediately gratifying."

Smenkhkare sprang. He took everyone by surprise, except the Lord Ay, who simply was not where he had been before. He stood out of the king's reach, sighing and shaking his head. "Ah, my lord, such energy, such temper! The Two Lands could make excellent use of both, were they applied to suitable ends."

"I am king," Smenkhkare said with the stiffness of great anger. "I do as I please. You will go, and quickly, before I remember all that a king may do to those who provoke him."

Lord Ay bowed as a high lord bows to his king, no more and no less. There was no fear in him that Nofret could detect. "My lord," he said, and went as he was bidden.

■ ■ ■

Nofret caught him far down the corridor that led from the king's bath. She had no clear memory of willing to do that; she had simply done it.

Once she was level with him, she did not know what to say. He regarded her as calmly as he had the king, with a brow lifted in polite inquiry. She searched his eyes for signs of temper, but found none. "How can you be so calm?" she demanded of him.

Most great princes would have dealt her a blow for her presumption. Lord Ay answered her as if she were entitled to speak to him at all. "I've served three kings. One learns serenity early, or one leaves the royal service."

"I haven't learned it yet," Nofret muttered, "and I'm still here."

"Ah," he said, amused, "but you serve a queen, and a most unusual one at that."

"Oh, yes," said Nofret. "It's clear that queens don't do all the work she does unless they're distinctly odd. She's killing herself, my lord. She won't listen to anyone who tells her so."

"That is the privilege of queens," Lord Ay said, "and of kings: not to listen to anyone unless they please."

He sounded more wry than bitter. Nofret eyed him narrowly. "It's not just pity for her that moves you, is it? I'd have thought that lords and princes would prefer a king who doesn't pay attention to ruling—who doesn't interfere with them—to one who has his eye on everything at once."

"Certainly," said Lord Ay. Probably it amused him to be direct for once instead of princely complicated. "A king who does nothing is an invitation to the princes to do as they please. But we've had one king who not only discarded the cares of kings, he discarded the gods as well. Now we have a king who cares nothing for either gods or kingship."

He was not looking at her any longer but at the air above her head, frowning as he spoke thoughts that maybe had festered in him for long and long. "You may not understand this, foreign-born as you are; or if you do, you may not realize what it means. The king is more than a man who wears the Two Crowns and carries crook and flail and does as he pleases in the Great House. The king *is* the Two Lands. At each waking he brings the sun into the sky. What he does in the day, and again in the night, embodies the strength of the kingdom.

"We had a king who denied the gods but who exerted himself unceasingly to serve the one he set in their place. He was hated for what he did, but he was indisputably king. He lived as a king should live, and for long years he performed his duties as a king ought.

"This king that we have now neither serves the gods—not even his brother's one god—nor chooses to serve the kingdom. His beauty and his bodily strength may be enough, he thinks, to sustain us all. But beauty fades, and strength is too easily weakened. We have a weak king, and worse than that, a king who refuses to be strong."

Nofret was very quiet. She dared not say what she thought now. If all of what Ay said was true, then Egypt was in worse case than he could have dreamed. Smenkhkare was not only a weak king, he was a king who fancied himself alone. But Akhenaten was not dead. He had left his crown and his throne, cast them off as useless, as no other king in Egypt had ever done.

What if he could not actually do it? What if his being alive and pretending to be dead did something to the heart of Egypt—to the power that made it strong? He had denied Egypt's gods. They might not care who held the throne now. They might take revenge on the man who sat in it— and then turn their eyes on the one who had abandoned it.

Good riddance to a bad lot if they did as much, but Ankhesenpaaten was kin to both. She could be the sacrifice. And then—

Lord Ay had wandered away, murmuring to himself. He had forgotten Nofret completely. She was rather glad. Slaves who knew too much did not live long.

CHAPTER THIRTY

▲

THE queen had worked herself into a fever. Nofret put her to bed, assisted—silently, irresistibly—by Leah, and coaxed a cup of herb-brew into her. She made a face at it but drank a sip or two. Her flushed cheeks and unpainted eyes made her look even younger than she was. She lay back and pretended to sleep, a pretense that Nofret allowed. Better that than sitting up chattering of everything and nothing, trying to summon clerks and ministers who should long since have gone to their own beds. She was

like a horse that had run too long, that kept trying to run
even when its legs had failed.

Nofret put out the lamps, all but the one that was always
lit beside the bed, and sat by her lady. She had taken to
doing that since the king pretended to die, and often fell
asleep so, head on folded arms, half on her lady's bed and
half on the floor.

Tonight Leah sat on the bed's other side, shadowy in
her black robes, with the black veil over her hair. Only her
face was clear to see, familiar and yet strange, as if the
skull had come clearer under the soft wrinkled skin.

Nofret wanted to ask her why she was there, why tonight of all nights, the night of the day when Lord Ay had
as much as said that Smenkhkare was no king in Egypt.
Silence held her. The weight of the night was heavy, bearing her down. It was not sleep; she was wide awake. It
was a heaviness of the limbs, a dullness of the mind and
spirit. She could only sit and wait, and watch for what
would come.

■ ■ ■

The wailing had grown terribly familiar since the year of
the plague. One could listen, could train the ear to its direction, could mark the place and the intensity.

This was wild, more a shriek than a formal cry of grief.
It came from the north, from the king's palace. Someone
there was dead, or dying fast.

Shouts, cries, sound of running feet. The queen, asleep
at last, heard nothing. Nofret moved to shield her. As if
anything could protect her from what came: darkness visible, embodied in a Nubian maid—Tama who had served
Meritaten since the queen was a child, recognizable only
for her size and her black skin. Her face was all twisted,
bleeding where she had rent it with her nails.

She stopped within the door, staring at Nofret and at
Leah as if she had never seen them before—even Nofret

who had been her friend. She did not seem to see the sleeper between them.

When she spoke it was with quiet that shocked Nofret. It was so ordinary to speak such words as it spoke. "They are dead," she said. "My lady, my lord."

Nofret did not understand. "Someone in the court has died?"

Tama shook her head, hard, side to side. "No. No, no, no. Are you a fool, then, after all? They died in the night. They lie in one another's arms, stiff and growing cold. It was the wine, I think, that they had before they slept. Or maybe the dainties she fed him one by one. Or nothing but air and spellcasting. I fed a cake to the cat—it hardly turned a whisker. I drank the dregs of the wine. There's no pain in my belly. But someone killed them. Someone wafted poison across their faces."

At last Nofret's staggering wits caught up with her tongue. "Smenkhkare? Smenkhkare's dead? And Merita-ten? But—"

Tama nodded. Her nod became a stagger. Nofret sprang to catch her, crumpled under her massive weight. Her face was grey, her lips blue-tinged. She was gasping, shudder-ing. Her tongue had grown thick, but Nofret understood her. "Wine. It was the wine. Tell—if anyone—it was the wine!"

"I'll tell whoever will listen," Nofret said. Her heart was cold, colder than the body that shivered in her arms. Weeping might have eased it, but she could never summon tears when she needed them. She kept on thinking, kept on yattering inside her head.

Tama died in Nofret's arms. Nofret knew the precise moment, though the shivering went on for a little while longer, the body empty of soul but the cold still in it, coming to possess it wholly. She looked up just then into Leah's face, the dark eyes shadowed under the dark veil, the whole like an image in an old, old temple. It seemed no more human than that.

"You knew," Nofret said.

"As did you," said Leah. "In your heart, where all true knowledge is."

"No," said Nofret, but she barely heard herself. She was not denying what Leah said. She was refusing to hear it. Hearing it meant that she had known, and shut off the knowing. She did not want to be a prophet as Leah was.

"It's not," she said, maybe to herself, maybe to Leah, maybe to the woman who lay dead in her arms, "that I can see. It's that I can't act on what I see. I knew—my heart knew that they would try to kill him. But I said nothing. I wouldn't even listen to my heart."

"Maybe you wanted him dead," Leah said.

Nofret sucked in a breath. It was hot, like the anger in her. "I know who did it."

"Do you?" asked Leah.

Nofret wavered. That made her angrier, but Leah's eyes on her were steady, compelling her to think—to use her wits. Lord Ay had seen a way to perceive Smenkhkare as something less than a true king in Egypt, but could he have killed his sister's son and his daughter's eldest child, both together, with a single draught of poison?

Then who? Who would want Smenkhkare dead?

"Anyone," said Leah as if Nofret had spoken aloud, "who could see a way to do it without angering the gods. He was king, but not full and sole lord of the Two Lands, not till the elder king comes out of the house of purification. He was less than king, in that he refused to perform his duties to god or kingdom. Better no king at all than one who fell so far short of what a king must be."

"But if people can think like that," Nofret said, "then anyone can kill a king any time he pleases, simply because that king isn't precisely what he wants a king to be."

"Yes," Leah said. "And from there he can wonder why

one needs a king at all, if a king is such a simple thing to do away with.''

Nofret shivered. She laid Tama down very carefully, not for horror of the dead, but for the cold that was on her in thinking what she was thinking. ''They killed a king and a queen both. If they wanted to dispose of this other queen, too, the one of them all who ever did anything fitting to a queen . . .''

She leaped toward the cup that lay on the table by the bed, the cup into which she herself had poured herb-brew from the flask that the king's physician had given her. The cup was still mostly full. The potion in it smelled faintly bitter, faintly green. She sipped, and grimaced. Bitter, yes. But not deadly. Not poisoned. She had tasted it herself before she made her lady drink of it. Her stomach was hollow, clenched in on itself, but that was grief and fear, not poison.

Still she was afraid. She could not stop herself. There had been intrigues in Mitanni. No one drank from a cup that had been left to itself, or that one's enemy might have touched. But in Egypt she had forgotten what it was to live on the edge of slow and secret death.

''Stop that,'' said Leah gently, but Nofret felt it with the force of a blow. ''If you're going to have hysterics, put them off till this is over. A king and a queen are dead. There's now no king in Egypt.''

''Do I care for that?'' Nofret shook her head. ''No. No, don't say it. I know I should, because my lady must.''

''What? What must I know?''

Nofret whirled. The queen was sitting up, heavy-eyed with sleep and yet dismayingly alert. ''What's happened?'' she demanded. ''Why are you whispering? What's that noise outside?''

Her eyes shifted from Nofret's face. Nofret moved too late. The queen saw Tama. There could be no mistaking that she was dead.

It was Leah who spoke to her, gentle as ever, and merciless. "Your sister and your sister's husband áre dead. Poison took them. It was Amon, I think, and some in the court who have tired of kings who will not conduct themselves as kings should do in Egypt."

The queen scrubbed sleep out of her eyes, childlike and yet not a child at all. She said nothing either foolish or expected. She rose and reached for the robe that Nofret lacked the wits to hold for her. She wrapped it around herself.

Whether it was prescience or whether a god guided her, she was ready, armed as a woman could be in white linen and royal pride, when men ran through the door. They were her own guards, and others with them, and in their midst two who were unarmed and unarmored. Lord Ay led a child by the hand, a boy of some eight or nine years, well grown and limber-strong.

He came under protest, flushed and irritable as if he had been roused from a sound sleep. While Lord Ay was distracted, disposing his guards about the room and sending most of them back to guard the door against the invasion that must inevitably come, the boy pulled free. He was in a fine temper.

Then he caught sight of the queen standing by her bed, stiff and still. His face lit like a lamp. "Lotus Blossom! You look terrible. Did they tell you the lie too? That somebody killed Smenkhkare?"

"It's not a lie," said the queen. She seemed to believe it only because she had said it.

"It is a lie," the boy insisted. "People can't kill him. He's the king."

"Still," she said, "they have." She held out her hands. "Come here, lion-cub."

The lion's cub, who was her uncle Tutankhaten, came to take her hands. He had been receiving tutelage in being a man: he did not break down as a child might have, nor fling himself on her and beg her to make it all better. "But if my brother is dead," he said, "then who's to be king?"

"You are," said the queen. "There's no one else."

"But," said Tutankhaten, "I can't be king. I'm not married to someone who has the king-right."

"I have the king-right," said the queen.

"Well," said Tutankhaten. "Then I had better marry you if I have to be king." He frowned at her. "I do have to, don't I?"

"I'm afraid you do," said the Lord Ay behind him. To the queen he said, "Lady, I judged it best to bring him here. There are those in the palace now who would be excessively eager to get possession of the only possible heir to the throne."

"And those who are in the palace would not think as even an eight years' child does, that while he may be the heir, the right to rule resides in one of the royal ladies?" The queen spoke as she had since she woke, cool and quiet, as if she felt nothing at all. "Grandfather, have you secured your wife and your daughter?"

"My lady and my lovely Mutnodjme are taking the air at my estate outside of Memphis," said the Lord Ay. "You may reckon it a pleasant coincidence that a company of my personal guard is in residence at that same estate."

"You knew," said the queen.

"Let us say," he said calmly, "that when your father died, I found it expedient to move my ladies out of harm's way. I would have done the same for you, Granddaughter, if it had been possible."

She inclined her head, gracious as ever, even in this extremity.

Tutankhaten still held to her hands, looking from her to her grandfather, who was also his uncle. He had been kept close among his nurses and his tutors; Nofret had not even known he was in Akhetaten, though he could hardly have remained in Thebes while his eldest brother was king. He was not the plump brown-cheeked child she remembered. He had grown tall for his age, slender but strong, and beautiful as he had promised to be. He looked like Smenkhkare, but Smenkhkare blessed with quickness of wit. "Will it protect you," he said, "if you marry me? I'm going to learn the sword next year. I can shoot a bow, a little."

The queen did not smile as a woman might at a child's fancy. She answered him seriously. "It will protect us both. You because you will be king. Me because no one can be king unless I marry him."

"And," said Lord Ay, "a child-king may offer less of a threat than a man grown."

"Threat?" asked Tutankhaten. "What threat are we?"

"Why, a terrible one," the queen said. "My father killed all the gods. Then his brother refused to bring them back again, or even to think about them."

"That wasn't right," said Tutankhaten. "I know that there are gods. I hear them talking in the night when everyone thinks I'm asleep. They aren't dead at all, nor are they sleeping. Some of them are very angry."

"Yes," said the queen. "Some are angry enough to kill a king." She drew him to her and laid an arm about his shoulders, a gesture half of comfort, half of seeking comfort.

He hugged her tightly. "They won't kill us," he said. "I won't let them."

"Gods willing," said Ankhesenpaaten.

PART TWO

BELOVED OF AMON

How lovely the moment,
May it endure forever:
I have made love with you,
You have lifted up my heart.

—FROM THE SONGS OF ENTERTAINMENT

CHAPTER THIRTY-ONE

▲

IT seemed they were forever struggling up to the royal tombs, first with Akhenaten, then with Smenkhkare and Meritaten; that the only banquets in the palace of Akhetaten were funeral banquets, and the only sounds those of mourning. But when the kings were laid to their rest, when the weeping was done and the priests left to perform the rites of the dead in peace, there was a new king raised up in the Two Lands, and a royal wedding, and what to some was a promise of new things. The king after all was a child, nor was his queen much more than that. He might be more malleable than either of his brothers had been.

Ankhesenpaaten ruled for him. Lord Ay led the council of his ministers in advising both the queen and the young king. The king himself seemed inclined to do as he was told, to learn all that he could learn, and to oppose nothing that his counselors proposed.

Nofret did not commit the error of thinking him too easily led. Far too many people did. Enough of that might have torn the Two Kingdoms apart, but Lord Ay was strong in his quiet way, and kept the council firmly behind him; and Ankhesenpaaten had learned the arts of queenship from Ay's sister Tiye. They held on. The court followed them as much for laziness as for any other cause.

The rest of Egypt seemed willing to wait and to be patient. The king, at his counselors' urging, did not wall himself in Akhetaten as both his brothers had, but went on royal progresses, traveling the length and breadth of the Two Lands, making his face known to the people and establishing his presence in the kingdom. He always came back to Akhetaten, always spent at least part of the year there in the palace that his brother had built.

Egypt watched and waited and was patient. The temples had been opened again and priests worshipped their gods with impunity, although neither Smenkhkare nor Tutankhaten had unmade the decree against them. Only Amon in Thebes kept his gates sealed.

Amon's priests came to Akhetaten in the first year of the reign of Tutankhaten, came and saw and went away unmolested. They did not request audience. They did not, as many had feared, cast a new curse on this new king. They would bide their time, it was clear, and see how this child-king went about his kingship.

Akhetaten was dying. It had been ill since well before Akhenaten left it through the door of the house of purification, but under Tutankhaten it faded perceptibly. The court lingered perforce, and the functionaries who lived and died by the king's will, but the lifeblood of the city, the common people who filled its walls and made it sing, had drained away. The strength of the Aten was not enough to hold them, nor could it grant life and substance to a city built on emptiness.

■　■　■

In the fourth year of the reign of Tutankhaten, the priests of Amon returned to Akhetaten, where the king was living during the river's flood. They bore with them a gift of tribute and a plea that was in fact a summons. "Come back to Thebes," said the chief of them, bowing low at the young king's feet. "Come back to the place where you were born, to the city of your forefathers. Leave forever this bleak and desert place. Let it fall into the sand from which it rose, under the sun for whose glory it was made."

He spoke in the great hall of the palace before the gathered brilliance of the court, a figure stark in the simplicity of white linen and clean-shaved skull. The king, seated beside his queen on the dais in a glittering army of courtiers, regarded the priest in silence. Tutankhaten was no longer a child, though not yet a man: boy maturing into youth, with a face like a golden mask, beautiful and impenetrable. But he had never quite mastered his eyes. Those were quick with intelligence, flickering from the priest's face to those of his following.

It was most often the queen who answered petitioners, or Lord Ay in his office of regent. But Ankhesenpaaten was silent, sitting rigid—whether with anger or resignation, Nofret, standing near her in the flock of maids and servants, could not tell.

Lord Ay stirred as if to speak. The king's hand lifted, stilling him where he stood.

Tutankhaten leaned forward. He lowered the crook and flail that he had been holding crosswise in the royal fashion. The crook he rested across his knees. He ran the lashes of the flail through his fingers, toying with them. They were precious and seeming useless, all lapis and gold, but Nofret suspected that they could deal a vicious blow before they shattered.

The king knew that very well. He was not being subtle. "I have been here seldom enough," he said. "I've traveled everywhere in the Two Lands."

"Everywhere but Thebes," the priest said.

"Thebes has made us unwelcome," said the king. "It tried to kill my brother. Can I be assured that it won't kill me?"

"Thebes will welcome you," said the priest, "in Amon's name."

The king sat back. Maybe he was pondering. Maybe not. After a while he said, "Suppose that I do as you ask. What will you do in return?"

"Why, serve you, majesty," the priest replied.

"And forbear to curse me? How generous." Tutankhaten left off playing with the flail. "What if I refuse?"

"That is your right, majesty," said the priest. "You may remain here in an empty city, where none but courtiers and their slaves have chosen to be. Or you may go back to a city that lives as it has lived for thousands upon thousands of years."

"I remember," said Tutankhaten, "how we left Thebes rather than be killed there."

"Your brother was cursed," the priest said. "You, majesty, are not. You may return and be welcome."

"May the Aten return? May he rule again outside of his own city?" The queen's voice held the stillness that meant, to those who knew, that she was deeply moved. Still Nofret did not know what moved her, whether she was angry or whether she was on the verge of surrender.

The priest addressed her with careful respect. "Lady, the Aten was never god to Egypt, only to a single king and to those who were his kin. Amon is lord in Thebes, and always has been."

"Therefore," she said, "to live in Thebes, we must bow to the rule of Amon."

"Amon has always ruled in Thebes," said Amon's priest.

"You ask," she said, "that we abandon all my father did, all he was. Will you have us forget even his name?"

The priest did not answer. His eyes had flashed as she spoke, briefly, but not too brief to see. Nofret shivered. Here was a man who hated, and whose hate would last. But he was subtle in it. He could wait, and be patient—as he had waited for long years, until Akhenaten was dead. Maybe he had had a hand in disposing of Smenkhkare. She did not know. No one did. They had never found the person who poisoned Smenkhkare and his queen. A slave or two had gone missing—maybe fallen prey to crocodiles, maybe disposed of for knowing too much.

Amon's priest would wait again if he must, but his patience was reaching its limit. Here was a child king, a court holding to its splendor in a dying city, a kingdom cut off from the one who ruled it. Nofret could not see what choices there were. Everything had led to this, from the moment Akhenaten sailed out of Thebes to build his city in the desert place.

The queen must see it: it was in her eyes, in the way she held herself, too stiff, too still. What Tutankhaten saw, Nofret did not know. He seemed transparent, a beautiful bright child who took an innocent pleasure in being king. But there was more to him than there had been to Smenkhkare.

He did not glance at Ay nor at his queen. He kept his eyes on the priest. He said, "We will think on it. You may go."

The priest bowed. His patience would endure for yet a while, the gesture said. But only for a while.

■　■　■

"What choice do we have?"

In the privacy of the royal chambers, in the comfort of plain kilt and few jewels, both the king and his uncle were free to speak freely. The queen, freed of crown and scepter and heavy wig, paced like a cat in a cage. It was she who had spoken, startling the other two. They had been talking round it, Ay because he fell into indirection when he was being king's counselor, Tutankhaten because he needed to think it through.

She met their stares with impatience that made them stare even harder. "No, I haven't gone mad, and there isn't a demon in me! I've been thinking. And not about going to Thebes, either. About living here, even for as little time as it's come to lately. I've been watching this city die by fingerbreadths. What can we do to keep it alive? Nothing! The Aten doesn't speak to us as he spoke to my father."

Nofret held her breath. No one knew that the queen's father was still alive. Only the queen and Nofret, and Leah, who was still the mistress of the queen's wardrobe when the queen was residing in Akhetaten.

Leah was standing in the shadow of a pillar, dark robe and dark veil, watching, listening. She only did that when there was something to watch and something to hear.

Neither the king nor his counselor seemed to hear anything odder in the queen's voice than that she spoke at all, and with such intensity. Lord Ay said slowly, "Yet if the Aten is the true god—"

"Maybe he is," she said. "Maybe he's not. He hasn't told me. Has he told you, my husband?"

Tutankhaten looked startled. "All he ever gives me is a headache." He flushed as if at his own temerity. "No. No, that wasn't fitting. He doesn't talk to me that I know of. There's only the brightness when I perform his rites, and the way the world seems darker after. Should I ask him, do you think? Should I beg him to answer, before we forsake him for the other gods?"

"I already have," said Ankhesenpaaten. "Every day, every night, since . . . since Father went into the house of purification. He never says anything. I think he died with Father."

No one seemed horrified to hear her say that. No wind howled out of the dark, no lightning struck.

"Only Father ever saw the truth," she said. "It was truth for him; we never had any doubt of it. But the rest of us . . . what did we have? The Aten never said a word to us."

Maybe she had not known herself that she would say such things, not until she said them. Once said, they were not to be unsaid. There was a world of bitterness in them, bitterness so old that it was turned to resignation. "A god who speaks only to one man cannot be god to a whole people," she said. "I remember, someone said that once. But if we give in to Amon, and Amon grows too powerful—"

"Amon was too powerful before the Aten came," Tutankhaten said. "You said so yourself, uncle, and others say so, too. The Aten shut down more than a temple. He broke the power of priests who were beginning to think themselves above kings."

"So he did," said the Lord Ay. "And yet you see what came of it. He went too far. Better if he had used his authority as king to rein in Amon's priesthood, than to shut it down altogether."

"Is that what you were thinking?" the queen asked him. "All those years, were you thinking that my father had done wrong?"

Ay looked on her in deep affection, but he did not make the mistake of addressing her as a troubled child. He spoke to her as to a woman and a queen. "Lady, a man's thoughts may be his own, even when he serves his king to the best of his ability."

She bowed to that, though she did not precisely forgive him. "You were loyal always. But now he's gone. What loyalty holds you now? Will you go over to Amon?"

"I will go where my king and my queen go," said Ay. "Wherever that may be."

"Even to death?"

His eyes were steady, his expression as calm as ever. "Even to death, my lady."

"And if we refuse what Amon offers—what he threatens?"

"Then I stay with you," said Ay.

"You want us to go, don't you?" Tutankhaten had sat to watch them talk, perching on a stool and tucking up his feet. "You think this place will be dead, with us or without us."

"What do you think, my lord?" Ay asked him.

He did not blink. Ay had always taught him so, by asking him to choose, even when everything had been decided already among the counselors. "I think," Tutankhaten said slowly, "that I want to let this place die. It's been trying to for so terribly long, and we've been refusing to let it. I want to leave it to crumble in peace—even if it means letting Amon have his way. We can bridle him, can't we? We can make him serve the king, no matter how powerful he wants to be."

"If Amon is restored," Ay said, "he may be amenable to the royal will, to a degree. But he will insist on one thing. He will demand that the Aten's worship be ended, and the Aten returned, if at all, to what he was before: a lesser aspect of a lesser aspect of Amon-Re."

"Amon hates the Aten," Tutankhaten said. "The priest tried to hide it, but he couldn't—not anything as strong as that. If we leave here, the Aten won't be god and king any longer. He'll be forgotten."

They both glanced at the queen, who had prowled to the wall and back. She stopped in the middle of the room, with lamplight turning her whole body to gold, limning the shape of it in her light linen gown.

Tutankhaten did not seem to notice either her beauty or her womanliness. He was still a child in that, still had not come to her bed as a husband should.

Nor was she thinking of it then. Her hands were fists at

her sides. "I think," she said, "that if the Aten wanted to live, he would say something to one of us. Will you come with me to the temple, lion-cub? Will you pray there with me?"

"One last time?" he asked. She nodded. He bent his head. "I'll go with you, then. To ask him, and to demand that he answer. And if he doesn't . . ."

No one finished the thought for him. No one needed to.

▪ ▪ ▪

It was dim in the temple, among the great courts and under roofs as high as the sky. The priests on night-duty were startled to greet the king and the queen and their small company of attendants: only Ay and Nofret and Leah quiet behind, and a handful of guards. The temple itself was empty of worshippers, but then it always was, except when the king was performing a rite that required an audience. The Aten had no followers so devoted as to pray to him in his own house, unless the king commanded it.

They went all the way through all the courts to the inner shrine. The altar was bare of gifts, those of the day before cleared away and distributed among the priests, those of the new day not yet offered—that was for the king to do at dawn. Here at midnight there was only the bare stone table and the golden image of the god, the disk of the sun with its many hands offering blessings to the painted figures of Akhenaten and Nefertiti and their children. Dead, all of them, except for Ankhesenpaaten.

She bowed with Tutankhaten before the altar, lifted her hands and prayed aloud, though in a formal rite it would more properly have been he who spoke. She named the Aten by all his titles and his beautiful names, taking care not to leave out one. But the heart of her prayer was brief, and simple. "Lord of light, if you truly are, if you are the one and only and truest god, speak to us now. Give us a sign. Tell us what we must do."

The echoes ran away to the roof. No bat fluttered there, nor any breath or spirit. The shadows were empty. There was nothing stirring in them. Not even the spirits of the dead that liked to spy on the living, sipping of their warmth: not even they lingered here.

Ankhesenpaaten waited long and long. She repeated her prayer three times, each time more clearly, till her voice rang among the pillars. But there was nothing to answer her. The god, if he had ever been in this place, was gone away.

Maybe, thought Nofret, he had gone into Sinai with his sole and most devoted servant. The one who had been king was there, or so Leah had told her, bringing word only once in four long years: a message of almost hurtful brevity. *We are in Sinai. We all live, we are well.* No more then, and no more since, not even rumor. The desert had swallowed them all, both the nameless man and the two Apiru who had spirited him out of Egypt.

Wherever he was, whatever had become of him, his god was nowhere in the temple.

"He is gone," said the queen at last, her voice a sigh.

"If he was ever here at all," said Tutankhaten.

She rounded on him in rare anger. "He *was* here! But he is gone. He's left us. He can't hear, nor will he answer."

"Even," asked Tutankhaten, raising his voice as if he wished the god to hear, "if his absence means that we go back to Amon?"

"Even so," said the queen in the ringing silence. "He was my father's god. It seems he has no inclination to be ours."

"Then we go to Amon," said Tutankhaten. He spoke boldly, though his eyes flickered toward the image of the god upon the wall, as if he expected it to reach out with its many golden hands and punish him for his presumption.

The Aten did nothing. The image glimmered in the gloom, receiving its eternal tribute from its only chosen servant. Those whom it had forborne to choose turned away from it and left it, not looking back.

CHAPTER THIRTY-TWO

▲

NEITHER the king nor the queen looked again on the image of the Aten in his temple that Akhenaten had built. In the morning they performed the rites of the dawn in the king's chapel in the palace. The god they invoked was Amon, and the hymn they sang was the hymn to Amon. It had an air of defiance, of daring the Aten to strike, but no ill fell on them.

It was Akhetaten that died. Emptied of its god, with its king and queen turned away from him, it withered like a flower in the sun.

The king went back to Amon, but not, till it well suited his pleasure, to Thebes. It was Memphis he chose, and to Memphis that he went. "Thebes would have been a killer of kings," he said, "and Amon cursed a king. I grant them their power, but I am king. And the king sees fit to rule in the north, under the protection of Ptah of Memphis."

Amon could hardly refuse him that, or even question it. He had his power back again. The king had proved it: he had altered his name, such an act as none in Egypt did lightly, for names were power. He turned his back on the Aten. He was Tutankhamon, and his queen, beside him in this as in everything, had become Ankhesenamon. It was, as she had said, an easier name to say, and more melodious. She professed to be fond of it. She would not answer to her old name, nor hear it spoken. She-Lives-for-the-

Aten was dead; she lived for Amon now, and worshipped in his name.

It was her way, Nofret thought, of sealing her father in his tomb. She rejected the name that he had given her and the god he had imposed upon her. She took back what he had taken away, the old gods of Egypt, and made them her own. If she regretted what she had done, or feared that her father would learn and somehow find a way to punish her, she did not speak of it to anyone. She had chosen as her spirit moved her. She did not retreat from the choice.

■ ■ ■

The king and the queen left Akhetaten on the festival day of Amon in Thebes, taking ship up the river with their court and their following and all of the city that could be lifted and moved. Everything went, living and not. Even the bodies of the dead would go, joining the long slow caravan that went down to the river and then upon it in boats.

Only the tomb of Akhenaten remained, sealed and forbidden, with the body in it that wore the king's name and his seals but had belonged to a nameless slave.

Nor did they take away his queen or his children. Ankesenamon forbade it. "This was their city," she said. "Let them remain in it after it is dead."

But everyone else came, and everything that could be moved. No one wanted to linger. It was as if the city had been a rootless thing, a plant of the desert that shriveled and faded, till the wind caught it and blew it far away.

■ ■ ■

Nofret stood on the deck of the queen's ship as it sailed away from Akhetaten. It was a splendid day, cool for the season in Egypt, the sun more warm than searing hot. People were singing on the water, a song not of grief but of rejoicing. It was like a holiday, this exodus from the Aten's city.

She did not know what she felt. Relief, yes, to be out of that place so like a tomb. But regret, too, and not a little sadness. She had come to the Horizon of the Aten as a slave among slaves, determined to be a queen's servant. Now she was that, and secure in it. She would never walk again in the palace at Akhetaten with its odd painted images and its beautiful courts, nor ramble the city, nor make the journey to the workmen's village to visit Johanan and Aharon and Leah.

Leah had not come in the queen's following. She had left as quietly as she had come, asking no leave of the queen. To Nofret she had said only that she was going back to her people. "We'll be going down to Thebes," she said, "whether the king will go there or no. There are tombs in plenty to build there, and hordes of the living to add to the ranks of the dead. Look for us in the western valleys, if you ever come back."

She did not even wait for Nofret to speak before she was gone. Farewells were not a thing she liked or did well, no more than did Nofret. Nofret would have to trust that Leah would do as she had promised, and that the king and the queen would decide in the end to forgive the city as well as its god and go back to Thebes, taking Nofret with them.

There was no telling if the Apiru were still in their village, or if they had left already. Maybe they would choose to walk rather than to go in boats, desert people that they were, with their flocks of goats and their sheep. The old he-goat was dead, but he had a son who had grown to be as cantankerous as his father. Maybe he would come to Thebes and be a terror to the workmen there.

The thought made her smile a little as she looked back up the river. They had come a remarkably long way in a little while. Akhetaten was far enough behind them to seem insignificant, a city made of clay and set up in a princeling's tomb for him to live in after he was dead. Its walls were high still, its roofs unbroken, and all of it whole and beautiful in the embrace of its cliffs, and yet it was no living place. It was empty, stripped of its god and its people. The desert would cover it. Men would forsake it. It would die as mortal things die, and be forgotten.

She turned to look at her lady. The one who had been She-Lives-for-the-Aten, now She-Lives-for-Amon, was a different person. It was still the same face, still the same slender body and elegant hands, but the spirit that lived inside it had changed. Ankhesenpaaten would never have smiled as she sailed forever away from the city that her father had built, but Ankhesenamon not only smiled, she snatched a garland of flowers and called to her maids, and incited them to wage fierce war on the king and his young men in the boat beside hers.

Nofret's cold, contained princess would never have done such a thing. When she turned away from the Aten, she seemed to have turned away from her old somberness, too, and become as lighthearted as her husband. He had a deadly aim with a fistful of lotus blossoms. She caught them, laughing, and flung them back over the narrow stretch of water.

Some of the maids were dancing on the boat's deck in the rain of blossoms. Nofret found herself alone behind the queen's empty chair. She felt old and cold, not a little like a tomb. If she had ever known how to laugh, still less to play as children played, then she had forgotten.

Maybe Ankhesenamon was just learning it. If so, she was an apt pupil. She had turned her back completely on Akhetaten and was caught up in her joyous battle with the king and his friends.

■　■　■

Egypt welcomed its young king with open arms, with cheering and singing and carpets of flowers. Its gods all came out to greet him, made richer already by his gifts of gold and silver and precious things. Their images were renewed, their temples built higher and prouder than ever. The coldness with which the Two Lands had regarded Akhenaten was all forgotten, their joy immeasurable. They had their pride back again, and their ancient ways, and the gods that had been theirs and their ancestors' from the morning of the world. ▪

By the time the king came to Memphis, most of Egypt must have been hoarse with shouting his name. That city, set for so long beside but just beneath Thebes in the hearts of the kings, was mightily proud to be this new king's chosen place. There had been war of words, rumor said, between the priests of Ptah of Memphis and those of Amon in Memphis.

Whatever the truth of the rumor, when the king came they were all sweet amity. It was to Amon's temple that he went first, and broke the seal on the gate, and with his own hands—and the assistance of a troop of stalwart priests—flung it wide. Half the city seemed to pour in after him, to hear the rite of Amon sung in Amon's temple as it had not been in ten years and more, and to see the priests returned to their duties and their offices. But it was from Ptah's temple that he spoke his proclamation, uttering it in his own voice, clear and yet unbroken, declaring the restoration of the gods to their thrones in the Two Lands. This was politic, poorly though it might please Amon's priests: for after all he was Lord of the Two Lands, north and south, Memphis and Thebes, Ptah and Amon, and not simply of one alone.

Ankhesenamon kept to the king's side, performed the queen's part, received homage as he did. No one mentioned her father's name or the name of his city. Those were forgotten. She was in Ptah's city now, with the blessing of Amon on her, and the priesthoods of both gods bowing low at her feet.

It must have been heady to be so loved when she had been hated for so long for her father's sake. Nofret could hardly blame her for letting him be forgotten—she would have done the same, and gladly.

▪   ▪   ▪

"They're going to kill his memory," said Ankhesenamon after all the feasting and singing were over, when she had gone to her chamber in the queen's palace to rest and perhaps to sleep. It was deep night, some while yet from dawn: the hour when all is silent, before the birds begin to sing. She had bathed and anointed herself lightly and was sitting naked on her bed. She looked hardly more than a child, though she was a woman grown, and well grown, too, for all her slenderness and smallness.

She spoke of her father as if he had been a king of ancient times, observing calmly, "They hate him so much—they'll pull his city down and carve out his name wherever they can find it. It's what those who come after always do, when a king has earned his people's hatred."

Nofret opened her mouth, closed it again. Since Akhenaten went away, his daughter had said no word of him, nor spoken of him by name except as the king who was dead. Maybe he was dead to her as to the rest of Egypt.

It was not Nofret's place to remind the queen that her father was alive. Not if the queen chose to forget.

Instead of saying what had first come to her, then, of a king who was no longer king, Nofret said, "You're not going to stop them from killing his memory."

"No," said Ankhesenamon. Her old chill remoteness had come back. "Call me coward if you like. I honored him while he was king. I did as best I could to serve him. But this is another age. We have a new king, and the old gods have come back again. If they choose to take vengeance on a name, who am I to stop them?''

"You are the queen," Nofret said.

Ankhesenamon's eyes glittered. No, she was not so cold after all, and not so remote. "The queen is nothing and no one in front of the great gods."

"Even though she's Amon's own many times great-grandchild?''

"Then more than ever," said Ankhesenamon. "What do you think a god thinks when his children turn against him, call him false and worship another? Do you think he'll forgive either easily or quickly?''

Nofret shook her head. Gods were unchancy beings at best, capricious and, she sometimes thought in the privacy of her self, much too powerful for anyone's good. She often thought that it might be wisest to bring herself to the notice of none, not even for protection against ill. A mortal without a god stood less chance of running afoul of the gods than a mortal who devoted herself to one in particular and made all the rest jealous. That had been Akhenaten's mistake. It had killed his kingship and most of his family. Now his daughter, to Nofret's mind, was being sensible.

"I don't know much of Egyptian gods," Nofret said, which was only partly true, but true enough, "but I do know this: you never laughed or even smiled in Akhetaten. You had no joy. Here you have it in all the measure you ever lacked. It makes the day brighter, somehow, and the night less dark.''

"Ah, a poet," said Ankhesenamon. "I never had time to laugh. I was too busy trying to be a queen.''

"That hasn't changed," Nofret said. "Not the being queen. But you have light in you. You never did before.''

Ankesenamon thought about that. Her eyes narrowed. She frowned, not to be grim, but because she was thinking. After a while she said, "I think the Aten was too strong for my spirit. Amon is strong and he can be vengeful, but

he doesn't oppress me. He shares, you see. He lets the
other gods be.''

"That does ease the burden," Nofret agreed.

Ankhesenamon drew up her knees and clasped them and
rocked as she had done when she was much younger. She
was still thinking aloud. "The Aten only ever spoke to
Father. He never spoke to me. I never knew if he was
pleased with me, or if he even knew that I existed. The
more I tried to serve him, the less I felt of his presence.
Whereas Amon is everywhere in the Two Lands, not only
in Thebes. He talks to his priests and he talks to his people.''

"Does he talk to you?"

Ankhesenamon shrugged, sighed. "I don't know. I suppose so. I feel the anger in him. He's not angry at me, I
don't think. I don't matter enough.''

"Or you matter too much," said Nofret. "You carry the
king-right. No one can take that away from you."

"But my life," said Ankhesenamon, "that, anyone can
take. The priests have learned that they can kill a king. I
doubt they'll forget.''

Nofret shivered. "Are you afraid for your king, then?"

"No," said Ankhesenamon, perhaps a shade too
quickly. "He's their darling and their delight. He undid all
that my father did. They'll cherish him and keep him alive
as long as he does what they want him to do."

Which was mostly to let Amon have all the power in
Egypt. Nofret knew what priests were like. They were men
like any others, and men always wanted power. It was their
nature.

What women wanted was a little simpler, and a great
deal more complicated.

"I want to live," said Ankhesenamon, "and to give my
husband a son when he's ready to come to my bed. Are
those such terrible things to want?"

"They make a great deal of sense to me," said Nofret.

"Ah, but you're a foreigner."

"Not any longer," Nofret said. "I can't remember what I was in Hatti. Everything I am, I take from Egypt."

"But you aren't Egyptian," said Ankhesenamon. "You don't think like us."

"I don't think like anyone." It was too old a thought to be bitter. Nofret knelt at her lady's feet, sitting on her heels. "I think I grew up twisted somehow. Or I was born that way. I think things that are never proper for a woman, let alone a slave. I used to wonder why I couldn't learn to fight like my brothers."

"That's not difficult to answer," Ankhesenamon said. "Women are weaker. Everybody knows that."

Nofret surged to her feet. "Look at me! Do I look weak? I'm as tall as most men in this country. I could lift an ox if I had to."

"But in Hatti men are bigger than you. It's always the biggest who win in fights, because they're strongest."

"Not always," Nofret said. "Often it's the clever ones who win, who wait while the strong thrash about, and then move in the perfect moment and strike too fast to see. I told my father I could learn to fight like that. He laughed at me. I was a girl. Girls don't fight, not anywhere that anyone knows of."

Ankhesenamon looked at her, quietly curious. "Do you want to wear armor and learn to carry a spear?"

Nofret sank down, disgusted with herself. "Of course not. It's years too late, even if I weren't a female. I'd look a right fool, trying to learn the arts of war at my age. I'd trip over my own spear or put an arrow in my foot."

Ankhesenamon did not smile at that, though Nofret had rather expected her to. "What do you want, then?" she asked. "Do you want to be free? To marry, have children?"

No one ever asked a slave such questions. Except Ankhesenamon, who was as odd in her way as Nofret was.

They were not questions Nofret much cared to think on.
"What would I do if I were free? Where would I go?"

"To a husband," said Ankhesenamon. "To have his
children."

"Who would marry me? I'm a great gawk of a Hittite.
What Egyptian would want the likes of me?"

"Why," said Ankhesenamon, "any man who fancies a
strong woman. And one who's not so ill to look at, either."

All this made Nofret uncomfortable. She had had men
enough pawing at her in corners, but no one she wanted
to lie with, much less marry. There was something wrong
with her in that, too, she supposed. The other slaves had
lovers, or let men lie with them for the simple pleasure of
it. Nofret never had. The closest she had ever come was
with that idiot in Mitanni, whom she had fought off with
every art and skill she had. No one since had pressed as
hard: maybe because in Egypt she was larger than most
women, and so plainly strong.

"I don't want to marry," she said. "I'm content where
I am."

"Everyone marries," said Ankhesenamon.

"I don't," Nofret said. "I said I was different. You
didn't believe me."

"I believe," said Ankhesenamon, "that you need to
learn how to be happy. I thought it was much more difficult than it is, before I came here. There was never enough
laughter in that other place."

"There was never any," said Nofret. "I think it's still
inside me. Or I never was very lighthearted."

"You could learn to be," said Ankhesenamon.

"Maybe," Nofret said.

CHAPTER THIRTY-THREE

▲

NOFRET was never one to do what someone else wanted of her, but it struck her as useful to be as her lady wished: to be happy. It was a simple exercise. First one learned to smile, then to laugh. After that one learned to play, and to be silly. Silliness was in great fashion in the court of Tutankhamon, where everyone was young, or pretended to be.

The queen became a great master of the art of being happy. The king taught her. He was a bright spirit, he always had been. Ankhesenamon, raised like a bird in a cage, wing-clipped and silent, learned under his tutelage both to fly and to sing.

They had married in sorrow while he was but a child, to give him the right to wear the Two Crowns. In the sixth year of his reign, in the fourteenth year of his age, when he was come to a man's age if not yet to a man's strength, they married in the body. Ankhesenamon, half a dozen years the elder, once already a wife and a queen, learned from him to be lover as well as wife. Wife she had been before, and mother; but she could not have taken much pleasure from it, as young as she had been, and forced to it by duty and by her father's will.

Now she was a woman, and ripe for loving. Her husband, young though he was, was eager; and he had loved her since he was small.

They were beautiful together, two slender elegant people, he growing tall, she not small but not large either, standing just as high as his chin. They loved to sit side by side, to link hand with hand, even when they were being king and queen. When one had to be without the other for whatever reason—duty, pleasure, the needs of the king-dom—each seemed, not diminished, but as if the other should be there; there was an emptiness that should have been filled.

It was not all light and laughter. Twice Ankhesenamon conceived. Twice the child was born too soon, in much pain, and died before it drew breath. It was as it had been with Akhenaten: only daughters, and those frail, unable to live.

The blood was too close. Nofret thought that but never said it, no more than anyone else did. One did not say such things to a queen.

Ankhesenamon carried each child in great hope and lost it in grief. They mourned together, she and the king, as she had never done with Akhenaten. Grief shared was grief halved, the old women said. Certainly it was easier to bear in a lover's arms.

"We'll make a son," Tutankhamon told his queen in Nofret's hearing, as they lay together chastely, her head on his breast, her cheeks still wet with weeping for the second of their children. He wept as he spoke, but his voice was steady. "This is our sacrifice, the price we pay the gods. Next time it will be a son, and he will live."

Ankhesenamon did not say anything. No more did No-fret, who should not even have been there. Maybe the king had foresight. He was god and king, Horus on earth. Maybe he knew what the gods wanted of them all.

"We'll pray," he said. "We'll make offerings to Amon and to Mother Isis, and to Taweret who watches over women in childbirth. We'll give them all rich gifts, and they'll give us a son."

They did as he had said, did it over and over. Maybe their prayers had one worthy result. Ankhesenamon did not conceive another daughter, nor lose her.

She conceived no son, either. But the king was young.

The gods had years yet to forgive him for his kinship to the Aten's servant, and to grant him his prayer.

■   ■   ■

Nofret found it no easier to grieve than to be happy. Both seemed arts that she had never quite mastered. Mostly she felt inept and a little empty. She did her duties well; she knew that. She was the chief of the queen's servants. She commanded and others obeyed; set the queen's palace in order and kept it so, a task that often took the whole of the day and part of the night. In the midst of that she fulfilled the promise that she had made to Amon of Thebes, and gave him his gift of bread and beer for raising her to this eminence: a gift that, for her own peace, she renewed at each passing of the moon. She had accomplished what she had set out to do when she was a tribute-maiden from Mitanni. She was happy in it, but the happiness felt hollow.

She was not one to be easily content, she supposed. Ankhesenamon had a gift for taking what she had and making the most of it. Nofret was always looking for something else.

Memphis was a splendid place to look. It was as old as Thebes—some said older—and fully as splendid, as befit the capital of the north. Where Thebes had its valley of the tombs of the kings, Memphis had a wonder of the world: the old tombs, the great tombs, the mighty Pyramids that shone blinding white in the sun, ghostly white in the moon, guarding the horizon of the west. Memphis was closer to Asia than Thebes by many a hundred leagues, and its streets were fuller of strangers than Thebes' had ever been, or even Akhetaten's. Among them all, Nofret found one face she knew: the beer-seller from Akhetaten who had gone back home and set up a shop with a table and a bench, and a room behind where a woman could entertain a lover of an afternoon.

Not that Nofret ever did such a thing, though the beer-seller winked and smiled and hinted strongly that she should. She went there sometimes to drink decent beer and to watch the people go by. Maybe once or twice she went back to the palace faintly tipsy. Mostly she brought bits of gossip to make her lady laugh, or a bauble from the market. It should have been enough to satisfy her. It never quite was.

The king might have made his residence in Memphis, but he traveled everywhere in the Two Lands, up and down the river, all the way downriver to the Delta and all the way up past Thebes to the borders of Nubia. Thebes itself he visited in the end, but only when it suited him, and only as a distant second to his residence in Memphis. He was having his tomb built in the valley that lay to the west of Thebes because his ancestors had done so, and not, he made it clear, because that city came first in his heart.

It was not completely politic, but the king was uncharacteristically obstinate. "Thebes will have exactly as much of the king as it is owed, and no more," he said. "I'll live there forever after I'm dead. While I live, I prefer to live elsewhere."

Even Lord Ay could not persuade him to be more politic. He listened to reason in everything else, but in this he would not budge. Since he was king, there was nothing anyone could do to force him—and no one yet had tried to kill him. His counselors sighed and let him be. Amon's priests said nothing, nor threatened him. They had their power back, and their god in his glory. They chose to be content, or to feign contentment.

When the king traveled in the Two Lands, unless—as happened more, the older he grew—he traveled in arms, his queen went with him. Nofret went too at first, but by the time their second child died, she had too much to do in the palace in Memphis.

Ankhesenamon could have commanded Nofret, and Nofret would have had to obey. But the queen was engrossed
in her husband and not taking great notice of her servant.
She sighed at Nofret's refusal but did not argue with it.
When she went on royal progress thereafter, she took a
chosen few of her maids and left the rest in Memphis with
Nofret.

Nofret did not go to Thebes at all. She did not bear it
the hatred that the king did, but she had no love for it,
either. Even to discover if Leah had come there after all
with the rest of the Apiru, she could not quite bring herself
to go.

Memphis with neither king nor queen in residence was
no quieter, but the palace seemed echoingly empty. Most
of the court was gone, either with the king or to their own
estates. The servants had the palace to themselves. They
might have taken the opportunity to be lazy or not to be
there at all, but Nofret quickly put a stop to that. Duties
were light in the royal absence, but floors still needed to
be swept, servants and animals fed, and other, heavier
tasks done that could be awkward when the palace was
full of people: taking up and cleaning the carpets, washing
the bed-linens, scrubbing and polishing the furnishings in
the royal apartments.

The servants glowered at Nofret, and some tried to slip
away before she could catch them and put them to work.
But once she caught those and mustered the rest, they
obeyed her. She used the whip when she had to, which
was not often. Mostly her voice was enough, and the terror
of her glare.

■   ■   ■

She rose of a morning, one day in Egypt's balmy winter
when the queen was gone again to the Upper Kingdom,
and did as she did at every waking, and had for so long
that it had set into habit: bathed in the deep basin that

servants brought in, combed out her thick long mane and plaited it, weaving in the amulets of Amon and of Sobek that she had bought so long ago in Thebes, and put on a clean linen gown. It was the only one left in the press. Today would be a washing-day, then, as well as a day for scouring and airing the queen's apartments.

As she smoothed her gown, she paused. She never took much notice of herself except as a body to be kept clean and clothed, but today her skin felt odd, tender. The slight roughness of linen in her gown was almost more than she could stand.

Her courses had ended only a day or two before. There was no storm coming: it was a fine clear morning and would be very hot later. No sign of the terrible storms that sometimes came in this season, fierce dry winds sweeping ahead of them a wall of dust, and lightnings cracking in it. The air itself had none of the sparking tension that would have signaled such a storm. It was all in her, on her skin and under it.

Anyone she might have asked would have said that she needed a man. She thought of that, of seeking out someone who had shown interest, one of the guards perhaps, the young one with the lovely eyes, who was almost as beautiful as the king. But the thought of a man touching her, running hands over her newly sensitive skin, made her shudder.

She began the day's work as she always had, gathering the queen's servants and meting out their duties. As she spoke she felt as if she drifted outside of her body, up near the roofbeams like a winged spirit, and listened to the stranger-self give orders. None of the servants seemed to notice anything odd. The stranger-Nofret said the words it said every morning, chose who would do this and who would do that, did everything without any interference from the wandering spirit.

Nofret had always been very much inside of herself, one

and undivided, body and spirit. It was strange to discover that the Egyptians had the right of it. They divided the spirit into seven, each a part of the whole, ka-spirit and ba-spirit, shadow, breath, heart and name, and the body itself that housed the rest. The part of her that wandered must be either the ka—the soul that lingered with the body beyond death—or the ba that flew free on falcon-wings.

Whichever it was, it watched the body complete its giving of orders and walk through the queen's rooms, overseeing their stripping and scouring. It was not minded to wander away. The body's presence bound it.

Separated from her body as if she wandered in a strange dream, Nofret watched herself all that morning. At midday, when even the most diligent rested in the heat, the body turned not toward its cool dim chamber and its couch but toward the air and the sun. The heat barely touched it, was more caress than hammering force. The body walked through the courts and up to the walls, eluding the guards who, like everyone else with sense, sought shelter in the shade.

At the very summit of the palace, high up over the city, Nofret's body perched on the parapet. The wind caught her spirit and tugged at it, toying with it, coaxing it to drift far out over the city's roofs, the glorious rich green of the tilled lands, the mud-brown of the river. And then, it wheedled, it would carry her right out of the lands of the living toward the tombs of the old kings, the Pyramids that seemed to send up shafts of light into the endless sky.

But the body, bound to it as with a thread, resisted. For a long moment the spirit was perfectly balanced, half in the wind, half in the body. Then the body reached out and drew it in, gulped wind and spirit both, and was abruptly, dizzyingly whole.

Nofret wavered on the edge of the wall. The wind buffeted her, suddenly strong. She braced against it, moving warily away from the edge. She was dizzy and sick, and more than a little scared.

"Lady, are you well?"

She started and spun. A man was standing there, wearing a helmet and a great bronze collar and a fine linen kilt, and carrying a spear. It was the handsome guard, the one all the maids sighed after. He did not look beautiful to her now, only strange. "You seem ill, lady," he said in his soft light voice. "Come, there's water in a jar by the tower. I'll fetch you a cup."

She wanted to refuse, but her tongue would not obey her. He led her to the tower that marked the southward corner of the wall, dipped water from a clay jar there, offered it to her. His face was all limpid concern.

Suddenly she was furiously angry. If he had seized her and tried to rape her, or even pressed his attentions on her, she would not have minded half so much. This chaste solicitude made her want to claw his eyes out.

Her body, disregarding the frantic spirit, took the cup, even smiled before it drank. He smiled back. He had a beautiful smile, of course. Everything about him was simply lovely. Nor did he have the air that many handsome men had, of knowing too well how good he was to look at. He knew, he could hardly avoid it, but it did not seem to matter to him. He was like the king in that, and like the queen.

She watched her hand reach out and brush his cheek. It was smooth, hardly bearded yet, and that well shaven in Egyptian fashion. He blushed lightly under the bronzing of sun and wind, but did not pull away.

The cup was empty. She had drunk the whole of it, not even aware that she was doing it. He took the cup from her hands and laid it aside as carefully as if it had been fine glass and not mere rough clay.

She could not even remember his name. Seni, Seti, something of the sort. Names were power in Egypt. She

knew that, whose birthname was hidden and all but forgotten. She groped for it, but it was nowhere in her. Had
she lost it this morning? Was that why she was all so
strange?

The guard's eyes on her had gone strangely soft. They
were reflecting her own, maybe. He leaned toward her. His
kiss was dry, warm, eager but restrained. How fortunate,
she thought, that chance and the gods gave her a man like
this and not one who would long since have knocked her
down and done as he pleased. This was a man of patience,
a gentle man. He was much better than she deserved.

The tower was empty, and dark after the searing brilliance of the sun. Her eyes came to themselves long after
her body did. It lay on something more hard than soft, a
reed mat perhaps, and its gown was lost somewhere. So
were his kilt and helmet, though he still had his bronze
collar. Its edge pressed on her breast, not quite painful but
too evidently there. He was a little shorter than she, a little
narrower. His body was shaved smooth all over, a faint
rasp of stubble on her skin, evident as the collar was, not
quite enough to repulse her.

A distant part of her wondered precisely what she was
doing here. The rest knew very well. She was lying with
the beauty of the guard, each of them sadly derelict in duty,
and neither caring in the least.

When he pierced her, the pain was sharp, and not remote
at all. She saw how his eyes widened. He had not expected
to meet that barrier—not in her who was notably older
than he. He started to recoil, but she caught him in strong
arms, wrapped legs about his hips, bound him to her. He
struggled briefly, by instinct, but another instinct was
stronger still. With a sigh he yielded to it.

She waited for the pleasure that everyone said came after the pain. The pain sank to an ache, but of pleasure there
was little, except in the rocking rhythm, the closeness of
another body, the sharp scent of sweat. His breath quick-

ened, his rhythm with it. Then abruptly he was done, rigid against her, and flooding warmth inside of her.

He held her tightly for a long moment. Then he let go, dropping down, already half asleep. That too everyone told of, how some men slept as soon as they were spent, and even a few women. But not Nofret. She lay motionless beside a sleeping stranger, with an ache deep inside her, and no sense that she had gained anything but a few moments' pain. The day's strangeness was unaltered. She was if anything even more alien to herself, though her spirit chose to keep its place and not go wandering again.

She got up slowly. There was blood on her thighs. She found a rag hung on a peg, wet it in water from the jar outside, washed herself carefully with hands that kept trying to shake. Then she washed out the rag with equal care, till all the blood was gone from it. She was still bleeding a little, as she did in her courses. She bound the clean wet rag in place, put on her rumpled gown, did what she could to make order of her hair.

The guard was still asleep, snoring softly. He would be reprimanded or worse if his captain learned that he had abandoned his post to lie with a woman. She should wake him, get him dressed and armed again, and send him back to his duty. But if she roused him he would want to kiss her again, and maybe go back to bed-play. Men did that, the maids had told her. Either they took what they wanted once and forgot the woman who had given it, or they kept coming back, pressing, insisting, being a nuisance.

This one would want more. She read it in the way he lay, loose like a child, smiling in his sleep. He was really quite lovely, a beautiful boy, with his smooth brown skin and his slender hands. She was moved to kiss him, simply because he was so pretty, but she did not.

She left his helmet and spear beside him and said a prayer to Hathor who watched over lovers, that he would wake in time to escape his captain's wrath. Then she left him, treading carefully lest she shake her spirit loose from her body. But it seemed firmly bound now, wound about the ache in her center. That much at least she had done: brought body and spirit together again, and kept them so, for all they tried again to scatter.

CHAPTER THIRTY-FOUR

▲

THE guard's name was Seti. He waited several days before he came round, but come round he did. He came in the evening when Nofret had won a few moments' quiet for herself, choosing his moment by good luck or careful inquiry. He brought a gift, a lotus bloom and a jar of date wine.

Nofret was mildly astonished to see him standing in the doorway of her cell of a room, looking lovely and shy but just a little cocky. She was supposed to be flustered and flattered and utterly delighted, no doubt, that he would not only remember her but deign to favor her with his presence.

Before she could order him out, he smiled a perfectly charming smile and said, "I don't suppose you want to see me, but I had to come."

She opened her mouth to say something terrible and unforgivable. But her tongue was of another mind. It said, "I hope you didn't get into too much trouble with your captain, for sleeping on duty."

He flushed slightly. "No. Oh, no. The gods were kind. I was awake and at my post before anyone knew."

"Good," said Nofret. She meant it. She did not bear him any ill-will. He was pretty, he was charming, he was much better than she deserved.

He bowed and offered her the lotus flower. She had to take it or see it dropped at her feet. Its scent was sweet. She sneezed. He laughed a little breathlessly; so, after a moment, did she.

Somehow they ended in her bed, with the flower forgotten on the floor, and his kilt and her gown beside it. Her body seemed to have a will of its own when it came to this of all men. She did not even know if he could carry on an intelligent conversation. Intelligence had very little to do with what he was doing to her, and she to him.

He seemed to think that that was enough. All the words he breathed in her ear .were the kind of words that the lustiest of the maids swore they prayed for. Silly words, ridiculous words, words with kitten-love in them. How he could be besotted with her she could not imagine, but so he seemed to be. Maybe it was simply that she was the chief of the queen's servants, and he gained honor among his fellows in adorning her bed.

■   ■   ■

She gained the envy of the maids, and at least one vow to take him away from her. She might not have minded if the woman had succeeded. It was all very awkward. She could not quite seem to confess that she felt nothing for Seti but a kind of bemusement. What he wanted of her in the body she found easy enough to give. She even had pleasure in it. It was shocking the first time, expected and yet beyond expectation. Thereafter, and as both of them grew more adept at pleasing one another, it was delightful. She began to think longingly of it when he was not there, though she never allowed it to obsess her. She was much too stubborn a creature for that.

He had the body, all that he could ask for, and yet he wanted something of the spirit, too, or said he did; and that she did not have.

There was no one to whom she could say such things.

The one she thought of was nowhere in Egypt. Even if he had been, he might not have understood. Friend or no, Johanan was a man. Men had dreams; they constructed whole palaces of fancy, with queens inside of them, and courts of airy love. Women had to be more practical. They drank their herb-brews, prepared their potions, kept vigilance lest they produce a child. What irony, thought Nofret, if her precautions failed and she produced the son that her lady had always dreamed of. Son of a slave and a guardsman—but son nonetheless.

Which the gods avert. She did not want her belly filled with Seti's offspring, however beautiful or charming it might turn out to be. She did the things that the maids prescribed, preposterous or repellent though they were. It seemed that they worked: her courses came in their ordered round, as regular as the moon. She thanked the gods for that, and vowed to send Seti away; but her tongue would never say the words. It, like the rest of her body, was much too fond of the things that he did and said to it.

And after all, what harm was there in it? He was happy. Her body had learned to sing deep in the bones, and more sweetly the longer he played on it. She kept her duties still, and so did he. They were not like the lovers of story who forgot everything in the intoxication of one another.

▪ ▪ ▪

She did not fail in her duty, not at all, but she discovered that it was taking less of her heart and her time. She found herself one bright and burning day with a whole afternoon to herself. Everything that could be done for the queen's return had been done. The palace was in order. She had set most of the maids free to take their leisure. Those who remained went drowsily about their few tasks, none urgent, and none that required Nofret's presence.

It was rather disconcerting to realize that she was not

needed, nor had she anything pressing to do. It was like old days in Akhetaten.

Seti was on guard duty and would not be free till evening. She had no particular desire to seek him out, nor any to take him away from his post. Before he mattered to her, she had done it; but not now. She knew too much of him: his mother in the city; who relied on his wages for her own bread and beer; his brother who dreamed of a post in the guard but who was too young yet to seek one; his sisters who would be wanting husbands when they were a little older. All that edifice of family would topple if Nofret tempted him again to be derelict in his duty.

It was an odd, free sensation to know that no one needed her, nor had she anywhere to be until the evening. She took it with her out of her little room, wandering as she used to do in Akhetaten, with no particular aim or purpose. She might go to the city; she might not. She might choose to stay in the palace, amid splendors grown almost comfortable with use.

She had a favorite place, a garden court with fruit-trees, and a fountain with fish in it. It was nothing to the magnificence of the gardens proper, nor was it much frequented. It was smallish and old and somewhat neglected. Some ancient queen had built it, had overseen the planting of the trees and the setting of the fountain. She was long gone to her tomb. Her courtyard lived still, the grandchildren of the grandchildren of her trees bowed under the weight of their fruit.

Nofret plucked a pomegranate from the one tree of its kind, a ragged and splintery thing with a propensity for dropping branches on the unwary head. But its fruit was sweet. She ate it sitting in the shade of a less unchancy tree, buried the rind carefully and with a prayer to the spirit of its mother tree, and sat licking the blood-red juice from her fingers.

A murmur of voices brought her to the colonnade. As

seldom as anyone came to this court, it was not far from the courts of welcome where strangers were received into the palace. Once or twice before she had been here when embassies came, and once greeted a lordling from a distant nome of Egypt, who had taken a wrong turning and was much dismayed to find himself in a deserted garden. She had salved his pride and set him on his way, and got no thanks for it either; but that was the way of it with even the least of princes.

Nofret would have lingered in the cool shade with the taste of pomegranate sweet on her tongue, but curiosity brought her out to the colonnade and thence to the outer court, the court of the foreigners. A numerous embassy milled and babbled there, with much clattering of horses' hoofs and shouting of men.

Her heart caught in spite of itself. Emissaries had come from Great Hatti before, and often: companies of tall broad pale-skinned men in long kilts and embroidered mantles, their thick curling hair grown long behind and shaved smooth in front, and their hands never far from hilt or haft of a weapon. Even weaponless in front of the king they managed to look as if they were armed to the teeth.

They never took notice of the queen's maids, nor cared that one of them was a Hittite. Nor should she care who they were or where they came from. She was bound to Egypt.

And yet whenever men from Hatti came to speak with the king, Nofret came over all strange. They were her people, and they were not. The language they spoke sounded strange to her, though she could understand it well enough. One could lose one's capacity to do such things, she knew: she had seen it in others of the tribute-slaves, who when their own people came before the king, wept because they could not understand the envoys, only the interpreters.

Nofret clung grimly to her birth-tongue. Part of it was pride, part stubbornness, and part conviction that it might prove useful. She could assure herself that the interpreters were honest; and so they had been when she was there to hear them.

Her lady had never asked her to play the part of interpreter. It was not something Ankhesenamon thought of or Nofret saw fit to propose. Nofret was a maidservant, not a speaker of tongues.

■   ■   ■

There were Hittites in the court of the foreigners, an ambassador and his train, carrying the seal of the King of Kings, the Great King of Hatti. It was still Suppiluliumas as it had been when she was taken away to Mitanni. He was one of the great kings, Nofret had heard Lord Ay opine, and not entirely with admiration. Great kings' could be a nuisance. They made war all too often, and thought too much of increasing their lands.

Nofret wondered if Suppiluliumas was in a conquering mood again. If he was, General Horemheb would deal with him. General Horemheb was commander of the king's armies in Asia now, a higher post than the one he had held in the Delta, and comfortably distant from Egypt.

She lingered in the shadow of a column, more idly curious than anything else, watching the Hittites. In the king's absence and outside of Nofret's jurisdiction the palace had become a bit slack: the minister in charge of welcoming embassies was slow in coming, and the grooms and servants were at somewhat of a loss.

Nofret shook her head. Idiots. Even she, who held power only in the queen's palace, knew where the stables were and how one welcomed ambassadors, and where one sent them to bathe and rest and refresh themselves. No one here seemed willing or able to do any of that. The Hittites were conspicuously patient, but the nobleman in the middle had begun to frown, black brows knit over his mighty arch of nose.

Queen's servant she might be, but she belonged to the palace, too. Its honor reflected on hers. More so maybe because she was Hittite, and Hatti would not think well of Egypt if it offered so poor a welcome.

She drew a breath, smoothed her gown, and stepped into the light. It struck hard, and with it the shouting of men, milling of horses, baying of hunting hounds, even the snarl of a lion in a cage: Hatti had sent the lion-cub of Egypt a most proper tribute. She wove her way through the hurtling bodies. Men were cursing. Some of the dogs had got into a fight. The ambassador, high in his chariot, looked ready to haul his horses about and send them galloping back to Hatti.

Armed men surrounded him. The king's minister should have seen to that, too: none but the king's men could go armed in the palace.

A woman alone could be in danger amid so many men, but Nofret had her own armor: her height and breadth of shoulder, and her haughty glare at any man who offered insolence. The wall of men about the ambassador was the only quiet thing in that place, but there was nothing harmless about their weapons.

Nofret parted a pair of spears as if they had been the leaves of a door. The spearmen stared at her. She stared back. They were young men, smooth-shaven like Egyptians, but otherwise utterly different. Their faces were Hittite faces, arch-nosed and full-cheeked. One had a scar on his chin. The other's eyes were peculiar, not brown or black as most men's were, but grey, and his hair had a reddish cast. It was uncommon coloring in Hatti, but not as uncommon as that. Nofret had it herself.

Still, she thought, there was something . . .

"Lupakki," she said suddenly. "What in the world are you doing here?"

Well, she thought. That settled the question of whether

she could still speak Hittite. It came rough, but it came clear enough.

Her third-from-eldest brother looked her over from head to foot. Maybe he did not remember her. Brothers could easily forget a sister who had been snatched away in childhood.

His grey eyes went wide—so wide they rolled white. He looked as if he had seen a ghost, or a dead woman walking. "Arinna," he said. The name shook her. It was a stranger's name, and yet it rang in her bones: her birthname, the name that she had made herself forget.

It woke something, some part of her that she had thought was gone. He said it again. "Arinna." He reached out to touch her arm, flinching a little, but holding firm. "Arinna, you were dead. We saw the place where they killed you."

That too she had thought forgotten: the hunt, the capture, the fierce and hopeless battle. "I stabbed a bandit," she said. "He bled like a pig."

"We thought the blood was yours." His fingers tightened on her arm, then let go, as if he remembered suddenly where he was and who was staring. "Great gods, little sister. We've been mourning you, propitiating your spirit, praying you wouldn't haunt us for not looking hard enough for your body. And all the while—"

"And all the while, I was in Mitanni, and then I was here." She lifted her chin. "I'm the chief of the queen's servants."

He did not say the word that some would have said, the word that was shame: slave. His lip curled faintly, maybe, at the fact of her servitude, but his voice was light, deliberately so. "You're higher up than I, then," he said. "I fight under the king's general."

Nofret tilted her chin toward the man in the chariot, who took no notice of her at all. He was much too lofty, of course, and much too far out of patience. "That one?"

"That," said Lupakki, "is my lord Hattusa-ziti, and he is much insulted."

"I can see that," Nofret said dryly. "Will you let me by?"

"Why?"

Oh, that was Lupakki: always a question and never a simple acceptance of orders. Nofret wondered how that served him in his lord's army.

She was steady. Her mind was clear. Duty helped, and numbness, the shock of a face that she had thought never to see again.

She stepped between her brother and the man beside him and caught the bridle of the horse who was nearest. The stallion was restive, but it was well trained; it dipped its head to her. She looked up past its ears to the ambassador's face. He greatly disliked the necessity of noticing her, but she had outraged his dignity: she had touched one of his horses. She addressed him direct and clear, with as much respect as she could manage. "My lord, I welcome you to Memphis. I beg you be not offended by my presence, or by the regrettable lack of efficiency that you see here. The king is away, you see, and his servants were not expecting your arrival."

Lord Hattusa-ziti came close to a sneer at such a confession of disorder. Nofret did not care if he despised her. She did care that he be got out of this place and settled somewhere where he could be appeased.

"It was known," he said haughtily, "that I was to arrive."

"My lord," she said, "your messengers were not precise as to the day and time. You traveled quickly. I trust you traveled well?"

He snorted like one of his horses.

She suppressed a sigh. This was not going well. She raised her voice. "You will please, my lord, to come down from your chariot. Rooms will be ready, and all that you desire for your comfort, you and the men with you." She held out her free hand, the one that did not rest on the stallion's bridle. "Come, sir."

For a wonder he did. Maybe it was startlement, or the novelty of taking orders from a woman and a slave, and one who wore the gown of an Egyptian and the face of a Hittite.

She bowed in front of him, low as befit the messenger of the King of Kings. "I am called Nofret," she said. "I am the chief of the queen's servants. I speak with her voice, and offer you the courtesy that she would offer were she here and not in the Upper Kingdom."

Courtesy begot courtesy. Hattusa-ziti was an ambassador; he was trained to it as a chariot-horse to the yoke. He unbent for her, enough at least to accept her guidance into the palace.

A few well-placed words sent servants racing ahead and roused the rest to remembrance of their duty. In remarkably short order, the embassy was escorted to a guesthouse, its horses stabled, its gifts taken to a place where they would be safe until they were presented to the king.

The minister in charge of receiving embassies appeared late and rumpled and reeking of perfume. He had obviously been enjoying his afternoon's rest. Nofret offered him no reprimand. It was not her place. She left it to Hattusa-ziti, who had a well-honed and exquisitely lethal tongue.

With Huy's arrival, Nofret's part in the proceedings was done. She withdrew gladly. Contending with Hattusa-ziti was rather like a duel with swords: sharp, short, and dangerous. She had held her own, she rather thought. But she was glad to hand him over to the one who should have dealt with him to begin with. She was even gladder to leave her brother behind. She needed time to think, to remember what she was and what she had been.

▪ ▪ ▪

Seti was waiting for her, warm and rather silly with the date wine he had drunk while he waited. He gave her no time to greet him, fell on her at the door and carried her to the bed, tugging at her gown and cursing it, but laughing, when it proved intractable. Her body arched toward him but her spirit recoiled. She was in bed before she knew it, while he rutted on top of her.

She was not innocent of it, either. She made no move to stop him. Her spirit was tugging free of her body again, trying to fly as it had flown on the day she first lay with Seti. It had taken her to him then. Now it wanted to take her away.

It was a fickle thing, her spirit. It was thinking of her brother Lupakki, and the Hittites lodged in their guesthouse near the king's palace. She had refused to think of any of her brothers, or her father either, while she was a slave in Egypt. Now one of them had come to her, right before her face as she did her duty.

Seti did not fall asleep as he usually did, but stayed awake and wanted to talk. Wine touched some men so; and maddeningly now, when Nofret would have preferred that he sleep. He did not seem to notice the shortness of her answers. He chattered happily of nothing and everything, bits of gossip, nonsense to which she paid little attention. She fed him wine while he babbled, but it only made him babble faster.

At long last and so abruptly that it caught him between one word and the next, he succumbed to the power of the wine. Nofret heaved a sigh of relief. She almost drained the winejar herself, but she had more sense than that.

She got up instead, washed, combed and plaited her hair. She hesitated between the gown she wore every day and the one she wore for festivals. It might be reckoned a festival to see her brother again and all unlooked for; but the gown was of transparent linen, and Hittites were modest people. She chose the lesser garment, which was clean and of good strong linen, if not so handsome as the other.

With that she put on a jewel or two, her pendant of malachite carved with the Eye of Horus that Seti had given her, and the earrings of gold and malachite that had been a gift from her lady. She looked well, she thought, peering at herself in her lady's fine bronze mirror. She was not beautiful as Egyptians were, but she was not ill to look at, either. She would not shame either herself or her lady in front of the Hittite embassy.

■ ■ ■

There were women with the embassy, lesser ladies of the household brought in curtained wagons for the ambassador's entertainment. There were none who would speak as an Egyptian woman could, with the voice of an equal. Even queens in Hatti, whose sons alone could be kings, kept silence before the men, and spoke only in the inner room, where their lords might listen or not, as they chose.

Nofret had never had any talent for effacement. She walked boldly to the guards on the gate, tall men in armor but with empty scabbards, and said to them, "I would speak to the warrior Lupakki."

One of them moved to thrust her away. The other stopped him. "No, let her be. She's his sister: I heard them talking. She belongs to the queen."

Nofret smiled sweetly. "I am the chief of the queen's servants. Is there anything your lord requires? Be sure to apprise my lord Huy."

"What, the old woman in the kilt?" The guard curled his lip. "It will be a pleasure to keep him at the run."

"By all means, keep him running," said Nofret. "It's his duty and his office." She lifted her chin. "Where is Lupakki?"

"Inside," said the guard who had recognized her, "in the guardroom." He grinned at her. "If you can't find him, come and find me. I'm off duty when the sun dips below the rooftree."

Nofret patted his well-muscled arm. "I already have a guardsman," she said.

The man laughed. "An Egyptian? When you could have one of us?"

"My brother can't defend my honor against an Egyptian," said Nofret with a flash of teeth. She left him to ponder that, and went to find her brother.

■　　■　　■

Lupakki was not displeased to be called away from the labor of settling in the guesthouse. He still had a little of the startled-deer look about the eyes, but he seemed to have overcome the first shock of the meeting. He greeted her with deliberate insouciance. "Ah, a rescue! If you hadn't come, little sister, I'd have been condemned to unloading baggage."

"You were lazy as a child, too," Nofret said to him as they walked through the court of the foreigners. It was empty now, its paving scoured, no sign of the throngs of men and beasts that had filled it. Lupakki gaped at the size of it, the pillars like the trunks of mighty trees, the length and breadth of it, larger than a lord's palace in Hatti. And yet it was one of the lesser courts in this palace.

"Egyptians build so big," he said. "How do they live in it?"

"As anyone does," she answered. "They eat, they sleep. Sometimes they quarrel."

"That must wake echoes," he said, "in halls as big as this, and ceilings so high."

He was half laughing, but half not. "Kings and queens don't raise their voices," said Nofret. "The angrier they are, the softer they speak."

"How alarming," said Lupakki. He stepped up to a pillar and tried to circle it with his arms. He was a big man and long-armed, but not long enough. He peered up at the top of the pillar, which was painted to look like a fan of papyrus. "Imagine if it all fell down on us."

"I would rather not," Nofret said. "How is our father? Is he well?"

Lupakki turned to face her. "He died four years ago."

Her heart stopped, then started again, staggering in her breast. She should have expected it. Warriors never lived long, and her father had been well out of first youth when he mourned her supposed death. And yet it struck her hard, cramping in her belly. She spoke through it. "He died in battle?"

He nodded.

She let her breath go in a long sigh. "That's well enough, then. He'd have hated to die in his bed."

"Unless it was with a woman." Lupakki smiled, maybe in spite of himself. "All the rest of us are alive. Piyassili's head of the family now."

"Is he as dull as ever?"

"Duller," said Lupakki, "and very dutiful. His wife is even duller than he. But their sons are hellions."

Nofret laughed painfully. "Then there's justice in heaven," she said.

"So we like to say," said Lupakki. He paused if to gather courage. "And you? You've been well?"

"Well enough." She began to walk, she did not care where. He followed. His silence expected a better answer than she had given. Because he was her brother, she said, "I wait on the queen. She's kind to me; she indulges my eccentricities."

"She must be an unusual woman," said Lupakki.

He was being facetious, a little, but Nofret was not. "No queen or king in Egypt is precisely ordinary," she said.

"You'll see her soon enough. She's coming back here before the moon wanes."

"And the king?"

"He'll be with her. They go everywhere together."

"Even to war?"

"Well," said Nofret, "no. But he hasn't gone to war yet. He has generals to do that for him."

Lupakki raised his brows. "They really are like that? It isn't noble here to be a warrior?"

"Egypt is old," said Nofret. "It's grown past the urgencies of youth." And why she was defending it, she could not tell.

"This king is young, they say," Lupakki said. "He must want to do what young men do, surely: love a woman, hunt a lion, fight an enemy."

"He loves his queen," said Nofret, "and he hunts lions—and kills them, too."

"Then he'll be wanting to fight," said Lupakki, "if he's as much a man as that."

"You are a bloodthirsty savage," Nofret said.

He grinned at her, showing strong white teeth, and one broken. She had done that, defending herself against him in an altercation: snatched a stone and hurled it at him, and struck better than she meant. She had got a whipping for that. Her father was fair: he whipped his daughters as he did his sons, if they happened to deserve it.

Lupakki seemed to bear her no animosity. Boys did terrible things to one another, dealt dreadful wounds in the name of manliness. They resented it deeply when a girl presumed to do the same, but Lupakki had been less proud about that than most. He had found her amusing then. So he seemed to now, regarding her with honest delight. "Gods!" he said. "If Father could see you now, he'd take a fit."

"Then it's well he's dead," said Nofret.

"Wait till I tell Piyassili," he said, oblivious to her grim expression. "Our little sister not only alive but standing at the right hand of Egypt's queen. Remember how he used to swear you'd die in a slave-pit with your tongue still wagging, flaying your master's hide as he flayed yours?"

That cut close to the bone. "My lady tells me that," said Nofret stiffly, "after she's invited me to speak freely."

"She *is* remarkable," said Lupakki. He was oblivious to her stiffness. "Is she as beautiful as they say?"

"More," said Nofret, letting go her stiffness with reasonably decent grace, all things considered. There never had been any profit in quelling Lupakki. He simply laughed and went on with whatever he had been saying to begin with. "She's her mother's daughter. There was never anyone more beautiful than Nefertiti."

"And you saw her with your own eyes," sighed Lupakki. "What fortune! It almost makes me wish I could have been a slave."

"You'd have been an even worse one than I am," Nofret said. She tugged him with her into the hall of audience. "Here. See how the echoes run."

He did, with delight. The hall was empty, lit only by shafts of sunlight through the louvers in the roof. His voice sent the echoes running from pillar to pillar, from paving-stone to roofbeam: the tones of the singer's scale, the yipping of a jackal, the baying exuberance of a Hittite war-cry.

Nofret's heart quivered at that. But there was no omen in it. Once and only once, invaders had ruled in Egypt. They had been driven out and all their names forgotten. Hatti would never do as they had done.

This was not mockery or defiance. It was exuberance: a young man's innocent pleasure in a place so foreign that he could only marvel at it.

Nofret had expected to feel old, looking at him: old and remote. Oddly, she felt neither. She was no longer of Hatti, nor could be, but this was still her brother. It was strange to know it. Strange and a little alarming, but somehow reassuring. She was more than she had thought. She had a place in the world, and kin, too, who had thought herself so perfectly alone.

CHAPTER THIRTY-FIVE

▲

THE king returned with his queen before the Hittites had been in Memphis a handful of days. There was strain between the two of them: that, Nofret noticed as soon as she saw them. It was not anything obvious; but they who had ridden had in the same chariot, his arms wrapped about her and both their hands on the reins, rode each in a separate chariot. They smiled as it had become their custom to do, walked side by side into their palace, performed every office of royal amity, but it had a distinct air of ritual and not of simple joy.

Nofret learned the cause not long after the day had waned. The king was going to war.

Ankhesenamon spoke of it with cool dispassion, addressing the wall rather than Nofret, as Nofret cleansed the paint from her face and readied her for sleep. "It's really quite simple," she said. "Hatti has attacked and overcome Mitanni. King Tushratta is dead. You knew that, yes?"

"Yes," said Nofret. Her voice was carefully colorless.

"I am sure," said Ankhesenamon, "that you were pleased to hear it. Hatti is now greater than it was before. This is difficult for us, however. Mitanni was our ally. Hatti, in destroying it, becomes our enemy."

"It rather hopes not," said Nofret. "It's sent an embassy. They're in the guesthouse, waiting to be summoned.''

"Carousing, I suppose,'' said Ankhesenamon, ''and making a great deal of noise.'' She shook her head. ''I don't think my lord will listen to them. They only came to Memphis. Someone else came all the way to Abydos and caught us as we celebrated the rites of the gods, clasped my husband's knees and begged him to aid his people.''

"And your husband raised him up and promised him every sword and spear in Egypt.''

Ankhesenamon shot Nofret a glance. ''Don't laugh at him. He told the petitioner to rest and refresh himself—and then he shut himself up with Lord Ay and the rest of the council.''

"And said that they could advise as they pleased, but he was going to fight in a war.'' Nofret arranged her lady's wig on its stand, smoothing the many beaded plaits. ''Who's the ally?''

"Have you heard of Ashur?''

"In Hatti they call it Assyria,'' Nofret said. ''Its king is no older than Egypt's. He's full of fight, they say. He thinks that if Egypt and Ashur wage their wars together, they can crush Hatti between them.''

"You've been talking to the Hittites,'' said Ankhesenamon.

"Is that treason?'' Nofret asked her.

She leaned forward in her chair, set elbows on knees and chin in hands. She sighed. ''I don't think I know what treason is. No more do I want my husband to go to war. You'd call me a bad wife for that, I suppose. All Hittite wives must be miserable if their husbands aren't out fighting like proper men.''

"As I remember,'' said Nofret, ''they didn't know that there was any other way for a man to live, except if he were a fighting man.''

"They never argued? They never begged him to stay home?"

"They wouldn't dare. That would make him a coward, the scorn of the people."

Ankhesenamon covered her face with her hands. Her voice came muffled but clear. "That's what he said to me. He said that I would keep him a child, stifle the breath from him, protect him till he died. A king must fight, he said. A king who doesn't fight, who leaves it to his generals, is not a king at all; he's a child dressed up in crowns and scepter and set on a mockery of a throne."

"He's come to a man's years," Nofret said. "Can you stop him from wanting what a man wants?"

"He wants to go away from me," said Ankhesenamon. "What if he's killed?"

Nofret bit her tongue. She had almost answered as a Hittite answers: that if a man was killed, his women mourned him. But Ankhesenamon had mourned enough. She had joy at last, and love with it. If he died, it was all gone. She might never know it again.

No. That was tempting the gods to take him. "He won't die," she said. "He may go to war, and he may ride into battle, but his men will protect him. He's their king, the life of the kingdom. They won't let him be killed."

She could taste the truth in it, though it was bitter beneath. The king would not die in battle, nor in Asia. Where he died, how he died . . .

She closed the eyes of the spirit. She did not want to see where or when the king would die. It was enough to comfort her lady now, that she could say what she had said. "He'll come back to you," she said. "His army will make sure of it."

Ankhesenamon did not argue further. Maybe she wanted to believe Nofret; maybe she was simply too tired to fight. She went to bed alone and slept alone. The king did not come to her bed, nor did she seek his.

■ ■ ■

The coldness between them persisted. Nofret hated to see it, but there was nothing she could do. She thought of approaching the king, but what would she say to him? That she had a gift of foresight, a Hebrew prophetess had told her so, and she had seen that he would come back—and had apprised her lady of it? He would curse her interference. It was for her lady to approach him, to mend what was broken; and her lady did not do it.

They were both too proud for decent sense. Both had the right of it, too. A young man wanted to fight; it was his nature. A woman, his wife, wanted him safe, to protect her, to hold his place beside her, to be father to such children as she might conceive. If the young man was a king and the woman his queen, their quarrel became a matter of state. If the king wished to fight on an ally's behalf and the queen wished him to remain safe at home, then Egypt itself would suffer the consequences of the choice.

They did not quarrel as lesser folk might have done. Their altercations were quiet, their voices calm. They were perfectly reasonable in their disagreement.

"I remember," said the king as they sat in the lotus garden of a drowsy afternoon, "when men spoke of your father, how he would never go to war though he wore the Blue Crown, the war-crown, and had himself painted as a lord of battles; how he was afraid of it, and kept to his temple and his courts, and never went anywhere that would threaten his life."

"He was not a coward," Ankhesenamon said. "His god consumed him, left him no mind or spirit for the things of earth."

"He did nothing to defend the Two Lands," said the king. "His armies did what they could, but without the king's presence or his countenance, theirs was lessened. They laugh at us in Asia, my lady. They reckon us weaklings, too feeble with luxury to defend ourselves in war.''

"War is a fool's pursuit," she said, "or a child's."

"Then I am a fool and a child," he said, rising from his seat. He had grown taller in this season, and leaner, and darker with sun and wind. It had been nigh on seventeen floods of the Nile since he was born in Thebes. He was a man by the Egyptians' count of years, and bound no longer to heed the advice of his council.

He was angry now with a young man's anger. He bowed stiffly, turned on his heel, and left her.

Not since they were wedded had he gone out of his lady's presence without a kiss or a caress. She was as angry as he: a delicate flush stained her cheeks, and her eyes glittered. If he had kissed her, no doubt she would have struck him.

He engrossed himself in the arts of war: archery, chariotry, practice with lance and sword. She flung herself into the arts of ruling, of being queen and mistress of a great household. It was a right and proper division, if they had been Hittite. In Egypt, where king and queen did everything side by side but fight in wars, it was distressing to see.

■　■　■

The Hittite embassy was in a difficult position. The king was preparing war against Hatti while Hatti's ambassador lingered in Memphis. Hattusa-ziti was admitted in time to the royal presence, his message heard with royal courtesy. He asked that the king reconsider his war, which of course the king would not do for a Hittite, no more than for his queen. The words they exchanged were as precisely ordered as a dance.

But like a dance, once those words were ended they lingered only briefly in the memory. Hattusa-ziti must return to Hatti before the king's army marched; the king would not refuse him that, nor hold him prisoner. It was the honor of kings, and of kingly war.

Nofret said farewell to her brother at dawn on the day he went back to Hatti. He had been carousing for most of the night, as all the Hittites had: the king had held a feast for them, a banquet of worthy enemies. The queen had not attended, and neither therefore had Nofret. Ankhesenamon had dined alone in her palace, refusing the company of her ladies. She had gone to her bed soon after, and feigned sleep so well that Nofret almost believed her.

Nofret was heavy-eyed with lack of sleep. Lupakki was disgustingly lively, the wine still working in him, and the joy of going home from this strange and burning hot country. He embraced Nofret with gladness that altered swiftly into wine-scented tears. "Arinna," he said. "Come back with me. We're enemies now to Egypt—there's no dishonor in taking you away where you belong."

Oh, names were power, and he had named her as she was before she was taken into Egypt. The name could not compel her. It was not hers any longer. And yet it had been once; it was still a part of her, the part that was of Hatti.

And what if she took it back? What if she forsook the part of her that had given itself to Egypt? To be among her own people again. To speak the language she had been born to. To live in the women's house, shrouded and veiled as a woman was privileged to be, married maybe to a warrior, weaving his war-cloaks and binding his wounds. To be all of that, and nothing that had ever been in Egypt.

She shuddered. "I belong here," she said.

Lupakki held her at arm's length. He seemed suddenly a stranger, a man utterly foreign to Egypt, with thick-fingered hands and a bull's shoulders. She blinked hard. Her brother stood in front of her again, handsome grey-eyed young man in Hittite battle-dress, with the wine wearing off, and anger taking its place. "Have you become a slave, then?"

"Our enemies captured me and sold me into slavery when I was nine years old," she said, snapping off the words. "And where were you? Why didn't anyone find me before I stood on the slave-block in Mitanni?" But then she stopped herself; she caught at the edges of his mantle and held him before he spun away. "No! I won't part in anger."

"You needn't part at all," he said.

"I can't go," she said. "I'm the queen's servant. It would be dishonorable if I left her."

He opened his mouth, perhaps to remind her that the queen was Hatti's enemy. But he did not say it. Honor was a great thing in Hatti. Nofret maybe had too much of it, or she would have let him carry her away, no matter what she went back to.

His duties were calling him: ranks forming behind the ambassador's chariot, waiting for Hattusa-ziti to emerge from the guesthouse. He lingered, and she held still to his mantle. Her eyes were burning dry, the way they always were when she should have been weeping. His had a wide, set look, not quite fixed on her face. "Gods keep you, sister," he said abruptly.

"And you, brother," she said.

He pulled away just as she let him go. He did not look back. She stayed where she was, in the dark by the colonnade, until the sun had risen and the Hittite embassy marched out of the gate, taking the long road home.

CHAPTER THIRTY-SIX

▲

MARRY me,'' said Seti.

Nofret spun, startled. She had been folding her lady's
gowns and laying them in their presses, unattended by others of the maids, who were all playing in the lotus pool
with the queen. Nofret was not in the mood for such frantic
enjoyment.

Nor was she delighted to be brought to earth by Seti.
He tried to seize her and flatten her in the heap of linen,
but she braced her feet. He tumbled her against the wall
instead, babbling through a spatter of kisses. "Marry me.
I'm going to war; the king has said it. I know in my bones,
if you wait for me I won't die in battle. Marry me, my
beautiful one.''

"I'm not beautiful,'' Nofret snapped, "and I'm not going to marry you. Let me go.''

He only held her tighter and kissed her more avidly.
"So bitter a tongue, but so sweet to taste. I'll live on the
memory of you when I'm fighting the war in Asia.''

"You can remember me as I am.''

"As my wife.'' He tangled fingers in her hair, which
she had plaited so carefully that morning. It was all out of
its braids now, tumbling on her shoulders and down her
back. He buried his face in it.

"Tell me,'' she said, tight and cold, "that you aren't
doing this because people are afraid I'll turn traitor. I'm
the enemy, after all. I come from Hatti.''

He drew back, half angry, half laughing. "Of course
nobody thinks that! You belong to Egypt. Hatti lost you
long ago.''

"Then why are you so insistent, if not because an Egyptian's wife is more to be trusted than a Hittite slave?"

"Because," he said, "I love you."

She twisted out of his hands, not without cost to her hair. The pain was less than the sharpness of temper, the sheer preposterous impatience that possessed her as she looked at him. He was as beautiful as a woman, more beautiful than she, and his whole heart was given to her. And she did not want it.

She had gone to him first because he was there. She had let him continue because he so longed for it, and because he gave her pleasure. The love that bound man and woman in Egypt had never been there, not in her. Maybe she was made wrong. Maybe Hittite women were different.

Whatever the right of it, she did not want to marry him. She did not even particularly want to take him to her bed, not now, when she had so much to do. She had learned too well the art of winning a man. Now she wished that she had studied the craft of getting rid of one.

Harsh words and scowls that would have succeeded admirably with a friend or even an enemy had no power at all, it seemed, over a lover. They only made him the surer that she needed his protection—that she even wanted it.

She put him out bodily and barred the door in his face. He hammered on it for a long while before he tired of the sport. She shut her ears to it, folded and refolded each gown, and then took out the bed-linens and smoothed and folded each one and laid it away in its chest of cedar. The warm red-brown scent soothed her. She breathed it in until Seti went away, and for a long while, after, till it filled the whole of her, and nothing else could enter.

▪ ▪ ▪

The men went off to war. The women remained at home, as women had always done and would always do. Ankhesenamon's farewell to her king was publicly and precisely correct. Nofret's farewell to her guardsman was as brief and as cold as she could make it. He wept into her hair, begging her yet again to bind herself to him. She pushed him toward his company: other men weeping on the shoulders of other women, and men standing alone, and men too eager for war to take notice of the mothers or sisters or wives who lamented their departure.

They all formed in ranks, at first with dragging slowness, but the end of it was sudden. One moment they were a milling crowd of men and horses and chariots, baggage-mules and carts. The next they were an army marching.

The king rode in his chariot at their head, his armor all of gold, and golden plumes on his helmet. He was beautiful, like a warrior god. He held the reins of his stallions in his own hands, and mastered them. His bow was slung behind him. His arrows were fletched with gilded feathers. His spear rode in its rest, his sword at his side, and his army at his back.

The people cheered him out of Memphis. His queen watched him go from the gate of the palace, standing erect and still under a golden canopy. She said nothing, not one word: not to him before he went, not to anyone who stood with her. Her face was perfectly still. Her hands were fists.

■　　■　　■

Egypt with the king gone to war was its ancient self, undiminished by his absence. His people were proud of him, pleased to have again a warrior king. His council that remained behind kept its fears to itself, nor said what was in all their minds: that he had left no heir to inherit if he should die in battle. There was no son of his line left alive. His queen carried no child; her courses came in the dark of the moon, two hands of days after he rode out of Memphis. She carried the king-right in herself, as did her aunt Mutnodjme, and the Lady Tey who was kin to her through the Lord Ay. But there was no man or manchild to take the king's place.

Lord Ay was gone with the king. Nofret missed his presence and his strength. Perhaps Ankhesenamon did as well. Since she had gone silent, there was no telling. She ruled capably as she had since she was a child, little discommoded it seemed by the king's absence.

The people loved her and called her their lady of the lotus-blossoms, for she was always seen to cradle one in her hand or to wear one in her hair. Her lord had begun that custom not long after they became lovers as well as wife and husband, crowning her with flowers in front of court and city. She continued it even through their quarrel and his departure, for habit perhaps, or hope, or even defiance. She professed to love the sweet scent and the cool softness of the petals.

Nofret's flower, if she had had one, would have been the flower of the bramble-bush that grew in Hatti. She was not ashamed of herself for failing to be in love with Seti, but it troubled her that she did not seem to be able to love a man in the way that women in Egypt did. She did not love anyone. Her brothers were in Hatti; she did not know them, except for Lupakki, and he had gone away as he must, and she had remained behind. Her lady was her lady. Love or even liking had little to do with what was between them. Everyone else was a stranger.

Sometimes she thought of Leah. No word had come from Thebes, not even whether Leah had gone there. Of Leah's kinsmen Nofret would not think at all. They were alive, she supposed, somewhere in Sinai, and a dead man with them, worshipping his god in the desert. They were nothing to her but names remembered.

She was growing smaller inside herself. It was strange to know it. Seti had given her body pleasure and diverted her mind. He had also, it seemed, kept her spirit whole, simply because he was there. Any man might have done, or any woman who could have been her friend.

There was no one here who could serve such a purpose. The maids were silly fools. With so few young men left in palace or city, they squabbled endlessly over nothing, and fought, sometimes bloodily, for the attentions of a fat scribe or a shaven priest. Ladies of the court were little better; those who might have preserved their intelligence were gone to their estates to manage them in their lords' absence. Ankhesenamon was doing much the same, though she lingered in Memphis, which after all was the king's capital.

■ ■ ■

The war in Asia was going well. Ashur had crossed the Euphrates unmolested and trapped Hatti's governor in his fortress. Egypt marched from its own borders into Kadesh and besieged the city. Victory, said the messengers, would follow swiftly. Hatti was taken by surprise.

"Hattusa-ziti was too slow to return to his king," said Ankhesenamon when she heard the news. "Is he dead, I wonder? Did our army catch him and hold him back before he could cross the border?"

"Whatever befell him," said the Lady Tey, who was in attendance on the queen in the Lord Ay's absence, "it's clear that the gods favor us."

"May it always be so," said Ankhesenamon.

■ ■ ■

Everyone said that Kadesh would fall, and Ashur would take and hold the province that Hatti had seized from Mitanni; and then Hatti itself would be conquered. It sounded both simple and swift. Nofret, who had heard her father's tales of long grueling marches and bloody battles, reckoned that there was more to it than anyone in Egypt knew.

Hatti had been taken by surprise, but its king was a great king, a lion in battle. He had teethed, it was said, on the thighbones of slaughtered enemies, and drunk the blood of war with his mother's milk. He would not cower in his palace while both Egypt and Ashur marched against him. He would muster his forces—no doubt had mustered them already—and go to war.

Egypt knew nothing of such a thing. Egypt was a kingdom of women and old men, its people innocents, untried in war. While they celebrated a victory that had not yet come and perhaps never would, Nofret retreated to the shelter of her duties. She was safer there in any event, if anyone remembered that she was Hittite and possibly an enemy.

The garden was her sanctuary, the forgotten queen's pleasure-place near the court of the foreigners. More and more often she retreated there when she had need of rest. Its bareness soothed her, its worn paving and its weed-tangled spaces where once had been a garden of flowers. She would sit on the fountain's rim with the tree shading her head, and watch the fish dart among the lilies. There was peace in it, a blessed emptiness of spirit.

One day when she had lingered there much longer than she should, even drowsing a little in the heavy heat of Memphis during Nile-flood, a stranger came into this place that she had taken to thinking of as her own. She was aware first of the footstep, the tread of callused bare feet on paving; then a shadow in the colonnade, too large and voluminous to be one of the maids or menservants. By the time the shadow took substance she was on her feet, too angry to be afraid.

Indeed it was a stranger—a foreigner, a savage from the desert in swathings of dusty robes, with dust in his matted beard and Nile mud staining his feet. He would have been a peculiar sight in the streets of Memphis, where all the world might choose to wander. In the heart of the palace, within so many guarded gates, his presence was an outrage.

She seized the first weapon that came to hand, a broken bit of paving stone, and tested the weight and the heft of it. It was heavy enough, but clumsy. If he was fool enough to attack her, she would break his head.

He did not seem inclined to do any such thing. He advanced only a step or two into the court, dark eyes fixed on her above a nose as noble as any Hittite's. He was not a Hittite: he was tall enough and wide-shouldered, but lean rather than bull-broad. And he was too dark, and he was bearded, and dressed in the robes of the desert.

He spoke her name, the one that was hers now and not the one that she had had in Hatti. "Nofret."

She kept her grip on the bit of stone. "Who are you? How do you know who I am?"

He raised his brows. His expression, as far as she could see it in the thicket of beard, was wounded, but his eyes were glinting. "Ah, so I've changed that much? You haven't. You're as sharp in the tongue as ever."

Very slowly Nofret's mind set name to the face. The voice was new, rich and deep, with an accent as pure as an Egyptian noble's. But the face, the way he stood, the expression that called to mind a certain half-grown boy . . .

"Johanan," she said. The stone had fallen from her fingers. She was moving, and no memory of the first step—walking, then running, hurtling into him.

He barely staggered as her weight struck him. He wrapped arms about her and whirled her in a laughing, dizzying dance.

They stopped laughing in the same instant, breathless, hiccoughing. Nofret groped for the dregs of her anger. They were nowhere that she could reach. He had spun them all out of her, every one.

He dropped bonelessly to the bit of turf under the tree. She tumbled down with him, hands locked in his. Neither was minded to let go.

They looked at one another, hard, without embarrass-

ment, recording every line and every alteration. Johanan
was taller than ever and broader-shouldered, and all his
coltishness was gone. He was a big man but graceful, as
a panther is.

Nofret, moving on impulse, dipped a corner of his mantle in the pool and washed his face with it. He grimaced
a little but endured, suffering her to cleanse the dust from
his cheeks. His beard, wetted, curled into ringlets; she
could see the strong line of chin beneath, and the long
mobile mouth. He had a fine brown skin, more olive than
the red-brown of Egyptians who lived long in the sun.
Where veil and headdress had shielded it, it was as fair
almost as her own.

Once his face was clean, she washed his hands and feet.
He had grown into himself, she noticed. His feet were
elegant rather than gawky, and his hands were long-
fingered but strong, with calluses that spoke of hard work.
Some might be weapons-calluses: mark of bowstring or
swordhilt or spearhaft.

He was not carrying a weapon now, except the small
knife in his belt, half-hidden in his robe. "Is Aharon with
you?" she asked him. "Is . . . ?" But that name she could
not say, even if she had known it.

He shook his head. "They stayed behind in Sinai. I
came to visit my grandmother."

"She's not here," said Nofret, irrationally annoyed.
"She's in Thebes."

"I know that," he said. He was amused, and not making
any effort to hide it. "Memphis is very much on my way
to Thebes. Do you object? Was I mistaken to stop here?"

"No!" She was shouting. She lowered her voice. "How
did you get in? The gates are all guarded."

"I went over the wall." She glared at his levity. He
widened his eyes, spread his hands. "Truly, I did. There's
a place where it's easy enough, provided the guard doesn't
look your way while you're in the middle of the climb.

Handholds everywhere. I'll wager there's many a young rake from the city who's come up that way to visit a pretty maid in the palace.''

"I should hope not," said Nofret. "My lady will want to increase the guard on the wall if the palace is so easily invaded.''

"Oh, but it's a friendly invasion," he said. "Anyone who came in arms would be caught before he passed the first court. I came in peace, and with extreme caution.''

"Then how did you know where to find me?" she demanded.

"I asked a maid," he said. "She told me I needed a bath, and offered her services.''

"They always do, with you," said Nofret sourly. She wrinkled her nose. "You do need a better bath than I can give you here. Come with me.''

He followed without protest. He was smiling, maybe: it was hard to tell behind the beard.

■   ■   ■

It was not Nofret who oversaw his bath, nor any of the willing maids, but certain of the king's menservants who had stayed behind in Memphis. He came out of it glistening clean and dressed in a linen kilt, with his beard tamed and trimmed and his hair confined in a fillet. His robes, said the chief of the king's bath-servants with delicate distaste, would be cleaned and returned to him as soon as might be.

He did not appear overmuch to miss them. He was covered from navel to knee, which was enough for Apiru modesty. The rest he had no shame of, nor any need of it.

While he was in the bath, Nofret had ordered a small feast laid for him in one of the smaller retiring-rooms, with a roast duck and three kinds of bread, cheeses and fruits and a jar of honeyed wine. He greeted it with pleased surprise. "What, am I royal, that you feast me royally?"

"You're an old friend," she said, "and I'm the chief of the queen's servants. Now eat. I don't want the cook to be insulted."

"By all means," he said, "we must not insult the cook."

Not that he needed much encouragement. He ate as if he were starving—and from the look of him he had been on short commons for a while; his ribs were more prominent than she liked to see. Gods alone knew what he had been living on in the desert, or on his journey into Egypt.

"You came alone?" she asked him when he paused, the edge taken off his hunger, to sip the dark sweet wine.

He set the cup down and nodded. "I was safe enough. A lone traveler is reckoned either mad or penniless, and bandits are minded to let him be."

"You have nothing? No baggage? Not even a weapon?"

"I have a little," he admitted, "in the house I'm staying in, in the city. A bow, arrows for hunting. A spare tunic. A measure or two of barley meal."

"So poor," she said. "And you were rich once, as tomb-builders go." Her breath caught. "Johanan! You were the king's man. As far as anyone knows or can know, you escaped from his service. If anyone thinks of that—"

"No one will," he said with lordly confidence. "Who knew me, after all, except as your friend who came to visit you in Akhetaten? Now I visit you in Memphis. There's nothing criminal in that."

Nofret shut her teeth on what she might have said. The queen knew the truth; if he was brought to her by a zealous minister, she would speak for him. Nofret would have to trust in that.

■　■　■

He ate everything he could hold, and sat back sipping wine, replete and smiling. At the sound of a step, he lifted his eyes. He was on his feet before Nofret turned to see who it was, and then on his face, bowing as low as man could bow.

The queen pulled him up with her own hands and with little subtlety. "Stop that," she said. "Tell me. How is he? Is he alive?"

Johanan was quick-witted: he was taken off balance only briefly. He stood towering over her, which neither of them could like overmuch; when he sank to one knee, she allowed it, for that set his head somewhat below hers, and their eyes level enough to converse. "He is well, great lady," he said, "and speaks often of you when he prays."

She stiffened at that. "He knows. He must."

"He understands that a queen must do what she must do," said Johanan.

"Then he has changed," she said.

"He has changed," said Johanan. He paused. When he spoke again, his voice was quiet and a little remote, as if he recalled things from long ago. "The Black Land, the land that you live in, is a soft land, and gentle. The desert, the Red Land, is different: harsher, grimmer, more exacting to the spirit. Your gods are gods of the Black Land. In the Red Land live your demons and your dead.

"The desert is a forge of souls. A man who goes to it willingly, who lives in it, who knows the hammer of the sun, is tempered in it, is altered, is made strong."

"And a king who is dead?" asked Ankhesenamon. "What does it make of him?"

"It makes him . . ." Johanan thought for a while, while she waited in tight-drawn patience. "It makes him something else. Something new. It teaches him to see more clearly. And yes," he said with a swift glance at her face, "it teaches him to forgive what he might have regarded as a betrayal."

"I betrayed everything that he lived for," said Ankhesenamon.

"No," Johanan said. "You served the one thing that was strongest in him. You served the kingdom."

"I bowed to Amon. I still bow to him. My very name—"

"He knows. He understands."

"How can he? He knows no god but the one. I've turned my back on that one to worship the many—to be false, as he would think of it."

"And by that falsity you preserve the Two Lands of Egypt. He does understand that. He could never do it, but he knows that you do what you must."

"How weak he must think me," said Ankhesenamon.

Johanan held her up when she tried to sink down, and helped her into the chair that he had vacated. She looked small and delicate there, child-small, too desolate for tears. He knelt in front of her and took her hands in his. "Lady," he said, "never believe that he has forgotten you, or that he despises you for your courage. No, don't deny me! It took great bravery to surrender to the gods of Egypt so that Egypt could be strong again."

She stared at him, searching his face as if she could find something there, something that she had lost. "I don't understand you. Or him."

"That's because you haven't lived in the desert. Your soul is steeped in the rich earth of the Black Land. The Red Land demands a different spirit, a different way of looking at the world."

"A strange way," said Ankhesenamon. "A way that sees only one god, but forgives a woman for abandoning him."

"A woman who is a queen," Johanan said.

She bowed her head. When she lifted it her eyes were bright, maybe with tears. "He is well, then? He is . . . whole?"

"As sane as he can ever be," said Johanan. "He goes up on the mountain to worship his god. Some of our people follow him, at least to the lower slopes. His god is well shaped for the desert: a stern god, and just. He demands much of those who worship him.''

''And he—my father? What does the god demand of him?''

''Everything,'' said Johanan. ''Everything he is.''

Ankhesenamon sighed. ''He gave up everything when he died to Egypt. What is left?''

''Body,'' said Johanan. ''Soul. Breath. Spirit.''

''But not his name.''

''No,'' Johanan said. ''He had to leave that behind. Our people call him the prophet, the god's voice in the desert.''

''Then he has become nothing,'' Ankhesenamon said.

''No,'' Johanan said again. ''Our people have given him a name, of sorts. They call him the Egyptian—the man of the Two Lands. We have a word for that. Moshe.''

''Mo-she?'' Ankhesenamon frowned. ''What in the world is that?''

''Mose,'' said Johanan. ''So many Egyptians have that in their name, you see: Ahmose, Ramose, Ptahmose.''

''That's only the word for son,'' she said. ''It's not a name, not a whole one.''

''For him it is. He took it to himself. He's Moshe the Prophet, and he worships his god in Sinai.''

''We have not heard—'' Ankhesenamon stopped. ''No. No, someone told me . . . or I overheard . . .''

''A prophet in the desert,'' said Nofret, breaking in. ''It's idle gossip amid the marriages and the birthings. How the desert bandits have a new madman to lead them, or so it's said.''

''It is not said in the courts of the kingdom,'' said Ankhesenamon. ''Of course it wouldn't be. The courts concern themselves with wars and kings. What do they care for a rumor from the empty lands, unless it touches on their dignity?''

"That's well for you," Johanan said, "and for him. If it were known who he was—"

"It will never be known," the queen said with sudden fierceness. "I'll have you killed if you a breathe a word of it. Do you understand me?"

"Perfectly," he said, unruffled. "You need have no fear of me. I go to visit my grandmother in Thebes. She's old, and not as strong as she was. She needs her grandson beside her."

"Are you asking my leave?"

He looked her in the face. "I am not," he said, "great lady. Unless it pleases you to give it."

No one had ever addressed her so, calmly, boldly, and completely without defiance. He would do what he would do. She had no part in it.

It astonished her past even anger. She said, "If I gave you a safe-conduct throughout the Two Lands, what would you do with it?"

"Cherish it," he answered, "great lady."

"You are as impossible as he is." She said it without rancor, even with amusement. "No wonder he prospers so well among you. You're all like him."

"Well," he said, "after all, we're kin."

She laid a hand against his cheek, briefly, and smiled more briefly still. Then she rose. "When you go," she said, "my scribe will have it ready for you. Be sure to keep it safe. It will protect you wherever you are. Without it . . ."

"Without it I'm no more than a runaway slave." He grinned at Nofret, who glared back. "I understand, great lady. You've been most generous."

"I give you no more than your due." She dipped her head to him, which was a very great honor, coming from queen to Apiru slave. "Prosper well. Bear my greetings to your grandmother."

"Lady," he said, bowing low. When he rose, she was gone.

CHAPTER THIRTY-SEVEN

▲

JOHANAN left Memphis in the morning, with the queen's safe-conduct hidden in his robes. Nofret had fetched it from the scribe and given it to him before he left the palace. He lingered so long that she wondered if he meant to sleep in the room where he had eaten; but at last he rose from his seat.

His robes were waiting for him, clean and mended. He put them on. They changed him, made him both more and less a foreigner. They blurred the fine width of his shoulders, the narrowness of his flanks; but they were better fitted to his face, keen as it was, like a desert falcon's.

He hesitated, as if he wanted to speak but could not bring himself to begin. Nofret could not speak, either. She had been distressingly glad to be rid of Seti. This man, this stranger, this friend of her youth, who had never touched her as a man touches a woman, nor ventured such a liberty . . .

Except once. He had been leaving then, too, for years and perhaps forever. Anger surged up in her. It drove her forward, caught him in her arms, pulled his head down till their faces were level. Strange, to kiss a bearded man; neither pleasant nor unpleasant, simply different.

She pulled away first. He looked at her, his eyes dark, almost soft. "You have a lover," he said.

She caught her breath. "How can you—"

"I'm glad," he said. "I was afraid for you, so lonely as you can be, and so prickly-proud."

"You have a wife," she said. She did not know it, nor see. She only meant to wound.

The blow fell short of the mark. "No," he said. "I have no wife, nor lover either."

"Of course you do. You're a man grown. Every man marries, to sire sons."

"There's no one in Sinai," he said, "who makes my heart sing."

She glared at him. "What does that have to do with it? A wife is a commodity. She bakes your bread, weaves your robes. She gives you sons. What more do you need of her?"

"Nothing, I suppose," he said. He brushed her lips with his fingertip. Her lips were hot, his finger cool. "May the god keep you."

He was gone before she moved. She did not seek him out before morning. When her messenger found the house where he had been staying, he was set long since on the road to Thebes.

Nofret did not know why she was so angry. She loved him no more than she loved Seti. Less. Seti had been her lover. Johanan had never been anything but a friend. He was not even that now. He was a stranger, a wild tribesman, and nothing to her at all.

■　　■　　■

The war in Asia, as far as anyone in Egypt knew, was a mighty success, with victory after victory, and the king smiting his enemies wherever he went. War in Egypt could never go otherwise, nor could its king ever be seen to fail in anything he undertook. He was a god, after all, and infallible.

But other messages came to the queen, and from those Nofret, warrior-bred, could glean the truth. The king had won nothing but the right to return with his armies mostly intact. Hatti had risen to his goad, and had struck with all the force of which it was capable.

Worse, and rather insulting, Suppiluliumas had not

come himself to contend with the twofold threat of Egypt
and Ashur. He was engaged in matters of more importance
to his empire, far in the wilds of the north. He sent two
armies against the invaders. One drove the forces of Ashur
clear over the Euphrates and back to their own country.
Egypt, hearing of this, left the siege of Kadesh and retreated—foolish or not, coward or wise, it mattered little.
Hatti pursued, and did a thing it had done seldom before,
if ever: it crossed into Egypt's lands in Asia and took the
city of Amki, and took Egyptian prisoners, and drove them
to Hattusas.

This was a great shame and a clear defeat. But no word
of it was spoken outside of the queen's private chambers.
The scribes recorded a victory. The people welcomed the
army with cheers and rejoicing, flung flowers before its
feet, sang its triumph in the streets of every city.

It was a lie, but a beautiful one. The king himself
seemed to believe in it. He rode into Memphis in his
golden chariot, gleaming in his golden armor, all golden
himself as if gilded by the sun. He was grown a little taller,
a little wider in the shoulders, more distinctly now a man.

His queen waited for him where she had stood for his
departure, in the court of the gate, under a canopy, with
her ladies about her. She had taken great pains with her
appearance, more than Nofret had ever known her to take.
Her gown was spotless and perfectly pleated. Her jewels
were her best, like armor of lapis and gold. Her face was
painted as perfectly as ever face could be. Her wig, with
its uraeus crown, lay just so on her shoulders, its plaits as
even as the pleats of her gown.

She was as beautiful as an image of a goddess, and as
still. She sat a gilded throne; a little Nubian maid fanned
her with an ostrich-feather fan, for even in the shade the
air was heavily warm.

They heard the king's coming in the shouts and cheering
of his people, waxing as he drew closer, until they could

hear the rumble of his chariot wheels and the marching feet of his army. The court in its walls, with its forest of pillars, seemed deathly quiet, the people in it as immobile as the queen.

He burst into it like a lion on a herd of gazelles. Servants shrieked and scattered. He brought his stallions to a rearing halt full in front of the queen, leaped down from the chariot, and ran to take her in his arms. She was halfway toward him, throne and scepter and dignity forgotten, and perfect gown, too, rumpled beyond repair as he swept her up. They were laughing, she through tears, everything forgiven, everything forgotten but the joy of seeing one another again.

■　■　■

He had a scar or two, small ones: graze of arrow, glancing blow of swordblade. They all made much of him, his queen most of all. She bathed him with her own hands and dressed him in a cool kilt and led him to the feast that had been prepared. They went hand in hand as they had before they quarreled, with many pauses. If they had not been royal and bound to duty, they well might have abandoned the feast and gone direct to the bedchamber. But that luxury was not given a king or his queen.

It was a splendid feast, course after course, even to a whole ox, and a goose for every feaster, and mountains of cakes and fruit, and a different wine for every dish. The court, those who had remained at home reunited with those who had gone to war, fell to with a splendid will. They, like the king, seemed to have convinced themselves that they celebrated a victory. The tales that the returning warriors told were all of triumph, enemies defeated, plunder taken, cities sacked. Lies, every one. Grand lies, as if the repetition of them could transform them into truth.

In Hatti no doubt they were celebrating, too, with tales of their triumph over Ashur and mighty Egypt. Truer tales than were told here, but no less embellished, the count of captives multiplied a hundredfold, and of the slain by a thousand and more, and plunder such as no king could have amassed, however rich he might be.

Lies, like blood, were part of war. Without them it would have been a squalid thing, blood and pain and sudden death. With them it was glorious.

■　■　■

Seti was not waiting for Nofret in her chamber when she came to it, dizzy with the little wine she had drunk and ready to quell his importunings with kisses. Marry him she would never do, but she would keep him in her bed. She needed him for that. His warmth, his presence, the pleasure he gave her . . .

But there was no sign of him, nor did he come stumbling in late and reeking of wine. She slept alone, cold in the warmth of Egyptian night, and angry even in her dreams. Those dreams were none of Seti. The one who walked in them wore another name altogether, and another face: hawk-nosed, black-bearded, burnished with sun and wind. The things he did to her were things that Seti had done. But Seti was not there, not in waking and not in sleep.

She woke determined to forget him as he so clearly had forgotten her. No doubt he had found another woman, one willing to marry him. She would not quell her pride so far as to go looking for him. A woman abandoned could only make herself a laughingstock if she went blundering in search of her lover.

She held to her resolve for exactly half a day. That was how long it took her to realize that her lady would not be needing her—she was closeted with the king and would emerge, the guard said with a wink and a grin, when his majesty was pleased to let her go—and that everything was done as it needed to be done, and the maids could take their leisure.

A chief of servants could be too successful in the practice of her art. Nofret, intending to rest in her chamber, decided instead to seek out the garden court that had been her refuge. But that was tainted now with memory of Johanan. She had gone back once since he found her there, and been able to think of nothing but the touch of his hand and the sound of his voice.

She turned instead toward the house of the guards. It was beneath her dignity to enter, to lay herself open to the bawdry of idle men. But she could approach the man who hung about the door, polishing a helmet and yawning hugely though it was past noon. She could nudge him with a peremptory foot when he failed to look up quickly enough, and when he lifted wine-shot eyes, say to him, "I would speak with Seti the guardsman."

He frowned as if her voice was too loud or harsh for his ears, as the light must be too bright for eyes that had seen too much of lamplight and drowned too deep in wine. But he seemed to know her. He flinched from the knowledge— and no wonder, with him in such condition, and she so close to the queen. "Madam," he said. "Madam . . . I don't . . ."

"What, are you a stranger here?" she demanded of him. "Don't you know Seti?"

"Ptahmose," said a voice within. "What's the trouble?"

The man with the helmet turned with relief to the one who came out, an older man, somewhat battered and scarred and limping slightly. "She's looking for Seti," Ptahmose said.

The newcomer looked Nofret up and down. There was nothing lustful in his scrutiny, but something she could not read, an intensity that could have little to do with her beauty or lack of it. "Ah," he said at last with a lift of the chin. "The queen's servant. We know you, madam. We wish you well."

"I am looking," she said with careful patience, "for a guardsman who marched with the army. Seti is his name."

"We had several so called," he said. He was a captain, she realized. He was wearing a simple kilt and nothing to mark his rank, but his age and his bearing made it clear enough. "However," he added after a pause, "we do know which was yours. He was to marry you, yes?"

"No," said Nofret. Then, because perhaps she had spoken too quickly: "He thought so. He wanted it. I had no such inclination."

Both men exchanged glances. Nofret felt her back go stiff. "Well? Has he fled the guard? Did he dishonor himself in battle?"

"Of course not," said Ptahmose, as if stung to temper. "He fought as well as any man in the Two Lands. But—"

"But he died," the captain said, short and harsh. "He was killed in the siege of Kadesh. A stone flung from the walls caught him as he took his turn with one of the rams. He died quickly. We brought his body to his mother in the city. Were we in error? Should we have brought it to you?"

"No." Nofret's voice, even to herself, seemed thin and far away. "No, you did the proper thing. I wasn't his wife. You didn't know—you couldn't—"

"We knew," said Ptahmose in what he might have meant for gentleness, "that he lay of nights with one of the queen's servants. He was a quiet man. He didn't boast, even when the beer went round. When we told stories of women we had loved, he just smiled."

Nofret's throat was tight. Her eyes were dry. They burned. "Thank you," she said. "I thank you." She turned.

One of them—the captain: his voice was deeper—said, "Wait. We regret—"

No doubt they did. She kept on walking, neither fast nor slow, not dragging but not in haste, either. They did not try to follow. Men never knew what to do or say when a woman acted strangely.

She was very calm. She was not angry. She did not want to weep. It was hardly as if she had loved the man, or wanted to marry him. He had been the one she lay with on lazy afternoons, that was all. She had not even known that he died.

"Surely," she said, "if I had loved him I would have known. Wouldn't I?"

The person she addressed, the image of a king set up against a wall, regarded her in stony silence. He was dead—as dead as Seti. Of course he would have nothing to say to her.

The garden court was full of another man's presence. The wall where she had first lain with Seti was too far, and there was another man on guard there, diligent in his duty. Her own chamber was murmurous with memories: laughter and kisses, and Seti's shadow on the wall when the lamp was lit.

In the end she went to the lotus pool. The queen was closeted with the king, repairing the last of their quarrel. Her maids were wherever it pleased them to be while their lady had no need of them. There was only Nofret by the pool, and the ducks that swam in it and begged for bits of bread. She had none. They left her in disgust to attend their business on the far end of the pool.

She sat on the stone-paved rim. There was a colonnade to shelter her from the hammer of the sun, but she needed the force of it, beating on her head. She needed to lie in the merciless heat, to be sucked dry by it, but with her hand trailing in the cool water. The scent of lotus was strong. The ducks muttered among themselves. Far away she heard a voice singing, woman or eunuch, strong and sweet, words she could not catch, nor needed to. It was a love-song, a song of blazing noon. No death in it. No grief.

No one in Egypt ever forgot death or failed to give it

its due. But death to them was an image of life. They had made it so, and built their tombs to match it, if they had wealth enough, and foresight enough, to do as much.

Seti would have had neither. He was a common man, a soldier of the guard. He had all his fortune to make, and nothing left to build a house of the dead. His body would have been brought back among a hundred others, packed in natron to preserve it till it could be given to his kin. They would pay the embalmers what they could, for as much of the rite as they could manage—maybe all of it if his death in honor had gained him the wherewithal for a proper burial. Nofret did not know. It was not an aspect of the royal duty that she had ever studied.

She did not want to study it. Seti had been neither kin nor husband. She had lain with him, that was all, and refused him when he begged her to marry him. That warm body, those supple limbs, gone all cold and stiff—she could not remember him so. She would remember his hands on her, touching her secret places; his lips on her skin; the taste of him, his scent, his weight on her body, rousing all of it to pleasure.

But when she tried to see his face she saw that other, the one that for all she knew still lived.

"I should have known he had died," she said to the sun. "If I had loved him—if he had mattered enough—I would have known."

The sun had no opinion. It saw everything that passed under its face. It could not comprehend human blindness.

"I should have loved him," she said. "Instead—of—"

Instead of loving someone else.

How strange that it took a lover's death to recognize a truth. That he had had her body, but her spirit had wandered all the while, straying after one who wanted nothing of her but her friendship. He had not even asked her to go with him to Thebes. And why should he? She was like a sister to him. A sister stayed where she belonged, waiting on her lady, while he wandered where he would.

If it had been Johanan and not Seti who had shed her maiden blood, Johanan who had pressed her to marry him . . .

She would have refused him. She was all contrary. She did not want to marry. She wanted to be alone. Even a lover was not worth so much grief. A lover whom she had not loved—it was ridiculous. It was undignified. It was unworthy of his memory.

As well for him that his body had gone to his mother. Nofret could not have given it the honor it deserved. That woman in Memphis whom she had never met, the bronze-smith's widow, would mourn her son unvexed by a stranger's sorrow.

CHAPTER THIRTY-EIGHT

▲

NOFRET shared her grief with no one. The one whom she might have spoken to, Ankhesenamon, was in no mood to weep even for a friend, still less a slave. She had her husband back again. Their quarrel was forgotten. They were as they had been in the first days of their happiness, one heart and one soul together, and one body as often as they could accomplish it. They were the royal lovers, the beloved of Egypt, the delight of the Two Lands.

Nofret's heart was cold, but if it could have been warmed, so would it have been to see them. They had everything that human heart could desire: wealth, love, joy, youth and great beauty, and long life before them. No child had been given them, not since that second daughter who died aborning, but Ankhesenamon had great hope. She prayed in the temple of Isis and in the temple of Hathor and in Taweret's temple, and gave them rich offerings, and paid for the upkeep of their priesthoods. They would give her what she prayed for. She was sure of it.

Egypt was greatly pleased with its king. He had proved himself in war, or so they believed. He ruled well, with his queen at his side. He had restored the gods to their temples and made them wealthy. He was young and strong and would rule long. They had not had such a king since his father Amenhotep was young—not, some insisted, since the great Thutmose.

Thutmose by all accounts had been a gifted warrior and general. Tutankhamon, though not hopelessly inept, was neither. His intelligence did not center on the ordering of armies, nor overmuch either on the care of kingdoms. Those were duty for him, duty that he performed well, because he must. But his great gifts, if he had any, had not shown themselves. He was beautiful, amiable, a doting husband, a competent king. Brilliance he had none, nor seemed to need.

Nofret did not know why she should care. Greatness was rare in kings as in anyone else. Her lady was happy. Egypt was much enamored of them both.

The king had a throne made just then and set in place of the one that had been his father's: a beautiful gilded thing with lion-feet. On its back the limner had set the image of the king enthroned, and his lady in front of him, anointing him from a jar of sweet oil. It was a tender picture, and drawn from life. Just so were they with one another. Just so did they always intend to be.

Or at least until he spoke of going to war again. He showed no sign of it, devoted himself to the affairs of his kingdom and the happiness of his queen. Hatti did not press its advantage, that Nofret heard of. Horemheb the general was in Asia, making sure of it. She could not help but wonder if Horemheb preferred it so: to do his duty away from the king's interference.

■ ■ ■

The king, rested at last from the exertions of war, found in himself a great restlessness. He contemplated another royal progress, a triumphal procession through the Two Lands, with even a pause in Thebes to worship Amon in his own city. All the way to Nubia he would go, and then back, clear to the Delta, showing himself to all his people and receiving their homage. If he meant them to remember that his brother Akhenaten had not gone to them but had bidden them come to him to worship at his feet, then no one truly could fault him. Akhenaten had been at heart an indolent man. Tutankhamon had the strength of youth, and vigor that seemed unflagging. He was to Egypt like the cool breath of the growing time after the heavy heat of the river's flooding.

His processional took some time to arrange. His barge must be refurbished and newly brightened with gold. He had ordered a new chariot, and new horses had come to him, gift of a chieftain in Numidia: a pair of swift stallions like gazelles of the desert, with coats the color of the Red Land, but manes so pale a gold that they were nearly white. He loved their speed and their willingness, their lightness in his hands as they sped round the racecourse in Memphis.

While he waited for his servants to complete the muster of his court and kingdom, he proposed a hunt up the river toward the Delta. There were riverhorses in the reeds there, sluggish-seeming and slow but deadly when set at bay, and great flocks of geese and ducks to test an archer's skill, and even, for the bravest, lions in the coverts.

Nofret had been as sluggish as the king was restless, but when her lady prepared to accompany the king on his hunt, Nofret found herself adding her bit of baggage to the rest. Maybe it was the lure of the queen's chariot. The old gentle mares had been put to pasture not long ago. The new pair were sister-wives to the king's Numidian stallions:

silver as they were ruddy gold, dappled like the moon, with manes the color of smoke.

It would hardly be given to Nofret to drive them, but she could ride while the queen drove, and feel the wind in her face. She had not felt it in too long. It was a sudden need in her, to be out, away from the palace where she had taken a lover, and where she had learned of his loss.

They went by land into the Delta, with servants in boats bearing provisions and the baggage: all the servants, that is, but those granted the pleasure of riding with the princes. The king led as always, the queen beside him while the road allowed it, with a wing of his chariotry to guard him, and the court behind in their brightly painted chariots. They were the young and the bold, the intrepid hunters and racers, archers and spearmen, many with dogs running beside. Behind those came the people on foot: the beaters and drivers of game, the huntsmen with their hounds, the falconers with their birds, all the servants of the chase.

They went with much laughter and singing, no need for stealth till they came to the places of the hunt. They had new songs to sing, songs brought from Asia and rendered into the language of Egypt. Nofret recognized the bleached skeleton of a Hittite war-chant with Egyptian words hung on it, words that told of a lion-hunt and a kingly victory.

It was some days' journey to the place of the hunt, far up in the Delta. Although there were cities and villages in which they might have rested of nights, they chose to camp as armies did, under the stars. The king had a pavilion, of course, and the lords each a lesser one, with hangings of gauze to keep out the incessant, buzzing, biting swarms of the Delta. It was wetland here, fenland, and the Red Land far away: such country as was profoundly strange to the rest of Egypt.

Here the great river of the Two Lands divided into many streams, rich with beasts and birds, fish and crocodiles. Every night they feasted, now on fish, now on goose or duck, now on deer of the thickets. They were in no haste to come to the hunt itself; the journey was enough, and the lordly contests to find and slay food for the pot.

For Nofret it was a strange half-real passage through country as alien to Hatti as to the Egypt that she had seen till now. The best of it was that it bore no memory of Seti, not his face that her mind's eye had forgotten, nor the touch of hands that she too well remembered. Her sleep in this place was disturbed only by the buzzing of insects and the sting of the few that slipped through the gauze to taste of her blood.

She had the queen's pavilion to herself, for the queen slept in the king's, sharing his couch. The handful of maids who had come with her were asleep among the rest of the servants, and not all alone on their blankets, either.

Nofret did not want to be with them. She was content to lie alone, to let the dark cover her. When she slept, she dreamed nothing that she remembered. She was, perhaps, content.

■   ■   ■

At last and at their leisure they came to the place of the royal hunt. There was little to distinguish it from any other tract of field and fen along their way, except that the fields were wider, the fens more distant, and the river-reeds more crowded with birds. The beaters went out then, and the huntsmen, and the falconers brought the falcons to their lords and masters. The hunt went out in pursuit of its various quarry.

The queen had a fair hand with a bow and a quick eye for a bird in flight. For a good half of the day she and the king vied to fell geese for the evening's feast. When every bag was full and the cooks already returning to camp to pluck and clean the birds, one of the huntsmen came up panting to the king.

The king laughed and swung the man into his chariot,

steadied him and gave him a cup of water to drink. He took it gratefully, but he did not pause once he had drunk it. "Majesty," he said, still breathless. "Majesty, a lion— yonder."

The king came all alert. "Where?"

The man pointed with his chin. "There, my lord. Past the thicket, do you see the jut of rock?"

"I do indeed," said the king, peering under his hand. The land opened between the river and the thicket, and the rock was clear to see beyond that.

He sent up a sudden clear call. Lords who had wandered in search of game came hurtling back. Some of the huntsmen with hounds on leads brought their baying, lunging beasts to the king's side.

Nofret was in the chariot with the queen. Ankhesenamon held her mares in check, eyes on the king. Nofret wondered if he looked as odd to her lady as he did to her. He seemed to shimmer like a mirage in the desert. But the air here bred no such visions. It was too richly wet.

Other quarry a lady might pursue, but the lion was the king's prey. Even his lords did not venture to come before him. Ankhesenamon glanced back at the rest of the hunt. As she prepared to turn her horses, to leave the field to the men, Nofret's hands did a thing all separate from her will. They caught the reins and pulled the mares' heads about again, seized the whip and sent them leaping forward after the king and his huntsmen.

The huntsmen slipped leashes on the hounds. They cast about for a moment, searching for a scent. Then one yelped in excitement. The others crowded about it. From the thick of the pack rose a full-throated bay. They sprang into a run.

The king's stallions reared against the traces. He held them back as the hounds took the lead, then let them go. The rest pounded after, and the queen behind, and a straggle of followers.

The lion was waiting for them. It had made a kill: the young of a gazelle. It was a she-lion, and young herself, but strong—and in the lair behind her the hunters could see a flicker of movement, a gleam of eyes. She had cubs, then, to make her fierce.

Nofret, holding the rear with the queen clinging mute to the sides of the chariot, cast up a prayer to whatever god could hear. A massive old he-lion would have been far better, and safer too: slower than the lithe young lioness, and lazier, less inclined to attack before the first arrow struck him. A lioness with cubs was deadliest of all. She fought to defend her young, and she fought without quarter.

She knew that she faced enemies. She crouched over the body of her kill, teeth drawn back in a snarl. The dogs swarmed toward her, but none leaped on her. Not yet. They were wise dogs. They held her at bay for the hunters' coming.

The way to the lair was steep, but not too steep for a chariot or for the king's surefooted horses. He urged them up, not even pausing to see if the hounds would tear at her, weary her till she was easy prey. Headstrong, thought Nofret, and brave to folly. Just beyond the ring of dogs he pulled up his horses and leaped down, spear in hand.

Ankhesenamon's gasp was loud in Nofret's ear, but the queen said nothing, nor moved. No one did. This was the king's fight, by law and long custom.

He seemed utterly alone up there, armed only with a slender spear, and no shield but the dogs. He sent them forward with a cry not unlike a hound's bay itself. The lioness vanished in a seething mass of dogs.

The noise was indescribable: shrieking, yelping, baying, snarling. The lioness burst out of it in a storm of tawny hide, a scarlet flash of blood. A hound lay writhing, rent nearly in two. A snap of jaws broke another's neck. Just beyond that one was the king.

He stood light on his feet, spear poised, waiting as if he had all the time in the world. No tremor shook him.

The lioness crouched. The hounds circled again, yelling, but none moved close for the kill. Neither king nor lioness paid them any heed. Her tufted tail twitched. The great muscles of her haunches bunched. He balanced the spear in his hand, lightly, waiting.

The moment stretched. It ended with blinding swiftness. The lioness sprang. The king's spear caught her in the breast. She fought her way up the whole length of it, snapping, clawing, battling for her life and the lives of her young ones.

He braced against the spearbutt, held on with all his slender strength. Her claws raked air within a breath of his face. He held his ground. She gasped and coughed and died.

Carefully the king eased back. The lioness, convulsed in death, fought no longer against the spear in her heart. He drew a breath, the first perhaps since the lioness leaped on his spear.

From it seemed to rise the shouts of his people, cheering the victory: alone, with only a spear, against a lioness in defense of her cubs.

What had been stillness except for the battle of king and lioness, shattered into furious activity. The huntsmen leaped to gut and flay the body of the lioness. Some of the others scrambled for the cave to capture the spitting, snarling cubs—three of them in all, a he and two shes. The he-cub was presented to the king with ceremony. He wrapped it in a mantle that one of his princes gave him, and cradled the furious small bundle against his breast. He had an odd look, half exultant, half whitely shocked: the look of the warrior after battle, as Nofret too well remembered it.

The queen had not gone up on the rock with the rest. She remained below with her chariot, and her maids about her, all who had been swift enough to catch her. Her eyes on the king were full of light, the aftermath of deadly fear.

His grin flashed white as he seemed at last to see her. He raised the hand that did not grip the cub in its quelling mantle. In sudden exuberance he leaped, cub and all, into his chariot, took up the reins in his one free hand, and came hurtling down from the rock.

Nofret's heart thudded. He was taking no heed at all for the danger: such speed over ground so rough and so perilously steep. Escape from death could do that, convince a man that he was immortal.

King and god he might be, Horus incarnate, but not even kings in Egypt lived forever. That was only given to gods who were not born as men.

He had forgotten that. Nofret breathed easier as his chariot came to the level. It was flying, and he was laughing. The lion-cub, whether lulled by his exuberance or simply stiff with fear, had stopped its snarling.

The king's chariot roared and rattled past the queen's. She caught the wind of it and the gust of his joy: she laughed herself, breathless, and freed her eager mares to catch their brothers.

Nofret, robbed of the reins, clung desperately to the chariot's sides. Level the ground might be, but it was broken and stony, and they were going much too fast for safety. The wheels touched the earth perhaps one stride in three.

If the king's wheels touched it at all, she would be amazed. He raced at full speed, heedless of the broken ground, headlong as if he had been on the racecourse of his own city. His laughter floated back to them, a clear glad sound, wild and very young.

It happened suddenly and yet very slowly, as does everything that is inevitable. Nofret saw the whole of it without surprise. This, maybe, she had come to see; this had brought her on the hunt.

The stallions ran surefooted as ever, skimming the earth.

The chariot flew behind them. The stone that caught it was a little sharper than the rest, and jutted a fraction higher. The wheel jarred against it with force that must have rattled the king's teeth. Above the thunder of wheels and the roar of wind in her ears, Nofret heard a squall from the lion-cub. The king kept his balance: he was light on his feet and supple, and had taken worse blows than this on many a road.

But the chariot, his beautiful new chariot that he had had made for this very hunt, with its sides like gilded vulture-wings and its shafts tipped with electrum and precious silver, was not as robust as the man who rode in it. The wheel lurched against the traitor stone, and caught, and bent.

His body braced to balance the light weight of the chariot. The wheel steadied; he straightened. His horses slowed somewhat.

The axle snapped with a sound that Nofret could hear even from well behind. The chariot leaped like a live thing. The king, caught off guard, swayed too far and fell.

A charioteer learned how to fall. But the king had the lion-cub to think of. He coiled as he fell, protecting the bundle in his arms, heedless of his own head. He rolled and tumbled, limbs flailing, but clinging still to his burden.

In the last instant he lost it. It rolled squalling away as he dropped sprawling, the shards of the chariot long gone behind his maddened horses.

The queen halted her mares so hard that they surged up on their hindlegs. She was not aware of them at all. She flung the reins in Nofret's face and leaped down beside her husband. He lay utterly still.

So might any man if he had taken a fall, Nofret thought as she struggled to master the rearing, plunging horses. He would need a moment to recover himself; even to regain consciousness, as hard as he had come down and as fast as he had been going before he fell.

But he was lying very still. The queen knelt by him, touching his face with trembling hands, easing wig and helmet-crown from his head. He stirred under her hands, drew up a knee, let it slide down again.

Nofret got the mares in hand and secured the reins to the chariot-frame. They were wild to pursue their brothers, but training held them. They halted, snorting and tossing their heads but venturing no resistance against the tautness of the reins.

She climbed down and ran back toward her lady. The king had moved—he lived. "He's coming to," she said as she came up. "See, he stirs."

Ankhesenamon did not seem to hear her. It dawned on her, too slowly, that there was blood on the queen's hands, and on the linen of her gown where she cradled the king's head. His face was grey-pallid under the bronzing of the sun. He stirred again, but not as one who wakes: feebly, as if in convulsions.

Nofret dropped to her knees. The queen did not resist as she slipped a hand beneath the king's head. It was sticky-wet. But blood meant little to her who was a warrior's child. Worse by far was the thing that her fingers felt, the narrow sliver of stone broken from the greater one, that pierced his skull as an arrow might, and dealt just such a wound, to just such deadly purpose.

Others were coming, the ones behind still whooping and cheering but the ones in front aware, if much too late, that the king had fallen. There was none whom Nofret wanted to see, no physician or priest, only useless silly fools, princes with nothing in their heads but wine and the hunt. She rose to drive them back, as if she alone, afoot, could do any such thing to a mob of lordlings in chariots. She stumbled on something soft that yowled.

Blindly she gathered up the lion-cub in its wrapping of linen. By some jest of the gods, it was still securely bound. She was safe from its claws, and if she took care, from its infant teeth. She held it because she could think of nothing else to do.

Ankhesenamon sat on her heels, stroking her lord's face over and over. He was greyer than he had been. Tremors ran through his body. His kilt was stained: he had soiled himself.

"Maybe," said Nofret, stammering it. "Maybe—maybe he's only in shock. So hard a fall—so fast—"

"He is dead," said Ankhesenamon.

The bare bald words made no sense to Nofret. "Of course he isn't. He's hurt, and badly. He needs a surgeon. But he's moving, see. He's alive."

Ankhesenamon shook her head. "He is dead," she said again. "His spirit is flown. The body clings to life, but no soul dwells in it."

"No," said Nofret. Not to deny any kind of truth, but because Ankhesenamon saw so cruelly clear. Not for her the blessedness of oblivion, however brief. She knew exactly what she saw and what it signified.

The first of his princes plunged to a halt nearly on top of him. He was still alive in the body, whatever had become of the souls. There were tremors in it still, a likeness of life.

Ankhesenamon's terrible clarity of mind was not to be blurred by any idiocy of prince or courtier. She saw her lord lifted and carried slowly on foot back to the place where they had camped. There were still few who believed that he was dead. They thought him simply unconscious, and carried him so, without the wailing of grief that might have broken the queen's composure.

They would do what they could to bring him back to life. One or two had servants who were of some use, who could tend him while he lingered, unable quite to give himself up to death. But he was dead. Ankhesenamon had seen it, nor would she refuse it.

Nofret followed the procession back to the camp, leading the queen's horses. She had laid the cloak-wrapped cub in the chariot. She did not know what she would do with it. It could be said to have killed the king, since he broke his head defending it from harm. But she could not leave a young thing to starve, as this cub surely would, for it was too young to hunt on its own.

She had been empty of spirit when she went on this hunt. She was no less so now. But her mind was working, and it kept careful watch on the queen. Ankhesenamon had seen so much death, and held fast through all of it. She had proved her strength over and over, and never more so than now, when she kept order in hunt and camp and saw that there was no panic, no outburst of grief on the king's behalf.

She was too strong. Strange that it could seem so, but Nofret's bones knew what they knew.

Nofret tended the lion-cub as she might, found a leash for it and a maid to nurse it with milk from a she-goat that someone had bought in a village and brought to provide balm for a delicate stomach. The cub needed it more than milord Rahotep did. Nofret left maid and goat and cub to their preoccupation and went to tend her lady.

CHAPTER THIRTY-NINE

▲

THE king died indeed, and not only to his queen's perception, long before he came back to Memphis. He lingered for a handful of days, bleak days all, tempting the ignorant with false hope. But by the time he returned to his city, Egypt knew that its king was dead. It was a funeral procession that came to the city, however roughly formed, however hasty. Egypt mourned its king, and that mourning, as far as Nofret could see, was heartfelt.

She grieved for him, too. She had known him since he was a young child, all bright eyes and questions. She had been fond of him then, and no less so as he grew older: a charming youth, a sweet-spoken and often sweet-tempered man, no great model of kingship but ample for the purpose. And he had loved his queen.

Ankhesenamon was as brittle as an image carved in wood, painted and gilded to seem a living woman. She oversaw the embalming of the body and the transformation of the royal progress into a funeral cortege.

"There's no help for it," she said. "We have to go to Thebes. Kings of our line are buried there. He wanted it; he shall have it."

"But his tomb," said Lord Ay: "he was so young; he had no time. It's barely begun."

"Then we shall make do," she said.

He could not deny the necessity of that, but he could say, "If need be, he can be buried here in the old house of everlasting and taken to Thebes when his tomb is ready."

"No," said Ankhesenamon. Nor would she be moved. The king would be buried in Thebes. His tomb would be a hasty thing, ill-made perhaps and without distinction, but his body would reside with the rest of his line, all but his elder brother, who slept forever in the hills beyond Akhetaten. Even Smenkhkare was in Thebes: he had been brought there with the rest of the dead after the Horizon of the Aten was abandoned. Tutankhamon had insisted on it. Akhenaten he would not move, but the second of the brothers would go where the rest of the kings of their line had always gone.

Ay surrendered to the queen's will, though he found himself in a position that perhaps he had never looked to hold. He was the heir of Tutankhamon. There was no one else. When the king was laid in his tomb, Ay would open the mouth of the dead and take the Two Crowns and be king in Egypt.

What was not spoken of, not yet, not in the queen's silence, was that his lady wife might bear the king-right by her kinship to the line of Nefertari, but the chief bearer of it was the queen herself. The father of Nefertiti, to be properly king in Egypt, must be wedded to Nefertiti's daughter.

Nofret found no horror in it as she had when Akhenaten sought heirs in desparation and wedded daughter after daughter, begetting daughters on daughters, till the gods rebelled. Lord Ay was a gentle man for all his soldier sternness. He understood what he did and why, and why he must. He would do nothing to harm his beloved young queen.

■　■　■

She was in great haste to come to Thebes, such haste that she would not leave the body of her king in the house of embalmers in Memphis. Once the preparations had been made, when the king could be laid in his bed of natron, she had a house of purification built on a barge that could be rowed up the river, attended by priests well versed in the rite. They would accompany him to Thebes and complete the ceremonial there, then surrender him to the priests of the tomb.

No one but Ay dared to contest the queen's will. Even the embalmer priests gave way to her, a thing unheard of. But Ankhesenamon, for all her delicacy and her seeming gentleness, had a core of forged bronze. She was queen and goddess. She would have what she would have.

"And why?" Nofret was not arguing. She wanted to know. Everything was ready; they would leave Memphis in the morning.

Tonight the queen had gone early to her chambers, performed the rituals of the evening but not lain down on her bed. She had not slept since the king died. Most nights, as now, she prepared to spend in reading from the books that the scribes had copied for her, or in listening to musicians who would do turn and turn about as the night spun into dawn.

But the players on harp and flute, drum and sistrum, had not yet come. Ankhesenamon held the book in her lap but did not read from it. It was a book of spells, she had told Nofret once, and prayers to guide the dead through the ordeals of the netherworld. Some of it she had read to Nofret on other nights, but tonight she did not seem inclined to. Nofret was glad. Her lady said that spells only had efficacy if they were spoken in the proper time and place, with the proper intonation, but spells were spells, in Nofret's mind. They were best not spoken or even left open for strangers' eyes to see, lest they escape and do untold harm.

Nofret spoke in part to keep Ankhesenamon from reading the book. "Why so much haste?" she asked. "Why can't he stay in Memphis till his tomb is all built and the tomb-furnishings ready?"

"Because," said Ankhesenamon, rather to Nofret's surprise: she had not looked disposed to answer. "I want him safe in his house of everlasting, and all the prayers said, and the priests on guard."

"But why?" Nofret persisted. "He wasn't hated. Egypt doesn't want to gnaw his bones."

"Egypt," said Ankhesenamon, "no."

Nofret frowned. "Who else is there?"

"The one who killed him."

There was a silence. Nofret could think of nothing to fill it, except the painfully obvious. "He wasn't killed. His chariot hit a stone."

"His chariot broke its axle on a stone that should hardly have nicked the wheel-rim."

"Chariots," said Nofret, "are rickety things, even the

best of them. And he was racing over rough country, with no regard for life or limb."

"His axle broke," Ankhesenamon said. "It should never have broken. Someone saw to it that the wood was weak; that it would crack and then shatter when he could do nothing to defend himself."

Nofret bit her tongue. Here then was Ankhesenamon's necessary madness, the break in her composure. She could not believe that her king had died of ill luck and his own folly. He must, like Smenkhkare, have been murdered.

"The one who would kill him," said Ankhesenamon, "would stop at nothing. If he's buried, his tomb well hidden, all his house of eternity made safe—"

"From whom?" Nofret demanded.

Ankhesenamon looked sane enough, except for the hands knotted in her lap on top of the rolled book. "This I know," she said. "I know it in my bones. One wanted my father's death, and saw that Smenkhkare died, and my sister, too. And when they were gone, there was my king still, to bar the way to the throne."

Nofret's eyes widened. "Lord Ay? He would never—"

"No," said Ankhesenamon. "The general. Horemheb."

Nofret went stiff. But that was years ago, and the kings whom Horemheb wanted dead had been Akhenaten and his brother, Smenkhkare who had styled himself the Beloved of Akhenaten: no less than the title that Nefertiti had held before him. Vain folly, like the man himself, and sore temptation to those who hated him. Nofret remembered as clearly as if there had been no years between, the temple of Amon in Thebes, and Horemheb face to face with its priest, speaking of the death of kings.

Tutankhamon had given Amon all that he could wish for and more. There had been no cause to cut short his life.

Unless Horemheb truly meant what he had hinted then,

that he fancied himself as Lord of the Two Lands.

"It can't happen," Nofret said. "He'd have to marry you, and you won't have him."

"No more will I," said Ankhesenamon with grim purpose. "Maybe I'm a fool. Maybe he's my loyal servant. My bones can lie, or fear too much. But I want my lord in his tomb where no one can touch him, before Horemheb comes back from Asia."

"If he comes," Nofret said. "You can command him to stay. He's needed there, with Egypt robbed of its king, and its enemies too likely to take advantage of its weakness."

"He won't stay," said Ankhesenamon. "He'll make sure my messengers never reach him. Do you understand? I must carry my king to Thebes, and take my king's heir as husband in Amon's own house, so that Amon may defend me. If I fail—if he moves too swift and catches me—"

Nofret did not believe it, nor did she want to. Horemheb would not force matters. He was too practical a man. Ay was strong but he was old, and he well might die soon. Then Ankhesenamon would be ripe for any man's taking.

But Ankhesenamon was quite beyond reason. Something—god, demon, plain blind grief—had fixed itself on Horemheb and named him enemy. She would defend herself and her king as best she might, even if it meant that his mansion of eternity was a gilded hovel in the cliffs to the west of Thebes.

CHAPTER FORTY

▲

THE king's boat of eternity floated up the river under oar and sail. The people bade it farewell as it went, wailing their grief, singing songs of his youth and his beauty and his untimely death. The queen could not hasten any of that, nor alter the river's current, nor grant limitless strength to the rowers. The embalmer-priests would not suffer more haste, either, than the queen had already forced upon them. It was not seemly, they said, in the passage of the dead.

Nofret did not think that Ankhesenamon would fear to be haunted by the king's spirit. If he visited her in dreams she welcomed him gladly, and wept when she woke, because he had departed. The priests' threat of his anger left her unmoved. But they could resist and did, and slowed the king's passage to a more fitting pace.

She had learned in a hard school that it did a queen no good to grow wild with impatience. She paced the cabin of her boat at night, or the floor of her chamber if they had paused in a city. By day she preserved a hieratic stillness, set upon her throne in her queenly finery, making her slow way toward Thebes.

■ ■ ■

The city of Amon waited for her and for her king. The viceroy of the Upper Kingdom stood on the quay in a great crowd of lords and ministers, servants and lesser folk, and the rabble of the city come to gape at their sad young queen. They could not have been much satisfied: she was as royally remote as ever, no sign of emotion in the mask of her face.

She was stony still. Nofret saw why as her eyes ran over the officials gathered to welcome the queen. There were a large number of soldiers, more than she remembered seeing before. And among the princes, close by the governor, one who must have stilled Ankhesenamon's heart in horror.

It was not impossible that Horemheb could have come from Asia to Thebes while the queen made the much shorter journey up from Memphis. Horemheb could move at soldier-speed. The queen had had to advance as a funeral cortege must, even the most urgent. Of course he was here to greet her, to add his words of condolence to the rest, to bow low and offer all goodly aid to a queen bereft of her king.

She could not bring herself to feast among the court of the Upper Kingdom. That was forgiven her, Nofret could see, for her youth and her grief and the many things that she had endured since she was a child. Men knew great pity for a lady so lovely and so sad.

She was not sad. She was furious. "He came to claim me," she said, fiercely quiet, when she was alone in her chamber with Nofret, and all the rest of the servants banished. "He thinks that until Ay is crowned, the field is open; he can ride in and seize the prize."

"Lady," Nofret said, not wisely maybe, but she was tired, "why would he possibly want to defy the Lord Ay? What can he gain?"

Ankhesenamon rounded on her. "What can he gain, you ask? Are you blind? Witless? There's all of Egypt. He wants it. I know he wants it. I can see it in his eyes."

"Maybe he only wants you," said Nofret.

That was even less wise than what she had said before. Ankhesenamon turned from her in white rage and ran from the room.

She could not go very far. There were the outer rooms, or the baths or the gardens. The last were most inviting to a queen in a temper. It was early still, an hour at least till sunset. No one wandered the carefully tended paths, nor did a gardener vex the queen's solitude.

Nofret chose wisdom, rather too late perhaps, and waited by the garden gate. It was quiet there and almost cool. Unless someone came over the wall, her lady was safe.

Ankhesenamon remained in the garden till full dark. Just as Nofret was about to go in search of her, torch in hand, she came walking slowly out of the twilight. She was calm, her anger quieted. It was not gone: Nofret saw flickers of it still in her eyes. But she had made her peace with it.

Well enough for her that she had won that battle. For when she came to her outer chamber, Horemheb was sitting in it with a cup of wine at his elbow and an air of considerable ease.

Ankhesenamon stopped in the doorway. Nofret, behind her, heard the catch of her breath, saw how her shoulders stiffened. He would not have marked it, maybe. It was very subtle.

When she walked forward she was calmed, composed, royally polite. "My lord general," she said in her low sweet voice. "To what do I owe the honor?"

"Lady," he said, rising and bowing.

Ankhesenamon sat in the chair that he had vacated. There were others in the room, but none that he had claimed for his own.

He could not but comprehend the gesture. He accepted it to all appearances as right and proper. He did not venture to sit, since she did not invite him, but knelt on one knee before her.

Nofret, unregarded in the doorway, observed that he was not as old as she persisted in thinking him. His stern expression made him seem older than he was. He was still more young than old, a man in his prime, strong, honed in war. A fine figure of a man, a Hittite would say.

Ankhesenamon had chosen to blame him for all her sorrow. It was a pity, rather. A strong man, young but not too young, would do well for Egypt.

If the queen had known what Nofret was thinking, she would have called Nofret traitor. Nofret kept her tongue between her teeth. She was there only on sufferance. If she moved or spoke, she might be dismissed.

Or she might not. If Ankhesenamon truly feared Horemheb, she would want another there, a witness, perhaps a defender—though what Nofret could do against a man trained in battle, she did not know.

Horemheb was speaking while Nofret's wits wandered, something of sorrow, and of offering his aid however the queen might choose to accept it. The queen said nothing at all. She stared past him, stone-faced.

He ventured a very great liberty. He took her hands in his. "Lady," he said. "Look at me. You're shaken beyond bearing. I know it, we all do. But Egypt won't wait for you to recover, nor will any of the lands about it. Egypt needs you to be strong."

"I have always been strong," she said in a still, cold voice.

"And maybe you're tired of it," he said. "Any woman would be. Any man, too. You lost a husband whom you loved. You—"

"You never loved him," she said. "He was nothing to you."

"Lady," said Horemheb. "Lady, he was my king."

"You were contemptuous of him. Weak child, you thought him. Vaunting boy. Useless in war, interfering when he were best to remain at home and leave the fighting to those who were fit to do it."

Horemheb did not seem appalled by the queen's quiet venom. Nofret wondered if anything at all disturbed him. "Lady, you wrong me," he said, "and you wrong him. He was a good fighting man."

"But a terrible general. He was, wasn't he? He had to lie to have a triumph in Egypt. He lost the war in Asia. You could have won it."

Horemheb drew a slow breath: Nofret saw how his breast lifted, then sank again. With it he seemed to draw in resolve. "Lady, if you want to hear the truth, yes, I could have won that war—and would have, if he hadn't run home too soon. He knew no better. He was only a boy, and untried; but he was king."

"You want to be king, don't you?" She leaned forward, setting face to face. "You think you could be better than any who's ruled since my grandfather died.''

''What a man wants, or thinks he wants, is of no worth if he's not born to the proper eminence.''

Ah, thought Nofret: a crack in the armor. A suggestion of bitterness.

Ankhesenamon perhaps could not perceive it. She had never been less than royal. She had never known what it was to want to rise higher than the station the gods had given her. She said, ''A man need not be born to kingship. He can marry it.''

Horemheb's eyes sharpened. ''Are you saying that I can try?''

She tensed to surge to her feet, but he held her hands too tightly; he trapped her. She spoke through clenched teeth. ''Why did you come here tonight?''

''I came to comfort you,'' he said.

''Ah,'' she said with a twist of the mouth. ''Comfort. I know that comfort. Why should I want it?''

''Because,'' he said, ''you need a strong man. You've never had one, have you? Your first husband was too god-ridden, your second too young. You're not the child you were when you married each of them. You're a woman now. Isn't it time you had a man beside you?''

''So I shall have,'' she said. ''I shall have the Lord Ay.''

''Your grandfather.'' Horemheb shook his head. ''He's a good man, but he's old. There's no sap left in him.''

''He might surprise you,'' said Ankhesenamon.

''I doubt it,'' Horemheb said. ''You're thinking he's safe, aren't you? He's too old to trouble you in the bed-chamber. He has another wife to oblige him if by some chance the urge strikes. Don't you wonder what it will be like, having no one to keep you warm of nights?''

''The nights are often too warm in our country,'' she said.

Horemheb laughed, a short bark with little mirth in it.

"I should take you to Asia. There's snow on the mountain peaks there. Do you know what that is?"

"I know what it's said to be," she said. "I have no desire to see it."

"What, none? Haven't you ever wanted to travel?"

"I've traveled much," she said, "throughout the Two Lands."

"You have an answer for everything," he said. He seemed amused by it. "You know of course that your would-be consort is old. He'll die. Then who will be king?"

"I'm sure you think that it will be you."

"There is no heir. Will you try to give him one?"

"If I am not capable," she said with utmost steadiness, "of bearing a son, or indeed any child who will live and grow strong, then what makes you think that I can give you an heir, either?"

"Maybe," he said, "because I'm not your close kin. I've seen it with horses and with hunting dogs. You can breed strength to strength and beget greater strength, but weakness crossed on weakness weakens the line to breaking."

"Are you calling me weak?"

"I am saying that your line should look beyond itself if it's to continue. It will end, lady, whatever you do, when Lord Ay is dead."

"Then you may claim me," she said, "if you can."

"I'd rather not wait," he said. "Egypt needs strength now. It needs a man who is young, who is vigorous, who can both fight in battle and lead an army to victory. Hatti has seen that we're weak. It will act on it, you can be sure."

"But," she said, "Lord Ay has been a soldier and a general. And he'll have you to fight in Asia for him. What do we lose if I send you away?"

"Time," he said. "Wisdom. A chance at a son of your own body, to hold in your arms."

He had struck home: Nofret saw the quiver in her. But she was set against him. She turned her face away. "Go," she said, remote and chill, as if his hands were not gripping her still, and his body barring her escape.

"No," he said. "I'm not going to go. Your loyalty becomes you, but it's not wise. Be a queen now, and think. What is best for Egypt?"

"It is best," she said, "that you leave me."

His patience snapped so suddenly that it took Nofret by surprise. He surged up, and the queen with him, drawn as if she weighed nothing. He set her on her feet with a jolt that must have rattled her teeth in her skull, and set his mouth on hers. It made Nofret think of a lion going for the throat of its prey: so fast, so fierce.

She tensed to spring, but there was nowhere to go. Her lady was caught. Nofret had no weapon, no strength or skill to set her free. She could only watch, poised, alert for any opening.

Ankhesenamon twisted in protest, but he held her fast. The growl of his voice was like a lion's too, but with words in it, words that must have terrified the woman in his grasp. "Little minx. Little lioness. You can hate me, you can fear me, but you will give way to me. You know there's no one more fit to claim you."

"There is," she said, no more than a gasp. "And I will have him."

"Then you're a fool."

She laughed. It was cruel, and not wise: his face suffused with anger. "I, a fool? Then what are you? You have no right to claim me. You're no more than a commoner. How dare you dream that you can be king and god?"

"Maybe the gods dare for me," he said. He sounded as cold as she, but his face had grown no calmer and no paler. "I will be king, lady. Of that you can be certain."

"But not," she said, "while I live to resist you."

He looked at her, level and long. The color had left his cheeks at last, left them pale beneath the weathering, and very still. "So you say now," he said. "What will you say when your so-safe Lord Ay is dead?"

"That you killed him," she said, "as you killed two kings before him."

"I won't need to do that," he said. "Time and the gods will do it for me."

"Then you did kill them." Ankhesenamon caught him in a moment of distraction: twisted free and escaped to the inner door. Foolish, Nofret thought, if he was minded to pursue her; though at least Nofret could be a shield for her there. A bit of handy rape might be just what a soldier thought advisable to subdue a stubborn woman—but he would have to begin with the slave. The queen would have time to escape.

But Horemheb stood where the queen had left him. He was astonished, maybe, or appalled.

"You killed them," said Ankhesenamon. "You did. I see it in your eyes. You won't kill a third king. I'll see that you don't."

"How? By killing me first?"

She laughed, high and a little wild. "Oh, no! I'll let you be. We need you, after all, to protect our lands in Asia. But we know you. We know what you want. I'm on guard. I'll defend us all against you."

"You're mad," he said: Nofret's thought exactly.

"Probably," said Ankhesenamon. "Madness can see the truth sometimes, if the gods guide it. I'll be sane when you've gone out of my sight."

"I'll have you in the end," he said.

He was a soldier: he knew when to leave the field. Ankhesenamon stood immobile until he was gone. Then, and only then, she answered him. "I think not," she said.

CHAPTER FORTY-ONE

▲

AFTER Horemheb was gone, Ankhesenamon paced for a long while, twisting her hands and muttering to herself. She looked quite lunatic. Nofret could not persuade her to stop or rest, or even to slow her perambulations.

When at last she did stop, it was to smile in a way that chilled Nofret. "A strong man," she said. "A man who can fight. Who can defend Egypt." Her smile widened. She darted toward the clothing-chest that stood by the door, and from it snatched a mantle. Nofret tried to catch her as she ran past, but caught only the edge of the cloak, which slipped from her fingers.

The queen went swiftly, not running, but not walking either. Nofret had to trot to keep pace. There was no use in trying to pull her back. She was like one of her chariot mares with the bit in its teeth, running blindly where her will bade her run.

She went to the house of scribes, to the place where they slept, and roused a startled, blinking, shaven-headed old man from what no doubt was well-earned rest. "Bring me a man who writes the words of Hatti," she said imperiously.

The scribe was taken by surprise, but his wits were quick. He rose from his pallet, wrapped a length of linen about his middle, bowed to the floor and said, "Come, I'll fetch Meryre."

Meryre was a younger man with a long lantern jaw and world-weary eyes. He reminded Nofret forcibly of the lost Akhenaten. Ankhesenamon seemed not to think so, or not to notice. Likely she did not even see him except as a shadow and a pen. "Write a letter for me," she said.

The man did not answer, only bowed and reached for the palette and pen that were by his bed. He brought out and opened a new roll of papyrus, spreading it on his knees. Nofret could not tell if he was mute or merely taciturn. When he was ready, he poised pen above papyrus and waited.

Ankhesenamon spoke quickly, as if the words she spoke were learned by heart—and yet she could only have conceived them since she left her chambers. A god guided her, or perhaps something worse than a god.

"Write to the king of Hatti," she said. "Write well and write fair. Here is what the queen of Egypt says to the one who calls himself King of Kings:

"My husband is dead. I have no son. But you, it is said, have many sons. Give me a son of yours, and I will make him my husband. Never will I choose a servant of mine to be my husband—no, never, for I trust none of them. Save me, king of Hatti, for I am afraid."

The scribe's pen scratched out the words in the Egyptian picture-writing. Then, expressionless, he rendered them in the style that Hatti had taken over from the old peoples of Asia, the swift stab of wedge-writing that was best done with stylus in wet clay. So it would be, once it was completed, so that it could be sent to Hatti.

If it was sent. Nofret had heard it, therefore she had to believe it. Ankhesenamon was doing a thing that no queen of Egypt had done before: she was asking a king of a foreign country to send her a son to be her consort. Nor was it any king or any country. It was the very country that had been, indeed still was, Egypt's enemy in Asia.

She seemed oblivious to the enormity of what she did. She watched the letter written in both Egyptian and Hittite, and saw it limned in clay, too. Then she said to the scribe, "I need a messenger, one who is swift and safe and secret.

He'll be paid in gold and in royal favor when he comes back with the Hittite prince.''

The scribe bowed and did as she bade him. Nofret wondered what he thought of it all. His face betrayed nothing. He did not try to dissuade her, nor beg her to reconsider, or at least to wait until morning. He went and fetched the messenger while she waited. She gave the man the sealed tablets from her own hand and bade him give them at whatever cost into the hands of the king of Hatti himself. Both scribe and messenger obeyed her, blindly as it seemed, and without thought.

It was all mad. It was like a nightmare, a dream of perfect illogic, no reason in it, and silent figures moving as they were told, without question. Morning would find Nofret in her bed and none of it true.

She felt very much awake. The tiredness that dragged at her bones was real. So was the dread in her. ''You can't go this far,'' she said to her lady as they stood in the scribe's sleeping-room. He was gone with the messenger. She did not know if he would be back. Maybe not while the queen occupied his cell. ''You can't hate the general so much. This is betrayal of your own kingdom.''

''It is protection,'' said Ankhesenamon with awful serenity. ''You don't see, do you? And you a Hittite. I thought better of you.''

''I've been in Egypt too long,'' said Nofret. ''Tell me what I should see.''

''It's simple,'' Ankhesenamon said. ''Too simple almost; I nearly missed seeing it. I can hardly fault you for thinking me reft of my wits.''

''I know you are,'' said Nofret. ''You're making no sense at all.''

''I'm making a great deal of sense. Think, Nofret. Lord Ay isn't safe if Horemheb sees him crowned king. He'll be killed as the others were. But if he's not crowned, if another is—a warrior of a warrior race, raised to be a king in his own country—then we have what Horemheb wants: a soldier king. And more than that. Who is the enemy we most fear? Hatti. But Hatti will have a prince on the throne of Egypt. Egypt will be safe from Hatti, and Ay from Horemheb, and I . . . I will have a strong husband as our so-wise general has advised.''

''I think,'' said Nofret carefully, ''that Egypt will never accept a foreigner on its throne, even if that foreigner marries a bearer of the king-right. Better a commoner than that, Egypt will say.''

''Egypt will accept whatever I bid it accept,'' said Ankhesenamon. Her arrogance was as perfect as her father's had ever been.

''Of course,'' she said after a pause, ''we can't allow this to be known till the prince is here and ready to take my hand in marriage. Ay will have to go on thinking that he'll be king. He'll open the mouth of my husband who is dead. He'll play the part of the heir. But I'll put off the wedding. I'll plead exhaustion and excessive grief. I'll go to Memphis, I think, and leave him in Thebes to look after the Upper Kingdom. When the river's flood has been and gone, then, I'll tell him, we can marry.''

''Oh?'' demanded Nofret. ''And what's to keep Horemheb from killing the old man while you're away from him in Memphis?''

''He won't do that,'' said Ankhesenamon. ''He'll wait till Ay is king. I'm protecting him, you see? Horemheb likes to kill kings. He won't kill a lord of the kingdom who hasn't yet worn the Two Crowns. And meanwhile Hatti will be sending a prince to save us all.''

''You can't be sure of that,'' Nofret said. She wanted to seize her lady and shake her, but that would not have been wise: it would have been too much like Horemheb. Nofret had no desire to confirm her in her lunacy. She tried words instead, and the force of reason. ''Hatti may think you've set a trap. And what if Horemheb gets wind of it?''

"He will not," said Ankhesenamon. "I will not allow it." She swept her mantle about her. "Come. It's late. I think, now I've done what's needful, that I can sleep."

"Now you've done what's absolutely mad," muttered Nofret. If Ankhesenamon heard, she gave no sign.

■　■　■

Most likely, Nofret thought, Hatti would not respond at all. Or if it did, it would be to refuse what anyone could see was an act of perfect folly.

In any case it would be days, weeks, before the messenger could reasonably be expected to reach Hatti, and weeks more before a reply could come. In that time Ankhesenamon exercised the royal art of patience. Maybe, if fate was kind, she had forgotten her night's lapse from reason; but Nofret set no hope in that. There was too much to remind her.

■　■　■

Nebkheperure Tutankhamon, beloved of Amon, protected of Horus, Great House, Pharaoh, Lord of the Two Lands, king in Egypt, went to his tomb in the west of Thebes with such state as haste and a queen's distraction could muster. All the great ones who could be in Thebes went in processional behind the king's bier, in a wailing of women and a great proclamation of the king's deeds and his virtues. They began in the eastern city, passed through it with the people following, gaping and wailing and, if they were devoted, smearing their faces with the mud of mourning.

The queen herself walked behind the bier with its yoke of white she-cattle like images of horn-browed Hathor. She was all alone, her face unpainted except with earth, her breast bare, her gown torn as grief demanded. She allowed herself the cries of mourning and the upflinging of hands, the rending of cheeks and breasts, all the excesses that queenly restraint heretofore had forbidden.

At the river's bank the funeral boats were waiting. No other boats sailed the river of Thebes that day, by the queen's own order; only those that served the king's last journey. He rode in his catafalque with the yoked cattle and a single oarsman and a company of women wailing the dirge, his barge drawn behind a many-oared ship. The rest embarked on the other boats, crossing the river in their sorrowful fleet.

Ankhesenamon cried the words that set them on their way, words as old as Egypt and as young as her grief: "O my brother, O my husband, O my sweet friend! Stay, rest with me. Leave me not alone; do not cross the river. O you oarsmen, why such haste? Let him linger awhile. You may return to your homes, but he must go to the house of eternity."

For response she gained nothing but the striking off of the boat. The last of her cry was wordless, a long wail of loss. Her women held her while she wept, until she quieted; until they had come to the western bank.

Ministers of the dead waited there where the Red Land rose stark beyond the queen of the river's edge. The bier took its place again at the processional's head, the bearers of grave-goods behind, and the queen and the rest. She walked now as she must, as she had no choice but to do, onward, in silence amid the keening of the women.

They went from the city into the valley of the dead, from the Black Land with its dark earth and its green riches to the bleak barrenness of the Red Land. It was meant to strike them with the force of the contrast: from green land into wasteland, from life into death. The heat of the sun made it stronger, and the length of the journey. It was a suffering, a sacrifice that they made in honor of the king who was dead.

His tomb was a pitiful thing beside the tombs of older kings. Some lord or nobleman had been building it but had failed maybe of his wealth, or died too soon to finish it.

The queen's servants had done what they could in too little time and with too much of ritual and courtesy to weigh upon them. The grave-goods that they brought to it were hurled together as best might be from his own belongings, castoffs of his father and his brothers, bits and pieces of what, for all Nofret knew, were other burials. They were all reckoned necessary and even indispensable, since a king must keep such state in death as he had kept in life, or he gained no respect among his kind in the dark lands.

Such haste could do him no good, Nofret reflected as she struggled along behind her lady. Ankhesenamon was close and yet unspeakably far away, aware of nothing, it seemed, but the dead. Did she care that the magic could not be done properly, that too much was being done too quickly, that the house of eternity was a frail and rickety thing with crooked walls and a mismatched roof?

Maybe it did not matter. Maybe appearance was enough, and grief paid and paid again.

■　■　■

At the edge of the Red Land, where the road grew too steep and stony for the slow feet of cattle, men took over the burden of drawing it upward, and left the cattle to rest as they might. A priest led the way with ewer and censer, driving off spirits of ill. But one spirit came forth to his call, a solid and living one, wearing the heifer-mask of Hathor. It spoke the welcome to the houses of the dead in the voice of a mortal man, but one with good strong lungs. It was more a bull's bellow than a heifer's lowing.

This apparition withdrew to let them pass. They struggled onward and upward, directing themselves toward the tomb that was open, that waited for one to be laid in it.

Time now was short, here on the threshold of eternity. Strong servants raised the king's coffin from the catafalque and set it upright against the tomb's stone. Ankhesenamon knelt, as graceful as a dancer in a dance, and laid her arms about it, embracing it. It must have been cold after the warmth of the living body, hard and unyielding as death must always be.

The shrieking and wailing rose to a crescendo. It rang in the cliffs, soared up to the sky.

When the echoes had begun to die, the priests of the dead stirred where they stood before the tomb. Here was the great working, the magic above magics, the rite that would grant the dead the memory of life, and free him to live in the land beyond the west. They would give him back his body, his strength, his heart and soul and voice. Their power would let him see again and hear, and taste and touch and smell—all his senses restored to him in the house of everlasting.

Chief of the priests was the Lord Ay in a mantle of leopardskin. He wore the Blue Crown that was given only to the king. He stood erect and stiffly strong, and yet, thought Nofret, he had grown old. They called him that in the palace, spoke of him as an old man, but to her he had always been a man just past his prime.

No longer. He was shrunken in his skin, his face deep-lined, the blade of his nose more prominent than ever. He looked like an old eagle, crooked-clawed, half-blind, clinging to its rock with grim persistence.

So he clung now to the office that fate and the gods had thrust on him. He spoke the words that opened each of the dead man's senses. He performed the rite with precision that only made clearer the mumbled haste of the other priests. They committed errors, Nofret suspected, from the way people stirred and muttered; but Ay did not. The king's senses were opened with full and proper ceremony by one who had loved him in life and cherished him still in death.

It might not be such a blessing, if his house was so feebly made, that he should have full use of his faculties therein. But it was not Nofret's place to say so. She watched in silence as the king was taken at last into the small mean tomb that had been found for him, laid in it with the hasty heaps of his belongings, and sealed in his sarcophagus for all of eternity.

The last memory she had of the tomb was of the lamplight burning low in it and the glitter of gold crowded all about it, and atop the massive bulk of stone that housed his body, the one frail and living thing that would remain in that place: the garland of flowers that Ankhesenamon had borne with her. She laid it there as she left him, brushing it with fingers that trembled, smoothing the petals that already were wilted in the heat of the Egyptian sun.

Then she was gone, out into the light, and he was left behind in the endless dark. She ate what she could of the funeral feast among the mourners and the princes. He would feast there below, or so the Egyptians believed, on the great store of provender that they had brought to supply him for his journey among the dead. But there would be none living to keep him company. Even the priests of his tomb would serve his memory under the sun, beyond the seals and the spells and the great wards and guardings that were laid on the houses of the dead.

He was gone, except in memory. There was no calling him back. Not even the priests of Egypt, who claimed mighty magic, could restore the dead to life.

CHAPTER FORTY-TWO

▲

THE queen left Thebes for Memphis without actually marrying Lord Ay, and therefore without granting him the right to wear the Two Crowns. It was said that she was distracted, and that she was prostrated with grief. But since the kingdom went on being ruled as before, with Lord Ay in Thebes serving as chief counsellor and regent, and the queen in Memphis being queen as she had been for the half of her life, no one could properly object.

Nor did anyone appear to suspect what the queen had done, what letter she had sent under cover of night and with the knowledge of two scribes who had been well paid to say nothing. She herself said no word of it.

Nofret did not make the mistake of thinking that Ankhesenamon had forgotten. The demon that had possessed her to do it was not a demon of oblivion. It had persuaded her that she did the right thing, the logical thing. There was no purpose in fretting over it, since it was done, and done as well as it might be.

Nofret herself had nothing to say. Her lady had turned to Nofret's own birth-country for help. Egypt would look on it with horror. Nofret, the Hittite slave, could find it in herself to wonder what a son of the Great King of Hatti would do if he were set on the throne of Egypt. Egypt would hate him for his very foreignness, but if he was anything like his father, he would find a way to win hearts even in this most foreigner-hating of kingdoms.

For Ankhesenamon it was a waiting time. The flood of the river receded as it did every year, leaving its riches behind, the black mud that was the life and strength of Egypt. In the first of the sowing time, which in Hatti would have been the beginning of winter, came the ambassador of the Hittite king with his company of guards and attendants.

It was the same man who had come before, Hattusa-ziti the king's chamberlain, with much the same men at his back. But there was no Lupakki. He had married, Nofret discovered, and his wife was highly placed. She had won him a position in the king's own household.

Nofret could hardly be disappointed. It was well for her

brother that he had risen so high, and so quickly, too. But she would have liked to see him again.

If she was fortunate, and there was a Hittite king in Egypt, she might do better: she might win leave to go to Hatti and visit him there. And her other brothers, too, if it suited her. They could not look on her in scorn if she came as a woman of consequence, chief servant of the queen's household.

That was not to happen quite yet. Before the eyes of court and kingdom, Hattusa-ziti came bearing condolences on the death of the king. It could be suspected also that he had come to take the measure of Egypt, to discover who would be king. It was reasonable and wise, and well might be expected of so canny a monarch as Suppiluliumas.

The queen received him in court as she did every embassy, with the same words and the same gestures, the same ancient ritual that said everything and nothing in the turn of its formal phrases. She betrayed no anxiety. He offered no suggestion that he was present at anyone's wish but that of his king.

It was beautifully played, a regal dance, she in her golden finery, he in the most splendid of Hittite court robes and a high conical hat that made him tower even taller than he was. His attendants made a martial display: great broad shaggy-breasted men who could each have made two of the queen's slender countrymen, ringing in bronze armor and crowned with tall helmets. The queen matched them with a company of Nubians, coal-black giants with nuggets of gold and amber woven into the black fleece of their hair.

But when the words were all said, the gifts given and received, the ambassador dismissed and the queen retired to her chambers to rest, as she said, from the day's exertions, the queen met with the ambassador in a small and secluded chamber. It was not in the queen's palace but near it, in a wing that was then little used. She had had it prepared, cleaned and refurbished, so that it would be fit for a queen and for a king's ambassador. There was wine waiting, and delicacies from the palace kitchens, even a dainty or two that was said to be much favored in Hatti.

While Ankhesenamon waited for Hattusa-ziti to appear, she eyed the bowl of stewed mutton in barley with some distaste. "They eat this? Without spices or any savor?"

"It's subtle," Nofret said, "but it does please the tongue, if one has grown up eating it."

Ankhesenamon shuddered delicately. "I think your people lack sophistication of taste."

"It's only youth," said Nofret, "compared to Egypt."

There was no one there but the two of them. The queen did not trust her maids to keep quiet to their friends or lovers. She was not afraid that the Hittite would betray her or do her harm. Nofret hoped that it was trust in Hittite honor. More likely it was arrogance, and the conviction that only an Egyptian had the wit or the daring to kill an Egyptian queen.

The Hittite envoy came likewise attended only by a single man, a large and quiet one who effaced himself by the door. There was no interpreter, except for Nofret. Queen and ambassador were alone and quite private as royalty would think of it.

Nofret, endeavoring to be invisible at the queen's back, was aware of the Hittite's eyes on her. They weighed, they judged; they drew conclusions. They could hardly escape it, since she was the voice of her lady, and she wore a face that would be all too familiar in line and contour.

The first words that either queen or envoy spoke after the words of greeting were Hattusa-ziti's, asking Ankhesenamon, "She who is with you—that is one of ours, surely?"

Nofret thought briefly of failing to render the words in Egyptian, or else of inventing further greetings and fabricating a reply. But her wits were too slow for that. She asked the question as Hattusa-ziti had phrased it, as if it had nothing to do with her at all.

Ankhesenamon shot Nofret the briefest of glances, but answered as if Nofret were no more than a voice. "Yes, my maid is a Hittite. She was a captive, I'm told, taken and sold into Mitanni. Have her people been hunting for her?"

She knew perfectly well that they had not, but Nofret's place was to be silent except when she was being the voice of one or the other of them. Hattusa-ziti frowned and tugged at his chin. "Indeed, majesty, the truth escapes me. Shall I undertake to discover it?"

"Perhaps," said Ankhesenamon, "at another time."

She went silent then as queens could do, and queens in Egypt best of all. It was a silence that sucked at the will, that opened mouths that had been locked shut and made people babble simply to be spared the weight of royal patience.

Hattusa-ziti was schooled in the art, that was clear: the king in Hatti must be a master of it himself. Nonetheless he was the king's ambassador and not the king himself, and he had a message to convey. He did so simply, with directness that befit a man of a warrior people. "Lady, our king, the Sun, has received a letter that purports to be from the queen, the Sun's wife of Egypt."

Ankhesenamon waited, silent still, but the silence had changed. There were edges in it now.

"The letter says," said Hattusa-ziti, "that the god's wife of Egypt, whom we call Dahamunzu, is in much grief and is afraid, because her husband is dead and she had no sons."

"My husband is dead," said Ankhesenamon, low and quiet, like an echo, "and I have no sons. You know that, king's man of Hatti. You were here when we were happy. You know that there are no sons."

"Sons may be born while a man is traveling from realm to realm, lady," said Hattusa-ziti. "Or sons may be concealed from kin who wish them ill. That was so with your father the king, the Sun, was it not? He was brought from his mother's house when his elder brother died untimely, and set before the people, and made their king."

"Everyone knew that he had been born," said Ankhesenamon, "and many had seen him in his mother's house."

"Even so," said Hattusa-ziti. "Our king finds your request most strange. Is there no prince in Egypt to whom you would give the right of throne and scepter?"

"No," said Ankhesenamon. "And if there were, he would die as untimely as did my beloved."

Hattusa-ziti's brows rose slightly. "You have reason to fear?"

"I have reason to fear," said Ankhesenamon.

She did not look afraid. She looked royally remote. That was her defense, the mask that she wore.

Hattusa-ziti seemed to understand that. He had been standing till now, since the queen had not invited him to sit. He looked about, found a chair that was lower and less ornate than the queen's, inclined his head toward it. "Lady?"

She nodded with a touch of impatience.

His attendant brought the chair and set it opposite the queen. He sat in it, made himself comfortable, moving without haste but not excessively slowly. He was making himself, not her equal, never that, but something more than the menial of a foreign king.

Ankhesenamon's eyes glittered, but she offered no objection. In inviting Hatti to present her with a consort, she had made the Hittite king a kinsman. His envoy therefore stood higher than a mere tributary or petitioner.

At length, when he was well settled, Hattusa-ziti spoke. "Lady, may I be outspoken?"

To his patent astonishment, Ankhesenamon laughed. "Oh, do!" she said. "Please do."

Nofret, in translating, could not help it; she had to explain, or try to. "Lord," she said, "my lady expects it of us Hittites."

Hattusa-ziti frowned as if in puzzlement, but then he grinned, as startling as Ankhesenamon's laughter. He looked like a boy, and a wild one, too. "Ah, she does, does she? Good!" He set fists on knees and leaned forward. "Well then, lady, let me tell you that when our king read your letter, he was hard put to believe a word of it. He thought it might be a trap. 'What if there are sons?' he asked us in council. 'What if she means to mock us all, and to lure us into some deadly foolishness?' "

"I suppose," said Ankhesenamon, "that that's to be expected. We've been enemies, after all. Nobody in Asia is stronger than Hatti, or bolder in confronting Egypt."

"So why did you do it? Why a Hittite? Why no one in Egypt, or even in Mitanni, or Nubia? Why an enemy and not an ally?"

"Because our allies are weak," said Ankhesenamon. "They're cowed. I need a man who can face the strongest men in the Two Lands, and be stronger than they."

"Is that what your maid has told you of us Hittites?"

"She hasn't needed to. I can see it for myself."

Hattusa-ziti looked her over. "Lady, if it's as bad as that here, and you've got people murdering kings, what's to keep them from murdering a king's son out of an enemy country?"

"Nothing," she said, "but his own strength and his bravery. Hittites are brave, they say. They're warriors born. Your king has a whole army of sons, but only one of them can be king after he dies. Doesn't one of the others fancy a throne for himself? Even if he dares death to get it?"

"That's for my king to say," said Hattusa-ziti, "and

my king's sons. First he needs to know that you wrote in good faith: that you weren't plotting treachery, or thinking to get revenge for the war in Asia.''

"I wrote in good faith,'' said Ankhesenamon. "I am afraid here. Any man I take for my king will die soon or late, but always before his time.''

"Who will kill him?''

"One who has strong allies. Who wants the throne for himself, but who knows that he can never get it if he must get it through me.''

"He could kill you,'' said Hattusa-ziti. "That would remove the obstacle, wouldn't it?''

Ankhesenamon nodded. She was not afraid. Not of that. "Oh, he could, and if he were completely wise he would. But he's a stubborn man. He wants the throne in right and proper wise, through me.''

"And maybe he wants you for yourself,'' said Hattusa-ziti with a tilt of the brows. "You're a beautiful woman. More beautiful I've seldom seen, and I've seen half the beauties of the world. A man would be glad to take a kingdom that came with such a queen.''

"Or,'' she said, "he would be glad to take me, because in taking me he subdues all that has ever tried to master him. He's killed two kings. He'll kill a third, unless that king is stronger than any man in Egypt.''

Hattusa-ziti pondered for a while in Ankhesenamon's tight-drawn silence. So many silences, Nofret thought, and every one of them different.

"It could still be said,'' he said at last, "that Egypt, having killed two kings of its own, thinks to take one from Hatti and kill him too, and prove to Hatti that its princes are no safer than anyone else's. It would be a fine and subtle vengeance.''

"We aren't that subtle,'' said Ankhesenamon. "Not outside of our own people. I tell you truly, I would rather a Hittite consort than an Egyptian, because if he dies, it's no kin or friend of mine, but a stranger who was an enemy. But if he lives—and I wager my life and honor that he does—I have myself a strong king from a strong people, and one who can stand fast against the malice of that one Egyptian and his allies.''

"That Egyptian,'' said Hattusa-ziti. "He wouldn't be a soldier, would he? Or a common man who's risen high and hopes to rise higher?''

"He might,'' said Ankhesenamon.

"Ah,'' said Hattusa-ziti as if she had just explained everything. "Ah, indeed. Yes, I see that you have reason to be afraid. And no sons, either—or are you bearing any—?''

Ankhesenamon's hand went to her belly. Her voice was remote again. "The gods have not favored me.''

"They well may, if one of our young stallions comes to be your consort,'' said Hattusa-ziti.

"So I should hope,'' she said. "I gamble on it. There's no other heir whose life I would venture, and none who's strong enough to face . . . that one.''

Hattusa-ziti nodded abruptly, rose, knelt in homage that looked heartfelt. "Lady, by your leave I'll linger a bit, to look unsuspicious. Then I'll go back to Hatti.''

"And?''

"And,'' he said, "I'll tell my king that if he's minded, and if he has a son with a taste for adventure, he could do worse than be father to the king of Egypt.''

CHAPTER FORTY-THREE

▲

IT was well the queen had had long training in patience. The Hittites lingered, it seemed, endlessly. They could not go back to Hatti in the height of winter, when the snows could close the roads for months on end, and the winds were bitter beyond the belief of homebound Egyptian. In Egypt winter was growing time, sowing and harvest time.

The Hittites did not linger the whole while in Memphis. They traveled about, hunting and sightseeing, visiting this temple and that ancient city. Some said they were spying. Had anyone known what they had truly come for, that suspicion would have been certainty, and the embassy might have been set upon with stones and clots of dung or worse.

When at last they left, it was harvest time in Egypt and spring in Hatti. They would travel as quickly as they might. Hattusa-ziti promised this. By Nile's flood, or not long after, the queen might look for a Hittite prince to come to Memphis, if the king was well minded. Hattusa-ziti thought that he might be.

Ankhesenamon determined to make sure of it. She sent a letter with him, and a messenger with the letter, a man named Hani. He was one of her advisors, one whom Nofret did not know well, but Ankhesenamon trusted him, perhaps because he was besotted with her. He could never say no to her, even when the rest of the council resisted to a man.

His one virtue was that he knew how to keep his counsel. He would not betray his queen, Nofret did not think.

The messenger was soft-spoken and much enamored of his lady. The letter was considerably blunter. "Why do you not believe me?" she ordered her scribe to write. "Why do you say that I deceive you? If I had a son, do you think that I would have betrayed to a foreigner my shame and the shame of Egypt? How dare you disbelieve me? My husband is dead. I have no son. I shall never take one of my servants and make him my husband. No other king has had such word from me, only you. They say you have many sons. Give me one of them. He will be my husband, and king in Egypt."

With that missive, and with Lord Hani traveling discreetly in the middle of his escort, Hattusa-ziti led his embassy out of Memphis. The queen waited as she had waited since her king died, in tight-drawn patience. Her council and messengers from the council in Thebes had begun to weary of their own waiting. They requested, ever so politely, that she consider ending her time of mourning and accepting a new king. It was understood that that king would be the Lord Ay.

When pressed too hard, she invoked the presence of the Lady Tey. "It grieves me to displace her," she said.

"She understands the needs of kingdoms," they responded with growing impatience. "And these two kingdoms need a king. They cannot prosper until they have one."

She did not fail to point out that Egypt prospered as well as it had since she was queen. The harvest was rich, and the river's flood looked to be a strong one, with a great wealth of water and a greater one of black earth left behind for the next year's harvest. But that could be a false promise, her advisors insisted: the gods' jest before they laid the kingdom low for failing to provide it with a king. The kingdom could not prosper when ruled by a queen alone. Even the woman-king whose name was no longer spoken had ruled as regent for a prince who became himself a great king.

There was no defying the gods, as all believed. Ankhesenamon knew that. She did not tell them that she was going to give Egypt a king, but one of her choosing, and one whom they would never have expected. She had sanity enough left to keep her counsel till the man himself was there and inarguable and well fit to rule at her side.

For Nofret too it was a waiting time. Ankhesenamon waited for the world to be bright again, for a strong man to sit the throne beside her and defend her against the demon of her own mind that she had given the name and the face of Horemheb. Nofret waited for the storm to break.

She went about her days' duties as she always had, day blurring into day. One day it rained: a rarity, and everyone was out in it, dancing, laughing, getting gloriously wet. They all took it as an omen, a promise of joy. She hoped that it was that, and not a warning of storms to come.

■   ■   ■

The last of the harvest was taken in and stored. The river rose. Land that had been fertile cropland gave way to creeping water. Egypt retreated to the edges and to a well-earned idleness, growing fat on the riches of its harvest.

There was a strange comfort in this ancient round of the year. No other country lived so bound to its river, dependent on it for its very existence. Without the river Egypt would be all barren Red Land and no Black Land. Without the river's floods there would be no sowing, and never any fruits of the sowing.

Ankhesenamon's own planting brought its harvest in the second month of the flood. A messenger came to her in secret—that same one whom she had sent into Hatti with her letter that begged the king for one of his sons. Lord Hani was on his way, the man said, and with him a prince of the Hittites.

For the first time in many months, Ankhesenamon's face was a living woman's face and not an ivory mask. She could not be said to be eager, but her voice held something of animation. "What is his name? What is he like?"

The messenger was pleased to answer. "Lady, his name is Zennanza. He looks much like his father. A big man, but then Hittites are, and of course he has the Hittite face: the eagle's profile that no one can mistake. His skin is fair. His hair is red like your maid's, lady, but not as dark. His eyes are the color of the river in flood, neither brown nor green but something of both."

"Is he a handsome man?" she asked.

"Women seem to think so," the messenger said, "and in Hatti they call him that. He's his father's favorite, which honors you greatly. And young—he is that. He can't be more than nineteen summers."

"Young," said Ankhesenamon, "is all to the good. Is he strong? Does he fight well in battle?"

"Exceedingly well," the messenger answered, "and as for strength, he's the champion of Hattusas in wrestling hand to hand, as his father was in his own youth."

"A favorite son," Ankhesenamon mused. "But not the eldest. Not the heir."

"A king would hardly send the prince-heir to a foreign country, to be king there and not in his own place."

Ankhesenamon shook her head. "No. No, that's very well. A royal heir might think to be king of both kingdoms, and to make of them an empire. A younger son is much more to my taste. *He* need have no ambitions beyond the throne that I can give him."

She sent the messenger away to well-deserved rest, with a rich payment in gold for his trouble. For a long while after he had gone, she sat in her privy chamber, chin in hand. Her expression was one she had not had before. Dreaming; smiling; not content, she could not be that until the Hittite prince arrived in Memphis, but well pleased with her vision of him.

He probably was as lovely as the messenger had said. Suppiluliumas was a splendid figure of a man by all accounts, and his sons were said to be the image of him. Nofret had not heard of Zennanza—he would have been a toddling child when she was taken out of Hatti. She wondered what he was thinking, how he hoped to get on in Egypt, which was so different from anything he could have known.

She had managed it. He would, too, and with far more help than she had had. He would learn Egyptian, of course, if he had not already, much though it might prick his princely arrogance to have to speak any other language than his own.

There: she was dreaming, too, if considerably less sweetly than her lady. A Hittite prince in Memphis, crowned with the Two Crowns. Improbable dream. Preposterous, she would have said, if she had not seen and heard it for herself.

Ankhesenamon shook herself awake. A smile lingered about the corners of her mouth, but the rest of her was itself again, queenly somber. "By the full of the moon," she said to no one in particular, "there will be a king in Egypt."

■ ■ ■

A hand of days before the full of the moon, General Horemheb came to Memphis. He had been at his post on the border between Egypt and Asia, and safely so, the queen had thought. He came so boldly that she was much angered, marching in with a company of soldiers, and himself in a new and magnificent chariot drawn by horses that were not the light-boned beauties of the Two Lands. These were larger beasts, heavier and stronger. Such animals drew war-chariots in Asia, and in Great Hatti.

Horemheb requested—it might even be said demanded—an audience with the Lady of the Two Lands. She did not wish to grant him one. She sent word through her chamberlain that she was indisposed.

His messenger came back almost at once. "My lord says," he said, "that the Lady of the Two Lands would perhaps be less indisposed if she knew what service my lord has done her."

"He has done me no service," said Ankhesenamon, and sent the man away again.

That was before the sun came to noon. Near its setting, when Horemheb had established himself in the palace, nor had anyone seen fit to object, his messenger returned yet again. He found the queen new come from her bath, conferring with the goldsmith regarding the design and fitting of a pectoral. She would not receive the interloper, no more than she had before: it was Nofret who ran the messages back and forth.

Nofret had not been easy since Horemheb appeared in the city. This latest of his messages disturbed her unduly. She did not know why. It was mild and seeming harmless. It said simply, "My lady may do as she pleases, but it would please her well to speak with my lord."

Ankhesenamon returned no answer. She went to her bed at the same hour as always, rose and did as she did every morning, broke her fast, was dressed and wigged and anointed, painted her face and her eyes, prepared herself for the duties of the day. First were the rites of the gods: Amon as always, and Mother Isis, and Horus to whom she prayed for a strong husband well able to protect both his queen and his kingdom.

Horemheb was waiting in the temple of Horus. He said nothing, nor moved, but stood where she could not help but see him. And when she returned to the palace for the morning audience, his messenger was there, waiting.

She could outwait him, and meant to. But the messenger said, "My lord bids me tell you, O queen, that the word he bears for your ears alone were best not cried aloud in the nomes of the Two Lands."

That was a threat, and barely veiled. Ankhesenamon stiffened at it. Her pride might have been stung, but she could not fail to remember as Nofret did, where Horemheb had been. Prince Zennanza would have had to cross the borders that he guarded.

He had come, or would come, in the company of a lord of Egypt, with the queen's own safe-conduct and the promise of her countenance. Horemheb might have detained him, then, and come to Memphis to vex the queen with it.

But why come himself, Nofret wondered, and not send a messenger?

Perhaps he meant to claim the queen before the Hittite prince could do so. Perhaps he intended to face her himself, knowing that she would receive no emissary of his, but that his living and persistent presence might be more than she could withstand.

It was not Nofret's place, and in everything else she had learned to keep silence. But she bent and said in the queen's ear, "That's a threat, my lady. He knows—if not everything, then enough. You should see him."

The queen did not move, did not even glance at her. But she said to the messenger, "We will speak with him in the hour before sunset. Let him come to us in the lesser hall of audience."

The messenger bowed. It was not sufficient, his manner said, but it would have to do.

■   ■   ■

Ankhesenamon, having granted an hour of audience, seemed to forget it and its cause completely. A queen could do that. A queen's servant must remember, and must be certain that the lesser hall was prepared as the queen would wish. It would be a coldly formal audience, with few in attendance: a handful of the maids, a larger handful of guards, and of her counsellors only the oldest, the deafest, and the most easily lulled to sleep. They must gather a good hour and more before the queen appeared, so that they would be well advanced in boredom and little inclined to heed anything that the queen said to the general of her armies in Asia.

The queen herself arrived late and at her leisure. Horemheb cooled his heels in an antechamber. He could not but be sensible of the insult, but he betrayed no sign of it.

She was not reasonable, but with Horemheb she never had been. A queen could do such things. Whether he for-

gave her, Nofret did not know. She doubted it. Horemheb
was not a forgiving man, even of beautiful women who
were queens and the daughters of queens.

When Ankhesenamon was well ready, and only then,
she had the general brought before her. She sat her lesser
throne with her maids behind her and her guards along the
wall, and her troops of ancient counselors drowsing in their
places. Her expression granted nothing. She was queen and
goddess. He, mere mortal, must worship at her feet.

He was pleased, or amused, to do so. One of the men
behind him, Nofret noticed, carried a casket of bronze as
if it were a gift or an article of tribute.

When the words of greeting were spoken, words that
were as hollow as the death-mask of a king, the queen fell
into a silence that she had used before. She would give
nothing, the silence said. Let the petitioner speak and have
done. It was not her task to ease his burden or to aid him
in the laying down of it.

Horemheb took his time in speaking. During it he studied her, amused still, an amusement that undertook conspicuously to avoid anger. He indulged her, his expression
said, because she was queen, and because he found her
beautiful, and, yes, desirable.

At length, through the rasp of the counselors' snoring,
he said, "Lady, we bring you a gift." He nodded to the
man with the casket. The man, expressionless, set his burden at the queen's feet and lifted the lid.

The odor that rose from within was potent and sickly
familiar. It was the odor of the house of purification, of
natron underlaid with the stink of death. One or two of the
maids shrieked. One fainted.

The queen herself did not move. She could see into the
casket, as could Nofret if she craned a little. The objects
laid within on what seemed a dark, folded cloth were more
nondescript than alarming: something roughly globular and
two shriveled shapeless objects of no color in particular

and no great distinction—until the eye met the mind and knew them for what they were. The head and hands of a man. And the cloth on which they seemed to rest was a plaited coil of hair, ruddy brown, thick and shining.

There would be little mistaking the man, even without the peculiar color of the hair. The nose in the dried dead face was as noble as any in Hatti, and more princely than most.

"This man," said Horemheb, "rode past the border of Egypt with the fair beginnings of an army, with footsoldiers and chariotry, and every weapon honed and gleaming. His heralds told a preposterous tale, a lie that only a barbarian and an enemy would dare. He was, they declared, a prince of princes of the Hittites, and he came at Egypt's urging, to take the throne of Egypt and the hand of its queen."

Horemheb paused. The silence was enormous. Ankhesenamon said nothing, nor moved.

He shook his head as if in disbelief. "Lady, can you credit that? Hatti saw a kingdom without a king, and sent one of its own to claim it—for all the world as if the Two Lands were a barbarian fief, and their queen, their goddess on earth, a prize to be taken and given to the highest bidder. Only a barbarian would offer you such insult.

"Why, lady," he said, "he insisted that you yourself had begged him to come, had beseeched his father for a son of royal Hatti to be your king, because you would have no man in Egypt. Was there ever such presumption? I gave him what he deserved. I fell on him and destroyed him, and took his head and hands for a gift to you. It's a poor enough payment for the dishonor he did you, staining your name with treason."

Ankhesenamon could not seem to take her eyes from the casket. Her face was stark white under its paint. She breathed too light, too fast: Nofret heard the catch and release of breath in her throat.

She must have feared this, foreseen it, dreaded it—else why be in such fear of Horemheb? Now all her fears were proved true.

Nofret had been the fool after all. Ankhesenamon had seen clear from the first. Horemheb was much as ever, briskly efficient, cool and practical. And very, very dangerous.

The words he spoke were reasonable words. He had simply been doing his duty, protecting the borders of Egypt from invading armies and defending his queen's honor against a terrible slander. Yet he knew. It was in his eyes, clear to read. He knew that Prince Zennanza had told the truth. He had discovered everything that the Hittites knew, that they told him in all innocence, not suspecting that there was danger in the queen's man if the queen herself had bidden them come to her. They had told him everything, as trusting as children, and he had turned on them and slaughtered them.

"Of course," he said, "once I had disposed of our so-clever invaders, I had to make sure that they weren't leading the whole army of Hatti against us. I forayed some distance into their country, sacked and burned a village or two, left them a message that they couldn't mistake. They won't try any such audacity with us again. Claiming that you had invited one of them to be king in Egypt—how blind did they think I could be?"

"Do you expect," asked Ankhesenamon, so low that Nofret could barely hear her, "that I should reward you for this gift?"

"I expect nothing," said Horemheb, "but what is my due from the Lady of the Two Lands."

She bent her head. It might have been a nod. It might have been weariness beyond endurance, bowing under the weight of the crown. "You will receive your due," she said, a little louder than before. "You may felicitate me on my marriage to the Lord Ay, and the Lord Ay on his accession to the throne. Both will be done as soon as he arrives in Memphis.''

Horemheb's eyes narrowed. "I felicitate you, lady,'' he said with a suggestion of clenched teeth, ''and your lord. Does he know yet of his good fortune?''

"He fully expects it,'' she said. "Your excellence in defense of these kingdoms must be well recompensed. Go now, while we consider how best to go about it.''

■ ■ ■

Long after he was gone, her maids and servants dismissed, the counselors sent stumbling and yawning to their own houses, Ankhesenamon sat in her chair of audience with the bronze casket open at her feet. Prince Zennanza's face stared up at her in mild astonishment, as if it had not quite dawned on him that he was dead. He must have died quickly and in little pain: there was no fear there, no sign of anguish. It was little enough mercy in the circumstances.

"His father will be very angry,'' said Ankhesenamon. She sounded perfectly cool and rather remote. Inside, Nofret knew, she was weeping and raging.

"It will serve that man right,'' Nofret observed, "if he's got us into a war with Hatti.''

Ankhesenamon slanted a glance at her. "So you think I'm not so foolish after all? But I am. He spoke this much truth: that I did ill in asking a foreign prince to protect me from him. I never thought that prince would be caught and killed. There are always people coming across our borders, traders, embassies, traveling lords and princes. No one stops them, no one prevents them, even when they seem to come in arms. And I was so careful. I kept my secret. I knew that if he guessed, if he discovered—''

She stopped. "Do you think . . . were we betrayed? Did he let it all happen, letters and embassy and all, simply so that he could do this to me, bring me the head of my husband-to-be as if it were a gift and a tribute?''

"I don't know," said Nofret. "I think he guessed at the very least, and when the prince came, he asked and was answered. He did his duty to the letter, knowing what it would mean to you."

"He has a peculiar way of showing me that he wants me," said Ankhesenamon. She rose, stiff as an old woman, and laid down her scepter, and knelt to close the casket. The sound of the lid's shutting was distinct and somehow final.

She stood. "He will never have me. That I swear to you. If I have to lock myself in my own tomb in order to escape him, then I will do it."

A practical servant might point out that Horemheb was clearly stronger than a Hittite prince and more likely to be able to rule Egypt. But Nofret was done with being practical. She had seen the look in Horemheb's eyes when he gave his gift to the queen. It was the look of a man who does exactly as he pleases, when it pleases him, and calls it duty and honor; who acts on behalf of kingdoms, but whose actions always and ultimately serve himself foremost.

Such men made great kings and strong generals. They made the kingdom's good their own, and defended it fiercely. But they were never to be trusted. If Horemheb decided that the kingdom—by which he meant himself—was best served by the queen's death, then he would have her killed. He had done just that, she suspected, in disposing of Smenkhkare and Meritaten. Tutankhamon . . . who knew? It had seemed to be an accident. Perhaps it was. Perhaps the queen saw true, and it was Horemheb's design and his will to be rid of the last obstacle to the throne of Egypt.

"But," said Nofret out of the depths of her reflections, "what of the Lord Ay? He'll die, too, if you marry him."

"I must marry someone," said Ankhesenamon. "He expects it. I'll give it to him. And warn him, and pray that he can defend himself. He was a lord in the Two Lands long before Horemheb came out of his father's hovel to be a king's soldier. Maybe he'll be stronger after all than a foreigner could be, even a Hittite prince.''

She spoke firmly, but her hands were trembling. She looked about as if distracted. ''Oh, I hope he can be stronger. Did you see that man's eyes? He wants more than the throne. He wants my soul. He'll take it unless I fight him. He'll devour it whole.''

''He's not as bad as that,'' said Nofret. ''He wants to be king, that's all. And you carry the king-right.''

''No,'' said Ankhesenamon. ''He's an eater of souls. He's hungry for mine. I can feel him sniffing about me, gnawing at my edges.''

Nofret, listening to her, began to grow alarmed. The queen had been troubled, but in reasonable fashion; afraid, but with cause, after what she had done in summoning an enemy of Egypt to be her consort. One would expect that she would fear for herself now that she was discovered.

But this was more than plain human fear. It was obsession. She was trembling as if with cold, but her skin was burning hot. She had fretted herself into a fever.

Nofret coaxed the queen out of the hall of audience and down the passage into her private chambers. There were maids hovering. Nofret drove them out. She undressed her lady by herself, washed her with water scented with green herbs, dressed her in a light linen robe and persuaded her to lie down on her resting-couch.

She lay rigid, shivering in spasms. ''He'll consume me,'' she said over and over. ''He means to. I know it. I feel it. Can't you feel it, Nofret? Can't you feel it in your bones?''

CHAPTER FORTY-FOUR

▲

THE queen was ill, if not to death, then close enough that
Nofret took it on herself to send a swift messenger to
Thebes, bidding the Lord Ay come to Ankhesenamon in
Memphis. The man carried a warning likewise for Ay's
ears alone: to fear Horemheb and to trust no one.

Nofret thought long on poison or on dark magic as a
cause of Ankhesenamon's sickness. She had the skill to
detect neither, nor was there anyone in Memphis whom
she dared ask. She could think of no one there whom she
could trust, not one, except Ankhesenamon herself. Leah,
if she still lived, was in Thebes. Of Johanan she knew
nothing—and what could he do? He was too conspicuous
to conceal himself among the servants. He had no arts that
she knew of, except the overseeing of stonecutters and the
crossing of deserts and the shooting of a bow. None of
those could be of use in the close and stifling confinement
of the queen's palace.

She was alone in the royal city, alone and surrounded
by strangers. All the years she had lived there, she had
made no friends, nor known she needed any. Now when
her lady was ill in the spirit as in the body, she did not
even trust the maids who flocked about, alternately weeping and chattering. Any one of them might have dropped
the poison in her lady's cup, or helped to make the magic
that cast her down living and aware into the dark.

None of them seemed suspicious of anything but fever
and grief excessively prolonged. They talked about it in
Ankhesenamon's presence, where she could hear if she
roused from her dream. "She must marry again," they

said. "She gnaws herself with grief for her husband. A new husband, a young one maybe, and strong, will teach her to forget that poor lost boy."

They could not know that she had tried to do just that, and been forestalled by the one man she feared most. She did not babble in her fever as most people did. She lay silent, barely moving except to draw a breath. Her lips were tight shut. Her eyes opened on occasion and stared blindly into the dark, before they closed again in the sunken sockets.

One deep night when the maids were asleep and the shadows chittering among themselves, Nofret unwound the amulets of Amon and of Sobek from the plaits of her hair and bound them about her lady's neck. The queen was armored in amulets already, images of every god and power that priest or physician could think of, but Nofret's spirit wanted to believe that her two had some power that the others lacked. Loyalty, maybe. Love for her lady, whom she did not quite call friend—part of herself, rather, like a second shadow.

The rest of the amulets were set to cure the queen of sickness. On these Nofret laid a simple prayer: "Free her from fear. Bring her back to me alive and whole."

It was a paltry thing, but it was all Nofret could do till the Lord Ay came. If he would come. She was sunk as low as that: she wondered if even he could be trusted, who had always been purely loyal to the children of his daughter Nefertiti. What if after all he were in league with Horemheb, with the Two Crowns for their prize? Power could twist even the best of men, could transform him into a parody of himself.

Nofret shut down the thought. She must go on hoping, and hope lay in the Lord Ay. He was old, and there were rumors that his health was no longer of the best, but he was wise and canny and he loved his granddaughter. He would know what to do.

■ ■ ■

Nofret had been braced for the sight of him after the tales that she had heard. Even so she was shocked when he came from his boat into the palace, not even pausing to change out of his traveling clothes before he looked on the queen. As old as he had been when he wore the Blue Crown at the burial of Tutankhamon and performed the rites of the royal heir, now he was ancient. He was still tall, but his back was bent and stooped, and his face was deeply scored with age and weariness. His teeth, that had been strong for an Egyptian's, were gone; his lips had fallen in, his speech grown slurred and soft.

But the eyes were still clear in the altered face, and the mind had not failed of its keenness. He looked long at the queen lying all but lifeless in her bed. Then he dismissed the servants and the hangers-on, all but Nofret, and sent his own attendants to prepare chambers for him as near to the queen as might be.

There would still be listening ears. There was no avoiding them in palaces. He spoke to Nofret in a language she had not known he knew, though considering his father and his history he certainly must: the speech of the Apiru. She spoke it middling badly but understood it well enough. "Tell me now," he said, "and be quick. Is she poisoned?"

His speech was crisper in the Apiru tongue, even through toothless gums. Nofret shook her head in answer but said as best she could, "I don't know. Sometimes I think yes, sometimes no. Or maybe it's an ill magic."

"I have priests with me," he said, "and physicians, and masters of magic both good and ill. They will do their duty as they can. But I ask you. Do you think someone has endangered her?"

"I think one man or more than one would be pleased to see her dead," said Nofret. "The more so if word gets out of what she tried to do."

"The prince from the north?" Ay shook his head. "That was very ill thought of."

"But how did you—"

Nofret broke off, but Ay had heard enough to answer. "Very little in the Two Lands can be done completely in secret. I heard of it too late, from one who knew I could be trusted. I would have stopped her if I could."

"I couldn't," said Nofret. "She's my lady and my queen."

"And you come from his country," Ay said. "No one will hold you at fault. But she did an unwise thing."

"She was afraid," Nofret said.

"So should she have been," said the Lord Ay. He paused as if considering what he should say—perhaps determining whether she could be trusted. At length he said, "Her fears were well founded. Her error was to believe that no one in the Two Lands could be trusted, and that only a foreign king—a king who had but lately been our enemy in war—could protect her from the one she feared most of all."

"He is to be feared," said Nofret. "I thought not, but then I saw his face when he stood in front of my lady. He wants what he should never think to have."

"After me," the Lord Ay said, "there may be no one more able to hold it."

"He is dangerous."

"He is a man who believes himself fit to be king. He well may be. He's an excellent general, a strong commander of men. We've lacked such a one for too long."

"But you—" Nofret began.

"I grow old," he said, dispassionate. "I'll die in a year, two, three. Someone has to come after me."

"Then you would advise her to accept the suit of a man who may intend to kill her once he has her?"

"He won't kill her," said Ay. "In his way he wants her as much as a man can want a woman."

"And she hates the sight of him."

Ay sighed. "It was never ordained by any god that the human heart should be a reasonable thing. She loved her husband. She believes that he died at an enemy's instigation. So he may have done; but a queen must be practical."

"You won't marry her yourself? She thinks you can protect her."

"I can protect her till I die," he said. "And maybe that will be long enough for her to recover from her beloved's death, and to see reason. I hope it will be long enough."

"He might try to kill you," said Nofret.

"He may try," said the Lord Ay with a flicker of his old fire.

▪ ▪ ▪

Ankhesenamon seemed to gain strength from her grandfather's presence. His priests and physicians were no more illustrious than her own, but with so many in attendance, besieging the gods and invoking the powers, she had no choice but to rally. By the evening of Ay's second day in Memphis, she came to herself enough to open her eyes and look at him and whisper, "Grandfather?"

He clasped her fragile hand in his own that though gnarled and old was still stronger than hers. She clung like a child, eyes fixed on his face, seeming to see nothing in it but what she had always seen: strength, and a bulwark against fear. He spoke softly to her, as he would soothe a restive mare. "Yes, child, I'm here. Are you going to wake now and be strong?"

"I am awake," she said in a thread of a voice. "Is *he* here?"

Ay understood her. He said, "I won't let him harm you."

"Make him go away," she said. "Send him to the ends of the earth. Forbid him to come back."

"Hush," he said. "Hush."

She struggled to rise. Her voice rose to almost its old clarity. "I command you!"

A gaggle of priests and physicians leaped to subdue her. Ay waved them back. He held the queen by the hand, supporting her, speaking firmly. "You will rest, and you will recover your strength. Then you may command as you judge best."

"I can judge now," she said. "I want him sent away." But she sounded sulky rather than imperious, and she lay back when he urged her, subdued by his gentle compulsion. Under it she sipped a cup of water and ate a little broth with herbs in it, and suffered a round of prayers and incantations. Ay kept those brief, though the priests and physicians would have made of it a high rite. He knew as well as Nofret did that the queen was not strong enough for such a carrying on.

When she slept she was still fevered, but much less than before. Nofret began to believe that the only poison was fear, and the only sickness in her spirit. Such could kill her just as surely as either plague or potion. That was frightening, but not in the same way as if it had been Horemheb's hirelings conniving in the queen's death.

CHAPTER FORTY-FIVE

▲

QUEEN Ankhesenamon married the Lord Ay quietly in deference to her recent illness, and crowned him with her own hands, setting on his head the Two Crowns of the kings of Egypt. He bore the weight and the honor with becoming dignity and no great excess of arrogance. "I stand between the worlds," he said to his queen. "Soon I become Osiris. Then, lady, look you well to the one who may be Horus after me.''

Ankhesenamon inclined her head, but that was respect, no more. She did not look at Horemheb, who attended the ceremony in his office of General of the Armies. Nor did he betray anger that she had so defied him. He could wait, his stance said. The old man would die. Then he would have what he had always wanted.

He had betrayed nothing of what she had done to evade him, nor could anyone prove that his servants had let slip the knowledge. Maybe the scribes talked. Maybe the messengers were indiscreet over their wine. However that might be, it was known in Egypt that the queen, desperate to escape an Egyptian marriage, had sent to an enemy and begged him for a son. The charitable ascribed it to a madness of grief. Most were not so swift to spare her, even as lovely as she was, and as frail still from her sickness.

She was not too frail to be bedded on her wedding night, but Nofret had reason to believe that they did no more than sleep chastely side by side. Lady Tey had remained in Thebes, discreetly out of the way; but her presence loomed large in everyone's memory. Ay had neither put her aside nor repudiated her. He had chosen as a king might, to have two wives: one of the heart, and one who was his queen.

Certainly, after the first few necessary nights, Ay kept to the king's palace and Ankhesenamon to the queen's. In the day they shared the ruling of Egypt, side by side on slightly mismatched thrones. Tutankhamon's had gone to the tomb with him. Ay's was new, Ankhesenamon's the one she had always had, that no doubt would be buried with her.

They pretended that all was well, but they moved in a cloud of whispers. The queen in her wedding procession, as brief as that had been because of her frail health, had been carried in a chair outside of her palace so that the people might see her. They saw her indeed, and a rash few hurled stones that by good fortune flew wide. Those less rash settled for mutters in much the same words wherever they were: "I'll wager she wishes that was a nice big Hittite buck and not an Egyptian up there beside her."

"Ay's half a foreigner himself," someone recalled in Nofret's hearing. "We're slipping back, I say: back to the Shepherd Kings."

The snarl at that raised her hackles. Egypt had cast out a nation of invaders whose name they never spoke, but whose memory they cherished in infamy. It was their only shame in their thousands of years, the only foreigners who had ever laid claim to the throne of the Two Kingdoms.

And Ankhesenamon had tried to give Egypt a foreign king—had, too many insisted, done so indeed, though Ay was half Egyptian by breeding and all Egyptian in speech and in spirit. Some even muttered that the queen herself was Ay's grandchild, and not full Egyptian either.

It was an ugly thing, that river of rumor. It swelled with time and feeding. Maybe Horemheb had nothing to do with it: maybe he did not need to. The simple truth with which it had begun, Ankhesenamon's letter to the Hittite king, was enormity enough.

They had hated Akhenaten for robbing them of their gods. They remembered that, too, and cast all their resentment on his daughter's head—his daughter who had told a foreign king that she would have no Egyptian for a husband.

She could hardly be oblivious to flung stones, to hissing when she went to one or another of the temples to pray and to bless them with the royal presence, to backs turned and even, once, an arrow that flew over her head while she stepped out of her chair in front of Hathor's temple. A moment earlier and it would have pierced her eye.

She neither wept nor flew into a panic. She went in calmly while her guards hunted down the archer and disposed of him. She was praying ostensibly for a son, an heir at last for the dying royal house. Nofret believed it more likely that she prayed to any god who would listen, to take Horemheb and devour him before he seized the throne.

As she emerged from the temple, the captain of her guard brought word that the archer had been found dead on a rooftop with a dagger—evidently his own—in his throat. She accepted the news without expression, thanked the captain for his services, mounted her palanquin and rode back silently to the palace. No stones flew from among the people, and for once no one said anything. The arrow had been eloquent enough.

▪   ▪   ▪

Ankhesenamon let slip her composure only when she was safe in her own rooms, with the daymeal long past and her maids dismissed to their beds. Ay had not come to do his husbandly duty, even in seeming, nor was he expected. The queen was as solitary as she could be. Nofret of course was no one, or near enough: the queen's shadow, too long familiar to be noticed.

Ankhesenamon sank to a chair that she favored, where sometimes she read of an evening or listened to a player on harp or flute. She lowered her face into her hands and sat so for a long while, not moving, not seeming to weep.

When she spoke, she took Nofret by surprise. Her voice was clear and calm. "I think," she said, "that I would like to die."

Nofret held herself still, sitting on her heels near the chair, the servant's position that with use had grown comfortable. She did not speak. She made herself even more invisible than before.

"After all," Ankhesenamon said as if there had been a response, "what more is there for me? Ay can only protect me for a little while. The gods will give me no son of his begetting. Our line ends with us; there can be no more.''

''You can't know that,'' said Nofret, forsaking invisi-
bility almost as soon as she had assumed it. ''For that
matter, if Ay's seed is dried and barren, what's to keep
you from finding someone younger to father Ay's son and
heir? It won't be the first time, I shouldn't think. There
are some who say your mother did the same, because your
father could never raise his shaft, let alone beget so many
daughters.''

Ankhesenamon favored Nofret with a long, dark stare.
''My father's weaponry was small and not excessively
keen, but it was sufficient for the purpose. He needed no
one else to father his daughters.''

''But a son,'' said Nofret, ''since the need is so
great . . .''

''Perhaps I should raid the slaves' quarters,'' Ankhesenamon said, ''and find me a strong and lusty boy-baby.
An Apiru, maybe, of my own kin. I could pretend to be
with child, and go into confinement. Or I could seem to
find a royal infant in a basket in the river-reeds, a gift of
the gods, with the gods' seal on his brow.''

''You are quite mad,'' said Nofret.

''I rather think I may be,'' Ankhesenamon said. ''My
foresight failed me, you see. I knew—I *knew*—that I
would have a son, and that my beloved, my king and god,
would be his father. I saw us growing old together. I never
knew that he would die so young and give me no more
than two poor tiny twisted girl-babies who could never
have lived past infancy. I didn't see, till it was far too late,
that someone else wanted to be king, and would do anything to make sure of it. Maybe the gods themselves didn't
know.''

''The gods know. The gods know everything.'' Nofret
shivered. The night air was always full of whispers, but
tonight it seemed to be clamoring on the edge of hearing,
as if the spirits of the dead and the unborn had gone to

war. Ankhesenamon spoke through them. "I do think I want to die. Unless I can find a boychild in the reeds. Should I hunt for him? Would it matter at all?"

"You should sleep," said Nofret for lack of anything better to say.

Ankhesenamon sighed. "Oh, I can sleep. I can dream. I see him there. The one who died—the other one. The prince who came to be my savior. Would he have been gentle, do you think, or would he have been hard-handed and cruel?"

"I think he would have been in awe of you," Nofret said. She did not want to close her eyes. The Hittite prince's face was there, too, as it must be for her lady. It was not a thing one could ever forget.

"Awe can be cruel, particularly if it's in a man and it makes him afraid. I wasn't wise to send for him. But I wonder . . . if . . ."

Her voice drifted off. The whispers in the air seemed to fade into it.

She had fallen asleep sitting up in her chair. Nofret eased her into her arms. She was a light weight, no heavier than a child, murmuring as a child will, frowning and curling into herself when Nofret had laid her in her bed.

Nofret snuffed the lamps, all but the one that burned nightlong, and sought her own pallet in her cell of a room. She had thought not to sleep, but sleep was waiting, lying in ambush as Horemheb's men had done to the prince from Hatti. Dreams were in it, nightmares, memories that were best forgotten. Morning was a blessing, even with the rumbling in it, the thunder that was like Akhetaten before the old king went away from it.

■　■　■

The queen was quietly out of her mind. She did her duties as she always had, as she had been trained to from a child. But as her father had done before her, when she was not needed to be queen, she vanished from her chambers.

Sometimes Nofret found her in the garden by the lotus pool where she had idled so often with her young king. More frequently she was not to be found, not anywhere that a queen should be. Nofret trailed her down to the river and the beds of rushes, where the servants did not go for fear of crocodiles. The queen had wits enough not to trail hands or feet in the water, but she wandered often far down the stream, searching, one would think, for a basket with a baby in it.

There never was one. Nofret doubted that she had expected it. It was a dream she had, a haunting of the spirit. She wandered away from herself, from all that she was, searching for what she could never find. A Hittite prince had only been the beginning of it.

Maybe most of all she was seeking what her father had found. Death that was not death. Escape from an office that had become intolerable.

She might find death in truth if she kept wandering so close to the water. Nofret watched from concealment, braced to leap if she stumbled or fell. Or if—and this was dangerously likely—someone tripped her and flung her in. Horemheb was a patient man, and he wanted Ankhesenamon alive, with the king-right she carried. Others might not be as willing to let her be.

When Ankhesenamon grew tired of walking along the river, she took to commanding that her horses be harnessed to her chariot, and to driving out wherever her whim took her. Guards rode behind, unnoticed and unforbidden, as was Nofret herself in the queen's chariot. Nofret carried a knife, and no matter what some might say of slaves and deadly weapons.

She might have done better to carry a bow and a full quiver, but archery was not an art she had ever studied. The guards in the chariots behind carried spears, little use as those would be if an arrow flew to strike the queen.

Stones did fly, and more than once, out of a faceless crowd. None struck home, though one or two dented the chariot's rim, and once one clipped the rump of the left-hand mare. She shied and sprang forward, dragging the right-hand mare with her. But Ankhesenamon, for all her slenderness, was a strong charioteer, and skilled. She gentled the frightened mare and brought both horses back to their former courtly gait.

Ankhesenamon would not hear of keeping to the palace, not even with such threats as stoning. "My father faced worse before he fled Thebes," she said. "These don't mean to kill me, only to make me afraid. Him they wanted dead."

"You might wonder why they want to frighten you," said Ay. He still dreamed of swaying her with reason, though she was as far beyond that as her father had ever been.

She did not hear him, of course. She said placidly, "They are angry because I tried to set a Hittite over them. That is ended, with thanks to General Horemheb. You rule, and you they can endure."

"And when I die? Will you send for another Hittite?"

She regarded him with wide eyes, so wide they seemed blind. Certainly she saw him no more clearly than she heard him. "I'll die before you," she said.

CHAPTER FORTY-SIX

▲

NOFRET rested little in those days. At night she slept as best she could on the floor of her lady's chamber. Mostly she lay awake, missing her own bed. She had lost the art of sleeping wherever she could.

Her only peace of mind came when the queen was in court with the king beside her. Ay was old and had lost the strength of his arm, but his presence was potent and his guards were many, and they were fiercely loyal. It would take more rashness than Nofret thought any Egyptian had to menace the queen there.

While Ankhesenamon heard petitioners and received embassies and saw to the rule of the Two Kingdoms, Nofret could snatch a little sleep, or simply rest. She would take refuge in one of the gardens, or put on her plainest gown and plait her hair behind her and walk in the city, and maybe she would go to the seller of beer and buy a jar and sit for a while. She did not always drink the whole jar. Many times she fed the remnants to the beer-seller's dog. It was a fat, sleek, tipsy animal, much like its mistress, and it lived chiefly on beer and on leavings from the butcher down the way.

She was feeding most of a jar of beer to the dog, one day of Egyptian summer, when the river was full in flood but just beginning to slacken. The air was thick with the river's presence, thick enough almost to drink, and the flies were swarming. The beer-seller had a curtain of gauze to keep the worst of them out, which darkened the little cell of a place to a twilight gloom but little relieved by a lamp hanging from a rafter.

At this hour Nofret was the only person there, Nofret and the dog. The beer-seller was outside hawking her wares to passersby. Nofret heard her singing the song she sang, a song of beer and of the joys it brought. People laughed at some of the verses, and bought a jar or two on the strength of them.

One man who paused had a glorious deep voice, and towered over the rest of the people in the street. He was a foreigner, a robed and bearded tribesman, wide in the shoulders, with an eagle's arch of nose: like a Hittite and yet unlike.

Nofret's mind lagged far behind her eyes. It did not even catch up when, having conferred with the seller of beer, he ducked through the curtain and loomed in front of her. The room could hold a dozen and more without crowding, but he filled it. He went on doing that even when he hooked a stool with his foot and sat facing her, jar of beer in hand. "Share with me?" he asked.

"Johanan." Nofret did not know why she should be so angry. He had done nothing that she knew of to offend her.

That was precisely why she was angry. Because he had done nothing. She had heard no word from him since he passed through Memphis on his way to visit his grandmother, while Tutankhamon was alive. When she was in Thebes he had made no effort to seek her out. She had thought him gone. Maybe he had been. Maybe he had gone back to Sinai, and now returned to Egypt. Maybe . . .

She took the jar of beer because he was thrusting it at her, and drank deeper than perhaps she should. It was a strong brew as Egyptian beer went, strong enough to dizzy her a little. Johanan's face wavered in front of her. He looked thinner than she remembered, and darker, burned black with the sun. His hands that took the jar back were roughened as if he had been at hard labor.

He saw her eyes on them. "Stonecutting," he said without shame, "carving tombs in Thebes."

"You never had much skill in that," she said. "I thought your greater gift was for commanding men."

He shrugged and drank less deep of the beer than she had, but with more apparent relish. When he had wiped the foam from his beard with the edge of his sleeve he said, "I did what work was to be had. Thebes isn't as Akhetaten was. The men in command are Egyptians. They aren't fond of foreigners. Particularly foreigners who once enjoyed the patronage of the fallen one of Akhetaten."

"Is that what they call him in Thebes? He's never mentioned at all in Memphis."

"Thebes will be the last to forget him," said Johanan, "though it's already undertaken to forget his name. They had me carving it out of inscriptions. It amused them, I think, to make me undo what my people did so much of, not so long ago."

He did not sound bitter. Nor was he resigned, not as a man is who has given up his pride and his will.

"You didn't see me while I was in Thebes," Nofret said.

"The slaves of the tombs aren't given leave to visit servants in the palace."

That, now, was bitter. Subtly so, but clear to her ear. Her throat tightened. "Leah. Is she—"

"She lives," he said. "She's here. I left her in the lodging, to rest from the journey. She's much as she ever was, but traveling has never been easy for her."

Nofret stared at him. "You weren't let go, were you? You escaped."

"We never considered ourselves slaves. We were kin of the king. But the king is dead and his kin are not loved."

"And you ran away. The rest of your people—are they—"

"They wouldn't go. It's not so bad, they say. They have to work harder and the hours are longer, but they're still paid their bread and beer. No one's taking their wives and daughters or threatening them with anything worse than a touch of the lash now and then, when there's an example to be set."

The way he said that made her leap to her feet. The jar would have gone flying if he had not caught it. She seized his robe and tugged hard.

It was good wool, well woven but much worn and faded. It gave way with a sigh, baring his shoulders. They were as dark nearly as his face, what she could see of them.

There were scars on scars, and half-healed wounds on top of those. Her hand dropped as if burned.

He shrugged his robe back into place as much as he could. His face was calm, even amused. His eyes were too dark to read. "I take direction badly," he said. "I'm much better at giving it. That's not an advantage in a slave."

"They were going to kill you," she said.

"So my grandmother said," said Johanan. He did not seem to care, still less to be afraid. "She wanted to leave. She said it would only get worse, and we would bear the brunt of it, since I can never hold my tongue. I was in the desert too long. I've forgotten how to speak soft to a haughty master."

"You should never have come here," said Nofret. "You shouldn't have come back to Egypt at all. If word is out that you've fled—if anyone is looking for you—"

"Grandmother says not," he said. "We went into the desert, and we seemed to go south. They won't look for us in the north."

"They will unless they're perfect fools. They know what you are."

"They haven't followed me." He would not hear more of it: there was a set to his mouth that said so. "We kept to the desert while we could, but Grandmother said we had to stop here. Will you come and speak to her?"

Nofret drew a breath. She was going to refuse, to plead that she must return to the palace, that it was late, that if she did not go back, her queen might wander without her and be hurt or killed. But she heard herself say, "Where is she? Take me there."

▪   ▪   ▪

He led her to a travelers' lodging deep in the city, where the faces were more foreign than Egyptian. People there spoke every language that the world knew. Nofret heard Hittite, and the singsong strangeness of the sea-rovers from the north of the great sea, and Nubian and Libyan and the dialects of Mitanni and Canaan and Ashur, and yes, Apiru, too, both the raiders of the desert and the tribesmen of Sinai who were kin to the kings of Egypt.

Leah was resting in a dim rear chamber of the lodging. It was so much like the room that she had so often waited in in the workmen's village of Akhetaten, that Nofret felt herself taken back there. The walls, of plain mudbrick like all poor dwellings in this country, were hidden behind draperies that transformed the place into a tent in the desert. There were no chairs, but rugs and cushions in plenty, and a bronze ewer for water, and a jar of date wine and little cups, and a bowl of dates steeped in honey.

Leah had not changed as the Lord Ay had. She had always seemed ancient to Nofret, but strong, like a gnarled and venerable tree. Her skin was still soft, still barely wrinkled. Her back was straight, her eyes bright, resting on Nofret with the familiar welcome. Nofret's eyes filled, astonishing her. She had given up weeping on the day she was captured and taken to Mitanni.

She sat where she had always sat, on a heap of rugs facing Leah, and poured date wine from the jar, a cup for each, and for Johanan too as he came in behind her. "We only need Aharon," she said, "to make the gathering complete."

She had meant it lightly, but it came out somber. Neither of the Apiru smiled. Leah nodded. "Aharon would be welcome," she said. "We're going back to him, to the place he's made among the people of Sinai."

Nofret had expected it. There was no safe place for them in Egypt. "But if you go," she said, "I'll never see you again."

"Unless you go with us."

It was Leah who said it. Not Johanan, who had never

in any way intimated that she should accompany him any-where.

Through the anger that had no reasonable cause, Nofret forced herself to think, to say what was best to say. "You know I can't leave my lady. Now least of all."

"Why?" asked Leah.

Nofret stared at her, narrow-eyed. She stared back without flinching. "If you can see truth," said Nofret, "or even hear what everyone in Egypt is saying, you know that she's not loved and in many places is much hated."

"Because she did a thing that no queen should do." Leah nodded. "Yes, I've heard what everyone says. How much of it is true?"

"You can't see?"

"Tell me," said Leah.

"That she sent for a Hittite prince," Nofret said after a pause, "that is true. So is it true that she refused to marry any man of hers in Egypt, till she was compelled by the death of the prince who had been sent to her. Then she took what she had to take. She ventured her grandfather's life against the one who she believes has killed two kings already and is prepared to kill a third."

"And will that one do it?"

"I . . . think not." Nofret stopped, considered altering what she had said, left it as it was. "He knows his time is near. Lord Ay is old. Time and the gods will dispose of him before his rival grows too greatly impatient. And meanwhile there's Hatti to engross him. It can hardly have submitted meekly to the murder of its prince."

"That it has not," said Leah. "But all wars end, and soldiers come home. Is that what your lady fears?"

"My lady is beyond fear," Nofret said. It was almost like peace to be able to say so; to go on, and to say what she had said to no one else, not even the Lord Ay. "She's as mad as her father ever was, but without a god to give her grace. She thinks that if she could just find a son, any son, from anywhere, she will be safe.''

"You know that can't be," Johanan said, "unless she finds a man grown, and one honed in war, too. Like that Hittite prince. It's a pity he was killed. Egypt would have hated him, but from all I know of his kin, he would have stood rather well against his lady's enemy.''

"He wouldn't have lasted long," said Nofret. "She needs an Egyptian, and young, and strong enough for her purpose. She's found none. All the ones suitable are dead or far away. They've been disposed of one by one, year by year. And no one saw but my lady. My poor lady, whose mind has broken.''

"Has it?" Leah asked. "Or is she seeing clear, and that clarity terrifies her, and she runs away from it? She saw the enemy before anyone else did. What if she sees more than that? What if she knows what is to come?''

"She never has seen that clear before," Nofret said.

"Grief can open the eyes of the heart," said Leah, "and she has had more grief in her brief years than most women know in a lifetime.''

"And yet," said Nofret, "she's not herself. She wanders the riverbank looking, she says, for a child in a basket. She tells tales to herself of the sons of slaves and servants, of seizing one and commanding that all the rest be put to death lest he contest the right of the one to be king. She tells wild stories, flights of fancy such as no sane woman would indulge in.''

"And yet she continues to rule, and that not badly, or people would be remarking on it.''

"No one needs to remark on it. She sent to Hatti for a husband. That's madness enough for all the rest.''

Leah shook her head. "I think you underestimate her. She's in great danger, and well she knows it.''

"Then why," Nofret demanded with sudden heat, "does she ride about in her chariot as if she were immortal, and wander by the river, taunting the crocodiles?''

''Maybe she wants her enemies to believe her less than she is.''

''She feigns it too well,'' Nofret said. ''She wants to die. She says so, and she's speaking the truth.''

There was a silence. Nofret realized that she was gripping her cup of date wine as if she would crush it. She unlocked her fingers, moved to sip, set the cup down again untouched. Its sweetness would have gagged her.

Slowly, after what seemed a long while, Johanan said, ''He said that we would speak of this. That when the god willed it, she would become as you say she is: weak in spirit, frail, and in great danger. He said that she would die; that when the enemy had what he wanted, he would dispose of her and take a wife more tractable, who had not been raised to be a queen.''

''Who said that? Who told you such a thing?'' But Nofret knew. She shook the knowledge out of her head. ''Was it the dead man? Does he still babble of everything and nothing? Was he in Thebes, then? You left Sinai years ago!''

''He knew,'' said Johanan. ''He's always known. His god shows him everything. It would break the mind of a lesser man.''

''But his mind is already broken.'' Nofret spat, deliberately vulgar. ''So he foresaw this. What did he say we should do about it? Kill her before her so-loyal general does it for us?''

''She will die,'' said Leah, ''if she remains here. She has no friends, no one who will protect her once her husband is dead. She has no son; and if she bore one now he would be easy prey for the enemy. Children die so easily, and she has never borne one who lived past infancy. She has no defense and little enough hope. Her lord will die and the other will take her. No prince from afar will come to defend her.''

"He won't kill her," Nofret said. "He's ruthless, yes, but he wants her for herself as much as for the kingship that she carries." She was echoing Lord Ay, and why not? He was a wise man.

"She carries kingship, but no son for a king. Once he has the Two Crowns he'll look for a woman who can give him an heir."

"The gods might be kind," said Nofret. "Or he can take a concubine. Sons of lesser queens have taken the kingship before now."

"All that might happen," Leah conceded. "Or it might happen as she foresees it. She sees only death. If she had not sent to Hatti . . . maybe. Or maybe Egypt would remember her father, and what he did to its gods."

"Egypt is restless," Johanan said. "It's learned that kings can die of other means than war or age or sickness. That people can grow weary of them and dispose of them, and set up kings who suit them better. Now it sees itself subjected to an aged king, a man too feeble to beget a living son, and a queen whose children have all died. The king and the queen are the life and spirit of the kingdom. If they are frail, then what of the land they rule? How long can it go on before it totters and falls? And when it falls, to whom can it fall but the nation to which its queen sent for a king, the foreign nation, the nation that would be its conqueror?"

Nofret clapped her hands over her ears, but his voice went on, quiet, relentless, speaking the truth in all its merciless clarity. When it stopped, she lowered her hands. He was bent over his own, rocking as he used to do when he was young and in some trouble of the spirit, some slight thing that was all the world to a boy. Now he was a man, and she could almost believe that he grieved as much as she. "Then we have no hope," she said. "No choice but to play it out."

"Her father didn't think so," Johanan said.

Nofret opened her mouth, shut it again. "Are you saying . . ."

"He said to me," said Johanan, "that when the time came, when I was no longer welcome in Thebes, when Egypt lay under the rule of an old man and a woman who had sought a king from another kingdom, then I was to carry hope to the queen of Egypt. I was to set her free."

"To kill her?"

Johanan tossed his head, as impatient as he had ever been in youth, and scornful, too. "Are you blind, or are you only afraid to see what's as plain as your face?"

"She can't do what her father did," Nofret said. "Only luck and his god kept him from being discovered. We can't be sure that we can do it again."

"And it does lack a certain imagination," said Leah. She met both their stares with equanimity. "She won't want to go, either. Her father belonged only to his god. She belongs always and forever to Egypt. She'll never leave of her own will."

"She'll die here," said Nofret. "She wants to. She insists on it."

"And you're going to let her?" Johanan flung up his hands. "Grandmother, you were the one who made us come here! Now you tell me it's useless."

"Did I say that?" Leah was maddeningly composed. "I didn't say you should kill her either, or let her be killed."

"Then how—" said Nofret and Johanan together. They stopped, disconcerted alike, furious alike.

Leah laughed, sweet as a girl. "Oh, you children! Open your eyes and see. The queen will die if she stays. She won't go, because she is queen, and she knows no other thing to be. She has no god to guide her. Her father would do it if he could, but his time is not yet come. He's far away in Sinai, where his god has bid him stay. You heard the god, Johanan. He called you out of Thebes. He brought you into Memphis."

"You brought me into Memphis," said Johanan, not a little sullen.

"You followed where I led, where you knew the god was."

Nofret looked from one to the other. She had never seen a great likeness between them. Johanan favored his father, and Aharon the long-dead father before him, she had always thought. And yet they were alike after all. They had the same eyes.

The same light in them, too, full day in Leah's, a slow and reluctant dawn in Johanan's. "You didn't mean—for us to—"

"It is outrageous," said Leah. "It may even be mad."

"As mad as she pretends to be." Johanan glanced at Nofret, then back at his grandmother. "Is she, then? What will she do if—"

"You know she won't ever go of her own will," Leah said, "no matter how much you may have hoped for it."

He shook his head. "No. No, we can't do it. Not if she resists us. She'll betray us at the first guardpost, condemn us to death with a word."

"I think not," said Leah.

"Then how are we to do it? Drug her and carry her like baggage?"

Nofret listened in growing incredulity. She had not understood at first, then not wanted to understand. They were speaking of abducting the queen of Egypt. Of seizing her and carrying her away into the desert, where no doubt her father was waiting, with his god beside him.

"You can't do that," she said. "The wrath of all the gods will follow you. Egypt's armies will hunt you down and destroy you—you and the woman you think to snatch away. The one who wants the throne so badly will have all the cause he could ever wish for, to hunt her to her death."

"Not while she carries the king-right," said Johanan.

"She's not the only one," Nofret said. "Everyone thinks so, because the Lord Ay has been so careful to protect his own. But he has a daughter, a sister of Nefertiti, younger than she, young enough still to bear a child. She's never married. She lives in seclusion, or in Amon's temple in Thebes, where she is a singer. She'll be remembered, you can be sure of that. She'll do more than well for what that man needs of her."

"You see," Johanan said, "that your lady has no hope here."

Nofret rounded on him. "Whose side are you taking? You've been arguing against this!"

"I don't have to like what I see," he said. "And for a fact I hate it. It's perfect insanity."

"There is nothing else to do," said Leah. "Not if she's to live. Egypt is close to destroying her. She knew it when she sent to Hatti. That sending made it a surety."

"I don't think," said Nofret, "that anything she did could have been the right thing. But how in the name of all the gods can we abduct a queen and carry her all the way to Sinai, and not be caught and killed?"

"The god knows," Leah said. "Open your eyes and see."

"I see nothing but death," said Nofret.

"Then you are blind." Leah leaned forward and stretched out her hands. They were warm on Nofret's face, dry and thin, an old woman's hands. But there was tremendous vitality in them, tremendous strength of spirit. Nofret recoiled by instinct, but they followed. She could not get away from them.

"Open your eyes and see," said Leah.

Nofret squeezed them shut, but the light would not go out of them. Light like a burning brand, like a column of fire in the night. Light such as had filled the king who was gone, the dead man who yet lived, who was a prophet in Sinai.

She set her teeth. "I don't want to know this god."

"It's not a matter of wanting," Leah said. "Open. See."

"No," said Nofret.

"See," Leah commanded her, no gentleness now, no yielding. "Open and see."

CHAPTER FORTY-SEVEN

▲

NOFRET never really saw anything but hopelessness, a queen whose mind was broken and whose people had come to hate her. She might be strong enough to overcome it all, even the man who would have her, the strong man, the soldier who was never so weak as to succumb to mercy. Everyone knew that when Ay was dead, Horemheb would be king. It was as certain as the river's flood.

He was still in Memphis. He came often to the hour of audience, to stand in the place allotted the General of the Armies, to show his strength by the simple fact of his presence. The queen conducted herself as if he had not been there at all. The king acknowledged him when it was proper. He had not laid claim yet to the name of heir. But no one else contested him for it, nor would. Everyone in Egypt was afraid of Horemheb.

He did not look so terrible, if one knew nothing of him but his face. He was a handsome man, no longer in first youth but far from old. He carried himself as a soldier will, erect, poised, alert for any danger. The men who accompanied him in court, the guards who strode behind him when he traveled in palace or city, were warriors bred and born. They were beautiful and dangerous, like hunting cats, but so were warriors in Hatti. They might not mean harm to Nofret's lady. Their lord might even, against all hope, be the husband that she needed to restore her to herself.

Nofret had difficulty, watching him in court and about the palace, in remembering that he was her lady's enemy. He had brought Prince Zennanza's head and hands in a casket, certainly, but that was the old Egyptian way when a man had destroyed an enemy. By his own lights Horemheb had done nothing but good for the Two Lands, had prevented the ascent of a foreigner to the throne, and protected a queen from her own folly. He could hardly be faulted for the fact that Egypt had learned of what she did, and loathed her for it. Even if he had taken advantage of it to gain power over the queen's life and fate—who could blame him, after all? He only did what any strong man would.

Egypt needed a strong king. Ay had said it, who was too old and too worn to be as strong as Egypt needed. He would not dispose of the man who meant to be his heir. He was too wise a man, too devoted to Egypt.

Sometimes Nofret was sure that she was going as mad as the queen. There were Leah and Johanan in the city, waiting for her to do what they had agreed on in that room in the travelers' lodging—what they had imposed on her by sheer force of will. There was the queen, wandering distracted by the river, driving her chariot headlong in and about the city, sitting in court like a painted image, and never a moment's true thought in her.

And there was Nofret, doubting everything, knowing nothing, and too much the coward to move. She could refuse her part in the Apiru plot—for plot it was, and high treason, and if it were known, she would die, and not either slowly or easily. She could trust that her lady's fears after all were false, and she was in no danger; she would mourn the Lord Ay when he died, accept his heir as her king, and be queen as she had been for so long, whole and sane and freed at last from grief.

Nofret could hope for such a thing, but Leah had seen otherwise. Leah was the seeress of her people. She had seen a soldier without mercy, who lived only for the power that he could gain; who would take a poor distracted queen, and use her, even treat her kindly since it served his purpose, but in the end, when she failed to present him with an heir, he would dispose of her and take a wife who would do what she could not. He might even love her in his fashion, but love to such a man was as nothing beside his yearning to be king.

Nofret had seen what he was. She had heard him in Amon's temple so long ago, and seen his face when he came bearing Prince Zennanza's head and hands. That was the man unmasked. No other was the truth.

Yet even if she held herself to that, there was still the enormity of what she proposed to do. Ankhesenamon would never consent to be anything but queen. She had lived so, and so she would die. She would never take the road that her father had taken. It was not in her.

If Leah and Johanan had their way, Nofret would force it on her. Nofret had insisted that she have time to speak to her lady, to persuade her if she could, to lead her away of her own will. But looking at Ankhesenamon in court, crowned with plumes of gold, cradling the scepter, she could see nothing else, not even the woman who roamed the riverbanks in search of a thing that could not be.

And when Ankhesenamon transformed herself from queen to distracted woman, Nofret could say nothing to her that she would hear. It was the chariot today, careening through the city with reckless disregard for anyone who got in her way, then out into the Red Land, the desert shimmering under the pitiless sun. Nofret had the parasol, clutching it against the wind of their speed, and was nearly flung out of the chariot for it. The guards were well behind, their horses laboring to catch the queen's swift mares. Even those were taxed by the pace she set: their coats were sodden with sweat, silver-white darkened to the blue-black of the skin beneath.

Ankhesenamon had some remnant of sense left: she slowed the horses as a charioteer does, little by little, letting them come down to a walk. They trod lightly still, but their sides were heaving, dripping with sweat and foam. The queen turned them slowly. They walked back to the city, meeting the guards on the way, with their blown and stumbling horses. They were walking, leading the beasts, to spare them the weight of armored men in the chariots.

Ankhesenamon did not even glance at them. Her eyes were fixed on the city's walls, on the gate that was open, waiting for her to ride in. Nofret wondered how it seemed to her: welcoming or threatening or simply there, without significance except as a barrier to be passed.

There was no telling what she thought. Once Nofret would have known or been able to guess. She was blind now to her lady's heart as to everything else—everything but the Apiru's god, the god that she would not worship, because he was no god of hers. He reared behind her eyes like a pillar of fire. He willed her to do what every grain of wit and sense cried out against, because it was mad; because it was death if she failed. And even if she did not . . .

She was a coward. She had never thought she would welcome the name. She could not do it. She could not snatch her lady away and carry her off into Sinai, where her father waited, and his god with him, and the people that he had made his own.

∎   ∎   ∎

Ankhesenamon handed her chariot and her horses to those who could best tend both, and went to her bath to scour away the dust and sweat of her wild ride. There was blood on her cheek: stone flung up by the wheels or stone flung by someone in the city, Nofret did not know and could not remember. She cleansed it carefully while Ankhesenamon sat unresisting, not caring even for her vanity, nor asking if the cut was deep, or if it would scar. In fact it was slight, a scratch only; but a woman with all her wits about her, a woman who was beautiful and knew it, would at least have asked.

She wandered away almost before her bath was done. There was court still to come, but she refused the court dress, indicating instead a simple linen gown, little better than a servant's. "I must look," she said. "The river—I must—"

Now, if Nofret was to do it, she must move. But she could not bring herself to follow. She did something that she had not done before: she sent a guard in the queen's wake, with orders to let her be but to protect her if she should fall into danger.

That was a refusal, as complete as could be, of everything that Leah had wished on her. And yet she felt as if she had done nothing but what was sensible—too sensible. Nothing was done that could not be undone. There was time still. Years, if foresight was true, before Ay went into his tomb.

Could Leah wait that long? Could Johanan, with his Apiru face and his scarred back, who might even now be hunted down and killed for escaping the tomb-building in Thebes?

They would leave. Nofret would be in peace. Ankhesenamon would live as she could. Nofret would guard her. Horemheb would be no danger to her while Nofret lived.

■　■　■

Ankhesenamon came back from the river with mud on her feet.

"She tried to wade in," the guard said. "She said she saw a boat."

"Not a boat," said Ankhesenamon, startling them both. "A basket. I saw a basket."

Nofret caught the guard's eye. "A duck had a nest in the reeds," he said.

"It was a basket," said Ankhesenamon, "woven of rushes from the riverbank and caught in the reeds. I tried to fetch it. He stopped me. You will have him whipped."

His eye rolled white. Nofret shook her head at him. He did not look greatly comforted. She waved him out. He fled without shame, escaping to the safety of his guard-room.

As Nofret had expected, Ankhesenamon forgot him as soon as he was gone. She fretted over the basket that she had lost, but she made no move to go back for it. Nofret coaxed her into yet another bath and yet another linen gown—it was too late by far for her to grace the court with her presence. There was still the day's feast, but Nofret chose not to remember it. She had food fetched from the kitchens, dainties to tempt a delicate appetite, some of which Ankhesenamon even nibbled on. The wine was heavily spiced and dosed with a potion that would calm her and help her to sleep. It was not the strong drug that Leah had given Nofret to give the queen. That was hidden among Nofret's belongings, wrapped and wrapped again in the scraps of linen that she used to stanch the blood of her courses.

Tonight and every night till she brought the queen to him drugged and compliant, Johanan would be waiting with a boat to take them away down the river. If he was caught he would be killed. A renegade had no life worth mentioning, nor any hope, once he was discovered.

Nofret watched her lady slip into a drowse. It was a rare peace for her, a rare moment of rest. She did not fight it. She seemed barely aware of it. Her mind was still fixed on the basket that she fancied she had seen in the reeds. "It had a baby in it," she murmured. "It did. I saw him move. He babbled like water running, no fear in him at all. He'll make a king, that bold child. He'll make a king indeed.''

''Yes,'' said Nofret to soothe her. ''Yes, lady.''

Ankhesenamon sighed and closed her eyes. Her breathing steadied and deepened. She had fallen asleep.

Nofret watched her for a while. She did not move or wake. There were guards on the door, and maids in their gaggle outside. Nofret left them with some reluctance. But tonight was her night to bathe, and she needed it badly after her ride in the queen's chariot. She could trust so many guards and servants, surely, to look after one small sleep-sodden woman.

■　■　■

Nofret lingered in the bath, in the quiet and the deep pleasure of warm water on her skin. She even washed her hair, then with the help of a little Nubian maid she combed out all its tangles. The maid was enthralled with it: it fell to her hips, and it was thick, and its color was the darkest of reds. Nubians never grew such manes; their hair was like fleece or like black smoke, and they cropped it short or else grew it only long enough to plait with beads and feathers.

Sunset had come and gone before Nofret returned to her post. Her hair, still damp, was demurely plaited. She had put on a new linen gown. She felt cool and clean and almost content.

When she came to her lady's chamber, the bed was empty. The maids were asleep or playing at hounds and jackals in one of the lesser rooms. Nofret asked them nothing. There would be no answer, no more than there would be from the guards. The queen was gone, and no one had seen her go.

Johanan had come, or Leah. They had taken her without Nofret's aid, knowing that Nofret would prove a faintheart.

She should go to her room and sleep and pretend that she had seen as little as the maids or the guards. And then when morning came and there was no lady to wake and to prepare for the ceremonies of the sunrise, Nofret would be as innocent as anyone else.

But what if it had not been the Apiru? What if Horemheb had had his own plot to be rid of the queen who hated him, who did her best to stand in the way of his rise to power? And if it was not Horemheb, what of any number of other people in Egypt, high and low, who called her traitor and worse for what she had done with the king of Hatti?

Nofret went out quietly. Every bone and muscle screamed at her to run, but that would have attracted suspicion. Until she knew who had taken the queen, she would tell no one. She would discover it for herself, and then choose whether to raise the alarm or to pretend that she knew nothing. If Ay or Horemheb resorted to torture of the servants . . .

She would not think of that until she must. She walked as slowly as she could bear to. The river first, in case it was Ankhesenamon who had taken herself away, and gone back to hunt for the imagined child in his duck's-nest basket. She would think of crocodiles no more than she thought of the torments that Egypt could inflict on a servant who had failed to guard her mistress.

There was no moon tonight. The stars were hazed with the river's moisture, swimming as through water. They shed no light worth the name. Nofret groped as best she could out of the palace and through the gate in the wall to the open lands along the river. She dared not bring a torch from one of the guardposts; that would be a beacon to draw the guards to her.

Luckily she knew the way. Her eyes, growing accustomed to the dark, were able to pick out the paler glimmer of the path through the shadow that was the growth of reeds along the riverbank. The water itself gleamed faintly in the starlight. She heard the whisper of it as it lapped its expanded bank. In winter there was a whole great elaborate garden running down to the diminished river, but now, in the full of the flood, the garden was a narrow stunted thing and the river as great as a sea under the stars.

Once or twice she glanced back. The white walls of Memphis loomed behind. There was nothing ahead but river. No living thing moved. No night bird called, nor did a jackal cry in the place of tombs away to the west, on the other side of the city. There was only the sound of water and the whisper of wind in the reeds.

The queen had not come here, or if she had, she was long gone. Nofret wavered, turned to go back, but paused. Down along the river's edge, something rustled. A shadow stirred within shadow. Faint, so faint it was all but invisible, she saw a glimmer of paleness. It might be a spirit wandering lost, but spirits did not rattle the reeds, nor stumble and utter a soft cry. Nofret heard distinctly the sound of a body falling.

She had never moved so fast or with such surety in the dark. She nearly fell over the crumpled shape. It was a good body-length yet from the water, half in and half out of a bed of reeds. She hauled it back with desperate urgency, away from the gods knew what danger in the water.

It was Ankhesenamon. She was alive, breathing deep, but unconscious. Nofret, groping along the length of her, found her hand. There was a bottle in it, loosely stoppered. The scent that rose from it made her gasp. "How in the world—"

The scent of Leah's potion was on Ankhesenamon's lips, too. Her fingers were locked about the bottle. However she had found it, whatever had led her to it, she had brought it down to the river and drunk from it, as if she thought it poison and meant to drink it till she died, there by the river that was the life of Egypt.

She had drunk most of it, unless some had spilled when she fell. Leah had assured Nofret that the drug would do no harm, but she had also urged that it be given to the queen in wine, and a few drops only, not the whole drunk undiluted from the bottle.

She was all slack, as if her bones had turned to water. Nofret gathered her up, slight weight as she was, but awkward. The palace—she should go back there, call for the physicians. But what if they were not to be trusted? What if one of them had somehow discovered the bottle and coaxed the queen to drink from it?

So many questions. And no answers but this: a nearly empty bottle, a woman collapsed from the power of the drug, night and the river and death by drowning or in a crocodile's jaws had she fallen a body-length closer to the water. Nofret began to walk, but not toward the palace.

She walked down the river, north as the water ran, between the wall and the water. Maybe a god guided her feet. She wore Sobek's amulet with Amon's: Sobek, crocodile-god, protector of travelers along the river. He might well have chosen to direct her on the right path and to make light the burden she bore, the dreaming body of her lady. But the god she went to was none of Egypt.

She could turn still, go back to the palace, trust that her fears were false and blind chance had caused the queen to search Nofret's belongings for a vial of what well might be poison.

She could not trust so far. All that she trusted, either she carried in her arms or she expected to be waiting in the place that had been agreed. It was not too far to carry a drugged and dreaming woman, but far enough in the dark, on uneven ground, with fear riding her shoulder: that she was followed, that it was a trap, that what would be waiting was not a big black-bearded man in a boat but a company of soldiers.

The quiet of the night was profound. Nofret could not

ever remember such a silence. Even the water's murmur was muted. The wind had died. The only sound was the pad of her feet on the path, and the whisper of reeds when she brushed them. If anyone pursued her, he did it in perfect silence. She could have heard him breathing, so still was the night. But she heard nothing. Nothing at all.

This must be what it was to be in a god's hand, surrounded by his protection. Perfect; absolute. Terrifying. The conviction grew in her that if she turned back, Memphis would be gone. There would be no city, no palace; only the dry land, the abode of the dead.

She could only go forward. All doubt was gone, and irresolution with it. The palace was lost to her. The choice was made, and by no will of hers. The queen herself had made it.

■　■　■

Half lost in a dream, Nofret nearly passed the place of meeting before she remembered what it was. It was a pier built on the flood, little more than a raft of reeds, a place to tie a boat to for a moment or an hour. Fishermen used it, and people who hunted birds along the river, to pause before they ventured the city's greater harborages, or else to conceal the best of their catch from officials who might demand tribute. At night it was deserted, or so Johanan had assured her.

It was deserted now, except for a single boat. It was small, nondescript, such a boat as a common man in Egypt might use to move about on the river: narrow prow and stern, tented deck in the middle, one long oar in the rear to steer and guide it. Nofret could not see if it was painted or ornamented. She suspected not. It must be perfectly anonymous.

Though how anonymous it could be with such a boatman as rose up in it, she could not imagine. Big broad-

shouldered bearded men in desert robes were seldom seen
in Egyptian boats.

He had put off the robes and put on a scrap of loincloth.
The rest—

She gasped, loud as a shout in the silence. "Johanan!
What do you do to your beard?"

"Hush," he said, far softer than she. He held out his
arms. "Give her here. Careful now. Don't rock us till we
sink."

Nofret surrendered her burden as blindly as she had
brought it here. Only when she was relieved of it did she
think to resist. Johanan, his shorn face a dim blur in the
gloom, carried the queen back to the tent and vanished
beneath it. Nofret stumbled after, rocking as the boat
rocked, clumsy on the water as she had not been since she
was a very young tribute-maid in Egypt.

He emerged so suddenly that she nearly cried out,
caught her arm and steadied her, and eased her gently but
firmly to the deck-planking. "Stay there," he commanded
her, soft as a lion's purr.

There was a spell on her: a spell of obedience. She sat
where she was set. He moved back lightly along the boat's
length, cast off its mooring, took up the steering oar and
swung into motion. She was numbly surprised to see how
well he managed it. There seemed to be little that he could
not do, even sail a boat on the river of Egypt.

The boat might seem a small and common thing, but it
was light on the water and remarkably swift. It caught the
current with marvelous smoothness and rode it as lightly
as a falcon rides the wind.

Nofret wavered between the deck-tent and the man in
the stern. Both, then, but the man first. She was steadier
now, more her seamanlike self, moving back toward him
where he stood at the oar.

He loomed above her, broad shoulders and proud head
crowned with stars. His beard was shaven but he had kept

his hair: all of it, braided and wound like a helmet over the pale oval of his face. "Vain," she murmured, looking up at him, "after all."

"Practical," he shot back. "And short of time. There were soldiers roving the city today. Looking for nothing in particular, people said. But searching faces, and pausing when they found a man from the desert."

"Someone knows," Nofret said, "or suspects." She paused. It seemed foolish to keep whispering so far out on the wide expanse of the river, but they were still in Memphis, with far to go before they were away from it. And sound carries over water. "Johanan, I didn't drug her and bring her out here. I found her already by the river, with the bottle in her hand."

"Did you tell her, then? As you were threatening to do?"

"No." She almost said it aloud. She reined her voice back in and went on as softly as she could. "I was a coward. I didn't do anything. But somehow she knew. Somehow she found the bottle, and knew where to go. If this is a trap—"

"God guard and defend us," breathed Johanan.

"I think we should make all the speed we can," Nofret said. "In case—if someone heard us somehow, spied on us, and told—someone—"

"Anyone in Egypt," he said, "would call us traitors and kill us on sight." He paused, head up as if testing the air. "It's dead calm. We can't rig a sail."

"We'll row," she said. "We can take turn and turn."

"I think . . ." He broke off. "Go. Talk to Grand-mother."

"She's here?" Nofret's heart thudded. Leah had insisted that she would not go with them; she would only slow them. She would stay in Memphis, she had said, with some of the tomb-workers who were Apiru or their kin. Later, when it was safe, she would take some of them for guides and venture the desert.

But she was on the boat, in the tent, lit by the faintest flicker of a lamp that after the black night was as bright as day. Ankhesenamon lay soft on heaped rugs and cushions, the bed that had been prepared for her. Leah sat beside her, upright under the low ceiling of the tent, hands folded in her lap, as serene as ever.

There was just room for Nofret in the tiny space, if she sat on her heels and did not jostle the sleeping woman. For she did sleep: her breast rose and fell, and her face had the flush of life.

"She drank most of the bottle," Nofret said by way of greeting. "By herself, without my urging. I don't even know how she found it."

"The god directed her," Leah said. "Oh, child, how you tremble! Were you so afraid?"

"I'm furious," Nofret gritted. "I imagined—gods, horrible things. You can't tell me she knew exactly where to look, and what to do with what she found."

"And yet it seems she did."

"Unless there was a spy, and he—or she—led her, and will lead an army to capture us."

"That could be," said Leah. "There were spies, certainly, and soldiers hunting for us. But she had no part in that. Sometimes the mad see what the sane can perceive only dimly, and hear the gods full and clear."

"But if a god guided her away from Egypt," said Nofret, "she would resist him. She's queen first and always."

"I would wager that the god said nothing of going away, and something of going down to the river, where she would find what she had been seeking."

Nofret pondered that. "Yes," she said at length. "Yes, that would be like a god. Gods always speak the truth, but they never speak it plain."

"On the contrary, child, their truth is the plainest of all.

So plain that no mortal can understand it. Mortals always lie. To themselves, to each other, to the gods. It's the gods who never tell anything but the truth.''

"Truth so perfect it's a lie." The taste on Nofret's tongue was bitter. "I told Johanan as plain a truth as a woman can tell. I didn't mean to come here. I followed my lady, and found her by the river just as the drug took her. I wasn't going to do it at all."

"Of course you were," said Leah. "You simply wouldn't admit it."

"I wasn't," Nofret said fiercely. "I couldn't do it. I didn't want to."

"You did it as you were meant to." Leah's voice was tranquil. "Lie down now and sleep."

"I can't sleep. If we've been spied on, if there are troops waiting for us—"

"The god will guard us," Leah said.

She sounded so like the old king that Nofret could have hit her. Rather than do such a fearful thing, she crawled back out of the tent, into the dark and the stars and the surprising comfort of Johanan's presence. She sat on the deck where he had made her sit while he cast off, clasped her knees and rocked with the slow rocking of the boat on the river. Maybe she slept. Maybe she dreamed. Maybe the whole of it was a dream, and when she woke she would be in her own bed in Memphis, with the queen rousing for the sunrise rite.

But the dream went on and on. Darkness, stars. Scent of water. Boat skimming over it, riding the current, guided lightly by Johanan's oar. The walls of Memphis fell slowly behind. Ahead was the broad black gleam of the river, and the night, and freedom.

Freedom. She had never even let herself think the word. Not for herself. Freedom only to die, most likely, as one who had stolen away the queen of Egypt.

But as she huddled on the deck of that boat in the night,

with long hours yet to dawn and the dread of discovery, she knew a sudden, irresistible elation. Free, however briefly. Free as she had not been—sweet heaven, as she had not been since she was a child, hunting oryx in the hills of Hatti.

Even if she died come morning. Even if she died in pain. It was worth it after all, to remember what she had so long forgotten. To be free.

CHAPTER FORTY-EIGHT

▲

NOFRET must have slept at last, for she dreamed that there were troops waiting downriver of Memphis, a whole flotilla of them, and armies lining the banks, waiting to seize the queen. But when she started up, tensed to warn Johanan before he sailed right into the fleet, the river was empty of anything but a flock of wild geese. She could see them clearly. The light was the pale clear light that comes just before sunrise, when the shadows are long still and black, but water turns bright silver, and the sky is blood-scarlet in the east, deep luminous blue in the farthest west.

Everything was water and sky. From where she crouched she could see no land nor any human thing. The river had carried them far down from Memphis. The air seemed richer here and warmer. Its weight even in the cool of morning was heavy, as if there would be heat later, humid and oppressive.

"Are we going all the way to the ocean?" she asked Johanan.

He was still at the oar. Guilt smote her, hours too late, as he answered her question. "We're going where it's safe to go."

"The sea is safe?"

He stared at her for a moment, maybe incredulous, maybe only too tired to gather the words together. "We're not going to the sea. There's a landing—a village, but it's safe, some of our people are in it. They'll be waiting for us."

"Nothing is safe," Nofret said.

He did not seem to hear her. She straightened stiffly, feeling bruises where she had slept on the hard planking. When her knees had unlocked and her back unkinked, she crawled through the flap of the deck-tent.

Leah was asleep, sitting upright with her chin on her breast. Ankhesenamon had not moved all night long. She lay still as Johanan had laid her, on her back with her arms at her sides. She was alive; she breathed as before. Nothing at all had changed.

Nor did anything change while they made their way down the river in the rising heat of morning. It was strange; Lower Egypt was quite a populous country, at least in the region of Memphis; but that morning no one was minded to set sail on the river. They were all alone in what seemed an endless sea, no company but the water birds, no pursuit but a lone crocodile that drew its wake after them till a flurry of ducks distracted it.

Near noon Johanan bent the boat away from the middle of the stream. So broad as it was there, it seemed to have no shore, but as they curved eastward Nofret saw a line of green that must be land, and red beyond that that must be desert. In the middle of the green was a cluster of brown, the houses of the village that Johanan had spoken of.

It was a mere speck of a village, so small that it did not even boast a temple, though it had its rich man in his house of six whole rooms with a garden in back of it. He was not Apiru but his wife was, and some of her kin had settled in the village. They were not stonecutters like the Apiru of the tombs, but something closer to their world of the desert: herders of goats and sheep, shearers and weavers of wool, makers of a sharp pungent cheese that went surprisingly well with the eternal Egyptian bread and beer.

Nofret never learned what the village was called. It must have had a name—no place in Egypt could be without one—but no one spoke it where she could hear. It was simply *here*, the place where she had come, where she was fed and offered bath and bed. She took food and bath but refused the chance to sleep. The others took it. Ankhesenamon, who had not roused even when she was carried from the boat into the rich man's house, slept as she had since Nofret found her. They had got a little water into her, and a bite or two of bread, which she chewed and swallowed in her dream; but she never woke.

Nofret had nothing to say to the people who lived in this house. They had little to say to her. It was clear that the husband thought her less than nothing, since she was a slave. The wife seemed shy to speechlessness, a little brown mouse of a woman who would not meet Nofret's eyes. Neither appeared to know who slept in the best bed with Leah beside her, nor overmuch to care. Johanan had mumbled something about a cousin and a sleeping sickness before he tumbled headlong into sleep himself. That seemed to be enough.

Nofret felt as if she should stand guard. Once or twice she wandered as far as the door, but she did not go out. Mostly she stayed with Leah and with her lady, watching them sleep, shutting away vision after vision of lovely horror. All of them had to do with being caught, named, condemned for the highest of high treason.

Maybe the god did protect them. No soldiers burst in, no official came to denounce her. No one came at all. It was as if she was alone and perfectly unknown, perfectly safe.

■　　■　　■

"It's the garrisons we have to worry about," Johanan said. He had roused near sunset, eaten voraciously, and announced that they were leaving as soon as it was full dark. Their hosts uttered weak protests, but Nofret could see the depth of their relief. Unsuspicious they might be, but they were inconvenienced by the presence of so many guests.

Johanan bought from them a donkey that might have been near kin to the one that carried the old king away from Akhetaten. It was just as small, just as motheaten, and just as cantankerous. It came laden with waterskins and carrying a substantial sack, but even so burdened it managed to support the slack weight of Ankhesenamon. She was wrapped in robes that must have been Leah's, and veiled as an Apiru woman preferred to be when she went abroad, a faceless, shapeless bundle of black wool amid the other bundles on the donkey's back.

Nofret must have cut a similar figure herself, but afoot, dressed in an old robe that had belonged to the rich man's wife. It reeked of the musky scent that the woman preferred, but it was decently woven and not too threadbare, and it was voluminous: it covered her from head to foot. With a veil over her face she was well concealed, like a taller, broader shadow of the swaddled bundle that was Leah.

There was no one to bid them farewell, no gawkers, not even a child lingering in a doorway. As they had been on the river, they were alone in the world under the vastness of heaven.

From Black Land to Red Land was a single step, from rich earth to bleak desert, sand and stones and sky. Johanan took the lead with a staff in his hand and the donkey on its rope beside him. Leah walked as strongly as Nofret, and maybe with more ease in the shifting landscape of sand and rock. Their pace was steady, set as much by the donkey as by anything else, middling slow walking pace that paused rarely to rest or to drink or to eat.

They went by the stars, tracking east toward Sinai. Johanan walked as if he knew the land well, marking the path by means invisible to Nofret. She was a creature of the mountains and the plains of Hatti, and then of cities. Desert was all strange to her. Its landmarks shifted eternally as sand will. In deepening night it was simply a shadow lit by stars, but a shadow that to Johanan must be as distinct as the streets of Memphis in the dusk.

She had to trust that he would lead them well, and not cast them far out of the way or else stumble into a guardpost full of soldiers who answered to Horemheb. Her own instincts were useless here. Those all cried to her to wait for daylight, to take the roads, to follow the well-marked ways into the hands of the enemy.

She prayed a great deal as she trudged through the night, following the others more by scent and sound than by sight. Leah was just ahead of her, a waft of sandalwood, a whisper of feet in sand. The donkey's four-footed step-and-glide shifted to a soft clatter on stone, but Leah's footfalls then were all but silent.

Nofret prayed to no god in particular. Egypt's gods held power here, for this was still Egypt, but they were changed as the land was changed, no longer gentle, no longer propitious, but fierce and cold and strange. Amon was the hammer of the sun. Horus was the blind eye of the moon and the soar of the falcon at sunrise, beautiful but unreachably remote. Nut, whose domain was the night, whose body was the arc of heaven set with stars, arched higher and farther than ever she had above the Black Land.

Nofret prayed to all of them and none, blind wordless prayers compounded of fear and hope and desperation. She did not feel free here as she had on the river. She felt terribly trapped, lost in a land that was all alien to her, bound in the company of people so foreign that they worshipped but one incalculable god, drawn along with them by no will of her own. But for her lady she would have dug in her heels and refused the whole of it, demanded to be taken back to places she knew, and no matter how she suffered for it.

This was not even the world of the living. Egyptians set the abode of the dead in the west beyond the horizon of the Red Land, but who was to say that it had not extended itself into the eastern desert? Except for the lone falcon in the sunrise, she saw no bird, no animal, and certainly no human creature. Sometimes, far off, she heard the howling of jackals. But jackals were the guides of the dead, servants of Anubis whose body was a man's but whose head was a jackal's.

Soon after sunrise of that first long night, Nofret stumbled into an obstacle that yielded and turned, catching her when she tried to push on. She stared blankly into Leah's face. It looked as haggard as she felt. Dust was thick on it. She scrubbed at her own face, grimacing at the grittiness of sand on skin.

Over Leah's shoulder she saw that Johanan had stopped and was lowering Ankhesenamon to the ground. One of the donkey's bundles was a tent, no more than an outsize cloak or blanket of woven goat's hair, with Johanan's walking-staff for its tentpole. It was cramped beneath, but it was shelter. Nofret was glad of it in the cold of dawn, and would be gladder of it, no doubt, in the full fierce heat of the day.

They ate in silence, barley bread and goat cheese and an onion each, and water from the donkey's burden. Nofret coaxed a little water into Ankhesenamon. Much of it dribbled out, but some went down: her throat worked as she swallowed.

"Will she ever wake?" asked Nofret. Her voice was rough with dryness and disuse. None of them had said a word since they left the village; strange to know that now, and for the first time. Silence and the desert were inextricably a part of one another.

"She'll wake when the god wills," Leah said.

"You mean you don't know." Nofret was too tired to be angry. But dismayed—yes, she was that. "What if she dies out here? If a physician could save her—"

"The god guards her," said Leah.

Nofret turned her back on Leah, lay down beside her lady and covered her eyes with her arm and set her teeth. She wanted to cry, loud and long and utterly useless. She had come to this place as if driven, without will or wit to resist. There was no going back. Only going forward.

Johanan was outside: on guard, she supposed. There was no room for him in the tent. She wished him well of the donkey's company.

Sleep was slow in coming. Ankhesenamon lay unmoving beside her. Leah slept, snoring softly. The sun came up, and with it the heat. The tent kept out the worst of it, and most of the flies that rose with the day.

Both struck her with breathtaking force when she crawled out. She had to relieve herself; and she could not sleep. Johanan had set up a smaller tent beside the larger one: his mantle propped on a bit of bush. The donkey, hobbled, grazed in a patch of thorny scrub.

The sun's light was blinding, stunningly strong. She rested briefly in the shade of a rock. A flicker of movement made her start: a lizard on the track of a beetle. The lizard blurred into motion, but the beetle darted into a crevice too narrow for the lizard to enter. The lizard paused, mouth open. It seemed to be panting as a dog does; or maybe it was a silent scream, frustration as complete as Nofret's own.

She crawled back into the tent. It was hot and still and redolent of musk and goat and human sweat, but it was shade. She sipped a mouthful of still-cool water, held it for a long while on her tongue, let it sink in as water seeps into sand.

■   ■   ■

Night found them on their way again, taking advantage of
the cool and the darkness. Nofret had slept a little after all,
enough to go on with. Her eyes were gritty, her mind
blurred and slow, but it took no great power of intellect to
follow Leah, who followed the donkey, who followed Johanan eastward by the stars.

She had made no great study of maps or journeys. The
tribute-train from Mitanni had come to Akhetaten by the
royal road and then on the river of Egypt. Nofret remembered little but heat and dust, endless walking and too-
brief pauses. There had been a garrison, she remembered
that. And when they came to Egypt they had kept pausing
in this city or that so that the envoy could worship in every
temple there was time for. He had been a religious man,
and superstitious. Everything he saw or heard or fancied
was an omen for good or ill. He had worn so many amulets
about his neck that he seemed to be wearing a huge clashing collar.

She still had her amulets of Amon and of Sobek. She
took to touching them as she walked, stroking the smooth
carved surfaces. She sensed no power in them, no spark
of divinity. They were only stone. But they comforted her
in their small way.

She was clutching them in her hand in the deep night,
the fourth from the village north of Memphis, when Johanan led them straight to a camp of soldiers. He had not
lost his bearings, surely not, and he was as remote from
any garrison as his craft could take him, but there were
soldiers in that wadi in the deep desert. What they were
doing there, Nofret could not begin to guess. Hunting,
maybe: lion or gazelle or some beast more fabulous than
either. Prospecting for copper or for turquoise—did they
not mine turquoise at least in Sinai? Or else, and worst of

all, they were lying in wait for an escaped queen and her accomplices.

Ankhesenamon by this time was conscious enough to sit up on the donkey's back for an hour or two at a time, though she seemed tranced or spelled. Her eyes though open were blurred as if with sleep, and her face wore no expression. In the days she lay so, open-eyed, barely blinking, neither speaking nor seeming to notice where she was. She would eat if fed, and drink, and relieve herself when she was led apart. She would not answer when questioned, though she responded to the sound of a voice. Any voice, saying anything, and even the howl of a jackal.

For all Nofret knew, her lady's mind was gone, lost among the dead or wandering her palace in Egypt. An Egyptian would have said that the ka, the double, was apart from its body. Whether it would come back, Nofret did not know, nor would she ask Leah. It was petty, that refusal, but there was no accounting for the heart's foibles.

With Ankhesenamon awake but unaware and the rest of them grown incautious with safety, they were nearly in the camp before any of them realized what they were doing. Outside of storm season travelers often walked in the wadis, the dry sandy riverbeds that were as smooth as roads in the stony waste. These soldiers, trusting in a clear sky and an empty land, had made camp in a broad turning where the sand was wide and clear. Elsewhere the banks were cut deep, but here the wadi's eastern edge eased into the desert, a low hill of firm sand that was not ill climbing for a fit man.

The camp seemed as little concerned for trouble as the travelers themselves had been. There were fires lit without concealment, and tents in a rough circle about them, each with its thicket of spears thrust into the sand. There was a chariot beside the largest tent, with a pair of horses tethered by it, nibbling on a heap of dry fodder. Men must have had to carry the chariot into the wadi: the sand was deep, and would have caught the wheels till they stuck fast.

Right on the edge of the camp, just out of reach of the outermost fire, the travelers stood as if they had forgotten how to move. The camp filled that part of the wadi, but there was room to skirt it if they were careful. Nofret was about to say so when one of the horses whinnied.

The donkey brayed a reply. It was a she-donkey and those were stallions. They must have caught wind of her: they began to fret and tug at their tethers. Men came stumbling out of tents, cursing the racket. One of them had a brace of hunting hounds on leads. They began to bay, leaping and plunging against their collars, one toward the horses, the other toward the dark where the travelers stood rooted.

The donkey, being a donkey and contrary, had fallen silent after that one, betraying call. She would not move, either, though Johanan tugged at her rope.

The light of the camp flowed out toward them, borne by men with torches. Nofret would have dived for cover, but Ankhesenamon on her donkey was as deeply tranced as ever, and neither Johanan nor Leah seemed able to move. Johanan, having done what he could to budge the donkey, stood still in the torchlight, looking taller and narrower than ever, a shape of robes and shadow.

One of the Egyptians called out as he approached, in what he no doubt fondly fancied was the language of the desert tribes. It sounded like, "Who what name give you?"

"Sirs!" Johanan called back in Egyptian, but with such an accent as she had never heard in him before: a tribesman's accent, and reasonably convincing, too. It would hardly do for a man in desert robes to sound like a nobleman from Thebes. "Sirs," he said again, "well met on a dark night. We're travelers into Sinai. My grandmother is tired and my sister is ill. May we rest awhile under your protection?''

Nofret held her breath. Shyness had never been a flaw of Johanan's, nor had she known him for a coward. But this was bolder even than she would have ventured.

It had its effect. The soldiers glanced at one another. After a moment one said, ''Better ask his lordship.''

''By all means,'' said Johanan, ''consult your commander. You'll not want to take in guests for an hour without his say-so.''

Again the soldiers exchanged glances. The one who had spoken before said, ''Come with us.''

▪   ▪   ▪

Nofret would not have put it past the gods to set Horemheb himself here in the desert far from any city, lying in wait for three runaway slaves and a runaway queen. But the man in the largest tent was a stranger, thickly built for an Egyptian, with a broad, solid-jawed fighter's face. He was surly with being waked so deep in the night, but he had a great deal of native courtesy. He poured wine for Leah with his own hands, and had his cook prepare a meal for them as if they had been princes and not mere wanderers in the waste.

The Apiru seemed not at all dismayed to be the guests of an Egyptian commander and his troops. Ankhesenamon was oblivious as ever. She ate, drank, but said nothing. To Nofret's anxious eye her bearing and her face were unmistakably royal, but in her robes and veils she must have seemed no more than a simple desert woman, mute and not greatly gifted with wit. She attracted no notice.

None of the women did. Johanan kept their eyes on himself, chattering endlessly of everything and nothing. He managed to say very little of consequence, and nothing at all of where he had come from or where he was going. Mostly he regaled them with tales of hunting lions, which was what the commander was doing here, and trading for purple in Tyre, and searching out new oases in the wilderness of Gaza.

"There's one," he said, "deep in, where even the wolves of the desert fear to go; where, it's said, the dates grow already dipped in honey, and the trees pour forth sap that's pure sweet milk. A goddess blessed it long ago, they say, and promised that any traveler who was worthy could rest there for the span of a night and a day. But only as long as that. Anyone who overstays his time wakes on the second morning to find the dates turned to stones and the milk of the trees to ashes, and even the water in the well is foul."

"That's a marvel, to be sure," the commander said. He did not share the meal but he was clearly fond of wine. He was on his second cup. "Tell me, have you ever been there?"

"Alas, not I," said Johanan, wide-eyed with innocence. "But I met a man who had, and who was no fool. He left within the time allotted, and he swears that he's never since found milk or honey to equal what he tasted in the oasis. Everything he's eaten and drunk since, he says, has been a disappointment."

"One could call that a curse," the commander said.

"So one could," said Johanan amiably.

■　■　■

They escaped near dawn. Johanan wanted to reach an oasis that he said was within reach before the day's heat overtook them. He was remarkably vague about its location, while seeming to give the commander precise directions. They parted with an exchange of gifts: a skin of the commander's wine for a finely woven rug that had been one of Ankhesenamon's saddlecloths.

It was by no means a fair exchange, in Nofret's estimation. The commander must be grinning at the gullible tribesman. The tribesman seemed disgustingly pleased with himself, calling out cheerful farewells to the whole camp, including the dogs and the horses.

"He cheated you," Nofret said when the camp was well behind.

Johanan's grin was clearly visible in the early-morning light. "He did, didn't he? He's congratulating himself on it, too."

"You could have given him something less valuable, and still left him feeling as if he'd got the better of you."

"Oh," he said, "but this convinces him completely that I'm a fool and all tribesmen are idiots. He didn't even notice you, let alone your lady. He was too busy being the mighty, the noble, the infinitely superior Egyptian."

"And not thinking that maybe we're worth inquiring into further." Nofret shook her head. "There's such a thing as being too clever."

"And may the god protect me from it," he said, still grinning.

CHAPTER FORTY-NINE·

▲

AFTER the camp of the soldiers they met no human creature. The desert was empty of men though full of living things: birds, lizards, snakes, jackals hunting in the night. The night after they left the camp, Nofret glimpsed movement as she trudged over yet another hill of sand and stones. A lean prick-eared shape loped ahead of them, seeming for a moment to be leading them, guiding Johanan who was their guide in the waste.

It glanced over its shoulder. Its eyes were lambent in the gloom, not green or red as other animals' would be, but frosty white like stars. She blinked hard. For an instant the creature ran not on four legs but on two: a man's lean body but jackal-headed, jackal-eyed, with fangs that gleamed as it smiled at her.

Jackal-headed Anubis was guide of the dead, and Egyptian dead at that. She was all too much alive. She ached in every bone. Her feet were raw with night after night of walking in thin-soled sandals. She was thirsty, hungry, tired beyond belief. Leah must be even worse, though she walked with apparent ease. She would not let herself be mounted on the donkey behind Ankhesenamon. She could walk, she insisted. She would not hear of anything else.

They found water that night, a well in the desert, so small and so secret that not even a tussock of grass marked it. There was not enough water in it to fill more than one of the donkey's waterskins, but it would do.

Johanan would not say how much farther they had to go to be with his people in Sinai. They were far out of traveled ways, out of the world even, though not—Johanan said firmly—lost. Even if Nofret had known any map or road of this desert, she would not have known where they were, except that they were north and east of Egypt.

She had not known there was so much desert in the world, or that she would have to walk over it. It was tumbled, broken, barren desert, and mountains looming against the sky. Each night they loomed closer. Each night Ankhesenamon came more to herself, but never completely. Never enough that she seemed to know where she was.

If her spirit was gone and did not come back, Nofret did not know what would become of her. She was meek, who had always been royally imperious; docile, who had accepted no one's will but her own since her father went to the house of purification in Akhetaten. It hurt to watch her, to see the face so lovely and so empty, the eyes unseeing, staring out over the dry land as if it had been the green richness of her garden.

Maybe she was in comfort. She knew no pain. No memory vexed her. She was a body without a spirit, going wherever she was led.

"Did he come this way?" Nofret asked Johanan as they walked almost easily on a stretch of level sand. "Was he as far out of himself as she is? Did he ever come back?"

Johanan did not need to ask whom she meant. "He led us, with the god in front of him."

"Of course," said Nofret after a pause. "And she follows, as blind as she ever was."

"It's better so," said Johanan. "When we come to the place of the tribes, she'll wake."

"Do you know that?" she demanded of him. "Can you be sure of it?"

"I was promised," he said. "As I was promised that no danger would touch us. Haven't we come safe through the lions' country, and through the burning land, and through the camp of the soldiers?"

"We're not there yet," she muttered. "At this pace we may never be."

"Have hope," said Johanan.

"Hope is for fools." Nofret speeded her pace till she was well ahead of him, keeping a straight path from sand to stones to trackless waste. She heard the others behind her. A shadow came and went in front of her: the jackal again, or one of its kin. She knew nothing better than to follow it, though it might do no more than lead her to its den.

■　■　■

It led her to the dawn, to a hollow in a hill of stones, where a spring bubbled from the rock, and on the wan grass beside it they could slake their thirst and rest and even sleep.

The others slept, even Ankhesenamon. Nofret lay awake. In the shade of the stones she had chosen not to take shelter within the tent where Leah and Ankhesenamon were. Johanan had set himself on guard: sitting up against a rock, shrouded in his robes and veils, watching the sun rise and with it the hammering heat.

It was not so terrible here. The water's presence cooled the air a little. She laved her face and cooled her aching, blistered feet, sighing with the simple pleasure of it.

There were eyes on her. She looked up from the water to Johanan's face. He had let fall his veils. His beard was coming back, black and thick already, but the shape of his jaw was still clear to see. His eyes were dark, shadowed under the strong brows.

She flushed and looked down again to the water, and to her feet in it, raw white and raw red, nothing lovely about them at all. She withdrew them hastily and tucked them under her skirts.

What in the world was she doing? She had walked naked through the great cities of Egypt, and here in the desert, under one man's eyes, she went all modest like a wild tribeswoman.

Deliberately she thrust her feet out again and dipped them in the water, washing her ankles too, and her legs to the knee. She was filthy inside and out, though she had been scrubbing herself as desert people did, with sand. But nothing cleansed deeper or better than clear water on the skin.

Her temper was up, and the water was here, clean and plentiful. She stripped off all her robes, every reeking one of them, and washed herself as best she could from head to foot. She did not care if he watched. She rather hoped he would. He had offered nothing but what was most proper and most brotherly since he returned to Memphis.

A splash beside her made her start. He was there, his robes in a heap beside hers, but unlike her he had kept a rag knotted about his loins. Pity, that. The scars on his back flexed and shifted as he moved. Some were barely healed: they had opened not long ago. He had betrayed no sign, nor seemed to be in pain.

He scoured himself as she had, with sand from the verge and water from the spring. He even loosed his hair from its plaits and washed that, working out knots and tangles with fierce concentration. He had a great deal of hair, almost as much as Nofret had, and nearly as long.

She saw the moment when he lost patience. She was clean herself and had given up on her hair: she was thinking rather longingly of Egyptian cleanliness, a skull shaved smooth and free of itches and vermin. But that would have to wait till she came to a civilized place, if there was any such thing in this bleak outland of the world.

She moved in behind him, plucked the comb from his fingers, began to ply it. It was a rich thing, carved of white bone and ornamented with the heads and horns of gazelles. He must have kept it from the time when he was a prince of tomb-builders in Akhetaten.

He sighed and leaned into her hands. No shyness in him, or none that he would let her see. She thought of tugging till he yelped, but her hands were cruel enough as it was.

He endured in silence. He had mixed a bit of herb from the poolside with the sand; he carried its sharp green scent over the musk of humanity. It was a pleasant mingling, more pleasant than any unguent she could remember.

She combed and coaxed his hair till it was smooth. Then sitting on her heels she plaited it in two long braids and wound it about his head as it had been before. He was asleep sitting up, or so she thought, breathing deep and slow, the long muscles of his body seeming longer with ease. She smoothed her hands across the width of his shoulders, careful of the scars, those that were healed and those that were rough still and scabbed.

"If I had ointment," she said, "I could soften these."

She had been talking to herself, but he heard her. He glanced over his shoulder. His eyes were bright, unclouded with sleep. "In the donkey's pack," he said, "wrapped in a bit of wool."

She resisted moving, but curiosity thrust her up. She had to hunt among a remarkable variety of things, most of which she did not remember seeing before, but in the end she found it: a packet wrapped in faded black wool. Inside was a jar of pale chalcedony with a seal on its lid. She knew the symbol on the seal.

As she went to kneel behind him again she said, "You don't buy anything but the best, do you?"

"It was a gift," he said, "from a man who was a king."

Akhenaten, he must mean. Nofret broke the seal and lifted the lid. A glorious scent rose to surround her, the scent of the richest of ointments, compounded of myrrh and aloes. It was made to soothe the skin of queens, and to delight princes with its fragrance.

A pair of slaves could take pleasure enough in it, when all was considered. Nofret smoothed it into Johanan's scars, one by one and as lightly as she could. He did not gasp or flinch. His skin around the scars was softer than one might imagine a man's could be. Soft, she thought, as sleep. She laid her cheek against it.

He turned so smoothly that she was not caught off balance at all. His breast was rougher than his back, thick with curly hair. She worked her fingers into it. His voice rumbled under her ear. "You understand that if we go on, there'll be no hope for you—for either of us. I'll name you my wife in the assembly of my people."

She stiffened, but she could not bring herself to pull away. "How many wives do you have already?"

"None," he answered.

"Not even a concubine? No one at all to keep you warm of nights?"

"I only need one woman," he said. "I've never needed more."

"I'm surprised no one's married you off. Aren't you a prince among your people?"

"Who would try? Grandmother knows who was meant for me. She warned Father long ago not to try to find me a wife among the Apiru."

"And you? Are you so blindly obedient?"

"If this is obedience," he said, "then I embrace it."

"Maybe I don't want you," said Nofret.

He laughed under her ear, with his arms about her and his body warming to her. She had not embraced a man so in a long stretch of years. Not since Seti died.

Poor Seti. She could not remember his face nor the sound of his voice. She could barely remember the feel of his body against hers.

Then even that was gone. Her only memory was this: this man, this body. His loincloth had vanished, fallen and forgotten. She gasped as he passed the gate, not for pain but for the intensity of her pleasure.

■   ■   ■

They woke in the cool of evening, tangled in one another. Nofret had a brief and piercing memory of waking beside another man, of the stab of impatience mixed with affection that had always struck her when she lay with Seti. but this was no one who mattered so little to her as Seti had. This was the half of her soul.

This big raspy-bearded man with his surprisingly delicate touch, this stranger whom she had barely seen since he was a child. This slave of a god whom she did not know. She tensed to recoil, found herself clinging tighter, winding limbs with his, as if she could sink into him, make herself a part of him.

It was like a sickness; but sweet—honey-sweet. "I want all of you," she said. "Every living part of you."

"It's been yours since we were children," he said.

"No," said Nofret. "If I didn't know, you couldn't, either."

"Some of us are slower than others," he said.

He was laughing at her. He usually was. Damnable, maddening man. She kissed him so deep he gasped, and bit him—but not quite hard enough to draw blood. He kept right on laughing.

■ ■ ■

Leah knew, of course. Ankhesenamon knew nothing, no more than she had since Nofret found her by the river in Memphis. Neither of them said anything. In the days they kept to the tent, and Nofret lay with Johanan in what shade they could find, sometimes no more than their two mantles draped over the skeleton of a bush. Once it was merely the donkey's shadow as it dozed hipshot in the sun. However slight the shelter, it was always enough. They made it so.

In the nights they walked hand in hand. Often a jackal guided them, servant of Egyptian Anubis in the wilderness of Sinai. They were happy, there in the desert where it seemed no living thing could endure. Yes, even Nofret, who had been certain that she would never be more than vaguely content.

CHAPTER FIFTY

▲

ONE night as they walked under a moon that had swelled to the full, they followed it and their jackal-guide straight into the dawn. There in the wan light was a hollow in a hill of stones, and beyond it the loom of a mountain. In the hollow was a cluster of tents, a dog or three, a flock

of goats and sheep. Their center was a green place, a tree,
a well ringed with stones as carefully carved and joined
as any in Egypt.

Nofret halted on the camp's edge, caught in confusion.
Johanan's hand had slipped from hers. The jackal was nowhere that she could see. The dogs came barking and
clamoring, but there was no snarl in it, no flash of teeth.
They were all leaping about Johanan, who was laughing,
ruffling the ears of a grey-muzzled bitch, while the others—her pups, no doubt—sniffed eagerly at his robes.

He turned still laughing. "Grandmother, Nofret, look!
It's Tirzah. She remembers me."

"So I see," said Leah. She had gone wrapped and
shrouded in veils since she left Egypt. They were lowered
now, and she was smiling. She looked as young as Nofret
had ever seen her, tired though she was and worn thin with
traveling.

People were coming out of the tents, drawn by the dogs'
barking. They were familiar people though Nofret had
never seen them before: tall, most of them, and strongly
built, with proud faces. Apiru faces. But these were not
the slaves of the tombs. These were the wild tribesmen,
the people of the desert.

They flocked about Johanan as the dogs had, sweeping
his grandmother with them, chattering too fast for Nofret
to understand. She was left outside of them, a stranger,
alone and forgotten. Somehow she had got hold of the
donkey's rope. Her lady sat mute on the beast's back, staring as she had stared for days and nights out of count,
seeing nothing but her own dream.

Nofret knew the instant when her eyes changed. When
she drew herself erect. When she saw.

A man was coming down off the mountain, walking
through the camp. His stride was long and easy, the gait
of a man who walks often and walks far. He carried himself erect, so that he seemed much taller than in fact he

was. Not that he was a small man, not by any means, but compared to the one who walked behind him he was no more than middling tall.

Nofret would not have known him at all without his companion. Johanan grown older, beard grown to his breast and shot with grey, would look exactly so: just as Aharon did, and not so much different than he had when he left Egypt. The other man could only be her lady's father.

He was profoundly different. His hair had grown long, and his beard, concealing the long narrow skull, the long jaw. The stubble of them had been black when Nofret knew him; now they were whitened to silver. The nose was as long as ever and as haughtily arched, with the same scornful flare of nostrils. So too the eyes, long, heavy-lidded, seeming to regard the world down the length of that royal nose.

But their expression had changed beyond recognition. They were awake; aware. They had lost their dreamer's look. They saw clearly, a clarity that was no more sane and no more simply human than their vagueness had been before.

This was not a king who refused to be a king. This was a seer of the desert people, the prophet of Sinai. People murmured as he came through them. "Moshe. Moshe the prophet."

Ankhesenamon made a sound, not a word, nothing so coherent. She had slid from the donkey's back. She stood beside it, swaying but erect. Her face had come alive, but the life that was in it was terrifying: half anger, half horror. "You are dead," she said in a clear and carrying voice. "You died."

"Here in Sinai," he said, "I live."

His voice was more like his old self than any of the rest. It was still light, still too weak to carry far. He still stammered, though less than before. Death, it seemed, could alter a man's face, but not the voice the gods had given him.

The gods. His god. The Apiru had drawn back, leaving him face to face with his daughter. He took no notice of them.

She noticed them too well. She looked about in incredulity, as one who wakes from a long and sodden sleep to find herself transported to a place so strange as to be incomprehensible. "Who are these people? How did I come here? Have I died?"

"You were brought here," her father said. "The god led you. He guarded you. He guided you to me."

Ankhesenamon shook her head. "No. I'm still in Memphis. I'm dreaming this. Or I died. Is this my punishment for a life ill lived? Am I to spend my death in this desert, among these savages?"

Nofret trampled in, though she knew it was folly. "You haven't died. You aren't in the land of the dead. You're in Sinai. We brought you out of Egypt before you were killed or worse."

Ankhesenamon rounded on her. "What is worse than death? Than this?"

"Slavery," Nofret shot back. "Servitude to the will of a man you hated, who had killed kings to gain the kingship. Imprisonment in your palace, surrounded by people who had no love for you. Danger—"

Ankhesenamon shook her head. Her face was closed, her eyes flat. "You abducted me. You laid a spell on me. Treason—betrayal—"

This was worse than Nofret had feared. Shock, yes, she had expected that. Anger, certainly: she had robbed the queen of her queenship and taken her away from all that she had known. But this cold and royal fury was out of her reckoning.

"Take me back," said the queen of Egypt. "Take me home where I belong."

"There is no going back," said the king who had died and come to live in Sinai. Moshe, they called him here; Moshe the prophet. Nofret must learn to call him that.

Ankhesenamon shook her head. She was set in her fury, blind with it. "I do not wish this. Take me back!"

"No one can take you back," he said, gently inexorable. "You are dead by now in Egypt; dead and vanished. They would have found a scrap of your garment in the rushes by the river where the crocodiles come to feed. They've taken you out of the count of the living. They've mourned you, transformed you into a memory. You'll not live again in the Two Lands."

"No," she said. "You're lying to me. You're envious, you who are dead. You hate me because I am alive. Because I keep my name when yours is all forgotten."

"You're as dead as I," he said.

"No," said Ankhesenamon. She said it over and over.

Her mind was breaking—if there was anything left of it to break. Nofret moved to touch her, to shake her, to rouse her from her stupor. But Moshe was there before her. He laid his hands on his daughter's shoulders.

She struggled. He did not seem to move, but nothing she did sufficed to win her free. When she subsided, gasping for breath, his hands were on her shoulders as they had been before, and his eyes were fixed on her face. "Child," he said in the gentlest of voices, and no stammer in it. "Child, look at me."

She who was no child, who reckoned herself still a queen, resisted his compulsion, but he was too strong. "The god led you to me," he said. "He brought you out of Egypt, from the shadow of your death. He preserved your life against the terrors of the desert. Have you no thanks to offer him? Are you bereft of gratitude?"

"I am not grateful," she said through clenched teeth. "I do not thank him for robbing me of all that was mine."

"You loved him once," her father said.

Her head shook hard. "I never loved him. I loved you, but you are dead. I have forgotten your name."

"My name is Moshe," he said.

She stared at him. For the first time she seemed to see him: not the voice, not the eyes, but the man who stood in front of her. The stranger, the man of the desert. She reached up with a hand that trembled just visibly, and touched him: half on the cheek, half on the bristle of his beard.

She began to shake, not only her hand, but all of her. She looked about. Her eyes were wild. "I don't want to be dead. *I don't want to be dead!*"

He folded his arms about her. She shrank in them, but she did not try to escape. The strength had gone out of her. Her knees buckled. He lifted her as lightly as if she had been the child he called her, cradled her as he must have done when she was small. "Come, child," he said. "Rest. Have peace."

■　　■　　■

He carried her away to a tent that stood apart from the others. Nofret took a step to follow, but could not make herself take the next, or the next. She was still attached to the donkey. She could not see Leah. Johanan was half-hidden in a crowd of people and dogs.

She had no place here. All of them, even Ankhesenamon—they belonged here. Not she. She was a foreigner, no kin to them at all. She had brought her lady where the god willed. Now, for very truth, she was free.

She looked back toward the desert. North and east somewhere was Hatti. The donkey would keep her company. It did not seem greatly overjoyed to have come to this camp, nor overmuch eager to linger. Dogs vexed it. Children were deplorably inclined to swing from its tail. It would be glad to go back to the wilderness.

She turned its head about and began to walk.

A hand closed over hers on the donkey's rope. A body made a wall of itself between Nofret and the desert. Johanan demanded, "Where are you going? Won't you even stay to greet my father?"

"I'm going home," Nofret said.

"Home is here," said Johanan, "at the feet of our holy mountain."

"For you it is," she said. "Not for me. I come from Hatti. Now it's time I went back there."

He was not laughing now, nor looking on her follies with lordly amusement. He was afraid—bold brash Johanan, afraid. "Do I matter so little to you?" he asked her. His voice was almost gentle.

"You matter the world to me," she said. "But I don't belong here. There's no place for me."

"There is a place," he said. He laid his arm about her shoulders. "Here, where you were meant to be."

"I was not—" Nofret broke off. That was not true. But it was not all of it, either. "I can't be one of your modest women. I was never made to be."

"You are what the god made you," he said.

She pulled free. "I have to go."

"And what is there for you in Hatti? Will you be any less a stranger there than you are here where you have friends who love you? Where you have me?"

She could feel herself wavering. She stiffened her resolve—but for what? For misplaced pride?

For shyness. For fear. If he came in front of his people and named her what he insisted on naming her, and if they rejected her—

"They will accept you," he said, reading her heart as he always had. "I told them long ago that I had chosen my wife, and that she was a woman of the Hittites, a foreigner and an unbeliever."

"And were they angry?" she asked.

"Furious," he said. "For a while. Then they grew resigned to it. After a while they even convinced themselves that they wanted it. They're waiting now to welcome you. You're the guest they've long awaited.''

''I, and not my lady?''

''Your lady, too, but for a different reason. I won't be marrying her,'' said Johanan with a flicker of his old humor.

Nofret's breath caught. ''Oh, gods! Her father—when he went away, he was—her—''

Johanan shook her till she stopped babbling. ''Hush now. Hush. All that is forgotten. Better than that: forbidden. He brings laws down off the mountain, the word of the god to us his people. One of them is that no father take his child to wife, and no son may wed his mother. He'll not break his own law, beloved. Even if he had another law before.''

''I wish I could believe you,'' she said.

''Believe it,'' said Johanan. ''The man who was king in Egypt is dead. Moshe the prophet welcomes his daughter as daughter only, beloved and protected. He'll teach her to be whole again.''

''I don't know if anyone can do that,'' said Nofret. She was walking under Johanan's gentle guidance. Away from the desert. Toward the camp of his people.

Strangers. Foreigners.

And had she ever known otherwise since she was taken out of Hatti?

Strangers, yes. And kin. And beloved.

She looked up past the tents to the slope of the mountain. Mount Horeb, that was its name: the mountain of their god. The sun had topped its summit at last and leaped blinding into the sky. In Egypt it was god and king. Here in the wilderness it was another thing, both lesser and greater: no god itself but servant and creation of the god who ruled the Apiru. They knew one god only, and no other before him.

"You are no god of mine," she said to him, "and your people are no people of mine, except that they will it so. But for love of your servant, and of my lady who needs me still, I will stay. I will do your will—not because you wish it, but because I choose."

The god did not blast her where she stood, nor strike her blind. Nor did he drive her any madder than she was already. He knew that he would gain no more of her than that, nor compel her to serve him in any greater capacity.

It was enough. She linked arms with Johanan and firmed her grip on the donkey's rope, and led them both into the camp.

PART THREE

THE LORD OF HOSTS

The Lord is my strength and song, and he is become my salvation: he is my God, and I will prepare for him an habitation; my father's God, and I will exalt him.

—Exodus 15:2

CHAPTER FIFTY-ONE

▲

ANKHESENAMON was in no way resigned to her exile. She had not willed it. She had not chosen it. The arrogance of her servants had thrust it upon her, snatched her away from everything she knew and flung her headlong into a place and a position she hated.

For she did hate it. With all her heart. Nofret was in no doubt of that. Ankhesenamon made it abundantly clear with each morning's waking. She demanded that she be served as a queen was served, however difficult that might be in a camp of wandering tribesmen. She would do no work in the camp, though every hand was needed, even that of Moshe the prophet. He was one of their herdsmen, guarding the flocks that grazed on the slopes of the mountain.

"How have the mighty fallen," said Ankhesenamon with a delicate sneer, when it was made clear to her that her father himself undertook to be of use to the tribe.

"The crook that the king carries in Egypt is a shepherd's crook," Nofret reminded her.

She arched a brow. "The Lord of the Two Lands is a shepherd of men. Not," she said, "of smelly sheep."

Nofret told herself that Ankhesenamon was shocked to the bone, taken out of place and time and made to be something that she had never desired to be. The god had not called her, not in any way she would accept. Even her father was no longer the man she had known.

The first day in the camp she discovered how different he was, when he carried her to his tent. Nofret, coming later, found Ankhesenamon crouched against the far wall, staring at an Apiru woman as if she had been a cobra reared to strike. It was an utterly unremarkable woman, swathed in veils as they all were, but with her face uncovered here in the shelter of the tent. She had no beauty at all, and no distinction. A plump naked boychild clung to her skirts, fist in mouth, brown eyes wide. From the curve of the belly under the robes, there was another coming, and not long for it either.

When Nofret came in, blinking in the sudden gloom after the dazzle of daylight, Moshe was saying, "This is Zipporah. My wife. And this," he said, swooping down, swinging the child laughing into his arms, "is my son. His name is Gershom. Gershom, greet your sister."

The child mumbled something around his fist. Ankhesenamon shrank back even farther, blankly and starkly appalled.

Time was, Nofret thought, when the very thought of a son for this man would have sent his daughter into transports of joy. But now, when he was dead to Egypt and she was dead also and against every wish of her heart, to see him happy, possessed at last of an heir, and from such a mother . . .

Zipporah seemed a shy brown mouse of a woman, but she had a core of strength. She would have to, to be married to this man. She said in a soft voice, a voice that was beautiful as her face was not, "Lady, I welcome you to the tents of my people."

Ankhesenamon flung up her head. "And who are you, to welcome me?"

"My father is a priest of the people," Zipporah said calmly, "and I am the eldest of his daughters, wife to the prophet of Sinai. You, lady, I know. You are most welcome here."

"I do not wish to be welcome," said Ankhesenamon.

No more did she. She demanded and received a tent to herself. She expected that Nofret share it with her. Nofret chose for a while to humor her. Johanan did not like it, but he had his own duties, his own place among the tribesmen. Nofret was not surprised to see that it was a high place. His father was what they called a Levite, a member of the priestly caste, and he stood high in it. Johanan, as his eldest son, performed the office of the heir.

For long and long he had been the only son, born of a mother who died bearing him. But Aharon in Sinai had taken not one but two wives. They were sisters; by some intricacy of Apiru law he had had to marry both if he was to marry either. They seemed quite pleased with the arrangement, and were happily presenting him with a tribe of sons. There were half a dozen that Nofret counted, and another coming.

She grew to know all of them, and well. Ankhesenamon could not keep her shut up in the tent for every hour of every day. She had to go out at least for water, and to gather and prepare food, and to wash her own and her lady's clothing in the little river that ran through the field of the flocks. She managed thereby to be out of the tent for most of the day while Ankhesenamon sat inside it, immobile as she had ever been upon her throne, refusing to move, or to speak except in command.

"It's a great shock for her," said Korah. The younger

of Aharon's wives was also by a little the prettier—though they were both very pretty, round and ruddy like ripe apples, and apt for laughter. They did not laugh at Ankhesenamon. They pitied her.

"Poor thing," said the elder, Elisheba. They were all washing clothes that day, beating them on the rocks. Some of the women were singing. The rest were gossiping with the comfortable air of women who knew everyone and everything and had an opinion on it all.

Elisheba tucked a stray curl under her veil and scrubbed at a particularly stubborn stain. "Poor lost lady, she went to sleep a queen and woke up a desert savage. All her world's turned upside down."

"I could be less charitable," said one of the other women, one whose name Nofret had not yet learned. "She's obviously too good for the likes of us."

"And isn't she?" asked Korah. "Remember who she was."

"I know what she is now." The woman shot a glance at Nofret and shut her mouth with a snap.

The others were less shy of the Egyptian woman's servant. Everyone knew that she would marry Johanan when the time came for marrying. If there were objections, Nofret did not hear them. It was too clear to most people, as Zipporah had explained, that the god meant the two of them to be mated.

The god was everywhere for these people. He oversaw everything, knew everything, missed nothing. He was like every god that Egypt or Hatti had, all together and in one. Nofret wondered how he could bear to be god of everything and anything that was.

He seemed not only to bear it but to revel in it. He would have no other god before him, the women told her. Any who tried was promptly put in his place—even, they whispered, destroyed. People could fashion no image of him, nor even call him by name. He was simply Adonai,

Lord. He was more powerful than any name.

"Does that mean he has none?" Nofret asked.

"Of course not," said Zipporah. Women could not be priests here, no more than they could in Egypt, but they were allowed to share some of the secrets. The men could hardly prevent them—not if they wanted their clothes washed and their meals cooked and their children tended.

Zipporah was the eldest daughter of a priest who had no sons. She was the one who knew about the god. She did not make a brag of it, nor did she chatter idly about him, but when Nofret asked she would answer. "He has a name," she said, "but only the chosen may know it. None may speak it. Its power is too great. With it one can shatter a world."

"One would think," said Nofret, "that men might go to war to gain the power of that name."

Zipporah's eyes went wide. "Oh, no," she said. "No man would dare. A man who misuses it, you see—he dies the death."

There was a pause. Its heart was chill. Nofret broke it with an effort. "Such a god would be too terrible for me. I'd rather one who was a little more human—who had some mercy on his servants."

"The Lord is merciful always," said Zipporah. "Even his justice he tempers with mercy."

"Except when someone makes free with his name."

"Then he is just," Zipporah said.

▪ ▪ ▪

Ankhesenamon saw no justice in anything that she suffered. When she woke in the camp she had awakened wholly, not only to awareness but to sanity. It was a cold, harsh, bitter clarity for her who had been lost for so long in a dream.

Bitterness first made her silent, then drove her to speech. Nofret had never heard so many words from her as she did once the dam had broken. Bitter words, furious words. Words that poured out of her in reckless profusion. More words than Nofret had known she knew, and not only in Egyptian, either. Before the camp she knew no other language. Within the tent she spoke Apiru quite as well as Nofret did, perhaps even a little better.

She remembered every moment of her life in Egypt. Princess and queen, daughter of the apostate king, Great Royal Wife to him and to his successor and to the one who came after, she ran through them all. Sometimes she wept. More often she sat in a tight knot of anger, spitting out the words, counting the memories like beads on a string.

Nofret stopped listening early on. She could go about her business, even sleep, while the recitation unwound itself. It lulled her to sleep of a night, woke her in the morning. If Ankhesenamon slept in between, Nofret did not know of it.

She did not know how tired she was becoming until they moved camp. Apiru were wanderers; they went from pasture to pasture and from stream to well as the moon wore on its round. Who decided it, and how, she did not yet know. The elders, maybe, who met in council—mostly to sit about and drink date wine and gossip as the women did at the riverbank, but sometimes to decide this matter or that.

However it was done, one morning everyone moved at once to fold the tents, to load them on the backs of donkeys or of strong women. The herdsmen gathered the herds and drove them milling and bleating in the track of the tents. By full light the whole camp was in motion, the fires shut up in the firepots, and only the trampled ground to show where they had been.

Ankhesenamon did not want to go. Nofret had to strike the tent around her, load it on the donkey that had carried her out of Egypt, and gather everything else she could. Ankhesenamon sat throughout, immovable as a stone. "I will stay here," she said in the most maddeningly royal of voices.

"No, lady," said Johanan, appearing out of nowhere. "You will not." Before either of them knew what he was doing, he had swept Ankhesenamon up and deposited her on the donkey, and slapped it on the rump to startle it into a trot. Ankhesenamon had to cling to its neck or be flung off.

The donkey slowed when it reached the herd of its fellows. Nofret, cursing, sprang in pursuit. Johanan caught her arm and brought her up short. "Let her go," he said. "She's safe enough. The whole tribe will see to it."

"But she's my—"

Johanan cut her off. "Not for the moment she's not. Here, walk with me. I haven't seen you in half of eternity."

"You saw me last night," said Nofret impatiently. "I fed you bread that I'd baked myself."

"It was good bread, too," he said. "Will you bake more for me tonight?"

"It there's any way to bake it," she said, "yes."

He wound his fingers with hers, matching her pace, falling in among the last of the Apiru on the march. Her eye, anxious, kept seeking and finding Ankhesenamon among the people on donkeys. She was hard to mistake, as straight as she sat, and as rigid with anger.

"Everything she does is angry," said Johanan, "and every thought she thinks is bitter. She's a massively spoiled child. If I were her father I'd take a stick to her behind."

"One does not take a stick to the behind of the queen of Egypt." Nofret said it as stiffly as was proper, but her heart was a traitor: it agreed with him. "One has to pity her. All that she was, all that was taken away from her—"

"—was a madness of grief, and certain death." Johanan scowled at the figure on the donkey. "She wasn't going anywhere but into the river the night she was taken away. We gave her life. We gave her the freedom to be furious.''

''Maybe you should have let her die.''

Johanan stopped. Nofret, handlinked with him, stopped perforce. ''Maybe we should have,'' he said. ''I think not. The god has more for her to do than to sulk in her tent and bewail her lost throne. The sooner she sees it, the happier we'll all be.''

''I wish . . .'' said Nofret. But she did not go on. She was still her lady's servant. There were still some things that she could not say, even to Johanan.

He said them for her. ''We all wish she'd get on with it. Pity only takes us so far; compassion is wasted on a woman who spits on it. Maybe, after all, that stick to the behind . . .''

''No!'' Nofret tried to pull free, but he was too strong. ''You can't talk like that. No matter what you think of her, she's still queen and goddess. She can't be anything else.''

''She won't,'' he said. ''In the end she'll have to. Even if it kills her.''

''You think it won't?''

''I admit,'' he said, ''sometimes I hope it will. She was never a very likable creature.''

''She never knew how to be.'' Nofret found that if she walked with sufficient determination, she pulled him along with her. Only the rearguard of the tribe was behind them now: the young men with their bows and their spears, on guard against raiders, either animal or human. Johanan himself had a bow slung behind him, and a quiver of arrows.

She felt safe, if exasperated. Exasperation edged with a peculiar, distant grief. ''One doesn't *like* a princess. One worships her. How could she ever know how to make people like her?''

''Some people come by it naturally,'' Johanan said. Once he was set in motion he stayed there, walking easily beside her, matching stride for stride. So they had wandered through the wilderness, with the same equality of pace, the same comfort in one another's presence—even at the moment, when they were close to quarreling.

"I am," Nofret admitted after a few dozen strides, "tired. I could be happy if I weren't bound to serve my royal lady."

"And are you?" Johanan asked her. "Are you bound?"

"I gave my word," said Nofret.

"When? When you were given to her as tribute? She's no longer a queen. You're no longer her slave."

"Except in the heart," Nofret said. "I can't abandon her."

"No more will you. But if she's to grow out of herself, she has to be left on her own. You can't nursemaid her. If she wants to eat, she can earn her bread, and bake it too. If she wants her tent set up, she can set it up. If she wants her clothes washed, she can wash them. She can do everything that any other woman does among the people."

"Men don't do any of that," said Nofret.

He flashed a grin at her. "So, then. If she doesn't want to be a woman, she can be a man. She can guard the flocks and fight off lions and defend the people."

"And sit in the tents at night, drinking date wine and telling extravagant stories." Nofret shook her head. "That might suit her better, but I don't think she'd want to spend her days in the sun. It would ruin her complexion."

"There, you see. She'll have to learn to be a woman instead of a queen."

"She won't learn."

"If she has to, she will."

Nofret fell silent. Johanan did not press her. That was one of his great virtues: he knew when to be quiet. They walked the road that the Apiru had walked since the world was young, following the flocks from pasture to pasture.

CHAPTER FIFTY-TWO

▲

ANKHESENAMON learned what she was forced to learn. That first night, when Nofret did not go to set up the tent, it was as bitter for Nofret as for her. She was too proud to send a messenger. Nofret turned again and again toward the edge of the camp where the small figure sat erect and alone, waiting to be waited on. Each time Johanan's eye caught hers, or Leah called her to a gathering by one of the fires, to settle a dispute over something small but pressing.

Ankhesenamon slept on the ground that night, cold and supperless. No one brought her a blanket. No one fed her. Someone—not Nofret, who was prevented each time she tried—set a waterskin where she could reach it if she exerted herself.

In the morning they moved camp again. It was three days' journey to the place of the green pastures, Nofret had been told. She dreaded to discover that Ankhesenamon was not among the people, but when she looked, the erect small figure was sitting on the donkey, riding as she had ridden the day before.

That night she set up her tent. She was sore taxed by it, though it was a small tent, and light; she had never troubled to learn how best to go about it. Nofret had to sit on her hands to keep from hastening to help, even when it was clear that Ankhesenamon would only eat if she humbled herself to approach the nearest fire and ask for bread. Water she had, and a few dates that Nofret had gathered the day before they left the mountain. If she ate them, she did it in the tent where no one could see.

No one spoke to her. It was not a thing that anyone decided to do; it was accepted, that was all. She must speak if she wished to be spoken to. She would earn her place or have none.

It was not in her to weep, even when she felt cruelly used. She presented a proud cold face to the tribe. When at last she asked for bread, she did so with frigid courtesy. She was given it with warmth that was a rebuke, and an invitation to tarry by that particular fire. It happened to belong to Korah and Elisheba. Aharon was not with them: he was sitting with Leah and Johanan and Nofret, sharing a haunch of gazelle that Johanan had shot on the day's journey.

The other haunch roasted over his wives' fire. They offered Ankhesenamon a choice cut of it. She refused, drawing back, retreating to her cold fireless tent and her haughty solitude.

Aharon, watching, shook his head and sighed. "It's hard to be human," he said, "when one's been a god."

"One learns," said Leah, "or one dies." She was watching another fire altogether. Moshe sat by it with his son in his lap and a handful of the elders about him. He was talking as he usually was, undeterred by the stammer that had been his curse from childhood. The elders nodded at whatever he was saying. Sometimes they argued, but at the moment they were all in agreement.

He was talking about the god again, Nofret supposed. When they argued, it was usually because he had bethought himself of some new law that his god would wish to decree, and they took issue with it. Apiru were wonderful people for arguing, even with their god or his prophet. Only when he talked directly about the god did they fall silent and listen. The god spoke to everybody, they believed. But he spoke most clearly to Moshe the prophet.

■ ■ ■

Nofret, denied her lady's tent, found shelter in Leah's. Johanan had his own, but she was not allowed in there. It was not proper. They were betrothed as the Apiru thought of it, but until they married they were not to share a tent.

There was nothing to prevent Leah from lingering by the fire with others of the women, or Johanan from slipping under the back of the tent and into Nofret's blankets. The first time he did it, she almost thrust him out again for startlement. He was ready for that: he wound his long arms about her and held fast till she stopped struggling. By the time she thought to cry out, he had stopped her mouth with a kiss.

It was a long while before he would let her speak. When he did, she was laughing too hard at first to begin. "Oh!" she gasped. "Oh, you! Is this at all proper?"

"Not in the least," he said cheerfully. "But it's perfectly well expected."

"So when do we make it proper?"

"Well," he said. "That's a bit difficult. In the ordinary way of things, you see, my father would approach your father and offer him a reasonable price. He'd turn it down, of course, and propose one that he reckoned more reasonable. My father would howl at the enormity of it, and so they'd go on, till they settled on the sum they both knew they'd come to before they began. Then they'd hammer out the marriage contract."

"That's like enough to what I remember from Hatti," said Nofret. "But since I have no father here to speak for me, and no brothers—" She sucked in her breath. "Johanan! You're not telling me we can't marry."

He kissed her so hard she gasped. "There now. Stop that. Of course we'll marry. Grandmother's going to speak for you. She drives a wonderfully hard bargain. She's only waiting for the time to be right and proper."

"Which could be never," she said sourly. "But suppose it does come—what then?"

"Then they seal the contract and Father pays the bride-price, whatever it may be: sheep usually, and fine fleeces, and a tent for us to live in, with all its fittings. Then we have the wedding."

"Gods," said Nofret. "What are we thinking of? A wedding. Do we have to be so hideously obvious?"

He laughed so hard he rolled out of the heaped rugs and fleeces and lay naked on the floor. She scrambled after him with as many of the rugs as she could gather, flung them all over him and herself with them, clamping a hand over his mouth. "Stop that! The whole camp can hear you."

He took his time, but in the end he stopped. When he could talk again he said, "You'd better get used to it. I don't intend to be one of those husbands who spends more time with the sheep than with his wife."

"I should hope not," she said tartly. "I should also hope that you can preserve at least the appearance of dignity."

"What, must I?"

"You know you do."

He sighed heavily. "O hard taskmaster. If you're so cruel now, what will you be when you're a wife?"

"Worse," said Nofret. "Infinitely worse."

■　■　■

The place of the green pastures was breathtakingly true to its name. It was a deep valley in the barren hills. A river ran through it. There were orchards and vineyards, and a village of Apiru who remained settled there and did not wander.

It was quite astonishing and quite perfectly hidden. From the summit of the ridge above it one could see the mountain of the god. From its heart, from the river that flowed even in summer, one saw nothing but greenness and peace.

For all its appearance of innocence, it was well guarded. The slopes of its sides were sheer, the way in both narrow and steep. A chariot could not come down that track. A donkey could, and a long line of people on foot, and their surefooted herds.

There were men on the heights, archers with strung bows, who called greetings to their kin, but none left his post. Nofret wondered how many more there were whom she did not see, concealed in the tumbled stones. Peace in this country was a fragile thing, and green grass and water more precious than gold.

The chief of the elders of the valley was Zipporah's father Reuel the priest. He welcomed the travelers with open gladness. They set up their tents downriver of the village, making a village of their own, doubling and trebling the numbers of those who inhabited the valley.

This, Nofret understood, was the heart-home of the tribe. Those who wandered did so to spare the grazing in the valley, and to follow the paths of their god. They had gone to the mountain that they called Horeb, so that they might worship in the holy place. Their return would endure for the rest of that season; then they would go out again on the round of the year, as constant as the moon, and as bound by necessity.

Those who wandered were not always the same. Sometimes former wanderers stayed and others went out: particularly the very old, the very young, the women with child. The priests went as their god called them, or stayed in this place that was blessed.

They were strong, they believed, because they were both a settled people and a people who wandered where the wind and the god took them. If ever they built a city and lived bound to it, with a king over them, their strength would fail. They must have the freedom of the desert, and with it the peace of their hidden place—both equally, and both alike. If they chose one over the other, then that one in the end they would lose. Their god had decreed it, they said, in the morning of the world.

■ ■ ■

On the morning of Nofret's wedding to Johanan ben Aharon, Ankhesenamon gained for herself a name among the Apiru. She had been sitting in front of her tent, alone as she always was. The children of the wanderers had learned not to circle round her and stare, but to the children of the valley she was still a new thing. It was beneath her dignity to dismiss them, but neither would she acknowledge them, nor answer their stream of questions.

One of the elder children was more outspoken than most. "Mother says that you are bitter," she said, "like wormwood. Why are you bitter? There's no place sweeter than this."

"That's what she is," said one of the others. "The bitter one. Miriam. Is that your name, stranger-lady? Are you Miriam?"

"I am—" Ankhesenamon shut her mouth. When she opened it again, it was to say in a faint, cold voice, "I am nothing and no one. You may call me what you please."

Miriam it was, then, and by evening everyone was calling her that. It was easier on the tongue than the name she had had in Egypt, and truer to the woman that she was: Miriam, the bitter one, the rebellious, who would not be resigned to her exile.

She came to the wedding. Nofret was too startled to be pleased. No one had expected Ankhesenamon that was, Miriam as she had become, to take part in any joyous thing, especially the wedding of the servant whom she blamed for her exile.

But she was there, dressed as somberly as she ever was. She had no other clothing, no jewels, nothing either bright or beautiful. If she was offered any such thing, Nofret was sure that she would refuse it.

A touch made Nofret jump. Leah, behind her, had brought her back to the world of the living. She was the bride in her splendor, set up in front of the people. And there was the bridegroom under the canopy, beautiful in a new robe, waiting for her to come and be joined to him. The priest of the joining was white-bearded Reuel, and Moshe and Aharon behind him, prophet and priest-prince. They were all waiting, all the people with their black robes laid aside, bright as a field of flowers.

She who had known the somber builders of tombs and the black-robed wanderers of the desert saw now what they were when they were contented and at peace. They looked on her with lively curiosity, though most of them had seen her already. None was hostile, foreigner though she was and thief as she might be thought of, who had taken the son of Aharon from the women of the people.

Today at least they were glad of and for her. They sang and danced and clapped their hands. Their maidens danced before her, casting flowers at her feet. She walked slowly through the throng of them, self-conscious as she had never been when she was chief of the queen's servants in Egypt. She had not been the focus of all eyes then, not she herself, apart from her lady and queen. It was terrifying.

She fixed her eyes on Johanan. The sight of him made her strong. He seemed at ease, but then he would: this was his own place, his own people. When she came to him at the end of this procession that seemed endless, she too would belong to them. She would be Apiru. Adopted; accepted. Made one of them.

Her heart tightened in her breast. She blinked hard. If she broke down and wept in her wedding procession, it would be the most dreadful of omens. She swallowed the tears although they gagged her, lifted her chin and firmed her stride and walked straight and strong to her husband's side.

■ ■ ■

"You could change your name, too," he said. They were in their own tent in their own blessed solitude, with the wedding going on outside. It had a lazy drunken air to it, the last and most dedicated of the revelers still clinging to their revelry, while the rest slept where they had fallen, or else had retreated to their beds and their own wives and husbands.

They were prisoners here, the two of them. They would not be allowed to go out till evening. It must be a full and perfect consummation, the women had told Nofret, for the good of the tribe and the pleasure of the god.

They had made a very good beginning. He was resting from his exertions, propped on his elbow, smiling lazily at her. She reached to ruffle his beard. "Don't I have enough name to go on with?" she asked him.

"It's not the one your father gave you."

"I'm not the child my father named," she said.

"And are you still the woman who was given an Egyptian name from a long list of them, handed out to her like a ration of barley?"

"I chose to keep it," she said.

"Even now?"

"Why?" She rose on her own elbow, face to face with him. "Does it so displease you to call me by it?"

He seemed taken aback by her sharpness. "I only thought—"

"It's because it's Egyptian, isn't it? How you must hate Egypt! Would you come to hate me, because you have to use their language whenever you name me?"

"No," he said. "No, damn it. I thought you only took the name because you didn't want Egypt to have your real one—your real soul."

"My real soul," she said, "became that name long ago. Egypt won, you know. I never meant it to, but it did."

"You could change it. Egypt is far away. You're Apiru now; you're of our people."

She shook her head. "I don't think so. I'm still the Hittite woman, the Egyptian queen's slave."

"And the wife of Johanan ben Aharon."

"All of that," she said. "Every one."

She knew why she loved him: he did not press her further. Much later, and when he patently had put it out of mind, she asked, "What would you have called me? If I'd wanted to be someone else?"

He had to stop, to shift his mind and body, to answer, "I don't know. I was asking you."

She hissed in exasperation. "You weren't even going to give me a name?"

"I thought you'd be sick of that: first your father, then whichever scribe or servant it was who wrote you into the list of royal servants. This time I thought you'd want to name yourself."

"Names don't work like that," she said. "They come as the gods send them."

"The god has sent you none?"

"The god has left me as I am. Nofret. The Hittite woman, the Egyptian slave."

"And my beloved."

"And your beloved," she said.

"My beautiful one. My bride." His voice went sweet, like the beginning of a song. "I will go up to the mountain of myrrh, and to the hill of frankincense."

They were all poets, these Apiru. Poets and dreamers and madmen. And beautiful, all beautiful. The wine she had drunk at the feast was long gone, but she was dizzy all over again. He had always been able to do that to her.

"If I didn't love you to distraction," she said, "I think I could very easily hate you."

"What, for being so importunate?"

"No," she said. "For being so perfectly irresistible."

"Then that's a hate we'll have to share," said Johanan.

"A wife," she said solemnly, "should share everything with her husband."

"Indeed," said Johanan. "And she should obey him in everything."

"Oh, no," Nofret said. "Share and share alike. Obedience for obedience."

"That's not—"

"That is my vow to you," she said.

"Are you marrying me all over again? With new words?"

"Every day," she said. "Every night. The same vows. The same conviction."

She had caught him; held him. He had been barely so intent when she spoke the words that the Apiru priests bade her speak, words very like these, but much more in them of yielding to her husband's will. She would do that, yes. But when she had sworn it before the people, she had sworn in her heart, before the god, that Johanan would do it, too: that he would be to her as she was to him.

Now she held her breath. If he had sworn no such vows in his own heart, nor wished to, then she did not know that she could remain his wife. It was late to think such a thing, too late as the Apiru would say, but she could not help herself. She had to think it.

He was long in replying, so long that her eyes went dim and her lungs cried for air. Then at last he said, "Obedience for obedience. Love for love."

"The gods will witness it," said Nofret.

"One god," said Johanan, "for them all."

She drew breath to differ, but chose instead to keep silence. Was that obedience, then? It was fair enough, she supposed. He had yielded to her, after all, in the changing of their vows.

CHAPTER FIFTY-THREE

▲

ANKHESENAMON that had been, Miriam as she was now, might have sunk to nothing among the Apiru, if it had not been for Leah. Nofret tried, but she could not be what she had been: forever the loyal servant, devoted to her lady. She was a married woman, welcomed among the women, accepted into their councils. She had her husband, the keeping of his household, and her own stubborn insistence that when she needed to wander afield she would, no matter what a proper woman did among these people. Then when the babies came, they were all-engrossing.

For whole days and weeks at a time she managed to see no more of Miriam than a figure sitting alone by its tent on the edge of camp or village. She would urge herself guiltily then to visit, and sometimes she even did. But there was never anything to say. Miriam would not care for gossip: this baby born, that one sick and like to die, this woman marrying and that one cuckolding her husband, all the daily ordinariness of life among the common folk. Still less did she need to hear how Nofret doted on Johanan even when he was being a perfect idiot, or what prodigies his children were.

For of course there were children. Nofret had come late to it, was nearer thirty than twenty when she began, but her body was strong. It was made for bearing babies.

First came the son of their hearts, whom his father named Jehoshua. That was a great name, a name of power. " 'God is salvation,' it means," Johanan said. "And so he is. Our son will be one of those who prove it."

Nofret foresaw no such thing. Her sight was as clear as

it had ever been, but it had narrowed. She saw her husband, her children, even a glimpse of her children's children. But no more. She needed to see no more, in this time and place.

She muttered of arrogance and presumption, but she liked the sound of her firstborn's name. It did suit him, when she thought about it. When she turned it on her tongue, she knew no shiver of fear, merely a sense of rightness. So he was Jehoshua, and he was given the name before the people, and taken into the tribe as one who would grow to be a man among the Apiru.

When Jehoshua was weaned, three years almost to the day since the wedding in the valley, the twins were born, a boy and a girl. Nofret named them, since Johanan had named the eldest. She thought of Hittite names, and of Egyptian ones, but these were too distinctly Apiru children. She called her daughter Anna, because it was both simple and beautiful, and her son Ishak, because even as a young child he was always laughing.

Miriam was there for each of the births. She did not come into the light nor offer assistance to the midwives, but she came, and Nofret knew. Each time she left before Nofret could call to her, after the babies were born but before they had been taken out to their father.

She never spoke. She did not say anything when later Nofret visited her, though she had sent gifts: a blanket that she must have woven herself, a gourd that rattled, a little man made out of wood, with legs that bent and arms that could be raised and lowered. Small things, but useful, and valued for that.

It was Leah who drew Miriam out of the self into which she had retreated. Leah had her son and her grandsons and now her great-grandchildren, but her office and her dignity set her apart. She would seek out Miriam, or summon her—and for a wonder Miriam would accept the summons. They were often together. When the elders met in council, Leah as prophetess met with them, and Miriam sat mute behind her, eyes lowered, hands folded in her lap. There were no queenly posturings, no flashes of arrogance. Whether by Leah's teaching or by her own lateborn wisdom, Miriam had learned to keep at least the semblance of humility before the Apiru.

It was a comfort to Nofret to know that they were both looked after, each by the other. Bitter Miriam seemed to have grown, if not resigned, then less openly resentful of her lot. She did not smile that Nofret ever saw, but then she never had, except when she was queen and beloved of Tutankhamon.

All that she seemed to have forgotten, or buried deep. Her beauty had faded not at all—if anything it was more piercing than ever with neither paint nor wig to mask it. Time only fined it, made it shine clearer. But no man dared to offer for her, nor would she have accepted him if he had. She was as remote from the yearnings of the body as living thing could be. Dead, that part of her, and withered. Her beauty was as pure and terrible as a sword, and no more humanly warm.

Among another people she might have been worshipped as a goddess. Here she was accepted calmly as the god's child. Her own father seemed happily earthbound beside her, with his sweet-faced plain wife and his much-loved sons. But it was he who wandered in the desert, following his god's call, and he who went up on the holy mountain and spoke to his god. Sometimes Aharon went with him, and on occasion Johanan. Most often he went alone. Never with Miriam. She kept to the camp or the village, and to Leah's side.

■ ■ ■

They were encamped by the mountain of the god, one unusually wet spring. That year it rained almost every day, and even the most barren hills were touched with tentative green. Jehoshua was old enough to carry on a quite cogent conversation, if somewhat slanted toward his enthusiasm of the hour, which just then was the bow that his father had made for him. The twins were almost ready to be weaned. Ishak, grinning, had just bitten his mother and been slapped smartly for it. Anna, actually the more outrageous of the two, showed signs of fury that she had not thought of it first.

Nofret had banished them to the tent where they would nap under the eye of the old dog Tirzah's eldest pup, now well along in years herself. Tirzah the younger had raised many a litter and was heavy with the latest, most likely her last. She knew well how to look after a pair of human pups.

Nofret lingered outside in the relative quiet, rubbing her throbbing breast. At this hour of the day all the women were busy with children or with washing. The men were out with the herds or up on the mountain. Johanan had gone hunting, taking Jehoshua with him, the son riding with enormous pride on his father's shoulders.

She smiled at the memory. That was a strong line, the line of Levi the priest. All its men looked remarkably alike, even as babies: big, broad-shouldered, hawk-nosed. Ishak was the same. Anna, bless the luck, had inherited beauty from somewhere, maybe from Leah. And she had her mother's hair, which pleased Johanan to no end.

They were a handsome family. Sturdy, too. She shaped a sign for protection, in case something of ill-will was listening. The Apiru god seemed to have no objection to happiness among his people, but other powers were not so generous.

She sighed, stretched, luxuriating in the movement. She was not getting any younger, but by good fortune she had kept her teeth, all but the one that the midwives called the child-toll, lost while she carried the twins. Her waist was thickened, her breasts no longer high and firm; but she had never been a lissome beauty, nor did her big broad Hittite bones look well without a decent padding of flesh.

Her husband professed himself satisfied. She felt as strong as ever. It was amazing how robust a woman could be, chasing after lively offspring and hefting them two at a time, and carrying water in heavy jars to and from well and river, and beating the washing on the stones, and doing all the things that a woman did where even the rich labored beside their servants.

She had a girl who came for part of the day to look after the children and to do what needed doing: a younger daughter of a family excessively blessed with daughters. Their mother had been trying to urge a second on Nofret, even a third, but she did not see the use in that. If she had had a house in a village, yes, certainly, but not in a tent of the wandering Apiru. Nor was she about to give up her wandering. She liked it; she thrived on it. Her children were growing up sturdy and strong, if somewhat obstreperous.

She was content. More than content. Happy.

It was becoming an accustomed state, one that would have seemed so strange once as to be impossible. She stretched again in the warming sunlight, loosening the kink in her back that was there more often since the twins were born. Maybe she would bathe in the river, in the pool that the women had claimed for themselves. A bath would be pleasant. If she washed her hair, too, and scented it with herbs, then tonight . . .

She shook her head ruefully. She knew too well where that led. Another daughter, maybe. Everyone wanted sons, but she was odd in that as in everything else. Sons went to their father when they were old enough. Daughters stayed with their mother till they were women themselves. If she was lucky the friendship endured even after they were married, when they went to their husband's tent and set themselves under the authority of his mother.

Nofret slipped into the tent to gather the things that she needed for bathing. As she came out with the bundle in her arms, she nearly fell over someone who was sitting in front. At first she thought it one of the children, a girl new come to womanhood and wearing a woman's robes and veil. But the face that turned upward was not a child's face.

Nofret stopped short. "Lady!" She had never got out of the habit of that, nor seen why she should. "You startled me. Have you come to visit the children? They're asleep now. Zillah's looking after them. If you want to go in and see—"

"No," said Miriam. Her familiar word, her familiar soft remote voice. "Leah asks to see you."

Nofret's mind did not want to shift. "Leah wants to see the children? If she waits till tonight, we should have a gazelle, or if my husband's luck fails, the black-spotted kid—"

"She wants to see you," said Miriam. "Now."

Something in her expression stilled the rest of Nofret's babbling. When she rose and walked quickly away toward the edge of the camp, Nofret followed.

▪ ▪ ▪

Nofret had visited Leah only a day or two before. Or three days, maybe—the twins were teething, it was hard to remember. Four days? Five? Not so long. Not long enough for Leah to have changed so much.

She had been old since Nofret first knew her. She was very old now, but had been still hale, still able to follow the tents and the herds. A season or two ago, some of the elders—men and women of grey age themselves, but younger than she—had tried to persuade her to stay in the valley. She had laughed in their faces. She could outwalk them, outlast them, outdo them in any feat they chose.

Somehow, in the few days since Nofret was in her tent,

drinking date wine and eating the wonderful sweet cakes that Leah made with raisins and honey, she had grown shrunken and frail. Her skin was waxen, her hands shriveled. She lay on her bed of rugs and blankets, and even her eyes had grown dull. Till Nofret knelt beside her: then they came alive, as darkly bright as ever, but with a look in them that Nofret did not want to know.

Unfortunately for her own complacency, Nofret had never been adept at clouding her own sight. What she saw, she saw clear. And in those eyes she saw death.

She took Leah's hands in hers. All the strength was gone out of them. "How?" she asked. "How so soon?"

"It's a gift," said Leah in a thread of a voice. "The Lord gave it to me from a child: to be strong to the end, but when that end came, to go quickly."

"No," said Nofret. "Quickly is in your sleep, between one breath and the next, and no failing of strength till all strength is gone."

Leah smiled. "So it is. But one should have some warning, you see. Time to settle one's affairs. To say goodbye."

Nofret's eyes were burning dry. She was no better at weeping now than she had ever been. "What if I won't let you?"

"You wouldn't be that foolish." Leah tightened her fingers on Nofret's. "Listen to me. I'll see the sun go down— I've been promised that. But there's much to do before then, many people to see. You're the first, except for my daughter here."

Nofret glanced where Leah's eye slid, at Miriam sitting on her heels just within the tentflap. Miriam wore her old royal mask, the one that could hold steady even when her heart was breaking.

Leah was still speaking, wasting strength on words that she need not have said. "You too were a daughter to me, a granddaughter, beloved of my grandson whom I loved.

It gives me joy to see you now so happy, so beautifully content.''

"I know all that," said Nofret, not graciously, but she had never lied to Leah. "I don't want to hear it. I want you to get up, walk out of here, be as you always were."

"I don't," said Leah. "I'm going home. The god is calling me. He's held back for so long . . . Did you know that all my family are dead, all who were alive when I was young? I'm the oldest in the tribe. The elders themselves were born after I grew into a woman."

"You're not as old as that," Nofret said. "Aharon can't be more than—"

"Aharon was the child of my age. He was my Ishak: the impossible one, the one who was born when I should have been past bearing." She laughed, a catch of breath, no more. "Don't look so shocked, child! It's not indecent to have a baby when you're past forty. Simply . . . unexpected."

"You can't be that old," Nofret protested.

"But I am," said Leah. "They thought I was barren, did you know that? And so did I. My husband took two other wives, and they bore him sons, and they were his heirs. Then Aharon was born, our beloved, our prince of the people. He was our great joy. My husband died in the fullness of his age, but I lived to see my son's son and his grandsons. Few women are given such a gift."

"Then why are you giving it up?"

"Because," said Leah, "it's time. The old order is gone, the one that went into Egypt with Yuya and his brothers, and the one that lives here by the mountain of God. Both of them were sundered. Now they'll be one again. Moshe will lead them, and Aharon, and our Johanan. Your Jehoshua, too, your savior of the people."

Nofret's skin was cold, a cold that had nothing to do with the air of Leah's tent. That if anything was too warm.

"I've seen it, too. A little. None so clearly that I could be sure of it."

"You will," Leah said, "when the time comes. Your children absorb you now, and so they should. Your husband needs you to love him, and not to give yourself up to the people."

"But if I have to," said Nofret, "if it's laid on me—since I can see—"

She did not want to say it, but it was not a matter of wanting or of not wanting. This had been coming on her since first she met Leah in Akhetaten, when she learned that she could see what others could not see.

"It is not laid on you," Leah said. "Not yet."

Nofret stared at her. "It's not—"

"In your time," said Leah, "you will be a seer of the people. But the time is not now. Now you are the wife of Johanan ben Aharon, and the mother of Jehoshua and Anna and Ishak. They bind you. They cloud your sight on behalf of the people."

"But I have it," Nofret said. "I do have it."

Nor had she ever wanted it, either—but it was there. It was hers. Who was Leah to take it away from her?

"I take nothing from you," Leah said, reading her as she always had, with effortless ease. "I give you a gift, a blessing. A life of peace while your children are young."

She wanted that. Oh, she wanted it. But she was angry nonetheless, with the perfect lack of reason that seemed to be the lot of the human creature. Especially, Johanan would tell her, human woman.

Johanan could be insufferable when he chose to be. So could his grandmother, even dying. "What if I don't want the gift?" Nofret demanded.

"It's not yours to accept or refuse," said Leah. "Do be sensible now, and think."

"I am thinking," Nofret shot back. "I think that the people need you. That you can't just abandon them."

"Of course I can't," Leah said. "There is one to follow me."

"But you said that I—"

Nofret broke off. Miriam had not moved, had done nothing at all, but Nofret's eyes had fallen on her and held.

Clouded the sight might be, shrunk to the compass of her own near kin, but it was clear enough to see what sat in front of it.

"She doesn't have the eyes," Nofret said. "She never did."

"The queen of Egypt saw only her own kin and kind," said Leah, disturbing echo of Nofret's own thoughts. "When those were gone, then her eyes opened and she could see."

Nofret's throat constricted. What she felt did her no credit at all. Sheer sea-green jealousy. She was jealous of her own poor exiled lady, her lost queen whom she had taken out of Egypt. The one she pitied when she took time to think of her at all. Who was to be the prophet of the people, the seer of the Apiru, because Nofret was not ready.

It was hard to face that, harder to face herself. She did not like what she saw. Time was when it was right and proper that her lady be set over her. Had not the gods done it since they both were born?

She had grown proud among the Apiru. Married to one who was as close to a prince as they had, mother of his children—she had come to think of her lady as the lesser. The god of the Apiru had little patience with mortal pride, and less with mortal foolishness.

This was gentle as such things went. The ill spirit in her wanted her to get up and walk out without another word. Plain sense held her where she was. It made her say, "Lady. I—"

"Miriam," said her lady. "I'm called Miriam now. I've no more rank than you have."

If, it was clear, no less. Miriam had lost nothing of pride, either, since she was queen of Egypt.

Nofret smiled thinly. They were more equals now than they had ever been. She wondered what Miriam thought of that. No more, probably, than she herself did. "Miriam," she said. "Are you whole, then? Heart-whole?"

"No," said Miriam. "But it will do."

Nofret bent her head, raised it again. She understood.

She was still holding Leah's hands. They were thin and cold. Colder than they should be. She gasped. "Leah!"

Leah's eyes flickered under lids gone near transparent. She drew a breath, another. She swam up as if from deep water, looked into Nofret's face, smiled. "Go, child. Your children are calling you."

Her children were sound asleep. She opened her mouth to say so, but closed it again. She bent, kissed the hands that lay so limp in hers, laid them gently on the shrunken breast. "May your god keep you," she said.

CHAPTER FIFTY-FOUR

▲

LEAH died at evening in sight of the holy mountain, cradled in the arms of her son, with her kin about her. It was a good death. They mourned her for the full length of their rite, and buried her upon the mountain, in a place where the sun shone bright in the morning. A spring bubbled from a rock not far from her grave, covering it with green, and in spring with a carpet of flowers.

It was a blessed place. Nofret went there often, and sometimes her children with her. There was no daughter after the twins, after all; but she did not grieve too much. She was not past bearing yet, nor would be for a while.

Miriam proved to be a strong seer of the people. It should not have surprised anyone: a queen in Egypt was remarkably like a prophetess of the Apiru. She did not have to believe in their god, either, that Nofret could discern. It was Moshe who was the god's slave in heart and soul. Miriam served the gift of her own sight, and the people on whose behalf it was given her. She said nothing of any god or spirit.

Nofret could hardly quarrel with it, since she would have been much the same. They had even less to say to each other now than they had before. Miriam moved among the councils of the elders. Nofret's place was among the women and within her family's tent. When she departed from it, it was to go up to Leah's grave, or to walk the paths of the desert with one of Johanan's dogs to guard her.

She did not think of these wanderings as anything unusual. She had always gone off by herself when she could. Apiru women did not do it, but their men often did. They heard their god more clearly, they said, under the sky.

Nofret was not listening for a god's voice. She went for the silence. There was never any of that in camp, even in the deep night: there was always a baby crying, a goat bleating, a dog whimpering in its sleep. Away from all of that, in the desert or on the mountain, there was no sound but the wind's song, and now and then the call of a bird.

Once in a great while she met Moshe out wandering, too. He had no dog to guard him, nor carried any weapon but the staff that he had carved for himself soon after he went out of Egypt. It was a remarkable thing, a straight stave of some dun-golden wood, its head carved in the image of a cobra reared to strike. It was the same serpent that guarded the crown of Egypt, the uraeus-serpent, defender of the Lower Kingdom. No one seemed to think it odd that the prophet of Sinai should carry such a thing as if he were still the Lord of the Two Lands.

When they met, they sometimes spoke. He lost his stammer in speaking to one woman alone, but he kept his old courtesy, his princely politeness that let him ask after herself and her family. She could be startled into answering him, and thence into conversation. He was saner than she ever remembered, more honestly human: a man, not king and god. Only when he spoke of his god was he the man that he had been in Akhetaten: bound, enslaved, obsessed.

But it was a gentler enslavement than it had been. There was less desperate urgency in it. Here the people believed as he believed. He was not a king imposing an alien faith upon a reluctant people, but a prophet among the chosen of his god.

She was not disconcerted therefore to be clambering up a particularly interesting slope, the year they went late to the mountain pasture because the rains were late in coming, to come upon Moshe clambering ahead of her. He had gone all grey since she came to Sinai, and his beard was of noble and venerable length, but he was as nimble as a young man. He needed his staff only rarely to steady his steps.

She had been moved of late to explore beyond her wonted paths. A restlessness had been growing in her, mildly preposterous in a woman of forty, mother of children who grew tall, and the eldest already a man in the eyes of the Apiru. She could not say that her sight was growing any clearer. Miriam was still incontestably the seer of the people. But something was changing. Maybe it was only her body, warning her that her days of childbearing were ending.

If that was what it was, then she was some distance yet from proof of it. The Apiru had a custom of setting their women apart during their courses, which had come on her a handful of days ago. Rather than go into the house of the women, she had chosen to wander on the mountain. Tomorrow, that being the end of the time that the Apiru called unclean, she would go back down to the camp.

She should not be following Moshe now. He was become so perfectly Apiru that he would reckon himself stained by her presence. But he climbed with such concentration and such clear sense of purpose that she could not help but scramble after him.

She had never climbed so high. The Apiru did not go up on the mountain that they called the mountain of God, not unless they were summoned. As far as she knew, only Aharon had ever had such a summons, and of course Moshe, who had been known to dwell for days on or about the summit, communing with the god.

What the god would think of an unclean woman in his holy place, she could too well imagine. But if he had not wanted her here, would he have let her see his prophet, or tempted her to follow him?

The slope that Moshe chose was one of the steepest. He did not seem aware that he was followed. He had a fixed and eager air, as if someone were calling him, beckoning him to the mountain's top.

In fact he stopped short of the summit. The slope grew ragged there, and on one side a great jut of rock reared up against the sky. There was a twisted knot of brush on top of the rock, clinging grimly to its high perch, bent and tangled by the force of the wind. The sun, rising above the mountain, seemed caught in the branches.

Moshe had stopped at the foot of the rock. Nofret, near blind with the effort of matching his pace, nearly ran him down. She dropped just in time to the dubious shelter of a tumble of stones.

She could have danced around him and flung sand in his face, and he would not have noticed her. All his being was focused on the slope above him. The sun was dazzling. Nofret narrowed her eyes against its glare, shading them with her hand.

Moshe was a shadow in the brightness, but she could

see that he stared straight into it. He was talking to it. He
spoke the language of the Apiru as he always did now,
reckoning it the only fit tongue for addressing the Apiru
god.

"I'm here," he said.

His head tilted as if he listened. He moved toward a
track that wound up along the rock. The glare had grown
blinding. Nofret's eyes streamed with it. She had to lower
her head and draw her veil over her face. But she did not
leave. She was too stubborn.

"I'm here," Moshe said again. He bent. He was taking
off his sandals, she saw, setting them tidily side by side.
She thought he would go on up the rock, but he stayed
where he was, face bared and eyes wide open to the sun.

Through the screen of her veil she could see well
enough. Moshe was sidewise to her. Expressions played
across his face like light on water, each of them remarkably clear to read. Intent concentration; slow dawning of
understanding; incredulity. "But," he said then, "my
Lord, who am I, that I should do this?"

Nofret could have answered that herself: the prophet of
Sinai, who was once king in Egypt. Maybe the god said
the same. "And you?" Moshe asked the immense and
speaking silence. "By what name shall the people call
you? I knew you in the Two Lands, or I thought I did.
Here I am a stranger. The people will never name you to
me. They say that I know your name; there's no need to
ask it, or ever to speak it."

The silence thrummed deep. Nofret could feel the force
of it in the earth. She had not felt anything so strong since
she came to Thebes where the gods of Egypt were, when
the Aten had cast them all down and sealed their temples.
There was godhead here. The air was ablaze with it, a scent
like heated bronze, a light too fierce to bear.

She should not be here. She was alien, interloper. The
fire would destroy her.

But she was whole, and remained so. She could not hear the god's words, if truly he spoke any. Only the words of his prophet. "My lord," he said. "What you ask . . . I have no strength. My tongue stammers; my voice is frail. I had never the gift of leading men, even—when—"

His voice faded. He sank down. He was trembling. "My lord, they will never believe me. None of them will follow me. You know how I tried, how I failed. My city is dust already, my name and my laws forgotten."

But not here. Nofret heard it as clearly as if a voice had spoken it. Not in Sinai. The Apiru believed him, and knew his god.

"But will they follow me?" cried Moshe.

The air rang like a shield smitten with a spear. The god smote his prophet to the ground, weak protesting mortal that he was, all kingship and godhood long since gone from him.

But Moshe had a little strength left, and enough resistance to gasp, "Lord, I beg you. Send another man!"

Moshe was the one whom the god had chosen. Nofret, cowering in her inadequate shelter, knew it as clearly as he. No protests, no weakness, could shift that crushing burden from Moshe's back. He was a weakling, a coward. He had fled from Egypt when he grew weary of it to take refuge in Sinai. Now Sinai proved itself no haven. The god had seized him and would not let him go.

She did not even know what the god wanted of him. Something dreadful, no doubt. Something divinely appalling.

She knew the moment when the god left that place. The blaze of light had grown but little less. The air was still fierce with heat even so far up the mountain. But the terrible weight, the odor of hot bronze, was gone. The earth was earth again, holy because a god had touched it, but freed from the god's presence.

Slowly, creaking like an old woman, Nofret got to her

feet. She could barely see; when she turned too quickly, spots danced in front of her eyes. Fear stabbed, fear that she would be blind.

It nearly drove her away. But Moshe was lying where the god had abandoned him. His breath came harsh, with a rattle in it that she did not like.

Time was when she would have left him there, and never mind pity. But she was friend to his wife, and she was deeply fond of his sons. They loved their father to excess; if they discovered that she had left him alone on the mountain, maybe to die, they would hate her.

For their sake and not for his own, she made her stumbling, half-blind way to the man who lay at the foot of the rock. From there, looking up, she could see what he must have seen: the thicket above, the branches that for so endless a moment had caught and held the sun.

His breathing had quieted. There was a fever on him, but she had known worse in one of her children. She laved his brow and cheeks with water from the skin that she carried, and persuaded him to drink a little.

As she withdrew the waterskin he came to himself, or as much of himself at least as he had shown in Akhetaten. He did not seem to see her at all. His eyes were full of light. He struggled up, groping for the staff that had fallen when he fell. He found it with a cry and clutched it, clasping it to his breast as if it had been a living thing.

His steps when he began to walk were weak, wavering. Nofret set her shoulder next to his. He saw her no more clearly than he had before, but he accepted her steadying hand.

She thought more than once, and nastily, of letting him fall. But she lacked the fortitude to do such a thing. It was a failing in her character. She got him down off the mountain, and a long bitter road that was, and not a glance or a word of thanks did she get for it. His god possessed him utterly. He saw, heard, knew nothing else.

She did not even know for certain what it was that he saw. The god had not seen fit to speak to her, only to Moshe. She could be bitter, she supposed. Or she could shrug and do as the god clearly intended her to do: look after his prophet as women had been looking after men since the world was made, and see that he came safe to the camp of the people.

Servitude at least she knew, though she had got out of the habit of it. "And don't think you'll get this from me every day," she said somewhere along the way, half to the man she led, and half to the god who dazzled him. The man did not hear her. The god did not choose to.

Very well, she thought. She would know soon enough what it was that so frightened Moshe that he lost all sense of where to put his feet. It was not a war, she hoped, or something equally disruptive of the women's peace of mind.

CHAPTER FIFTY-FIVE

▲

It was not war. It was, if anything, worse.

The god, Moshe declared to the gathering of the elders, had bidden him return to Egypt. Not, he was swift to assure them, to be king again. Never that. But the god had grown weary of the cries of his people, the tribes and clans left behind, children of those who had come with Yuya out of Sinai. The god had in mind to set them free, to return them to the desert, far away from the power of Egypt's king.

"But why now?" the elders demanded. They had gathered willingly at Moshe's summons, expecting some revelation from the mountain, some new word of the law that

Moshe brought down from the hand of the god. This was as far out of their reckoning as it had been out of Nofret's. "Why does he summon you now?" they asked him. "Why so late, when you've had so many years among us? Why not when you were in Egypt already, and in a position to set all of them free?"

"The Lord told me," said Moshe, stammering as badly as Nofret had ever heard him, "that I—I must—" He had to stop, to master his tongue, before he could go on. "Now is the fullness of time. Now, and not then. Now that I'm one of you, bound in heart and soul to this land and these people."

"It's got worse, hasn't it?" That was Johanan, come in late and from the hunt, in the tunic he wore to hunt in, with his hair bound up in a fillet. He had left his bow and quiver outside the tent of gathering, but there was still a knife at his belt. He set himself in front of Moshe, fists planted on hips. "It was bad when I left—Lord of Hosts, has it been ten years? Fifteen? How much worse could it be?"

"Very much worse," said Moshe. "I was given to see . . ." He closed his eyes, swaying. Hands leaped to prop him up. He eluded them with surprising, boneless ease. "Horemheb is dead."

The sound of that name, even after so long, could freeze Nofret where she sat, far on the edge of the gathering. She had no proper place there, but she had brought Moshe down off the mountain; she was determined to hear what he would say.

Horemheb was dead. How strange to hear such a thing. He had become king after Ay died; had won at last the throne and the crowns for which he had intrigued for so long. He was a strong king, harsh as many said, but after so many years of weak kings, Egypt was glad of him.

But now he was gone. He had had no son. That had been a great grief to him, no doubt, if not to the Apiru.

His heir had been, like Horemheb himself, an ambitious man who seized and held the office of minister for the Two Lands.

"Ramses," Aharon was saying. "That would be his heir. A hard man, they say, as hard as Horemheb ever was."

"Hard indeed," said Moshe, "and strong, and no lover of our people. They remind him that our god endures, the god of the horizon, the one who is above all gods."

"And I suppose," said Johanan, "he finds them stiff-necked and often difficult, but strong workers, too skilled to lose."

Moshe regarded him without comprehension. Gods did not care for the concerns of practical men. "They must be set free. The Lord has chosen me to do it. He hears none of my objections, nor any that you may raise. I must go. I must lead the people out of Egypt."

"Alone?"

Moshe turned to face Aharon. "No, my brother. When I cried out to him that I am weak of mind and body, stammering of tongue, unfit to lead men or to speak before them, he gave me one to speak for me. One who has the voice that I lack, and the presence, and the cleverness with words. He gave me you."

A murmur went up at that. But Aharon was smiling. "Did he indeed?"

Moshe nodded. He looked hardly fit to cross the tent, let alone to make the long journey into Egypt. "I asked him," he said, "why, if you were to speak and lead and do all the rest that I lacked the strength or the wits to do, you could not simply be the one, the chosen of the Lord. He replied in his ineffable wisdom, 'I chose as I chose. Go now into Egypt, and take your brother with you.'"

None of them showed the least sign of objecting to their god's high-handedness. They accepted that he would send his prophet where he pleased, with a prince of the people to fetch and carry for him. The cry that went up was for those who would follow the two of them: every one of the elders, if they had their way, and half the women, and most of the tribe behind them.

It was Johanan who shouted them down, who beat as much sense into them as anyone was going to. There would be an embassy, it was decided: Moshe, Aharon, a handful of the elders, and a company of young men under Johanan, to defend them and to give them consequence.

"And what of your wives? What of your children?" Nofret was driven out of all caution. She faced Johanan in front of the elders. "Will you simply abandon them?"

"Beloved—" Johanan began.

"We will go," said a clear cold voice. Miriam had been silent throughout that long strange council, shadowed and all but invisible in a corner. Now she gathered them all to her as she had learned to do when she was queen: caught their eyes and held them. "Those of us who came up from Egypt—we will go as you go."

"But," said Johanan. "The children—"

Nofret leaped on the words. "Exactly! Are you going to abandon your sons, and your daughter who loves you?"

"Are you?"

Miriam stepped between them. "The children will stay among the people. Zipporah, Korah, Elisheba—they have mothers in plenty, and sisters and brothers, as many as they could ask for. They'll be well looked after."

Nofret found that her mouth was open. She shut it. The last thing that she had ever wanted was to see Egypt again. She had been happy in Sinai among the Apiru. Egypt was slavery, misery, death.

"It will know," she said, "who comes back to it. The dead walking. Forgotten king, long-vanished queen returned alive—the land will rise up against you. Unless . . ." She paused. "You don't actually intend to—"

"I laid down the crook and the flail," said Moshe. "I'll

never take them up again. I belong to the people of God. He bids me lead them out of Egypt."

"And what if someone recognizes you? What then?"

"I think," he said with surprising gentleness, "that I may have changed since I died in the Two Lands."

It was difficult to deny that. The man who had sat enthroned in golden splendor, crowned with the Two Crowns, bearing the crook and the flail, bore no resemblance to this prophet of the Apiru with his flowing white beard. The long disdainful mouth was hidden, the long nose shrunken between luxuriance of beard and curling fullness of hair. As for the eyes, and the voice with its light timbre, its frequent hesitations . . .

"It was long ago," Miriam said, "and long forgotten. Egypt will know the prophet of the Apiru, but never the one who died in Akhetaten."

"It does have to be you," said Johanan. "Doesn't it? Because Egypt will never let so many go, not as valuable as they are. But because you were what you were, both of you, you can compel the land itself, and the gods, and even the king."

"Or they'll kill you." Nofret looked from one to the next. Not one could meet her eyes. They could argue freely among themselves, and would, when it came time to prepare the journey. But they would not contest the will of their god. He had chosen. They would do as he bade.

Johanan, too. Johanan most of all. "I never knew," she said to him, soft, for only him to hear, "that you hated Egypt so much."

"Not hate," he said. "Inevitability. What was done to me before I left Thebes—that was a small thing. Some of our people have died for the whim or the malice of their masters."

"People always die," said Nofret.

"Not that way," he said. "Not my people."

She knew that look in his eye, that set to his chin. There was no shifting him. He would go.

She nodded abruptly. "Very well. There's much to do. Are you going to stay here blathering, or will you help me with it?"

He seemed briefly ready to remonstrate, but something stopped him. Maybe she wore the same expression he did: the same immovable obstinacy.

■ ■ ■

Once Nofret made up her mind to a thing, she could do it without hesitation and with as little regret as she could manage. She prided herself in that. But she had never had to do a thing so difficult. To go away from the place that had become home. To abandon her children.

That was even harder than she had thought it would be. The twins did not weep. They had seldom cried even as babies; and now, as they made clear to their mother, they were much too old for tears. Ishak had been hunting with the men for a good handful of years. Anna was becoming a woman. All too soon she would be wanting to marry.

Not so soon, Nofret told herself sternly. She would have returned long before her children were grown.

Jehoshua presented a wholly separate difficulty. He was grown, at least in the eyes of the Apiru. He had reached the years of manhood and been taken among the young men. As his mother and his father gathered their belongings for a journey of indefinite length and no little danger, he betrayed remarkably little dread of their departure. He was even lighthearted, coming to their fire at night and sharing their supper as he still did more often than not— his mother's cooking, he was fond of saying, was a fair deal better than the fare at the young men's fire.

Nofret ought to have been comforted, if somewhat dismayed. Her eldest was a man, and conducting himself with manly fortitude. Instead she was suspicious. She watched him with what she hoped was well-veiled wariness, listening to the things that he did not say. He was the image of his father at that age, all knobs and angles, with eyes that had never known how to lie.

She caught him by the fire on the night before they were to leave. By chance there was no one else about. The twins were with Aharon's brood, playing with a lamb that had been orphaned and was being raised as a pet. Johanan was with the elders, arguing no doubt, as they had been arguing since Moshe came down from the mountain. It had got down to the matter of how many donkeys the embassy was to take, and which, and whether they should wear their best harness out of the camp or wait to put it on till they were in Egypt.

Nofret intended to walk, not to ride a donkey. Her beast of burden had a perfectly decent harness that would do very well both in the desert and in the court of the Egyptian king. She had already sat through the discussion of which robes for the embassy and when, and how many jewels, and how soon to put them on. She was glad of the peace of her own fire, the pot simmering over it, a rich scent rising from it. In a little while, when the light was out of the sky, they would all be gathering in the middle of the camp, where an ox was roasting, and a fat sheep.

This end of the camp was almost empty. Everyone was crowded round the roasting-pit. Some people had got into the wine; they were singing, and a skein of them wound in a dance.

She was a little surprised that Jehoshua stayed with her. He had come ostensibly to fetch his hunting horn, which made a fine accompaniment to some of the young men's songs. He lingered to poke his nose in the pot and to investigate the cakes baking in the ashes. She slapped his hand when it crept toward one that was done and cooling on the good bronze platter.

He looked at her with big starving eyes. "Just one?"

he begged. "To see if they're fit for a feast?"

Nofret snorted. "The day one of my cakes isn't fit for a king's banquet, you'll be sure it's time to wrap me in my shroud."

His hand flashed, casting aside the omen. Nofret eased another cake or two from the ashes, and shifted the rest to catch the best of the coals. While she did that, she kept the corner of her eye on Jehoshua.

He squatted on his heels to watch her as she watched him. He had grown again: his limbs seemed inordinately long, his coat rather excessively short. Nofret would have to—

She caught herself. Someone else would let out the sleeves and add a strip to the hem. She was going to Egypt with his father.

He got up after a while, darted past her, snatched a cake and bolted laughing. She shook her fist at him, but her heart was not in it.

▪   ▪   ▪

"He's not grieving," she said to Johanan. They were wrapped in each other's arms. The twins slept near them, or pretended to. In a little while she would get up and stir the fire for the last breakfast that they would take together. She did not know that Johanan would come. No more did she know that he would not.

"He's too full of himself," she said. "You'd think he didn't believe we were going."

"He believes it," said Johanan. He had not been sleeping any better than she had. The nightlamp showed the hollows under his eyes, the deepening lines from nose to mouth. She smoothed them with her fingers. He darted a kiss at them, but his mind was not on it. "Do you want him to weep and wail and make a spectacle of himself?"

"No," Nofret said. "I want him to stop acting as if he's coming with us."

Johanan widened his eyes. "What makes you think—"

She surged up. "I knew it! You knew. Damn you, Johanan, you can't let—"

"Hush," he said. "You'll wake the children."

She lowered her voice a fraction, but she did not abate the force of it at all. "You will go out there now and tell our son that he is staying here."

"I can't do that," said Johanan.

She nearly hit him. "You are his father! You can command him. He has to obey."

"I can't," he said. "Jehoshua's bidden to come."

"By whom?"

"By the Lord," he said.

"By Moshe," said Nofret. "It's Moshe, isn't it? He thinks he'll keep us happy, let us have our firstborn with us, let us watch him—die—"

"Jehoshua will not die in Egypt," said Johanan.

"You don't know that," Nofret said. "Get out there and forbid him to go."

"No," said Johanan.

She drew away from him, muscle by muscle. It had been clear for longer than she would admit, that Jehoshua expected to go to Egypt with the rest of them. Certain knowledge of it moved her remarkably little. But that his father knew, and would not deny him—that, she could not accept.

"You know," she said, "that I want my children here. No matter what it costs me, no matter how long I'm forced to be away. They're safe here. No one is safe in Egypt."

She hoped, prayed, that he would not say the one thing, the thing that she would not forgive.

Of course he said it. He was Apiru. "The Lord will protect him," he said. He believed it without question, who questioned everything else under the sun.

Nofret's throat burned with bile. "You are blind," she said. "All of you. Stone blind."

"You needn't go," he said. "If you're afraid—if you don't believe—"

"What does believing have to do with it? I'll go. Jehoshua will not."

"Jehoshua must."

She looked at him as if she had never seen him before. There was a core of stone obstinacy in every Apiru. It was buried deep in Johanan, but now she saw it clear. For anything else she asked of him, he would yield. For this, no. Not if his god compelled him.

She should forgive. No Apiru would go against his god. Even for his wife. Even to protect the life of his son.

She had never worshipped this god. She acknowledged his existence—she was no such fool as to deny it. But she would not name him sole and only god, and no other before him. There *were* other gods in the world. She had felt their presence, heard their voices.

None of that would matter to Johanan. He knew just as surely that his god was one and alone. That was the prayer of his people, the children of Yisroel as they called themselves before their god.

She had lived for fifteen years among these people. She had married one of them and borne his children. She did not know them at all. No more did they know her, to think that they could take her son as they had taken her husband—as they had taken her. Her son would have no part of this.

And what could she do? He wanted it, the idiot boy. No one else would stop him. She could try, but she had bound herself to go. Short of knocking him down and sitting on him, she would never keep him here. He was as stubborn as both of his parents put together.

Defeat had never come easily. She got to her feet, stiff and aching, as if in that brief moment she had grown old. Johanan might have said something, reached for her— something to lessen the cold distance that had opened between them. She did not hear, nor did she see.

Morning was coming. The camp was rousing, groaning, sodden with wine and dancing. Women stirred up the fires, set the bread to bake. Over by the westward edge, the embassy had begun to gather: the guards with their weapons, the pack-animals, the elders dressed to travel, with their finery packed away till they came to Egypt.

Nofret moved with deliberate slowness. She did the things that she did every morning: waking the fire, baking the bread, milking the she-goat and filling the cups with warm rich milk. The twins came stumbling out, rubbing sleep from their eyes. She sent them to wash and to comb out their tangles. Ishak protested. Anna looked stubborn. Nofret overpowered them both with a glare.

They would do nothing differently now than they ever had. Not till the moment when the ram's horn lowed, calling them to the gathering. At the sound of it Nofret froze. Johanan was on his feet, the last round of bread abandoned, bow and quiver in hand, half-running toward the muster. Nofret would have gone slowly even if two solid young bodies had not flung themselves on her. They still refused to weep or plead. The weight of their unshed tears dragged her down.

With all the strength she had, she tore herself free. She must remember why she went. If there was a reason—if it was not plain obstinacy, and refusal to let her husband out of her sight.

No, there was more to it than that. This embassy of madmen and visionaries needed someone whose eyes were clear, whose mind was unblinded by the light of their god. Maybe it was a summons of its own, this conviction that she must go.

Jehoshua was standing among the young men, armed as they were, full of himself as they all were, lifting his chin as her eye caught his. His expression dared her to call him out, to forbid him to go.

She would not give him the satisfaction. She had no particular, ordained place in the caravan, but there was one that seemed proper: beside and a little behind Miriam, who walked in front with her father. Johanan was well back with the guard where he belonged, as she belonged here.

The twins, bless their good sense, did not run yelling after, pleading to be taken as their brother was. Nofret could see them through the blurring of sudden tears, two tall and upright figures in the midst of a flock of children: Aharon's, Moshe's, a shifting crowd of others. She saw no tears on their faces. Only a white, stark stillness.

Brave children. Braver than their mother, who was within a hair's breadth of bawling like a bullcalf.

People were singing as they went out. They were glad, or pretending to be. They sang praise to their god in sight of his holy mountain, naming him the holy one, the mighty one, the one who would bring his people out of Egypt.

Nofret had no song in her. She walked grimly out of the camp, away from her joy and her freedom, back into slavery. Not because any god called her. Because she was a fool. A headstrong, purblind, gods-blasted fool.

CHAPTER FIFTY-SIX

▲

FOOL or not, Nofret was set on the road to Egypt. She had nothing to say to Johanan. If he had anything to say to her, she did not hear it. She shared a tent with Miriam, walked with her, waited on her in a pattern that she thought forgotten. It came back with disturbing ease.

They went by far less secret ways than Johanan had taken in bringing the queen out of Egypt. They took the royal road through Sinai, traveling openly as an embassy well might. By night they camped in oases or in encampments of their people, and as they reached the royal road, in garrison towns and in caravanserais among other embassies and among the traders passing back and forth. They did not trumpet their errand to all who could hear, but they did not conceal that they were an embassy from the tribes to the king of Egypt.

This country in name was Egypt. It had been conquered long since, secured with garrisons that ran in a skein along the border of Canaan. But it was not Egypt proper. Egypt was the Two Lands, Upper and Lower. Its shape was as a lotus blossom on a stem that stretched from Nubia to Memphis. Its flower was the Delta, the many mouths of the river that opened on the sea.

All else, and Sinai itself, was conquered country. Egypt, Red Land and Black Land, was the heart of the empire. Its gods were strongest there. Its earth was different underfoot.

Nofret knew when they passed into Egypt proper. The desert was desert still, bleak Red Land. The Black Land and the river that begot it were far away. But this was Egypt.

It knew who had come back to it. Moshe, who wore his god's light like armor, felt nothing that Nofret could discern. Miriam frowned as she walked, but then she always did. Only Nofret seemed to notice how the air quivered, how the sun seemed to peer closer, marking the dead who had returned.

In the desert of Sinai they had gone as all travelers did, on guard against thieves, falling into company with other travelers as occasion warranted. The beasts of the desert shunned them, even among their tents at night.

In Egypt they had companions on the road—not human companions as they had had before, but creatures of the desert. At night a tribe of jackals was always about them. The guards would have driven them off, but Johanan stopped them. "They do no harm," he said. "They might even help. Anyone who tries to break through their circle will get such a welcome as to rouse the whole camp."

No one seemed to find it odd that they were so accompanied—so guarded. Some of the Apiru seemed to decide that Egyptian jackals were a kind of wild dog, and to treat them accordingly.

Nofret kept her tongue between her teeth. If those who ought to know better did not see fit to enlighten the innocents, she was not about to do it for them. Egypt's gods were here, watching. The god of the Apiru might be stronger than they, or he might not. That war was not for Nofret to fight.

Egypt bided its time. She perforce did the same. She wore again the amulets that she had kept for so long hidden in her tent, the little images of Amon and of Sobek, the blue glass and the green stone, plaited into her hair. She doubted that either would care if she invoked him, not with the company she kept, but she felt safer with them than without.

■　■　■

Moshe in the Red Land lost little by little the humanity that had been his in Sinai. Without his wife to woo him with her gentleness, without his sons to draw him away from contemplation of his god, he became as Nofret had known him in Akhetaten: dreamer and prophet, remote and more than a little mad. He could be coaxed out of it, particularly by the young men, who asked him endless questions and argued happily with the answers. But the closer he came to Memphis, the more distant he seemed.

Miriam at least was as much herself as ever. Nofret had had no hopes of this journey, nor was she disappointed that Miriam offered none of the intimacy that an Apiru woman would have done, sharing a tent and a cookpot, night after night. Miriam preferred silence to the easy chatter of women. She did not expect servitude, nor servility either, which suited Nofret perfectly well. They were two women traveling among the elders and the young men, sharing company but not confidences.

Nofret did not know that Miriam had ever had the art of friendship. It was late for her to begin. Nor would Nofret help her, or press her to be other than she was.

The elders lacked Nofret's circumspection. They had all heard Moshe's declaration before the mountain, that he would not be king again in Egypt. Now that they were come to Egypt and were soon to come to Memphis, they pricked at him, urging him to reconsider.

"Just think," they said. "Here you are, and here is the kingdom. The man who rules it is your heir only by distant courtesy. The line of kings has broken. Won't you restore it? You even have sons to inherit after you."

Moshe seemed not to hear them. He was sitting cross-legged by the fire under the vault of stars that in Egypt was thought to be a goddess' body, listening to the song of the jackals. With firelight on his face he looked nothing at all like the king who had ruled in Akhetaten: that long-chinned strange man with his mouth set forever in disdain.

"If you could see," they went on, talking as much to hear themselves as to be heard. "Our people are beaten down by kings who both fear and despise them. If one were to come, to proclaim himself king, to set our people free to rule beside him—"

That had gone too far. Miriam spoke with more warmth than Nofret had heard in her since Tutankhamon died. "You do not know what you say. Egypt will never endure a foreign king or the rule of a foreign people. It suffered the Shepherd Kings—and it has never forgotten it. Why do you think this king sets his foot so heavy on the people's necks? He remembers that Egypt was conquered once, and could be again."

"Is it conquest," asked one of the elders, "for a king

to come back to the throne that is his by right of birth?''

''If that king is dead,'' she answered, ''and he comes back leading a tribe of foreigners, yes, it is conquest.''

Heads shook round the circle, beards wagging, chins setting firm against her too excellent sense. ''Why would a king trouble to free slaves who are both numerous and useful, even if their kinsmen come to beg him? How much better if that king were disposed of and one set up in his place who has reason to favor our people.''

''The god has commanded no such thing,'' Miriam said with a snap in her voice. ''We are bidden to free the people from the hand of Pharaoh, and to lead them out of Egypt. Not to claim Egypt's throne.''

''Yet,'' said the elders, ''if we did—''

''You will not,'' said Miriam. ''I was driven into exile because I tried to set a foreign prince on the throne beside me. If I were to come back from the dead, and my father with me, and a pack of shepherds at our backs, Egypt itself would kill us, without need for its king to raise a finger.''

The Apiru did not believe it. None of them but Aharon and Johanan had lived in Egypt. They were all men of the free desert, innocents in the ways of the Two Lands. They argued it over and over, while Moshe ignored them and Miriam stalked away in disgust.

■   ■   ■

Miriam kept her anger even when she had gone to her bed in her half of the tent. She was quiet, but Nofret felt it: a heaviness in the air, a tautness like a bowstring about to snap. Nofret spread her blankets, slipped out of her clothes, lay down in the dim light of the lamp that hung from the tentpole. She could see Miriam wrapped in her own blankets, a tousle of hair, a small closed face in the center of it, eyes open, dark, staring at nothing.

''I would think,'' Nofret said after a long while and much thought, ''that you would be glad to hear them talking so. Don't you want to be queen again?''

Somewhat to her surprise, Miriam answered her. "What I want is of no consequence whatsoever.''

"So you do,'' Nofret mused. "But not badly enough to think you can have it.''

"I want nothing,'' said Miriam, "but to do what I've been bidden to do, and to get it over.''

"And then to die?''

Miriam's eyes flashed to Nofret's face. Nofret withstood the heat of them with the fortitude of a woman married to a man with a temper, mother of children with worse tempers yet. "What else is there to do?'' Miriam demanded of her.

"Live,'' said Nofret. "Be happy. Worship your god if you choose.''

"Nothing is ever so simple.''

"Sometimes it is.''

"For you, maybe.'' Miriam set in that all the arrogance of a daughter of kings.

Nofret laughed, which was not wise, but she could not help it. "You make everything so complicated. No wonder people think the god has forbidden you to smile. If you do, they say, you'll be afflicted with leprosy, or something even worse.''

"That is nonsense,'' said Miriam.

"Isn't it?'' Nofret propped her head on her hand. "I think you're afraid to smile. Your face might crack. Or someone will smile back. What if it's a man? What if he's good to look at? What if he takes your heart out of the mummy-jar that it's been pickled in for so long, and warms it, and brings it to life again?''

"My heart is not—'' Miriam's mouth snapped shut.

"I should have said this to you years ago,'' Nofret said, more to herself than to Miriam. "You're mummified, do you know that? You live and walk and breathe, but you've been dead since your young king died.''

Miriam lay still. Nofret had driven her behind her barriers. They were high, as high as years could make them. What was behind them, Nofret could not know for certain. But she hoped suddenly, out of nowhere, that it was a young girl, the third princess of Akhetaten, naked and supple and endlessly curious. That princess had not yet learned to be a queen, to wear a mask that was proud and hard and cold. She was young; her heart was whole, if still a green unripened thing.

There was little to be seen of her in this quiet bitter woman with her beauty that had never faded or grown stale. Strange, thought Nofret, how the beauty endured even after the heart had withered.

"You've forgotten how to live," Nofret said. "Now you can't even remember what it is to want to. This madness of your father's, that you abetted him in—you hope he'll fail, and you'll be killed."

"I do not," said Miriam. There: Nofret heard the child, petulant maybe, but present. "You are presumptuous."

"Aren't I?" said Nofret. "I always was. You gave me permission to be, long ago. Do you remember?"

Miriam did not answer.

"I was the one who could say the things that you couldn't, because you were too proper a princess. Now let me say what you won't say. You won't mind in the least if you die in Egypt."

"Do you fault me for that?"

Nofret sat up and clasped her knees. Her hair, plaited for the night, slipped over her shoulder. She noticed distantly that it was shot with grey. Miriam's was still as black as ever.

Some women had all the luck.

"Look at you," Nofret said. "The rest of us show the weight of years. My hair's going white, my breasts are starting to sag, my bones ache in the mornings. You've hardly aged a day since you were a girl. You're still as lissome as ever, your hair's still black, your face hasn't gained a line. And you want to die. Why? What's the use in that, except to make a beautiful corpse?"

"What have I to live for?" Miriam demanded.

She thrust herself up in her blankets, facing Nofret across the width of the tent. Nofret was surprised to see how much animation was in that face, even if most of it was temper.

"I thought you had your god," Nofret said, "and your prophecies. And, if they aren't enough, your father."

"My father doesn't need me. He has sons."

"Are you jealous, then?"

Miriam glared. "I am glad for him. But what use am I, the last of all his daughters, when he has menchildren to prove that he's a man?"

"Well," said Nofret, "for one thing, you're the eldest who's still alive, the one who's known him best. You loved him enough to let him die to Egypt. You've pleased him in no little degree since you came to him in Sinai."

"What, I, the one who turned on him after he was gone, and brought back the old gods? I, the bitter one, the one whose face can sour a festival?"

"You, the clear-eyed seer, the mirror of his god."

"You sound," said Miriam, "exactly like Leah."

Nofret blinked.

"She rallied me endlessly," Miriam said. "Rebuked me, remonstrated with me, made it abundantly clear that I was a self-pitying fool and a waster of the god's gifts. Of which she said I had many. I never saw them, nor knew what they were. In the end I think she despaired of me."

"Hardly," said Nofret, "if she made you her successor."

Miriam's mouth twisted. "That was her revenge on me for being so intransigent."

"I don't think so," Nofret said.

"You may think as you please."

"Why, thank you, your majesty," said Nofret.

Miriam regarded her in incredulity too perfect even for anger. "Will you never forgive me," she asked at last, "for having been your queen?"

"Never," said Nofret.

Miriam pondered that: her eyes were dark, turned inward. After a while she nodded as if in agreement. She lay down, her back to Nofret, and wrapped herself again in blankets.

Nofret did not know what she was feeling. Not satisfaction, she did not think. Certainly not regret. She had seen wounds pierced when they had begun to suppurate, the evil pouring out of them till the clean blood ran. Then the wounded one recovered—unless the lancing came too late, when at least he died in less pain and squalor than if he had been left alone.

She could hope that Miriam would not die of the truth; that she might heal, if only a little. Her wound was old and very deep. Deep enough that scars had thickened over it, but it was as bitter as ever beneath.

And maybe Nofret was wounded, too, by years and neglect, anger and old resentment. Miriam had struck close to the bone when she spoke of being forgiven for having been Nofret's mistress. For having kept her as a slave, and never, of her own will, set her free.

Egypt would heal them both, or it would kill them. At that particular moment, Nofret did not even care which.

CHAPTER FIFTY-SEVEN

▲

ANCIENT Memphis had changed but little since Tutankhamon was king. Its white walls were perhaps a little whiter, polished anew by the new king. The great tombs beyond its western edge were very slightly more worn by the passage of years. And of course the name carved and painted on decrees and proclamations had altered: no longer Nebkheperure Tutankhamon as it had been so long ago but another, just lately crowned, Menpehtire Ramses who had been high minister under Horemheb.

Horemheb had had no son to be his heir. One might think that that was the gods' justice on the man who had taught Egypt that a king, like any mortal, could be killed for a man's convenience. He had gained the throne he sought, but sired no son to take it after him. He had, like Ay, like Tutankhamon himself, to surrender it in death to a man who—for all anyone knew—had wished him as ill as Horemheb had wished Smenkhkare and Tutankhamon.

Nofret drew a long breath of relief when Miriam read the name on the cartouche of the new stone that had been set up before the gate of Memphis. She had not believed that Horemheb still lived. News of his death had run down the trade-roads, as had the news of a new line set up to rule in the Two Lands, a line that did not take its king-right from the daughters of Nefertari. That much of the old law Horemheb had submitted to. Ramses had cast it aside perforce. There was no living child of Nefertari in Egypt, that anyone knew of.

It was astonishing how much Nofret remembered as she walked beneath that gate, trying not to shrink from the guards with their spears and their expressions of settled boredom. It even mattered that a king of Egypt should have broken the line and begun a new one, with a son to hallow it.

The gods of Egypt, it seemed, looked with favor on their new Horus. The people had an air of gladness that Nofret had not seen in them before, a lightness, as if a great weight had left them. The world, old as it was, had been made anew under its new king.

■ ■ ■

There was a protocol for embassies, even a ragtag gathering of savages from the desert. The faces of the palace servants were eloquent of contempt, lips pursed and noses lifted as if in disgust at the stink of goats. The Apiru in their best finery, washed meticulously in a traveler's lodging, combed and anointed with sweet oils, lifted their own noses even higher and swept into a palace of such grandeur as only Johanan and Aharon, Miriam and Moshe, had ever seen.

No nose could be raised more haughtily than an Apiru's, except perhaps a Hittite's. They put the Egyptians to shame. The Egyptians yielded to it. Their manner did not soften, but when they spoke again thereafter, they spoke with decent respect, all things considered.

Aharon spoke for the Apiru in his pure Egyptian accent with its intonation of princely Thébes. That subdued the servants even further and won his companions admittance to a lodging of somewhat greater consequence than they might have been judged to deserve. It did not win them immediate audience with the king. Even a royal embassy from Hatti or from Punt would not be granted such a concession.

■ ■ ■

They settled to wait. The elders had studied patience, and were unabashedly glad to rest in such luxury: rooms as wide as half a dozen tents laid end to end, and if possible higher; a garden to walk in, with fountains, and trees laden with fruit; servants alert to their every need. The young men, separated from their weapons, and not willingly either, allayed their restlessness by roving the city.

Moshe seemed oblivious to anything but the voice of his god. Memphis had been no capital of his, nor had he ruled from its palace. It could mean little to him even if he had cared to remember what he had been.

For Miriam it was torment. She had been queen within

these walls. Here she had known both her greatest happiness and her greatest grief. And the palace did not know her. It had forgotten her as it forgot all those who died to it. It could do no other, not as ancient as it was, overburdened with memory.

Nofret saw that she suffered, but there was nothing that anyone could do. To speak might be to betray her. To admit that she should care where she was, she who was known in this life as the prophetess of the Apiru, would be to recall the one who had died, who must not be allowed to live again.

For Nofret it was a life remarkably like the one she had lived in Egypt before: waiting on her lady, who was mostly too stunned or too sullen to speak, and watching Moshe wander about in a god-begotten fog. The Apiru were a difference, but they were inclined to keep to themselves. They did not eat as people ate here, and they prayed to their god in their own way, going apart to do it.

Johanan did not seek Nofret's company. Nofret made no effort to look for him. She supposed that he kept Jehoshua within sight. She did not know. Her son did not visit her, either, or send to see how she did. Their quarrel had grown in silence till it was like a wall, dividing them on the journey and sundering them here in Egypt.

She told herself that she did not care. There was an emptiness in her, a hard cold stillness. The outside of her was as it had always been, in Memphis as in the desert: walking, talking, eating and breathing, waiting on her lady. She had no desire to wander afield, not even to explore Memphis. For all she knew the beer-seller was still there, still brewing a stronger brew than most, and serving it in the same battered cups.

It was not as if her whole self depended on Johanan's goodwill. He could be as massive a fool as he pleased, cast his own son—her son—into danger, kill them both and be damned to him. She had lived well enough before she married him. She could live as well again, in Egypt as easily as anywhere else.

She felt strange, thinking that. As if there was no stretch of years ahead of her. Every morning came like the edge of the world, shifting always just enough that she did not fall. What was beyond it, truly beyond, she did not know.

In Sinai she had thought she knew how the years would pass. They would be many, she could hope, and long; her children growing up, marrying, presenting her with grand-children; the round of the year with its journeys from pasture to pasture. Death in the end, of course, but not before Johanan, when both of them had come to a great and venerable age. Egypt had been no part of it, nor dying still almost young, nor losing Jehoshua before he was even a man. His beard was no more than a shadow on his upper lip; his voice had barely broken; and he was strutting about like a lord of warriors.

So for that matter was his father, who should have known better. She nursed her quarrel with fastidious care. It kept her from making a fool of herself, chasing after a pair of heedless men and begging them to take her home.

And where was home, if they were not in it? She was not Apiru except by courtesy. Egypt knew nothing of her. Hatti had forgotten her. She had nowhere to be but here, nothing to do but stand companion to a woman who neither needed nor heeded her.

Nofret despised self-pity. She knocked it down and trampled it. Still it kept rising again, taking her by surprise, laying her low.

■   ■   ■

In the fullness of time a messenger came to the Apiru. The king would see them in audience among the rest of the embassies that had come in since last the moon was full. There were a surprising number, most come to welcome the new king to his throne and to take his measure on behalf of their own kings and chieftains.

They were all gathered in the hall of audience, ordered according to the whim of an august official with a golden-headed staff. He had not been the minister of protocol when Ankhesenamon was queen, but Nofret knew him. He was much older and more portly than the lithe young underling that he had been. He still had the cast in his eye, and the way of tilting his head that he thought concealed it.

She kept her head down and her veil up. It had been slow to occur to her that she and not her lady might betray them all. Servants were invisible, true enough, but the queen's Hittite, her chief of servants, might actually be remembered. Nofret had to hope that her veil was concealment enough, and that no one would ask how an Apiru woman could be grey-eyed.

No one seemed to see her. She was only one of a throng of foreigners. Those from Punt were much more notable, women and men, naked, coal-black, ornamented with feathers and hung about with amber and ivory. There were tattooed Libyans, bearded and brocaded princes from Asia, even a company of thickset, heavy-muscled men from Ashur with a gift of lionskins. No Hittites. Hatti was slow to know that Egypt had a new king, or else bided its time, waiting to see how he would conduct himself toward a nation that had been both ally and enemy.

The hours passed slowly. Each embassy brought forward its gifts or its tribute, delivered its speeches, offered its respects in the fashion of its country. The Apiru, well back in the ranks, could see little but a forest of pillars and the heads of the embassy in front of them. They could not crane into the aisle: the king's guards prevented them. They were expected to keep their places, to advance in their proper order, and not, under any circumstances, to object.

It was one of the more grueling ordeals that Nofret could remember, more so even than the day she came to Akhetaten and was presented as tribute to its king. Either she had forgotten how tedious it was to wait on kings, or there was a difference in the tedium when one was privileged to stand at the head of the hall among the royal attendants. One could slip out then without colliding with an armed guard, and rest or relieve oneself, eat or drink, and return with no one the wiser.

The king was so privileged, but those who came to his audience were not. When he took his recess they remained in their ranks, hungry, thirsty, yearning for a privy. Nofret heard a whisper behind her that sounded very much like Jehoshua, hissing loud enough to be heard across the hall: "God of Hosts, but I have to *go!*"

Another whisper, a fraction less penetrating, responded, "Water a pillar. Who'll notice?"

Someone else hissed them into silence and, Nofret hoped, restrained them from committing a violence to the sanctity of the hall. That would be Johanan, she supposed. She refused to look back, to be certain.

This king was old, though she had not seen him yet, and needed to excuse himself remarkably often. While he was gone, time stretched to an image of eternity. She caught herself wondering if the courts of judgment were like this in the life after Egyptian death. So many bodies crowded together, such a reek of sweat and unguents, wool and ill-washed flesh. Even as airy as the hall was built to be, the sun held at bay by a mighty thickness of walls, the atmosphere was close, too warm for the swathings of desert robes.

Nofret dared not shed hers, though she itched formidably. The Asiatics ahead of them were not clean. It would be like the gods' humor to have afflicted her with fleas, and when she had just bathed, too.

She glanced at her companions. The elders had settled

in a circle. Some of them were snoring gently. The young men were on their feet, and Moshe leaning on his staff, and Miriam. They all seemed lost in a trance of waiting, even the young men, though Jehoshua had a faintly mulish look.

If any of them had been apprehensive, that was long lost in boredom. What Moshe would say, what he would do, no one knew, not even Moshe. The god would guide him, he had said. It might well be the god's intention to betray him in the heart of the kingdom that he had once ruled, before the face of its king.

She should have bolted while she still could—or stayed in their lodging, from which at least there was some hope of escape. Here there was none. Every door was guarded. There was no way out except past the king.

At long last they made their way to the front of the hall. By degrees Nofret could see the high ones in their places, rank on glittering rank, and all their attendants, from the little naked maids to the haughty chiefs of servants. She had leisure—far more than she wanted—to study faces. Many were familiar, too many not. Not all were too young to have stood in court when Tutankhamon was king. This new king had brought his own people to power, friends and allies who had been too lowly or too far out of favor to stand before Tutankhamon.

The king himself sat on the dais in the place that was most hauntingly familiar. His throne was new, but it stood where a throne had been since Memphis was a village on the banks of the river. It stood alone, no queen's throne to bear it company. His queen was dead, nor had he taken another, though it was said that his lesser ladies were numerous. Likewise his daughters, many of whom stood among those nearest him, and one, the eldest, only a little less near than his young and surprisingly attractive son. The woman was old enough to be the boy's mother, but

that was not said of her, that she had borne a son to her
father.

They both bore a notable resemblance to the king. Nofret had known him vaguely, more a name than a face in
the following of Horemheb. Pa-Ramses, he had been then,
one of the general's many allies, ambitious as most of them
were. He had been a chief of works, she recalled from
some deep font of memory, a great builder in the Delta,
much given to proposing new cities and renewing old ones.

He must have been not much younger than Horemheb.
He seemed as old as Ay had been when he took the Two
Crowns, gone to flesh as many did in Egypt, but condemned by custom to wear the garments that needed a
young man's body to set them off. His dressers had done
what they could in binding his kilt tight and somewhat
high and adorning him with a splendid mass of jewels:
bracelets, armlets, a pectoral as broad as a general's breast-
plate. None of it could disguise the soft swell of his arms,
or the veined hands that clutched the crook and the flail.

She looked last at his face. It was the familiar royal
mask under the two tall crowns, White nested within Red;
painted like a woman's, heavy with white lead, the eyes
drawn large and long with kohl and malachite. Still she
saw the heavy jowls, the downward turn of the mouth, the
deep lines clotted thick with paint.

He was much more beautiful on his stelai. But then all
kings were, except Akhenaten, who had taken a rebel's
pride in his ugliness.

■　■　■

The Asiatics delivered their gifts and their speeches, both
profuse and prolix. The king actually yawned in the middle: subtle, disguised as an inclination of the head, but
Nofret had learned in youth to penetrate a king's subter-
fuges. This king was less subtle than he might have been
had he been born to it, less practiced in his deceptions.

After an endless while the Asiatics were ushered out, one of them still trying to babble. The Apiru drew taut, rousing from a near-doze to sudden, fierce alertness.

Moshe barely waited for the king's minister to call him forward. The space before the dais was the brightest part of the hall, so lighted that the king had clear vision of any who stood there. Moshe entered it with his head up and his stride firm. His hair shone silver-bright, his beard flowing white on his breast. His robe was his best, woven of new wool, pure and undyed. The only color in him was in the head of his staff, the serpent's head glowing, gold washed thinly over bronze.

Aharon behind him, his robe striped with crimson and gold, seemed somehow the more subdued. The rest in black were like shadows, a guard of honor as it were, arranging themselves in a rough circle.

They brought no gifts for the king. That was uncommon enough to raise the royal brows; the court muttered, naming them ungracious, a company of savages, to come empty-handed before the Lord of the Two Lands.

Unless of course the company of young men was the gift, or the staff in the elder's hand. Nofret saw how they stared and speculated, as idle minds will.

Moshe sharpened their attention by failing to fling himself at the king's feet. He stood erect, did not even bow; looked up at the man on the dais with such focus and such intensity that the king actually seemed to recoil. Nofret, edging round till she was almost among the courtiers, saw enough of Moshe's face to know that it was calm, that it even smiled. The god was in his eyes.

The king's minister of protocol was the first to recover from the general astonishment. His brows were knit, his mismatched eyes almost equal in their focus, fixed on this man who refused to behave as a petitioner should. He had raised his staff of office, might even have struck Moshe with it, had Moshe not raised his chin a fraction and said,

"My lord of Egypt. Do you know who I am?"

Nofret's heart stopped. Her glance leaped to Miriam. There was nothing to be read at all in a face veiled to the eyes, and those eyes wide, blank, completely without expression.

But nobody cried the name of Akhenaten, nor even the titles that they had given him after he died in his city: the fallen one, the rebel of Akhetaten. No one named him king and god, still less a god who had died and presumed to return to the house of the living. The king regarded him in haughty astonishment, the hauteur rather clumsily played to eyes that knew the true royal pride.

Such eyes were rare here, or did not accept the truth. Moshe stood as a king stands, looking this king in the face, saying lightly, serenely, "I see that you do not know me. You hold my people captive, my lord of Egypt. They build your city for you, your Pi-Ramses, who once built tombs for kings and princes."

The king's eldest daughter leaned close, whispering in his ear. The king's frown deepened even further. He was perhaps being advised not to speak: Nofret saw how his jaw tightened. The woman saw it, too. She drew back with an expression that said clearly, *On your head be it.*

The king spoke abruptly in a harsh, old man's voice, much louder than Moshe's but no more penetrating. "Yes, I do know you. You would be the prophet from Sinai, the one who brings visions to the tribes. Have you brought me a vision? Is that your gift to me?"

"Perhaps," said Moshe. "Our god is given more to words than to images. He feels the want of worshippers; he bids you set my people free to go into the desert, to celebrate his feast and his sacrifice."

"What," said the king, "your god commands? And who is this god, that he should set his will on the Great House of Egypt?"

"He bids you let them go," Moshe said, "to serve him

as he decrees. Three days' journey, he bids you, three days into the desert, to worship him with prayer and sacrifice, or he will strike his people with pestilence.''

The king snorted explosively, nearly dislodging the Two Crowns. ''That is preposterous! What is this god to me, that I should disrupt the building of my city, put my overseers out of work, and set my slaves free to roam where they please? Does he take me for a fool, then, that I'll expect any of them to come back once their festival is over? They'll vanish into the desert, every last man and woman and child of them, and leave my city unbuilt.''

Moshe bore the king's temper with remarkable aplomb. When it had sputtered itself out, he said, ''My god is greater than you can know. Will you defy him? Have you no fear?''

''I fear nothing that comes from the desert,'' snapped the king.

Moshe nodded slowly. ''You have your own gods. You think that they protect you. But my god is stronger than they.''

''So strong, no doubt,'' said the king, ''that he drives you mad before my face.''

Moshe smiled. It was a sweet smile, with nothing gentle in it. He beckoned. Aharon came forward as if drawn by the hand. Moshe gave him the staff. The serpent's head seemed to stir, its hood to widen. The gilt was less bright now, the bronze more darkly distinct. Its shape and curve mirrored exactly that of the uraeus-serpent in the king's crown.

Aharon flung the staff at the king's feet. It should have clattered, but it fell soft, as if it were a living thing and not a shape of wood and gilded bronze. As it lay on the paving, it seemed to writhe.

The court gasped. There were shrieks, and not all of them were women's. The king drew back as far as the throne allowed.

A strong voice called out from among the king's attendants. His was a new face, and young, but the linen robe and the emblem of Amon named him priest, and a high one at that. He spoke with the strength of his god, and no little mockery in it. "What, prophet! Is your god so feeble? That's a trick as old as Egypt. See, we match it."

Every priest who could come forward cast down his own staff. Many of them laughed as they did it. The things writhed as they fell, seemed even to hiss.

Trickery. Jointed wood, cleverly forged bronze, a bit of priestly subterfuge.

Moshe smiled. Aharon spoke, but not to anything human. "Go," he said. "Feed."

Moshe's staff coiled as if it were alive, and struck swift as a snake strikes: here, here, here. It ate the priests' staffs one by one, swallowed them whole. When the last was gone, it sank down on the paving. It died, one might almost have thought: went stiff and still, was simple wood and bronze again. And no other staff anywhere, though the priests searched with mounting urgency.

"Clever," said the king. "Entertaining in its fashion. Shall we hire you for our banquets, then? A diversion between the meat and the wine, a bit of sorcery to make our ladies shriek and tremble?"

"My god is not mocked," said Moshe, cold and clear. "Will you set my people free?"

"What, no word now of a rite or a sacrifice? Is it freedom in full that you ask for?" The king shook his head. "You are mad, sir. Amusing, but quite mad. Will you go, or must I have you removed from my presence?"

"I will go," said Moshe. "But my god is not finished, nor will he be until his people are freed."

"Then it's fortunate," said the king, "that gods live forever."

"But kings," said Moshe, terribly gentle, "do not."

CHAPTER FIFTY-EIGHT

▲

Moshe the prophet had threatened the Great House of Egypt. There was no other way to regard it, and no hope for it either.

And yet he was not hauled off in chains. He was allowed to walk out of the king's presence as he had walked in, free and unhindered. He went to the place of their lodging with the others straggling behind him, shocked into silence by the words he had spoken. Fools, thought Nofret, and in that she included herself. They should have known that Moshe would do the unthinkable.

He secluded himself deep in the guesthouse. The others huddled in the gathering-room, even Aharon, who looked wan and old. Nofret had not till then remembered that he was older than Moshe. Now she saw it in his face.

"We should go elsewhere," Nofret said when the silence had grown huge enough to suffocate. "We're not safe in the palace. If the king takes it into his head that we mean to attack him—"

"We're safer here than anywhere." Those were the first words Johanan had spoken directly to her since they left Mount Horeb. "These are strong walls, and guarded. The king will spy on us—he'd be a fool if he didn't—and that will put his mind at ease. Whereas if we pack up and go elsewhere, he'll know that we mean him harm, and follow us, and dispose of us somewhere suitably secret."

"He can dispose of us here, and no one the wiser."

"The whole palace would know," he said. He prowled the edges of the room. The others watched him, trapped in immobility as he was in restlessness.

Nofret seemed the only one with wits to speak. "The palace may not care if we live or die. They'll be laughing at us now, if they're not in a rage: a gaggle of desert savages who vexed the Great House with insolence. Even our magic is a tawdry thing, a charlatan's trick, as common as bad beer in the market."

"The Lord commanded," said Aharon wearily. "We did as we were told."

"And does your god intend for all of us to be laughed out of Egypt?" Nofret demanded.

"Inscrutable is the mind of the Lord," said Aharon, "and incalculable his ways."

The others murmured pious agreement. Nofret shook her head in disgust and thrust herself to her feet. She refused to pace as Johanan did. She went out instead; it did not greatly matter where.

There were guards outside the door, big burly Nubians in the king's livery. They understood no Egyptian, or none that they would admit to. She could pass, they made it clear, but only if one of them went with her. For her own safety, of course.

She retreated, snarling to herself. The garden at least was empty of armed men, its walls too high to climb. She had not noticed before how small it was, how circumscribed its limits.

She was not remarkably surprised to find that she had a companion. Johanan was less restless here than he had been within, but still too restless to sit. He stood in the shade of the pomegranate tree, looking up at the branches, searching for ripe fruit maybe among the green.

"It's too early," she said to him.

Johanan glanced at her. His eye was cold, as if he were a stranger. He could hold a grudge, too, damn him. "Maybe it's too late," he said, "to win our people's freedom."

"Maybe they should never have come to Egypt."

"They hadn't much choice. There was drought, famine. Our pastures were bare. Egypt had grain for our flocks, and water enough from its river to keep us all alive. And our kinsman was here, the man whom the Egyptians called Yuya, brought to Egypt as a slave and raised to be a prince of the realm. He offered us sanctuary."

He spoke as if he had been alive through all of that. But it was all done before he was born: born in Egypt, a prince of his blood, forced from birth to labor for his living.

"We were not slaves," he said. "We owed our livelihood to the king, yes; we had a debt which we undertook to pay. But he never owned us."

"Then how," asked Nofret, "did your people come to this?"

He dropped down under the pomegranate tree. For a moment she saw not the tall princely man with the glint of silver in his beard, but the long-legged boy he had been. He spoke more than half to himself. "We are a fecund people. Even in exile, even bound to a king by a debt that seemed to grow larger the more we paid it back, we were fruitful; we multiplied. Our children had to be fed. They needed roofs over their heads. Somehow we had to pay for that. So we sold ourselves, not only our labor but our bodies that performed the labor." He caught the flash of her eye. "No, I didn't! But when I went back to Thebes after I'd been in Sinai, I found that there were no free men left. All my people were bound—for convenience, the overseers said. To make it simpler in ordering this tomb or that. Then after I left, the tomb-workers were told to pack up and go. They were needed; there was a city of the living to build."

"Pi-Ramses," Nofret said. "Ramses' city. So he owns you all."

"So he imagines," said Johanan.

"You don't really think he's going to set you all free just because you ask."

"He would do better to give way," Johanan said.

Nofret looked at him as if she had never seen him before. "Even you believe that? Two dozen boys and a handful of elders and a pair of priests who know the trick that every priest in Egypt learns in his cradle—what in the world makes you think that you'll move the might of Egypt?"

"That trick," Johanan said with a slight curl of the lip, "was simply to prove that yes, our priests are priests, too. It was only the beginning."

"It may well be the end," she said, "after what Moshe said to the king."

"I doubt that," said Johanan. "He must be as incredulous as you are. Maybe he's even diverted, now his temper's had time to cool. He'll be curious to see what else we can do."

"What, more tricks? The leper's hand that the priests of Set and Sobek use to horrify the gullible? Water to wine, maybe, or to blood if you're ambitious? There's nothing you can do that will convince him to free so useful an army of slaves."

"You think so?" Johanan stood. "I'll lay you a wager."

"I didn't know you gambled."

"Of course I do," he said. "I came to Egypt twice. I married you."

"Well then," she said. "A wager. If I win, we die here. If you win . . ."

"If I win, we go free. Either way, we do it together."

"Only if you send Jehoshua back to Sinai."

The air that had warmed between them went cold again. "It's too late for that," he said. He left her sitting there, glaring at the place where he had been.

■   ■   ■

On the day after the audience with the king, a messenger came to speak, as he put it, to the priests from Sinai. He was a priest himself, the young man of Amon's following who had matched the trick of the staff with a trick of his own. His name was very long; he gave them leave to call him Ramose—Ramses, like the king.

The message that he brought came direct from the Great House. "My lord Horus had pondered upon your people's plight," he said in his beautiful voice. "He has considered what he best may do to honor your request. It grieves him to lose workers of such excellence, so numerous and so splendidly suited for the work of building his city. Yet if your people wish truly to be free, it is a simple matter to assure it. You need but pay the price of each of his slaves, such as they would fetch in the market of Memphis, so that he may purchase new laborers in the place of those whom he must lose."

He stopped while they unraveled the elegance of his speech, those who spoke princely Egyptian translating for those who did not. Nofret heard Johanan convey it most succinctly, almost spitting it. "He says that we can free our people if we simply buy them back."

One or two of the elders brightened at that. "So simple? A ransom only, and they are ours?"

"A ransom indeed," said the priest Ramose, thereby betraying his knowledge of Apiru. He spoke in Egyptian, however, as if he understood the language of the desert but did not trust himself to speak it. "For every man, woman, and child, at such value as each would fetch in the market of Memphis."

They all fell silent. Some counted on their fingers. Nofret watched the truth dawn on them, and with it dismay. "That would take a king's wealth in gold!"

"But you see," said the priest, "they are a king's wealth. How can he lose them?"

"They belong to our god," Miriam said. Moshe was

still shut up in the inner room, but she had come out, heavily veiled, at the priest's coming. Her voice was as cold as it could well be. It was hardly human.

The priest seemed unperturbed. "Your god, then, gave them into our king's hands. He will sell them as he is entitled to do. But he cannot give them away."

"Our god lent them for his own purposes, for his glory and the glory of his people. Your king too is an instrument. See, priest, how our god hardens his heart against us. That is to temper us like iron in the forge."

"Our king and god," said the priest of Amon, "submits to the will of no mere spirit of the desert."

"Indeed," said Miriam. "His own pride serves our god's will."

The priest seemed much amused. "I see that your god turns every chance to his advantage. Still, lady, he would do well to offer greater signs than we saw before the king. Such things are the stock-in-trade of any petty godlet. A great god, a true god, must do more."

"Our god is greatest of all," said Miriam. "And so you shall see."

"I shall be intrigued," he said, smiling, bowing to her as if she had been—still—a queen.

CHAPTER FIFTY-NINE

▲

WHILE the Apiru were shut up in the guesthouse of the palace in Memphis, receiving messengers and idlers of the court and waiting for Moshe to finish his fasting and praying, another messenger came under cover of night. He had traveled hard and far, nor had he eaten, nor drunk more than a sip of water by the wayside. There was no mistaking what he was: he had the face of the Apiru, and his back was more deeply scarred even than Johanan's.

His name was Ephraim. He had had word of the Apiru in Memphis. "Slaves have nothing but know everything," he said with a wry humor that he kept even in his fear and exhaustion.

For he was afraid: terrified. Fear had brought him to Memphis, even into the king's hands if so the god willed it, to speak to the prophet of Sinai. "I don't speak for the elders in Pi-Ramses," he said, "even if all of them had tongues to speak, which too many don't: they protested the latest outrage and were deprived of the means to protest further." He did not wait to hear their gasps of outrage but went on, "I came because I could escape, and because the Lord allowed it. I came to ask the prophet a question."

"The prophet is praying to the Lord," Miriam said. "Is this a question I can answer? People call me the seer of the Apiru."

Ephraim shook his head. "I have to ask the prophet."

Nor would he budge for any persuasion. They fed him, bathed him, rid him of his vermin as best they could, and put him to bed in the young men's barracks. He slept there as if he had not slept in days out of count, safe in the protection of his kin.

■　　■　　■

Ephraim in daylight, rested and fed, was thin and drawn but not likely to fall over dead of weariness and starvation. "They feed us just enough to keep us working," he said as he broke his fast with all of them but Moshe. "If we slacken we're flogged. Not to death, not nearly—that's not what's wanted of us. We're more valuable alive, they tell us. The king needs us to build his city."

"And the women?" Nofret asked. "The children? Do they suffer, too?"

"The women work beside the men," he said. "The children too, if they're old enough. If they're not, their mothers carry them on their backs. Or—'' He broke off.

''Or?'' asked Nofret.

He did not want to say it, but the force of all their eyes was too strong for him. ''Or they're sold. The boychildren, the ones who are born strong, once they're old enough to be weaned—they're taken. Older ones, too. Up to the boys who are almost men, but not quite. They're taken away. There are too many of us, the Egyptians say. They can't feed all of us. So they sell the ones who will fetch a good price, but who are too young to work as well as the men grown.''

Small wonder, thought Nofret, that he had hesitated to speak. Slavery was terrible enough, and anger enough even for her who had been a slave. But that the menchildren should be taken and sold, that was more dreadful than simple servitude.

''They're taken from among the kindred,'' Aharon said for them all, ''and raised among strangers—people who know nothing of our way or our god.'' He flung back his head as if he were under the sky and not shut within a roof, and cried out, ''O Lord, my God, how can you endure it? How will we find them?''

''I would imagine,'' said Miriam, soft after that great outcry, ''that the Lord will guide us to them, or them to us, when the time is come.''

''Sometimes I weary of trusting in the Lord,'' said Johanan, half wry, half deadly serious.

His tone matched Ephraim's expression. ''I remember,'' Ephraim said, ''when it wasn't so bad to be building a city. We were slaves, to be sure, and some of us were a little too well acquainted with the lash. But we were fed, and we had houses that were better than some the free men had, and no one kept us from worshipping our god as we chose. I don't even know when it changed. It was slow. A little here, a little there. Maybe . . .''

"Maybe when Pa-Ramses knew he was going to be king?" Nofret asked.

"Maybe," said Ephraim. "He used to be the king's builder. You know that, I suppose. He lived in Pi-Ramses. He'd come out to watch us. Sometimes he'd ask us questions: how we did, were we getting enough to eat, did we want a day free to worship the Lord. Sometimes he gave us what we asked for. When he didn't, for all we knew he couldn't. But when the king grew older, the king's builder stopped coming so often. He was with the king, we heard, making himself secure so that he could be king himself."

"And one of the things he did," Nofret said, "was to prove to Horemheb that he could be harsh enough when he needed to be. Even sell your children if he reckoned there were too many."

Ephraim nodded. "We knew the old king didn't love us. Our overseers were supposed to watch us, because we might be rebels like the king whose name no one remembered—the fallen one, the servant of the Aten. We had to be careful that we didn't talk to Egyptians about our god, or say anything that might make him seem too much like the fallen one's god. That wasn't easy. All anyone needed to do was call him the One, the only god."

"I should think," said Nofret, "that you'd be no threat to the gods of Egypt. They conquered the Aten, destroyed him completely. Why would they fear your god? He's not even one of theirs."

"Fear doesn't have to be comprehensible," Miriam said. She was safe with Ephraim to sit unveiled as Nofret did. But he did not stare at Nofret as he did at Miriam. Nofret was a rather ordinary woman of a certain age. Miriam was beautiful as the old royal blood could be. Her remoteness only made her beauty the greater.

He was gaping at her. She did not seem to know it. "One can be afraid," she said, "and know no reason for it, except that it is."

"Memory would be reason enough," Johanan said. "Gods don't forgive. Even when they're strong, they can be afraid of others who are stronger. They know—and their servants fear—that our god is not only greater than the Aten ever was; that he's greater than they."

"But if they don't exist—" Nofret began.

Johanan turned on her. "The god who is above gods simply *is*. The gods of men live in men's minds, feed on men's fears, live by men's belief. If one of them loses his worshippers, he loses himself. He ceases to be."

"But—" said Nofret.

"There is fear," Johanan said. "Fear for one's very existence. And if a king is one of those gods, then his fear is a real and present thing. Such fear can enslave a whole people."

"Such thinking would mark a madman in most parts of the world," said Nofret.

"Then our whole tribe is mad," said Johanan.

"I don't doubt it," Nofret said dryly.

■　■　■

Moshe came out of his seclusion with the air of one who wakes from a long and restful sleep. He found them all still together, the remains of their breakfast in front of them. They stayed where they were, knowing better than to ask him what had come of his vigil, but Ephraim scrambled to his feet.

It was Jehoshua who pulled him back down again. He struggled, but Jehoshua was bigger than he was, and stronger.

Moshe took no notice. He sat where there was a space in the circle. The man nearest him reached for the basket of bread and pushed it toward him. Someone else fetched the bowl of fruit and the cheese, and the last of the lamb from the night before.

He ate with care as one learned to do who fasted often,

but his hunger was clear to see. He drank, too, water cooled in an earthen jar, and a little of the thin Egyptian beer.

When he had eaten and drunk as much as he dared, he seemed to come to himself. He looked about. He saw the stranger in the ranks. Ephraim, who at first could not meet his eyes, after a little stared boldly back and said as if he had said the words over and over to himself and could no longer keep them in, "I came to ask you. Why do we suffer so? Why does the Lord allow it? We belong to him!"

"That is why," said Moshe. He never had been offended by difficult questions, not even when he was king. He received this one calmly, as if he had expected it. "No one else can hear him, you see. Only our people. Every other tribe and nation shut its ears to him long ago, invented its own gods and forgot how to listen to his voice. Only we can hear."

"Then," said Ephraim, "the Lord should protect us. He should smite any man who does us harm."

"So he does," Moshe said. "So he intends to do."

"He should have done it long ago," Ephraim said.

Moshe spread his hands. "The Lord does as he wills. Who are we to judge him?"

"We belong to him," Ephraim said. "He named us his own."

"And should a child question its father's will?"

"If that will causes pain, he well should."

"But if the pain has a purpose beyond that child's understanding—what then? Should the father give way to the child?"

"The father should teach the child to understand."

"If the child's understanding is sufficient, so he should. But if the child is too young or his wits too frail, best then that the father simply say, 'Do it, because I will it,' and

the child obey. So are we with our God, who surpasses
human understanding.''

■   ■   ■

The Apiru capacity for theological argument surpassed Nofret's outland comprehension. She swallowed a yawn and
began to gather plates and cups and bowls. The servants,
hearing the clatter, came hastily to do their duty.

She would have withdrawn then, but Moshe, for a wonder, had said all that he intended to say. She had never
known him to be so brief. He washed his hands in the
water-bowl and stood, and beckoned to Aharon. ''Come,''
he said.

The others followed, some so quickly that they left behind their sandals. Even Ephraim went in his borrowed
shirt, barefoot and astonished.

The guards on the door drew back before so many of
them, but fell in behind as they had been commanded to
do. Some of the young men seemed to regret the loss of
their weapons, but they offered no insolence. Moshe's
presence quelled them, and the authority of his stride, leading them all through the courts and corridors of the palace.

They went by the straightest way to the gate, and no
matter what anyone might think of that. Moshe was a
prophet. Prophets had their gods to guide them; they knew
where all roads led, and how to follow them.

No one ventured to stop them. The king's guards had
orders only to watch them. Moshe, surrounded from birth
by armed men in royal livery, must have found nothing
odd in such an escort.

He led them down to the river. It was high morning, the
ways of the city thronged as always. There was a great
crowd by the water, with music and the chanting of priests.

Nofret was mildly startled to recognize the pattern of
the ceremony. They were marking the end of the river's
flood, the point at which it had completed its inundation

of the Black Land and returned to its winter bed. A like ceremony marked the height of the flood, when they measured it on the great column and proclaimed the extent of its blessing.

Now that blessing was all given. The waters had receded. The rich black mud had dried; the time of sowing was long since begun, the fields already growing green. The priests and their king gave thanks to the god of the river for his ancient gift, and honored him with prayer and sacrifice.

It was not permitted to any common person to approach the gathering of priests and princes. And yet the Apiru came to stand full beside them on the still-damp bank. Here the reeds were cleared away and a platform set up for the high ones, to keep their feet dry. The Apiru stood in the mud and reeds, taking no great heed of it as it sifted through their toes.

Nofret kept watch for crocodiles. She had never known them to attack so many people crowded together, but crocodiles were unpredictable creatures. Her hand slipped beneath her veil to the plait of hair wound about her amulet of Sobek.

The rite on the dais wound to its end. The people on the bank applauded, crying homage to the king: "Thousands and thousands of years! May you live forever!"

The king, who had stood to offer the sacrifice, had returned to his throne under its canopy. His bearers took their places and bent to the carrying-poles.

Aharon's great voice halted them as they stooped. "My lord of Egypt! Will you still defy our god?"

Amid the general astonishment, the sheer white shock that anyone would dare address the king, Moshe sprang up on the platform with Aharon on his heels. White-bearded elders that they were, they moved like boys. Aharon towered over the priests and the princes. Moshe, tall for an Egyptian, stood above anyone near him.

The king's guards, recovering their wits, surged forward. Moshe raised his staff. "No," he said mildly. They stopped as if at a wall.

The priests and princes likewise seemed to lack the power to move. Moshe smiled at them, a deadly sweet smile, but addressed his words to the king. "My lord king, Great House of Egypt, Lord of the Two Lands, do you yet mock the Lord of Hosts?"

"I do not know your god," the king said. His voice was harsh, grating, as if he had lost the power to sweeten it.

"You know him," said Moshe, still softly, but no one seemed unable to hear him. "He has spoken to you night and day since you made his people your slaves."

"I do not hear him," said the king.

"You hear," said Moshe. "You refuse to acknowledge him. He frightens you. And well he should, who is mightier than all the gods of Egypt."

The king raised the hand that held the flail. Either that gilded symbol of kingship was wrought of stone, heavier even than gold, or his hand struggled against some unseen weight. But he lifted it and pointed it at Moshe. "Strike him," he said. "Strike him down."

No one stirred to obey. The guards could not pass the wall that Moshe's staff had raised. The priests either could not or would not move.

A deep crimson flush stained the king's cheeks under the paint. "Your spell will fail," he said to Moshe, "as all spells do. Then you shall die."

"Spell?" Moshe seemed baffled. "I am no sorcerer. I serve my God, no more. It is his hand that lies upon you."

"Your god is a lie and a dream. I invoke Amon against you. I invoke Ptah and Thoth, Osiris and Isis, Horus, Set . . ."

Moshe heard the litany of gods with unruffled composure. When the king had run out of names to say, Moshe said, "My Lord is One, and mighty is his name. Will you set my people free?"

"I do not free slaves who are yet of use to me."

"It is the Lord who makes you intransigent," said Moshe. "Look. See the proof of his power."

"What," the king demanded, "more tricks? The leper's hand? The water into blood?"

"Ask," said Moshe, "and it shall be given you." He turned to face the river, and bent his staff along the line of it. "See."

For a stretching while there was nothing to see. If the guards could have fallen on Moshe, they would have done it. The priests gazed where Moshe pointed, as if their wills were subjugated to his. Only the king was strong enough to resist. He had half risen from his throne, battling the hand of power that was on him, when a long murmur ran down through the crowd. Those that were farthest upriver had begun it, and others, farther up, who had not come to the king's ceremony. For all Nofret knew, that sound, half groan, half cry, ran all the way down from Nubia.

The river, eased from its flood, flowed blue under the sky and brown in shadow, a deep brown, the color of the Black Land. Sometimes, under trees or among reeds, it was green; once in a great while it was grey under clouds or white-flecked with wind.

Now a new current ran in it. The cry from upriver came clear as it drew closer: "Blood! The river is turned to blood!"

It was, she supposed, more nearly red than brown. She had seen earth so colored, red earth; and seafarers spoke of the sea running red in certain seasons. Fish died, she had heard them say, and men who ate of them died too of a griping in the belly.

"Water into blood," said Moshe, quiet yet clear under the outcry of the people, "is, as you say, a simple trick, a charlatan's trick.'' He paused. ''Will you set my people free?''

The king's eyes were fixed on the river, set in a kind of horror; but the clearest emotion in them was rage. ''No,'' he said. ''I will not.''

CHAPTER SIXTY
▲

ALL water that flowed in Egypt flowed from the river. Its fields were watered from the river, and its wells were filled with the river's water. Every well and cistern therefore, every field, every channel, was filled with water that was red, like blood.

It lacked the thickness of blood, but it had the iron stink. Only the water that people had chanced to draw before the river changed was still clear, still untainted. Those few jars and waterskins were all the water in Egypt that was safe to drink, all the water that anyone would have for themselves or their animals, until the God of the Apiru saw fit to lift his curse.

They were saying as much in the city and even in the palace. Nofret caught rumors of it. She had left the riverside with the rest of the embassy, walking behind Moshe. It would not have surprised her if the crowd had fallen on them all and rent them to pieces, but no one moved. A path was open for them as for a king's procession, all the way from the river to the palace.

She would not have chosen to go back there of all places, but it was Moshe who led them, and Moshe who seemed unable to understand why the palace might not be the best refuge. It was his upbringing, she thought. Palaces had always sheltered him. He could not see the use in going anywhere else if there was a king's house to rest in.

They were not harmed. No one approached them, no one stopped them. When, much later that day, she happened to look out of the door, there were no guards standing in her way. That whole part of the palace seemed deserted except for the Apiru.

The water in the guesthouse was clean, likewise that in the cistern behind it. Jehoshua, foraying afield, came back with a string of fat geese, plucked and cleaned, and word that the rest of the palace was not so fortunate. The geese were a gift, he said, from a frightened functionary. "He wants us to take the curse off his well," he said.

"The Lord will do as the Lord pleases," Moshe said. He had prayed for a while, alone but for Aharon, but then he had come out to talk to Ephraim. No one asked him what he had done to the river, or how. No one needed to. They were Apiru. They worshipped the god who spoke through him.

Nofret did not know what to think. She was stubborn, she knew that, and not much less intransigent than the king. If she had been Ramses, she would have been no more willing to give way to a pack of desert bandits.

The king's men were abroad in the Two Lands, reassuring the people, praying and propitiating the gods who, they said, had visited this trial upon the kingdom. They spoke no word of the god of the Apiru.

Moshe maintained his serenity. "The Lord has only begun," he said.

■ ■ ■

For seven days the river ran red, the water fouled beyond hope of cleansing. Men hoarded what little clear water they had. There were battles in the marketplace and in the fields. Cattle ran wild in search of water, for they would not touch any that came from the river.

In the river itself the fish died, and the water-birds died

of eating them. Only the crocodiles seemed proof against the foulness. They ate the fish and the birds. They drank the water and seemed to take no ill from it.

At dawn of the seventh day a new cry went up along the river. Nofret heard it in the depths of a dream-ridden sleep. At first she thought it another dream, a confused murmur as of wind in trees or a battle far away. But the wider awake she was, the clearer she heard it.

She thrust herself up from her bed beside Miriam's. Miriam was gone. So were the rest of the embassy. She found them on the roof of the guesthouse, which backed against the palace wall. From there they could see the river and the crowd of people along it. Some of them were in it—splashing, shouting, defying rotting fish and crocodiles.

The water ran broad and brown as far as she could see. The blood-tinge was gone. It would be gone, she suspected, from Nubia to the Delta, from all the wells and cisterns, and from the fields that stank of long-dead fish.

People were dancing, singing, praising the gods. None of them looked toward the palace, or toward the foreigners on its wall. Nofret was glad of that. Better to be ignored than to be blamed for their suffering.

"It is not over," said Moshe.

■　■　■

The river flowed clear again, but the numbers of fish that had died were too great even for the crocodiles to dispose of. Farmers made the best of it: there was no better fodder for young crops than the corpses of fish. The stink was indescribable.

Out of the stink came something new, something unlooked for. It wriggled in the new-cleansed pools. It seethed in the river. It hopped and croaked out of the crowded water onto the land. It was in every place where the water had run red as with blood: wells, cisterns, fields and channels.

Frogs. Frogs of every size and shape. Frogs no larger than a lady's fingernail. Great deep-croaking frogs that would barely have fit onto a platter at a king's feast.

The water bred them. They were born of blood and reeking death. They overran every house in Egypt.

Every house but a house in which Apiru were living. They were even in the king's palace, filling his water-jars, teeming in his bed. A white-faced, trembling-handed servant brought Moshe to him with some of the embassy behind, stepping gingerly lest they set foot on a wriggling body.

The frogs seemed to shy from the feet of the Apiru, but they fairly leaped to sacrifice themselves beneath the Egyptian's sandals. They made an appalling noise as they died, half croak, half scream.

Nofret found herself taking pity on him. Egyptian he might be, servant of a king who would not give the Apiru what they wanted, but he had done no harm in himself.

The god of the Apiru did not seem to understand pity. She followed his prophet, thinking her own thoughts, resolving to make her own bargains with the gods she knew.

■ ■ ■

The king was in his private receiving-room. Only a few servants attended him, and a handful of his daughters, and a guard or two.

The room had been a pleasure-chamber when last Nofret was in it. The walls still carried their painted image of the hunt: a supple young king in his chariot, bringing down lions to the lively admiration of his queen. Miriam, Nofret saw, glanced once at the walls and then away. Her memories must be bitter.

The king who sat in the tall carved chair was nothing like the one whom Miriam would be remembering. He was dressed as a king at leisure, his kilt plain, his ornaments few. He wore the Blue Crown, the cap in the shape of a helmet that marked a warlike king, or a king who wished to be in comfort beneath the burden of his office.

It was little enough comfort, with frogs hopping everywhere about the room. His servants were hard put to maintain their dignity. More than one strangled shriek marked a frog that had done its best to climb a man's leg. There were frogs even on the dais, and frogs about the throne. One great wise-eyed green-and-brown-spotted creature sat in state at the king's feet. As the embassy approached, it stirred once from its stony immobility: darted a blinding-swift tongue, snared a fly, subsided once more into stillness.

The king ignored the great frog with teeth-gritted determination. He addressed Moshe as soon as the prophet had come before him, wasting no time in waiting for an obeisance that was not forthcoming. He said, "Remove this curse from us, and I will set your people free."

Someone near Nofret let out a long sigh. Nofret was still holding her breath. So, she noticed, was Moshe, till he had to speak. "Indeed, my lord," he said. "Will you abide by your word?"

"Just rid me of these monsters!" snapped the king.

Moshe inclined his head. "It shall be as my lord wishes. My God will remove the curse. You will free our people to offer him their sacrifice."

"Just do it," the king said, biting off each word.

"Indeed, my lord," said Moshe, "it is done."

The king opened his mouth as if to speak again, but no words emerged. The floor that had writhed with life went slowly still. The silence was immense. Nothing croaked, nothing screeked.

With utmost care, in taut-drawn revulsion, the king stretched out his foot. It touched the great frog. The creature did not stir. He kicked it with sudden force. It flew from the dais and fell at Moshe's own feet, pale belly uppermost, stiff and lifeless.

Moshe looked from it to the king's face. "Tomorrow," he said, "we depart for Pi-Ramses. When we come there, our people will follow us, out into the desert."

The king said nothing. Moshe left him so, sitting on his throne amid the heaped corpses of frogs.

■   ■   ■

Between the stink of rotting fish and the stink of rotting frogs, the air in Memphis was foul beyond belief. It was clean only within the walls of the guesthouse. There was no reek more pungent there than well-worn wool, and the scent of flowers from the garden, faint and sweet.

The young men were laughing and dancing, singing the victory. Ephraim was in the center of them. He had become one of them, taking to their freedom of speech and movement as if he had been born to it. But then, thought Nofret, all Apiru were heart-free. None of them was fit to be a slave.

The elders were a little silly themselves, giddy with triumph. All but Miriam, and Moshe who had retreated to his meditations. Miriam kept no festival. She ate and drank sparingly and went early to bed.

Nofret followed her. She was awake, lying on her back, hands folded on her breast. "You haven't packed yet," Nofret said. "Shall I do it for you?"

"No," said Miriam.

Nofret hesitated on the verge of speech, shrugged, sighed and said nothing. She gathered her own belongings, as few as those were: a clean undergarment, a second pair of sandals, a bag of oddments. She had bought nothing in Memphis, nor did she intend to. She would leave as she had come, traveling light.

"I wouldn't trouble," Miriam said.

Nofret paused. "What are you saying?"

"I wouldn't bother," said Miriam.

"Miriam," said Nofret, "the king said—"

"A king need not be honorable," Miriam said.

Nofret sank down on the heap of her possessions. It was barely enough for a cushion between herself and the floor. "He's not going to let them go."

"He only wanted to be rid of the frogs," said Miriam.

And once he was rid of the frogs, he had no need to honor the bargain. Nofret laughed weakly, without mirth. "Such innocents we are, to trust him."

"We trust in the Lord," Miriam said, "who is more powerful than any king."

Indeed. And was the king wondering as Nofret did, whether it was the Apiru god at all, or a mingling of luck and sorcery? Rivers had run red before. Frogs might well be born out of the foulness, and die as they had come, poisoned by their own fecundity. There might be nothing divine in it at all.

CHAPTER SIXTY-ONE

▲

IN the morning when the Apiru readied to depart, they found the doors barred and a double complement of guards in front of them. The king had broken his word. No slaves would be set free, nor would the embassy be leaving Memphis. They would stay, heavily guarded, and among the guards a company of priests to protect against the threat of sorcery.

Moshe was as serene as ever, trusting in his god. Some of the young men gathered themselves to escape, but Aharon forbade them. "The walls are doubled and trebled," he said. "Can't you smell the stink of magic?"

"I smell the stink of death," said Jehoshua, gagging on it. "*Feh!* The whole country reeks."

It was worse on the roof, to which they were allowed to go since the wall was too high for escape. People were raking the dead into heaps, burying some, burning the rest. The city had come to a standstill. Its markets were a charnel-house of frogs. Its streets were thick with them.

"Your god does nothing by halves," Nofret said to Miriam, who happened to be standing beside her.

Miriam nodded slightly. "More will come," she said, "again and again till Pharaoh sets our people free."

■　■　■

Hard upon the frogs came a plague of stinging gnats and a plague of flies. The burial-parties knew it first: black and swarming clouds, blinding them, pursuing them as they fled.

The cattle suffered worse than the men who tended them. Their bellowing reached even to the palace walls, the stamping and furious squealing of horses, the blatting of sheep, the braying of donkeys driven to madness. No house was safe, no door or window proof against the swarms. Gnats buzzed and stung. Flies crawled on every surface. No one could eat without swallowing a mouthful of flies, nor drink but that the cup was full of them. They were ravenous, voracious: the gnats for blood, the flies for anything that could be eaten or drunk.

Still the king would not yield. The Apiru were held prisoner in the guesthouse. From its roof they could see Egypt through a cloud of buzzing, stinging tormentors—tormentors that never came close to them nor troubled them. Their house was a haven of clear air in a kingdom gone foul.

As the gnats wearied of their endless assault and the flies dropped sated, too bloated to take to the air, the beasts in the fields began to move about erratically, lowing or blatting or braying. First one and then another stumbled and fell. For a while they struggled to get up. Then they grew too feeble even for that. They lay gasping, tongues protruding, blackened with sickness; and after a while they died.

The Apiru's donkeys lazed in their stable, untouched by the pestilence that beset the rest of Egypt. Nofret went down to see, breath held against the stench of death. But the only scent in the stable was that of dung and donkey, cut reeds spread for their bedding and sweet fodder in their mangers. She stood rubbing the withers of the one that had carried her tent from Sinai, a pretty dove-grey creature with exceptionally large and well-formed ears. It glanced at her now and then as it nibbled on its dinner.

Nofret let herself rest against its warm solidity. "Even supposing," she said to it, "that the river was about to turn to blood by some force of nature, and Moshe happened to have word of it from far to the south and to exploit it for his own ends—even supposing that, and concluding that the rest was an inevitable consequence of the river's fouling—there is still the fact that we suffer nothing while Egypt rots and dies. The king can see it as well as we can. How long before he acts on it? How long before he has us killed?"

"He won't touch us," Johanan said behind her.

She glanced over her shoulder. Johanan was alone. She was a little surprised. She might have expected Jehoshua to be with him. Then they could both have gloated that they were here together after she had been so insistent that they be parted.

That was not charitable. She made herself look on Johanan with a calm face. "Don't tell me that the Lord defends you. I've heard that till I choke on it."

"Very well," he said. "I won't. I'll say that the king is trapped by his own pride. If he has us killed, it's an admission that we're to blame for Egypt's troubles."

"Where's the shame in that? It's the truth."

"He maintains," said Johanan, "that our prophet has a

trick or two in his arsenal, no more. He's done nothing that any sorcerer can't do."

"If a sorcerer did to Egypt what your god is supposed to have done, that sorcerer would be executed in the most public way possible, an example to any and all of his kind who might think to cow a king with their arts. Black arts," said Nofret. "Arts that destroy. Does your god care nothing for Egypt?"

"Egypt defies him," Johanan said.

"Egypt's king refuses to free an army of useful slaves. Should his people suffer because he's too stubborn to give way?"

"The king is Egypt," said Johanan.

She stared at him. "I don't know you," she said after a while. "I wonder now if I ever did."

He met her stare without flinching. She looked for any regret, any softening, but there was none. He was as much his god's slave as Moshe himself. They all were. All but Nofret.

"I don't believe," she said, "no matter how much I see. That he's a god, I know; I feel his strength. But there are other gods. He's not alone."

"He is above all gods," said Johanan.

"I don't know that," she said. "I'm not one of you. If I went out there I'd be eaten alive by gnats. My cattle would die. I'd be in no better case than any Egyptian."

"Then why don't you go?"

She showed him her teeth. "Because I'm a coward."

"Oh, no," he said as if he meant it. "Not you. You do believe, I think. You just don't want to admit it."

"Your god won't admit it, either. He's not a forgiving god, is he? He wants all of a man's soul, not just the part of him that's left when the other gods are done."

"The other gods are lies, the children of men's minds. Our god is the true one, the one who is above gods."

"So I've heard before," she said. "So far he hasn't done anything that any god can't do."

"But," said Johanan, "has any god tried to stop him?"

That made her pause. But an answer came to her. "The gods don't meddle. They let the world go as it will."

"That's not what the priests say."

She shook her head to clear it. "You say your god is meddling. The king says your prophet is taking advantage of a run of ill fortune. I don't know what I should say. Maybe Egypt's gods agree that Egypt's king needs humbling."

"That would be unusual," he conceded: "gods allowing their own people to be destroyed because it suits their purposes. Suppose that that were so. Our god is still our god. He's still working great wonders to sway the king's mind, to win his people free."

"But the king won't be swayed. He doesn't want to be. He's saying all that I've said. There will be priests hung from spikes before this is over, for letting this go so far without their gods' intervention."

"Priests have already died," Johanan said. "The rest are praying night and day, trying to fend off what they persist in seeing as a work of magic."

"And it isn't?"

"Magic is what men do to force the world to their will. This is greater than magic. This is the work of a god."

"But it looks like magic," Nofret said. "It's nothing that a sorcerer can't do—or a whole tribe of priests invoking their god in temples from Nubia to the Delta."

"Here," he said, "it's one man."

"One man, yes," she said. "A man who once was Egypt. What if he still is? What if he can do this not because his god is greater than the others, but because he himself was a god?"

Johanan did not want to hear that. His eyes narrowed; he shook his head. "That's all past. He died."

"Egypt remembers," said Nofret. "What if it becomes a contest not of a king against a tribe of slaves, but of king against king? Kings are gods here. If the elder king and god is alive and raising the power in Egypt, what's to become of the later king? Is he really king at all, or only a pretender?" By now he was not even listening: she knew that shuttered look, that set of the jaw. But she had to say it, all of it. "He's done nothing so far that a king can't do. He's set his hand on the weaving that is Egypt and plucked out a thread, and all the rest has unraveled. That's a king's power, Johanan. That's what a man can do who is the heart and soul of Egypt."

"It is what our God can do," Johanan said, low and tight. "You call him unforgiving—and say things that only a god would be great enough to forgive."

"I say what I see," said Nofret.

"You're as obdurate as the king," he said.

She raised her brows. "Am I? Indeed. Which one?"

That rid her of him. He walked away without another word. She was glad—or tried to be. The center of her heart was a dark, cold thing. But then it had known neither light nor warmth since she quarreled with him beside Mount Horeb.

CHAPTER SIXTY-TWO

▲

PESTILENCE begot pestilence. Foul water, plagues of frogs and gnats and flies, murrain on the cattle, all so poisoned air and land that no man was either safe or clean. Amid such filth, so many carcasses, first those compelled to dispose of them, and then their wives and families, and in time the princes set over them, were laid low with such eruptions of the skin that no one was free of them.

Except the Apiru. They were immune as always, clean and in comfort, their bodies unmarred.

It was strikingly evident as the guards burst in one white-hot morning, seized them all and brought them before the king.

He was on his throne in the great hall, as if he could do battle with splendor against the open weeping sores that disfigured him as they did every other man and woman about him. Paint was no protection. Courtiers of both sexes hid behind feather fans and wrapped their bodies in heavy linen, robes of a fashion more apt to the desert than to the court of the Black Land.

The king himself had resorted to an older fashion than was his wont, a robe like a priest's, with a mantle over his shoulders and arms. But there was no concealing the hands with their suppurating wounds, nor the face, the black eyes staring out of it from a mask of scarlet and stark white. His head could not bear the weight of a crown; he wore the light headdress that was permitted the king, with the uraeus-serpent on the brow.

They all saw how the Apiru walked without flinching, and how their hands and faces were free of sores. The murmur that ran through the court had a distinct edge of anger.

The king's speech was slow and somewhat slurred: his tongue too suffered. "We are told," he said, "that your people are spared even the lightest brush of every curse that has been laid on us."

"It is so here," said Aharon. "I trust that it is so in Pi-Ramses."

"It is so wherever your people are," said the king. "They walk safe. Their water is clean, no vermin beset them. Their flocks and herds continue to prosper while ours die in pain."

"Surely," said Moshe, "that would prove to you that

our God is angered at Egypt, that it will not permit his people to worship him in his holy place.''

''And may they not worship in the city that they build?'' the king demanded. ''I never forbade them to give their god such honor as they pleased.''

''But our god's honor requires that they be free,'' said Moshe, ''and able to travel into the desert where they can celebrate his rites under the sky.''

''If we let them go,'' the king said, ''what surety have we that they will ever return?''

Moshe was silent at that.

The king stretched his bleeding lips over teeth that had seen much better days. It was not a smile. ''I think that your god would like to trick us into sending away the best and strongest of our slaves. He lays a potent curse, I grant him that, but not potent enough that I'm willing to surrender my will and power. Our gods in the end will triumph as they have before.''

''But at what cost?'' Moshe asked him. ''How far must my God go before he convinces you to yield?''

''You told me before,'' said the king, ''that your god makes me obdurate so that he can prove his power. If this is his doing, then let him play out the rest of it. If this is not, then let him test us till our own gods rise up in wrath.''

''Take care,'' said Aharon, ''that that wrath is not directed against you. Egypt has not fared well through your resistance.''

''The fault is yours,'' the king said. ''You forced me to it. The gods know. They'll see that you pay.''

''Egypt has already paid,'' said Moshe, ''and will continue to pay until you yield.''

''I am Horus, Great House, god and king, Lord of the Two Lands. I will not give way before the likes of you.''

■   ■   ■

The worst of it, Nofret thought, was that the court did not turn on him for this pride that was destroying them. They were all proud to folly. Egypt would not surrender to the will of any foreign god. The Apiru were sent away as before, with their petition refused, their people still bound in servitude.

She wanted to scream at them, to shake them till they saw sense. Was it so impossible a thing to set a few hundred slaves free, turn them loose in the desert and tell them never to come back? They were no great nation, no tribe of warriors who would turn on Egypt and conquer it as the Shepherd Kings had done before them. They only wanted to wander the desert, tend their flocks, worship their god.

Well, and maybe some of them wanted more. The young men talked a great deal about a place of their own, a kingdom, cities and all the rest of it. They had some claim on Canaan, from what they said. But not on Egypt. They did not want it. They only wanted to be free of it.

It was no use for her to say anything. She was a foreigner to all of them, Egyptian and Apiru alike. She kept her thoughts to herself, did what needed doing in the guesthouse since the servants had vanished—nursing their wounds, she supposed, and cursing the people who had inflicted them. Sometimes she thought of simply walking out. The guards, having brought the embassy before the king, had not returned to their post. She could leave if she pleased.

It might be worth it, even if she fell prey to the Egyptians' curse. There might be somewhere that she could go. Maybe she should begin brewing beer, set up a stall, sell it to anyone who was left when the god of the Apiru was done with his smiting of Egypt.

She was almost ready to do it when Moshe himself went out. He did not go in front of the king this time, but walked into the city with Aharon close behind him. The elders, tired or frightened, stayed in the guesthouse, but most of the young men followed, and Miriam, and Nofret last of all. She nearly did not go, but she had already made up her mind to walk out. She shrugged and went.

People who might once have sprung on the Apiru and destroyed them were now so weakened as to fall back in fear. A few approached, crying out for relief. They were brave, or too far gone in pain to care what became of them. Moshe did not pause for them, seemed unaware that they existed. It was Nofret who said over and over, "Go. Make yourself a salve. If you can find oil of aloes, or an unguent made of it, it will ease the pain."

It was less than nothing, but people seized her hand and wept on it, incoherent with gratitude. She had to pull herself away and run to catch the rest of the procession. Over and over, surreptitiously, she inspected her hands. They were the same as ever, whole and unharmed, except for a bruise where one man had pressed too hard.

Moshe went as if led by the hand, straight to the temple of Ptah. The chanting of priests rolled forth from it, and clouds of incense, and the cries of beasts brought to the sacrifice. Fools, Nofret thought, to kill the few healthy animals that were left. The gods could not be pleased by that, unless they were greater idiots than she had taken them for.

There was power in that place: a thrumming under her feet, a prickling of her skin. She had felt no such thing through all the evils that had fallen on Egypt. They grew out of the land and the air, as inevitable as corruption in a corpse. This that lay on Ptah's temple was power clear and distinct, power apart from the common run of earth. Magic.

As Moshe drew near to the great gate of the temple, the power thrummed deeper. The chanting rang louder, as if with desperation. He wavered not at all, nor seemed to notice that there was a great working raised against him.

The air where he was was quiet. The ground where he walked was still. Magic might not have existed, for all the power it had over him.

None of the Apiru seemed to know what they did. They followed Moshe, that was all, gaping at the temple. It was vaster than the palace, and more imposing. Egypt built nothing on a merely human scale. Everything was immense, like the work of a god.

Their god, the Apiru would say, needed no such pretenses. He was great in himself. Those who believed in him need fear no other god, no other power, not even magic.

Moshe halted on the porch of the temple. A crowd had gathered in the great square, men following him as blindly as a sheep follows its shepherd. He turned to face them, leaning lightly on his staff with its bronze serpent. Their faces, blotched and glistening with sores, might have touched even his cold heart: his face was somber, his eyes dark with what could have been sorrow. When he spoke, Aharon echoed him, playing the herald in that glorious deep voice.

"People of Egypt," he said. "Your king will not be moved. He persists in his pride; he delights in his obstinacy. Till now my God has been gentle with him, and with you who are his servants. Now he is moved to anger."

No one spoke. No one begged to differ. No one even contended that their suffering till now had been remarkably like the wrath of a god. They were mute, caught by the spell of his words.

They were not particularly eloquent words, but they had a certain power in their simplicity. "My God grows angry," Moshe said. "He tells me now that for your king's great folly he will smite these two kingdoms as they have never been smitten before. Take shelter, people of Egypt, with all your servants and children, and your flocks and herds that survived the pestilence. See that your roofs are strong against the storm that my God will raise.

"For you see," he said, "my God is merciful. He will take the life of no man in Egypt, not if that man is wise and obeys his warning." He raised his voice, and Aharon his own in turn, till the sky echoed. "Go! Protect yourselves! See my Lord, how he comes!"

He flung up hand and staff. People craned, turning their faces to the sky.

The sky in Egypt was a changeless thing, a vault of cloudless blue by day, a vault of stars by night. Now and then it suffered the presence of a cloud or two. Once in a great while there were more clouds than blue; and sometimes, though it was a rarity, it rained.

Storms when they came were swift and violent. That which gathered now was swifter than Nofret had ever seen in any country, even Great Hatti where the storms came often and could be terrible. These clouds boiled like water in a cauldron, black shot with the deep blue of lapis, fanged with lightnings.

"*Go!*" Moshe's voice was a shriek, Aharon's hardly less shrill.

The people milled like a flock beset by wolves. Some at length mustered wits to bolt out of the square. The rest streamed after.

A chill wind had begun to blow. It smelled of rain in the desert: a hot, dry smell, more dust than water. Moshe walked calmly through it, but he was not walking as slowly as he might.

It seemed a very long way to the palace. The streets were choked with people. Most of them lacked the sense to take shelter, or were caught far from their houses. Among them, to make it worse, were the doubters. "It's only a storm," they said. "Only rain. It falls every day in Asia."

That was an exaggeration, as some people pointed out. Too many listened, and hindered those who would not.

The confusion in its way was as deadly as the storm.

Moshe did not let himself be stopped, nor did he yield the way to anyone. The palace gates were open, the guards beset with people trying to crowd in. Moshe penetrated the throng, sweeping his people behind him, even Nofret the doubter, who lacked the courage to escape while she still could.

■   ■   ■

Even in the guesthouse the wind's voice was distinct, a rising howl interspersed with the drumroll of thunder. If the wrath of a god had a voice, it was that: wind, thunder, crack of lightning.

Then came the rain, and hard on the rain the hail. This time their house was not spared. Maybe the god did not choose to; maybe it was too much trouble amid so terrible a storm, to pass by one smallish roof. It was like a battlefield, a mighty clatter and clamor, a rain of stones as great as a man's fist. Any man or beast caught out in it would fall stunned to the ground and die, beaten as if with cudgels.

Even the Apiru were cowed by that relentless buffeting, struck to silence, huddling together in the center of the house. If the roof broke above them, it would fall on the upper floor, and the hail with it. The second roof, the ceiling directly over them, was sturdy, but they shot frightened glances at it, the more frightened the longer the hail fell.

It fell for the half of an age. It was an hour, perhaps, from beginning to end, but that hour was as long as years. They were deafened, pummeled by the sound alone, beaten down by the wrath of their god.

Only Moshe held himself erect. Only Moshe betrayed no fear. But he was paler than Nofret had seen him before. Maybe even he had not known how truly terrible his god could be.

CHAPTER SIXTY-THREE

▲

THE silence after the storm was immense. Nofret emerged with the others, climbing up on the roof that had borne the assault with only one breach, a stone the size of a man's head that had pierced the westward corner. They blinked astonished in sunlight, looking on a world that glittered with hills and mountains of crystal.

Already it was melting, running with clear water on the parched and tormented land. The wall of cloud had run away down the river, north toward the Delta—toward Pi-Ramses, thought Nofret. She wondered if the Apiru there would be safe, since the prophet and his people in Memphis had not been. No doubt their god would warn them, and see that they were all in shelter when the storm struck.

Here in Memphis was devastation. Houses in the city had fared well enough, but the huts of farmers along the river were beaten down. Any who had been caught in the fields was dead or dying. And the crops, the flax in bud, the barley in the ear, were pounded flat, were destroyed. Only the spelt was safe, for it had not yet sprouted. There would be precious little linen spun in Egypt this year at harvest time, and bread and beer only from stores that had been laid aside in case of famine—if the storehouses had not been breached, their contents ruined by rain that had fallen amid the hail.

The sun seemed a mockery, the sky cloudless blue once more, the heat rising after the chill of the storm. It had done one good thing for Egypt: it had cleansed the land, and washed away the stink of death that had lain on it for so long.

■ ■ ■

It was only a respite. The king would not be moved. His priests strove even more strongly to raise their magic against the power of the Apiru's god. Nofret could have told them that their efforts were useless. No matter how great their working, no matter that now it thrummed from end to end of Memphis and arched above the city like a vault of light, it could not touch the god who was beyond all mortal magic. His prophet and his people could not be touched by it, neither harmed nor diverted from their course.

Maybe it was that Nofret was Hittite that let her know what the magic was, yet kept her from succumbing to it. Her skin tightened in its presence and her feet tingled when they touched unshielded earth, but her mind was unclouded. She could think as well as ever, for what that was worth.

She had gone beyond rebellion to a kind of fixed and steadfast incredulity. She disbelieved because she did not know how to believe. What she saw about her, what she felt, touched her body and her wits but not her heart. A madman from the desert had walked into Egypt and defied its king and gods, and they did nothing while his god destroyed the land with a sheer and bloody ruthlessness that no man could match.

Such a god might in time win her belief. But she could not love him. Far better the little gods that the Apiru said were the creation of men's minds. Those could be appalling, some beyond all reason, but there was a certain humanity in them: a part of them that she could touch, that was like herself. This One True God with his insistence upon no other before him was nothing that she could talk to or lay hand on or understand.

When she could be by herself, when she was in the room she slept in and Miriam was elsewhere, praying as the

Apiru did at every opportunity, she unplaited her two amulets from her hair and held them in her hands. They had never been much more than glass and stone somewhat crudely carved, cool in her palm and smooth. Yet they comforted her.

■   ■   ■

It was well she had something to cling to. Her kin were sundered from her, those in Hatti and those in Sinai and those who were here in Egypt. She had no friend; certainly not Miriam, who had retreated again into herself, too far for Nofret to follow.

The memory of the hail was fading, though it would never vanish from the mind of anyone who had lived through it. The flax and the barley were lost. The spelt however sprouted and grew, and those fields at least were green again, a fragile and tentative green that farmers nurtured as tenderly as their own children.

But the king would not give way. Of a morning then, just when the crop was high enough to be strong, a new cloud came out of the south. It came swift and it came dark, with a humming in it like nothing else that Nofret had ever heard. Something of it was like the humming of flies, but flies grown huge.

Egypt, so terribly battered and yet unyielding, wailed in a wholly new despair. The old remembered and the young had been told often enough of this new scourge, this plague that came out of the south.

The locusts came in swarms so thick that they darkened the sun, so vast that they filled the sky. They came and they paused and they settled. And where they settled, they devoured.

They ate the crops in the fields. They ate the fruit from the trees, what little the hail had left, and the leaves, and such branches as were tender enough for their taste. The carcasses of cattle that remained, dried to leather in the sun, they stripped to the white and gleaming bone. They ate everything that could be eaten—even, it was said, the kilt from a man's body.

They ate the earth bare, scoured it clean, left not one thing that was not walled and barred from them. Even the granaries were their prey, those that the hail had pierced, or that had not been secured in every cranny. They were merciless as only a god, or a god's instrument, could be.

■ ■ ■

In the humming of locusts, in the sound of uncounted jaws grinding as they devoured everything that could be devoured, a maidservant came to the Apiru in their guesthouse and asked for the prophet's sister. She was scarred with sores, trembling, barely able to speak. But she made it clear that she came from Pharaoh's daughter, and that the prophet's sister, by whom she meant Miriam, was not to come attended. The other woman could come, she said. No more.

The Apiru did not like the sound of that at all, but Miriam took up her veil and prepared to go where the maidservant led. Nofret followed in silence. She scented nothing of a trap, in spite of the men's outcry. The king held hostage the whole nation of Yisroel in Egypt. He did not need any more of them, even if they were close kin to the prophet.

The maid led them as Nofret had expected, to the palace that had been the queen's and belonged now to the king's daughters. Only one of them was waiting, with maids in attendance. Nofret knew her from their audiences with the king: the eldest daughter, the one who looked most like her father.

It was not a fortunate resemblance. The woman's body carried the weight of flesh with somewhat more grace, but the face with its heavy jowls would have been better suited to a man. Her name was Nefer-Re, Beauty of Re: a commentary on the god, surely, and not on her own loveliness.

She did not try to feign what she did not have. She wore the paint and the wig of Egyptian nobility, and the linen gown and the jewels as befit her station, but there was no excess of ornament. She seemed in fact a solid, practical woman.

She received the strangers with courtesy, without either fear or effusiveness. She bade them sit; she offered wine, cakes, whatever they wished. Miriam refused. Nofret was neither hungry nor thirsty. The buzzing of the locusts had set in her bones. It left no room for anything else.

Nefer-Re spoke first, since neither of the others was inclined to. She was direct as her father was, brusque for a fact, for all her careful politeness. "I asked you to come here, lady—ladies—to talk to you as women can talk even when their men are quarreling. My father is caught, you see, trapped by his office, bound to do what he's been doing. He can't yield, or in his way he's given up the rule of Egypt."

"He may think so," said Miriam without expression.

"He knows so," said Nefer-Re. "His heart weeps for his people—but how can he give way?"

"Easily," Miriam said. "Let our people go. Forget them. Devote himself to the restoration of the Two Kingdoms."

"Nothing is so easy," said Nefer-Re, "or so simple."

Miriam raised her brows but said nothing. Nefer-Re poured wine into a cup, drank deep. She filled it again and sipped more slowly. The color had risen to her cheeks. She shook her head. "You don't understand. How can you? It takes a king to understand, or a king's daughter. The kingdom lives by the king's strength. Can you see how this spate of dying, these plagues and pestilences, set all that he is at naught, and prove his kingship a mockery? He says that you intend this. I don't think you do. I think that all you see is your people's slavery. You want them free, no more and no less. You don't care what you have to do to bring it about.''

Miriam still did not speak. Her eyes had flickered when Nefer-Re addressed her as if she were a commoner, a child of slaves, but she was wise enough not to betray the truth. In this life she was a child of the desert, a stranger to palaces.

Nefer-Re seemed undismayed by the silence. ''Suppose that I could bring my father round to your way of thinking. Would you be able to take away the curse?''

''I have no such power,'' said Miriam, ''but my father does.''

Nefer-Re's eyes widened slightly. ''Your—?'' She broke off. ''I was told that you were his sister.''

''He has no sister,'' Miriam said. ''I am his daughter. Your father has given you leave to treat with me, it seems. Mine has done no such thing. I can only be a messenger. I can promise nothing.''

''Nor can I,'' said Nefer-Re with the ghost of a smile, ''but I have a certain degree of influence. And Egypt is suffering.''

It was difficult to see whether she honestly cared for that. Her face and manner were not suited to the expression of delicate emotion.

''Then this is no better than a gathering of women by the cookfire while the men hold council in the tent,'' Miriam said.

''But women can sway their men,'' said Nefer-Re, ''and my father listens to me.''

''Mine listens to his god,'' said Miriam.

Nefer-Re leaned toward her. ''Your father is asking that your people be allowed to go into the desert to worship your god, yes? My father refuses, partly for pride and partly for suspicion. How can he be sure that his slaves will come back once they've done their duty to their god?''

"If we give our word," said Miriam, "we will keep it."

Nefer-Re nodded. "Yes, I believe that. I also believe that my father can be persuaded—if your people are willing to make one small concession."

Miriam sat still. Her eyes had sharpened, Nofret noticed, but her face was as serene as always. She refused to ask the inevitable question.

Nefer-Re, unperturbed, asked it for her. "Yes, what concession? It's not a great one. It's even wise, if you consider the danger of bandits, lions and jackals, storms in the desert." She paused. Miriam watched her in silence. She let it out perhaps more quickly than she had meant, and more bluntly. "Leave your children behind. Let them stay in Pi-Ramses while their elders worship the god. They'll be safe, protected, well looked after. No one will threaten them. And no one," she said strongly, as if it were a telling point, "will remove them. They'll be there and waiting when their kin come back."

Nofret's back tightened. There was nothing of reason in it. Those were nearly the precise words that she had spoken when she left her children behind in Sinai—that she had flung in Johanan's face when she saw that her firstborn would come with them into Egypt. It was a greater pain than she had thought it could be, a sharp and stabbing anguish, a yearning beyond measure for Anna and Ishak. She could see their faces as she walked away from them, brave as befit the children of Yisroel, but with eyes full of tears.

The pain was so fierce that for a long moment she neither saw nor heard. When she was aware again of where she was, Miriam was speaking. She knew that soft, bitter voice far too well. "And do you think that we will abandon our children to your tender mercies? Swear any oath you please. Give us your word from here to the ends of the earth. We'll never trust you. We'll never give our young ones to you who have already sold the best of them away from their people.''

Nefer-Re seemed taken aback. People always were when Miriam let slip the mask she wore, the gentleness that ran no deeper than the skin.

''We have no reason to trust you,'' said Miriam. ''Not your honor, not your good faith. You took our people who had been servants of the king, free men who worked for wages, and made them slaves. You sold their children into a deeper bondage. Now you ask that we go away from those of our children who are left, abandon them, leave them ripe for your plucking.''

Nefer-Re had been startled, but her wits were quick. ''You would only say such things,'' she said, ''if you yourself were prepared to break your word. You want your children with you, because you don't intend to come back. Once you've gone into the desert, Egypt will never see you again.''

Miriam met her eyes. There was no mask now, no pretense. She was all imperious, all queenly proud. ''Do we owe you honor who so dishonored us?''

''If we are to speak of honor or of owing,'' said Nefer-Re, ''then what of Egypt stripped bare, our people facing famine? Slaves you might have been, you Apiru, but we never starved you.''

''No. You whipped us, tortured us, sold off our children. You make our laborers labor with bare hands, without the tools they need, or compel them to forge those tools but give them no time for the forging. Whatever they do to satisfy your overseers' demands, you add to those demands without taking away. You do your best to break my people. All for a petty vindictiveness, a memory of a time when the gods of Egypt were subject to one great god. If our people worshipped half a dozen false divinities, they would still be free men building tombs in Thebes and herding flocks in the Delta. They would not be penned together in

Pi-Ramses, building a city for a king who both fears and hates them."

Nefer-Re rose slowly. "You are a stiff-necked people," she said. Her voice was carefully controlled. "You are proud, nay arrogant. You are all that my father condemns you for."

"Certainly," said Miriam. "We're very like him."

For a breathless instant Nofret was sure that Nefer-Re would strike Miriam. But a lady, even a lady as manly forthright as this, did not resort to blows. Her weapon was the tongue. "I see that you are no better than your father. Go, exult with him over Egypt's suffering. Praise your god of cruelty, your jealous god who will have no other god beside him."

"You too," said Miriam, "are your father's image. If you would but set us free, Egypt would be spared its suffering. All that it endures, your father has laid upon it with his intransigence."

Nofret discovered that she had been holding her breath. She let it out slowly. The two of them, princess now and queen who had been, stood face to face, eye to burning eye.

There was no remedy but surrender, and it must be absolute. Kings or queens, they were all the same.

Wives, too, and husbands. War was the way of the world. Even gods fought one against the other.

Miriam parted from Nefer-Re with remarkable civility. That was an attribute of kings. They would speak softly to those whom they would destroy, and offer royal courtesy to their enemies, and end a battle with the strict forms of politeness. If Nefer-Re wondered where the seer of the Apiru had learned such things, she did not speak of it.

▪ ▪ ▪

When there was no green thing left in Egypt, a wind came out of the west and blew the locusts away, swept them clean, all the way to the sea that lay between Egypt and Sinai.

But the wind itself was a terrible thing, like the hand of the god. With the locusts it blew the black earth of Egypt, the gift of the river that was the wealth of the Black Land. Mingled with it was the Red Land itself, a storm out of the desert, dry as dust, dry as sand, alive with lightning.

Black Land and Red Land had gone to war along the river. For three days the sun could not pierce the cloud of dust and earth. The only light was lightning. All else was darkness. Night was but a fraction darker than day; day was a dim brown glimmer, a hint of the brightness that shone beyond the cloud.

Then at last the king broke. Maybe his daughter had a part in it. Maybe she had no need.

He was still proud; he would not come to Moshe like a beggar at a king's door. He had Moshe brought to him as before, in a company of guards, with a prince of servants to guide him. The hall was ablaze with lamps, the court huddled as close to one another as they could be. They had even brought their dogs, their golden-earringed cats, their pet monkeys and gazelles and their birds in cages, all their living chattels, as if this were a city under siege.

"I yield," the king said to Moshe. "I yield to your god. Your people may go."

The young men of the Apiru grinned at one another. They had grown cocky in the darkness, determinedly undismayed by it, calling it the Lord's cloak and walking boldly abroad in it. Now they were proved right: the king had given in. Their people were free.

"Nine times your god has spoken," said the king. "Eight times I have defied him. No longer. My kingdom is in ruins. We look on famine, on starvation, all by your god's will. Let it be as he commands. Let your people take their belongings and go. Let them go far, and let them go long. Let them worship him as and where they well please.''

''My lord is generous,'' said Moshe, ''and ultimately reasonable.''

''What choice have I?'' the king asked bitterly. ''Go. My boat is waiting to carry you to Pi-Ramses. When you come there, gather your people. Take them out of Egypt.''

''So we shall,'' said Moshe. But he did not turn, nor did he go, though he had clearly been dismissed.

It was Miriam who spoke for him, and not Aharon, who seemed as pleased as the young men. She spoke delicately, with exquisite politeness, in her pure Theban accent. ''Your boat, my lord? Surely you mean your boats. We have baggage, and beasts to carry it.''

''Ah,'' said the king. ''Yes. But you see, we need those animals. Your god has destroyed the great part of our herds. There are too few oxen for the plowing, too few asses to bear burdens; the sheep and the goats are sorely depleted. I'm afraid we must keep any that we can, whether here or in Pi-Ramses.''

Miriam regarded him without surprise. Her eyes did not shift to the woman who stood among his attendants, Nefer-Re, erect and expressionless. Whether this was her doing or her father's own, there was no telling.

Miriam said to the king softly, reasonably, ''We must have our herds. They are our livelihood. Without them we will starve.''

''Surely,'' said the king, ''your god will provide.''

''Our god provides only what we fail to provide for ourselves,'' said Miriam. ''We are shepherds and keepers of flocks. We cannot live without them.''

''Neither can we,'' said the king, ''and we are more numerous and more deeply in need. Your people may go— isn't that what you wanted? I'll not even ask that you leave your children behind, as might have been safest. But the animals that you keep, that alone escaped the pestilence, those we must have. Our children are starving, lady. Without those flocks and herds, they die.''

"They are ours," Miriam said. "Our god has preserved them for us."

"You too are intransigent," said the king. "Will you deny your people freedom for the sake of a few goats and sheep?"

"Those few goats and sheep," said Moshe, "are the life of our people, their sustenance in the dry land. Their wool weaves our tents and covers us with our mantles and our robes. On their meat and milk do we live. And," he said, "their unblemished young are our sacrifice to the Lord of Yisroel."

"Ah," said the king. "Your god, your lord of wrath and vengeance. No, you must not anger him. I leave you one goat, then, for every household, and one lamb for sacrifice. The rest we must keep. Your god took away our own. We will have yours in recompense."

"We cannot do that," Moshe said. "The Lord has been most clear. All of us must go, and all our goods and chattels, our herds, everything that is ours. Nothing less will content him."

"Then you are a fool," said the king, "and your god is a monument to avarice. You may go, I set you free. But your flocks will stay."

"Without our flocks we cannot go," said Moshe. "The Lord has forbidden us."

"Then stay!" roared the king. "Stay and be damned!"

CHAPTER SIXTY-FOUR

▲

FROM every other audience Moshe had come forth almost serene, wearing his god like a cloak. From this one he came shaking, though whether it was anger or terror, Nofret could not tell. When he sat down in the guesthouse

and wept, it was the kind of weeping that besets a man
when he had come to the end of his endurance: dry and
hurting-hard.

He did not seem to notice that the others hovered and
fretted. He spoke to no one that Nofret could see, with
none of the forms or gestures that other men used in converse with their gods. He simply spoke as to another man,
albeit one older and higher than he, a father perhaps, or a
master of slaves. "O Lord, my God, how much longer will
you test us? How much more must the Two Lands suffer?
When will you set us free?"

There was no answer that Nofret could hear. She was
tired to the bone. The darkness had crept into her heart
and settled there. The sun would never shine again. They
would all live and die in the dark, without even stars to
comfort them.

■ ■ ■

Nofret woke from a heavy, sodden sleep. At first she did
not know what had roused her. There was light—lamplight, but unnaturally bright. She sat up blinking.

Sunlight. Daylight. The darkness was gone from the sky.

Indeed. But not from her heart. It was as deep there as
ever.

She got up, pulled on what garments came to hand. Her
body felt like a stranger's. It was heavy, stiff. Moving it
was like moving a wooden image.

She walked out of the room in which she had slept, into
tumult. All the embassy were gathered together, and all
their baggage. She saw her own among the rest—numb
and blind, she must have been, not to see that it was gone.

"What—" she tried to say.

Jehoshua appeared in front of her. He had a white, wild
look. "Come," he said. "Come quickly."

She did not have to dig in her heels to keep him from
dragging her off. She was made of wood, of cedar from

the Lebanon. She was much too heavy for him to lift. "Tell me why," she made herself say.

His head tossed with impatience. "Mother! We have to go. We have to go now. The Lord says so."

"Moshe says so." That was Johanan with a pack on his back. "The king summoned him again when the sun came up. There was shouting and worse. We're ordered to leave Memphis or die."

"But where—"

"Pi-Ramses," said Jehoshua. It was like hearing an echo, the son so like the father that if she let her eyelids fall half-shut she could not tell them apart. Johanan was bigger and his beard was blacker, thicker and longer. She must remember that.

"The Lord is angry," Johanan said. "Truly angry. The land and its creatures have suffered and died for the king's obduracy. But no man of Egypt, no woman or child, has been slain at the Lord's hand."

"That mercy is ended," said Jehoshua. "Mother, wake up. Hurry. We have to be in Pi-Ramses when the Lord's wrath falls."

"We have a little time," Johanan said. He caught his son's eye. "But not much. Come, beloved. We have to go while we still can."

■ ■ ■

There was a boat waiting for them on the river, a barge to carry their beasts and their baggage. The bargemen had Apiru faces though they wore the loincloths that were the only sensible working-clothes under the sun of Egypt. The Lord had provided the boatmen, Nofret supposed, as he provided the food and water that were on board the barge, and protection from the king's guards. Some of those were watching from the walls or the bank, but they did not interfere.

By the time the boat had cast off from the shore, Nofret

was fully awake, though her body still felt strange. She sat under the striped linen canopy with the elders and Moshe and Miriam. The young men and Johanan, and Aharon with them, took turn and turn among the barge's crew. She did not ask acidly, as she thought to do, why the Lord had not given them a swift sailing ship and a crew of oarsmen. The lovely sleek river-ships could not carry a herd of donkeys in comfort.

They went swiftly enough with the aid of current and sail. Where the bank was level, the young men sprang out and rigged lines to tow the barge. Night's coming did not stop them, although they slowed, guiding themselves by starlight and lanternlight and, for all Nofret knew, their god's light that she alone of them all could not see.

They said little, and most of that was prayer. Silence in the Apiru was an alarming thing, like meekness in a lion or abstinence in a crocodile. Their silence had weight. It dragged her down.

Moshe's was most massive of all. His god-inspired trances had always had in them an element of exaltation, of being lifted up. When he chose to die to Egypt, to set aside his kingship and become the prophet of Sinai, he had gone to his seeming death with something close to joy.

Now there was no joy in him. He was about to win the battle to set his people free, that much Nofret understood. But the thing that his god would do, the things that his god had done, were rending him with grief.

When Tutankhamon was king, Nofret had ridden on the river or taken the road beside it, traveling from Memphis into the green lands of the Delta. She could remember still how rich the country had been. Pastures full of flocks and herds, fields of barley and of flax, orchards, vineyards, great wealth and beauty. The air had been full of birds, the water teeming with fish.

Now it was all barren. The green was devoured. The black earth was turned to dust and blown far away. The once-great herds were shrunk to a heap of white bones in the blackened remnant of a field, and a lone emaciated heifer lowing pitifully beside a farmer's hut.

The god of the Apiru had done this. Egypt was laid low. Its people huddled in their villages, staring bleakly at ruin.

Moshe's stare was no less bleak. Sometimes Nofret heard him murmuring to himself in Egyptian. "O my kingdom. O my people. How you have fallen!"

She had never credited him with love of the Two Lands that he had ruled so poorly. And yet it seemed he had loved them. It was bred in him, she supposed.

But then she had no cause to love Egypt, and she grieved for it. Kings and gods: they were a plague and a pestilence. Better for the world if neither of them had ever been.

Moshe wept as the boat carried him down the river to Pi-Ramses. His daughter did not weep, nor did she speak. The Apiru were grimly silent.

Only Nofret did not know what took them to Pi-Ramses. Nor would she ask. It was a kind of cowardice. The less she knew, the later she discovered it, the better for her heart's peace.

▪ ▪ ▪

Pi-Ramses—the house of Ramses, beloved of Amon, great in victory—was one of the king's treasure-cities, a city of storehouses and granaries, treasuries and temples. It was a fortress already before the Apiru were shut up in it, a walled city set on the shore of a lake called the Sea of Reeds. A far eastern branch of the river of Egypt flowed past its walls. The road into Asia began there. There was the edge of Egypt, the last of the green land between the Delta and the desert.

The city crouched like a stone lion amid the deep green of vineyards, their beauty untouched by the plagues that had destroyed the rest of Egypt. The sweetness of wine wafted from it. One could almost imagine that this was a city of peace; but there was a scent of cold stone beneath, and an iron harshness that was blood.

Nofret would always remember Pi-Ramses so, not by sight but by the mingled scent of wine and blood. Old blood as well as new. The Shepherd Kings, those invaders whose name was forgotten, had ruled here. Now another race of shepherds, their distant kin perhaps, were held captive beneath the yoke of Egypt, bound in slavery, forced to build the king's treasure-houses under the lash of his overseers.

As greenly placid as the land seemed, the city had the same bleak lost look as the rest of Egypt. Egyptians, even armed guards, shied away from the Apiru. The Apiru huddled in their own quarter, crowded together with their sheep and goats, their children, their belongings.

There were boats moored at the quay, but no one in them. People in the city had retreated to their houses. Guards stood stiff at their posts, but made no move to stop the strangers.

Moshe entered the city almost quietly. There could be no concealing a whole embassy of Apiru, complete with donkeys and baggage, but no one came out to watch them. There was no greeting-party at the quay, either to welcome them or to drive them out.

In the quarter of the Apiru, people were waiting. Frightened people, people so beaten down by years of servitude that they had forgotten how to stand straight. They walked bent, with their eyes fixed on their feet.

But a remarkable number still held their heads high. Apiru pride: it put Egyptian royalty to shame. They came forward to the gate that barred their dwellings from those of Egyptians, and stood in a ragged rank between the strangers and the rest of their people. They might be on guard. They might be warding the strangers against their own people's fear.

Ephraim, who had come to Memphis from Pi-Ramses, had so far forgotten his shyness among the bold young men from Sinai that he stepped in front of Moshe himself, between the prophet and the people of the city, and said to the man foremost, "Shmuel, what are you doing? Let us in."

Shmuel appeared to be an elder of these people. He was perhaps no older than Nofret, but thin and grey, worn to the bone by hard labor. Unlike many of the others however he seemed the stronger for what he had endured. He stood upright, faced Moshe, and said clearly, "You may be all that rumor makes you. I know nothing but that your coming has made the Egyptians angry."

"They were angry before he came," said Ephraim hotly. "Shmuel, let us in. The Lord is waiting."

Shmuel looked to be at least as stubborn as the king. Nofret wondered if the Apiru god would smite an Apiru for standing in the way of his prophet.

She never did discover whether he would do such a thing. Before Shmuel could speak, Aharon advanced to Ephraim's side. He had never failed to take advantage of his size and breadth where it would serve him: as much here as in the king's court. His voice was soft, gentle, deep enough to rumble in the earth. "We come to set you free."

"And what is freedom?" Shmuel demanded. "Starvation in the desert?"

"By the Lord's grace," said Aharon, "no."

"The Lord will give us a land of our own," a new voice said. Nofret started. Jehoshua was standing at Aharon's shoulder. How had he grown so tall? He was growing into his grandfather's voice, too, that beautiful rich timbre which made Aharon so powerful a herald for his prophet.

Jehoshua was still young, still no more than a boy. He had a boy's eagerness, half clumsy, half captivating. "We've been promised. When we come out of Egypt there will be a country for us, a land that will be ours. You'll see. You'll look on it with the rest of us and be glad.''

"If any of us lives to see it," said Shmuel.

"We will live," said Jehoshua. "The Egyptians—"

"The Egyptians will know the Lord's wrath." Moshe had spoken at last, freed for once from his stammer. "Come to the gathering place, quickly. Time is short."

Diffident as Moshe could seem, light-voiced, hesitant, lacking the power of presence that was so distinct in Aharon, still he could lead men when he chose. Even reluctant Shmuel gave way before him.

■   ■   ■

They all gathered in the place that would hold them, the market-square now emptied of stalls. Goats and sheep were penned in the corners of it, but the center was open. The people poured into it until they filled it, a greater throng than Nofret could have expected. There were hundreds of them, of every age, from doddering ancient to babe at the breast. They were a great army, if anyone had had the will to muster them and train them for war.

There was nothing warlike about them as they gathered in front of Moshe. They were slaves, cowed and trembling, too full of their own fears to listen to him. Aharon had to raise his voice to a battlefield bellow before they would stop babbling among themselves.

Even then they could not all hear Moshe. Aharon spoke the words as he spoke them, transmuting their hesitance into firmness and strength.

"The Lord is angry," he said. "He sent me into Egypt to set you free, but the king of Egypt persists in holding you captive. His land is destroyed, his people cast into famine, but still he holds fast. His pride rules him. He will not give way.

"And now the Lord has come to the end of his patience. Nine times he has shown his power. Nine times the king has turned his face away. But from this, children of Yisroel—from this, even the Great House of Egypt cannot escape.''

He paused. The crowd was silent. A mere prophet could not still their chatter, but mention of their god quelled even the children.

Moshe's head bowed with the weight of the world. He spoke slowly now, measuring the words one by one. ''The Lord has spoken. The children of Yisroel must obey every word as he has uttered it. Listen, my people. Listen and remember.''

Aharon's voice rose to fill the sky. Moshe's was dim beneath it. Dimmer still, maybe, was the voice of the god of whom they were only heralds.

''This shall be the first month of the first year,'' they said. ''The first day is past: that day when the Lord bade me stand before the king and convey the last of his warnings. When the tenth day comes, the Lord bids you seek for each household an unblemished lamb: a male, a yearling, no older, no younger. Take that lamb; feed it. Consecrate it. And on the fourth day thereafter, in the first fading of evening, let it be sacrificed before the people. Let each of you take a bundle of hyssop; dip it in the blood of the lamb, and spread it upon the doorposts and the lintel of each house in which dwells man or woman or child of the Apiru.

''Then go within, my children, and eat of the lamb, roasted whole with all its limbs and organs, and no bone broken. Eat it with bitter herbs and with unleavened bread. Eat it standing, clad for travel, with your staffs in your hands; but take great care that none of you come forth till morning.

''For at the stroke of midnight,'' they said, echo within echo, ''I shall pass over the land of Egypt. Every house that is sealed with the blood of the lamb, I shall not touch. But every other house, every stable, every barn and byre, shall know the stroke of my hand. Death shall smite them, my children, death of their firstborn, whether they be princes or slaves, lords in their palaces or beasts in the fields—aye, even to the king himself, for whose pride I have ordained this scourge upon the land and the people of Egypt.''

If the silence had been deep before, now it was absolute. No one moved. No one breathed.

Moshe lifted his head. Tears were running down his cheeks. ''But you, my children,'' he said—his god said— ''I shall spare. When the morning comes, take the leavings of the lamb; burn them all, to the last of them. Then you shall be free; then you shall go forth from the place of your captivity.

''Do this,'' he said. ''Do this, and remember it forever.''

CHAPTER SIXTY-FIVE

▲

I wish I could believe that he wasn't going to do it,'' Nofret said. ''I wish I could believe that he lacked the power.''

She had gone with the rest of the embassy to the largest house in the slaves' quarter, which happened to belong— ironically enough—to Shmuel the doubter. She was not greatly surprised to discover that he was Ephraim's father. Strength of will and purpose seemed to run in that family. Its direction differed, that was all, and the manner of its expression.

Shmuel might not be greatly happy, but he knew the requirements of courtesy. And he had heard the voice of his god. Even Nofret had done that, and she was a for-eigner.

His wife was a hospitable woman, less dour than her

husband, undismayed to find herself guesting a small army of strangers. She, with her gaggle of yet-unmarried daughters, was glad of Nofret's help, and of Miriam's: a prophetess, she said, was a woman like any other, and well for her if she could bake bread for three dozen.

It was to Miriam that Nofret spoke while the two of them mixed water into barley flour. They were not to leaven it, for this was the night when the god would pass over. If she strained she could hear the bleating of lambs where they were gathered together. At sunset the sacrifice would begin.

Miriam glanced at her. "Will you be worshipping the Lord, then, since you believe in him?"

"No," said Nofret.

"Do you fear for your firstborn?"

Nofret surged up, but caught herself before she leaped. She sank down again, breathing deep. "My firstborn will sleep—if he can—behind a gate warded with blood. Your god demanded only that; not that everyone within be his devoted slave."

Miriam shrugged. She worked water and flour together, but carefully, lest in kneading it she cause it to rise. It was a peculiar prohibition, like the god who required it. It signified haste, Moshe had said; time shortened to nothing as the people fled out of Egypt.

Bread unleavened and baked flat would have little enough savor. Roast lamb at least they would have, fragrant with herbs. Women had been out gathering them, in some fear of the Egyptians, but those who did not flee the Lord's people were well enough disposed toward them. Some had been coming to offer gifts of gold and silver for the journey, precious vessels, jewels, a trove of treasures useless to a wandering people. Moshe had not forbidden them to take such booty—bribery, Nofret thought it, to win immunity from the god's last curse. But only the blood of the lamb could do that, and no Egyptian could ransom himself so.

A commotion brought her rather gratefully to the door. It was open on the street, to let in what air there was. People were running past, babbling incoherently. But she only needed a few words to know what had set them off.

The king was in Pi-Ramses. He had come by swift boat like a courier, attended by the eldest of his daughters. An army marched behind him. They would be in the city in a day or two. Then no doubt the Apiru would be slaughtered.

But not yet. There were not enough soldiers in the city to muster an attack against the Apiru. Johanan, anticipating trouble, had already gathered every man who could wield a weapon. The result was an army indeed, hundreds strong, standing guard by turn and turn.

The number of their weapons was a matter of some surprise to Nofret, who knew how difficult it could be to arm a company of warriors. There must have been swords hidden in the clothing-presses or buried under the floors of houses; bows kept for hunting, with arrows made and fletched and put away for the time of need. Any man who lacked either had found himself a spear, taken from a soldier maybe, or preserved from long ago.

Whether their god or their own swords defended them, they would suffer nothing that night from the king of Egypt. Nofret heard Aharon's voice quieting those who had run in panic. Another great voice from another part of the quarter must be Johanan's, or possibly Jehoshua's: his had a piercing quality that the older men's lacked, like a trumpet ringing far away.

By the time the bread was made and taken to the oven that the women shared, the sun had sunk below the city's walls. The sky was still bright but the streets were dim, night falling early among the houses of the Apiru. They had all gathered where Moshe had spoken to them of the god's passing over, where priests had set up altars and begun the round of the sacrifice. As each man of the household presented the lamb for slaughter, a priest slit its throat and directed its blood into a bowl that was held by a son or daughter of the house. Then when the lamb died it was borne away to be skinned and roasted, its blood painted on the door for a ward against the god's destruction.

There was a strange, somber joy in that rite. The reek of blood and death, the holy stink of sacrifice, must have gagged the priests, who were little accustomed to such a plenitude of slaughter. The people sang the praises of their god, drowning out the lambs' bleating. The god, it seemed, was not a practical deity. He had not thought to silence the victims who came later to the sacrifice and were dismayed by the sight and sound and scent of those that died before them.

■　■　■

Aharon was among the priests of the sacrifice, and Johanan bloodied to the elbows. They finished after dark had fallen, cleansed themselves and their altars, prayed whatever prayers their god demanded, and returned to the house in which they were lodging.

Nofret had gone back long ago, with the young men carrying the four lambs that they had reckoned for so many: Shmuel's household, Aharon's, Moshe's, Johanan's, with all the servants and the elders and the embassy. It was Miriam who had limned the door in blood, stretching high to mark the lintel. It was beautiful, bright scarlet; nor did it dry and darken as blood should properly do. Every door and lintel was so in that part of the city: framed in blood-red, unmistakable.

When the priests returned, the tables were laid within, the feast prepared. The bread, hard dry rounds of it, was baked and ready, most laid aside for the journey, the rest on the table to be eaten on this night of all nights.

All the lamps were lit, prodigal of oil, for they could

not carry it all where they were going. The great room of
the house was a haven of light. The dark was shut out.
Here was the scent of lamb and herbs, the savor of unleavened bread, the murmur of prayer and praise to the
Lord of Yisroel.

There were no battles tonight. No one argued. No one
cast doubt on what they did. Fear was banished with the
dark.

Somewhere between the lamb and the wine, someone
began to sing. The wine was strong sweet wine of Pi-
Ramses, heady and potent after the bitterness of captivity.
They all drank deep of it, sending the cups round and then
round again.

They passed the night in wine and in song, safe behind
their warded door. None spoke of the world without, or of
death, or their god's anger. They were safe. He protected
them.

■   ■   ■

Nofret drank as much as anyone, but her head remained
stubbornly clear. She had eaten enough to satisfy hunger,
but no more. She was cold inside, a cold that did not warm
for anything she did.

She was as safe here as anyone else. But her eyes kept
returning to Jehoshua, as if he would stiffen suddenly and
fall, destroyed because his mother would not worship one
god above the rest. And Johanan—he too was the firstborn
of his father. He too could die.

They were not afraid. They sat side by side among the
men, sharing a cup as often as not, so like to one another
that her eyes stung with tears.

She left them on a pretext. The winejar would be empty
soon, and wine, like oil, was awkward to carry far in the
desert. But instead of seeking out the room where the wine
was stored, she took a lamp and went up on the roof.

This was mad. Moshe, or his god, had bidden all his

people to keep safe within, not to dare the night air while his spirit of death passed over.

It was cool for Egypt, almost cold. The stars were blazing bright. A vast quiet lay over the city. No light shone, not even in the governor's palace, where tonight the king was lying sleepless. Perhaps he too held off the dark with wine and lamplight, music and song.

And maybe the god had no power to do what he threatened. Maybe the king was here to set the Apiru free.

Maybe Nofret was grasping at something, anything, to deny what she knew was true. Death walked the night in Egypt. Almost she felt the brush of its wings. Almost she heard the sound of its footfall, soft and yet immense.

For a moment it seemed that the stars were blotted out, that the dark was absolute. She shuddered in her bones. But the death had not come for her. She was the sixth of her father's children, the third of his daughters. If this had been Great Hatti—if any Hittite had been as great a fool as the king of Egypt—her brother Piyassili would have fallen down dead, but none of the rest.

Maybe after all this was a merciful god. An unmerciful one would have killed every living thing in Egypt, from the least to the greatest: not simply one in each generation, the first to be born, the eldest and the first in inheritance.

She felt rather than saw the one who came up behind her, knew him by the sound of his step and the warmth of his body even across the width of the roof. She whipped about. "Get below! It's death for you here."

Johanan came to stand beside her, face turned to the sky. The stars were clear again, the shadow gone, if in fact it had ever been. "It's past," he said. "We all felt it go."

"You were too far gone in wine to feel anything."

"The Lord is stronger than wine," said Johanan. He was close, almost touching. He did not presume to lay an arm about her shoulders.

They had not stood so near to one another since they

left Sinai. Nofret fought compulsion, but in the end she yielded; she circled his waist with her arm and leaned lightly against him.

He did not stiffen, she noticed. His arm settled where it belonged, around her shoulders. She sighed. "If Jehoshua comes to any danger, any whatsoever, before we come back to Sinai, I honestly will never forgive you."

"That's fair, I suppose," he said.

"It's not fair at all," said Nofret. She completed the circle of her arms, burying her face in his breast. She could see nothing, not even stars, but the night was less dark, the wings of death less softly terrible as they fell upon the firstborn of every living creature in Egypt.

He carried her down from the roof into the guarded fastness of the house. Everyone was in the hall; the singing had shifted from hymns to songs more secular by far. The sleeping-rooms were empty. Even the servants were partaking of the wine, holding off the night and the fear.

If the Lord of Yisroel objected to such comfort as two people could find on the night of his wrath, he forbore to smite them for it. "He bids us be fruitful," Johanan said somewhere in the night, "and multiply, and have joy in it."

"I don't remember the joy," she said, "when that law was declared to the people."

"It went without saying," he said.

CHAPTER SIXTY-SIX

▲

THE Apiru crept out in the first light of morning, venturing one by one through doors on which the blood had gone dark at last. Their quarter was deathly quiet, but beyond it they heard the sound of wailing.

The Lord had done as he promised. In every house the eldest child, the firstborn, lay dead, struck down by the hand of the god. The king sat on his throne with his firstborn in his arms, his daughter Nefer-Re whom he loved. He would not let her go. But the people who had caused her death, the slaves whom he had held captive for so long, he sent away in a great howl of rage and grief. "Go!" he cried to Moshe and to the few who had been brought to the governor's palace in the first hours of the morning. "Go, and never come back!"

The children of Yisroel took him at his word. Obedient to their god's command, they burned the leavings of the feast, gathered all their belongings, their flocks and herds, and went out of Pi-Ramses. The gates were open for them. The guards were dead or fled. No throngs accompanied them, no crowds of the curious ran behind to see where they went. No one had heart or leisure for such a thing. Every house in Egypt was a house of mourning.

Only the Apiru were glad. They went forth singing, driving their beasts before them. They were a great multitude, a whole nation freed at last from its captivity.

■   ■   ■

Nofret was in front with Moshe and Aharon, Miriam and the rest of the elders from Sinai. For all their gladness, for all the Egyptians' prostration, Johanan and Jehoshua had mustered the armed men and set them on guard to front and rear and sides. They traveled from the city as their kin wandered through the desert, armed against attack.

They had been slaves. They understood caution and knew the uses of wariness. But most had little acquaintance with wandering, nor knew how best to preserve their strength or their provisions. Nofret saw how many of them were prodigal with their water, drinking much too often from their families' supply, and spilling it as if they needed only to walk down to the well for more.

That would have to stop once they came to the desert. Here they were still in civilized country, on the road through the outposts of Egypt. They could not take to the open desert with so many people, so many of them children or the old.

The eastward way, the way into Canaan, might have been simplest, for there were cities, and oases between, and no lakes or seas to cross. But the people there would not take kindly to the coming of a whole nation, a tribe in arms that might be taken for an invading army. Therefore they went south and east on the desert road, the road that led to the eastern sea.

That was Moshe's doing. No one sane would have done it, and no one sane would have followed anyone else who led the people that way. But Moshe was the prophet of their god. The god guided him, he said. Therefore they followed.

■　■　■

So many people, so little accustomed to the ways of wandering in the desert, traveled much more slowly than the tribes in Sinai. By midday they were still in sight of the green shimmer of the vineyards about Pi-Ramses. By sunset they were on the desert's edge, looking out across the Red Land.

They camped there. Some of them had still enough strength to sing. Most were weary and footsore, the children whining, begging to be carried, but they were happy. They were free.

There was dancing round the fires that night. The young in particular were resilient, and with a little rest and a sufficiency of water and food they were apt for another night's revelry. Tonight the stars were clean. No death walked the dark. They needed no protection but their own young men, archers and spearmen set on guard as was only sensible in the desert.

The elders were either sleeping deep or dancing with the young men. But Moshe and Aharon and Miriam held council instead of festival. Nofret was of a like mind. So, she noticed, was Johanan; and Jehoshua, having proved to the youths of Pi-Ramses that he could leap twice as high over the fire as any of them, came to drop laughing at his mother's feet.

His laughter died quickly. They were eating sparingly, drinking watered wine. "Tomorrow," Johanan said, "these people will learn the beginnings of wisdom. We'll gather all the food and water, set men in charge of it—"

"Women," said Miriam. "Let women command the food. We have to cook it, after all."

"Women, then," Johanan said amicably. "We'll choose the elders and those with authority, and set them to meting out a set portion each day. There'll be fighting else, and hunger and thirst among the improvident."

"Some will be out of water by tomorrow," Jehoshua said. "I saw one man bathing in his. He'd dug a basin in the sand and lined it with goatskins, and was swimming in it like a pharaoh in a pleasure-pool."

"No one stopped him?" Nofret asked, incredulous.

"Who would know to? People laughed and asked if they could go after him. They don't understand that water's not to be had for the asking, not here."

He did not understand such people, he who had been raised in the camps of Sinai, but he was trying. Nofret was proud of him.

"They're going to learn," said Johanan, "that they're not people of the cities, not any longer. They belong to the desert, and to the Lord of hosts."

Moshe nodded by the fire. Miriam, beside him, said, "There may be no need for any of that. We have escaped the city, but not yet the king."

"The Lord has laid him low," said Jehoshua. "He's let us go."

"Grief laid him low," Miriam said. "Pride will master him once more and send him in pursuit of us. He had no love for us before. Now he hates us. Now he has his daughter's death to avenge."

"His son and heir still lives," said Jehoshua. "Surely he doesn't—"

Nofret cuffed him, to his startlement and sudden anger, and said to him, "If you were a girl, my fine young lion, I would be no less devastated to lose you." He was growing abashed, she could see, but he was stubborn. She cuffed him again. "Open your eyes, child! He loved his daughter and valued her: she was the chief of his counselors. Without her he has a son to inherit the throne, but no mind to match his."

Jehoshua looked down, not at all willingly, but he was at heart a sensible young man. "Very well. So you think the king is going to come after us."

"I know he is," Nofret said before Miriam could speak. "He'll think to trap us by the sea, since we chose this of all roads."

"The road into Canaan is a warrior's road," Johanan said. "We aren't a warrior people, not as many as we are."

"Nor are we gods or spirits, to walk dry-shod across the sea," said Nofret.

"The Lord will guide us," Moshe said.

Not even Johanan believed that. But it silenced him and drove Jehoshua into speechlessness. When next anyone spoke, it was Jehoshua, calling back to one who had called to him from another fire, leaping up and running to the dance.

▪ ▪ ▪

Moshe wept for Egypt. He alone of them all had wept when they left Pi-Ramses, wept as he had done on the river out of Memphis, for the dead and for the sorely battered kingdom. While his people sang, he mourned. He knew no delight in the victory, only grief.

Some of the elders from Sinai came to him that first night, warm with wine and laughter. They had a new plan, a plan that they reckoned inspired. "Egypt is weak," they said, "and the king is gone from Memphis. Let us go there and take the city and be kings in it."

"That," said Miriam, "is the wine speaking. Go, sleep it off. We leave at dawn."

They paid no heed to her. They pressed close round Moshe as he sat by the fire. "Don't you want to be king again? Isn't it time and past time, since you've shown the might of the Lord? We can rule as the Shepherd Kings did, but more strongly than they. After all, our king will be king by right in Egypt."

"We told you long ago," said Miriam, "that a king who has died cannot be made to live again."

She was outside of their circle, invisible, inaudible, disregarded. "Lead us to Memphis," they said. "Isn't that what you're doing, taking us south instead of east? Let's turn west. Let's go to the king's city."

Moshe rose, startling them. He walked straight through the circle and out into the dark. They gaped. One or two rose as if to follow, but met large and glowering obstacles: Johanan and Aharon, barring their way.

An elder needed no courage to hold the office, nor even much wisdom, simply the good fortune to have outlived his agemates. These were brave enough to enter Egypt, but not to face two men both tall and strong. Aharon and Johanan stared them down, sent them slinking back to their own campfires and the solace of the wine.

"They won't ever stop that, will they?" Nofret said to Miriam as the elders beat their retreat.

Miriam shrugged. "When we're out of Egypt and away from temptation, likely they'll forget this silliness."

"Is that what it is?" Nofret asked her. "Aren't you

tempted yourself? You could be queen again if you cared enough to try.''

For a moment Miriam's face was open, the mask of indifference laid aside. Nofret saw the raw longing, the pain of memory, the regret that, in the end, was less than it well might have been. "I don't care to try," she said, soft and steady.

"Truly?''

Miriam's eyes glittered, but she kept her temper. "Not enough, my friend. Not nearly enough.''

The name of friendship took Nofret slightly aback. She had not thought of them as friends; but what else could one call it? Not lady and slave, certainly. They had a certain comfort in each other's company. They knew the quality of one another's silences.

They shared no confidences as women did among the Apiru. But then they did not need to. They had known each other from childhood. None not kin had known Nofret for as long as Miriam had known her; Nofret had known Miriam since she was a small naked princess, the third daughter of forgotten Akhenaten.

They looked at each other in the firelight. Miriam nodded slightly, turned, went into the tent that she shared with her father.

Nofret did not follow her. If Miriam needed to weep, she would want to do it in solitude. Difficult as it had been for Nofret to return to Egypt, it had been more than bitter for that one who had been queen and goddess and was become nothing but air and a voice.

Nofret turned slowly on the edge of the light. Aharon and Johanan were sitting again by the fire, talking quietly. Jehoshua was dancing with the young men, leaping high and then higher, laughing as he did it. Some of the girls from Pi-Ramses were watching, giggling behind their veils.

Of Moshe she saw nothing. And yet her bones knew

where he had gone. He was walking in the desert, wrapped in his god as in a cloak. The night spirits walked wide of him. The creatures of the dark shrank from his presence.

It dawned on her that she was seeing and perceiving things that were hidden, that simple human eyes could not see. She had always been able to sense the presence of gods and powers; magic had been as clear to her as fire in the dark. But this was a new clarity. It was more a knowing than a seeing, less of the eyes than of the bones—not wholly then the gift that Leah had had, that Miriam seemed to have. Nofret was something other than they. But then she was a foreigner, no kin to the Apiru.

Time was when she would have refused this gift, turned against it with all the power of her native obstinacy. But here in the Red Land, on the road from Pi-Ramses, she was emptied of resistance. She could not say as the Apiru might, "The Lord's will be done." But she could bow to the inevitable.

She wandered a little way from the fire, on the track that Moshe had taken but not in pursuit of him. She went only far enough to escape the light. The clamor of the camp was muted. She heard the cry of a jackal. The gods of Egypt were there, watching, lifting no hand against the interloper from Sinai.

There was someone else, too, someone who believed himself to be both king and god. He was still in Pi-Ramses, but he had given the order: in the morning his army would march. Every man of it mourned a kinsman or a friend or a comrade in arms. There were gaps in the ranks, men who had been the first of their fathers' children.

The king's daughter had been taken at last to the house of purification. Ramses wept for her, shut up in his chamber, sleepless and raging. The pride that had brought his kingdom such sorrow was stronger in him than ever. It possessed him as a demon will, beyond reason or logic. The god of the Apiru had resorted to murder. The king of

Egypt would destroy the people who worshipped that god.

It would be a just execution, he was thinking. He was past caring that in slaying so many, he was destroying the wealth of a nation in slaves. They had destroyed the land's wealth of Egypt, and the wealth of its eldest-born.

Nofret returned to herself with a shock, as if she had plunged into deep water and come near to drowning. Nothing that she had ever done was like this. There were tales, whispers of the priests' arts, spirits that could wander wherever their master directed. If this was what it was, then it was simpler than the priests would ever admit.

She turned back blindly to the light. The camp had quieted, abruptly it seemed, till she looked up at the stars. They had wheeled a whole hour's span in the moments since last she had seen them.

Her breath shuddered as she drew it in. Her body shook with shivering. Somehow she got herself to the fire and huddled by it, drawing from it all the warmth she could.

Johanan's arms folded about her. Slow warmth seeped into her. She sighed.

He did not ask her why she was so cold in the desert night. Even when she said, "Pharaoh means to follow us. He's in a deadly rage."

He nodded, unsurprised. Of course: Moshe and Miriam had foretold it. When he gathered her up, she protested only feebly. He carried her into their tent and laid her in their bed.

There at last she was warm enough. She almost forgot, for a while, what she had seen and foreseen.

CHAPTER SIXTY-SEVEN

▲

THE king would not come upon them that day, or the next, or the one after that. He was too far away, had waited too long to take his army out of Pi-Ramses. Duty shackled him, and kingship, and the offices of mourning. But when at last he could set out, he could not fail to know where the Apiru were: they left a track as broad as the river of Egypt.

They were if anything an even more untidy mob as they broke camp than they had been in departing from Pi-Ramses. Two nights of carousing had left too many of them barely able to move. Already some were going thirsty: they had wasted all their water. There were loud outcries when it was brought home to them that there would be no water on the road, and none where they were most likely to camp for the night. A smaller company or a swifter one might have found one of the oases, but not this whole nation.

The worst of the stragglers were those who refused to leave camp at all. They would stay, they insisted. If the king came in pursuit of them, which they preferred to doubt, maybe he would pass them by. They did not seem to understand that their god had destroyed any hope of their remaining in Egypt, nor could they ever return there. They could not go back, only forward.

They needed the overseer's whip. Instead they had their own young men and the men from Sinai with swords and spears, lifting them if they stumbled, carrying them if they resisted. The whole nation of Yisroel went out of that camp in the dry land, whether it would or no.

■ ■ ■

The day before, they had marched in a haze of wine and joy. Now people were waking and realizing where they were and how they had come there. The way was hard. The sun beat down. No one knew for certain where they were going. Sinai, they supposed, but Sinai to most of them was a dream or a myth.

"Desert," some said. "Nothing but sand and rock as far as anyone can see, with a high mountain in the midst of it, where the Lord lives."

"No, no," others argued. "It's a land of beauty, green and rich, overflowing with milk and honey. Our flocks will grow fat there; our herds will prosper and multiply."

They disputed as they marched, till their mouths grew too dry for speech. Only one thing they agreed on: that this country was dreadfully harsh, and that there was not enough water. Those who dreamed of green pastures looked about them at the Red Land and despaired. Those who foresaw nothing but desert places and lives of hardship were loudly convinced that this was only the beginning. "We'll wander in the desert forever," they said. "We'll never see green grass or running water again."

"You will when we come to the sea," Nofret told one of them.

"Yes," the woman shot back, "and how are we going to cross that, I ask you? Will there be boats waiting for us? Is there a bridge?"

Nofret had no answer. Moshe did, but it was the same as always: "The Lord will provide."

■ ■ ■

The nation that called itself Yisroel, that being the name of the ancestor from whom they all claimed descent, was the most stubborn, argumentative, indomitably mule-headed collection of people that Nofret had ever run afoul of. And yet somehow it managed to keep marching, even to keep some semblance of order. People—not enough, but a surprising number—were beginning to measure out the water that they had left, and to be less prodigal of their provisions.

By evening they were well ready to stop and rest. The vanguard of Johanan's troops—mostly his own men from Sinai, with the rest scattered among the rearguard—had gone ahead to find a camping place. When the rest of the marchers came to it, they found the young men waiting, ready to take charge of the packtrain, the water, and the provisions. People were to pitch tents, build fires as they could, see themselves settled. Then they would be given the wherewithal to eat and drink.

The complaints were loud and long, but no one was lively enough to rise in revolt. That would happen later, Nofret suspected, when they were rested and toughened to the rigors of the march. For now they grumbled, and some even tried tears, but they did as they were told.

"That's wise," she said to Johanan when he came to the fire at last, tired and ruffled and more than a little surly. "Set your will on them when they're too tired to fight, and by the time they've rested it's too late; they're in the habit of acting like an army instead of a ladies' walking-party."

"They'll never be an army," he said grimly. "I'd settle for a reasonably decent tribe of desert rovers."

She set a cup in his hand, filled with heavily watered wine, and fed him roast kid wrapped in bread and herbs. He had little appetite at first, but after a while he grew hungry.

When he had eaten as much as he would eat, he looked about in some surprise. "We're all alone here."

She nodded. "The elders are in council again. Moshe's laying down the law. Better now than later, he says. This has to be something other than a rabble by the time the king finds us.''

Johanan leaped to his feet, or tried. He stumbled with weariness. She steadied him, and held him when he tried to pull away. He scowled at her. "What are you doing? I have to be there.''

"You can rest a bit," she said. "They'll be blathering for half the night.''

"I have to blather with them. We're going to have a revolt if we do again what we did tonight. We had to do it, mind you, and quickly, but after this, people will want a say in whatever we do.''

She could not stop him by force; he was too much stronger than she. She let him go, but followed, toward the middle of the camp and the largest fire, where the elders were gathered.

There was no carousing tonight. The camp was almost quiet. Many were sleeping, some where they had fallen after pitching their tents. Most of those who were awake were somewhere in sight of the elders' fire, craning to hear whatever they could.

It was blather, as Nofret had known it would be. Most was a continuation of the argument on the march: green pastures against bleak desert. The elders from Sinai seemed to have roused at last to the understanding of what they had done in bringing so many hundreds out of Egypt, all of whom needed to be fed and housed and provided with the means to live. Their own country supported, with difficulty, those who were in it already. Now a whole new nation was coming to live among them.

Moshe was saying nothing. Nor was Miriam. At first Nofret could not even see them, but they were there, not far from the fire but in shadow, silent, seeming oblivious to the clamor around them. It was Aharon who said, "The Lord has taken thought for this. Wait and be patient. First we get out of Egypt; then we go to the country that the Lord has prepared for us.''

"And where is that?" one of the elders demanded. Nofret knew the voice and the face: Shmuel from Pi-Ramses, as contentious as ever. "I say we go back to Egypt. It's clear enough that we can't leave it—either we have to fight our way out or we have to learn to swim across a sea.''

"We can't go back," Aharon said. "The Lord has made sure of it.''

"The Lord has shown the king how strong he can be. The king needs us to build his city. He knows that we won't be beaten and starved, and we won't have our children taken away from us. Let us work for him as men do for wages. There are no better builders than we are—if there were, would he have refused for so long to let us go?''

"The king was too proud to let you go," said Johanan, shouldering in beside his father. "That pride will kill you if you try to go back. He wants you dead now, dead and rotted, for what the Lord has done to him and to his kingdom.''

"Kings' memories are short," Shmuel said. "The works of their glory are long and dreadfully expensive. He needs us, and he knows it. Without us he'll be hard put to finish his city in the time he's got left to live.''

Johanan flung up his hands. "Go then! Go back to him. He's not a day's journey behind, with soldiers and chariots. Go and throw yourself at his feet. All the easier then for him to hack your head off and name you first in the count of Egypt's revenge for its firstborn.''

"I always said," someone muttered not far from Nofret, "that that was going too far. Plagues on the land and the livestock are very well, but killing people's children—''

The rest was overrun by a babble of voices. Everyone was shouting at once, some for going back, some for going forward, some—still—for taking Memphis and setting up a king.

A great bull-bellow rose above them all. It did not quell them, but that was not its purpose. Men came running from all over the camp, some dressed and armed, others hastily pulling on tunics and unsheathing swords. Another roar of command from Johanan and they were in ranks, the men from Sinai leading, those of Pi-Ramses following in reasonable order, advancing into what was rapidly becoming a mob.

Nofret took what shelter she could. It was only the patch of shadow where Moshe and Miriam were, and neither of them seeming to notice anything but the visions that formed and faded behind their eyelids. But it was an island of calm in the torrent. No one entered that shadow, nor did anyone try to seize one or the other of the prophets and hold a hostage.

Soon enough, though it seemed horribly long in the doing, Johanan's men had restored order. Shmuel himself was gently but firmly restrained by his own son. There was much glaring and no little muttering, but the shouting had died. Those who had come to blows were held apart from one another, and no matter how they struggled.

Johanan regarded them all with fists on hips, eyebrows raised. "And these," he said with astonishing mildness, "are the wise men of Yisroel. Two days out of captivity and already you're at war. Have you all forgotten why it is that we are here and not safe and soundly flogged in the king's treasure-city?"

Eyes lowered at that, and some of the muttering faded.

"My people," he said. His voice was almost tender, as it could be when one of the twins had done something appalling and been thrashed for it, but he could not help but betray that he loved them still. "O my people, if we are to live until we come to Sinai, we must be strong together. We can't be fighting over every step and every choice. The Lord leads us out of Egypt and into our own country.''

Several voices rose at that. His eyes flashed on the speakers, silencing them. ''No, it might not be in Sinai. Yes, we have to go through Sinai in order to come there. We can't turn back. We can't throw ourselves on the Egyptians' mercy. There is none. The king of Egypt is behind us, my people, and he is angry. When he catches us, he will do his best to kill us.''

A wail went up, a cry of sheer wordless terror. Johanan's voice lashed across it. ''*Stop that!* We are in danger, yes. Some or all of us could die. But we are the Lord's people. He chose us. He guides us. While we are strong, he will not let us die at the hands of the Egyptian king.''

''And if we can't be strong?'' Shmuel again, as truculent as ever.

Ephraim answered for Johanan. ''We have to be. There's nothing else we can do.''

''Lord of hosts,'' sighed Shmuel. He shook himself out of his son's grasp and raised his arms. ''Then pray, my people. Pray that we're not all mad, and led by madmen!''

First a few, then several, then a great number of those about him began to pray as he prayed, arms lifted, swaying, crying aloud to the Lord. It was a hideous discord, a clamor without either beauty or coherence, and yet it had power in it. The power of desperation, perhaps, but power nonetheless.

One sound, nearer than the rest, startled Nofret into speechlessness. Miriam was laughing. Softly, as if she could not help it, but without a doubt.

When the gust of it had passed, Miriam looked up at Nofret, smiling such a smile as Nofret had never seen in her. It had tears in it, but they were tears of mirth. ''Such people,'' she said. ''Such persistence. Who else would obey a god so perfectly but with such a mighty outcry?''

''We would,'' Nofret said.

Miriam laughed again. "So we would! Is this our pun-ishment, do you think? Are we here among them because we deserve them?"

"I think," said Nofret after a pause, "that their god has a finely honed sense of fitness, and a broad streak of cru-elty."

"No, not cruelty," said Miriam. "Humor. I never laughed, you see, when I was young. Now that I begin to grow old, I'll laugh or die. That's the doom he's laid on me."

Nofret sat on her heels beside Miriam. The praying went on in the light. Moshe, sitting beyond his daughter, was as immobile as a stone. His god held him captive. He would not be let go until morning. She was as private with Miriam as if they were alone.

"You think we're going to die," she said.

Miriam regarded her in something like curiosity. "Do you think so?"

Nofret opened her mouth to snap that she did, but closed it again. Did she? Slowly she said, "I don't know what I think. I know the king is on our track. He'll find us when we come to the sea. We're numerous, but most of us are women and children and men too old to fight. He can run right over us with his chariots and his bowmen."

"So he can," said Miriam. "He can certainly try. Don't you trust the Lord to save us?"

"Do you?"

Her own question, turned back on her. She shrugged under the weight of it. "He has before. I hope he will again."

"I don't even know what I know," said Nofret, "still less what I believe. If I look ahead, I see water and I see dry land. I see Sinai and the mountain of the god. I see years, Miriam. Years in the desert, always wandering, never stopping, hunted wherever we go. No one wants us. We're too many; we need too much. The only hope for us is to take and take again, whatever we must, however we may. Or to die on this side of the sea, at the hands of the Great House of Egypt.''

''Death is hope?'' Miriam pondered that. ''I suppose in its way it is. Maybe the dry land that you see—that I see— is the land of the dead. They wander forever, it's said, unless they're so blessed as to have been buried in houses of eternity. There will be no such thing for us. We'll bleach our bones under the sky.''

She did not sound as horrified by that as she might have once, when she was Egyptian, raised to believe that the body must endure so that the soul might live. She was the seer of the Apiru now. The Apiru set no value on the body once the soul had fled from it. They buried it, mourned it, forgot it.

This whole nation might die on the shores of the sea. Nofret had walked the edge of death's country before, had seen far too many who stepped over and could not return. This was different. This was an entire people, a tribe and a nation, escaped from captivity only to fall into danger of death.

And did Nofret want to die with them?

She did not want to die at all. If she had to . . . better here than alone among strangers. Her husband and her son would die with her. The rest of her children were safe if their god allowed, far out of reach of Egypt's king.

It could be worse. She shrugged, sighed, got to her feet. Miriam wanted to stay and pray. Nofret needed to sleep. Soon enough—tomorrow or the next day or the next— they would come to the sea, and the king would come upon them. Then she would need all the strength she had, to fight or to die.

CHAPTER SIXTY-EIGHT

▲

THE nation of Yisroel rested a long night in their second camp. They slept well into the morning, by their leaders' decree. When at last they rose and broke camp and readied for the march, Aharon said to them, "The king is behind us. He has chariots; we have flocks and children. From here we march in the night as well as in the day. We must reach the sea before him."

Sleep had weakened their resistance. Fear roused them to an effort that a day ago they might have refused. By taking turn and turn riding the pack animals that were not too heavily laden, and by stopping for long enough to eat, drink, sleep briefly, they pressed on swiftly toward the sea.

Moshe led them as always. Sometimes Nofret fancied that she saw a guide ahead of him, a bank of cloud by day, or a column of smoke; by night a pillar of fire. She could not always see it. She would have thought that she imagined it, except that she heard others speaking of it, calling it by the title that they gave their god: Adonai Elohenu, the Lord, the One.

It had been as strange as this when she first escaped from Egypt, when there were only the four of them: Johanan, Leah, her lady, herself. Now as then, she felt as if they had gone out of the world that simple men lived in. They were in the gods' country, with a god in front of them, showing them the way.

The way was no easier for that, the sun no less hot, the stones' edges no less sharp. Sleeping in snatches, marching in the dark as in the light, she lost all sense of where she was or what she did. She marched, that was all. Fear drove

her as it drove the rest. She more than most had reason to
be afraid: the dark behind her eyes was full of blood and
slaughter, the vision that was in the king's mind, the thing
that he would do when he caught them.

He was refining it as he pressed in pursuit. Now he
would only destroy the men, and such of the women and
boys as resisted him. The rest would be brought back to
Egypt and bound in deeper slavery even than they had
been before. He particularly desired to take Moshe alive,
to torment him until he died: and part of the torment would
be to see his daughter killed as the king's daughter had
been, but never so swiftly or so mercifully.

Nofret tried to shut her eyes to that, but the eyes of the
mind had no such escape. Waking and sleeping, the king's
thoughts followed her, the king's hate and his yearning for
revenge.

Sometimes she had relief when Johanan could walk with
her, or when he could be spared from guarding the camp
and roving with the scouts to rest for an hour beside her.
It was all she could do to keep the pace of the march. He
was tireless, commanding the armed men, sending out
companies before and behind, helping to choose the places
where they would pause. His god sustained him, or he was
simply too stubborn to admit that he was exhausted.

"When we've crossed the sea," he said, "then I'll sleep
for days. But not before."

"You still don't know how we're going to do that," she
said.

"I trust in the Lord," said Johanan.

■   ■   ■

When he was not with her, somewhat to her surprise Jehoshua was. Her son had been much caught up in his
young manhood, his training in arms and his place among
the fighting men. On this march, when he was not needed
on guard or among the scouts, he chose to walk with his

mother. He never said much. He had that habit of silence from her: certainly no Apiru could keep quiet for as long or as comfortably as he did.

Somewhere between Sinai and this desert, he had grown taller than she. Rather notably so. He looked as his father had when she first met him, all arms and legs and angles. Watching him, she remembered a great number of things: the color of the sky over Akhetaten, the scent of its air, the grit of sand underfoot as she walked from the city to the laborers' village. She even remembered the horrible great he-goat that had been a terror to the town. He was long gone to dust, as Akhetaten was.

As she grew more weary, she stumbled more often. Jehoshua was always there to steady her steps. The latest of many times that he did it, she lashed out at him. "What, do you think I'm too infirm to walk by myself?"

"I think you're too tired to see where you're going," he said with some of his father's maddening complacency. "Or you're seeing things. You are, aren't you? Miriam looks just like you. But she's steadier on her feet."

"She's had longer to learn how to do it," muttered Nofret.

He did not ask what it was that she saw. That was the Apiru in him: she could never have swallowed her curiosity so easily. An Apiru simply knew that it was something to do with the god, and left it at that.

"I don't want to be a prophet," Nofret said. "I thought I did once, when Leah died and left her place to Miriam. Now I know I don't want it at all. I'd rather be a plain woman of the people."

"You were never that," Jehoshua said. "You're the Hittite woman, the one who sees the truth."

Nofret shook her head so hard she staggered. "I'm not seeing it now. I'm feeling it. It's in me. She's the one who sees—Miriam, who is what Leah used to be. I just know things in my bones."

His hands were strong, holding her up. She looked into wide brown eyes. His father's eyes. The light that dawned in them was blinding in its brilliance. "You aren't like the others either, are you?" she said, half in pride, half in sadness. "You can see, too. Your bones know."

He nodded. He was calm about it. Of course he would be: he was half Apiru. Nothing their god did dismayed them. "The Lord is in me," he said. "He chose me."

She shook him, or tried. He was like a stone, rooted in the earth. "Don't you grow proud," she said. "Don't you get so full of yourself you can't see what's below your nose."

A flash of sulkiness recalled the boy he had been and still was. The sudden smile was pure Jehoshua. "Oh, Mother! You know I'll never do that. You'll always be there to bring me up short."

"I hope so," she said grimly. "Just remember it. Not," she mused, "that you may have to remember long. We could die when the king drives his army against us."

"The Lord—"

"—will protect us," Nofret finished for him. "Maybe he will and maybe he won't. I won't expect either until it's been and gone."

He laughed, which did nothing to cool her temper. "O unbeliever," he said, both mocking and tender. She nearly hit him, but he was too quick to dart away.

She was exhausted, footsore, sunburned, and terrified, but for an improbable moment she was happy. She could believe just then that they would live through this; that they would come to Sinai, and she would see the rest of her children again.

It was a pleasant dream to wander in. More pleasant than the desert, and the shimmer on the horizon that opened at last into the broad blue expanse of the sea.

■   ■   ■

A cry went up behind them, a long and swelling wail. "Egypt! Egypt has come!"

From the front of the march Nofret could see nothing but the wall of people behind her. But her bones knew. The king had caught them. He was in sight of the rearguard and closing fast.

He had taken his time in coming. He had chariots; he could ride more swiftly than any nation could walk. He had only to wait till they were trapped with the sea at their backs, and close for the kill.

Nofret had never had much hope, even with visions to tempt her, but she was too stubborn for despair. She simply kept on walking because everyone else did. Moshe strode ahead of her, making nothing of the deepening sand, the long rolling descent to the shore. Above the murmur of wind in stones she heard the sigh of waves. It was a sound that she had seldom heard, and never since she was taken out of Mitanni. River-water flowed differently: smoother, steadier, like a serpent's glide. The sea was like a great beast breathing in and out, endlessly.

The sun sank as they descended to the sea. The long column that had wound through the desert spread wide along the shore, driven by the army behind it.

But they were not defenseless. They had an army of their own, hundreds strong, set in order between them and the enemy. When the call went out to camp for the night, it was a guarded camp ringed with sentries, its heart the children and the flocks that would be their wealth in Sinai.

The king did not press battle. He saw maybe that they were defended, and that they could not retreat from him, not unless they could walk on the water. He made camp along the summit of the descent to the sea, just out of bowshot. Lesser camps sprang up to the north and south, surrounding the people of Yisroel, cutting them off from escape.

The deep desert night came down, and with it the cold

after the heat of the day. They could not wander far to find fuel for the fires, but there was enough wrack on the shore to serve the purpose. There was a half-ring of fires about them, and a glitter of weapons. The neighing of horses was distinct in the stillness.

They sang in their beleaguered camp, songs of praise to the god, songs of defiance, songs of protection against the dark. There was no song in the Egyptian camp. It was silent but for the calling of stallion to stallion, or the squeal of a mare. Without the horses the army would have been utterly, deathly silent.

The Apiru fought silence with clamor. Even their animals were unwontedly noisy tonight, bleating and blatting and braying. Children shrieked as they played. Babies cried. Men called out to one another. And everyone sang, the louder the better, to drown out the stillness of the night.

Nofret's head was ringing. She crawled into her tent and hid under all her blankets with her veil stuffed in her ears, and she could still hear the uproar. It bade fair to go on all night.

So would Johanan's stint on guard. He had seen to it that the rest had at least part of the night to sleep, but he would not practice the same wisdom for himself. He would pace the night through from guardpost to guardpost in sleepless vigilance.

The Egyptians would not trouble to attack at night, not with a sitting target that would wait till the morning. But they might be fools, or some hothead might take a notion to try a raid while the Apiru were sleeping. Johanan's sentries stood on guard against that. It did not harm them, either, to be seen as watchful and to display their weapons.

Nofret could not sleep alone. It was too cold, as much in the heart as on the skin. After a while she got up, wrapped her mantle about her, and went out into the light of the fires.

The noise had died down somewhat. People were being

persuaded to sleep. Miriam was in the midst of that. Nofret watched her briefly, sighed, lent her own voice to the chorus. "Come now, rest as you can. It's a long way till morning, and you'll want to be strong for it."

"For what?" one woman demanded of her. "To die?"

"If need be," said Nofret. "Or to escape, if the god wills it."

"We're not escaping that," another woman said, jabbing her chin at the fires strung on the hilltop like jewels on a thread. "If we run, we run right into Egyptian spears."

"We have spears, too," Nofret said, "and men who know how to use them. Trust them. Trust the god. And sleep."

There were others too who followed Miriam's lead, a skein of women and a few men coaxing the Apiru to their beds. Nofret was reminded of mothers with recalcitrant children, restive offspring who, though yawning, insisted that they were wide awake. The same persuasions prevailed on them, the same threats.

Little by little the camp quieted. On its edges the fires still burned. The men still sang softly as they stood guard. Within, the people slept.

Even Moshe was asleep in his tent. Miriam crouched in front of it, prodding at the fire, banking it till morning.

She looked as wide awake as Nofret felt, not tireless but shut away from sleep. Nofret sat on the sand that kept still the day's warmth, clasping her knees. She rested her forehead on them—rather proud that she was still limber enough for that—and closed her eyes. Just for a while. Just until Miriam went to her own bed.

■ ■ ■

When she opened them she was lying in a hollow in the sand, and the fire was grey ashes over a faint glimmer of coals. The sky was the same, like a reflection in water.

The waves sighed on the shore. Their scent in the air was salt, like tears.

She unfolded limb by limb, groaning with stiffness. The women were awake, stirring fires, setting bread to bake in the coals. She heard the sleepy murmur of children, the wail of a baby cut off as its mother thrust the nipple in its mouth. Her own breast tightened in sympathy, though it had been years since she nursed a child.

The stars were fading. Eastward over the water, the sky had grown pale. She could see the line of hills beyond, for the sea was narrow here, the desert of Sinai close, with its stark ridges and sudden valleys. On that side Egypt had power only to threaten, not to conquer.

On this side the king's army roused and took up weapons, hitching horse to chariot, setting soldiers in their ranks about the camp of Yisroel. They were shadows in the dawn light, shot with a cold gleam of metal: bronze and iron, edged and forged for war.

They waited now, spears at the rest, horses fretting against the bit but holding still till they should be freed to gallop down the long slope upon the camp below. A thin line of armed men defended it, motionless as the king's men were, seeming even to be at ease. That would be Johanan's training. He taught his young men never to waste their substance in fretting, but to rest as they could, and to wait in trained patience. It was hunter's wisdom, such as Nofret herself had had once, before she was taken captive and sold into slavery.

She still had a little such wisdom left. She found it buried deep and lured it into the light. It was just enough to calm her thudding heart and to let her mix and bake the morning's bread, take count of the provisions, fill a cloth with bread and goat cheese and the last of the honeycomb.

■　■　■

Johanan was crouching in a circle of men with bows and spears, drawing battles in the sand. None of those seemed to bear much resemblance to this trapped hopelessness. They were proper battles, with armies on open plains or armies besieging cities or champion fighting champion on the field between their armies.

Nofret slipped through the circle and crouched beside him, and set his breakfast where he could see it. He finished what he was saying—yes, it was a lesson in warfare, not a plan for battle here—then offered the bread and cheese to any who would take it. He would have kept none for himself if she had not stopped his hand and met his glance with a glare. "Eat," she said, "or you'll die of hunger before an Egyptian can get an arrow in you."

He ate, but not before she had eaten half of what she reckoned to be his share. There were grins round the circle, boys whom she had known since they were clinging to their mothers' skirts. By evening they might be dead with Egyptian arrows in their hearts.

A roar from the camp brought them all about. Fast upon it came a runner, a swift-footed child who cried out as he ran, his voice as shrill as a trumpet's call: "Moshe calls you to gathering! Everybody come—even the soldiers."

Johanan rose. Some of the young men protested: "But if we go, there's no one to defend us."

"We'll go on guarding the edges of the people," he said. "We'll just do it from the middle of the camp."

That was sense enough to silence them. They all went together, taking their weapons and such belongings as they had with them. Nofret, following, glanced at the Egyptian army. They were staring, glancing at one another, wondering what led the Apiru to abandon their defenses and gather in the camp's center.

The middle of it was open—those whose tents had been in it had struck them and loaded them on mules and donkeys. Moshe was standing where his own tent had been, and Aharon beside him. The ground rose a little there, not so much as to be a proper hill, but enough that people on the edge of the crowd could see them both.

Aharon spoke for Moshe as he did so often, the voice as strong as ever, reaching easily to the place where Nofret stood. There was nothing behind her but a bit of camp and the stretch of sand and the king's army.

She should have felt naked and undefended. Strangely, she did not. Maybe this was what it was to be Apiru, to know always that one's god stood at one's back.

The great beautiful voice rolled over her. It had a surge like the sea. "We will gather," it said, "as we have gathered every morning, each household in its place, each tribe in its rank and order. Let no possession be forgotten, no child left behind. Then when we are ready, we will march."

Someone must have shouted near the front: the inevitable question.

"Where?" Aharon echoed it. He swept about, robes flaring, arm outflung. "There!"

Their eyes followed the sweep of his arm. There was nothing to see but a narrow strip of sand, and beyond it the water, broad and gleaming, blue in the morning light. A flock of birds wheeled and cried above it, seabirds, white and grey like clouds, or like foam on the sea.

"We will march," said Aharon. "The Lord will show us the way. Trust in the Lord and be not afraid."

CHAPTER SIXTY-NINE

▲

THE people of Yisroel trusted in their god as always and as in nothing else. Nofret could feel their fear, see their glances at the army on the hill and at the sea in front of them. Some of them were weeping with terror. But

Aharon's voice roused any who faltered. Moshe and Miriam went among them, lending a hand here, offering comfort there.

It was strange to see them, to remember what they had been: royal, hallowed, set apart. They were hallowed still, but they were of these people, standing on the same earth, eating the same bread, lifting the same burdens that any mortal could carry. There was no divine kingship among the Apiru. Only their god was granted divinity.

Breaking camp was always a lengthy undertaking. This morning they had begun late, and they were afraid, even where they trusted in their god. Children and animals were unwontedly fractious. It was nearly noon before all the tents were taken down and packed, the pack animals laden and led to their places, the flocks and herds gathered, the people set in marching order. Their backs were to the Egyptians, their faces to the sea. Their own army, Johanan's young men, stood between the last of them and the Egyptian chariots.

Nofret was in the rear with Johanan and Jehoshua. It was not a proper place for a woman, but she was past caring for that. They knew better than to object. She had taken charge of the mule that carried their waterskins and such of their weapons as they could not both carry and fight: spears, quivers of arrows, even a packet of bowstrings. She was useful, since she set one more of them free to fight rather than to tend the mule. And she was where she needed to be.

The king was biding his time. He stood on the hill beside the golden glitter of his chariot, watching, as curious perhaps as she was, to discover what the Apiru would do.

She was far in the rear and Moshe was in the front, on the water's edge. Her eyes could not see him, but eyes had little to do with such sight as she had. She knew that he stood in the sand with the waves surging and subsiding about his feet.

He had his staff in his hand. The gilt had long since worn off the serpent that crowned it, baring the bronze. The rearing cobra seemed a living thing, supple and darkly gleaming.

He raised the staff and stretched it out over the water. If he spoke, she did not hear the words. She only saw how he stood as if rooted, with the waves now washing about the hem of his robe, now sinking far back along the sand.

The small wind that had played about them through the morning had died as the sun touched the zenith. Now it rose again. In the morning it had been a restless, playful thing, dancing from everywhere and nowhere. This new face of it was steadier. It came from the east across the water, ruffling the waves, toying with Moshe's beard, catching at his sodden robe and tugging against the water's resistance.

He might have been carved in stone, so still as he stood. His staff never wavered. The wind swelled and freshened. Nofret's body, far back along the shore, felt it on its face. The mule's head was up, its long ears alert, nostrils flaring as if to drink the wind.

It was a strong east wind. Such were not rare in Egypt, nor unexpected on the shores of this sea. But its steadiness, its sheer unvarying persistence, was not so common.

Nofret could not tell if the god rode on it. Perhaps he had no need. As with much else that Moshe had done in Egypt, any middling capable sorcerer could call up a wind. But to keep it blowing into a gale—that took such power as was only given to prophets, and to kings.

The king of Egypt was doing nothing to stop it, nor if he had priests in his army was any of them offering to come forward. Most likely he had left the priests behind, disgusted with their failure to protect the Two Lands against this one nameless god and his stammering fool of a prophet.

Nofret braced her feet against the wind. Sand whipped

her cheeks. She raised her veil and fastened it tightly. The men were doing the same, she noticed, but keeping hand to weapon and an eye warily on the army that was growing less visible as the sand rose into a cloud. The Egyptians faded to shadows and vanished behind the red-dun wall.

The sand that swirled about them stung unprotected cheeks, but it was nothing to the storm that raged behind them. Before them was clear air and windblown spray, and a murmur of wonder.

It began as a strangeness in the heave and surge of the waves. They swelled and rose and broke, ran back, gathered strength, swelled again as they had since the sea was made. But the wind drove through the midst of them, pressing like a hand, driving them down and down.

Or, thought Nofret, like a child playing with a shallow basin, blowing hard along it till the water was cloven in two. Only that child was a god, and the god wielded the wind to drive back the waters. He veiled his people in a cloud of dust and sand, protected them through the long slow hours. Maybe too he calmed them, bound them in a spell, so that even the beasts and the children were quiet, waiting in unnatural patience.

Nofret watched the sun sink slowly from the height of heaven. The waters divided with mighty dignity. Little by little a road came clear, a broad track of glistening sand. On either side was the sea, a wall of deep blue water, higher than any wall that men could raise. The road between ran straight from shore to shore.

It was a greater wonder, maybe, and more fearful, for a god to destroy the firstborn of every house in Egypt. But this was power bare. This was impossible, unimaginable, terrible and splendid.

In the midst of the road between the walls of water rose a dazzle of light. Nofret might have taken it for a stone or a pillar uncovered by the waters' parting, but it was nothing so solid or so earthly. It was a pillar of fire, growing brighter as the daylight waned.

Moshe stood at the beginning of the road. He had lowered his staff, grounding it in the wet sand. "Go," he said to Aharon in a voice taut with effort and exhaustion. "Go quickly."

■　　■　　■

It was Aharon who led the people of Yisroel out upon the road that had been the sea. They went blindly, most of them, shrinking between the walls of water. They were near witless with awe and terror. Those who hung back were herded forward by the throng of people behind.

They went in such order as they might, as they had on the march from Pi-Ramses. They were not what anyone would call swift, but neither did they drag their feet. The sand was firm underfoot, scattered with weed and shells. Here and there a fish flopped stranded, or a creature of the deep scuttled from the touch of human foot where none had ever been or been dreamed of.

The elders and the leaders of the people urged their charges on. Moshe stood silent as they passed, with Miriam behind him. They did not have the air of sorcerers maintaining a great working, but neither were they wholly in the world as others knew it. Moshe's eyes were as full of the god as they had been while he was king in Akhetaten. Then he had been alone in his devotion. Now he spoke for his god before a whole people.

His god not only spoke; he showed himself in signs and wonders. Most of those were turned against Egypt. Revenge, Nofret supposed, for its refusal to accept one god above the rest.

She was more fortunate than Egypt. She was beloved of a man who worshipped the god, mother of his children. She still could not make herself worship this one god of them all. She was stubborn, she knew it very well. She had lived so, and so no doubt would she die.

But not on this day that moved now swiftly into night. The people of Yisroel followed their guide, the towering fire that even she could see. Their armed men hung back until the last, till every tribe and clan had passed down the god's road, walking dry-shod across the bottom of the sea.

■ ■ ■

When all the people were set on the road, their defenders followed. It was full dark now. Fear was a dim and distant thing, but still they strung their bows and kept their guard.

With the coming of night, the cloud behind had begun to fade. As the last of them advanced between the waters, they saw behind them a glimmer of flames: campfires, Nofret thought at first, but campfires did not shift and waver. They were torches. The army of Egypt was mustered behind them. Perhaps it was afraid to venture that road between those walls; but it was fast gathering courage.

She was the last to set foot on the road through the sea. It would have been Moshe, but Johanan had seized him bodily and all but carried him ahead of her. Johanan was moving swiftly, almost running. Nofret struggled to keep up. He had heard what she had: the bray of a war-trumpet.

It was hard going. The road was dry, but it was sand, and deep. Within a few strides she was winded, but she quickened her pace as best she could. Behind her a horse neighed. "Onward!" a man's voice bellowed in Egyptian. "Take them!"

She slipped, scrambled, stumbled and almost fell. So many feet passing for so many hours had pocked and pitted the sand till it was all but impassable. She gasped—prayer, curse, she did not know—and pressed on.

A strong arm caught her up. The touch of it was so familiar that she nearly fell, limp with relief. But Johanan was ahead of her, driving Moshe before him. The arm about her belonged to Jehoshua.

Her body was caught in a black dream. As in a dream, it struggled forever and seemed to advance not at all. Her back was taut with dread of an Egyptian arrow.

But none flew. The Egyptians' great advantage was in their chariots, in swift horses and swift wheels. Horses that wallowed and struggled in the sand even as did she, and wheels that caught and mired.

She would have laughed if she had had breath for it. The curses of the Egyptians were horrific, shouts and clashing of armor, cracking of whips as charioteers drove their teams forward against the suck and drag of the sand. She was faster on her staggering feet, because she was lighter, and had her son to bolster her.

Much too soon the Egyptians woke to sense and abandoned the chariots, forging ahead on foot. None of them seemed to be an archer, or perhaps it was too dark for shooting. They had spears and swords: she saw the gleam of metal in the torchlight.

All at once her feet left the ground altogether. Jehoshua was carrying her, grunting with effort but too stubborn to let her go. Johanan dragged Moshe just ahead, and one of the young men—Ephraim; she recognized the shock of wild hair that would never stay confined—had flung Miriam over his shoulder and was bounding like a stag through the sand.

In the dark, lit by the fire ahead and the torches behind, they might have been on any road that ran beside a sea. The murmur of the waters above had grown louder; or maybe that was the roar of blood in Nofret's ears. Was the road narrower? Had the walls drawn closer? She could not tell.

Jehoshua surged upward suddenly, scrambling up a brief, sharp slope. Then at last he would let Nofret down, but dragging her still, running with renewed vigor. People were running ahead of them, crying out. Some were trying to turn back, to ready weapons, to fight the enemy that followed. But Johanan, and Moshe recovered from his stupor, drove them onward, Johanan with the flat of his sword, Moshe with his staff.

Moshe halted so abruptly that Nofret nearly collided with him. The sweep of his arm sent her half-running, half-flying after the rest of the Apiru.

Sheer weight of obstinacy brought her to a halt. And something else, something that had changed. The wind had died.

She could see Moshe, she realized. He was a grey dim figure, but clear, with the staff upraised in his hand. Beyond him, shadowy in the dawn, was the cloven sea, and the road that had been laid bare by the waters' parting. The whole army of Egypt was on it. Even as she stared, the vanguard set foot on the slope that slanted steeply up to the eastern shore.

With a sound half like a sigh, half like the sea's roar heard far away, the walls of water let go their strength and fell. They crashed like a great wave on the right hand and on the left, down and down upon the heads of the Egyptians. They stood like men who neither believed nor comprehended what had befallen them: mute and motionless, staring upward, helpless in the face of their death.

The horses had more wit and sense than their masters. Some of the chariots had struggled in the rear, bearing the king and the loftier of his princes. As Nofret watched, the king's pale-coated stallions surged up in the traces. She saw the charioteer struggling, fighting the fear-maddened beasts. They wheeled, half-falling, dragging the chariot. The king's helmet fell from his head, baring the shaven skull. He had the reins in his own hands—the charioteer had been thrown from the chariot, or the king had thrust him out. He lashed the team into a wallowing, stumbling run. Away from the sea that had come to claim its own.

Toward the distant shore, the shelter of Egypt, the dry land that he had, like a fool, forsaken.

The walls of water crashed together upon the army of Egypt. Men howled. Horses screamed. But louder than they, louder by far, was the roaring of water.

CHAPTER SEVENTY

▲

THE sun rose, serene and vastly remote. The sea's surge had quieted. Of the army of Egypt there was nothing left, not even a scatter of stormwrack. The water had taken them all, weapons and armor, horses and chariots.

All but one. One lifeless body washed up on the shore, rolling slack in the waves. Its helmet was gone, its gilded armor and its ornaments stripped from it, but there was no mistaking the face. The Great House of Egypt, the Lord of the Two Lands, lay dead at Moshe's feet.

The king who had died and lived in Sinai looked down at the king who had died and would live only in memory. He bent down even to his knees and wept. "We were enemies," he said. "He defied my God. And yet we were kin. He knew—he too, he knew the weight of the crowns."

■   ■   ■

They laid Egypt's king to such rest as they might, there on the shore of the sea, on the westward edge of Sinai. Egypt would come to claim him, Moshe said. Nofret did not doubt it. Gods had a way of looking after their own.

For this brief time he was laid in a cairn of stones, wrapped in fine linen that had come from Egypt with the children of Yisroel, with such spices as they could spare.

Moshe crowned the cairn with the helmet-crown that Nofret had seen fall from the king's head before the waters
drowned him—and maybe the sea had brought it, and
maybe the god had set it in Moshe's hand. She was no
longer certain of anything but that she was alive, and every
man and woman and child of those who had escaped from
Egypt; but the army of Egypt was destroyed.

■   ■   ■

"Not all of it," Johanan said in their tent, when at last
they had marched far enough from the sea to camp in
safety. "Not even the half or the third of it. This was a
raiding party, a vengeance-expedition. The heir wasn't
with them, did you notice? He's safe in Memphis, I'll wager, and ready to claim the throne that his father was fool
enough to run away from."

"He's like to come after us," Nofret said, "once he
knows that his father is dead."

"I think not," said Johanan. "Seti struck me as a sensible man, from what I saw of him. He'll be hard put to
undo all the damage that the Lord did to his land and
people. Best for them all if he forgets us."

"As Egyptians forget?" Nofret asked. "By forgetting
our names and our very existence?"

He shrugged. He was going out again, as weary as he
was, because they could not leave the people unguarded.
He put on a clean tunic, washed in the sea that had destroyed the Egyptians, and said, "They may forget us, but
the Lord remembers."

She pulled on a robe herself, went to the tentflap, opened
it and peered out. Their tent stood on the camp's edge,
looking out on the desert of Sinai. Although the sun had
set, the sky was still full of light. It washed the stark land
with blood and gold.

Johanan knelt beside her. She leaned briefly against him,

not to tempt him back to bed, but simply for the comfort of his presence.

They could hear the people singing. The song had begun as they marched away from the sea, leaving the king in his cairn behind them. It had gone on without pause ever since.

Without saying anything, without either asking the other's leave, they followed the singing to its source. This camp was a great circle, its center left open so that the people might gather. A fire was built high in it, and there were dancers and singers and players on harp and timbrel.

Moshe was among the singers. His voice was weak in song as in speech, but true, and when he sang he suffered no stammer. He had laid aside his staff and his dignity; he was laughing as he sang, praising his god.

The strange unbeautiful man whom Nofret had first known was truly dead. This was the god's great servant, messenger to a people who welcomed him and reckoned him one of them. Egypt was all gone from him, as he was gone from Egypt.

He seemed to know no regret for what he had lost. But then he never had. He had gone willingly into Sinai. Now he had returned to it. His wife and sons were waiting for him, and the people whom he had made his own.

Nofret's throat tightened. She too had children whom she longed to see. As for what came after that—she had wandered all her life among these people. She would wander again and always, wherever their god took her. Even . . .

She shut her mind's eye to foresight. Time enough for that when they were set upon that road: when the nation that had come out of Egypt left the desert and advanced in conquest against the cities of Canaan.

Now they were still a wandering people, new come from their captivity. Their joy tugged at her.

And was she not glad? Her husband was beside her. Her

son was among the dancers. Her younger children waited in the green valley to which this road would lead her. She had gone twice into Egypt, and twice she had escaped. There would be no third such journey. She was free now and forever from the gods and the bindings of the Two Lands.

Johanan drew her toward the fire and the dancing. He was needed to stand guard, nor had he forgotten it, but duty could wait for yet a while.

The dance that leaped and spun in the firelight was a men's dance, a dance of the hunt and of war. Johanan was whirled irresistibly into it, leaving Nofret alone but not forlorn. She loved to watch him dance. He was beautiful always, but in the dance he was splendid.

This night he danced the escape from the land of Egypt, the god's great power and terror, and the people's joy in their freedom. No one leaped higher than he, or spun with more grace.

The women were frank in their praises. Nofret caught herself blushing like a girl, and she the mother of a grown son. She retreated with the rags of her dignity toward a bit of shadow and an eddy of quiet.

There was someone in it, as she had half expected. What she had not expected was the smile that warmed Miriam's face, brightening it even in the dimness.

They sat side by side, companionable as they could sometimes be. Nofret was content in the silence. So, for a while, was Miriam.

Then she said, "I feel so strange."

Nofret glanced at her. She looked much the same as ever. Lighter, maybe. Less somber.

She looked as Moshe did. Free, and freed.

Nofret said so. Miriam nodded. "That's what it is. That is the name of it. Free. When the waters parted, my heart was torn asunder. When they crashed together, they made it all anew. Egypt is gone, Nofret. I can remember it, but the memory is dim, as if it came to me through deep water.''

"That's the god's doing," Nofret said.

"Do you forgive him for it?"

That was utterly like Miriam, to ask such a question. But there was no bitterness in it.

Nofret shook her head. "There's nothing to forgive. I see you well. I actually saw you smile. Can you do it again, do you think? Would it tax you sorely?"

Miriam laughed. She stopped abruptly as if startled. "What in the world—"

"You laughed," Nofret said.

Miriam frowned at her. "Yes, I laughed. I know what that is. But—"

"But you didn't expect to do it just then." Nofret was smiling herself, and not because she could help it. "We may have to change your name," she said. "From the bitter to the sweet. From—"

"I would thank you," said Miriam with the full measure of her old royal stiffness, "to leave my name alone. It suits me. I choose to keep it."

"As my lady wishes," said Nofret, bowing her head.

Miriam glared. Nofret laughed at her. Oh, she was altered indeed: her glare transmuted into astonishment, and thence into mirth. "But I am not your lady!" she said in the midst of it.

"Old habits die hard," Nofret said, unrepentant.

"So do queens," said Miriam. She leaped up, light as a girl. "Look, it's time for the women's dance. Come and dance with me."

Nofret dug in her heels. "I don't dance."

"Tonight you will." Miriam had her by the hand. And there was Johanan, flushed and sweat-streaming and more beautiful than ever, grinning at her and daring her to try.

The singers had rested while the men danced. Now they

raised their voices again, pure voices of women, deep voices of men.

All ye peoples, clap your hands; shout to God with cries of gladness!

The women spun in a skein, in the clapping of hands, the stamping of feet, the whirling of skirts and veils and braided hair.

Miriam had snatched up a timbrel, beating on it as she danced, singing in her pure trained voice.

Sing ye to the Lord, for he hath triumphed
  gloriously:
The horse and rider he hath thrown into the sea.

Into the sea, the women echoed her in their sweet descant.

Nofret, who did not sing, or dance either, found that she was doing both. It was a fever in the blood, a white heat of gladness.

Who is like to thee, O Lord, among the gods?

She almost stopped then, almost argued with it—she, the foreigner, the Hittite woman, who would not worship this one god alone. But the dance was too strong, the music sunk too deep into her bones. She was a part of it whether she would or no: she and all of them. They were the god's people. He had made them his own.

Even she. She could do battle with it till she died, or she could surrender to it. Or—and at that she smiled a broad and fang-edged smile—she could dare the god to refuse her.

"I won't be yours," she said to him as she whirled round the fire. "I'll make you mine. Not your slave, my lord, but your free servant."

He did not strike her dead where she stood. Nor did he turn his people against her. He was too high for that. Or, perhaps, too much amused.

The dance cast her out, dizzy and breathless, into her husband's arms. "What," she gasped, "still here?"

"Still and always," said Johanan.

There was her answer. Holding her up, grinning at her, tempting her to do something utterly improper in front of the whole nation of Yisroel.

And why not?

She whirled him about, set lips on his and pulled him down into the shadow beyond the firelight.

Still the children of Yisroel sang as they had sung since the dawn and for all the day and night thereafter.

Who is like unto thee, O Lord, among the gods?
Who is like thee, glorious in holiness, terrible in
praise, doing wonders?
Thou in thy mercy hast led forth the people which
thou hast redeemed:
thou hast guided them in thy strength unto thy holy
habitation.

Johanan echoed them softly, even as distracted as he was, ending the song, greeting the new dawn:
The Lord shall reign for ever and ever.

Nofret forbore to sigh. The god might have Johanan's soul, and welcome to it. But she had his body and his heart. She was well content with her part of the bargain.

Warm in his arms, tired beyond need of sleep, and ineffably happy, she watched the sun rise over the hills of Sinai.

Author's Note

▲

There are few periods in Egyptian history more widely known than the Eighteenth Dynasty, and few pharaohs more familiar to the general public than the "rebel" Akhenaten and his successor Tutankhamon (they ruled, in sequence, from approximately 1358–1331 B.C.). Akhenaten's reign even rates its own archeological epoch, the Amarna Period—Amarna being the modern name of the site on which he built his city, Akhetaten, the Horizon of the Aten.

Akhenaten himself has been a figure of endless fascination to modern readers and scholars. He has been called the first true individual, the first monotheist, the first honest monomaniac on the human record. Sigmund Freud in *Moses and Monotheism* went so far as to propose him as the mentor and teacher of Moses.

Even more outrageous from the standpoint of biblical scholarship is the theory set forth by Ahmed Osman in *Moses: Pharaoh of Egypt* (London, 1990). By tweaking and fiddling with the chronology of the Exodus, selecting carefully from the archeological record, and citing not only the Pentateuch but the Koran, Osman manages to construct the thesis that Moses was not simply the pupil of Akhenaten but was in fact the exiled and discredited pharaoh. His thesis requires a great deal of stretching and adjustment of the historical and scriptural evidence—but from the novelist's perspective it is pure gold. To go even further, to propose that Moses' sister Miriam could have been Akhenaten's daughter and wife (since in Egyptian the same word can be used for both sister and wife) Ankhesenamon, seems a natural progression.

In Osman's chronology, Akhenaten feigned death

around about the age of thirty-two, went into exile in Sinai, and returned some thirty years later, after the death of his enemy Horemheb, perhaps to reclaim his kingship, perhaps simply to free the Israelites from bondage. The Israelites themselves, Osman proposes, were the kinsmen of Joseph, whom he identifies as Yuya, Commander of Chariotry to Akhenaten's father Amenophis III. We have Yuya's mummy (thereby, if Osman is correct, negating the statement in the Book of Exodus that Joseph's body was carried back with the Israelites in the Exodus); he was indeed a Semite and not an Egyptian, a strikingly handsome, eagle-nosed man whose mummified face preserves the dignity it must have worn in life.

Yuya, according to standard Egyptological thinking, was the father of Queen Tiye, who was the mother of Akhenaten. He may also have been the father of Ay, and Ay in his turn may have been the father of Nefertiti—the evidence is confused on this point; Ay could also have been Nefertiti's brother. I have chosen the former as the more dramatically useful.

In any case, if Yuya was the biblical Joseph, then Akhenaten was related by blood to the Israelites. Osman finds various ways to accommodate the story of Moses to the biography of Akhenaten as it is known to Egyptologists—it can most conveniently be read in two recent versions, that of Donald B. Redford, *Akhenaten: the Heretic King* (Princeton, 1984) and that of Cyril Aldred, *Akhenaten, King of Egypt* (London, 1988)—and through this accommodation to construct his equation of the Hebrew prophet and the Egyptian king.

I have made liberal and sometimes quite broad use of Osman's chronologies and theories in the latter portion of this novel. In earlier portions however I have adhered more faithfully to the Egyptological and historical view. For chronology and identification of principals, including the ages of Akhenaten's daughters, I have chosen to follow

Aldred; for the sake of dramatic effect I have simplified the chronology in some cases, notably in the deaths of Nefertiti and her three daughters, and the death of Tiye. In fact these deaths may not have occurred in the same plague, but over a period of years. Likewise I have conflated Meketaten's childbirth and death with the childbirth of Meritaten, and disposed of Ankhesenpaaten-ta-Sherit a year or two earlier than may actually have been the case.

In other controversial issues I have chosen among often widely divergent theories, again for the sake of the most effective story. I follow Redford's suggestion that Akhenaten's secondary queen and favorite, Lady Kiya, may have been a princess of Mitanni—perhaps that Tadukhipa or Gilu-khepa whom we have on record in the king's harem. Likewise I have chosen to present Smenkhkare and Tutankhamon as Akhenaten's brothers rather than his sons as some scholars believe, and proposed that they were all sons of Tiye. Further, I grant Smenkhkare no independent reign; I dispose of him shortly after Akhenaten's putative death, and bring Tutankhamon immediately to the throne.

I have done nothing with some of the wilder theories about Smenkhkare: that he was a woman, a eunuch, Akhenaten's boy-lover, perhaps even Nefertiti in male disguise. There is another book in all of that, but not, unfortunately, this one.

Nor have I made Nefertiti the conniving figure that she has sometimes been portrayed. Theorists who believe that Akhenaten's peculiar physical appearance was the result of a medical condition, believe that that condition would have precluded his producing any children—in which case none of his six putative daughters was in fact his offspring. It has also been proposed that Nefertiti vanished from the archeological record not because she died but because she turned against her husband, or else refused to participate further in his experiment at Amarna—including Akhenaten's marrying his daughters in order to produce the son and heir whom she had failed to give him. These options, while intriguing, again belong in another novel.

I have taken liberties, some of them extensive, with the geography of Amarna/Akhetaten, notably the palace and the workmen's village. Akhenaten's tomb is as described, although there is no evidence that its builders were Hebrews.

■   ■   ■

For the reign of Tutankhamon, again I have followed the orthodox historical view. The circumstances of his death are my own invention. That he died by violence is a fact; the wound in his skull appears to be that of an arrow. He might have died in battle, or he might have been assassinated. If the latter, it is possible that Horemheb was involved—he does appear to have intrigued for the throne.

Theories again are numerous, and books thereon proliferate. Among them is Nicholas Reeves' glossy and lavishly illustrated *The Complete Tutankhamun* (London, 1990). If nothing else, it is a testimony to the splendor of the young king's relatively shabby and hastily cobbled-together tomb and grave-goods.

That Tutankhamon's wife was Akhenaten's daughter is not contested. What happened to her after the pharaoh's death, however, is a mystery. She appears to have married Ay, who became pharaoh for a brief time—four years at most: he was an old man, and apparently died a natural death. Long before Ay died, however, Ankhesenamon vanishes from history. The last evidence we have of her is not Egyptian at all, but an account in the memoir of a Hittite king.

The Deeds of Suppililiuma as Told by His Son Mursili II (edited and translated by Hans Gustav Guterbock in the *Journal of Cuneiform Studies,* volume 10 [1956]) is a remarkable document, an eyewitness account of the events of the period. Among these is an unusual incident, the arrival of a letter and an embassy from the queen of Egypt, requesting a thing that had never been requested before: a husband to be her consort, to sit the throne of Egypt. I have quoted this letter and its sequel verbatim, as it is recorded in Guterbock's translation.

We know that the Hittite prince Zennanza was sent to Egypt. We also know that he was killed—probably by Horemheb. What we do not know is what became of the queen thereafter. She simply vanishes. Most probably she was disposed of for what was, after all, an act of treason. My proposal in the novel is an extension of Osman's theory regarding Akhenaten—and in fact it was remarkably simple to transform Akhesenamon the queen into Miriam the prophetess of the Israelites.

■   ■   ■

Along with Osman I find it fairly simple, and quite dramatically useful, to equate the Pharaoh of the Exodus with Ramses I. His reign was short, and seems to have been cut off rather abruptly. Why not, then, by the waters of the Red Sea? That he was also a great builder, and had been master of works under Horemheb, is even more convenient in the context of the Book of Exodus.

As for Johanan and Leah, Aharon and Jehoshua, I have made quite free with the biblical characters. Johanan is my invention, as is Leah. Aharon and Jehoshua of course are not, but there is no evidence that they were related in the degree that I have depicted. I have made similarly free with the geography of Sinai and the location and composition of the Hebrew tribes therein.

What is remarkable is that I have had to invent or to alter so little—that it all fits together so well. Errors, omissions, heresies and heterodoxies are my own; but the story, the history, is very much itself, and happened very much as I have written it.

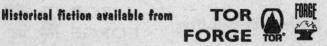

Available by mail from

1812 • David Nevin
The War of 1812 would either make America a global power sweeping to the Pacific or break it into small pieces bound to mighty England. Only the courage of James Madison, Andrew Jackson, and their wives could determine the nation's fate.

PRIDE OF LIONS • Morgan Llywelyn
Pride of Lions, the sequel to the immensely popular *Lion of Ireland,* is a stunningly realistic novel of the dreams and bloodshed, passion and treachery, of eleventh-century Ireland and its lusty people.

WALTZING IN RAGTIME • Eileen Charbonneau
The daughter of a lumber baron is struggling to make it as a journalist in turn-of-the-century San Francisco when she meets ranger Matthew Hart, whose passion for nature challenges her deepest held beliefs.

BUFFALO SOLDIERS • Tom Willard
Former slaves had proven they could fight valiantly for their freedom, but in the West they were to fight for the freedom and security of the white settlers who often despised them.

THIN MOON AND COLD MIST • Kathleen O'Neal Gear
Serving in the trenches as a Civil War Confederate spy, a woman of the West makes her way alone towards the promise of the untamed Colorado frontier—until her new life has room for love.

SPIRIT OF THE EAGLE • Vella Munn
Luash, a young woman of the Modic tribe, tries to stop the Secretary of War from destroying her people.

THE OVERLAND TRAIL • Wendi Lee
Based on the authentic diaries of the women who crossed the country in the late 1840s. America, a widowed pioneer, and Dancing Feather, a young Paiute, set out to recover America's kidnapped infant daughter—and to forge a bridge between their two worlds.